IN A DRY SEASON

AND

DRY BONES THAT DREAM

The Inspector Banks series

GALLOWS VIEW

A DEDICATED MAN

A NECESSARY END

THE HANGING VALLEY

PAST REASON HATED

WEDNESDAY'S CHILD

DRY BONES THAT DREAM

INNOCENT GRAVES

DEAD RIGHT

IN A DRY SEASON

COLD IS THE GRAVE

AFTERMATH

THE SUMMER THAT NEVER WAS

PLAYING WITH FIRE

Peter Robinson grew up in Yorkshire, but now lives in Toronto.

His Inspector Banks series has won numerous awards in Britain, Europe, the United States and Canada. There are now fourteen novels in the series.

PETER
ROBINSON

IN A DRY SEASON

DRY BONES THAT DREAM

INSPECTOR BANKS MYSTERIES

PAN BOOKS

In a Dry Season first published in Great Britain 2000 by Macmillan
First published by Pan Books 2003
Dry Bones that Dream first published 1995 by Constable, London.
First published by Pan Books 2003

This omnibus edition published 2004 by Pan Books
an imprint of Pan Macmillan Ltd
Pan Macmillan, 20 New Wharf Road, London N1 9RR
Basingstoke and Oxford
Associated companies throughout the world
www.panmacmillan.com

ISBN 0330 43265 6

1 3 5 7 9 8 6 4 2

A CIP catalogue record for this book is available from
the British Library.

Typeset by SX Composing DTP, Rayleigh, Essex
Printed and bound in Great Britain by
Mackays of Chatham plc, Chatham, Kent

IN A DRY SEASON

For Dad and Averil,
Elaine and Mick,
and Adam and Nicola

The past is a foreign country; they do things differently there.

L. P. Hartley, *The Go-Between*

PROLOGUE

AUGUST 1967

It was the Summer of Love and I had just buried my husband when I first went back to see the reservoir that had flooded my childhood village.

I made the journey only a few months after Ronald and I had returned from one of our frequent long spells abroad. Spells which had suited me well for many years. Ronald, too, had suited me well. He was a decent man and a good husband, quite willing to accept that our marriage was one of convenience. I believe he saw me as an asset in his diplomatic career, though it was certainly neither my dazzling beauty nor my sparkling wit that snared him. I was, however, presentable and intelligent, in addition to being an exceptionally good dancer.

Whatever the reason, I became adept at playing the minor diplomat's wife. It seemed a small price to pay. In a way, I was Ronald's passport to career success and promotion, and – though I never told him this – he was my passport to flight and escape. I married him because I knew we would spend our lives far away from England, and I wanted to be as far away from England as possible. Now, after more than ten years abroad, it doesn't seem to matter very much. I shall be quite content to live out the rest of my days in the Belsize Park flat. Ronald, always a shrewd investor, also left me a tidy sum of money. Enough, at least, to live on for some years and to buy myself a new Triumph sports car. A red one. With a radio.

And so, singing along with 'All You Need is Love', 'Itchycoo Park' and 'See Emily Play', listening to the occasional news bulletins about Joe Orton's murder and the closing-down of the offshore pirate radio stations, I headed back to Hobb's End for the first time in over twenty years. For some reason I have never been able to explain, I enjoyed the raw, naive and whimsical new music the young people were listening to, even though I was in my early forties. It made me long to be young again: young without the complications of my own youth; young without the war; young without the heartbreak; young without the terror and the blood.

I don't think I saw another car after I left the main road outside Skipton. It was one of those perfect summer days when the air smells sweet with the perfume of cut grass and wild flowers. I fancied I could even smell the warm exhalations of the dry-stone walls. Berries shone like polished garnets on the rowan trees. Tewits soared and tumbled over the meadows and sheep bleated their pitiful calls from the far dalesides. The colours were all so vibrant – the green greener than ever, the blue of the sky cloudless and piercingly bright.

Not far beyond Grassington I lost my way. I stopped and asked two men carrying out repairs to a dry-stone wall. It was a long time since I had heard the characteristic broad speech of the Dales and at first it sounded foreign to me. Finally, I understood, thanked them and left them scratching their heads over the strange middle-aged lady with the sunglasses, the pop music and the flashy red sports car.

The old lane stopped at the edge of the woods, so I had to get out and walk the rest of the way along a crooked dirt path. Clouds of gnats whined above my head, wrens flitted through the undergrowth and blue tits hopped from branch to branch.

At last I broke out of the woods and stood at the edge of the reservoir. My heart started to pound and I had to lean against one of the trees. The bark felt rough on my palms. For a moment, skin flushed and fingers tingling, I thought I was going to faint. But it passed.

There had been trees long ago, of course, but not as many, and most of them had been to the north of the village, in Rowan Woods. When I had lived there, Hobb's End had been a village in a valley. Now I gazed upon a lake surrounded by forest.

The water's surface, utterly still, reflected the trees and the occasional shadow of a gull or a swallow flying over. To my right, I could see the small dam where the old river narrowed as it flowed into Harksmere. Confused, unsure what I was feeling, I sat on the bank and stared over the scene.

I was sitting where the old railway branch line used to run, the train I had travelled on so often during my childhood. A single track that ran to and from Harrogate, the railway had provided our only real access to the larger world beyond Hobb's End during the war. Dr Beeching had done away with it three or four years ago, of course, and already the lines were overgrown with weeds. The council had planted weeping willows on the spot where the old station had stood, where many a time I had bought tickets from Mrs Shipley and waited on the platform with rising excitement to hear the distant chugging and whistling of the old steam engine.

As I sat there remembering, time went by. I had started out late and the journey from London was a long one. Soon, darkness infused the woods around me, filling the spaces between the branches and the silences between the bird calls. A whisper of a breeze sprang up. The water caught the fading light in such a way that its slightly ruffled surface looked as if it had been sprinkled with salmon-pink powder. Slowly, even this darkened, until only a deep inky blue remained.

Then a full moon rose, scattering its bone-white light, in which I fancied I could see clear through the water to the village that used to be there, like an image preserved in water-glass. There it was, spread out below me, darkly glittering and shimmering under the barely perceptible rippling of the surface.

As I stared, I began to feel that I could reach out and touch it. It was like the world beyond the mirror in Cocteau's *Orpheus*. When you reach out and touch the glass, it turns to water and you can plunge through it into the Underworld.

What I saw there was a vision of the village as it had been when I lived there, smoke curling from chimneys over the slate and flagstone roofs, the dark mill on the hillock at the west end, the squat church tower, the High Street curving beside the narrow river. The longer I looked, the more I imagined I could see the people going about their daily business: shopping, making deliveries, gossiping. In my vision, I could even see our little shop, where I met her for the first time that blustery spring day in 1941. The day it all began.

1

Adam Kelly loved to play in the derelict houses, loved the musty smell of the old rooms, the way they creaked and groaned as he moved around inside them, the way the sunlight shone through the laths, casting striped shadows on the walls. He loved to leap the gaps between the broken stairs, heart in his mouth, and hop from rafter to rafter, kicking up plaster dust and watching the motes dance in the filtered light.

This afternoon, Adam had a whole village to play in.

He stood at the rim of the shallow valley, staring at the ruins below and anticipating the adventure to come. This was the day he had been waiting for. Maybe a once-in-a-lifetime opportunity. Anything could happen down there. The future of the universe depended on Adam today; the village was a test, one of the things he had to conquer before advancing to the Seventh Level.

The only other people in sight stood at the far end, near the old flax mill: a man in jeans and a red T-shirt and a woman all dressed in white. They were pretending to be tourists, pointing their video camera here and there, but Adam suspected they might be after the same thing he was. He had played the game often enough on his computer to know that deception was everywhere and things were never what they seemed. Heaven help us, he thought, if *they* got to it first.

He half-slid and half-ran down the dirt slope, skidding

5

to a halt when he reached the red, baked earth at the bottom. There were still patches of mud around; all that water, he supposed, wouldn't just evaporate over a few weeks.

Adam paused and listened. Even the birds were silent. The sun beat down and made him sweat behind his ears, at the back of his neck and in the crack of his bum. His glasses kept slipping down his nose. The dark, ruined cottages wavered in the heat like a wall behind a workman's brazier.

Anything could happen now. The Talisman was here somewhere, and it was Adam's job to find it. But where to begin? He didn't even know what it looked like, only that he would know it when he found it and that there must be clues somewhere.

He crossed the old stone bridge and walked into one of the half-demolished cottages, aware of the moist, cool darkness gathering around him like a cloak. It smelled like a bad toilet, or as if some gigantic alien creature had lain down to die in a hot, fetid swamp.

Sunlight slanted in through the space where the roof had been, lighting the far wall. The dark stones looked as slick and greasy as an oil spill. In places, the heavy stone flags that formed the floor had shifted and cracked, and thick gobbets of mud oozed up between them. Some of the slabs wobbled when Adam stood on them. He felt poised over a quicksand ready to suck him down to the earth's core if he made one wrong move.

There was nothing in this house. Time to move on.

Outside, he could still see no one. The two tourists seemed to have left now, unless they were hiding, lying in wait for him behind the ruined mill.

Adam noticed an outbuilding near the bridge, the kind of place that had perhaps once been used to store coal or keep food cold. He had heard about the old days before electric fires and fridges. It might even have been a toilet. Hard to believe, he knew, but once people had to go outside to the toilet, even in winter.

Whatever it had been, The Destructors had left it largely alone. About seven feet high, with a slanting flag-stone roof still intact, it seemed to beckon him to come and vanquish it. Here, at least, was a structure he could mount to get a clear view. If the pretend-tourists were hiding nearby, he would see them from up there.

Adam walked around the outbuilding and was pleased to see that on one side a number of stones stuck out farther than others, like steps. Carefully, he rested his weight on the first one. It was slippy, but it held fast. He started to climb. Every step seemed solid enough, and soon he was at the top.

He pulled himself on to the roof. It only slanted at a slight angle, so it was easy enough to walk on. First, he stood near the edge, cupped his hand over his eyes to shield out the harsh sun and looked in every direction.

To the west stood the flax mill, and the strangers were now nowhere in sight. The land to both the north and south was covered in woods, so it was hard to see anything through the dense green foliage. To the east lay the teardrop shape of Harksmere Reservoir. On The Edge, which ran along the south side of Harksmere, a couple of car windscreens flashed in the sun. Other than that, there was hardly any movement in the world at all, hardly a leaf trembling.

Satisfied he wasn't being watched, Adam struck out over the roof. It was only about four or five feet wide, but when he got to the middle he felt the faintest tremor, then, before he could dash the short distance to the other side, the thick stone slabs gave way beneath him. For a moment, he hung suspended in air, as if he might float there for ever. He stuck his arms out and flapped them like wings, but to no avail. With a scream, he plunged down into the darkness.

He landed on his back on a cushion of mud; his left wrist cracked against a fallen flagstone and his right arm, stretched out to break his fall, sank up to the elbow.

As he lay there, winded, looking up at the square of blue sky above him, he saw two of the remaining roof slabs tilt and fall towards him. Each one was about three feet square and six inches thick, enough to smash him to a pulp if it hit him. But he couldn't move; he felt trapped there, spellbound by the falling slabs.

They seemed to drift down in slow motion, like autumn leaves on a windless day. His mind emptied of everything. He felt no panic, no fear, just a sort of acceptance, as if he had reached a turning point in his short life, and it was out of his hands now. He couldn't have explained it if he'd tried, but at that moment, lying on his cot of warm mud watching the dark stone flags wheel down across the blue of the sky, young as he was, he knew there was nothing he could do to avoid whatever fate had in store for him; whichever way it went, he could only go with it.

This must be the Seventh Level, he thought as he held his breath, waiting for the impact, waiting to feel his bones breaking, grinding against one another.

One slab fell to his left, embedded itself in the mud and tilted against the wall like an old gravestone. The other fell to his right and cracked in two against one of the floor flags. One half tipped towards him, just grazing his upper arm, which was sticking out of the mud, and raising a few drops of blood.

Adam took a few deep breaths and looked up through the roof at the sky. No more slabs. So he had been spared; he was alive. He felt light-headed. There was nothing seriously damaged, he thought, as he started to move his limbs slowly. His left wrist hurt a lot, and it would probably come up in one hell of a bruise, but it didn't feel broken. His right arm was still thrust deep in the mud, and the slab chafed against his grazed elbow. He tried to wiggle his fingers under the mud to find out if he could still feel them, and they brushed against something hard.

It felt like a cluster of smooth, hard spindles, or a bundle of short rods. Curious, he pushed his arm in deeper and grasped it tightly, the way he used to hold his mother's hand in town when he was very small and frightened of all the crowds; then he leaned his weight back over to the left, gritting his teeth as the pain seared through his injured wrist, and tugged.

Inch by inch, he dragged his arm free, keeping a firm grasp on his prize. The mud made sucking, slurping sounds as he pulled. Finally, he was able to free the object he was holding. He rested it against the slab and edged back towards the far wall to study it.

The thing lay against the flagstone in the dim light, fingers hooked over the top, as if it were trying to pull itself out of the grave. It was the skeleton of a hand, the bones crusted with moist, dark earth.

●

Banks stepped back to survey his handiwork, whistling along with the habanera from *Carmen*, which was playing loudly on the stereo: Maria Callas past her best but still sounding fine.

Not bad for an amateur, he thought, dropping the

paintbrush in a bowl of turpentine, and a definite improvement over the mildewed wallpaper he had stripped from the walls of his new home yesterday.

He particularly liked the colour. The man at the do-it-yourself centre in Eastvale said it was calming, and after the year Banks had just suffered through, he needed all the calming he could get. The shade of blue he had chosen was supposed to resemble that of oriental tapestries, but once it was on the wall it reminded Banks more of the Greek island of Santorini, which he and his estranged wife Sandra had visited during their last holiday together. He hadn't bargained for that memory, but he thought he could live with it.

Pleased with himself, Banks pulled a packet of Silk Cut from his top pocket. First, he counted the contents. Only three gone since morning. Good. He was trying to restrict himself to ten a day or less, and he was doing well so far. He walked into the kitchen and put on the kettle for a cup of tea.

The telephone rang. Banks turned off the stereo and picked up the receiver.

'Dad?'

'Brian, is that you? I've been trying to get in touch with you.'

'Yeah, well . . . we've been on the road. I didn't think you'd be in. Why aren't you at work?'

'If you didn't expect me to be in, why did you call?'

Silence.

'Brian? Where are you? Is anything wrong?'

'Nothing's wrong. I'm staying at Andrew's flat.'

'Where?'

'Wimbledon. Look, Dad . . .'

'Isn't it about time your exam results were out?'

More silence. Christ, Banks thought, getting more than a few words in a row out of Brian was as tough as getting the truth out of a politician.

'Brian?'

'Yeah, well, that's why I was calling you. You know . . . I thought I'd just leave a message.'

'I see.' Banks knew what was going on now. He looked around in vain for an ashtray and ended up using the hearth. 'Go on,' he prompted.

'About the exams, like . . .'

'How bad is it? What did you get?'

'Well, that's it . . . I mean . . . you won't like it.'

'You *did* pass, didn't you?'

''Course I did.'

'Well?'

'It's just that I didn't do as well as I expected. It was really hard, Dad. Everyone says so.'

'What did you get?'

Brian almost whispered. 'A third.'

'A *third*? That's a bit of a disappointment, isn't it? I'd have thought you could have done better than that.'

'Yeah, well, it's more than you ever got.'

Banks took a deep breath. 'It doesn't matter a damn what I did or didn't get. It's you we're talking about. Your future. You'll never get a decent job with a third-class degree.'

'What if I don't want a *decent job*?'

'What do you want to be then? Another statistic? Another cliché? Another unemployed yobbo?'

'Thanks a lot, Dad. Nice to know *you* believe in me. Anyway, as a matter of fact, I'm not on the dole. We're going to try and make a go of it. Me and the band.'

'You're *what*?'

'We're going to make a go of it. Andrew knows this bloke who runs an indie label, and he's got a studio, like, and he's said we can go down and make a demo of some of my songs. You might not believe it, but people actually like us. We've got gigs coming out of our ears.'

'Have you any idea how tough it is to succeed in the music business?'

'The Spice Girls did it, and look how much talent they've got.'

'So did Tiny Tim, but that's not the point. Talent's got nothing to do with it. For every one that makes it, there's thousands who get trampled on the way.'

'We're making plenty of money.'

'Money's not everything. What about the future? What are you going to do when you've peaked at twenty-five and you don't have a penny in the bank?'

'What makes you an expert on the music business all of a sudden?'

'Is that why you got such a poor degree? Because you were too busy wasting your time rehearsing and going out on the road?'

'I was getting pretty bored with architecture anyway.'

Banks flicked his cigarette butt in the hearth. It scattered sparks against the dark stone. 'Have you talked to your mother about this?'

'Well, I sort of thought, maybe . . . you know . . . you could do that.'

That's a laugh, Banks thought. *Him* talk to Sandra? They couldn't even discuss the weather these days without it turning into an argument.

'I think you'd better ring her yourself,' he said. 'Better still, why don't you pay her a visit? She's only in Camden Town.'

'But she'll go spare!'

'Serves you right. You should have thought of that before.'

The kettle started whistling.

'Thanks a lot, Dad,' Brian said, his voice hard-edged with bitterness. 'I thought you'd understand. I thought I could depend on you. I thought you *liked* music. But you're just like the rest. Go see to your *fucking* kettle!'

'Brian—'

But Brian hung up. Hard.

The blue of the living room did nothing to soothe Banks's mood. Pretty sad, he thought, when you turn to DIY as therapy, house decoration to keep the darkness at bay. He sat for a moment staring at a brush hair stuck to the paint above the mantelpiece, then he stormed into the kitchen and turned off the kettle. He didn't even feel like a cup of tea any more.

'Money isn't everything. What about your future?' Banks couldn't believe he had said those things. Not because he thought that money *was* everything, but because that was exactly what his parents had said to him when he told them he wanted a weekend job in the supermarket to earn some extra money. It frightened him how deeply instinctive his whole response to Brian's news was, as if someone else – his own parents – had spoken the words and he was only the ventriloquist's dummy. Some people say that the older we get, the more we come to resemble our parents, and Banks was beginning to wonder if they were right. If so, it was a frightening idea.

Money isn't everything, his father had said, though in a way it *was* everything to him because he had never had any. *What about your future?* his mother had said, her way of telling him that he would be far better off staying at home studying for his exams than wasting his weekends making money he would only use to go hanging around billiard halls or bowling alleys. They wanted him to go into a nice, respectable, secure white-collar job like banking or insurance, just like his older brother Roy. With a good degree behind him, they said, he could *better himself*, which meant he could do better than they had done. He was bright, and that was what bright working-class kids were supposed to do back in the sixties.

Before Banks had a chance to think any further, the phone rang again. Hoping it was Brian ringing back to apologize, he dashed into the living room and picked up the receiver.

This time it was Chief Constable Jeremiah 'Jimmy' Riddle. Must be my lucky day, Banks thought. Not only was it *not* Brian, the new call also meant that Banks couldn't even dial 1471 to get Brian's Wimbledon phone number, which he had neglected to ask for. 1471 only worked for the last *one* call you received. He cursed and reached for his cigarettes again. At this rate he'd never stop. Bugger it. Extraordinary circumstances call for extraordinary measures. He lit up.

'Skiving off again, are you, Banks?'

'Holiday,' said Banks. 'It's official. You can check.'

'Doesn't matter. I've got a job for you to do.'

'I'll be back in the morning.'

'Now.'

Banks wondered what kind of job Jimmy Riddle would call him off his holidays for. Ever since Riddle had had to reinstate him reluctantly after dishing out a hasty suspension the previous year, Banks had been in career Siberia, his life a treadmill of reports, statistics and more reports. Everything short of going around to the schools giving road-safety talks. Not one active investigation in nine months. He was so far out of the loop he might as well have been on Pluto; even the few informers he had cultivated since arriving in Eastvale had deserted him. Surely the situation wasn't going to change this easily? There had to be more to it; Riddle never made a move without a hidden agenda.

'We've just got a report in from Harkside,' Riddle went on. 'A young lad found some bones at the bottom of Thornfield Reservoir. It's one of the ones that dried up over the summer. Used to be a village there, I gather. Anyway, there's nothing but a section station in Harkside, and all they've got is a lowly DS. I want you down there as senior investigating officer.'

'Old bones? Can't it wait?'

'Probably. But I'd rather you get started right away. Any problem with that?'

'What about Harrogate or Ripon?'

'Too busy. Don't be such an ungrateful bastard, Banks. Here's the perfect opportunity for you to drag your career out of the slump it's fallen into.'

Sure, Banks thought, and pigs can fly. He hadn't fallen into the slump, he had been *pushed*, and, knowing Jimmy Riddle, this case was only going to push him even deeper into it. 'Human bones?'

'We don't know yet. In fact, we know nothing at all so far. That's why I want you to get down there and find out.'

'Harkside?'

'No. Thornfield bloody Reservoir. You'll find the local DS already at the scene. Cabbot's the name.'

Banks stopped to think. What the hell was going on here? Riddle was clearly not doing him any favours; he must have got tired of confining Banks to the station and thought up some new and interesting way to torture him.

A skeleton in a dried-up reservoir?

A detective chief inspector would not, under normal circumstances, be dispatched to the remote borders of the county simply to examine a pile of old bones. Also, chief constables *never* assigned cases to detectives. That was a job for the superintendent or chief superintendent. In Banks's experience, CCs usually restricted their activities to waffling on the telly, opening farm shows and judging brass-band competitions. Except for bloody Jimmy Riddle, of course, Mr Hands-On himself, who would never miss an opportunity to rub salt in Banks's wounds.

However busy Harrogate and Ripon were, Banks was certain they could spare *someone* qualified to do the job. Riddle obviously thought the case would be boring and unpleasant, or both, and that it would lead to certain failure and embarrassment; otherwise, why give it to Banks? And this DS Cabbot, whoever he was, was probably as thick as pigshit or he would have been left to handle things himself. Besides, why else was a detective sergeant stuck in a section station in Harkside, of all places? Hardly the crime capital of the north.

'And, Banks.'

'Sir?'

'Don't forget your wellies.'

Banks could have sworn he heard Riddle snicker like a school bully.

He dug out a map of the Yorkshire Dales and checked the lie of the land. Thornfield was the westernmost in a chain of three linked reservoirs built along the River Rowan, which ran more or less east from its source high in the Pennines until it turned south and joined the River Wharfe near Otley. Though Thornfield was only about

twenty-five miles away as the crow flies, there was no fast
way, only minor unfenced roads for the most part. Banks
traced a route on the map with his forefinger. He would
probably be best heading south over the moors and along
Langstrothdale Chase to Grassington, then east towards
Pateley Bridge. Even then it would probably take an hour
or more.

After a quick shower, Banks picked up his jacket and
tapped his pockets by habit to make certain he had car
keys and wallet, then walked out into the afternoon sunshine.

Before setting off, he stood for a moment, resting his
hands on the warm stone wall and looked down at the
bare rocks where Gratly waterfalls should be. A quote
from a T. S. Eliot poem he had read the previous evening
came to his mind: 'Thoughts of a dry brain in a dry
season'. Very apt. It had been a long drought; everything
was dry that summer, including Banks's thoughts.

His conversation with Brian still nagged on his mind; he
wished it hadn't ended the way it had. Though Banks
knew he fretted more about his daughter Tracy, who was
at present travelling around France in an old van with a
couple of girlfriends, that didn't mean he wasn't concerned about Brian.

Because of his job, Banks had seen so many kids go
wrong, that it was beyond a joke. Drugs. Vandalism. Mug-
ging. Burglary. Violent crime. Brian was too sensible to do
anything like that, Banks had always told himself; he had
been given every possible middle-class advantage. More
than Banks had ever got. Which was probably why he felt
more hurt than anything by his son's comments.

A couple of ramblers passed by the front of the cottage,
heavy rucksacks on their backs, knotted leg muscles,

shorts, sturdy hiking boots, Ordnance Survey maps hanging in little plastic holders around their necks in case it rained. Some hope. Banks said hello, remarked on the good weather and got into the Cavalier. The upholstery was so hot he almost jumped out again.

Well, he thought, fumbling for a cassette to play, Brian was old enough to make his own decisions. If he wanted to chuck everything in for a shot at fame and fortune, that was up to him, wasn't it?

At least Banks had a real job to do. Jimmy Riddle had made a mistake this time. No doubt he believed he had given Banks a filthy, dead-end job, full of opportunities for cock-ups; no doubt the dice were loaded against him; but anything was better than sitting in his office. Riddle had overlooked the one overriding characteristic Banks possessed, even at his lowest ebb: *curiosity*.

Feeling, for a moment, like a grounded pilot suddenly given permission to fly again, Banks slipped Love's *Forever Changes* in the cassette player and drove off, spraying gravel.

●

The book-signing started at half past six, but Vivian Elmsley had told her publicist, Wendi, that she liked to arrive early, get familiar with the place and have a chat with the staff.

There was already a crowd at quarter past. Still, it was only to be expected. All of a sudden, after twenty novels in as many years, Vivian Elmsley was a *success*.

Though her reputation and her sales had grown steadily over the years, her Detective Inspector Niven series, which accounted for fifteen of the twenty books, had recently made it to the small screen with a handsome lead actor, glossy production values and a big budget. The first three episodes had been shown, to great critical acclaim – especially given how bored many television critics had become with police dramas recently – and as a result Vivian had become, over the past month or so, about as familiar a face to the general public as a writer ever is.

She had been on the cover of *Night & Day*, had been interviewed by Melvyn Bragg on the 'South Bank Show' and featured prominently in *Woman's Own* magazine. After all, becoming an 'overnight success' in one's seventies was quite newsworthy. Some people even recognized her in the street.

Adrian, the event organizer, gave her a glass of red wine, while Thalia arranged the books on the low table in front of the settee. At half past six on the dot, Adrian introduced her by saying that she needed no introduction, and to a smattering of applause she picked up her copy of the latest Inspector Niven story, *Traces of Sin*, and began to read from the opening section.

About five minutes was enough, Vivian reckoned. Anything less made her look as if she couldn't wait to get away; anything more risked losing the audience's attention. The settee was so soft and deep that it seemed to enfold her as she read. She wondered how she would ever get out of it. She was hardly a spry young thing any more.

After the reading, people formed an orderly queue, and Vivian signed their books, pausing to chat briefly with everyone, asking if they wanted any specific sort of dedication and making sure she spelled their names right. It was all very well if someone said he was called 'John', but how were you to know it wasn't spelled 'Jon'? Then there were the more complex variations: 'Donna', or 'Dawna'? 'Janice', or 'Janis'?

Vivian looked down at her hand as she signed. Talon-like, she thought, almost skeletal, dotted with liver spots, skin shrivelled and wrinkled over the knuckle joints, puffs of flesh around the wedding ring she could never remove even if she wanted to.

Her hands were the first to go, she thought. The rest of her was remarkably well preserved. For a start, she had remained tall and lean. She hadn't shrunk or run to fat like so many elderly women, or generated that thick, hard, matronly carapace.

Steel-grey hair pulled back tightly and fastened at the back created a widow's peak over her strong, thin face; her deep blue eyes, networked with crow's-feet, were almost oriental in their slant, her nose was slightly hooked and her lips thin. Not a face that smiled often, people thought. And they were right, even though it had not always been so.

'A steely, unblinking gaze into the depths of evil,' one reviewer had written of her. And was it Graham Greene who had noted that there is a splinter of ice in the heart of the writer? How right he was, though it hadn't always been there.

'You used to live up north, didn't you?'

Vivian looked up, startled at the question. The man appeared to be about sixty, thin to the point of emaciation, with a long, gaunt pale face and lank fair hair. He was wearing faded jeans and the kind of gaudy, short-sleeved shirt you would expect to see at a seaside resort. As he held the book out for her to sign, she noticed that his hands were unnaturally small for a man's. Something about them disturbed her.

Vivian nodded. 'A long time ago.' Then she looked at the book. 'Who would you like me to sign this to?'

'What was the name of the place where you lived?'

'It was a long time ago.'

'Did you go by the same name then?'

'Look, I—'

'Excuse me, sir.' It was Adrian, politely asking the man to move along. He did as he was asked, cast one backward glance at Vivian, then he slapped her book down on a pile of John Harveys and left.

Vivian carried on signing. Adrian brought her another glass of wine, people told her how much they loved her books, and she soon forgot about the strange man and his prying questions.

When it was all over, Adrian and the staff suggested dinner, but Vivian was tired, another sign of her advancing years. All she wanted to do was go home to a long hot bath, a gin and tonic and Flaubert's *Sentimental Education*, but first she needed a little exercise and some air. Alone.

'I'll drive you home,' said Wendi.

Vivian laid her hand on Wendi's forearm. 'No, my dear,' she said. 'If you don't mind, I'd just like a little walk by myself first, then I'll take the tube.'

'But, really, it's no trouble. That's what I'm here for.'

'No. I'll be perfectly all right. I'm not over the hill yet.'

Wendi blushed. She had probably been told that Vivian was *prickly*. Someone always warned the publicists and media escorts. 'I'm sorry. I didn't mean to suggest anything like that. But it's my job.'

'A pretty young girl like you must have far better things to do than drive an old lady home in the London traffic. Why don't you go to the pictures with your boyfriend, go dancing, or something?'

Wendi smiled and looked at her watch. 'Well, I did tell Tim I wouldn't be able to meet him until later. Perhaps if

I phoned him now and went to queue at the half-price ticket booth, we could get some last-minute theatre tickets. But only if you're *sure*.'

'Quite sure, my dear. Good night.'

Vivian walked out into the warm autumn dusk on Bedford Street.

London. She still sometimes found herself unable to believe that she actually *lived* in London. She remembered her first visit – how vast, majestic and overwhelming the city had felt. She had gazed in awe at landmarks she had only heard of, read about or seen in pictures: Piccadilly Circus, Big Ben, St Paul's, Buckingham Palace, Trafalgar Square. Of course, that was a long time ago, but even today she felt that same magic when she recited the names or walked the famous streets.

Charing Cross Road was crowded with people leaving work late or arriving early for the theatres and cinemas, meeting friends for a drink. Before getting on the tube, Vivian crossed the road carefully, waiting for the pedestrian signal, and strolled around Leicester Square.

A small choir was singing 'Men of Harlech' just beside the Burger King. How it had all changed: the fast-food places, the shops, even the cinemas. It wasn't far from here, on the Haymarket, that she had been to her first London cinema, the Carlton. What had she seen? *For Whom the Bell Tolls*. Of course, that was it.

As she walked back to the Leicester Square tube entrance, Vivian thought again about the strange man in the bookshop. She didn't like to dwell on the past, but he had pushed her into a reminiscent mood, as had the recent newspaper photographs of the dried-up Thornfield Reservoir.

The ruins of Hobb's End were exposed to the light

of day for the first time in over forty years, and the memories of her life there had come crowding back. Vivian shuddered as she walked down the steps to the underground.

2

Banks paused for breath after his walk through the woods. From where he stood on the edge of Thornfield Reservoir, the entire elongated bowl of ruins lay open below him like a cupped hand, about a quarter of a mile wide and half a mile long. He didn't know the full story, but he knew that the site had been covered with water for many years. This was its first reappearance, like an excavated ancient settlement, or a sort of latter-day Brigadoon.

He could see tangles of tree roots sticking out of the slope on the opposite embankment. The difference in soil colours showed where the waterline had been. Beyond the high bank, Rowan Woods straggled away to the north.

The most dramatic part of the scene lay directly below: the sunken village itself. Bracketed by a ruined mill on a hillock to the west, and by a tiny packhorse bridge to the east, the whole thing resembled the skeleton of a giant's torso. The bridge formed the pelvic bone, and the mill was the skull, which had been chopped off and placed slightly to the left of the body. The river and High Street formed the slightly curving backbone, from which the various ribs of side-streets branched off.

There was no road surface, but the course of the old High Street by the river was easy enough to make out. It eventually forked at the bridge, one branch turning towards Rowan Woods, where it soon narrowed to a footpath, and the other continuing over the bridge, then out of the village along the Harksmere embankment, presumably all the way to Harkside. It struck Banks as especially odd that there should have been a fully intact bridge there, under water for all those years.

Below him, a group of people stood by the other side of the bridge, one of them in uniform. Banks scampered down the narrow path. It was a warm evening, and he was sweating by the time he got to the bottom. Before approaching the group, he took a handkerchief from his pocket and mopped his brow and the back of his neck. There was nothing he could do about the damp patches under his arms.

He wasn't overweight, or even especially unfit. He smoked, he ate lousy food and he drank too much, but he had the kind of metabolism that had always kept him lean. He didn't go in for strenuous exercise, but since Sandra left he had got into the habit of taking long solitary walks every weekend, and he swam half a mile at the Eastvale public baths once or twice a week. It was this damn hot weather that made him feel so out of shape.

The valley bottom wasn't as muddy as it looked. Most of the exposed reddish-brown earth had been caked and cracked by the heat. However, there were some marshy patches with reeds growing out of them, and he had to jump several large puddles on his way.

As he crossed the packhorse bridge, a woman walked towards him and stopped him in the middle. 'Excuse me, sir,' she said, arm extended, palm out. 'This is a crime scene. I'm afraid you can't come any further.'

Banks smiled. He knew he didn't look like a DCI. He had left his sports jacket in the car and wore a blue denim shirt open at the neck, with no tie, light tan trousers and black wellington boots.

'Why isn't it taped off, then?' he asked.

The woman looked at him and frowned. She was in her late twenties or early thirties, by the look of her, long-legged, tall and slim, probably not much more than an inch shorter than Banks's five foot nine. She was wearing blue jeans and a white blouse made of some silky material. Over the blouse she wore a herringbone jacket that followed the contours of her waist and the gentle outward curve of her hips. Her chestnut hair was parted in the middle and fell in layered, casual waves to her shoulders. Her face was oval, with a smooth, tanned complexion, full lips, and a small mole to the right of her mouth. She was wearing black-rimmed sunglasses, and when she took them off, her serious almond eyes seemed to appraise Banks as if he were a hitherto undiscovered species.

She wasn't conventionally good-looking. Hers wasn't the kind of face you'd find on the pages of a magazine, but her looks showed character and intelligence. And the red wellies set it all off nicely.

Banks smiled. 'Do I have to throw you off the bridge into the river before I can cross, like Robin Hood did to Little John?'

'I think you'll find it was the other way round, but you could try it,' she said. Then, after they had scrutinized one another for a few seconds, she squinted, frowned, and said, 'You'll be DCI Banks, then?'

She didn't appear nervous or embarrassed about mistaking him for a sightseer; there was no hint of apology or deference in her tone. He didn't know whether he liked that. 'DS Cabbot, I presume?'

'Yes, sir.' She smiled. It was no more than a twitch of one corner of her mouth and a brief flash of light behind her eyes, but it left an impression. Many people, Banks mused, probably thought it was nice to be smiled at by DS Cabbot. Which made him all the more suspicious of Jimmy Riddle's motives for sending him out here.

'And these people?' Banks pointed to the man and woman talking to the uniformed policeman. The man was aiming a video camera at the outbuilding.

'Colleen Harris and James O'Grady, sir. They were scouting the location for a TV programme when they saw the boy fall through the roof. They ran to help him. Seems they also had their camera handy. I suppose it'll make a nice little item on the evening news.' She scratched the side of her nose. 'We'd run out of crime-scene tape, sir. At the section station. To be honest, I'm not sure we ever had any in the first place.' She toyed with the sunglasses as she spoke, but Banks didn't think it was out of nervousness. She had a slight West Country burr, not very pronounced, but clear enough to be noticeable.

'There's nothing we can do about the TV people now,' Banks said. 'They might even be useful. You'd better explain what happened. All I know is that a boy discovered some old bones here.'

DS Cabbot nodded. 'Adam Kelly. He's thirteen.'

'Where is he?'

'I sent him home. To Harkside. He seemed a bit shaken up, and he'd bruised his wrist and elbow. Nothing serious. Anyway, he wanted his mummy, so I got PC Cameron over there to drive him and then come back. Poor kid'll be having nightmares for months as it is.'

'What happened?'

'Adam was walking on the roof and it gave way under him. Lucky he didn't break his back, or get crushed to death.' She pointed at the outbuilding. 'The rafters that helped support the flagstones must have rotted, all those years under water. It didn't take much weight. I should think the demolition men were supposed to pull the whole place down before it was flooded, but they must have knocked off early that day.'

Banks looked around. 'It does seem as if they cut a few corners.'

'Why not? They probably thought no one would ever see the place again. Who can tell what's there when it's all under water? Anyway, the mud broke Adam's fall, his arm got stuck in it, and he pulled up a skeleton of a hand.'

'Human?'

'Don't know, sir. I mean, it *looks* human to me, but we'll need an expert to be certain. I've read that it's easy to mistake bear paws for human hands.'

'*Bear paws*? When was the last time you saw a bear around these parts?'

'Why, just last week, sir.'

Banks paused a moment, saw the glint in her eye and smiled. There was something about this woman that intrigued him. Nothing in her tone hinted at self-doubt or uncertainty about her actions. Most junior police officers, when questioned about their actions by a senior, generally either let a little of the 'Did I do the right thing, sir?' creep into their tone, or they became defensive. Susan Gay, his old DC, had been like that. But there was none of this with DS Cabbot. She simply stated things as they had occurred, decisions as she had made them, and something about the way she did it made her sound completely self-assured and self-possessed without being at all arrogant or insubordinate. Banks found her disconcerting.

'Right,' he said, 'let's go have a look.'

DS Cabbot folded up her sunglasses, slipped them in

her shoulder bag and led the way. Banks followed her to the outbuilding. She moved with a sort of loose-limbed grace, the way cats do whenever it's not feeding time.

On his way, he stopped and talked briefly to the TV people. They couldn't tell him much, except that they'd been exploring the area when they saw the lad fall through the roof. They rushed over immediately, and when they got to him they saw what he'd pulled up out of the earth. He hadn't seemed particularly grateful for their assistance, they said, or even pleased to see them, but they were relieved he wasn't seriously hurt. True to their profession, they asked Banks if he would mind giving them a comment for the tape. He declined politely, citing lack of information. As soon as he had turned away, the woman was on her mobile to the local news channel. It didn't sound like the first time she'd called, either.

The outbuilding was about six or seven feet square. Banks stood in the doorway and looked at the depression in the mud where the boy had landed, then at the two heavy slabs of stone on either side. DS Cabbot was right; Adam Kelly had been very lucky indeed. There were more slabs strewn around on the floor, too, many of them broken, some just fragments sticking up out of the mud. He could easily have landed on one and snapped his spine. Still, when you're that young, you think you're immortal. Banks and his friends certainly had, even after Phil Simpkins wrapped his rope all the way around a tree trunk, jumped off the top branch and spiralled all the way down on to the pointed metal railings.

Banks shook off the memory and concentrated on the scene before him. The sun shone on the top part of the far wall; the stone glistened, moist and slimy. There was a brackish smell about the place, Banks noticed, though there was no salt water for miles, and a smell of dead fish, which were probably a lot closer.

'See what I mean, sir?' said DS Cabbot. 'Because the roof kept the sun out, it's a lot more muddy in here than outside.' She swept some stray tresses from her cheek with a quick flick of her hand. 'Probably saved the kid's life.'

Banks's gaze alighted on the skeletal hand curled around the edge of a broken stone slab. It looked like a creature from a horror film trying to claw its way out of the grave. The bones were dark and clotted with mud, but it looked like a human hand to Banks.

'We'd better get some experts in to dig this place out,' he said. 'Then we'll need a forensic anthropologist. In the meantime, I haven't had my tea yet. Is there somewhere nearby we might be able to get a bite?'

'The Black Swan in Harkside's your best bet. Will you be wanting Adam Kelly's address?'

'Have you eaten?'

'No, but—'

'You can come with me, then, fill me in over a meal. I can have a chat with young Adam in the morning, when he's had time to collect himself. PC Cameron can hold the fort here.'

DS Cabbot glanced down at the skeletal hand.

'Come on,' Banks said. 'There's nothing more we can do here. This poor bugger's probably been dead longer than we've been alive.'

●

Vivian Elmsley felt bone-weary when she finally got home from the signing. She put her briefcase down in the hall and walked through to the living room. Most people would have been surprised at the modern chrome-and-glass decor in the home of a person as old as Vivian, but she far preferred it to all the dreadfully twee antiques, knick-knacks and restored woodwork that cluttered up most old people's houses – at least the ones she had seen. The only painting that adorned her plain white walls hung over the narrow glass mantelpiece, a framed print of a Georgia O'Keeffe flower, overwhelming in its yellowness and intimidating in its symmetry.

First, Vivian opened the windows to let in some air, then she poured a stiff gin and tonic and made her way to her favourite armchair. Supported by chrome tubes, upholstered in black leather, it leaned back at just the right angle to make reading, drinking or watching television sinfully comfortable.

Vivian glanced at the clock, all its polished brass-and-silver inner workings exposed by the glass dome. Almost nine. She would watch the news first. After that, she would have her bath and read Flaubert.

She reached for the remote control. After the best part of a lifetime's writing in longhand, with only an old walnut-cabinet wireless to provide entertainment, she had given in to technology five years ago. In one glorious shopping spree the day after she received a large advance from her new American publisher, she went out and bought herself a television, a VCR, a stereo system and the computer she now used to write her books.

She put her feet up and clicked on the remote control. The news was the usual rubbish. Politics, for the most part, a little murder, famine in Africa, a botched assassination attempt in the Middle East. She didn't know why she bothered watching it. Then, towards the end, came one of those little human-interest bites they use to fill up the time.

This one made Vivian sit up and take notice.

The camera panned a cluster of familiar ruins as the voice-over explained that the drought had brought this lost Dales village of Hobb's End to light for the first time since it had been officially flooded in 1953. She already knew that – this was the same film footage they had used when the story first made it to television about a month ago – but suddenly the angle changed, and she could see a group of people standing by the bridge, one of them a uniformed policeman.

'Today,' the voice-over went on, 'a young boy exploring the scene discovered something he hadn't bargained for.'

The narrator's tone was light, fluffy, the way so many of the cosy mysteries Vivian detested made light of the real world of murder. It was a mystery worthy of Miss Marple, he went on, a skeleton discovered, not in a cupboard, folks, but under the muddy floor of an old outbuilding. How could it have got there? Was foul play suspected?

Vivian clutched the cool chrome tubes at the sides of her armchair as she watched, gin and tonic forgotten on the glass table beside her.

The camera focused on the outbuilding, and Vivian saw the man and woman standing on the threshold. The narrator went on about the police arriving at the scene and refusing to comment at this early stage, then he brought the piece to a close by saying they'd be keeping an eye on the situation.

The programme was well into the weather by the time Vivian had recovered from the shock. Even then, she found that her hands were still gripping the chrome so tightly, even her liver spots had turned white.

She let go, let her body sag in the chair, and took a deep

breath. Then she reached for her gin and tonic, hands shaking now, and managed to take a gulp without spilling it. That helped.

When she felt a little calmer, she went into the study and dug through her filing cabinet for the manuscript she had written in the early 1970s, three years after her last visit to Thornfield Reservoir. She found the sheaf of papers and carried it back through to the living room.

It had never been intended for publication. In many ways, it had been a practice piece, one she had written when she became interested in writing after her husband's death. She had written it when she thought the old adage 'Write about what you know' meant 'Write about your own life, your own experiences.' It had taken her a few years to work out that that was not the case. She still wrote about what she knew – guilt, grief, pain, madness – only now she put it into the lives of her characters.

As she started to read, she realized she wasn't sure exactly *what* it was. A memoir? A novella? Certainly there was *some* truth in it; at least she had tried to stick to the facts, had even consulted her old diaries for accuracy. But because she had written it at a time in her life when she had been unclear about the blurred line between auto-biography and fiction, she couldn't be sure which was which. Would she see it any more clearly now? There was only one way to find out.

•

Banks had never been to Harkside before. DS Cabbot led the way in her metallic purple Astra, and he followed her along the winding one-way streets lined with limestone and gritstone Dales cottages with small, colourful gardens behind low walls. Many of the houses that opened directly on to the street had window boxes or baskets of red and gold flowers hanging outside.

They parked beside the village green, where a few scattered trees provided shade for the benches. Old people sat in the late-summer dusk as the shadows grew long, wrinkled hands resting on knobbly walking sticks, talking to other old people or just watching the world go by. At the centre of the green stood a small, obelisk-style war memorial listing the names of Harkside's dead over the two world wars.

The essentials were arrayed around the green: a KwikSave minimart, which from its oddly ornate façade looked as if it had once been a cinema, a Barclay's Bank, newsagent's, butcher's, grocer's, betting shop, Oddbins Wines, a fifteenth-century church and three pubs, one of them the Black Swan. Though Harkside had a population of only between two and three thousand, it was the largest place for some miles, and people from the more remote farms and hamlets still viewed it as the closest thing to the big city, full of sin and temptation. It was simply a large village, but most local people referred to it as 'town'.

'Where's the section station?' Banks asked.

DS Cabbot pointed down a side-street.

'The place that looks like a brick garage? The one with the flat roof?'

'That's the one. Ugliest building in town.'

'Do you live here?'

'For my sins, yes, sir.'

It was just a saying, Banks knew, but he couldn't help wondering what those sins were. Just imagining them gave him a little thrill of delight.

They walked over to the Black Swan, a whitewash-and-timber façade with gables and a sagging slate roof. It was dim inside, but still too warm, despite the open door and windows. Though a few tourists and ramblers lingered over after-dinner drinks at the rickety wooden tables, it was long past their bedtime. Banks walked to the bar with DS Cabbot, who asked the bartender if they could still get food.

'Depends what you want, love,' she said, and pointed to a list on the blackboard.

Banks sighed. The guessing game. He had played it often enough before. You walk in about ten minutes after opening time and ask for something on the menu, only to be told that it's 'off'. After about four or five alternatives, also declared 'off', you finally find something that they just might have. If you're lucky.

This time Banks went through tandoori chicken and chips, venison medallions in a red-wine sauce and chips, and fettucine alfredo and chips before striking gold: beef and Stilton pie. And chips. He hadn't been eating much beef for the past few years, but he had stopped worrying about mad-cow disease lately. If his brain was going to turn to sludge, there wasn't much he could do to stop it at this stage. Sometimes it felt like sludge already.

DS Cabbot ordered a salad sandwich, no chips.

'Diet?' Banks asked, remembering the way Susan Gay used to nibble on rabbit food most of the time.

'No, sir. I don't eat meat. And the chips are cooked in animal fat. There's not a lot of choice.'

'I see. Drink?'

'Like a fish.' She laughed. 'Actually, I'll have a pint of Swan's Down Bitter. I'd recommend it very highly. It's brewed on the premises.'

Banks took her advice and was glad that he did. He had never met a vegetarian beer aficionado before.

'I'll bring your food over when it's ready, dearies,' the woman said. Banks and DS Cabbot took their pints over to a table by the open window. It looked out on the twilit green. The scene had changed: a group of teenagers had supplanted the old men. They leaned against tree trunks smoking, drinking from cans, pushing and shoving, telling jokes, laughing, trying to look tough. Again, Banks thought of Brian. It wasn't such a bad thing, was it, neglecting his architectural studies to pursue a career in music? It didn't mean he'd end up a deadbeat. And if it was a matter of drugs, Brian had probably had enough opportunities to try them already. Banks certainly had by his age.

What really bothered him was his realization that he didn't really *know* his son very well any more. Brian had grown up over the past few years away from home, and Banks hadn't seen much of him. Truth be told, he had spent far more time and energy on Tracy. He had also had his own preoccupations and problems, both at work and at home. Maybe they were on the wane, but they certainly hadn't gone away yet.

If DS Cabbot felt uncomfortable with Banks's brooding silence, she didn't show it. He fished out his cigarettes. Still not bad; he had smoked only five so far that day, despite his row with Brian and Jimmy Riddle's phone call. Cutting out the ones he usually had in the car was a good idea. 'Do you mind?' he asked.

She shook her head.

'Sure?'

'If you're asking whether it'll make me suffer, it will, but I usually manage to control my cravings.'

'Reformed?'

'A year.'

'Sorry.'

'You needn't be. I'm not.'

Banks lit up. 'I'm thinking of stopping soon myself. I've cut down.'

'Best of luck.' DS Cabbot raised her glass, took a sip of beer and smacked her lips. 'Ah, that's good. Do you mind if I ask you something?'

'No.'

She leaned forward and touched the hair at his right temple. 'What's that?'

'What? The scar?'

'No. The blue bit. I didn't think DCIs went in for dye jobs.'

Banks felt himself blush. He touched the spot she had indicated. 'It must be paint. I was painting my living room when Jimmy Riddle phoned. I thought I'd washed it all off.'

She smiled. 'Never mind. Looks quite nice, actually.'

'Maybe I should get an earring to go with it?'

'Better not go *too* far.'

Banks gestured out of the window. 'Get much trouble?' he asked.

'The kids? Nah, not a lot. Bit of glue-sniffing, some vandalism. Mostly they're bored. It's just adolescent high spirits.'

Banks nodded. At least Brian wasn't bored and shiftless. He had a direction he passionately wanted to head in. Whether it was the right one or not was another matter. Banks tried to concentrate on the job at hand. 'I called my sergeant on the way here,' he said. 'He'll organize a SOCO team to dig out the bones tomorrow morning. A bloke called John Webb will be in charge. He's studied archaeology. Goes on digs for his holidays, so he ought to know what he's doing. I've also phoned our odontologist, Geoff Turner, and asked him to have a look at the teeth as soon as it can be arranged. You can phone around the universities in the morning, see if you can come up with a friendly forensic anthropologist. These people are pretty keen, as a rule, so I don't think that'll be a problem. In the meantime,' he said as his smoke curled and twisted out of the window, 'tell me all about Thornfield Reservoir.'

DS Cabbot leaned back in her chair and crossed her legs at the ankles, resting the beer glass against her flat stomach. She had swapped her red wellies for a pair of white sandals, and her jeans rode up to reveal tapered ankles, bare except for a thin gold chain around the left one. Banks had never seen anyone manage to look quite so comfortable in a hard pub chair. He wondered again what she could possibly have done to end up in such a God-forsaken outpost as Harkside. Was she another of Jimmy Riddle's pariahs?

'It's the most recent of the three reservoirs built along the River Rowan,' she began. 'Linwood and Harksmere were both created in the late-nineteenth century to supply Leeds with extra water. It's piped from the reservoirs to the big waterworks just outside the city, then it's purified and pumped into people's homes.'

'But Harksmere and Thornfield are in *North* Yorkshire, not West Yorkshire. West Riding, I suppose it was back then. Even so, why should they be supplying water to Leeds?'

'I don't know how it came about, but some sort of deal was struck between North Yorkshire and the Leeds City Council for the land use. That's why we're not part of the park.'

'What do you mean?'

'Rowandale. Nidderdale, too. We're not part of the Yorkshire Dales National Park, though we should be if you go by geography and natural beauty. It's because of the water. Nobody wanted to have to deal with National Parks Commission's rules and regulations, so it was easier just to exclude us.'

Like Eastvale, Banks thought. Because it was just beyond the park's border, the severe building restrictions that operated *inside* the Yorkshire Dales National Park didn't apply. Consequently, you ended up with monstrosities like the East Side Estate, with its ugly tower blocks and maisonettes, and the new council estate just completed down by Gallows View: 'Gibbet Acres', as everyone was calling it at the station.

Their meals arrived. Banks stubbed out his cigarette. 'What about Thornfield?' he asked after he had swallowed his first bite. The pie was good, tender beef and just enough Stilton to complement it. 'How long has it been there? What happened to the village?'

'Thornfield Reservoir was created in the early fifties, around the time the national parks system was established, but the village had already been empty a few years by then. Since the end of the war, I think. Used to have a population of around three or four hundred. It wasn't called Thornfield; it was called Hobb's End.'

'Why?'

'Beats me. There's no Hobb in its history, as far as anyone knows, and it wasn't the end of anything – except maybe civilization as we know it.'

'How long was the village there?'

'No idea. Since medieval times, probably. Most of them have been.'

'Why was it empty? What drove people away?'

'Nothing drove them away. It just died. Places do, like people. Did you notice that big building at the far west end?'

'Yes.'

'That was the flax mill. It was the village's raison d'être in the nineteenth century. The mill owner, Lord Clifford, also owned the land and the cottages. Very feudal.'

'You seem to be an expert, but you don't sound as if you come from these parts.'

'I don't. I read up on the area when I came here. It's got quite an interesting history. Anyway, the flax mill started to lose business – too much competition from bigger operations and from abroad – then old Lord Clifford died and his son wanted nothing to do with the place. This was just after the Second World War. Tourism wasn't such big business in the Dales back then, and you didn't get absentees buying up all the cottages for holiday rentals. When someone moved out, if nobody else wanted to move in, the cottage was usually left empty and soon fell to rack and ruin. People moved away to the cities or to the other dales. Finally, the new Lord Clifford sold the land to Leeds Corporation Waterworks. They rehoused the remaining tenants, and that was that. Over the next few years, the engineers moved in and prepared the site, then they created the reservoir.'

'Why that site in particular? There must be plenty of places to build reservoirs.'

'Not really. It's partly because the other two were nearby and it was easier for the engineers to add one to the string. That way they could control the levels better. But mostly I imagine it's to do with water tables and bedrock and such. There's a lot of limestone in the Dales, and apparently you can't build reservoirs on that sort of limestone. It's permeable. The Rowan Valley bottom's made of something else, something hard. It's all to do with faults and extrusions. I'm afraid I've forgotten most of my school geology.'

'Me, too. When did you say all this happened?'

'Between the end of the Second World War and the early fifties. I can check the exact dates back at the station.'

'Please.' Banks paused and tasted some beer. 'So our body, if indeed there is one, and if it's human, has to have been down there since before the early fifties?'

'Unless someone put it there this summer.'

'I'm no expert, but from what I've seen so far, it looks older than that.'

'It could have been moved from somewhere else. Maybe when the reservoir dried up, someone found a better hiding place for a body they already had.'

'I suppose it's possible.'

'Whatever happened, I doubt that whoever buried it there would have put on a frogman's outfit and swum down.'

'Whoever *buried* it?'

'Oh, yes, sir. I'd say it was buried, wouldn't you?'

Banks finished his pie and pushed the rest of the chips aside. 'Go on.'

'The stone slabs. Maybe the body *could* have got covered by two or three feet of earth without much help. Maybe. I mean, we don't know how much things shifted and silted down there over the last forty years or more. We also don't know yet whether the victim was wearing concrete wellies. But it beats me how a body could have got under those stone slabs on the outbuilding floor without a little human intervention, don't you think, sir?'

●

It was a blustery afternoon in April 1941, when she appeared in our shop for the first time. Even in her land girl uniform, the green V-neck pullover, biscuit-coloured blouse, green tie and brown corduroy knee breeches, she looked like a film star.

She wasn't very tall, perhaps about five foot two or three, and the drab uniform couldn't hide the kind of figure I've heard men whistle at in the street. She had a pale, heart-shaped face, perfectly proportioned nose and mouth, and the biggest, deepest, bluest eyes I had ever seen. Her blond hair cascaded from her brown felt hat, which she wore at a jaunty angle and held on with one hand as she walked in from the street.

I was immediately put in mind of Hardy's novel, *A Pair of Blue Eyes*, which I had read only a few weeks previously. Like Elfride Swancourt's, this land girl's eyes were 'a sublimation of her'. They were 'a misty and shady blue, that had no beginning or surface . . . looked *into* rather than *at*'. Those eyes also had a way of making you feel you were the only person in the world when she talked to you.

'Nasty out, isn't it? I don't suppose you've got five Woodbines for sale, have you?' she asked.

I shook my head. 'Sorry,' I said. 'We don't have any cigarettes at all.' It was one of the toughest times we'd had in the war thus far: the Luftwaffe was bombing our cities to ruins; the U-boats were sinking Atlantic convoys at an alarming rate; and the meat ration had just been dropped to only one and tenpence a week. But here she was, bold as brass, a stranger, walking into the shop and without a by-your-leave asking for cigarettes!

I was lying, of course. We did have cigarettes, but what small supply we had we kept under the counter for our registered customers. We certainly didn't go selling them to strange and beautiful land girls with eyes out of Thomas Hardy novels.

I was just on the point of telling her to try fluttering her eyelashes at one of the airmen knocking about the village – holding my tongue never having been my strongest point – when she totally disarmed me with a sequence of reactions.

First she thumped the counter with her little fist and cursed. Then, a moment later, she bit the corner of her lower lip and broke into a bright smile. 'I didn't think you would have,' she said, 'but it was worth asking. I ran out the day before yesterday and I'm absolutely gasping for a fag. Oh, well, can't be helped.'

'Are you the new land girl at Top Hill Farm?' I asked, curious now, and beginning to feel more than a little guilty about my deceit.

She smiled again. 'Word gets around quickly, doesn't it?'

'It's a small village.'

'So I see. Anyway, that's me. Gloria Stringer.' Then she held her hand out. I thought it rather an odd gesture for a woman, especially around these parts, but I took it. Her hand was soft and slightly moist, like a summer leaf after rain. Mine felt coarse and heavy wrapped around such a delicate thing. I always was an ungainly and awkward child, but never did I feel this so much as during that first meeting with Gloria. 'Gwen Shackleton,' I muttered, more than a trifle embarrassed. 'Pleased to meet you.'

Gloria rested her hand palm down on the counter, cocked one hip forward and looked around. 'Not a lot to do around here, is there?' she said.

I smiled. 'Not a lot.' I knew what she meant, of course, but it still struck me as an odd, even insensitive, thing to say. I got up at six o'clock every morning to run the shop, and on top of that I spent one night a week fire-watching – a bit of a joke around these parts until the Spinner's Inn was burned down by a stray incendiary bomb in February and two people were killed. I also helped with the local Women's Voluntary Service. Most days, after the nine o'clock news, I was exhausted and ready to fall asleep the minute my head hit the pillow.

I had heard how hard a land girl's job was, of course, but to judge by her appearance, especially those soft hands, you would swear that Gloria Stringer had never done a day's hard physical labour in her life. My first thought was an uncharitable one. Knowing farmer Kilnsey's wandering eye, I thought that, perhaps, when his wife wasn't around, he was teaching Gloria a new way of ploughing the furrow. Though I wasn't quite sure what that meant, being only sixteen at the time, I had heard more than one or two farmers use the phrase when they thought I was out of earshot.

But in this, as in most of my first impressions about Gloria, I was quite wrong. This freshness in her appearance was simply one of her many remarkable qualities. She could spend the day hay-making, threshing, pea-pulling, milking, snagging turnips, yet always appear fresh and alive, with energy to spare, as if, unlike the rest of us mere mortals, she had some sort of invisible shield around her through which the hard diurnal toil couldn't penetrate.

On first impressions, I have to confess that I did not like Gloria Stringer; she struck me as being vain, common, shallow and selfish. Not to mention beautiful, of course. That hurt, especially.

Then, wouldn't you know it, but right in the middle of our conversation, Michael Stanhope had to walk in.

Michael Stanhope was something of a character around the village, to put it mildly. A reasonably successful artist, somewhere, I'd guess, in his early fifties, he affected a rakish appearance and seemed deliberately to go out of his way to offend people.

That day, he was wearing a rumpled white linen suit over a grubby lavender shirt and a crooked yellow bow-tie. He also wore his ubiquitous broad-brimmed hat and carried a cane with a snake-head handle. As usual, he looked quite dissipated. His eyes were bloodshot, he had at least three days' stubble on his face, and he emanated a sort of general fug of stale smoke and alcohol.

A lot of people didn't like Michael Stanhope because he wasn't afraid to say what he thought and he spoke out against the war. I quite liked him, in a way, though I didn't agree with his views. Half the time he only said what he did to annoy people, like complaining that he couldn't get canvas for his paintings because the army was using it all. That wasn't true at all.

But he would have to walk in right then.

'Good morning, my cherub,' he said, as he always did, though I felt far from cherubic. 'I trust you have my usual?'

'Er, sorry, Mr Stanhope,' I stammered. 'We're all out.'

'All out? Come, come now, girl, that can't be.' He grinned and looked over at Gloria mischievously. Then he winked at her.

'I'm sorry, Mr Stanhope.'

'I'll bet if you looked in the usual place,' he said, leaning forward and rapping on the counter with his cane, 'you would find them.'

I knew when I was beaten. Mortified, blushing to the roots of my being, I reached under the counter and brought out the two packets of Piccadilly I had put aside for him, the way I always did whenever we were lucky enough to get some in.

'That'll be one and eight, please,' I said.

'Outrageous,' Mr Stanhope complained as he dug out the coins, 'the way this government is taxing us to death to make war. Don't you think so, my cherub?'

I muttered something noncommittal.

All the while Gloria had been watching our little display with growing fascination. When I glanced at her guiltily as I handed over the cigarettes to Mr Stanhope, she smiled at me and shrugged.

Mr Stanhope must have caught the gesture. He was always quick to sense any new nuance or current in the atmosphere. He fed on that sort of thing.

'Ah, I *see*,' he said, turning his gaze fully towards Gloria and admiring her figure quite openly. 'Do I take it that you were inquiring after cigarettes yourself, my dear?'

Gloria nodded. 'As a matter of fact, I was.'

'Well,' said Mr Stanhope, putting the brass snake-head of his cane to his chin as he reflected, 'I'll tell you what. As I very much approve of women smoking, perhaps we can come to some sort of arrangement. I have but one stipulation.'

'Oh,' said Gloria, crossing her arms and narrowing her eyes. 'And what might that be?'

'That you smoke in the street every now and then.'

Gloria stared at him for a moment, then she started to laugh. 'That won't be a problem,' she said. 'I can assure you.'

And he handed her one of the packets.

I was flabbergasted. There were ten cigarettes in each packet and they weren't cheap or easy to get.

Instead of protesting that she couldn't possibly accept them but thanking him for his generosity anyway, as I would have done, Gloria simply took the packet and said,

'Why, thank you very much, Mr . . .?'

He beamed at her. 'Stanhope. Michael Stanhope. At your service. And it's my pleasure. Believe me, my dear, it's a rare treat indeed to meet a woman as comely as thyself around these parts.' Then he moved a step closer and scrutinized her, quite rudely, I thought, rather like a farmer looking over a horse he was about to buy.

Gloria stood her ground.

When Mr Stanhope had finished, he turned to go, but before the door shut behind him he cast a quick glance over his shoulder at Gloria. 'You know, you really must visit my studio, my dear. See my etchings, as it were.' And with that he was gone, chuckling as he went.

In the silence that followed, Gloria and I stared at one another for a moment, then we both burst out giggling. When we had managed to control ourselves, I told her I was sorry for deceiving her over the cigarettes, but she waved the apology aside. 'You have your regulars to attend to,' she said. 'And these *are* difficult times.'

'I must apologize for Mr Stanhope, too,' I said. 'I'm afraid he can be quite rude.'

'Nonsense,' she said, with that little pixie-ish grin of hers. 'I rather liked him. And he did give me these.'

She opened the packet and offered me a cigarette. I shook my head; I didn't smoke then. She put one in the corner of her mouth and lit it with a small silver lighter she took from her uniform pocket. 'Just as well,' she said. 'I can see these will have to last me a while.'

'I can put some aside for you in future,' I said. 'I mean, I can try. Depending on how many we can get, of course.'

'Would you? Oh, yes, please! That would be wonderful. Now if I might just have a look at that copy of *Picture Goer* over there, the one with Vivien Leigh on the cover. I do so admire Vivien Leigh, don't you? She's so beautiful. Have you seen *Gone With the Wind*? I saw it in the West End before I went on my month's training. Absolutely—'

But before I could get the magazine for her or tell her that *Gone With the Wind* hadn't reached this far north yet, Matthew dashed in.

Gloria turned at the sound of the bell, eyebrows raised in curiosity. When he saw her, my brother stopped in his tracks and fell into her eyes so deeply you could hear the splash.

•

The first thing Banks did when he got back to the cottage that night was check the answering machine. Nothing. Damn it. He wanted to put things right after his miserable cock-up on the phone earlier that day, but he still had no access to Brian's number in Wimbledon. He didn't even know Andrew's last name. He could find out – after all, he was supposed to be a detective – but it would take time, and he could only do it during office hours. Sandra might know, of course, but the last thing he wanted to do was talk to her.

Banks poured himself a whisky, turned off the bright overhead light and switched on the reading lamp by his armchair. He picked up the book he had been reading over the past week, an anthology of twentieth-century poetry, but he couldn't concentrate. The blue walls distracted him, and the smell of paint in the deep silence of the countryside made him feel lonely and restless. He turned on the radio. Someone was playing the first movement of Tchaikovsky's Violin Concerto.

Banks glanced around the room. The walls did look good; they harmonized well with the ceiling, which he had painted the colour of ripe Brie. Maybe they were just a little too cold, he thought, though he needed all the air-conditioning he could get in this weather. He could always repaint them orange or red in winter, when the ice and snow came, and that would give the illusion of warmth.

He lit the last cigarette of the day and took his drink outside. The cottage stood on a narrow, unpaved laneway about fifty yards west of Gratly. Opposite Banks's front door was a sort of bulge in the low wall that ran between the lane and Gratly Beck. In the daytime, it was an ideal spot for ramblers to stop for a moment and admire the falls, but at night there was never anyone there. The lane wasn't a through road, and there was plenty of room for Banks to park his car there. Just beyond the cottage, it dwindled to a public footpath, which ran between the woods and the side of Gratly Beck.

Banks had come to see this area as his personal veranda, and he liked to stand out there or sit on the low wall dangling his legs over the edge late in the evening, when it was quiet. It helped him think, get things sorted.

Tonight, the stone was still warm; the smoke on his tongue tasted sweet as fresh-mown hay. A sheep bleated high on the daleside, where the silhouetted falls were only a shade or two blacker than the night itself. Sharp starlight pricked the satin sky, along with the lights of a distant farmhouse; a gibbous moon hung over Helmthorpe, in the valley bottom, and the square church tower, with its ancient weather-vane, stood solid against the night. This must have been what the blackout was like, Banks thought, remembering his mother's stories of getting around London during the Blitz.

As Banks sat by the dried-up waterfalls, he thought again about the odd way he had come to live in this isolated limestone cottage. It was a 'dream cottage' in more than one way: though he had never told anyone this, he had actually bought it because of a dream.

Over his last few months alone in the Eastvale semi, Banks had drifted so far from himself that he hadn't even cleaned or tidied the place since Christmas. Why bother? He spent most of his evenings out in pubs or driving the countryside alone, anyway, and his nights falling asleep half-drunk on the sofa, listening to Mozart or Bob Dylan, fish-and-chips wrappers and take-away cartons piling up in an ever-widening circle around him.

In April he seemed to reach his lowest ebb. Tracy, who had been to visit her mother in London that Easter weekend, let it slip over the telephone that there was a new man in Sandra's life, a photojournalist called Sean, and that they seemed serious. He looked *young*, Tracy said. Which was a hell of a compliment coming from a nineteen-year-old. Banks immediately began to wonder just how long this affair had been going on *before* he and Sandra separated last November. He asked Tracy, but she said she didn't know. She also seemed upset that Banks would even suggest it, so he backed off.

As a result, Banks was more full of anger and self-pity than usual that night. Whenever he thought of Sean, which was far more often than he would have liked, he wanted to kill him. He even considered phoning an old mate on the Met and asking if they couldn't put the bastard away for something. There were plenty of coppers on the Met who would jump at the chance to put someone called *Sean* away. But while he had certainly bent the rules occasionally, Banks had never yet abused his position for his own ends, and even at his lowest ebb he wasn't going to start.

His hatred was unreasonable, he knew, but when was

hatred ever reasonable? He had never even met Sean. Besides, if Sandra wanted to pick up some toy boy and take him home to her bed, it was hardly the toy boy's fault, was it? More likely hers. But reason didn't stop Banks from wanting to kill the bastard.

That night, after several whiskies too many, he had fallen asleep on the sofa as usual, with Dylan's *Blood on the Tracks* playing on the CD. Long after the music had finished, he woke from a dream peculiar only for its emotional intensity.

He was sitting alone at a pine table in a kitchen, and sunlight flooded through the open curtains, bathing everything in its warm and honeyed glow. The walls were off-white, with a strip of red tiles over the sink and counter area; matching red canisters for coffee, tea and sugar stood on the white Formica countertops, and copper-bottomed pots and pans hung from a wooden rack beside the set of kitchen knives. The clarity of detail was extraordinary; every grain and knot-hole in the wood, every nuance of light on steel or copper shone with a preternatural brightness. He could even smell the warm pine from the table and the fitted cupboards, the oil on the hinges.

That was it. Nothing happened. Just a dream of light. But the intense feeling of well-being it gave him, as warm and bright as the sunlight itself, still suffused him when he awoke, disappointed to find himself alone and hung over on the sofa in the Eastvale semi.

When Sandra decided a few weeks later that their separation was to be permanent – or at least that reconciliation wasn't imminent – they sold the semi. Sandra got the television and VCR; Banks got the stereo and the lion's share of the CD collection. That was fair; he had collected them in the first place. They split the kitchenware, and for some obscure reason, Sandra also took the tin opener. Books and clothes were easily divided, and they sold most of the furniture. All in all, there hadn't been a hell of a lot to show for over twenty years of marriage. Even after the sale, Banks didn't care much where or how he lived, until a few weeks in a bed-and-breakfast place straight out of Bill Bryson changed his mind.

He began to seek isolation. When he first saw the cottage from the outside, he didn't think much of it. The view of the dale was terrific, as was the seclusion afforded by the woods, the beck, and the ash grove between the cottage and Gratly itself, but it was a squat, ugly little place that needed a lot of work.

A typical Dales mix of limestone, grit and flag, it had originally been a farm labourer's cottage. Carved into the gritstone doorhead was the date '1768' and the initials 'J.H.', probably the time it was built and the initials of the first owner. Banks wondered who J.H. was and what had become of him. Mrs Perkins, the present owner, had lost both her two sons and her husband, and she was finally leaving to move in with her sister in Tadcaster.

Inside, the place didn't make much more of an impression at first, either; it smelled of camphor and mould, and all the furniture and decor seemed dark and dingy. Downstairs was a living room with a stone fireplace at one end; upstairs, only two small bedrooms. The bathroom and toilet had been tacked on to the kitchen at the back, as they often were in such old houses. Plumbing was pretty primitive back in 1768.

Banks was not a believer in visions and prescience, but he would have been a fool to deny that when he walked into the kitchen that day he experienced the same feeling of well-being and of peace that he had experienced in the dream. It looked different, of course, but he *knew* it was the same place, the one in his dream.

What it all meant, he had no idea, except that he had to have the cottage.

He didn't think he would be able to afford it; properties in the Dales were fetching astronomical prices. But fortune and human eccentricity proved to be on his side for once. Mrs Perkins had no love whatsoever for the holiday-cottage trade and no particular greed for mere money. She wanted to sell to someone who would actually *live* in the cottage. As soon as she found out that Banks was looking for just such a place, and that his name was the same as her maiden name, the deal was as good as done. The only black mark against Banks was that he wasn't *born* a Yorkshireman, but she took to him anyway, convinced they were related, and she even flirted with him in that way some old ladies have.

When she let him have the place for £50,000, probably about half of what she could have got, telling him it would be enough to see her to her grave, Dimmoch, the estate agent, groaned and shook his head in disbelief. Afterwards, Banks always had the impression that Dimmoch suspected him of exerting undue pressure on Mrs Perkins.

The cottage became Banks's long-term project – his therapy, his refuge and, he hoped, his salvation. In an odd way he felt working on the cottage was like working on himself. Both needed renovating, and both had a long way to go. It was all new to him; he had never had the faintest interest in DIY or gardening before; nor had he been much inclined to self-analysis or introspection. But somehow he had lost his way over the past year, and he wanted to find a new one; he had also lost something of himself, and he wanted to know what it was. So far, he had fitted some pine cupboards in the kitchen, like the ones in his dream, installed a shower unit to replace the claw-footed Victorian bathtub, and painted the living room. It hadn't kept the depression away completely, but made it more manageable; at least he always managed to drag himself out of bed in the morning now, even if he didn't always view the day ahead with any real relish.

A night bird called out far in the distance – a broken, eerie cry, as if perhaps some predator was threatening its nest. Banks stubbed out his cigarette and went back inside. As he got ready for bed, he thought of the skeletal hand, possibly human; he thought of DS Cabbot, definitely human; he thought of Hobb's End, that lost, ruined village suddenly risen from the depths with its secrets; and somewhere in his mind, in the darkness way beyond the realms of logic and reason, he heard an echo, a click, felt something intangible connect across the years.

3

Banks watched from the edge of the woods the next morning as the SOCOs slowly lifted the skeleton from its muddy grave under the expert direction of John Webb.

First, they had to take down the wall next to which the bones were buried, then they made a trench around the area and dug down until the bones were exposed, about three feet below the surface. Next, they slipped a thin sheet of metal into the earth under the bones, and finally they got it in place, ready to lift out.

The bones came up on the metal sheet, still packed in earth, and four SOCO pallbearers carried it up the slope, where they laid it out on the grass at Banks's feet like a burnt offering. It was just eleven, and DS Cabbot still hadn't shown up. Banks had already talked to Adam Kelly, who hadn't been able to add anything to his previous statement.

Adam was still shaken, but Banks sensed a resilience in him that he had also possessed as an early adolescent. Banks, too, had loved playing in derelict houses, of which there had been plenty in postwar Peterborough. The worst he had ever come away with was a scraped knee, but a pupil from the girls' school had been killed by a falling rafter, so he knew how dangerous they could be. The council was always boarding them up. Anyway, Adam's little adventure had done no lasting harm, and it would give him stories to tell well into the school term. He would enjoy celebrity status of a kind among his pals for a while.

Banks stared at the filthy, twisted shape at his feet. It hardly *looked* human. The bones had taken on the muddy brown colour of the earth they had lain in for so long; they were also crusted with dark, grungy muck. It stuck to the ribs the way a hearty stew was supposed to do, and it clung to various joints, clogging the cavities and crevices. The skull looked full of it – mud in the mouth, the nose, the eye sockets – and some of the long bones looked like old rusted metal pipes that had been underground for years.

The sight of it made Banks feel vaguely sick. He had seen much worse without throwing up, of course – at least there were no gaping red holes, no spilled intestines, no legs cut off at the thighs, skin riding up over the raw edges like a tight skirt – but he hadn't seen much uglier.

The SOCOs had already photographed the skeleton during every stage of its excavation, and once they had finished carrying it up the hill they went back down and started their detailed search of the area, digging deeper and farther afield, leaving John Webb to give it a poke here and a scrape there. Webb also searched through the dirt for any objects that had been buried at the same time – buttons, jewellery, that sort of thing.

Banks leaned back against a tree trunk, as if on sentry duty, kept his nausea under control and watched Webb work. He was tired; he had not slept well after his late-night musings. Most of the night he had tossed and turned, waking up often from fragments of nightmares that scuttled off into dark corners when he woke, like cockroaches when you turn on the light. The morning heat made him drowsy. Giving in to the feeling for a moment, he closed his eyes and rested his head on the tree. He could feel the rough bark against his crown, and the sunlight made kaleidoscopic patterns behind his eyelids. He was at the edge of sleep when he heard a rustling behind him, then a voice.

'Morning, sir. Rough night?'

'Something like that,' said Banks, moving away from the tree trunk.

DS Cabbot stared down at the bones. 'So this is what we all come to in the end, is it?' She didn't sound particularly concerned about it; no more troubled than she seemed about turning up so late.

'Any luck?' Banks asked.

'That's what took me so long. The university year hasn't started yet and a lot of profs are still away on holiday, or busy running research projects overseas. Anyway, I've tracked down a Dr Ioan Williams, University of Leeds. He's a physical anthropologist with a fair bit of experience in forensic work. He sounded pretty excited by what we've found. Must be having a dull summer.'

'How quickly can he get to it?'

'He said if we could get the remains to the university lab as soon as possible, he'd have his assistants clean them up, then he'd manage a quick look by early evening. Only a preliminary look, mind you.'

'Good,' said Banks. 'The sooner we know what we're dealing with here, the better.'

If the skeleton had been lying there for a hundred years or more, the investigation wouldn't really be worth pursuing with any great vigour, as they would be hardly likely to catch a living criminal. On the other hand, *if* it turned out to be a murder victim, and *if* it had been buried there during or since the war, there was a chance that somebody still living might remember something. And there was also a chance that the killer was still alive.

'Want me to supervise the move?' Webb asked.

Banks nodded. 'If you would, John. Need an ambulance?'

Webb held his hand over his eyes to shield the sun as he looked up. A few of the silver hairs in his beard caught the light. 'My old Range Rover will do just fine. I'll get one of the lads to drive while I stay in the back and make sure our friend here doesn't fall to pieces.' He looked at his watch. 'With any luck, we can have it in the lab by one o'clock.'

DS Cabbot leaned back against a tree, arms folded, one leg crossed over the other. Today she was wearing a red T-shirt and white Nikes with her jeans, her sunglasses pushed up over her hairline. Pretty loose dress codes at Harkside, it seemed to Banks, but then he was one to talk. He had always hated suits and ties, right from his early days as a business student at London Polytechnic. He had spent three years there on a sandwich course – six months' college and six months' work – and the student life fast made encroachments on his dedication to the business world. Everyone at the Poly was joining up with the sixties thing back then, even though it was the early seventies; it was all caftans, bell-bottoms and Afghans, bright embroidered Indian cheese-cloth shirts, bandannas, beads, the whole caboodle. Banks had never committed himself fully to the spirit of the times, neither in philosophy nor in dress, but he had let his hair grow over his collar, and he was once sent home from work for wearing sandals and a flowered tie.

'I need to know a lot more about the village,' he said to DS Cabbot. 'Some names would be a great help. Try the Voters Register and the Land Registry.' He pointed towards the ruins of the cottage near the bridge. 'The outbuilding clearly belonged to that cottage, so I'd like to know who lived there and who the neighbours were. It seems to me that we've got three possibilities. Either we're dealing with someone who used the empty village as a dumping spot to bury a body during the time it was in disuse—'

'Between May 1946 and August 1953. I checked this morning.'

'Right. Either then, or the body was buried while the village was still occupied, before May 1946, and the victim wasn't buried too far from home. Or it was put there this summer, as you suggested earlier. It's too early for speculation, but we do need to know who lived in that cottage before the village emptied out, and if anyone from the village was reported missing.'

'Yes, sir.'

'What happened to the church? I'm assuming there was one.'

'A church and a chapel. St Bartholomew's was deconsecrated, then demolished.'

'Where are the parish records now?'

'I don't know. Never had cause to seek them out. I imagine they were moved to St Jude's in Harkside, along with all the coffins from the graveyard.'

'They might be worth a look if you draw a blank elsewhere. You never know what you can find out from old church records and parish magazines. There's the local newspaper, too. What's it called?'

'The *Harkside Chronicle*.'

'Right. Might be worth looking there too if our expert can narrow the range a bit this evening. And, DS Cabbot?'

'Sir?'

'Look, I can't keep calling you DS Cabbot. What's your first name?'

She smiled. 'Annie, sir. Annie Cabbot.'

'Right, Annie Cabbot, do you happen to know how many doctors or dentists there were in Hobb's End?'

'I shouldn't imagine there were many. Most people probably went to Harkside. Maybe there were a few more around when everyone was working in the flax mill. Very altruistic, very concerned about their workers' welfare, some of these old mill owners.'

'Very concerned they were fit to work a sixteen-hour shift without dropping dead, more like,' said Banks.

Annie laughed. 'Bolshevik.'

'I've been called worse. Try to find out, anyway. It's a long shot, but if we can find any dental records matching the remains, we'll be in luck.'

'I'll look into it, sir. Anything else?'

'Utilities, tax records. They might all have to be checked.'

'And what should I do next year?'

Banks smiled. 'I'm sure you can conscript one of your PCs to help. If we don't get a break soon, I'll see what I can do about manpower, though somehow I doubt this is a high-priority case.'

'Thank you, sir.'

'For now, let's concentrate on the identity of the victim. That's crucial.'

'Okay.'

'Just a thought, but do you happen to know if there's anyone who lived in Hobb's End still alive, maybe living in Harkside now? It doesn't seem an unreasonable assumption.'

'I'll ask Inspector Harmond. He grew up around these parts.'

'Good. I'll leave you to it and see these bones off to Leeds with John.'

'Do you want me to go down there this evening?'

'If you like. Meet me at the lab at six o'clock. Where is it?'

Annie told him.

'In the meantime,' he said, 'here's my mobile number. Give me a ring if you come up with anything.'

'Right you are, sir.' Annie just seemed to touch her sunglasses and they slid down perfectly into place on her nose. With that, she turned and strode off into the woods.

•

Banks was an odd fish, Annie thought as she drove back to Harkside. Of course, before she'd met him she'd heard a few rumours. She knew, for example, that Chief Constable Riddle hated him, that Banks was under a cloud, almost lost *in* the clouds, though she didn't know why. Someone had even hinted at fisticuffs between the two. Whatever the reason, his career was on hold and he was not a good horse to hitch one's wagon to.

Annie had no particular liking for Jimmy Riddle, either. On the one or two occasions she had met him, she had found him arrogant and condescending. Annie was one of Millie's projects – ACC Millicent Cummings, new Director of Human Resources, dedicated to bringing more women into the ranks and seeing that they were well treated – and the antagonism between Millie and Riddle, who had opposed her appointment from the start, was well known. Not that Riddle was especially *for* the ill treatment of women, but he preferred to avoid the problem altogether by keeping their presence among the ranks to an absolute minimum.

Annie had also heard that Banks's wife had left him for

PETER ROBINSON

someone else not too long ago. Not only that, but there
were stories going around that he had a woman in Leeds,
had had for some time, even before his wife left. She had
heard him described as a loner, a skiver and a Bolshie
bastard. He was a brilliant detective gone to seed, they
said, over the hill since his wife left, past it, burned out, a
shadow of his former self.

On first impressions, Annie didn't really know what to
make of him. She thought she liked him. She certainly
found him attractive, and he didn't look much older than
his mid-thirties, despite the scattering of grey at the
temples of his closely cropped black hair. As far as being
burned out was concerned, he seemed tired and he
seemed to carry a burden of sadness in him, but she could
sense that the fire still smouldered somewhere behind his
sharp blue eyes. A little diminished in power, perhaps, but
still there.

On the other hand, perhaps he really *had* lost it, and he
was simply going through the motions, content to shuffle
papers until retirement. Perhaps the fire she sensed in him
was simply embers, not fully extinguished yet, just about
to cave in on themselves. Well, if Annie had learned one
thing over the past couple of years, it was not to jump to
conclusions about anyone: the brave man often appears
weak; the wise man often seems foolish. After all, enough
people thought she was weird, too, and it wouldn't be
hard to argue that she had been merely going through the
motions lately, either. She wondered if there were any
rumours about her going around the region. If there were,
she had a good guess what they would be: dyke bitch.

Annie parked on the strip of Tarmac beside the ugly
brick section station and walked inside. Only four of them
worked directly out of the station: Inspector Harmond,

Annie and PCs Cameron and Gould. Apart from Samantha, their civilian clerk, Annie was the only woman. That was okay with her; they seemed a pretty decent bunch of men, as men go. She certainly felt no threat from any of them. PC Cameron was married with two kids, to whom he was clearly devoted. Gould seemed to be one of those rare types who have no sexual dimension whatsoever, content to live at home with his mum, play with his model trains and add stamps to his album. She knew that in books such types often turn out to be the most dangerous of all, the serial killers and sexual deviants, but Gould was harmless. Even if he liked to wear women's underwear in private, Annie didn't care. Inspector Harmond was, well, *avuncular*. He liked to think of himself as a bit like Sergeant Blaketon out of *Heartbeat*, but he didn't even come close, in Annie's opinion.

Harkside police station might be ugly on the outside but at least inside it was a sparsely populated open-plan office area – apart from Inspector Harmond's office, partitioned off at the far end – and there was plenty of room to spread oneself around. Annie liked that. Her L-shaped desk was the messiest of all, but she knew where everything was and could put her hands on anything anyone asked her for so quickly that even Inspector Harmond had given up teasing her about it.

Annie's desk also took up a corner, part of which included a side window. It wasn't much of a view, only the cobbled alley, a gate and the back wall of the Three Feathers, but at least she was close to a source of light and air, and it was good to be able to see *something* of the outside world. Even if there was hardly any breeze these days, she loved each gentle waft of warm air through the window; it lifted her spirits. These little things mattered so much, Annie had discovered. She had had her shot at the big time, the fast track, with all its excitement, but it had ended badly for her. Now she was slowly rediscovering what mattered in life.

Harkside was generally a law-abiding sort of community, so there wasn't a lot for a detective sergeant to do. There was plenty of paperwork to keep her occupied, make her feel she'd earned her pay, but it was hardly a high-overtime posting, and there were slack periods. That also suited her fine. Sometimes it was good to do nothing. And why should she complain if enough people weren't getting robbed, killed or beaten up?

At the moment she had two domestic-violence cases and a spate of after-dark vandalism on her plate. And now the skeleton. Well, the others could wait. Inspector Harmond had increased patrols in the area most often hit by the vandals, who would probably be caught red-handed before long, and just now the wife-beaters were contrite and arranging to seek help.

Annie headed first to the coffee machine and filled her mug, the one with 'She Who Must Be Obeyed' written on it, then she walked over and knocked on Inspector Harmond's door. He asked her to come in.

'Sir?'

Harmond looked up from his desk. 'Annie. What is it, lass?'

'Got a minute?'

'Aye. Sit down.'

Annie sat. Harmond's was a plain office, with only his merit awards on the wall for decoration, and framed photos of his wife and children on the desk. In his early fifties, he seemed perfectly content to be a rural inspector for the rest of his working life. His head was too large for his gangly frame, and Annie always worried it might fall off if he tilted it too far to one side. It never had; not yet. He had a pleasant round, open face. The features were a bit coarse, and a few black hairs grew out of the end of his misshapen potato nose, but it was the kind of face you could trust. If eyes really were the windows of the soul, then Inspector Harmond had a decent soul.

'It's this skeleton thing,' she said, crossing her legs and cradling her coffee mug on her lap.

'What about it?'

'Well, that's just it, sir. We don't know anything about it just yet. DCI Banks wanted to know how many doctors and dentists lived in Hobb's End, and if anyone who used to live there lives here now.'

Harmond scratched his temple. 'I can answer your last question easily enough,' he said. 'You remember Mrs Kettering, the one whose budgie escaped that time she was having a new three-piece suite delivered?'

'How could I forget?' It had been one of Annie's first cases in Harkside.

Inspector Harmond smiled. 'She lived in Hobb's End. I don't know exactly when or for how long, but I know she lived there. She must be pushing ninety if she's a day.'

'Anyone else?'

'Not that I can think of. Not off-hand, at any rate. Leave it with me, I'll ask around. Remember where she lives?'

'Up on The Edge, isn't it? The corner house with the big garden?'

The Edge was what the locals called the fifty-foot embankment that ran along the south side of Harksmere Reservoir, the road that used to lead over the packhorse bridge to Hobb's End. Its real name was Harksmere View, and it didn't lead anywhere now. Only one row of cottages overlooked the water, separated from the rest of Harkside village by about half a mile of open countryside.

'What about doctors and dentists?' Annie asked.

'That's a bit trickier,' Harmond said. 'There must have been a few over the years, but Lord knows what's happened to them. Seeing as the village cleared out after the war, they're probably all dead now. Remember, lass, I'm not that old. I were still a lad myself when the place emptied out. As far as I remember, there wasn't any village bobby, either. Too small. Hobb's End was part of the Harkside beat.'

'How many schools were there?'

Inspector Harmond scratched his head. 'Just infants and junior, I think. Grammar school and secondary modern were here in Harkside.'

'Any idea where the old records would be?'

'Local education authority, most likely. Unless they were destroyed somehow. A lot of records got destroyed back then, after the war and all. Is there anything else?'

Annie sipped some coffee and stood up. 'Not right now, sir.'

'You'll keep me informed?'

'I will.'

'And, Annie?'

'Yes, sir?'

Harmond scratched the side of his nose. 'This DCI Banks. I've never met him myself, but I've heard a bit about him. What's he like?'

Annie paused at the door and frowned as she thought. 'Do you know, sir,' she said finally, 'I haven't got a clue.'

'Bit of an enigma, then, eh?'

'Yes,' Annie said, 'a bit of an enigma. I suppose you *could* say that.'

'Better watch yourself, then, lass,' she heard him say as she turned to leave.

•

Before I tell you what happened next, let me tell you a little about myself and my village. My name, as you already know, is Gwen Shackleton, which is short for Gwynneth, not for Gwendolyn. I know this sounds Welsh, but my family has lived in Hobb's End, Yorkshire, for at least two generations. My father, God bless his soul, died of cancer three years before the war began, and by 1940 my mother was an invalid, suffering from rheumatoid arthritis. Sometimes she was able to help out in the shop, but not often, so the brunt of the work fell to me.

Matthew helped me as much as he could, but university kept him busy most of the week and the Home Guard took up his weekends. He was twenty-one, but despite the call-up, the Ministry was encouraging him to finish the third year of his engineering degree at the University of Leeds. They believed, I suppose, that his training would come in useful in the forces.

Our little shop was a newsagent's-cum-general store about halfway along the High Street, near the butcher's and the greengrocer's, and we lived above it. We didn't sell perishable goods, just things like newspapers, sweets, cigarettes, stationery, jam and other odds and ends, tea and tinned goods – depending, of course, on what was available at the time. I was especially proud of the little lending library I had built up. Because paper was getting scarce and books were in short supply, I rented them out for tuppence a week. I kept a good selection of World's Classic editions: Anthony Trollope, Jane Austen and Charles Dickens in particular. I also stocked a number of the more sensational novels, Agatha Christie and the Mills and Boon romances, for those who liked such things – unfortunately, the majority of my customers!

Though most of the able-bodied men in the village had joined up and put on one uniform or another, the place had never seemed busier. The old flax mill was operating at full strength again and most of the married women worked there. Before the war, it had practically come to a standstill, but now the military wanted flax to make webbing for parachute harnesses and other things where a tough fibre was needed, like gun tarpaulins and fire hoses.

There was also a big RAF base about a mile or so away through Rowan Woods, and the High Street was often busy with Jeeps and lorries honking their horns and trying to pass one another in the narrow space. The airmen sometimes came to the village pubs – the Shoulder of Mutton just down the High Street, and the Duke of Wellington over the river – except when they went to Harkside, where there was much more to do. We didn't even have one cinema in Hobb's End, for example, but there were three in Harkside.

These things aside, though, it remains difficult to say exactly how much the war affected us in Hobb's End. I think that at first it impinged upon us very little. For those of us left behind, daily life went on much as normal. The first wave of evacuees came in September 1939, but when nothing happened for ages, they all started drifting home again, and we didn't get any more until the bombing started the following August.

Even with rationing, our diets didn't change as much as those of the city folks, for we had always been used to eating plenty of vegetables, and in the country there were always eggs, butter and milk. Our neighbour, Mr Halliwell, the butcher, was probably the most popular man in town, so we were occasionally able to swap any tea and sugar we might put aside for an extra piece of mutton or pork.

Apart from the feeling of waiting, the sense that normal life was suspended until all this was over, perhaps the hardest thing to get used to was the blackout. But even in that we were more fortunate than many, as Hobb's End had no street-lights to begin with, and the countryside is dark enough at the best of times. Still, that pinprick of light on the distant hillside was often the only thing to guide you home.

In the blackout, we had to tape up our windows to prevent damage from broken glass, and we also had to hang up the heavy blackout curtains. Every night, Mother used to send me outside to check that not a sliver of light showed because our local ARP man was a real stickler. I remember the whole village laughing the day we heard Mrs Darnley got a visit from him for blacking out only the front of her house, but not the back windows. 'Don't be so daft,' she told him. 'If the Germans come to bomb Hobb's End, young lad, they'll come from the east, won't they, not by Grassington way. Stands to reason.'

On moonlit nights, especially if there was a full moon, the effect could be spectacular: the hills were dusted with silver powder, the stars glittered like cut diamonds on black velvet, and the whole landscape looked like one of those black-and-white engravings or woodcuts you see in old books. But on cloudy or moonless nights, which seemed far more frequent, people bumped into trees and even cycled into the river with alarming regularity. You could use a torch if you wrapped the light with several layers of tissue paper, but batteries were scarce. All car and bicycle lights had to be hooded and masked with a variety of gadgets that let the light through only in muddied, useless slits. Needless to say, there were a lot of car accidents, too, until petrol became too scarce and nobody drove any more except on business.

Several events made the war more personal for us, such as the Spinner's Inn fire, or the Jowett boy getting killed at Dunkirk, but the day before Gloria Stringer arrived, something hit even closer to home: Matthew got his call-up papers. He was due to report for his medical in Leeds in two weeks.

•

Jimmy Riddle had once accused Banks of skiving off to Leeds to go shagging his mistress and shopping at the Classical Record Shop. He had been wrong that time, but if he had seen Banks nipping out of the Merrion Centre late that afternoon, a new recording of Herbert Howells's *Hymnus Paradisi* clutched in his sweaty palm, Riddle would have felt vindicated at least on one count. Not that Banks gave a toss. He didn't even bother to look furtive as he walked out past Morrison's on to Woodhouse Lane.

It was gone half past five. Shops were closing and office workers were heading home. Banks had driven to Leeds behind John Webb's Range Rover and stayed with him until they got the skeleton set up and secured in Dr Williams's lab, which turned out to be the first floor of a large red-brick house off the main campus. While there, he had called the forensic odontologist Geoff Turner again and persuaded him – at the cost of at least one pint – to drop by the following morning to examine the skeleton's teeth.

After that, Banks had watched the lab assistants start cleaning the bones, then he had gone out for a quick sandwich at a café on Woodhouse Lane, making a slight detour to the Classical Record Shop. He had been gone for about an hour and a half.

DS Cabbot was just parking her Astra when Banks arrived back at the lab. She didn't spot him. He watched her get out and look up at the building, checking with the sheet of paper in her hand and frowning.

He stepped up behind her. 'It's the right place.'

She turned. 'Ah, sir. I was expecting something a bit more . . . well . . . I don't know really. But not like *this*.'

'More labby?'

She smiled. 'Yes. I suppose so. Whatever that means. More hi-tech. This place looks like my old student digs.'

Banks nodded towards the building. 'The university bought up a lot of these old houses when the families and their servants couldn't afford to live there any more. You'd be surprised how many odd and eccentric departments are hidden away in them. Let's go inside.'

Banks followed her up the steps. This evening she was wearing black tights and shoes, a mid-length black skirt and matching jacket over a white blouse. She was also carrying a black leather briefcase. Much more business-like. Banks caught a brief whiff of jasmine as he walked behind her. It reminded him of the jasmine tea that Jem, his friend and neighbour in the Notting Hill bedsit, used to pour so fastidiously, as if he were performing the Japanese tea ceremony.

Banks pressed the intercom and got them buzzed in. The lab was on the first floor, up one flight of creaky, uncarpeted stairs. Their footsteps echoed from the high ceiling.

Dr Ioan Williams waited for them on the landing. He was a tall, rangy fellow with long, greasy blond hair. Wire-rimmed glasses magnified his grey eyes, and his Adam's apple looked like a gobstopper stuck halfway down his throat. Much younger than Banks had expected, Dr Williams wasn't wearing a white lab coat but was dressed casually in torn jeans and a black T-shirt advertising Guinness. His handshake was firm, and judging by the way he lingered over DS Cabbot, his mind was not one hundred per cent focused on science. Or maybe it was. Biology.

'Come in,' he said, leading the way down the corridor and opening the lab door. 'I'm afraid it isn't much to write home about.' Despite his name, Williams had no trace of a Welsh accent. He sounded pure Home Counties to Banks, or Oxbridge. Posh, at any rate, as Banks's mother would say.

The lab consisted of two rooms knocked into one. Apart from the long table at the centre, where the skeleton lay, there was nothing much to distinguish it. Bookcases lined one wall, a long lab bench another. On it lay various measuring instruments and pieces of bone with tags on them like shop-window goods.

Still, Banks thought, what more did Williams need? All he looked at was bones. No mess. No blood and guts to clean up, no need for dissecting knives, scalpels or brain knives. All he really needed were saws, chisels and a skull key. And, thank God, they didn't have to worry about the smell, though the air was certainly redolent of loam and stagnant mud.

There were a couple of posters on the walls, one of Pamela Anderson Lee in her 'Baywatch' swimsuit and another of a human skeleton. Perhaps, Banks speculated, the juxtaposition meant something to Dr Williams. A reflection on mortality? Or maybe he just liked tits and bones.

The bones on the table certainly looked different now that Williams's assistants had been to work on them. Much of the crusting remained, especially in the hard-to-get-at crevices, but the skull, ribs and long bones were easier to examine. They were still far from the sparkling white of the typical laboratory skeleton, more of a dirty yellow-brown in colour, like a bad nicotine stain, but at least the whole resembled something more like a human being. There was even a little matted red hair on the back of the skull. Banks had come across this sort of thing before, so he knew it didn't mean the victim had been a redhead; hair turns red when the original pigment fades, and even many of the 'bog men', Iron Age corpses preserved in peat bogs, had red hair.

'There are a number of odds and ends my lads found while they were cleaning up,' Williams said. 'They're over there on the bench.'

Banks looked at the collection of filthy objects. It was hard to make out what they were: pieces of corroded metal, perhaps? A ring? Shreds of old clothing?

'Can you get them cleaned up and sent over to me?' he asked.

'No problem. Now let's get down to work.'

Annie took out her notebook and crossed her legs.

'First of all,' Williams began, 'let me confirm, just for the record, that we *are* dealing with human remains, most likely Caucasian. I'll check a few things under the microscope tomorrow, do some more work on the skull dimensions, for the sake of scientific accuracy, but you can take my word on it at the moment.'

'What about DNA analysis?' Banks asked.

Williams grunted. 'People seem to think DNA analysis is some sort of miracle answer. It's not. Right now, I can tell you a hell of a lot more about what you want to know than any DNA could. Believe me, I've had plenty of experience in this field. May I continue?'

'Please do. But get a DNA analysis done, anyway. It might be useful for determining identity, or identifying any living descendants.'

Williams nodded. 'Very well.'

'And what about radiocarbon dating?'

'Really, Chief Inspector, shouldn't you leave the science to the scientists? There's too big a margin for error in radiocarbon dating. It's mostly useful for archaeological finds, and I think you'll find our friend here is a little more recent than that. Now, if there's nothing else . . .?' He turned back to the skeleton. 'The height of the subject was easy enough to determine in this case by simple measurement once we got the bones arranged in their original positions. A metre and a half – between a hundred and fifty-four and a hundred and fifty-five centimetres.'

'What's that in feet and inches?' Banks asked.

'Five foot two.' Dr Williams looked over and smiled at DS Cabbot. 'But I can't be sure about the eyes of blue.'

Annie gave him a chilly smile. Banks noticed her roll her eyes and tug her skirt lower over her knees when Williams had turned away.

'Also,' Williams went on, 'you are dealing with the remains of a young woman.' He paused for dramatic effect.

Annie shot him a quick glance, then looked down at her notebook again.

'Go on,' Banks said. 'We're listening.'

'In general,' Williams explained, 'a male skeleton is larger, the bone surfaces rougher, but the main differences are in the skull and the pelvic area. The male skull is thicker.'

'Well, what do you know?' Annie muttered without looking up.

Williams laughed. 'Anyway, in this case, the pelvis is intact, and that's the easiest way for the trained eye to tell.' Williams reached over and put his hand between the skeleton's legs. 'The female pelvis is wider and lower than the male's, to facilitate child-bearing.' Banks watched as Williams ran his hand over the bone. 'This pubic curve is definitely female, and here, the sciatic notch.' He touched it with his forefinger. 'Also unmistakably female. Much wider than a male's.' He hooked his finger in the sciatic notch, then looked at DS Cabbot again as he caressed the skeleton's pelvic area. Annie kept her head down.

Williams turned back to Banks. 'The symphyseal area here, as you can see, is rectangular. In males it's triangular. I could go on, but I think you get the point.'

'Definitely female,' Banks said.

'Yes. And there's one more thing.' He picked up a small magnifying glass from the lab bench and handed it to Banks. 'Look at this.' Williams pointed to where the two pelvic bones joined at the front of the body. Banks leaned over, holding the glass. On the bone surface he could just about make out a small groove, or pit, maybe about half an inch long.

'That's the dorsal margin of the pubis's articular surface,' Williams said, 'and what you're looking at is a parturition scar. It's caused by the stresses that attached ligaments put on the bone.'

'So she'd given birth to at least one child?'

Williams smiled. 'Ah, you're familiar with the technical terms?'

'Some of them. Go on.'

Annie raised her eyebrows at Banks, then got back to

her notes before Williams could nail her with his leering gaze.

'Well,' Williams went on, 'there's only a single pit on either side of the pubis, which would strongly suggest that she only gave birth once in her life. Usually, the more times a woman has given birth, the more apparent the parturition scars are.'

'How old was she when she died?'

'I'd have to do more comprehensive tests to be certain of that. With X-rays of the ossification centres – the centres that basically *produce* the calcium and other minerals that make up bone – we can make a reasonably accurate determination. We can also do a spectrographic analysis of bone particles. But all that takes time, not to mention money. I imagine you'd like a rough estimate as quickly as possible?'

'Yes,' said Banks. 'What do you have to go on at the moment?'

'Well, there's epiphyseal union, for a start. Let me explain.' He looked over towards Annie like a professor beginning his lecture. She ignored him. He seemed unperturbed. Maybe this sort of ogling was just a habit with him, Banks guessed, and he didn't even notice he was doing it. 'Here,' Dr Williams went on, 'at the very ends of the long bones in both the arms and the legs, the epiphyses have all firmly united with the shafts, which doesn't usually happen until the age of twenty or twenty-one. But look here.' He pointed towards the collar-bone. 'The epiphysis at the sternal end of the clavicle, which doesn't unite until the late twenties, has *not* united yet.'

'So what age *are* we looking at? Roughly?'

Williams scratched his chin. 'I'd say about twenty-two to twenty-eight. If you take in the skull sutures, too, you can see here that the sagittal suture shows some signs of endocranial closure, but the occipital and the lambdoid sutures are still wide open. That would also suggest somewhere in the twenties.'

'How accurate is this?'

'It wouldn't be very far off. I mean, this is definitely not the skeleton of a forty-year-old or a fourteen-year-old. You can also take into account that she was in pretty good general physical shape. There is no indication of any old healed fractures, nor of any skeletal anomalies or deformities.'

Banks looked at the bones, trying to imagine the young woman who had once inhabited them, the living flesh surrounding them. He failed. 'Any idea how long she's been down there?'

'Oh dear. I was wondering when you'd get around to asking that,' Williams folded his arms and placed his forefinger over his lips. 'It's very difficult. Very difficult indeed to be at all accurate about something like that. To the untrained eye, a skeleton that has been buried for ten years might look indistinguishable from one that has been buried, say, a thousand years.'

'But you don't think this one has been buried a thousand years?'

'Oh, no. I said to the *untrained* eye. No, there are certain indications that we're dealing with recent remains here, as opposed to archaeological.'

'These being?'

'What do you notice most about the bones?'

'The colour,' said Banks.

'Right. And what does that tell you?'

Banks wasn't too sure about the usefulness of the Socratic method at a time like this, but he had found from experience that it is usually a good idea to humour scientists. 'That they're stained or decayed.'

'Good. Good. Actually, the discoloration is an indication that they have taken on some of the colour of the surrounding earth. Then there's this. Have you noticed?' He pointed to several places on the bone surfaces where the exterior seemed to be flaking off like old paint.

'I thought that was just the crusting,' Banks said.

'No. Actually, the bone surface is crumbling, or flaking. Now if you take all this into account, along with the complete absence of any soft or ligamentous tissue, then I'd estimate it's been down there for a few decades. Certainly more than ten years, and, as we already know, it's unlikely she was buried after 1953. I'd go back about ten years from there.'

'1943?'

'Hold on. This is a very rough guess. The rate of skeletal decay is wildly unpredictable. Obviously, your odontologist will be able to tell you a bit more, narrow things down, perhaps.'

'Is there anything else you can do to get a little closer to the year of death?'

'I'll do my best, of course, but it could take some time. There are a number of tests I can carry out on the bones, tests we use in cases of relatively recent remains as opposed to archaeological finds. There's carbonate testing, I can do an ultraviolet fluorescence test, histologic determination and Uhlenhut reaction. But even they're not totally accurate. Not within the kind of time frame you're asking for. They might tell you, at a pinch, that the bones are either under or over fifty years old, but you seem to want year, month, date and time. The best you can realistically hope for is between thirty and fifty or fifty and a hundred. I don't want to appear to be telling you your job, but probably your best chance of finding out who she was and when she was killed is by checking old missing-persons files.'

'I appreciate that,' said Banks.

'Anyway, I'll need more information about soil, mineral content, bacterial content, temperature fluctuations and various other factors. Buried under an outbuilding floor, then flooded under a reservoir, you say?'

'That's right.'

'I'll visit the site first thing in the morning and take some samples, then I'll get working on the tests.' He looked at Annie. 'Perhaps DS Cabbot here would be willing to escort me there?'

'Sorry,' said Annie. 'Far too busy.'

His eyes lingered on her. 'Pity.'

'Visiting the site's no problem,' Banks said. 'I'll arrange for a car and make sure the SOCOs are expecting you. Look, we're already a bit suspicious from the way and the place the body was buried. I know you don't have a lot to go on, but can you tell us anything at all about cause of death?'

'I think I can help you a little with that, though it's not really my area of expertise, and you should definitely get your Home Office pathologist to confirm this.'

'Of course. We'll ask Dr Glendenning to have a look as soon as he can. I doubt that it'll be top of his list, though. What have you found to be going on with?'

'See those markings on the bones there?' Dr Williams pointed to several of the ribs and the pelvic area. As Banks looked more closely, he noticed a number of triangular notches. They weren't easy to spot because of the flaking and crusting, but once he saw them he knew he'd seen them before on bones.

'Stab wounds,' he muttered.

'Exactly.'

'Cause of death?' Banks leaned over and peered.

'I'd say so. See those little curls of bone there, like wood shavings?'

'Yes.'

'They're still attached to the bone, and that only happens with living bone. Also, there's no sign of healing, is there? If she'd remained alive after these injuries, the bones would have healed to some extent, starting about ten days after the injury. So, technically, she could have been stabbed anywhere from one to ten days *before* she died of something else. But, as I said, it's unlikely. Especially since the position of some of these wounds indicates the blade would most certainly have pierced vital organs. In fact, I'd conclude that she was stabbed quite viciously, more than once, almost certainly causing death. But please don't quote me on that.'

Banks looked at Annie Cabbot. 'Murder, then,' she said.

'Well, I'd hardly imagine the poor woman did it herself,' Williams agreed. 'Yes, unless I'm very much mistaken, it looks like you've definitely got yourselves a murder victim here.'

4

Annie drove up Long Hill the following morning to interview Mrs Ruby Kettering. It was another scorcher, she noted, rolling her window down. Devil-may-care this morning, she had decided not to bother wearing tights. They were damned uncomfortable in the heat. You'd certainly never catch men wearing anything quite so ridiculous.

Long Hill began at the village green and linked Harkside to the edge of Harksmere Reservoir. Close to the centre of the village, it was the busiest shopping street, with a jumbled mix of shops and pubs and most of the public buildings, including the borough council offices, the library, the Women's Institute and the Mechanics Institute. It was early for tourists, but the shops were open and the locals were doing the rounds, shopping bags hooked over their arms, standing gossiping in little knots along the pavement. The road was narrow and double yellow lines ran along each side. Towards the end, the buildings dwindled and finally gave way to half a mile of open countryside before the T-junction with The Edge.

Annie parked on the grass verge opposite the junction. From there, she could see the ruins of Hobb's End in the distance. Several tiny figures stood clustered around the outbuilding where the skeleton had been discovered, and Annie realized it must be the SOCO team still searching the area. She wondered if Dr Williams the skeleton-groper was there, too.

Annie crossed the road and opened the gate. Mrs Kettering was squatting in the garden spraying her dahlias. She looked up. Annie introduced herself.

'I know who you are,' the old lady said, placing her hands on her thighs and pushing herself to her feet. 'I remember you. You're that nice policewoman who found my Joey.'

Annie accepted the compliment with a brief nod. She hadn't actually *found* Joey herself. The budgie had been innocently standing on the village green, accepting the crumbs an old man was scattering, blissfully unaware that it was being watched by a gang of sparrows up in one of the trees *and* by a ginger tom lurking behind a bush not more than ten yards away. One of the local kids had noticed, though, and remembering the poster offering a five-pound reward for a missing budgie, he had carefully scooped up Joey and carried him to the police station. Annie had simply delivered Joey back safely into Mrs Kettering's hands. One of the many exciting jobs she had done since arriving in Harkside. It was, however, through this incident that Annie had received her first on-the-job injury. Joey pecked the base of her thumb and drew blood, but Inspector Harmond wouldn't accept her injury compensation claim.

Mrs Kettering was wearing a red baseball cap, a loose yellow smock and baggy white shorts down to her knees. Below them, her legs were pale as lard, mottled red and marbled with varicose veins. On her feet she wore a pair of black plimsolls without laces. Though a little stooped, she looked sturdy enough for her age.

'Oh dear,' she said, wiping the streaks of sweat and soil from her brow with her forearm. 'I hope you haven't come to arrest me. Has someone reported me?'

'Reported you? What for?' Annie asked.

Mrs Kettering glanced guiltily at the hose coiled near the front door. 'I *know* there's supposed to be a water shortage, but I can't just let my garden die. A garden needs a lot of watering when the weather's like this. I don't own a car, so I don't waste any on washing one, and I thought, well, if I used just a little . . .?'

Annie smiled. She hadn't washed her car in weeks, either, but that was nothing to do with the water shortage. 'Don't worry, Mrs Kettering,' she said with a wink, 'I won't report you to Yorkshire Water.'

Mrs Kettering sighed and put a gnarled, veiny hand to her heart. 'Oh, thank you, dear,' she said. 'Do you know, I don't think I could stand going to gaol at my age. I've heard that the food in there is absolutely terrible. And with my stomach . . . Anyway, please call me Ruby. What *can* I do for you?'

'It's about Hobb's End.'

'Hobb's End?'

'Yes. I understand you used to live there.'

Mrs Kettering nodded. 'Seven years Reg and me lived there. From 1933 to 1940. It was our first home together, just after we got married.'

'You didn't stay there till the end of the war?'

'Oh, no. My Reg went off to fight – he was in the navy – and I went to work at a munitions factory near Sheffield. I lived with my sister in Mexborough during the war. When Reg came back in 1945, we stayed on there for a while, then he got a job on a farm just outside Harkside, so we moved here. We always did like the country. Listen, dear, would you like a cold drink? Lemonade, perhaps?'

'Thank you.'

'I'm afraid there's not much shelter from the sun,' Mrs Kettering said, 'but we can sit over there.'

She pointed to the side of the garden that abutted Long Hill. A short path led to a flagstone patio where two red-and-green-striped deck-chairs sat, half in the sun and half out of it. Various creeping plants coiled around the trellises fixed to the wall, which provided a little shade.

'That'll be just fine,' Annie said, walking over and taking off her sunglasses.

Mrs Kettering disappeared inside the house. Annie settled herself into one of the deck-chairs, stretched out her legs and luxuriated. She could feel the heat on her bare shins, warm and sensuous as a lover's caress. The sensation took her back to the beach at St Ives, where she had grown up and spent many a summer's day with her father, whose job it had been to rent out deck-chairs to the holidaymakers. The memory of those summers took her back to Rob, too: his days off, when they used to go for walks along the cliff tops, sail around the headland in his small boat and make love in secluded coves as the sunset colours emblazoned the horizon and waves crashed on the beach. How romantic it had all been, and how long ago it seemed.

Annie inhaled the sweet scent of the flowers. Bees droned around her, gathering pollen. She opened her eyes again and saw gulls circling over Harksmere.

'Here we are, dear,' said Mrs Kettering, coming back out with a tray. First she offered a tall glass to Annie, then she took the other for herself, set the tray aside and sat down. The deck-chairs faced each other at an angle, so it was easy to talk without straining one's neck.

'Hobb's End,' Mrs Kettering said. 'That takes me back. I can't say I've really given the place much thought in years, though I can see it from the bottom of the garden now, of course. What do you want to know?'

'As much as you can tell me,' Annie said. Then she told Mrs Kettering about the skeleton.

'Yes, I saw something about that on the news. I'd been wondering who all the people were, coming and going.' Mrs Kettering thought for a moment. Annie watched her and sipped lemonade. A robin alighted on the lawn for a few seconds, cocked an eye at them, shat on the grass and took off again.

'A young woman, about five foot two, with a baby?' Mrs Kettering repeated, brow knotted in concentration. 'Well, there was the McSorley lass, but that was when we arrived. I mean, she'd have been well over thirty by the time we left, and she had three children by then. No, dear, I can't honestly say anyone comes to mind. The far cottage, you say, the one by the fairy bridge?'

'Fairy bridge?'

'That's what we used to call it. Because it was so small, only fairies could cross over it.'

'I see. That's right. Under the outbuilding.'

Mrs Kettering pulled a face. 'Reg and me lived at the far end, just down from the mill. Still, I must have passed the place a hundred times or more. Sorry, love, it's a blank. I certainly don't remember any young woman living there.'

'Never mind,' said Annie. 'What can you tell me about the village itself?'

'Well, however close to Harkside it was, it had its own distinct identity, I can tell you that for a start. Harksiders looked down on the Hobb's End people because it was a mill village. Thought they were a cut above us.' She shrugged. 'Still, I suppose everyone's got to have someone to look down on, don't they?'

'Do you remember any doctors and dentists who used to practise there?'

'Oh, yes. Dr Granville was the village dentist. Terrible man. He drank. And if I remember correctly there were two doctors. Ours was Dr Nuttall. Very gentle touch.'

'Do you know what happened to his practice? I'm assuming he's dead now?'

'Oh, long since, I should imagine. And Granville was probably pushing sixty when the war started, too. You'll be after medical and dental records, I suppose?'

'Yes.'

'I doubt you'll have much luck there, love, not after all this time.'

'Probably not. What other sorts of people lived in the village?'

'All sorts, really. Let me see. We had shopkeepers, milkmen, publicans – we had three village pubs – farm labourers, dry-stone wallers, van drivers, travelling salesmen of one sort or another, a number of retired people, colonels and the like. Teachers, of course. We even had our very own famous artist. Well, not exactly Constable or Turner, you understand, and he's not very fashionable these days. Come with me a minute.'

She struggled out of her deck-chair and Annie followed her into the house. It was hot inside and Annie felt the sweat trickle down the tendons at the backs of her ears. It itched. She was glad she wasn't wearing tights.

Because of the sudden contrast between bright sunlight and dim interior, she couldn't make out the furnishings at first, except that they seemed old-fashioned: a rocking chair, a grandfather clock, a glass-fronted china cabinet full of crystalware. The room into which Mrs Kettering led her smelled of lemon-scented furniture polish.

They came to a halt in front of the dark wood mantel-piece, and Mrs Kettering pointed to the large watercolour that hung over it. 'That's one of his,' she said. 'He gave it me as a going-away present. Don't ask me why, but he took a bit of a shine to me. Maybe because I wasn't a bad-looking lass in my time. Bit of a rogue, Michael Stanhope, if truth be told. Most artists are. But a fine painter. You can see for yourself.'

Annie's eyes had adjusted to the light, and she was able to take in Stanhope's painting. She had a passion for art, inherited from her father. She smiled to herself at Mrs Kettering's remark. 'Bit of a rogue.' Yes, she supposed that fitted her father, too. Annie also painted as a hobby, so she was intrigued to look upon the work of Hobb's End's neglected genius.

'Is that Hobb's End before the war?'

'Yes,' said Mrs Kettering. 'Just after war broke out, actually. It was painted from the fairy bridge, looking towards the mill.'

Annie stood back and examined the work carefully. The first thing she noticed was Stanhope's peculiar use of colour. The season was autumn, and he seemed to take the hues and tones hidden deep in stone, fields, hillsides and water and force them out into the open, creating such a pattern of purples, blues, browns and greens as you never saw in a real Yorkshire village. But it made perfect sense to the eye. Nothing seemed to be its true colour, yet everything seemed right somehow. It was uncanny, almost surreal in its effect.

Next, she noticed the subtly distorted perspective, probably a result of cubist influences. The mill was there, perched on the rise in the top left corner, and though it looked as if it *should* dominate the scene, somehow, by some trick of perspective over size, it didn't. It was just there. The church, just to the right of the river, managed much more prominence through its dark and subtly menacing square tower and the rooks or ravens that seemed to be circling it.

The rest of the composition appeared simple and realistic enough: a village high-street scene whose people reminded her of Brueghel's. There was a lot of detail; an art teacher might even describe the work as *too* busy.

The villagers were doing the normal things – shopping, gossiping, pushing prams. Someone was painting a front door; a man straddled a roof repairing a chimney, shirt-sleeves rolled up; a tall girl stood arranging newspapers in a rack outside the newsagent's shop; a butcher's boy was cycling down the High Street beside the river with his basket full of brown-paper packages, blood-streaked apron flapping in the wind.

The rows of houses on each side differed in size and design. Some were semis or terraces, front doors opening directly on to the pavement, while some of the larger, detached houses stood back behind low stone walls enclosing well-kept gardens. Here and there, on the High Street side, a row of shops broke up the line of houses. There was also a pub, the Shoulder of Mutton, and its sign looked crooked, as if it were swinging in the wind.

Normal life. But there was something sinister about it. Partly it was the facial expressions. Annie could detect the smug, supercilious smiles of moral rectitude or the malicious grins of sadism on the faces of so many people. And Stanhope had included so much detail that the effect had to be deliberate. How he must have hated them.

If you looked long enough, you could almost believe that the man on the roof was about to drop a flagstone on some passer-by, and that the butcher's boy was wielding a cleaver ready to chop off someone's head.

The only characters who looked in any way attractive were the children. The River Rowan was neither very wide nor very deep where it ran through the village. Children were playing in the shallows, splashing one another, paddling, the girls with their skirts gathered around their thighs, boys in short trousers. Some of them looked angelic; all of them looked innocent.

The more Annie looked, the more she recognized that there was something religious, ecstatic, in the children's aspects, and the link with the water also brought to mind baptism. It was a sort of religious symbolism reminiscent of Stanley Spencer, though not quite so blatant. Over it all, the church brooded with its sense of menace and evil. The mill was nothing but a husk.

Annie looked away. When she turned back, the scene appeared more normal, and she noticed the strange colours the most again. It was a powerful work. Why had she not heard of Stanhope before?

In the bottom right, just above the artist's signature, stood the outbuilding where the skeleton had been found, next to a small, semi-detached cottage. Beside the door, a wooden sign announced the name: BRIDGE COTTAGE.

'What do you think?' Mrs Kettering asked.

'Have you noticed the way everyone looks? As if—'

'As if they were all either hypocrites or sadists? Yes, I have. That's Stanhope's vision. I must say I didn't see Hobb's End like that at all. We had our share of unpleasant characters, of course, but I'd hardly say they dominated the place. Michael Stanhope was, in some ways, a very disturbed individual. Would you like to go back out to the garden?'

Annie looked at the painting once more, seeing nothing that she had missed, then she followed Mrs Kettering outside.

The sunlight came as a shock. Annie shielded her eyes until she got to the chair and sat down again. There was still an inch or so of lemonade in the bottom of her glass. She drank it down in one. Warm and sweet. For some reason, the painting had unsettled her in the same way some of her father's more disturbed works did; she wanted to know more about it, more about Michael Stanhope's vision of Hobb's End.

'How old was Stanhope at that time?'

'He'd be in his late forties when I knew him.'

'What became of him?'

'I think he stayed in the village until the bitter end, and then I heard he moved to a small studio in London. But he didn't do much after that. Didn't *achieve* much, I should say. I saw his name in the papers once or twice, but I think he was like a fish out of water when he left Hobb's End. I don't think he managed to find a foothold in the big city art world. I heard he was in and out of mental institutions during the fifties, and the last I saw was his obituary in 1968. He died of lung cancer. The poor man always seemed to have a cigarette hanging out of the corner of his mouth. It made him squeeze his eyes almost shut against the drifting smoke when he painted. I was convinced that must have affected his perspective.'

'Probably,' said Annie. 'What happened to his paintings?'

'I wouldn't know, dear. All over the place, I suppose. Private collectors. Small galleries.'

Annie sat quietly for a moment, taking it all in. 'Bridge Cottage,' she said, 'where we found the skeleton. It looked neglected in the painting.'

'I noticed that, too,' said Mrs Kettering, 'and it made me remember something. Now, I can't be certain of this, not after so much time, but I think an old lady lived there. Bit of a recluse.'

'An *old* lady, you said?'

'Yes, I think so. Though I can't tell you anything about her. I just remembered, looking at the painting, that some of the children thought she was a witch. She had a long, hooked nose. She used to scare them away. I think it was her, anyway. I'm sorry I can't be of much help.'

Annie leaned forward and touched Mrs Kettering's arm. 'You *have* been helpful. Believe me.'

'Is there anything else you want to know?'

Annie stood up. 'Not that I can think of. Not right now.'

'Please call again if you do think of anything. It's so nice to have a visitor.'

Annie smiled. 'I will. Thank you.'

Back in her car, Annie sat drumming on the steering wheel and watching the gulls' reflections on the water's surface. She had learned that the place was called Bridge Cottage and an old woman may have been living there in the autumn of 1939. Of course, she still had no idea *how long* the body had lain under the outbuilding floor, so she didn't know whether this new information helped or not.

Perhaps more important, though, she had got her first real *feel* for Hobb's End from the Stanhope painting, and that might come in useful farther down the road. Annie had always thought it important to develop a feel for a case, though she had never expounded her philosophy to any of her male colleagues. Why was it that *feminine intuition* sounded as insulting to her as *hysterical* and *time of the month*?

She turned round and headed back down towards the station, a long day on the telephone looming ahead of her.

•

When Matthew met Gloria that first time, I could feel their immediate attraction like that eerie electric sensation you get before a storm, when you feel jumpy and ill at ease for no apparent reason. It scared me; I don't know why.

Something about Gloria changed when a man entered the room. It was as if she were suddenly *on*, the way I feel when the curtain goes up on one of our amateur dramatic productions and the real audience is there to watch us at last. I don't mean to indicate that there was anything deliberate about this, just that a change came over her and she moved and spoke in a subtly different way when there was a man around. I even noticed it with Michael Stanhope. He must have sensed something, too, or he wouldn't have given her those cigarettes.

But with Matthew it was the real thing. From that first April meeting, events progressed quickly between them. That very afternoon, Matthew showed her around the village, what little there was to see. A few days later they went to the pictures in Harkside and then to the Mayday dance at the Mechanics Institute there. I was helping out behind the refreshments counter, and I could see the way they danced so close together, the way they looked at one another.

I wasn't at all surprised when Matthew announced that he had invited Gloria to tea one Sunday. It was the eleventh of May, and Mother was in one of her states, so the preparation all fell to me. I'm sure I could have got away with a plate of sandwiches, but I was a good cook and, more important, I was good at making the best of what little was available, and I suppose I wanted to show off my skills.

All day we had been hearing disturbing rumours of a terrible air raid on London. Some people claimed that the House of Commons and Westminster Abbey had been completely destroyed and that thousands had been killed. I had already learned to take these things with a pinch of salt. After all, one of the first casualties of war is truth, to paraphrase Hiram Johnson.

I was listening to 'The Brains Trust' after putting the rabbit stew on to simmer. Joad and Huxley were arguing about why you can tickle other people but not yourself, when Gloria popped her head round the door, Matthew right behind her. They were a bit early and Mother was still titivating herself in her bedroom.

Gloria's golden hair, parted on the left, tumbled in long wreaths of sausage curls over her shoulders. She wore very little makeup, just a dab of face powder and a trace of lipstick. She was wearing a blue blouse with padded shoulders and puffed sleeves tucked into a simple black skirt with silver buttons down the side. I must admit that I was surprised at her restraint; I would have expected something far more garish from her. Even so, I felt dowdy in my plain old pinafore dress.

'Look what Gloria's brought for us,' Matthew said, holding out a pint of milk and half a dozen eggs. I took them and thanked her. As soon as Mother saw the eggs, I knew, her eyes would light up. She would put them in water-glass, the way she always did. Suspended in the clear jelly, they would last for months. Seeing them like that always made me uneasy; they looked sinister floating there in the transparent space, like wombs forever on the verge of giving birth, but never quite managing it, trapped there instead, frozen for ever in stillborn becoming.

Sinister or not, though, the water-glass meant we always

had fresh eggs as well as the powdered stuff, which was only good for scrambling.

'Hello, Gwen,' Gloria said, 'I should have known you'd be a "Brains Trust" fan. Tell me, who's your favourite? Joad or Campbell? Surely not Huxley?'

'Joad.'

'Why?'

'He's the most intelligent, the best-read, the most eloquent.'

'Hmm. Probably,' said Gloria, sitting down on the sofa, carefully arranging her skirt as she crossed her legs. Matthew sat next to her looking like the proud new owner of . . . well, of *something*. 'I like Campbell myself,' she said. 'I think he's far more entertaining.'

'I wouldn't have thought you even listened to something like that,' I said, regretting my rudeness almost as soon as the words were out of my mouth. After all, this was the woman my beloved brother clearly adored.

Gloria just shrugged. 'I've heard it once or twice.' Then her eyes lit up in that way they had. 'But you're right. If I had a wireless, I'd listen to nothing but music all day long.'

'You don't have a wireless?' I couldn't believe it. We might have been short of food, but surely everyone had a wireless?

'Mr Kilnsey won't have one in the house. He's rather a strict sort of Methodist, you know. Thinks they're the devil's loudspeaker.'

I put my hand to my mouth and giggled, then blushed. 'Oh dear. I am sorry.'

'It *is* rather funny, isn't it? Anyway, I don't mind that much. All I do is work and sleep there. It's sad for Mrs Kilnsey, though. I don't think she'd mind a bit of music now and then to cheer her up, but, of course, if the wireless is the devil's loudspeaker, then music is his voice at its most seductive.'

'Oh, good heavens,' said Matthew, shaking his head.

Gloria nudged him. 'It's true! He really talks like that.'

'I must go see to the food,' I said.

First I put the kettle on to make us all some tea, then I peeled a few potatoes and prepared the carrots and parsnips. If I say so myself, it was a good meal I put together that Sunday. Matthew had caught the rabbit in Rowan Woods on one of his weekend Home Guard exercises, and there was plenty of meat on it to feed the four of us. We also had some onions from the garden, and some rhubarb for a pie. Talk about *Dig for Victory*!

The kettle boiled. I made tea and carried it through, along with a plate of biscuits. With rationing, you had to be sparing, and the tea was a lot weaker than we were used to. With sugar rationed at only a pound a fortnight, and most of that in the rhubarb pie, the three of us had all stopped taking it. I didn't know about Gloria, so I offered her some.

'I gave it up,' she said. 'Actually, I've got a far better use for *my* sugar ration.'

'Oh?' I said.

'Yes.' She shook her curls. 'If you mix it with warm water, you can use it as a setting lotion.'

That was something I had never thought about, my rather fine and mousy hair being short, in the pageboy style, at the time. 'It must make your head feel terribly sticky,' I said.

She laughed. 'Well, sometimes it's hard to get my hat off, I can tell you. But that can be quite a blessing in the wind we get up at the farm some days.'

At that moment, Mother made her grand entrance. She walked slowly because of her arthritis and her stick tapped against the bare floorboards, so you could hear her coming long before you saw her. She was wearing one of her old flower-patterned frocks and had taken the trouble to curl her hair, though I doubt she had used sugar and warm water. Mother never wore makeup. She was a small, rather frail-looking figure, a little stooped, with a round, ruddy, pleasant face. It was a kind face, and she was a kind woman. Like me, though, she had a sharp way with words sometimes. Whatever the arthritis had done to the rest of her body, it hadn't progressed as far as her tongue. I expected fireworks when she met Gloria for the first time, but then I had been wrong about a lot of things lately.

'What a lovely blouse, my dear,' Mother said after the introductions. 'Did you make it yourself?'

I almost choked.

'Yes,' said Gloria. 'I managed to scrounge a bit of parachute silk, then I dyed it. I'm glad you like it. I can make one for you, if you like. I've got a bit more put away up at the farm.'

Mother put her hand to her chest. 'Good heavens, my dear, you don't want to waste your time making fancy clothes for an old crippled woman like me. No, what I've got will do to see me out.' Typical Mother that, the world-weary tone, as if we might well 'see her out' in the next few minutes.

'The Brains Trust' ended and a special about Jerome Kern came on. Gloria liked that better, all the songs she had heard in her beloved Hollywood musicals. She hummed along with 'A Fine Romance', 'You Couldn't Be Cuter' and 'The Way You Look Tonight'.

You could have knocked me over with a feather when Mother and Gloria got talking about how they both loved Fred Astaire and Ginger Rogers in Swing Time. It was time to serve tea and I was feeling really sick by then.

Jerome Kern finished and we turned the wireless off

while we ate. 'So, my dear,' said Mother when the stew was served, 'tell us all about yourself.'

'There's not much to tell, really,' Gloria said.

'Oh, come, come. Where are you from?'

'London.'

'Oh, you poor girl. What about your parents?'

'They were both killed in the bombing.'

'Oh dear, I'm so sorry.'

'A lot of people have died.'

'When was this?'

'Last year. September. I'm all alone now.'

'Nonsense, my dear,' said Mother. 'You've got us.'

I almost choked on my rabbit. 'It's not as if we're adopting her or anything, Mother,' I managed.

'Don't be so rude, Gwen. It's wartime, in case you hadn't noticed. People have to pull together.'

'Anyway,' Matthew said, 'Gloria's away from all that now, aren't you, darling?'

She looked at him with those big beautiful eyes of hers, adoration just dripping out of them like treacle. 'Yes,' she said. 'I am. And no matter what happens, I'm never going back.'

'Is there no one left?'

'No one. I was out visiting a friend a few streets away when the air raid came. We had no warning. My friends had an Anderson shelter in their back garden, so we went down there. I wasn't even worried. I thought my family would go to the underground or the church on the corner like we always did in air raids, but they didn't make it in time. Our house went up and the ones on either side along with it. My grandparents lived next door, so they were killed, too.'

We were all silent for a few moments, digesting the matter-of-fact horror of what Gloria had just told us.

Somehow it made us and our little rationing problems seem insignificant.

'What made you decide on a God-forsaken place like Hobb's End?' Mother asked.

'It wasn't my choice. That's where they sent me, the Land Army. I did my training at Askham Bryan, which isn't far away. Mr Kilnsey needs a lot of help since his boy joined up, and he's not getting any younger. I was just glad to get away to the countryside. I just couldn't stand the idea of working in a dirty, smelly munitions factory.'

'Still,' said Mother, 'farming's not an easy life.'

Gloria laughed. 'You can say that again. It's dirty and smelly, too. But I can cope. I've never minded hard work. Actually, I quite enjoy it.' She shot me a sidelong glance. 'This stew is delicious, Gwen. I really mean it. It's the tastiest meal I've had in a long time. Thank you very much.'

I felt absurdly pleased and struggled to stop myself from blushing, but you can't do it, like you can't tickle yourself. I blushed. 'My pleasure,' I said.

After the rhubarb pie, which Gloria once again was kind enough to remark upon, Matthew made more tea and we put the wireless on again for 'The Happidrome'.

I just caught the end of a news bulletin which confirmed that Westminster Abbey, the British Museum and the Houses of Parliament had been bombed, but only damaged, not destroyed. Still, you never knew whether to believe newsreaders or not, even though they had to say their names before each bulletin now, so we'd know the Germans hadn't taken over the BBC. After all, the Germans could listen to the broadcasts, too, and we didn't want them to think we were badly hurt or demoralized in any way. We had enough with Lord Haw-Haw doing that for us. Just the previous week he had actually said something about the Germans bombing the flax mill in Hobb's End, which nearly gave our ARP man apoplexy.

Over a cup of tea, Matthew and Gloria lit cigarettes. I knew Mother didn't approve of women smoking, but she said nothing. Then Matthew cleared his throat and said, 'Mother, I invited Gloria here tonight for a specific reason, because, well, we have something to tell you.'

Mother raised her eyebrows; my heart started to thump against my rib-cage.

'We want to get married.'

I gaped at Matthew: tall, dashing, handsome, that charming lock of dark brown hair always slipping over his eye, the dimples at each side of his mouth when he smiled, the clear eyes and strong chin. And then I looked at Gloria, saw her radiance.

Somehow, it was all so inevitable.

At that moment, I hated her.

'Ah,' said Mother, after a calming sip of tea. 'You do, do you?'

'Yes.'

'And you, young lady?'

'Very much,' said Gloria, leaning over and taking Matthew's hand. 'I know it's not been long that we've known one another, but it's wartime and—'

Mother waved her down. 'Yes, yes, my dear, I know all about that. Have you thought, though, that Matthew might be going far away soon?'

'We've thought about that, Mother,' he said. 'Even though I passed the medical, I'll still have my military training to do after the degree, and there's a good chance I'll be able to come home every weekend until after Christmas, probably, at least.'

'And the rest of the week?'

'I'll be working at the farm, as usual,' Gloria said, 'and Matt will be at university in Leeds until July, then he'll go wherever they send him for training. I know it's not perfect. We'd love nothing more than to be together *all* the time.' They held hands and she gazed at him. 'But we know that's not realistic. Not yet, anyway.'

I couldn't believe it; she called him *Matt*. How could she? He had always been Matthew to Mother and me.

'What about your studies?' Mother asked him.

'I'll be working just as hard as usual.'

'Hmph. A lot of couples are waiting to marry,' she said. 'Until times are less uncertain.'

'But a lot of people are getting married, too,' Matthew argued, 'making the best of the time they have. Yes, we know life is very uncertain now. But if anything happens to me in the forces, I'll die a far happier man for having been married to Gloria. Even if it was only for a day.'

'Don't talk like that, Matthew,' Mother said, putting her hand to her chest again. Then she glanced at me. 'What do you think about all this, Gwen?'

I swallowed. 'Me? Well, I suppose if it's what they really want to do, then there's nothing we can say to stop them.'

'Good old Gwen,' said Matthew. 'I knew I could depend on you.'

'Where will you live?' Mother demanded. 'Have you thought about that? It's not that we wouldn't have you, but there's not enough room here, you know, even if you *wanted* to live with Gwen and me. We don't even have enough room to take in evacuees. And you certainly can't both live at the farm.'

'Yes,' said Matthew, 'we've thought about that, too. That's why we want to get married as soon as possible.'

Mother frowned. 'Oh?'

'We're going to live in Bridge Cottage.'

'What? That run-down hovel by the fairy bridge?'

'Yes. It'll be big enough for us. And it'll be ours. Well, we'll only be renting it, but you know what I mean. As you know, it's been used for housing evacuees since old Miss Croft died. Anyway, I've talked to Lord Clifford's agent in Leeds, and he says that the people there now are moving out next week. It's a woman and her two children, evacuees from Birmingham. Apparently they're homesick and they're going home. I know it'll need a lot of fixing up, but I'm good with my hands. And it's only five shillings a week.'

'What about children? Have you thought about that, too?'

'I'm not having a baby, Mrs Shackleton, if that's what you mean,' said Gloria.

'Of course not, my dear. That's not what I meant at all. I wouldn't suggest such a thing. But if you *do* have a baby after you're married, the child's father will most likely be away and you'll have a lot on your hands.'

That sad look came over Gloria's face the way it did sometimes, a dark cloud blocking the sun. 'We haven't planned to have children,' she said. 'Not yet, anyway. I wouldn't want to bring a child into the world the way things are now, not after what I've been through.' Then the cloud passed and she smiled again. 'After the war, though, we'll see. Things will be different then.'

Mother was silent for a moment, then she grimaced as if in pain, which she probably was, and said, 'You've thought of everything, haven't you?'

Matthew beamed. 'Everything, Mother. We want to start having the banns called next Sunday. Please say you'll give us your blessing. Please!'

Mother held her cup out and I poured more tea. Her

hand was shaking and the cup rattled on the saucer. She looked at Gloria again. 'And you're an orphan, my dear? You have no living relatives?'

'None. But you *did* say I've got you, didn't you?'

Mother smiled. Only a little one. That's all she allowed herself those days. Little ones. 'I did, didn't I?'

'Oh, please, Mrs Shackleton, *please* give us your permission.'

'It doesn't look as if I've got much choice, does it? Go on, then, you have my blessing.' Then she sighed and looked at me. 'I suppose we'll have to start saving our coupons up, won't we, Gwen, love?'

•

Some mornings, especially when the weather was good, Vivian Elmsley liked to walk up Rosslyn Hill to the High Street, take a table outside one of the cafés and linger over her morning coffee. She walked slowly, finding her breath came with more difficulty these days.

One or two people on the street recognized her from her television and magazine-cover appearances, as usual, but the people of Hampstead took celebrity in their stride, especially the literary kind, so no one pestered her for autographs or 'simply had to' tell her how good or how bad her latest book was.

She found an empty table easily enough, bought her coffee and unfolded the *Times*. Her routine varied. Some days she found herself thinking about the book she was working on as she walked, hardly noticing the people in the street, unaware even of what season it was. On those days, she would sit down with her notebook and scribble a few ideas as she sipped. Today, though, the book was much farther from her mind than she would have liked.

Instead, she opened her newspaper. The brief item she was looking for appeared in a column on one of the inside pages usually reserved for news items from the provinces:

FOUL PLAY SUSPECTED IN
RESERVOIR SKELETON CASE

In a surprise statement given yesterday evening to local reporters, North Yorkshire Police indicated that the skeletal remains found under Thornfield Reservoir were those of a female murder victim. Detective Chief Inspector Alan Banks, in charge of the case, said that while police have not yet discovered the victim's identity, they do know that the body is that of a woman in her early twenties. All indications are that she was stabbed to death. How long the body has lain there, DCI Banks added, is much more difficult to determine, but preliminary information indicates that they are dealing with a twentieth-century crime. Thornfield Reservoir was constructed on the site of a village called Hobb's End, whose remains have now come into view for the first time since 1953. The skeleton was found buried under an outbuilding by a thirteen-year-old boy, Adam Kelly, while he was playing in the area. Anyone with information is asked to get in touch immediately with the North Yorkshire Police.

So they knew that much already. Her hand trembling slightly, Vivian put the newspaper down and sucked some of the frothy milk from the top of her coffee. She wouldn't be able to concentrate on the rest of the news now, or attempt the crossword. That little item had quite spoiled her day.

It was funny, she thought, how time played tricks. Over the years she had managed to distance herself from the past: the years with Ronald in Africa, Hong Kong, South America and Malaysia; her early struggles as a writer after his death; the rejections and humiliations; the flush of first publication; the slow rise to success; the television series. Before Ronald, she had thought her life completely blighted by fate. What she discovered instead, over the years, was that while it had been in some ways diminished, it had also been far more fulfilling than she could ever have dreamed. Time might not heal everything, but some things just die, dry up and flake off.

Of course, after Ronald's death, she had never been involved with another man. (One might say she hadn't even been involved with Ronald in *that* way.) But there is always a price to pay, and that was a relatively small one, far less than the nightmares and the deep, gnawing guilt that, while it fuelled her imaginative flights of fancy, crippled her in just about every other way and brought on black moods and sleepless nights she sometimes feared would never end.

Now this. She watched the innocent pedestrians passing to and fro on the pavement: a young woman in a smart grey business suit talking into her mobile telephone; a young fair-haired couple carrying rucksacks, Scandinavian tourists by the look of them, holding hands; a man with a grey beard, wearing a paint-smeared smock; two girls with green and orange hair and rings through their noses. Vivian sighed. The streets of Hampstead. 'All human life is here', as the old *News of the World* used to proclaim about itself. Well, perhaps not *all* – not in Hampstead, at least – but certainly the more privileged classes.

Were they all so innocent? Perhaps not. No doubt there

walked among the crowds of Hampstead a murderer or two.

Vivian gave a little shudder. She remembered how she had felt there was someone following her on and off over the past couple of weeks. She had put it down to an overactive imagination. After all, she made her living from writing about crime, and the same morbid imagination that made her so good at that also sparked off occasional panic attacks and fits of depression. They were two sides of the same coin; she profited from her fears, but she had to live with them, too. So perhaps she *had* been imagining it all. Who would want to follow her anyway? The police? Surely not. If they wanted to talk to her, they would approach her directly.

Vivian glanced back at her newspaper, folded open at the Hobb's End item, and sighed. Well, it shouldn't take them long now, should it? And then what would become of her hard-earned peace?

•

Banks started with Brian's university administration office, and ten minutes later, after a few white lies about the importance of the information he was requesting, he had managed to convince the assistant to break her 'strict code of privacy'. On the pad in front of him was the London telephone number of one Andrew Jones.

He paused before dialling, unsure of what he was going to say to Brian if he did get through. The only thing he knew was that they had to get beyond the argument, get to some position where they could talk like reasonable human beings. Still, both he and Brian had always been quick to forgive. Whenever they had disagreements in the past, one or the other would make a conciliatory move within minutes, and it was all over. Sandra was the one who kept things on a slow simmer; sometimes it took her a week of cool distance and moody silences before she let you know exactly *why* she was upset with you in the first place.

Whether Banks could manage reconciliation this time without slipping into the irate-father role, he wasn't sure. Besides, he had damn good reason to be irate. Brian had cocked up three years of higher education – which hadn't been easy on Banks and Sandra financially – and then he had bottled out of telling anyone for weeks, practically disappearing off the face of the earth.

As it turned out, Banks needn't have worried. When he dialled the number, no one picked the phone up, and there was no answering machine.

Next he phoned Annie, who seemed excited about a painting of Hobb's End done by an artist called Michael Stanhope. Banks couldn't share her enthusiasm, though he was glad to find out she had discovered the name of the cottage by the outbuilding.

Waiting for John Webb to call with an inventory of the material recovered at the crime scene, he examined the contents of his 'in' tray. Designs for new uniforms had been approved at a conference of the Association of Chief Police Officers. Fascinating stuff. Had they nothing better to do? What the hell did the top brass think the police force was, a bloody fashion statement? Soon they'd have PCs and WPCs flouncing down the catwalks in see-through uniforms with feather boas.

Under that was a copy of the latest report from Ms Millicent Cummings, Assistant Chief Constable, or Director of the Department of Human Resources, as her real title went. North Yorkshire had been under fire lately for its excessive number of sexual-harassment claims – accusations of bullying, sexual assault, discrimination and bizarre initiation ceremonies – and Millie had been brought in as the new broom. On a broomstick, too, so the lads had it. Banks liked Millie, though; she was a bright, fair woman with a tough job to do. As far as he was concerned, the more thugs and yobs kicked off the force, the better all round.

Banks turned to a report on tightening up alcohol sales. It included an incident report about a ten-year-old kid who got pissed on alco-pop and rode his bicycle through a shoe-shop window. Minor cuts and bruises. Lucky bugger. Which was more than could be said for the poor sales clerk who just happened to be bending over a prospective customer's feet with a shoehorn at the time. Instant haemorrhoid surgery.

Banks signed off on the reports and memos – including one that informed him CID was having its name changed to Crime Management – then he worked for a while on an article he was writing on policing in the nineties. One of the advantages of his new computer and his desk-bound existence was that he had written two of these over the past couple of months, and he found he enjoyed the process. He had also given a few talks and lectures and discovered he was good at that, too. There had been times when he had thought it might not be a bad idea to try for some sort of police-related teaching career, but the cards were stacked against him in the form of his education – or lack of it. Banks didn't have a university degree, as Brian had so cruelly reminded him the other day. He had come out of the Poly with a Higher National Diploma in Business Studies. It was supposed to be the equivalent of a pass degree, but only the *equivalent*. And that had been almost a quarter of a century ago. As far as he knew, such diplomas probably didn't even exist any more. A prospective employer would take one look at it and burst out laughing. The thought made Banks flush with shame and anger.

At least Brian had got a third-class honours, which beat a mere pass, or equivalent. Christ, it sounded like a poker game. Was he in competition with his son all of a sudden?

Luckily, the phone rang before he could frame an answer. It was John Webb.

'I've just picked up the stuff we dug up with the Hobb's End skeleton,' he said. 'Dr Williams's lads have given it a good clean.'

'What did you find? Not much after all this time, I imagine.'

'Actually, you'd be amazed at some of the things that *do* survive. It's all very unpredictable. I found a few buttons and some metal clips that look as if they might have come from a brassière or a suspender belt. I also found some small leather shoes which look as though they might have belonged to the corpse.'

'So you're saying she was buried in her clothes?'

'Looks like it.'

'Anything else?'

'Yes, some other material, black and heavy. Definitely not clothing.'

'Any ideas?'

'Some sort of curtains, perhaps?'

'Did you find a wedding ring, or anything that looked as if it might have been one?' he asked.

'I think so. I wasn't sure at first because of the corrosion, but that's what it looks like all right.'

'I don't suppose there's a name and date engraved on the inside, is there?'

Webb laughed. 'Even if there was, I wouldn't be able to read it after this long.'

'Thought not. Any sign of the murder weapon? Most likely some sort of knife.'

'Nothing like that.'

'Handbag or a purse? Anything with identification.'

'Sorry, no. Just what I've told you. And a locket, no inscription and nothing inside. Nothing that survived the years underground, anyway. If there *was* a photo or something like that, it probably disintegrated.'

'Okay, thanks a lot, John.'

'No problem. I'll have it sent over to you later today.'

Banks walked over to the window. The heat was still getting to him; he felt sleepy and woolly-headed, as if he'd had a couple of drinks, which he hadn't. The cobbled market square was chock-a-block with tourists, coaches from Leeds, Wigan and Scunthorpe, cars parked in every available nook and cranny, a riot of primary colours. All summer the tourist hordes had been coming to the Dales. Pubs, hotels, shops and B and Bs had all done record business. Of course, it hadn't rained in two months, and even before that there had been nothing much more than minor showers since April.

Though the health fascists had finally succeeded in banning smoking from every police station in the country, Banks lit a cigarette. He had been quietly ignoring the no-smoking order for a while now. In the larger open-plan stations, you couldn't get around it, of course; you simply had to go outside. But here, in the old Tudor-fronted warren, he had his own office. With the door closed and the window open, who would know? What did he care, anyway? What were they going to do, put him in detention?

Watching a couple of pretty young tourists dressed in T-shirts and shorts sitting eating ice lollies on the raised parapet of the market cross, Banks started to drift into pleasurable fantasies involving Annie Cabbot and her red wellies. He had been fantasizing a lot lately, and he didn't know whether it was a healthy sign or not.

Officially, of course, fellow police officers did not sleep together. Especially DCIs and sergeants. That was a real no-no. From one perspective it could be called sexual harassment, and from the other, sleeping your way to the top.

In reality, it happened all the time. All over the country, coppers were shagging one another like rabbits, fucking away like minks, regardless of rank. Murder scenes in particular got them going: sex and death, the old aphrodisiac combination.

Dream on, he told himself, snapping out of the fantasy. The truth was that Annie Cabbot wouldn't have him, and he wouldn't try it anyway. Any facility at chatting up women he might have had as a teenager had deserted him now. How do you start that sort of thing all over again? He was too old to go out on dates and worry about whether a goodnight kiss would be welcome. Or a nightcap. Or an invitation to stay the night. Or who should take care of the condoms. The whole idea made him feel nervous and awkward. He wouldn't know where to begin.

He had had only one sexual encounter since Sandra left, and that had been a complete disaster. In his cups at Susan Gay's farewell party in the Queen's Arms, Banks had picked up a woman called Karen something-or-other. Or perhaps Karen had picked *him* up. Either way, the beer was boosting his confidence, and Karen was tipsy and definitely frisky. Instant lust. Without much preamble, they went back to his place where, after only the briefest of hesitations, they got into a clinch and fell on to the sofa, clothes flying everywhere. Despite the booze, everything worked just fine.

Somehow, later, they must have crawled up into the bed, because Banks awoke around four in the morning with a pounding headache, a naked woman wrapped around him and a burning desire to be alone. He had used Karen – as perhaps she had used him – and now all he wanted to do was discard her. Instead, he lay awake beside her thinking gloomy thoughts until she stirred in the early dawn and said she had to go home. He didn't object, didn't show any tenderness on parting, and he never saw her again.

The telephone dragged him out of his depressing memory and back to his desk. It was Geoff Turner, the forensic odontologist. This reminded Banks that he had a dentist's appointment looming, and he had hated the dentist's since his school days. Maybe he would have an excuse to cancel if this case went anywhere.

'Alan?'

'Geoff. You're fast. Any news?'

'Nothing dramatic. Too soon for that. But I was keen to make a start. I've always been fascinated by skeletal remains.'

Banks thought of Dr Williams caressing the skeleton's pelvic region. 'Pervert.'

Turner laughed. 'Scientifically, I mean.'

'Go on.'

'I'm calling from the lab. What I wanted to do first of all was confirm Dr Williams's estimate of her age at the time of death. He's right. The third molars are up – that's wisdom teeth to you laymen – but the apexes haven't quite closed yet, nor have the medial sides of the incisal sutures. The third molars don't usually come up until your early twenties, so there's our first clue. Then the apexes are usually closed by the age of twenty-five and medials by thirty. Which makes her mid-twenties, give or take a year or two.'

'Thanks, Geoff. Any idea how long she's been down there?'

'Hold your horses. I told you I've only managed a quick look so far. What few fillings there are seem to indicate fairly recent dental work, if that's of any interest to you. And by recent, I mean twentieth-century.'

'Any closer? A rough guess?'

'By the look of the material and techniques, probably not later than the fifties, if that's any help.'

'Are you sure it's not more recent? Like nineties?'

'No way. You might not believe it when you're sitting in the chair, but dentistry's come a hell of a long way in the past thirty years or so, and this mouth shows no signs of that. No modern techniques or materials. And there are several missing teeth.'

'Could that have happened after death?'

'You mean could the killer have pulled her teeth out?'

'Could he?'

'Possible, but unlikely. They look like pretty clean extractions to me.'

'She can't have been buried between 1953 and this summer, if that's any help.'

'Then I'd say definitely before 1953.'

'Are you sure it couldn't just be someone who neglected her teeth?'

'It's not a matter of neglect, Alan, though I'll get back to that in a moment. It's materials and procedures.'

'Go on.'

'There's not much more to tell, really. Just a couple of vague ideas.'

'Where would we be in our business without vague ideas?'

Turner laughed. 'You shouldn't say that to a scientist. It's heresy. Anyway, I can't be certain until the X-rays, but we're not talking top-quality dental work here and we're also not talking regular visits. If I had to guess, I'd say this lass only went to the dentist's when she had a problem.'

'What do you mean?' asked Banks, who was beginning to feel even more empathy with the victim. He felt exactly the same way about dentists.

'The fillings might have lasted a few years longer, had she lived, but in one case the decay wasn't quite eradicated. That sort of thing. A bit sloppy. Also, as I said, there are signs of neglect, which may indicate we're dealing with someone from a poor background, someone who couldn't afford the best treatment. Quite often, you know, girls had all their teeth pulled out in their twenties and wore dentures for the rest of their lives.'

'Right. Thanks, Geoff.' Banks had always thought that the idea of *paying* for so much pain was the quintessence of masochism.

'Another possibility is wartime.'

'Really? Why do you say that?'

'Think about it. Most of the good young dentists and doctors were in the forces, and there were only old dodderers left. Poor equipment. Repairs were hard to get done. Military got priority over everything.'

'Right. I didn't think of that.'

'And there's another thing.'

'There is?'

'We didn't get the National Health Service until 1948. Before that you had to pay for dental work. Naturally, the working class had the hardest time of it.'

'Didn't they always,' said Banks, remembering his father coming home silent and exhausted after long shifts at the steel factory and his mother falling asleep in the evenings after spending her day cleaning other people's houses. 'So possibly wartime, possibly poor?'

'Right.'

'Thanks again. I owe you, Geoff.'

'It'll be my pleasure to collect. Of course, if you could track down her actual dentist, if there are still records . . .'

'We're trying,' said Banks. 'But it happened a long time ago. How long is a dentist likely to hang on to old records, even if he is still alive?'

'True enough. Best of luck, Alan. Talk to you later.'

Banks put down the receiver and leaned back in his chair to think about what he had just heard. Both Ioan Williams and Geoff Turner agreed that the skeleton had not been put there after Thornfield Reservoir dried up earlier in the summer, and Dr Williams had estimated the late thirties at the earliest. So the skeleton wasn't a hundred years old or more; it was more like fifty or sixty. Which meant that if the victim had been between twenty-two and twenty-eight when she was killed, she would probably have been between seventy and eighty had she lived. Not only might she still have been alive, then, but so might her killer, and so might a witness, or at least someone who *remembered* her.

This was quickly turning into a real case. What had been dug up from Thornfield Reservoir was no longer just a collection of filthy old bones; in Banks's mind, the woman was slowly assuming flesh. He had no idea what she had really looked like, but in his mind's eye he could already see a sort of amalgam of the wartime film stars in the fashions of the period: Greer Garson, Deanna Durbin, Merle Oberon. What he needed to know next was her name; that would make her even more real to him.

He looked at his watch. Just turned four. If he set off now, he could be in Harkside in an hour or so. Plenty of time to compare notes with Annie.

5

As weddings go, Matthew and Gloria's was a relatively small affair. A few family members came from as far away as Eastvale and Richmond, some of them distant uncles, aunts and cousins I hadn't seen for years. Gloria had no family, of course, so the rest of the guests were made up of people from the village. Mr and Mrs Kilnsey from the farm were there, though Mr Kilnsey looked terrified for his mortal soul to find himself in the Church of England, that hotbed of idolatry.

Gloria had also insisted on inviting Michael Stanhope, as they had become quite close friends, and he looked almost as uncomfortable as Mr Kilnsey to find himself in such hallowed surroundings. He was sober, though, and at least he had made the effort to shave, comb his hair and wear a decent, if rather frayed and shiny, suit. He also remembered to remove his hat during the service.

I must say Gloria looked radiantly beautiful. With her angelic face and earthly figure, she had a natural advantage to start with. Wizard that she was at making things, she had decided it was more expedient to buy her wedding dress. She had found one on sale at Foster's in Harkside for two pounds ten shillings. It was a simple white affair, neither voluminous nor trailing half a mile of material, both elegant and tasteful. She did, however, make her own veil out of lace, which wasn't rationed. Whether she had set them with sugar and water or not, I don't know, but her glistening blond sausage curls tumbled to her shoulders in an even more dazzling array than usual.

Gloria had bought her wedding dress almost as soon as Mother gave her blessing, so she was all right, but wouldn't you know it, clothes rationing came into force the Sunday before the wedding. Luckily, we had all got used to mending and making do by then. Matthew dug out his only suit and we had it cleaned and pressed. It would have cost him almost an entire half-year's clothes ration to get newly kitted out. Mother put on her best flowered frock, adding a belt here and a little lace there, just to make it look new, and she bought a new hat for the occasion, hats being one of the few items of clothing, along with lace and ribbon, *not* rationed.

Cynthia Garmen and I were bridesmaids and we wore matching taffeta dresses made out of some old curtains. Just for an extra-special touch, I cut up some lace to trim our knickers. I don't know about Cynthia – she certainly never said anything – but the things made my thighs itch through the entire service.

It was the seventh of June, 1941, and a lovely day, with clouds like trails of spilled milk spelling out Arabic characters in the sky.

The ceremony went smoothly. The Reverend Graham conducted the service with his usual oratorical skill and gravity. Barry Naylor, Matthew's best man, didn't forget the ring, and they all got their lines right. Nobody fainted, though it was exceedingly hot in the church. Mother shed a few tears. There was no confetti, of course, there being a paper shortage, and there was something else different that nagged away at the back of my mind, but I didn't remember what it was until much later that night.

We stood outside for photographs. Film was expensive and hard to obtain, but we weren't going to let Matthew's wedding day go by without some sort of visual record, and one of his friends from the Home Guard, Jack Cheswick, fancied himself as a bit of an amateur photographer. Mr Truewell, the chemist, was obliging, and the film cost us only twenty Passing Cloud cigarettes. Luckily for us, the pictures turned out all right, though the album got lost in one of the many moves that came later.

We held the reception in the church hall. Of course, I had done most of the catering myself, though I was able to leave the last-minute assembly to my helpers, Sue and Olive. We had to apply in Leeds for an allocation of rations, and Sue, who had got married herself just a couple of months earlier, had warned me it was advisable to double your estimate of the number of guests. Consequently, I said we were expecting a hundred people. Even so, we only got two ounces of tea, which we had to eke out with some of our own ration to make it even drinkable.

Luckily, our first American food on lend-lease had just arrived in the shop, so we had Spam for sandwiches, and tinned sausage meat, which was wonderful for making sausage rolls because you could also use the fat left in the tin to make the pastry. There wasn't much to drink, but we did manage to get a keg of watery beer from the Shoulder of Mutton and there was some sweet sherry we had been keeping in our cupboard. Mr Stanhope supplied a bottle of gin and some wine. The wedding cake was the biggest disappointment. Icing had been banned nearly a year earlier, so we had to make do with a cardboard-and-crêpe fake. Still, it looked nice in the photographs.

The highlight of the reception was the band. Matthew's friend, Richard Bright, played trumpet with the Victor Pearson Dance Band, so we got at least half the band to come and play for their supper.

Gloria and Matthew led off the dancing, of course, and a lump came to my throat as I watched them. After that, it was a free-for-all. The music was all right if you liked that sort of thing, but I found it all either too noisy and frenetic or too mushy and sentimental.

I talked to Michael Stanhope for a while and he remarked on how beautiful he thought Gloria looked and what a lucky man Matthew was. For once, he didn't say anything nasty about the war. Betty Warden, who had managed to wangle an invitation somehow, sat with her nose in the air most of the night, disapproving of everything and everyone, but I must say that when she danced with William Goodall, she seemed like a different person. So did he, for that matter. Almost human, both of them.

Alice Hill was cheerful and talkative as ever, and I rather think she developed a fancy for Eric Poole that very night. They certainly danced closely together often enough.

Gloria came up to me at one point – she had changed now into a long flared skirt and pink blouse – with a little sweat beaded on her brow and upper lip from dancing too energetically. Her eyes were shining. I think she'd had a drink or two.

She rested her soft, delicate hand on my arm. 'This is the happiest day of my life, Gwen,' she said. 'Do you know, just six months ago I thought I would never laugh or dance again. But thanks to you, your mother and, of course, dear Matt . . . Thank you, Gwen, thank you so much.' Then she leaned forward quickly and clasped me to her bosom, giving me a little peck on the cheek. It was awkward, and with her being so small, I had to bend. I could smell the gin on her breath. I'm sure I blushed, but she didn't remark on it.

'I haven't seen you dancing,' she said.

I shook my head. 'I don't. I mean, I can't.'

'I'll teach you,' she said. 'Not right now, of course . . . but I'll teach you. Will you let me?'

I nodded stupidly. 'Yes. If you want.'

'It's the *least* I can do.'

Then she excused herself and went to talk to Mother and Cynthia, smiling on everyone she passed with those Hardy-heroine eyes of hers.

I did my bit, moving from table to table, being polite to my distant relations, removing Uncle Gerald's hand from my knee without drawing attention to the fact that it was there.

The local people started to drift home around sunset to make sure they had all got their blackout curtains in place. Our relations were staying with friends in Harkside, so they began to leave, too, before it got too dark to see their way across the fields.

Matthew and Gloria went to Bridge Cottage for their first night together as man and wife. Whether this was their first *time* together, I have no idea. It may be hard to believe now, when everyone seems to be very sophisticated about sex, but I knew very little of such things back then. I had no idea, for example, what men and women actually *did* when they made babies.

The next day they were going to Scarborough for a three-day honeymoon. Matthew had already booked a room at a guest-house in St Mary's, near the castle. After that, it was back to university for Matthew – with his finals coming up soon – and back to Top Hill Farm for Gloria, though she would live at Bridge Cottage and walk or cycle to and from work.

Mother was talking to Sue and Olive at the door when I finally excused myself through tiredness and set off home alone. It had been a long, hard day.

Though it was late, a deep purple-and-vermilion glow

still lit the sky in the west, behind the dark mill. The streets were quiet, though I could still hear music coming from the church hall behind me. Back home, I made sure the blackout curtains were drawn tightly, then, weary to the bone, I went to bed.

It was only when I was on the very edge of sleep and heard the thrumming and droning of the bombers taking off from Rowan Woods RAF Base that I remembered what had bothered me so much outside the church after the wedding.

Not only had there been no confetti, there had been no wedding bells, either. All the church bells had been silent since 1940 and were only supposed to ring if there was an invasion. The thing was, I hadn't even noticed at first because I had got so used to the silence.

I thought that was very sad, and I cried myself to sleep that night.

•

Annie paused with the dusty file folder in her hands when she heard footsteps on the stairs. She hoped it would be PC Gould bringing her a cup of tea, so she was surprised when she saw, instead, DCI Banks.

'Inspector Harmond told me you were down here,' Banks said.

Annie turned her nose up and gestured around at the musty-smelling, ill-lit basement room. 'Welcome to Central Records,' she said. 'You can see how often we dip into our history around here.'

'Don't worry. One day it'll all be on the computer.'

'When I'm long since dead and buried.'

Banks smiled as he ducked under an overhead pipe and walked over to join her. 'Anything yet?'

'Quite a lot, as a matter of fact. I've been on the phone most of the day, and I was just checking some missing-persons files.'

'And?'

'It's a bit of a confusing period for that sort of thing. Just after the war. There were so many changes, so many people coming and going. Anyway, most of the ones who went missing seemed to turn up eventually, either dead or alive, or in the colonies. There are a couple of young women who fit the general description still unaccounted for. I'll follow up on them.'

'Fancy a pint? The Black Swan?'

Annie smiled. 'You took the words right out of my mouth.'

What a relief. If she had been hoping for a cup of tea, the prospect of a pint of Swan's Down was even more appealing. She had been in the stifling basement for the best part of the afternoon, and her mouth was full of dust, her contact lenses beginning to dry out. And it *was* gone five on a Friday afternoon.

Comfortably ensconced on a padded bench just a few minutes later, legs stretched out and crossed at the ankles, pint already half finished, Annie smacked her lips. If she were a cat, she would have been purring.

'I checked the Voters Register first,' she said, 'but the clerk in the council office told me it was frozen at the start of the war. The last person they've got listed for Bridge Cottage is a Miss Violet Croft. I had a bit more luck with the Land Registry. Violet Croft rented the cottage from the Clifford estate, and the manager kept impeccable records. She lived there between the fourteenth of September, 1919, and the third of July, 1940, so she must be the old lady Ruby Kettering remembered, the one the village kids thought was a witch. The cottage remained empty until June 1941, when a Mr and Mrs Shackleton took up residence there. It might have been requisitioned for the billeting of evacuees or military personnel in the interim period, but there was no record of that, and there's no way of finding out.'

'I doubt that many places stayed empty for long during the war,' said Banks. 'Maybe some soldiers got billeted there, killed a local tart in a drunken orgy and then decided to cover their tracks?'

'It's possible.' Annie gave a slight shiver.

'We're talking about wartime,' Banks went on. 'Army camps and air force bases sprang up overnight, like mushrooms. Evacuees came and went. It was easy to disappear, change identity, slip through the cracks.'

'But people had identity cards and ration books. The council clerk told me. He said there was a National Registry at the beginning of the war, and everyone got identity cards.'

'I imagine those sort of things were open to a fiddle easily enough. Who knows, maybe we're dealing with a Nazi spy done in by the secret service?'

Annie laughed. 'Mata Hari?'

'Maybe. Anyway, what happened to Miss Violet Croft?'

Annie flipped over a page in her notebook. 'I dropped by Saint Jude's next and found the young curate very helpful. They've got all the old parish registry records and magazines from Saint Bart's stored in the vestry there. Boxes of them. Violet Croft, spinster of the parish, died in July 1940 of pneumonia. She was seventy-seven.'

'That lets her out. What about the Shackletons?'

'Much more interesting. They were married at Saint Bart's on the seventh of June, 1941. The husband's name was Matthew Stephen Shackleton, the wife's maiden name Gloria Kathleen Stringer. The witnesses were Gwynneth Shackleton and Cynthia Garmen.'

'Were they Hobb's End residents?'

'Matthew Shackleton was. His parents lived at 38 High Street. They ran the newsagent's shop. The bride's listed as being from London, parents deceased.'

'Big place,' Banks muttered. 'How old was she?'

'Nineteen. Born the seventeenth of September, 1921.'

'Interesting. That would put her within Dr Williams's age range by the end of the war.'

'Exactly.'

'Any mention of children?'

'No. I looked through the registry of baptisms, but there's nothing there. Was he certain about that, do you think?'

'He seemed to be. You saw the pitting for yourself.'

'I wouldn't know a parturition scar from a hole in the ground. It *could* have been a post-mortem injury, couldn't it? I mean, these things are often far from accurate.'

'It could have been. We'll check with Dr Glendenning after he's done the post-mortem. Do you know what? I'm beginning to get a vision of St Catherine's House looming large in your future.'

Annie groaned. Checking birth, marriage and death certificates was one of the most boring jobs a detective could get. The only positive aspect was that you got to go to London, but even that was offset by the department's lack of willingness to grant expenses for an overnight stay. No time to check out the shops.

'Any luck with the education authorities?' Banks asked.

'No. They said they lost the Hobb's End records, or misplaced them. Same with the doctors and the dentist.

The ones who practised in Hobb's End are all dead, and
their practices went with them. Records, too, I imagine. I
think we can say goodbye to that line of inquiry.'

'Pity. What does your instinct tell you, Annie?'

Annie pointed her thumb towards her chest. '*Moi?*'

'Yes, you. I want your feelings on the case so far.'

Annie was surprised. No senior officer had ever asked
for her *feelings* before, for her *feminine intuition*. Banks
was certainly different. 'Well, sir,' she said, 'for a start, I
don't think it's a stranger killing.'

'Why not?'

'You asked for my feelings, not logic.'

'Okay.'

'It *looks* domestic. Like that bloke who killed his wife
and sailed off to Canada.'

'Dr Crippen?'

'That's the one. I saw Donald Pleasence play him on
telly. Creepy.'

'Crippen buried his wife under the cellar.'

'Cellar. Outbuilding. Same difference.'

'All right, I take your point. Conclusion?'

'Victim: Gloria Shackleton.'

'Killer?'

'Husband, or someone else who knew her.'

'Motive?'

'God knows. Jealousy, sex, money. Pick one. Does it
matter?'

'Did you ask Mrs Kettering if she kept in touch with
anyone else who lived in Hobb's End?'

'Sorry, sir. It slipped my mind.'

'Ask her. Maybe we can track down some people who
actually *knew* the Shackletons. Who knows where the old

residents live now? We might even get a weekend in Paris or New York out of this.'

Annie noticed Banks avert his eyes. Was he flirting? 'That would be nice,' she said, sounding as neutral as possible. 'Anyway, for what it's worth, I think it's more the kind of thing someone who lived there, or near there, would do. It was a good hiding place. I don't think anyone could have foreseen the reservoir, or the drought. Not that it would matter, really. I mean, if Adam Kelly hadn't been playing truant and larking about on that roof, we'd never have found out. You can't anticipate an accident of fate like that.'

'*Blackout curtains*.' Banks slapped his palm on the table.

'Come again, sir?'

'Blackout curtains. It's something John Webb told me. He said they found some heavy black material with the body. I didn't make the connection at the time, but it makes sense now. The body was wrapped in blackout curtains, Annie. And Geoff Turner mentioned wartime dental work. When did the blackout end?'

'At dawn, I suppose.'

Banks smiled. 'Idiot. I mean when was it no longer required?'

'I don't know.'

'We can find out easily enough, I suppose. Either the blackout material was left over – which I'd guess was unlikely, because from what I remember my mother telling me, *nothing* was left over during the war – or it was no longer needed for its original purpose, which might help narrow down the time of the murder even more. But I certainly think we're dealing with a wartime crime, and Gloria Shackleton fits the bill as victim.'

'Brilliant, Holmes.'

'Elementary. Anyway, before we go any further, let's find out all we can about her. What was her maiden name again?'

'Stringer, sir. Gloria Stringer.'

'Right. We already know she's about the right age, and we know she lived in Bridge Cottage during the war. She hasn't shown up as missing?'

'Not in any records I've seen. And hers was the first name I looked for.'

'Okay. If you can find no trace of her existence in the local records after, say, 1946, then we could narrow things down a bit.' Banks looked at his watch. 'How about something to eat? I'm getting hungry. I don't want to eat here again. Are there any decent restaurants in Harkside?'

Annie paused for a moment, thinking of every restaurant where she had found nothing she could eat but a salad, or meat and two veg without the meat, then she gave in to the little surge of devil-may-care excitement that tingled through her and said, 'Well, sir, there's always my place.'

•

After the honeymoon, Gloria continued to report for work at the farm every day at eight o'clock and she wasn't home until five or later. On weekends, she was at Bridge Cottage, looking fresh and beautiful, ready for Matthew's arrival. Matthew passed his engineering degree, graduating with first-class honours, as I knew he would, and started his military training at Catterick, which wasn't too far away.

Gloria had managed, I discovered one evening, to barter her needlework skills for an extra half-day off work at the farm, which gave her the full weekend. Her local area supervisor would be none the wiser, so long as the Kilnseys didn't tell. And while Gloria kept them in mended clothes they were hardly likely to do that.

Most days I was busy with the shop. In my spare time I was involved in the Harkside Amateur Players' production of a new J. B. Priestley play, *When We Are Married*, so I spent a lot of time in rehearsal.

Despite all this, we managed to get to the pictures in Harkside together a few times. Gloria just loved films and sometimes she didn't even have time to change out of her uniform before pedalling at breakneck speed to meet me outside the Lyceum or the Lyric. She always managed some little eccentricity in her appearance, like wearing a bright pink ribbon or a yellow blouse instead of the regulation green.

That summer, for the first time, we had double summertime, which meant it stayed light much later. In autumn and winter, though, it was always dark when we had to go home. Though it was only a mile or so from Harkside to Hobb's End across the fields, there was no marked path or road, and on a cloudy, moonless night you could wander for hours in the pitch-darkness and miss the place entirely. Unless there was a bright moon, we had to walk the long way home: all the way up Long Hill and then along The Edge, careful not to fall into Harksmere Reservoir.

Because it was much bigger, Harkside was eerier than Hobb's End in the blackout. For a start, they had street lamps, which we didn't, and though they weren't lit, of course, each one of them now had a white stripe painted up its length to help you see your way in the dark, the same way there were stripes of white paint along the kerbsides. People had also put the little dabs of luminous paint on their doorbells, which glowed like fireflies all along the streets.

Sometimes we accepted a lift with some of the RAF boys

from Rowan Woods, and we even became quite friendly with a couple of Canadian airmen attached to the RAF: Mark, from Toronto, and Stephen, from Winnipeg. Mark was the handsomest one, and I could have listened to his soft, smooth accent all night long. I could tell he liked Gloria by the way he looked at her. He even contrived to touch her in small ways, like taking her hand to help her step into the Jeep, and touching the spot between her shoulders if he opened a door for her and ushered her through. Gloria seemed amused by it all.

Stephen had a high, squeaky voice, ears that stuck out and hair that seemed glued on like handfuls of straw, but he was nice enough. Sometimes we let them take us to the pictures and they were both very well behaved.

For Gloria's twentieth birthday, in September, I took her to Brunton's Café on Long Hill, where we gorged ourselves on grilled sausage with mashed potatoes, braised butter-beans, followed by jam roll and custard. Matthew couldn't be with us because it was a weekday, but Gloria showed me the locket he had already given her as a birthday present. It was beautiful: dark gold with their names entwined on the heart and a photograph, cut out from one of the wedding pictures, of the two of them inside. After tea, holding our tummies, we went to the Lyceum to see *Ziegfeld Girl*, starring Jimmy Stewart and Lana Turner. It was so memorable that the next day I couldn't remember a single melody.

It was Gloria's choice, of course. Unfortunately, our tastes couldn't have been more different. Gloria liked empty-headed Hollywood musicals and romantic comedies with beautiful stars and handsome leading men, whereas I preferred something with a bit of meat on its bones, an adaptation of the classics, say. More often than not, I preferred to stay at home and listen to dramas on the Home

Service, where I very much enjoyed Mrs Gaskell's *Cranford* and Thackeray's *Vanity Fair*, among others.

Anyway, it was Gloria's birthday. She also liked the Lyceum best because of the red plush seats and the way the organ came rising up slowly and majestically through its trap-door, with the famous Teddy Marston, usually playing 'The White Cliffs of Dover', 'Shine On Victory Moon', or some such patriotic tune. Gloria would have tears in her eyes when she listened to that sort of thing. Then the lights dimmed and the heavy red velvet curtains parted slowly.

Sometimes Alice, Cynthia and Betty came to the pictures with us, even Michael Stanhope on occasion. While he often delighted us with his wicked critical commentary on the way home, he disappointed me in leaning more towards Gloria's sort of film than towards something with a bit more substance. After all, he *was* supposed to be a serious artist.

I often wondered what he and Gloria found to talk about when they went drinking together in the Shoulder of Mutton. I was too young to go with them, of course, not that they ever invited me. Anyway, I suppose they must have had long, intricate conversations about the deeper meaning of Hollywood musicals.

Matthew and Gloria tried to furnish Bridge Cottage as best they could. This was before the Government banned most furniture production, but even then the good stuff was either expensive or unavailable. You had to scrounge for the simplest of things, like curtain rods and coat hooks. They went to auctions some weekends, bought an old sideboard or a wardrobe here, a dresser there, and bit by bit they managed to furnish the house in a tasteful if not terribly elegant way. They made a home out of Bridge Cottage.

Gloria's pride and joy was the radiogram they bought from the Coopers after their son, John, was killed when the

Prince of Wales was sunk just before Christmas. It had been John's pride and joy, and his mum and dad couldn't bear to keep it around the house after he was gone.

Gloria honoured her promise to give me dancing lessons and I spent an hour or so over at Bridge Cottage each weekend while Matthew read the newspaper after dinner. It felt strange having her put her arms around me. Her body felt soft and I could smell her perfume, *Evening in Paris*. She was a good teacher, but with her being so much shorter it was awkward at first, having her lead me. I soon got used to it. I was a good pupil, too. Over the next couple of weeks I learned the waltz, the quickstep and the foxtrot. I actually tried out my skills at a Bonfire Night dance in the Harkside Mechanics Institute. We might not have been able to have bonfires during the war, but we still managed to celebrate Guy Fawkes Night. Anyway, I did very well at dancing, and that worked wonders for my confidence.

By Christmas, Matthew had almost finished his training, and there was talk of a posting. I asked him if he was going to be a commissioned officer and he said he didn't think so. He had been for an interview and was upset at the way the board asked him about what his parents did for a living and how often he rode with the local hunt. He said there wasn't much hope of a shopkeeper's son getting a commission.

It was also that Christmas, at a party Gloria and Matthew held, when I got my first real inkling of Gloria's problems with men.

•

Annie's place turned out to be a squat, narrow terrace cottage at the centre of a labyrinth. Banks left his car parked by the green and walked through so many twisting narrow streets and ginnels, by backyards where washing hung out on lines in the evening sun, where children played and dogs barked behind sturdy gates, that he was lost within seconds.

'Why do I keep thinking I should have left a piece of thread attached to the Black Swan?' he said as he followed her down a snicket narrow enough to pass through only in single file.

Annie cast a glance over her shoulder and smiled. 'Like Theseus, you mean? I hope you don't think I'm the Minotaur just because I live at the centre of all this?'

Banks's mythology was a bit rusty, but he remembered being impressed by an ancient vase he had seen on a school trip to the British Museum. It depicted Ariadne outside the Labyrinth holding one end of the thread and Theseus at its centre killing the Minotaur.

He had even seen what was left of the Labyrinth at the Palace of Knossos on Crete, where a pedantic guide inflicted with a serious case of synonymitis had explained it all to Sandra and him as they tried to hold back their giggles. 'And this is King Minos's throne, his regal seat, his chair of office . . . And they carried her body to the hill, the rise, the tor, the mountain.' He remembered the olive trees with their silver-green oily leaves and the orange trees lining the road from Heraklion.

But now wasn't the time to be thinking about Sandra.

He was about to say that he thought of Annie more as Ariadne, seeing as she was probably the only one who could get him out of there, but he bit his tongue. Considering what transpired between Theseus and Ariadne on Naxos, it didn't seem like a very good idea.

He followed Annie deeper into the labyrinth.

Her keys were jingling in her hand now. 'Almost there,' she said, glancing back at him, then she opened a high wooden gate in a stone wall, led him through a small flagged yard and in the back door.

'Where do you park?' Banks asked.

Annie dropped her keys on the kitchen table and laughed. 'A long way away. Look, it's tiny, there's not much of a view and very little light. But guess what? It's cheap, and it's mine. Well, it will be when I've paid off the mortgage. You must have been a DS once?'

'A DC, too.' Banks remembered the early days, scraping and saving to make ends meet, especially when Tracy and Brian were little and Sandra had to take extended periods off work. There were no maternity benefits back then. Not for dental receptionists, anyway. Even now, as a DCI, it was difficult making payments on the cottage. He also had to furnish the place by driving around to local auctions and car-boot sales. There would be no Greek holiday this year. 'At least you get overtime,' he said. 'You probably make more than me.'

'In Harkside? You must be joking.' Annie led him through to the living room. It was small but cosy, and she had decorated much of it in whites, lemons and creams because of the lack of outside light. As a result, the room seemed airy and cheerful. There was just enough space for a small white three-piece suite, the settee of which would probably seat two very thin people, a TV, mini-stereo and a small bookcase under the window. Several miniature watercolours hung on the walls. Local scenes, mostly. Banks recognized Semerwater, Aysgarth Falls and Richmond Castle. There was also one oil portrait of a young woman with flowing pre-Raphaelite hair and laughing eyes.

'Who painted these?' he asked.

'I did. Most of them.'

'They're very good.'

Annie seemed embarrassed. 'I don't think so. Not really. I mean, they're competent, but . . .' She put her hand to her head and swept back her hair. 'Anyway, look, I feel really grubby after being down in that basement. I'm going up for a quick shower first, then I'll start dinner. It won't take long. Make yourself at home. Open the window if you're too warm. There's plenty of beer in the fridge. Help yourself.' Then she turned and left the room. Banks heard stairs creak as she walked up.

This woman was an enigma, he thought. She had a DCI, her boss, as a guest in her house, yet nothing in her behaviour towards him indicated a deferential relationship. She was the same always, with everyone, not adapting herself to the various roles people play in life. He imagined she would even be the same with Jimmy Riddle. Not that she'd invite that bastard into her home, Banks hoped. He heard the shower start. Though it was small, the cottage wasn't particularly old – not like his own – and it had an upstairs bathroom and toilet. Even so, he guessed Annie must have had the shower installed herself, because it certainly wouldn't have come with the original building.

First, he did what he always did when left alone in a new room; he nosed around. He couldn't help it. Curiosity was part of his nature. He didn't open drawers or read private mail, not unless he thought he was dealing with a criminal, but he liked to look at books, choice of music and the general lie of the land.

Annie's living room was fairly Spartan. It wasn't that she didn't own books or CDs, but that she didn't have many of either. He got the impression that she might have had to pare down her existence at one time and everything that remained was important to her. There seemed to be no chaff. Unlike his own collection, where the mistakes piled up alongside the hidden gems. Discs he never listened to shared shelf space with some that were almost worn out.

First, he crouched down and checked the CD titles in the cabinet under the stereo. It was an odd collection: Gregorian chants, Don Cherry's *Eternal Now* and several 'ambient' pieces by Brian Eno. There was also an extensive blues collection, from Mississippi John Hurt to John Mayall. Next to these stood a few pop and folk titles: Emmylou Harris's *The Wrecking Ball*, Kate and Anna McGarrigle, some k. d. lang.

The books mainly centred around Eastern philosophy; it was a real sixties treasure trove, considering that Annie was a nineties woman. Banks remembered some of the titles. He had come across them first in Jem's room, in the Notting Hill days, and he had even borrowed and read some of them: Baba Ram Dass's *Be Here Now*; Gurdjieff's *Meetings With Remarkable Men*; Ouspensky, Carlos Castaneda, Thomas Merton, Alan Watts, and old blue-covered Pelican paperbacks about yoga, Zen and meditation.

Seeing them again took him right back to the dim, candle-lit room with the melting-butter walls and the jasmine joss sticks, to the first time he smoked hash, with Arlo Guthrie's 'Alice's Restaurant' on the stereo; earnest, all-night arguments about Marx and Marcuse, changing the system, love and revolution, with Banks, more often than not, playing the straight man, the devil's advocate. Gentle, sweet-natured Jem, his gaunt face always in shadows, dark hair spilling over his narrow shoulders, his soft, husky voice and his unwillingness to kill even the mice that sometimes walked across the room right in front of them as they talked. His record collection: *Rainbow Bridge*, *Bitches Brew*, *Live Dead*, *Joy of a Toy*.

Strange days. Old days.

Back then, Banks had spent half his time studying industrial psychology and cost accounting and the other half listening to Miles Davis, Jimi Hendrix, Roland Kirk and The Soft Machine. One way led to security and what his parents wanted; the other led to uncertainty and God only knew what else. Poverty and drug addiction, as like as not. Hard to believe now that there had been a time when it was all balanced on a razor's edge, when he could have gone either way.

Then Jem died and Banks joined the police, a third option he hadn't considered before, even in his wildest dreams.

The shower stopped, and a few seconds later Banks heard the roar of a hair-dryer. Shaking off the memories that seemed to cling to his mind like cobwebs, he wandered into the kitchen. Like the living room, it was decorated in light colours, white tiles for the most part, with chocolate brown around the work area, just for contrast. In addition to the small oven, fridge, sink and countertops, there was a dining table. It could probably seat about four comfortably, he guessed.

Banks opened the fridge and took out a bottle of Black Sheep. He found an opener in one of the drawers and a pint glass in one of the cupboards. Carefully, he poured out the beer so it had just enough head on it, then he took a sip and went back into the living room. The hair-dryer stopped, and he could hear Annie walking around upstairs. He took *Eternal Now* from its jewel case and put it in the CD player. He had heard of Don Cherry, a jazz trumpeter who used to play with Ornette Coleman, but didn't actually know his work.

The music started with strummed chords on oddly

tuned stringed instruments, then a deep, echoey flute-like instrument entered. Banks turned down the volume, picked up the CD liner notes and sat down to read while he waited for Annie, abandoning himself to the weird combinations of wooden saxophones, Indian harmoniums and Polynesian gamelans.

Before the first track had finished, Annie breezed into the room exuding freshly scrubbed warmth.

'I never took you for a Don Cherry fan,' she said, a wicked grin on her face.

'Life is full of surprises. I like it.'

'I thought you were an opera buff.'

'Been asking around?'

'Just station gossip. I'll start dinner now, if you want.'

Banks smiled. 'Fine with me.'

She disappeared into the kitchen. 'You can keep me company,' she called out over her shoulder.

Banks put the CD case back on the shelf and carried his beer through. He sat down at the kitchen table. Annie was bending over pulling vegetables out of the fridge. The jeans looked good on her.

'Pasta okay?' she asked, half turning her head.

'Great. It's a long time since I've had any home cooking. Mostly these days it's been either pub grub or something quick and easy from Marks and Sparks.'

'Ah, the lonely eater's friends.'

Banks laughed. It was funny, and rather sad, he had often noticed, how you saw so many young, single men and women wandering around the Marks food section just after five on a weeknight, reaching for the prawn vindaloo, then changing their minds, going instead for the single portion of chicken Kiev and the carton of mixed vegetables. He supposed it might be a good place to pick up a girl.

Annie filled a large pan with water, added a little salt and oil, then set it on the gas ring. She didn't waste a gesture as she washed and chopped mushrooms, shallots, garlic and courgettes. There was a certain economic grace to her movements that Banks found quite hypnotic; she seemed to possess a natural, centred quality that put him at ease.

She went to the kitchen cupboard, took down a bottle of red wine and uncorked it.

'Want some?'

Banks held up his beer. 'I'll finish this first.'

Annie poured herself a generous glass. Soon the oil was hot in the frying pan and she was dropping the vegetables in a handful at a time. When they were done, she added a cup or two of tinned tomatoes and a handful of herbs. Banks decided to make cooking his next project, after he had fixed up the cottage. Something else to keep depression at bay. He liked food, so it made sense to learn how to cook it properly now that he was alone.

About the time Banks finished his beer, Annie announced that dinner was ready and delivered two steaming plates to the table. Don Cherry finished, and she put on Emmylou Harris, whose voice seemed to catch on sharp notches inside her throat before it came out, singing about loneliness, loss, pain. All things Banks could relate to. He ground pepper and grated Parmesan on to the pasta and tucked in. After a couple of bites, he complimented Annie.

'See,' she said. 'It's not all salads and tofu. You learn to be more inventive in the kitchen when you're a vegetarian.'

'I can tell.'

'Wine?'

'Please.'

Annie brought over the bottle of Sainsbury's Bulgarian Merlot, refilled her glass and poured one for Banks. 'Plenty more where that came from,' she said. 'You know, I'd really like to find out more about this Hobb's End artist, Michael Stanhope.'

'Why? Because you think he's connected to the case?'

'Well, he might be, mightn't he? He *was* living in Hobb's End during the war. Maybe he knew the Shackleton woman. There may be other paintings. They might tell us something.'

'They might,' Banks agreed. 'Though I'm not sure how far art could be trusted as evidence, even if he painted the murder itself.'

Annie smiled. 'Not technically, perhaps. But artists often distort reality to reveal the truth about it.'

'Do you believe that?'

Annie's eyes, the colour of milk chocolate, shone in the failing light. 'Yes,' she said. 'I do. Not about my own work. As I said, I'm technically competent, but I lack whatever it is that makes a great artist. Vision. Passion. Intensity. Insanity. I don't know. Probably what most people call genius. But the true artist's reality is every bit as valid as any other. Perhaps more so in some ways because an artist struggles to see more deeply, to illuminate.'

'A lot of art is far from illuminating.'

'Yes, but that's often because the subject, the truth he's trying to get at, is so elusive that only symbols or vague images will do to approach it. Don't get me wrong. I'm not saying that artists are always trying to get some sort of deep message across. They're not preachers. What I'm saying is that Stanhope obviously perceived something odd about Hobb's End, something that went below the surface, beyond the superficial ideas of village life. He saw something *evil* there and maybe something redemptive in the children.'

'Isn't that a bit far-fetched? Maybe it was just because there was a war coming?'

'I'm not trying to make out he was a visionary. Just that he saw something a lot of other people would either not see or would gloss over. He really *looked* and maybe he saw something that might be useful to us. Damn!'

'What?'

'Oh, I just spilled some pasta sauce on my T-shirt, that's all.' She grinned and rubbed at the red mark over her breast. That only made it worse. 'I always was a messy eater.'

'I won't tell anyone.'

'Thanks. Where was I?'

'The artist's vision.'

'Right. It's got nothing to do with personality. In life, Stanhope might well have been a mean, lecherous, drunken slob. Believe me, I've known a lot of artists, and many of them have been exactly that. Talk about groups living up to their stereotypes.'

Banks sipped some wine. Emmylou Harris was singing about wearing something pretty and white. Banks thought he could detect Neil Young's high-pitched warble in the background. 'You seem to know a lot about the subject,' he said. 'Any particular reason?'

Annie fell silent for a moment, looking down at her empty plate, moving the fork around in her hand. Finally, she said in a quiet voice, 'My father's an artist.'

'Is he well known?'

'Not really. In some circles, perhaps.' She looked up and smiled crookedly. 'He'll never go down in history as one of the greats, if that's what you mean.'

'He's still living, I assume?'

'Ray? Oh, yes. He's just turned fifty-two. He was only twenty when I was born.'

'Does he have what it takes to be a great artist?'

'To some extent. But you have to remember, there's a big, big gap between someone like my dad and Van Gogh or Picasso. It's all relative.'

'What about your mother?'

Again, Annie was silent a few moments. 'She died,' she said at last. 'When I was six. I don't really remember her very well. I wish I could, but I can't.'

'That's sad. I'm sorry.'

'More wine?'

'Please.'

Annie poured.

'That oil portrait in the living room, is it your mother?'

Annie nodded.

'Your father painted it?'

'Yes.'

'It's very good. She was a beautiful woman. You look a lot like her.'

It was almost dark outside now. Annie hadn't put on any lights, so Banks couldn't see her expression.

'Where did you grow up?' he asked.

'St Ives.'

'Nice place.'

'You know it?'

'I've been there on holiday a couple of times. Years ago, when I worked on the Met. It's a bit far from here.'

'I don't get down as often as I should. Maybe you remember it was a magnet for hippies in the sixties? It became something of an artists' colony.'

'I remember.'

'My father lived there even before that. Over the years he's done all kinds of odd jobs to support his art. He might have even rented you a deck-chair on the beach. Now he paints local landscapes and sells them to tourists. Does some glass engraving too. He's quite successful at it.'

'So he makes a decent living?'

'Yes. He doesn't have to rent out the deck-chairs any more.'

'He brought you up alone?'

Annie pushed her hair back. 'Well, not really. I mean, yes, in the sense that my mother was dead, but we lived in a sort of artists' colony on an old farm just outside town, so there were always lots of other people around. My extended family, you might call them. Ray's been living with Jasmine for nearly twenty years now.'

'It sounds like a strange set-up.'

'Only to someone who hasn't experienced it. It seemed pefectly normal to me. It was the other kids who seemed strange. The ones with mothers and fathers.'

'Did you get teased a lot at school?'

'Tormented. Some of the locals were very intolerant. Thought we were having orgies every night, doing drugs, worshipping the devil, the usual stuff. Actually, though there always seemed to be some pot around, they couldn't have been further from the truth. There were a few wild ones – that kind of free, experimental way of life always attracts a few unstable types – but on the whole it was a pretty good environment to grow up in. Plus I got a great education in the arts – and not from school.'

'What made you join the police?'

'The village bobby took my virginity.'

'*Seriously.*'

Annie laughed and poured more wine. 'It's true. He did.

His name was Rob. He came up to see us once, looking for someone who'd passed through, one of the occasional undesirables. He was good-looking. I was seventeen. He noticed me. It seemed a suitable act of rebellion.'

'Against your par— your father?'

'Against all of them. Oh, don't get me wrong, I didn't hate them or anything. It was just that I'd had enough of that lifestyle by then. There were too many people around all the time, nowhere to escape to. Too much talk and not enough done. You could never get any privacy. That's why I value it so much now. And how many times can a grown person listen to "White Rabbit"?'

Banks laughed. 'I feel the same way about "Nessun Dorma".'

'Anyway, Rob seemed solid, dependable, more sure of himself and what he believed in.'

'Was he?'

'Yes. We went out until I went to university in Exeter. Then he turned up there a year or so later as a DC. He introduced me to some of his friends and we sort of started going out again. I suppose they found me a bit weird. After all, I didn't throw out the baby with the bathwater. I still had a lot of my father's values, and I was into yoga and meditation even back then, when nobody else was. I didn't really fit in anywhere. I don't know why, but being a detective sounded exciting. *Different.* When you get right down to it, most jobs are so bloody boring. I'd thought of becoming a teacher, but I changed my mind and joined the force. It was a bit impulsive, I'll admit.'

Banks wanted to ask her why she was in a dead-end place like Harkside, but he sensed that this wasn't the moment. At least he could ask a leading question and see if she was willing to be led. 'How has it worked out?'

'It's tough for a woman. But things are what you make them. I'm a feminist, but I'm the sort who just likes to get on with it rather than whine about what's wrong with the system. Maybe that comes from my dad. He goes his own way. Anyway, you know all about what it's like, about how *unexciting* it is most of the time. And how bloody boring it can be.'

'True enough. What happened to Rob?'

'He got killed during an armed drugs bust three years later. Poor sod. His gun jammed.'

'I'm sorry.'

Annie put her hand to her forehead, then fanned it in front of her face. 'Ooh, I'm hot. Listen to me go on. I haven't talked to anyone like this in ages.'

'I wouldn't mind a cigarette. Would you like to stand outside with me? Cool down a bit, if it's possible?'

'Okay.'

They went out into the backyard. It was a warm night, though there were signs of a breeze beginning to stir. Annie stood beside him. He could smell her scent. He lit up, inhaled and blew out a plume of dark smoke.

'It was like drawing teeth,' he said, 'getting you to talk about your personal life.'

'I'm not used to it. I'm like you in a lot of ways.'

'What do you mean?'

'Well, how much have you told me about your past?'

'What do you want to know?'

'That's not what I mean. You just wouldn't think of telling people about yourself, of letting someone in, would you? It's not in your nature. You're a loner, like me. I don't just mean now, because you're . . .'

'Because my wife left me?'

'Right. Not just because you're *physically* alone or

because you're living alone. I mean in your nature, deep inside. Even when you *were* married. I think you've got a lonely, isolated nature. It colours the way you see the world, the detachment you feel. I'm not explaining it very well, am I? I think I'm the same. I can be alone in a crowded room. I'll bet you can be, too.'

Banks thought about what Annie had said as he smoked. It was what Sandra had said when they had their final argument, what he had refused to admit was the truth. There was something in him that always stood apart, that she couldn't reach and he wouldn't offer. It wasn't just the Job and its demands, but something deeper: a central core of loneliness. He had been like that even as a child. An observer. Always on the outside, even when he played with others. As Annie said, it was a part of his nature, and he didn't think he could change it if he tried.

'Maybe you're right,' he said. 'Funny thing, though. I always thought I was a simple family man.'

'And now?'

'And now I'm not so sure I ever was.'

A cat miaowed in a nearby yard. Down the street, a door opened and closed and someone turned a television on. Emmylou drifted through the open kitchen window singing about losing this sweet old world. Banks dropped his cigarette and trod on the red ember. Suddenly a chill gust of wind rustled the distant trees and passed through the yard. Annie shivered. Banks put his arm around her and moved her gently towards him. She let her head rest on his shoulder.

'Oh dear,' she said. 'I don't know if this is a good idea.'

'Why?'

Annie paused. Banks could feel her warm shoulder under the thin T-shirt, the ridge of her bra strap.

'Well, we've both probably had too much to drink.'

'If it's the rank thing that's bothering you—'

'No. No. It's not that. I don't give a damn about that, to be honest. As I said, the Job's not my be-all and end-all. I still have a bit of the bohemian left in me. No, it's just that . . . I've had some bad experiences with men. I've been . . . I mean I haven't been . . . Oh, shit, why is this so difficult?' She rubbed her forehead. Banks kept silent. Annie sighed deeply. 'I've been celibate,' she said. 'By choice. For nearly two years now.'

'I don't want to pressure you,' Banks said.

'Don't worry. I wouldn't let you. I make my own choices.'

'I'll never find my way out of this labyrinth alone.'

'I'd lead you,' Annie said, facing him and smiling. 'If I really wanted you to go. But somehow I doubt whether you're in a fit state to drive. It's probably my duty to arrest you. Crime intervention.' She paused and frowned, then rested her hand lightly on his chest. His heart beat more loudly. Surely she could hear it, feel it? 'There are a lot of reasons for not taking this any further, you know,' she went on. 'I've heard you're a bad lot.'

'Not true.'

'A womanizer.'

'Not true.'

They looked at one another for a few moments. Annie bit her lip, shivered again and said, 'Oh, hell.'

Banks wished he hadn't just smoked a cigarette. He leaned forward and kissed her. Her lips yielded and her body moulded itself to his. Then he forgot all about cigarettes.

6

Matthew and Gloria decided to have their party on Christmas Eve, but first we all went ice-skating on Harksmere Reservoir. Already there were lots of people around and fires burned in braziers set up along the edges of the ice. It was dark and there was something hypnotic about the mix of ice and fire in the twilight – to me there was, at any rate – so I was skating in a sort of trance. If I shut my eyes I could see the flames dancing behind my eyelids and feel flashes of warmth as I sped by the bank.

People started drifting back to Bridge Cottage at about seven o'clock, then the other guests started to arrive, including more airmen from the base, some with their girlfriends. Alice's Eric was away in North Africa by then, but Betty's William hadn't passed his medical, which didn't surprise me at all, so they would only let him in the Home Guard.

Michael Stanhope came dressed in his usual artistic 'costume', including hat and cane, but he did bring two bottles of gin and some wine, which made him most welcome indeed. He must have had a cellarful of drink. Alcohol wasn't always easy to come by then, most of the distilleries having shut down, and it was very expensive if you could get it. I could picture Michael Stanhope, knowing a war was coming, hoarding his private stock away, bottle by bottle. I hoped he wouldn't run out.

Matthew and Gloria had decorated the tiny front room as

best they could, with balloons, concertina streamers and
fairy lights over the mantelpiece. The whole place had a
warm, cosy feel with the blackout curtains up, especially
when you thought of the icicles and the frozen puddles outside. There was also plenty of mistletoe and a fake Christmas
tree dressed in lights and tinsel.

The only cigarettes we had in stock were Pasha, and
Gloria said they tasted like sweepings from the factory floor,
which they probably were. The Canadians had some
Players, though, so the room soon seemed to fill with
smoke. Mark and Stephen had also contributed a bottle of
Canadian Club whisky.

Unfortunately for Gloria, John Cooper's musical taste
hadn't extended much farther than opera, so the record
collection she'd picked up along with the radiogram was of
little use to her. So far, she didn't have many records of her
own, so we listened to the radio. Luckily, there was a Victor
Sylvester concert on that night, and soon people were
dancing close together in the cramped space.

Matthew had hardly let Gloria out of his sight for a
moment all day, but as the tiny cottage grew more crowded
and noisy, it was harder for them to stay together.

Couples danced or chatted. Cynthia and Johnny Marsden
hogged the sofa and kissed one another. Once, I even saw
him trying to put his hand up her dress, but she stopped him.
Gloria drank too much Canadian Club and then switched to
gin. She wasn't loud or falling down or anything, but there
was a sort of glaze to her eyes and a slight wobble in her step.
It all got more pronounced as the evening wore on, as did
the way she held her cigarette slightly askew as she swayed
in time to the music.

I got distracted by an RAF radio operator, who first
dragged me under the mistletoe and gave me a kiss that

tasted of tinned sardines, then proceeded to explain the intricacies of radiolocation to me. I should have told him I was a German spy. Hadn't he seen those 'Walls Have Ears' posters everywhere?

It must have been close to ten o'clock by then, and the party was still going strong. I suppose quite a few people were already drunk. I had only been drinking ginger ale – well, I *did* have just a drop of Canadian Club – but I was feeling light-headed because of all the gaiety. When you had a party in wartime, especially at some important time like Christmas, the fun was just a little louder, a little gaudier and a little more desperate than at peacetime parties.

Michael Stanhope was holding forth to a young corporal about how artists had a duty to shun propaganda in their search for truth. 'If governments listened to the artists,' he said, 'there would be no wars.' The corporal would probably have moved on ages ago had Mr Stanhope not been topping up his gin every few minutes.

Matthew, I noticed, was leaning against the wall deep in conversation with two men in army uniforms, no doubt trying to find out what military life was really like once the training was over.

I realized I hadn't seen Gloria for a while and wondered if she was sick or something. She *had* been drinking quite a lot. I needed to go to the toilet anyway, so as gently and politely as I could, I disengaged myself from the radio-location lecture. It was cold and dark outside, so I put my coat over my shoulders, picked up the torch with its tissue-filtered light and headed out into the backyard.

Bridge Cottage had two outbuildings; one was the toilet and the other was used for storage. I could hear the radio-gram playing 'In the Dark' from inside the house as I made my way down the flags to the toilet.

Suddenly, I heard sounds nearby. I paused, then I heard them again, a grunt and a muffled little voice calling out. I couldn't tell where it was coming from at first, then I realized it was behind the outbuilding. Puzzled, I tiptoed over and pointed my torch at the wall.

What I saw made my skin tingle. Even in the poor tissue-weakened light, I could see it was Gloria pinned to the wall by Mark, the Canadian airman. Her back was against the large 'V' sign someone had chalked there during the summer *Victory* campaign. Her dress was bunched around her waist, and the pale white flesh of her bare thighs above the stocking-tops stood out in the darkness. I remember thinking she must be freezing cold. Mark was crushed forward into her, one hand over her mouth, the other fumbling at his waist.

Gloria was calling out in a muffled voice, 'No, please, no!' over and over again, trying to struggle against him, and he was calling her filthy names. When he saw my light, he swore at me and took off around the front of the house.

Gloria leaned back against the wall, gasping and sobbing, not looking at me, her hair and clothes in disarray. Then she straightened her dress, leaned forward with her hands on her knees and was sick right on to the garden. It was warm and made the ice crack. I could see the chalk dust from the 'V' on the back of her dress.

I didn't know what to do. I knew nothing about these things back then and I wasn't even sure what sort of scene I had witnessed – except that there was something very wrong about it.

All I knew was that Gloria looked hurt, upset and in pain. So I did what came naturally; I opened my arms and she fell into them. Then I held her close and stroked her hair and told her not to worry, that everything would be all right.

•

The birds struck up the dawn chorus first, then the milk-man's float rattled by, and soon Banks was listening to the myriad strange sounds of an unfamiliar street through the half-open window of Annie's bedroom. A baby cried for feeding; someone slammed a door; a dog started barking; a letter-box snapped shut; a motorcycle revved up. Everything sounded all the more foreign since Banks had got used to the silence of his new cottage.

Annie lay beside him breathing softly; she would be silent for a while, then let out a soft exhalation part-way between a sniff and a sigh. There was enough light through the thin curtains for Banks to see her. She lay on her side, curled away from him, hands clasped in front, where he couldn't see them. The single white sheet had slipped down far enough for him to see the curve of her waist, follow it up to her shoulders and hair. She had a small mole about halfway. Gently, Banks touched it. Annie stirred a little but still she didn't wake.

Banks lay on his back and closed his eyes. His only fear last night, what almost held him back until that intimate moment in the backyard, when his arm moved of its own volition, was that he would feel the same way he did when he slept with Karen. He should have known better; he should have known this was different. He *did* know. But the fear was still there.

Their lovemaking had been a little tentative at first, but that was only to be expected. It never happened in real life the way it did in movies, with both lovers exploding together in a climax of Wagnerian proportions as fire-works burst, orchestras crescendoed and trains rushed into tunnels. That was pure Monty Python. In real lovemaking, especially with people new to one another's bodies, there are disappointments, mistakes, hesitancies. If you can laugh at these, as Banks and Annie had, then you are halfway there. If you find yourself looking forward to the hours of practice it will take to learn to please one another more, as Banks did, then you are more than halfway.

Afterwards, skin warm and damp and tangy with sweat, she had rested in the crook of his arm and he knew then that he wouldn't wake with a burning desire to be alone.

Just for the briefest of moments he gave in to a wave of paranoia and wondered if this was a trap Riddle had set for him. A new approach. Give him enough rope to hang himself. Were there hidden cameras in the bedroom walls? Was Annie Riddle's secret mistress? Were the two of them plotting Banks's final downfall? The thoughts scudded across his mind like cloud shadows over the daleside. Then, as quick as it came, the paranoia was gone. Jimmy Riddle obviously didn't know who DS Cabbot was, or what she looked like. He clearly didn't even know her first name, otherwise he wouldn't have sent Banks within twenty miles of her.

Banks opened his eyes and looked at the Tibetan mandala on the wall, a circle of fire full of brightly coloured, intricately entwined symbols and mythological figures, some fearful, armed, some clearly benevolent. Jem had had a similar poster on his wall, too, Banks remembered. He had said that it was a map of stages you go through to reach a state of wholeness. According to Jung, Jem also said, people who were beginning to get themselves together would see mandalas in their dreams, without knowing anything at all about Tantric Buddhism.

That kind of thinking had been one of Banks's big problems with the whole sixties thing; he thought it was the mark of a brain softened by too much marijuana or LSD. In their long arguments about changing the system, Jem had always taken the view that you can't change the system from within; if you're in it, you become part of it; you become absorbed and corrupted by it. You end up with a *stake* in it. Maybe that was what had happened to Banks, but even back then he had never felt fully able to join in, especially with phoney let's-all-love-one-another togetherness. Annie was right; he was a loner. He had always kept his distance, even from Jem. Maybe if he hadn't, Jem might not have died.

Annie stirred and Banks ran his hand slowly all the way from her hip to her shoulder.

'Mmm . . .' she murmured. 'Good morning.'

'Good morning.'

'I see you're awake.'

'Have been for hours.'

'You poor man. You should have got up, made some tea.'

'I'm not complaining.' Banks hooked his arm over her side and rested his palm on her stomach, easing her closer. He kissed the soft flesh between her shoulder and neck, then slid his hand up to cup her small breast. Last night he had discovered that she had a tiny red róse tattoo just above her left breast, and he found it incredibly sexy. He had never slept with a tattooed lady before. Annie sighed and pushed herself further back towards him; curved bodies moulding to one another, skin touching everywhere it could touch.

Banks forgot about Jem now. He touched Annie's shoulder gently to turn her towards him.

'No,' she whispered. 'Like this is just fine.'

And it was.

•

'The other night,' said Gloria the next time I saw her alone. 'At the Christmas party. I want to thank you. If you hadn't come along, I don't know what would have happened. I just don't want you to think it was something it wasn't.'

'I don't know what I think it was,' I said. I felt embarrassed, her talking to me like this. Cold, too. We were in the High Street and the icy wind whistled through my old coat as if it were full of holes. Which it probably was. I pulled the collar up over my throat and felt my bare hands freezing around the handles of the shopping bag. Foolishly, I had forgotten my mittens.

'I was just going to the toilet,' she said, 'and he followed me out there. Mark did. I know I'd had a bit too much to drink. I didn't mean to, but I suppose I might have given him some encouragement. He called me a tease, said I'd been leading him on all night. Things just got a bit out of hand, that's all.'

'What do you mean?' I started shifting from foot to foot, hoping the movement would keep me warm. Gloria didn't seem to feel the cold at all. Still, the land girls were provided with warm khaki overcoats.

'Earlier in the evening,' she went on. 'He got me under the mistletoe. Everyone was doing it. I didn't think anything of it but . . . Gwen?' She chewed on her lower lip.

'What?'

'Oh, I don't know. Men. Sometimes, it's just . . . I don't know what it is, you try to be nice to them, but they get the wrong idea.'

'Wrong idea?'

'Yes. I was only being friendly. Like I am with everyone. I didn't do anything to make him believe I was *that* kind of girl. Men sometimes get the wrong impression about me. I don't know why. It seems like they just can't stop them-selves. They're so strong. And believe it or not, sometimes it's easier just to give in.'

'Is that what you were doing? Giving in?'

'No. I was struggling. I was trying to call for Matt, for anyone, to help me but Mark had his hand over my mouth. Maybe before, I would have given in. I don't know. But now I've got Matt. I love him, Gwen, I didn't want to cause a fuss, get Matt upset, start trouble. I hate violence. I don't know what would have happened if you hadn't come along. I didn't have much fight left in me. Do you know what I mean?'

'I think so,' I said. I had given up on ever getting warm now. Luckily, I was so numb I couldn't feel the cold any more.

'Can we just forget about it?' Gloria pleaded.

I nodded. 'That's probably for the best.'

She gave me a hug. 'Good. And we're still friends, Gwen?'

'Of course.'

•

After Banks had gone, Annie did her usual twenty minutes of meditation, followed by a few yoga exercises and a shower. As she dried herself, her skin tingled and she realized how good she felt. Last night had been worth the risk. And this morning. That celibacy business wasn't all it was cracked up to be anyway.

They definitely needed more practice. Banks was a little reticent, a bit conservative. That was only to be expected, Annie thought, after twenty or more years of marriage to the same woman. She thought back to her lovemaking with Rob, and how natural they had become. Even when they had been apart for a year or two, they had picked up the rhythm again without any trouble when they got together in Exeter.

How could so many people have read Banks wrong? she wondered. Gossip distorts the truth, certainly, but to such an extent? Perhaps he was the empty canvas people used to project their fantasies on to. Whatever he was, she hoped he wasn't the kind who felt a moral obligation to fall in love just because he slept with a woman. When it came right down to it, she hadn't a clue *what* she wanted from the relationship, if indeed there was to be a relationship. She wanted to see more of him, yes; she wanted to sleep with him again, yes; but beyond that, she didn't know. Still, maybe it would be nice if he did fall a little bit in love with her. Just a little bit.

Most of all, she hoped to hell that he wouldn't regret what they had done for *her* sake, wouldn't feel that he had taken advantage of her vulnerability or her tipsiness, or any of that male rubbish. As for the career business, surely he couldn't imagine she had only slept with him because he was her boss or because she was after advancement? Annie laughed as she pulled on her jeans. Sleeping with DCI Banks was hardly likely to advance anyone's career these days. Probably quite the opposite.

For the moment, another beautiful summer's day beckoned, and it was a great luxury not to have to make any more serious choices than whether to go and do her washing or drive to Harrogate and go shopping. She liked Harrogate town centre; it was compact and manageable. The cottage needed a tidy-up, true. But that could wait. Annie didn't mind a little mess; as usual, there were far more interesting things to do than housework. She could put the washing in before she went; there wasn't much.

Before going anywhere, though, she picked up the phone and dialled a number she knew by heart.

It rang six times before a man's voice answered.

'Ray?'

'Annie? Is that you?'

'Yes.'

'How are you doing, my love? What's happening? Having fun?'

'You certainly sound as if you are.'

'We're having a bit of a party for Julie.'

Annie could hear laughter and music in the background. Some retro sixties rock like the Grateful Dead or the Jefferson Airplane. 'But it's only ten o'clock in the morning,' she said.

'Is it? Oh, well, you know how it goes, love. Carpe diem and all that.'

'Dad, when are you going to grow up? For crying out loud, you're fifty-two years old. Haven't you realized yet that we're in the nineties, not the sixties?'

'Uh-oh. I can tell you're angry at me. You only call me Dad when you're angry at me. What have I done now?'

Annie laughed. 'Nothing,' she said. 'Really. You're incorrigible. I give up. But one day the police will come and bust the lot of you, mark my words. It'll be bloody embarrassing for me. How am I supposed to explain that to my boss? My father, the dope-smoking old hippie?'

'Police? They're not interested in a couple of teeny-weeny joints, are they? At least they shouldn't be. Ought to have better things to do. And a bit less of the "old", thank you very much. Anyway, how is my little WPC Plod? Getting any, lately?'

'Dad! Let's lay off that subject, shall we, please? I thought we'd agreed that my sex life is my own business.'

'Oh, you have been! You are! I can tell by your tone. Well, that's wonderful news, love. What's his name? Is he a copper?'

'*Dad!*' Annie felt herself blushing.

'All right. Sorry. Just showing a bit of fatherly concern, that's all.'

'Much appreciated, I'm sure.' Annie sighed. Really, it was like talking to a child. 'Anyway, I'm fine,' she said. 'What's Julie got to celebrate? Something I should know about?'

'Didn't I tell you? She's finally got a publisher for that novel of hers. After all these years.'

'No, you didn't. That's great news. Tell her I'm really happy for her. How about Ian and Jo?'

'They're away in America.'

'Nice. And Jasmine?'

'Jasmine's fine.' Annie heard a voice in the background. 'She sends her love,' her father said. 'Anyway, wonderful as it is to talk to you, it's not like you to phone before discount time. Especially since you moved to Yorkshire. Anything I can help you with? Like me to beat up a couple of suspects for you? Fake a confession or two?'

Annie fitted the receiver snugly between her ear and shoulder and curled her legs under her on the settee. 'No. But as a matter of fact,' she said, 'there is something you might be able to help me with.'

'Ask away.'

'Michael Stanhope.'

'Stanhope . . . Stanhope . . . Sounds familiar. Wait a minute . . . Yes, I remember. The artist. Michael Stanhope. What about him?'

'What do you know about him?'

'Not much, really. Let me see. He didn't live up to his early promise. Died in the sixties sometime, I think. Last few years pretty unproductive. Why do you want to know?'

'I saw a painting of his in connection with a case I'm working on.'

'And you think it might be a clue?'

'I don't know. It just made me want to know more about him.'

'What was it? The painting.'

Annie described it to him. 'Yes, that'd be Stanhope. He had a reputation for Brueghelesque village scenes. Touch of Lowry thrown in for good measure. That was his problem, you know: too derivative and never developed a uniform style of his own. All over the map. A bit Stanley Spencerish, too. *Haute* symbolism. Very much out of vogue today. Anyway, what could Michael Stanhope possibly have to do with a case you're working on?'

'Maybe nothing. Like I said, he just grabbed my curiosity. Do you know where I can find out more about him? Is there a book?'

'I don't think so. He wasn't that important. Most of his stuff will be in private collections, maybe spread around the galleries, too. Why don't you try Leeds? They've got a half-decent collection there, if you can stand the Atkinson bloody Grimshaws. I'd say they're bound to have a few Stanhopes, what with him being local and all.'

'Good idea,' Annie said, kicking herself for not thinking of it first. 'I'll do that. And, Ray?'

'Yes?'

'Take care of yourself.'

'I will. Promise, love. Come see us soon. Bye.'

'Bye.'

Annie looked at her watch. Not long after ten. She could be in Leeds in an hour, do her shopping there, instead of in Harrogate, have lunch and spend a bit of time in the art gallery. She picked up her car keys and her shoulder bag from the sideboard and set off through the labyrinth to her car, which was still parked outside the section station. She wondered if Inspector Harmond would make anything of that. Not unless he also knew that Banks's car had remained parked by the village green all night. Besides, she didn't care.

•

And friends we remained. We saw the New Year in together, linked arms and sang 'Auld Lang Syne'. Hong Kong had fallen to the Japanese on Christmas Day and the fighting in North Africa and in Russia went on as bitterly as ever. As the winter weather continued through January, British troops withdrew down the Malayan Peninsula to Singapore.

Though I often thought about what I had witnessed, I didn't begin to understand what had gone on against the outbuilding wall that Christmas night until much later, and even then I had no way of knowing how culpable Gloria had been. What had Mark been trying to do to her? To me, at the time, Gloria had seemed to be resisting, struggling, but when I discovered the act of sex for myself not so very much later, I found it could often be misleading that way; one often seemed to be struggling and resisting, especially during the wildest moments. Looking back now, I'd call it attempted rape, but memory, over time, has a way of altering its content.

So I did the best I could to put the whole episode out of my mind. I certainly agreed that Gloria was right not to involve Matthew. That would only have started a fight and upset everyone. His going away soon would have made it worse, too; he would be worried enough to leave her behind as it was.

Sometimes, though, at night in bed as I listened to the bombers drone over Rowan Woods, I would remember the scene, with Gloria's bare white thighs above the stocking-tops, and those strange muffled sounds she was making that seemed lost somewhere between pain and acquiescence, and I would feel a strange fluttering excitement inside me, as if I were on the verge of some great discovery that never quite came.

On the fifteenth of January, 1942, Sergeant Matthew Shackleton shipped out. He didn't know where he was headed, but we all assumed he would be going to North Africa to fight with the Eighth Army.

Imagine our surprise when Gloria got a letter from Matthew in Cape Town, *South* Africa, three weeks later. Of course, they could hardly sail through the Mediterranean, but even so, Cape Town seemed a long way round to go to North Africa. Then we got another letter from Colombo, in Ceylon, then Calcutta, India. What a fool I was! I could have kicked myself for not guessing earlier. They didn't need bridges and roads in the desert, of course, but they needed them in the jungles of the Far East.

•

The drive to Leeds took less time than Annie had expected. She parked north of the city centre and walked down New Briggate to The Headrow. The place was busy, pavements jammed with shoppers, all wearing thin, loose clothing to alleviate the blistering heat, which seemed even more oppressive in the city than it did out Harkside way. A juggler performed for children in Dortmund Square. The sun dazzled Annie, reflecting on shop windows, making it hard to see what was inside. Annie put on her sunglasses and set off through the crowds towards Cookridge Street. A little research after her chat with Ray had revealed that Leeds City Art Gallery had in its collection several works by Michael Stanhope, and Annie wanted to see them.

Once inside, she picked up a guidebook at the reception area. The Stanhopes were on the second floor. Four of them. She started up the broad stone staircase.

Annie had never liked art galleries, with their rarefied atmosphere, uniformed custodians and stifling aura of hush. No doubt this dislike was largely due to her father's influence. Though he loved the great artists, he despised the barren way their works were put on display. He thought great art ought to be exhibited on a constant rotation in pubs, offices, trattorias, cafés, churches and bingo parlours.

He approved of the Henry Moores standing out in open weather on the Yorkshire Moors; he also approved of David Hockney's faxes, photocollages and opera-set designs. Annie had grown up in an atmosphere of irrev-erence towards the established art world, with its stuffy galleries, plummy accents and inflated prices. Because of this, she always felt self-conscious in galleries, as if she were an interloper. Maybe she was being paranoid, but she always thought the guards were watching *her*, from one room to the next, just waiting for her to reach out and touch something and set off all the alarms.

When she found the Stanhopes, she was at first disappointed. Two of them were rather dull landscapes, not of Hobb's End, but other Dales scenes. The third, a little more interesting, showed a distant view of Hobb's

End in its hollow, smoke drifting from chimneys, the bright vermilions and purples of sunset splashed across the sky. A fine effect, but it told Annie nothing she didn't know.

The fourth painting, though, was a revelation.

Titled *Reclining Nude*, according to the catalogue, the painting reminded Annie of Goya's *Naked Maja*, which she had seen with Ray when it came briefly to the National Gallery in 1990. No matter what his opinions about galleries were, Ray certainly never missed the opportunity to view a great work.

The woman reclined on a bed in much the same pose as Goya's original, propped on a pillow, hands behind her head, looking directly at the painter with some sort of highly charged erotic challenge in her expression, bedsheets ruffled beneath her. Also, like the *Maja*'s, her round breasts were widely spaced and her legs bent a little, awkwardly placed as her lower half twisted slightly towards the viewer. Her waist was thin, her hips in perfect proportion, and a little triangle of hair showed between her clasped legs, connected to the navel by a barely perceptible line of fair down.

There were differences, though. Stanhope's model had golden-blond hair rather than black, her nose was shorter, her large eyes a striking blue, her lips fuller and redder. Even so, the resemblance was too close to be accident, especially the frank eroticism of her expression and the hint of pleasures recently enjoyed, conveyed by the rumpled sheets. Stanhope had obviously been strongly affected by Goya's original, and when he had encountered the same sort of sensual power in a model, he had remembered this and painted it.

But there was more to Stanhope's vision. As Annie

remembered, the background of the *Naked Maja* was dark and impenetrable; it seemed as if the bed were floating in space, the only important thing in the universe.

Stanhope hadn't given his model a realistic background either, but if you looked very closely, you could see images of tanks, aeroplanes, armies on the march, explosions and swastikas. In other words, he had painted the war into the background. It was subtle; the images didn't jump right out at you and dominate the work, but they were there, and when you looked closely, you couldn't ignore them: eroticism and weapons of mass destruction. Make of it what you would.

Annie glanced at the note on the wall beside the painting, then she stepped back with a gasp that made one of the custodians look up from his newspaper.

'Everything all right, miss?' he called out.

Annie put her hand over her heart. 'What? Yes. Oh, yes. Sorry.'

He eyed her suspiciously and went back to his paper.

Annie looked again. It wasn't mentioned in the catalogue, but there it was, plain as day, below *Reclining Nude*. A subtitle: *Gloria, Autumn 1944.*

7

On Monday morning, Banks looked again at the postcard reproduction of *Reclining Nude: Gloria, Autumn 1944* that lay on his desk. It was an uncanny and disconcerting experience to see an artist's impression of the flesh that had probably once clothed the filth-covered bones they found last week, and to feel aroused by looking at it. Banks felt an exciting flush of adolescent guilt, the same as he had on looking at his first pictures of naked women in *Swank* or *Mayfair*.

Annie had picked up several copies of the postcard at the art gallery and, thrilled by her discovery, phoned him late on Saturday afternoon. They met for dinner at Cockett's Hotel, in Hawes, with every intention of going their separate ways later, both having agreed that they shouldn't rush things, that they needed their time alone. After the second bottle of wine, though, instead of leaving, they took a room and woke to Sunday-morning church bells. After a leisurely breakfast, they left, agreeing to restrict their trysts to weekends.

At home, Banks had tried to reach Brian all weekend, without any luck. He knew he should call Sandra and find out what she had to say about it all, but he didn't want to. Maybe it was something to do with sleeping with Annie, or maybe not, but he didn't think he could handle talking to Sandra. He spent the rest of Sunday reading the papers and doing odd jobs around the cottage.

He walked over to stand by the open window. The gold hands against the blue face of the church clock stood at a quarter to eleven. Horns blared out in the street and the smell of fresh bread from the bakery mingled with the exhaust fumes. An irate van driver swore at a tourist. The tourist swore back and scurried off into the crowd. Another coach pulled up in the cobbled market square and disgorged its load of old ladies. From Worthing, Banks noticed, by the sign painted on the side. *Worthing*. Why couldn't the old biddies stay down there, maybe roll up their skirts and go for a paddle, stop and smell the seaweed? Why did everyone have to come to the bloody Dales? When it came right down to it, he blamed James Herriot. If they hadn't done that damn series on television, the place would be empty.

Banks lit a proscribed cigarette and wondered, not for the first time this past year, why he bothered with the job. There had been plenty of occasions when he felt like packing it all in. At first he hadn't done so because he simply couldn't be bothered. As long as people left him alone, it didn't really matter. He knew he wasn't working up to par, even on desk duties, but he didn't give a damn. It was easy enough to show up and push paper around without enthusiasm, or to play computer games. The truth was that he hurt so much after Sandra left that everything else seemed meaningless.

Then, when he bought the cottage and started pulling himself together, or at least managing to distance himself a bit from the pain, he seriously considered a career change, but he couldn't think of anything else he was qualified for, or even wanted to do. He was too young to retire, and he had no desire whatsoever to go into security work or a private detective agency. Lack of formal education had closed most other paths to him.

So he stuck with it. Now, though, partly because of this dirty, pointless, dead-end case – or so Jimmy Riddle must have seen it – Banks was finally getting back to some sense of why he had joined in the first place. When something becomes routine, mechanical, when you're just going through the motions, you have to dig down and find out what it was that you loved about it in the first place. What drew you to it? Or what obsessed you about it? Then you have to act on that, and to hell with all the rest.

Banks had cast his memory back and thought about those questions a lot over the past few months. It wasn't simply a matter of why he walked into the recruiting centre that day, asked for information and then followed up on it a week later. He had done that partly because of his disenchantment with the bohemian scene after Jem's death, partly because he hated business studies, and partly to piss off his parents. He and Sandra knew they were serious about one another by then, too; they wanted to get married, start a family, and he would need a steady job.

With Banks, it wasn't some abstract notion of justice, or being on the side of 'good' and putting the 'bad' guys away. He wasn't naive enough to see the police as good, for a start, or even all criminals as bad. Some people were driven to crime through desperation of one kind or another; some were so damaged inside that they were unable to make a choice. When it came right down to it, Banks believed that most violent criminals were bullies, and ever since he was a kid he had detested bullies. At school, he had always stuck up for the weaker kids against the bullies, even though he wasn't especially big or tough. He got frequent black eyes and bloody noses for his trouble.

In some way, it all came together with Mick Slack, fifth-form bully, two years older and six inches taller than Banks. One day, in the schoolyard, for no reason, Slack started pushing and shoving a kid called Graham Marshall. Marshall was in Banks's class and was always a bright, quiet, shy kid, the sort the others taunted by calling him a poof and a pansy, but mostly left alone. When Banks stepped in, Slack pushed *him* instead, and a skirmish followed. More by speed and stealth, Banks managed to wind Slack and knock him to the Tarmac before the teacher came out and stopped it. Slack swore vengeance, but he never got the chance. He was killed two days later on his way to play for the school rugby team, when his motorbike ran smack into a brick wall.

The strangest thing was, though, that about six months later, Graham Marshall disappeared and was never seen again. Police detectives came and questioned everyone in his class, asking if they had seen any strangers hanging around the school, or if Graham had told them about anyone suspicious, anyone who was bothering him. Nobody had. Banks felt especially impotent at being so useless to the police, and he remembered that feeling years later when he was on the other side of the interview table watching witnesses flounder as they tried to remember details.

The theory was that Graham had been abducted by a child molester and his body buried in some forest miles away. That made three deaths Banks had been exposed to as an adolescent, including Phil Simpkins, who had swung on to the sharp iron railings, but it was the ultimate mystery of Graham Marshall's disappearance that haunted him most of all, until Jem's death some years later, and in a way it was his curiosity and unaccountable feelings of guilt over it that were behind his decision to join the police years later.

All the petty duties and details of a policeman's job aside, Banks's obsession was with bringing down as many bullies as possible. When the victims were dead, of course, he couldn't defend them, but he could damn well find out what had happened to them and bring the bullies to justice. It wasn't foolproof; it didn't always work; but it was all he had. That was what he had to get back to, or he might as well pack it all in and join Group 7 or some other private security outfit.

He went back to his desk and sat down. As he looked at Gloria's pose again – beautiful, erotic, sensual, playful, but also challenging, mocking, as if she knew some sort of secret about the artist, or shared one with him – he felt that in this case he was needed as much as ever. He was convinced that Gloria Shackleton was the victim they had found buried at Hobb's End, and he wanted to know what she was like, what had happened to her and why no one had reported her missing. Did people just think she had vanished into space, been abducted by aliens or something? The bully who had killed her might well be dead, but that didn't matter a damn to Banks. *He needed to know.*

Dr Glendenning's call cut into his thoughts.

'Ah, Banks,' he said. 'Glad I caught you in. You're very lucky I happened to be in Leeds, you know. Otherwise you could have whistled for your post-mortem. There are plenty of fresh cadavers craving my expert attention.'

'I'm sure there are. My apologies. I promise to do better in the future.'

'I should hope so.'

'What have you got?'

'Nothing much to add to what Dr Williams told you, I'm afraid.'

'She was stabbed, then?'

'Oh, yes. And viciously, too.'

'How many times?'

'Fourteen or fifteen, as far as I can tell. I wouldn't swear to that, of course, given the condition of the skeleton and the time that has elapsed since death.'

'Is that what killed her?'

'What do you think I am, laddie? A miracle worker? It's not possible to say what killed her, though the knife wounds would have done the trick. Judging from the angles and positions of the nicks, the blade would almost certainly have pierced several vital organs.'

'Did you find evidence of any other injury?'

'Patience, laddie. That's what I'm getting to, if you'll slow down and give me the chance. It's all that caffeine, you know. Too much coffee. Try a nice herbal tea, for a change.'

'I'll do that. Tomorrow. But tell me now.'

'I found possible, and I stress *possible*, signs of manual strangulation.'

'Strangulation?'

'That's what I said. And stop echoing me. If I needed a bloody parrot I'd buy one. I'm going by the hyoid bones in the throat. Now, these are very fragile bones, almost always broken during manual strangulation, but I say it's only *possible* because the damage could have occurred over time, due to other causes. The weight of all that earth and water, for example. I must say, though, the skeleton was in remarkable condition considering where it's been for so long.'

'Would that make it more probable than possible?'

'What's the difference?'

'"When you have eliminated the impossible, whatever

remains, however *improbable*, must be the truth." Sir Arthur Conan Doyle.'

Glendenning sighed theatrically. 'And to think that fellow was a doctor. All right, shall we say it's certainly not impossible, and even quite *likely*, that the poor woman was strangled. Is that clear enough for you?'

'Before she was stabbed.'

'How would I know that? Honestly, Banks, you either have an overinflated opinion of the medical profession or you're being just plain bloody-minded. Knowing you, I'd bet on the latter. But let us, just for once, be reasonable about this, shall we, and apply a little logic?'

'By all means. My, my, you're grumpy this morning, aren't you, Doc?'

'Aye. It's what happens when my own doctor tells me to lay off the coffee. And I've told you before not to call me Doc. It's disrespectful. Now, listen. The way this poor woman was stabbed stopped just short of chopping her into little pieces. It would seem very unlikely to me – not *impossible*, but very improbable, if you like – that her killer felt any need to strangle her *after* he had done this. The degree of rage involved would probably have left him quite exhausted, for a start, not to mention the anger vented, the almost postcoital relaxation some killers feel after perpetrating extremely violent acts. So I'd say the strangulation came first and then, for whatever reason, the stabbing. That kind of thing is statistically more common, too.'

'So why the stabbing? To make sure she was dead?'

'I doubt it. Though it's true she may have still been alive after the strangulation, may just have lost consciousness. As I said, we're dealing with anger, with rage, here. That's the only explanation. In the vernacular, whoever did it got carried away with killing. Literally saw red. Either that or he knew exactly what he was doing and he enjoyed himself.'

'He?'

'Again, statistically more likely. Though I wouldn't rule out a strong woman. But you know as well as I do, Banks, that these sorts of things are usually lust-related. Either that or they stem from very strong passions, such as jealousy, revenge, obsession, greed and the like. I suppose it could have been a wronged wife or a woman spurned, a lesbian relationship gone wrong. But statistically speaking, it's men who do these things. I hesitate to do your job for you, but I don't think you're dealing with a run-of-the-mill sort of crime. It doesn't look like a murder committed during a robbery, or to cover up a secret. Of course, murderers can be damnably clever sometimes and disguise one sort of crime to look like another. Fault of all these detective novels, if you ask me.'

'Right,' said Banks, scrawling away on the pad he'd pulled in front of him. That was the trouble with computers; it was bloody awkward to write on them when you were speaking on the telephone. 'What about the parturition marks?'

'That's exactly what they are, in my opinion.'

'So there's no chance that they were also caused by the knife, or by time?'

'Well, there's always a *chance* that something else could have caused them, some animal, friction from a small stone or pebble, or suchlike, though given where she was found I say we can pretty much exclude the chance of scavenger activity. After so long, though, it's impossible to be a hundred per cent sure about anything. But judging by the distinctive position and appearance, I'd say they're parturition marks. The woman had a baby, Banks. There's no saying *when*, of course.'

'Okay,' said Banks. 'Thanks very much, Doc.'

Glendenning snorted and hung up.

•

All through February and March 1942, day after day, I followed the news reports. They were censored and incomplete, of course, but I read about the estimated sixty thousand British taken prisoner in Singapore, and about the fighting near the Sittang River, from where Matthew wrote Gloria another letter, telling her how things were pretty dull and safe really, and not to worry. Clearly, it's not only governments that lie during wartime.

Then, on the eighth of March, we heard about the fall of Rangoon. Our morale at home was pretty low, too. In April, the Germans gave up all pretence of bombing military and industrial targets and started bombing cities of great architectural beauty, such as Bath, Norwich and York, which was getting very close to home.

I remembered when Leeds, only about thirty miles away, had its worst raid of the war, about a month before Gloria arrived. Matthew and I took the train in the next day to see what it looked like. The City Museum, right at the corner of Park Row and Bond Street, had taken a direct hit and all the stuffed lions and tigers we had thrilled over on childhood visits hung in the overhead tram wires like creatures thrown from an out-of-control carousel. I wanted to go and see the damage in York, but Mrs Shipley, our stationmaster, told me York Station had been bombed, so no trains were allowed in. At least she was able to assure me that they hadn't destroyed the Minster.

It was a miserable spring, though we had the sunniest

April in forty years. There were the usual random shortages. Items simply disappeared from the shelves for weeks on end. One week you couldn't get fish for love or money; the next it was poultry. In February, soap was rationed to sixteen ounces every four weeks; the civilian petrol ration was cut out completely in March, which meant no more motoring for pleasure. We still managed to retain a small petrol ration, though, because we needed the van to make pick-ups from wholesalers.

I followed the news far more closely than I had before, scouring all the newspapers, from *The Times* and the *News Chronicle* to the *Daily Mirror*, the minute they came in on the first train, cutting out articles and pasting them into a scrapbook, spending hours tracing meandering rivers and crooked coastlines in the atlas. Even so, I never managed to get a true picture of what life was like for Matthew out there. I could imagine it from my reading of Rudyard Kipling and Somerset Maugham, but that was the best I could do.

I wrote to him every day, which was probably more often than Gloria did. She was never much of a letter writer. Matthew didn't write back that often, but when he did he would always assure us he was well. Mostly, he complained about the monsoons and the humid jungle heat, the insects and the dreadful terrain. He never said anything directly about fighting and killing, so for a long time we didn't even know if he had been in battle. Once, though, he wrote that boredom seemed the greatest enemy: 'Long stretches of boredom relieved only by the occasional brief skirmish' was the way he put it. Somehow, I had the idea that these 'brief skirmishes' were a good deal more dangerous and terrifying than the boredom.

As time passed, we got used to Matthew's absence and enjoyed what we could of him through his letters. Gloria would read bits from his to her (no doubt missing out all the embarrassing lovey-dovey stuff) and I would read from his to me. Sometimes, I sensed, she was jealous because he wrote to me more about ideas and books and philosophy and to her mostly about day-to-day things like food and mosquitoes and blisters.

That September, *Pride and Prejudice*, with Laurence Olivier and Greer Garson, finally came to the Lyceum. Gloria had just had a tooth extracted by old Granville after suffering toothache for several days. I told her I thought it was a crime the prices he charged for such poor work, but she countered that Brenchley, in Harkside, a notorious butcher, was even more expensive. As usual, Granville did more damage than good and poor Gloria had been bleeding from the torn gum for over a day. She was just beginning to feel a little better and I managed to persuade her to come to the pictures with me. As it turned out, she actually admitted to enjoying the film. That shouldn't have surprised me. It wasn't exactly the sharp-witted, ironic Jane Austen I knew from the books; it was far more romantic. Still, it made a nice change from all the silly comedies and musicals she had been dragging me to see lately.

Double summertime made it easy for us to see our way across the fields that night. It was a beautiful autumn evening tinged with smoky green and golden light, the kind of evening when I used to go out and enjoy the stubble-burning just after dark before the war, when you could smell the acrid, sweet smoke drifting in the air over the fields and see the little fires stretched out for miles along the horizon. Sadly, there was no stubble-burning in the war; we didn't want the Germans to know where our empty fields were.

This evening was almost as beautiful, even without the smoke and the little fires. I could see the purple heather darkening on the distant moor-tops to the west, hear the night birds call, smell clean, hay-scented air and feel the dry grass swish against my bare legs as I walked.

Despite the ravages of war and Matthew's being far away, I felt as deeply content as I had ever been at that moment. Yet as we came down towards the fairy bridge in the gathering darkness, I felt that chilling shudder of apprehension, as if a goose had stepped over my grave, as Mother would have said. Gloria, arm linked in mine, was chatting on and on about how handsome Laurence Olivier was, and she obviously didn't notice, so I let it go by.

As the weeks passed, I tried to dismiss the feeling, but it had a way of creeping back. There was plenty to rejoice about, I told myself: Matthew continued to write regularly and assured us he was doing well; the Red Army seemed to be making gains at Stalingrad; and the tide had turned in North Africa.

But after the victory at E1 Alamein that November, when I lay on my bed and listened to the church bells ring for the first time in years, all I could do was cry because Matthew had had no bells at his wedding.

•

'First off,' Annie told Banks over the phone later that day, 'I can find no official record of Gloria Shackleton at all after the wedding notice in 1941. There's no missing-persons report in our files and no death notice anywhere. The *Harkside Chronicle*, by the way, suspended publication between 1942 and 1946 because of paper shortages, so that's no use as a source. There's always the *Yorkshire Post*, of course, if they took any interest in the Harkside area. Anyway, it looks as if she disappeared from the face of the earth.'

'Did you check with immigration?' Banks asked.

'Yes. Nothing.'

'Okay. Go on.'

'Well, I was able to dig up a bit more about her life at Hobb's End, most of it pieced together from the parish magazine. She's first mentioned in the May 1941 issue, welcomed to the parish as a member of the Women's Land Army, assigned to work at a place called Top Hill Farm, just outside the village.'

'Top Hill Farm? Did you find out who owned the place?'

'I did. It was a Mr Frederick Kilnsey and his wife, Edith. They had one son called Joseph, who was called up. That's why they got Gloria. Apparently, it wasn't a very big farm, just a few cows, poultry, sheep and a couple of acres of land. Anyway, Joseph didn't come back. Killed at El Alamein. By then, Gloria was living at Bridge Cottage.'

'Still working for the Kilnseys?'

'Yes. I suppose it was a mutually convenient arrangement. They needed her, especially with Joseph dead, and she could live at Bridge Cottage and stay close to what family she had in Hobb's End.'

'All this from the parish magazine?'

'Well, I'm embroidering just a little. But it's remarkably informative, don't you think? I mean, it's easy enough to joke about how petty the news items they publish are at the time – you know, like "Farmer Jones loses sheep in winter storm" – but when you're looking back into something like this, it's a real treasure trove. Unfortunately, they also stopped publication early in 1942. Paper shortage again.'

'Pity. Go on.'

'That's about it, really. Gloria married the Shackletons' eldest child, Matthew. He was twenty-one and she was nineteen. He had a younger sister called Gwynneth. I assume she was the same one who witnessed the marriage.'

'What became of her?'

'She was still around in the last issue, March 1942, as far as I know. Wrote a little piece on growing your own onions, in fact.'

'How fascinating. What about Matthew?'

'The last time he was mentioned he was shipping overseas.'

'Where?'

'Didn't say. Secret, I suppose.'

'Any idea where any of these people moved when they cleared out of Hobb's End?'

'No. But I did ring Ruby Kettering. She knows two people still living who lived in Hobb's End during the war. There's Betty Goodall, who lives in Edinburgh, and Alice Poole in Scarborough. She thinks they'd be thrilled to talk to us.'

'Okay. Look, I've decided to send DS Hatchley to St Catherine's House tomorrow. Which do you fancy: Edinburgh or Scarborough?'

'Doesn't matter to me. Anything's better than checking birth, death and marriage records.'

'I'll toss for it. Heads or tails?'

'How can I trust you over the telephone?'

'Trust me. Heads or tails?'

'This is crazy. Heads.'

Annie paused a moment and heard a sound like a coin clinking on a metal desk. She smiled to herself. Insane. Banks came back on. 'It was heads. Your choice.'

'I told you, it doesn't really matter. I'll take Scarborough, though, if you insist. I like the seaside there, and it's not as far to drive.'

'Okay. If I get an early enough start I can be up to Edinburgh and back by early evening. Plenty of time for us to compare notes. I'd like to get something on tonight's news, first.'

'Like what?'

'I want to put Gloria's name out there, see if anything comes back. I know we might be jumping the gun, but you never know. We've got no idea what happened to the Shackletons, and Gloria may have had family in London who are still alive. They might know what happened to her. Or, if we're wrong about it all, she might drop by the station herself and let us know she's still alive.'

Annie laughed. 'Right.'

'Anyway, I'll try local television. That way I can get them to show the postcard.'

'What? Nudity on the local news?'

'They can crop it.'

'Let me know what time you'll be on.'

'Why?'

'So I can set my VCR. Bye.'

•

'So Jimmy Riddle thinks he's dropped you in the shit with this one, then?' said DS Hatchley after swallowing his first bite of toasted tea-cake.

'To put it succinctly, yes,' said Banks. 'I think he was also pretty sure this case wouldn't involve race relations or any of his rich and influential friends from the Lodge.'

'Oh, I don't know about that,' Hatchley said. 'I'd imagine quite a few of them have got skeletons in their cupboards.'

'Ouch.'

They were sitting in the Golden Grill, just across the

street from Eastvale Divisional HQ. Outside, Market Street was packed with tourists, jackets or cardigans slung over their shoulders, cameras round their necks. Like sheep up on the unfenced moorland roads, they strayed all over the narrow street. The local delivery vans had to inch through, horns blaring.

Most of the tables were already taken, but they had managed to find one near the back. Once the two of them had sat down and given their orders to the bustling waitress, Banks told Hatchley about the skeleton. By the time he had finished, their order arrived.

Banks knew his sergeant had a reputation as an idle sod and a thug. His appearance didn't help. Hatchley was big, slow-moving and bulky, like a rugby prop forward gone to seed, with straw hair, pink complexion, freckles and a piggy nose. His suits were shiny, ties egg-stained, and he usually looked as if he had just been dragged through a hedge backwards. But it had always been Banks's experience that once Hatchley got his teeth into something, he was a stubborn and dogged copper, and damned difficult to shake off. The problem lay in getting him motivated in the first place.

'Anyway, we think we know who the victim was, but we want to cover all possibilities. What I'd like you to do is take PC Bridges and go down to London tomorrow. Here's a list of information I'd like.' Banks passed over a sheet of paper.

Hatchley glanced at it, then looked up. 'Can't I take WPC Sexton instead?'

Banks grinned. 'Ellie Sexton? And you a married man. I'm ashamed of you, Jim.'

Hatchley winked. 'Spoilsport.'

Banks looked at his watch. 'Before you go, could you

put out a nationwide request for information on similar crimes in the same time period? This is a bit tricky because it's an old crime and they'll drag their feet. But there's a chance someone might have something unsolved with a similar MO on the books. I'll put someone on checking our local records, too.'

'You think this was part of a series?'

'I don't know, Jim, but what Dr Glendenning told me about the manner of death made me think I shouldn't overlook that possibility. I've also asked the SOCOs to broaden their search to include the general Hobb's End area. Given what I've just heard from Dr Glendenning about the way she died, I wouldn't like to think we're sitting on another 25 Cromwell Street without knowing it.'

'I'm sure the press would have a field day with that,' said Hatchley. 'They could call it the Hobb's End House of Horrors. Nice ring to it.'

'Let's hope it doesn't come to that.'

'Aye.' Hatchley paused and finished his tea-cake. 'This DS Cabbot you're working with down Harkside,' said Hatchley. 'I don't think I've come across him yet. What's he like?'

'*She*'s pretty new around here,' Banks said. 'But she seems to be working out okay.'

'She?' Hatchley raised his eyebrows. 'Bit of all right, then?'

'Depends on your type. Anyway, you seem to be showing a dangerous interest in these things for a man with a wife and child of his own. How are Carol and April, by the way?'

'They're fine.'

'Over the teething?'

'A long time ago, that were. But thanks for asking, sir.'

Banks finished his tea-cake. 'Look, Jim,' he said, 'if I've been a bit distant this past while, you know, haven't shown much interest in you and your family, it's just that . . . well, I've had a lot of problems. There's been a few changes. A lot to get used to.'

'Aye.'

Bloody hell, Banks thought. *Aye.* The word with a thousand meanings. He struggled on. 'Anyway, if you thought I ignored you or cut you out in any way, I apologize.'

Hatchley paused for a moment, eyes everywhere but on Banks. Finally, he clasped his ham-like hands on the red-and-white-checked tablecloth, still avoiding eye contact. 'Let's just forget about it, shall we, sir. Water under the bridge. We've all had our crosses to bear these past few months, maybe you more than most of us. Talking of crosses, I suppose you've heard they're changing our name to Crime Management?'

Banks nodded. 'Yes.'

Hatchley mimicked picking up a telephone. 'Good morning, Crime Management here, madam. How can we help you? Not enough crime in your neighbourhood. Dear, dear. Well, yes, I'm certain there's some to spare on the East Side Estate. Yes, I'll look into it right away and see if I can get some sent over by this afternoon. Bye-bye, madam.'

Banks laughed.

'I mean, *really,*' Hatchley went on. 'If this goes on they'll be calling you a Senior Crime Consultant next.'

The door opened and WPC Sexton walked over to them. Hatchley nudged Banks and pointed. 'Here she is. The belle of Eastvale Divisional.'

'Fuck off, Sarge,' she said, then turned to Banks. 'Sir, we just got an urgent message from a DS Cabbot in

Harkside. She wants you to get down there as soon as you can. She said a lad named Adam Kelly has something he wants to tell you.'

•

The telegram, in its unmistakable orange cover, came to the shop, for some reason. I remember the date; it was Palm Sunday, the eighteenth of April, 1943, and Mother and I had just got back from church. Gloria was working that day, so, heart thumping and heavy, I had to leave Mother to her tears and run up to Top Hill Farm. Though it was a chilly afternoon, the sweat was pouring off me by the time I got there.

I found Gloria collecting eggs in the chicken shack. She had one in her palm and she held it out to show me. 'It's so warm,' she said. 'Freshly laid. But what are you doing here, Gwen? You look out of breath. Your eyes. Have you been crying?'

Panting, I handed over the telegram to her. She read it, her face turned ashen and she sagged back against the flimsy wooden wall. A nail squealed in the wood and the chickens squawked. The sheet of paper fluttered from her tiny hand to the dirt floor. She didn't cry right there and then, but a soft moan came from her mouth. 'Oh, no,' she said. 'No.' Almost as if she had been expecting it. Then her whole body started to tremble. I wanted to go to her, but somehow I knew that I mustn't. Not just yet, not until she had let the first pangs of grief shake her and rip through her alone.

She closed her hand by her side and the egg broke. Bright yellow yolk stained her dainty fingers, and long strings of viscous glair trailed down towards the straw-covered earth.

•

The Kellys' house stood in the middle of a terrace block on the B-road east of Harkside. There was an infants' school across the road, and next to that a Pay and Display car park to encourage tourists not to clog the village centre. Beyond the car park, a meadow full of buttercups and clover descended eastwards to the West Yorkshire border and the banks of Linwood Reservoir.

Mrs Kelly answered the door and asked them in. Banks could sense the tension immediately. The aftermath of a scolding; it was a familiar childhood sensation of his, and the scoldings were usually dished out by his mother. Though it was never openly admitted, Banks knew his father believed that household discipline was a woman's job. Only if Banks cheeked her or tried to resist did his father step in and sort things out with his belt.

'He won't say owt,' Mrs Kelly said. She was a plain, harried-looking woman in her early thirties, old before her time, with limp, tired hair and a drawn face. 'I challenged him on it when he came home for his lunch, and he ran off up to his room. He wouldn't go back to school and he won't come down.'

'Challenged him on what, Mrs Kelly?' Banks asked.

'What he stole.'

'Stole?'

'Yes. I found it when I were cleaning his room. From that . . . that there skeleton. I left it where I found it. I didn't want to touch it. Anyone would think I haven't brought him up right. It's not easy when you're on your own.'

'Calm down, Mrs Kelly,' Annie said, stepping forward and resting her hand on her arm. 'Nobody's blaming you for anything. Or Adam. We just want to get to the bottom of it, that's all.'

The room was hot and a woman on television was explaining how to make the perfect soufflé. Because it was late afternoon and they were facing east, there was very little light. Banks was already beginning to feel claustrophobic.

'May I go up and talk to him?' he asked.

'You'll get nowt out of him. Clammed up, he has.'

'May I try?'

'Suit yourself. Left at the top of the stairs.'

Banks glanced at Annie, who tried to settle Mrs Kelly in an armchair, then he made his way up the narrow carpeted stairway. He knocked first on Adam's door and, getting no response, opened it a short way and stuck his head round. 'Adam?' he said. 'It's Mr Banks. Remember me?'

Adam lay on his side on the single bed. He turned slowly, wiped his forearm across his eyes and said, 'You've not come to arrest me, have you? I don't want to go to gaol.'

'Nobody's going to take you to gaol, Adam.'

'I didn't mean nothing, honest I didn't.'

'Why don't you just calm down and tell me what happened. We'll get it sorted. Can I come in?'

Adam sat up on the bed. He was a fair-haired kid with thick glasses, freckles and sticking-out ears, the kind who is often teased at school and develops an active fantasy life to escape. The kind Banks used to defend from bullies, perhaps. His eyes were red with crying. 'Suppose so,' he said.

Banks went inside the small bedroom. There were no chairs, so he sat on the edge of the bed, at the bottom. Posters of muscular sword-and-sorcery heroes wielding enormous broadswords hung on the walls. A small computer sat on a desk, and a pile of old comic books stood by the bedside. That was about all there was room for. Banks left the door open.

'Why don't you tell me about it?' he asked.

'I thought it were magic,' Adam said. 'The Talisman. That's why I went there.'

'Went where?'

'Hobb's End. It's a magic place. It were destroyed in a battle between good and evil, but there's still magic buried there. I thought it would make me invisible.'

'He reads too many of them comic books,' a voice said accusingly. Banks turned to see Mrs Kelly standing in the doorway. Annie came up beside her. 'Head in the clouds, he has,' Adam's mother went on. 'Dungeons and dragons, Conan the Barbarian. *Myst. Riven*. Stephen King and Clive Barker. Well, he's gone too far this time.'

Banks turned. 'Mrs Kelly,' he said, 'will you let me talk to Adam alone for a few minutes?'

She stood in the doorway, arms folded, then made a sound of disgust and walked off.

'Sorry,' Annie mouthed to Banks, following her.

Banks turned. 'Right, Adam,' he said. 'So you're a magician, are you?'

Adam looked at him suspiciously. 'I know a bit about it.'

'Would you tell me what happened at Hobb's End that day, when you fell?'

'I've already told you.'

'The whole story.'

Adam chewed his lower lip.

'You found something, didn't you?'

Adam nodded.

'Will you show it to me?'

The boy paused, then reached under his pillow and

pulled out a small round object. He hesitated, then passed it to Banks. It was a metal button, by the look of it. Corroded, still encrusted with dirt, but clearly a button of some sort.

'Where did you find this, Adam?'

'It fell into my hand, honest.'

Banks turned away to hide his smile. If he had a penny for every time he'd heard that from an accused thief, he'd be a rich man by now. 'All right,' he said. 'What were you doing when it fell into your hand?'

'Pulling the hand out.'

'It was in the skeleton's hand?'

'Must've been, mustn't it?'

'As if the victim had been holding it in her palm?'

'You what?'

'Never mind. Why didn't you tell us about it sooner?'

'I thought it were what I'd gone there for. The Talisman. It's not easy to get. You have to pass through the veil to the Seventh Level. There's sacrifice and fear to overcome.'

Banks hadn't a clue what the boy was talking about. In Adam's imagination, it seemed, the old button had taken on some magical quality because of how it had been delivered to him. Not that it mattered that much. The point was that Adam had taken the button from Gloria Shackleton's hand.

'You did well,' Banks said. 'But you should have passed this on to me the first time I came to see you. It's not what you were looking for.'

Adam seemed disappointed. 'It's not?'

'No. It's not a talisman, it's just an old button.'

'Is it important?'

'I don't know yet. It might be.'

'Who was it? Do you know? The skeleton?'

'A young woman.'

Adam paused to take it in. 'Was she pretty?'

'I think she was.'

'Has she been there a long time?'

'Since the war.'

'Did the Germans kill her?'

'We don't think so. We don't know who killed her.' He held out the button on his palm. 'This might help us find out. You might help us.'

'But whoever did it will be dead by now, won't he?'

'Probably,' said Banks.

'My granddad died in the war.'

'I'm sorry to hear it, Adam.' Banks stood up. 'You can come down now, if you want. Nobody's going to do you any harm.'

'But my mum—'

'She was just upset, that's all.' Banks paused in the doorway. 'When I was a lad your age, I once stole a ring from Woolworth's. It was only a plastic ring, not worth much, but I got caught.' Banks could remember it as if it were yesterday: the smell of smoke on the department-store detectives' breath; their overbearing size as they stood over him in the cramped triangular office tucked away under the escalator; the rough way they handled him and his fear that they were going to beat him up or molest him in some way, and that everyone would think he deserved it because he was a thief. All for a plastic ring. Not even that, really. Just to show off.

'What happened?' Adam asked.

'They made me tell them my name and address and my mother had to go down and see them about it. She stopped my pocket money and wouldn't let me go out to play for a month.' They had searched him roughly, pulling everything from his pockets: string, penknife, cricket cards, pencil stub, a gobstopper, bus fare home, and his cigarettes. That was why his mother had stopped his pocket money: because the Woolworth's store detectives told her about the cigarettes. Which they no doubt smoked themselves. He always thought that was unfair, that the cigarettes had nothing to do with it. Punish him for stealing the ring, yes, but leave him his cigarettes. Of course, over the subsequent years, he had come across many more examples of life's basic unfairness, not a few of them perpetrated by himself. He had to admit that there were occasions when he had arrested someone for a driving offence, found a few grams of coke or hash in his pocket and added that to the charge sheet.

'Anyway,' he went on, 'it took me a long time to work out why she was so upset over something so unimportant as a plastic ring.'

'Why?'

'Because she was ashamed. It humiliated her to have to go down there and listen to these men tell her that her son was a thief. To have them talk down to her as if it were her fault and have to thank them for not calling the police. It didn't matter that I hadn't done anything serious. She was ashamed that a son of hers would do such a thing. And worried it might be a sign of what I'd turn into.'

'But you're a copper, not a thief.'

Banks smiled. 'Yes, I'm a copper. So come on downstairs and we'll see if we can make your mother a bit more forgiving than mine was.'

Adam hesitated, but at last he jumped up from the bed. Banks moved aside and let him go down the narrow staircase first.

Adam's mother was in the kitchen making tea, and Annie was leaning against the counter talking to her.

'Oh, so you've decided to join us, have you, you little devil?' said Mrs Kelly.

'Sorry, Mum.'

She ruffled his hair. 'Get on with you. Just don't do owt like that again.'

'Can I have a Coke?'

'In the fridge.'

Adam turned to the fridge and Banks winked at him. Adam blushed and grinned.

8

Vivian Elmsley sat down with her gin and tonic to watch the news that evening. The drinks were becoming more frequent, she had noticed, since her memories had started disturbing her. Though it was the only chink in her iron discipline, and she only allowed herself to indulge at the end of the day, it was a worrying sign nonetheless.

Watching the news had become a sort of grim duty now, a morbid fascination. Tonight, what she saw shook her to the core.

Towards the end of the broadcast, after the major world news and government scandals had been dealt with, the scene shifted to a familiar sight. A young blonde woman held the microphone. She stood in Hobb's End, where crime-scene searchers in their white boiler suits and wellies were still digging up the ruins.

'Today,' the reporter began, 'in a further bizarre twist to a story we have been covering in the north of England, police investigating some skeletal remains found by a local schoolboy are almost certain they have established the identity of the victim. Just over an hour ago, Detective Chief Inspector Alan Banks, who is heading the investigation, talked with our northern office.'

The scene shifted to a studio background, and the camera settled on a lean, dark-haired man with intense blue eyes.

'Can you tell us how this discovery was made?' the reporter asked.

'Yes.' Banks looked straight into the camera as he spoke, she noticed, not letting his eyes flick left or right the way so many amateurs did when they appeared on television. He had clearly done it before. 'When we discovered the identity of the people living in the cottage during the Second World War,' he began, 'we found that one of them, a woman called Gloria Shackleton, hasn't shown up on any postwar records so far.'

'And that made you suspicious?'

The detective smiled. 'Naturally. Of course, there could be a number of reasons for this, and we're still looking into other possibilities, but one thing we are forced to consider is that she doesn't show up because she was dead.'

'How long have the woman's remains been buried?'

'It's hard to be accurate, but we're estimating between the early to mid-forties.'

'That's a long time ago, isn't it?'

'It is.'

'Don't trails go cold, clues go stale?'

'Indeed they do. But I'm very pleased with the progress we've made so far, and I'm confident we can take this investigation forward. The remains were discovered only last Wednesday, and within less than a week we are reasonably certain we have established the identity of the victim. I'd say that's pretty good going for this sort of case.'

'And the next step?'

'The identity of the murderer.'

'Even though he or she may be dead?'

'Until we know that one way or the other, we're still dealing with an open case of murder. As they say in America, there's no statute of limitations on murder.'

'Is there any way the public can help?'

'Yes, there is.' Banks shifted in his chair. The next moment, the screen was filled with the head and shoulders of a woman. Surely it couldn't be? But even though it wasn't a photographic likeness, there was no mistaking who it was: *Gloria*.

Vivian gasped and clutched her chest.

Gloria.

After all these years.

It looked like part of a painting. Judging from the odd angle of the head, Vivian guessed that Gloria had been lying down as she posed. Michael Stanhope? It looked like his style. In the background, Banks's voice went on, 'If anyone recognizes this woman, who we think lived in London between 1921 and 1941 and in Hobb's End after that, if there is any living relative who knows something about her, would they please get in touch with the North Yorkshire Police.' He gave out a phone number. 'There's still a great deal we need to know,' he went on, 'and as the events occurred so long ago, that makes it all the more difficult for us.'

Vivian tuned out. All she could see was Gloria's face: Stanhope's vision of Gloria's face, with that cunning blend of naivety and wantonness, that come-hither smile and its promise of secret delights. It both was and *wasn't* Gloria.

Then she thought, with a tremor of fear: if they had already discovered Gloria, how long would it take them to discover *her*?

•

'It only said he's *missing*,' Gloria insisted over two months later, at the height of the summer of 1943. We were standing by one of Mr Kilnsey's dry-stone walls drinking

Tizer and looking out over the gold-green hills to the northwest. She thrust the most recent Ministry letter towards me and pointed at the words. 'See. "Missing during severe fighting east of the Irrawaddy River in Burma." Wherever that is. When Mr Kilnsey's son was killed at El Alamein it said he was definitely dead, not just missing.'

What had kept us going the most since we heard the news of Matthew's disappearance was our attempt to get as much information as we possibly could about what had happened to him. First we had written letters, then we had even telephoned the Ministry. But they wouldn't commit themselves. *Missing* was all they would tell us, and nobody seemed to know anything about the exact circumstances of his disappearance or where he might be if he was still alive. If they did, they weren't saying.

The most we could get out of the man on the telephone was that the area in which Matthew had disappeared was now in the hands of the Japanese, so there was no question of going in to search for bodies. Yes, he admitted, an unspecified number of casualties had been confirmed, but Matthew was not among them. While it was still likely he might have been killed, the man concluded, there was also a chance he had been taken prisoner. It was impossible to get anything further out of him. Since the telephone call, Gloria had been brooding over what to do next.

'I think we should go there,' she said, crumpling the letter into a ball.

'Where? *Burma*?'

'No, silly. London. We should go down there and buttonhole someone. Get some answers.'

'But they won't talk to us,' I protested. 'Besides, I don't think they're in London any more. All the government people have moved out to the country somewhere.'

'There has to be *somebody* there,' Gloria argued. 'It stands to reason. Even if it's just a skeleton staff. A government can't just pack up and leave everything behind. Especially the War Office. Besides, this is London I'm talking about. It's still the capital of England, you know. If there are answers to be found, you can bet we'll find them there.'

There was no arguing with Gloria's passionate rhetoric. 'I don't know,' I said. 'I wouldn't have the faintest idea where to start.'

'Whitehall,' she said, nodding. 'That's where we start. Whitehall.'

She sounded so certain that I didn't know what to reply.

For the rest of that month I tried to talk Gloria out of the London trip, but she was adamant. Once she got like that, I knew there could be no stopping her getting her own way. Even Cynthia and Alice and Michael Stanhope said it would be a waste of time. Mr Stanhope had no time at all for government bureaucrats and assured us they would tell us nothing.

Gloria insisted that if I didn't want to come with her, that was fine, she would go by herself. I didn't have the courage to tell her that I had never been to London, not even in peacetime, and the whole prospect scared me stiff. London seemed about as remote to me as the moon.

It was finally arranged for September. Gloria decided it would be best if we went and returned by night train. That way she would only have to rearrange her one and a half days off for midweek rather than ask Mr Kilnsey for more time when things were busy. To her surprise, Mr Kilnsey said she could take longer if she wished. Since he had lost Joseph at El Alamein, he had become a more compassionate and sympathetic man, and he understood her grief. We still decided to stick to the original plan because I didn't want to leave Mother alone for any longer.

Cynthia Garmen said she would look after Mother and the shop while we were gone. She said Norma Prentice owed her a day's work at the NAAFI in exchange for babysitting the previous week, so it should be no problem. Mother offered to buy the train tickets and gave Gloria some of her clothes coupons to use down there if we had time to visit the big shops. Though she accepted them gratefully, for once clothes were the last thing on Gloria's mind.

•

It was about ten o'clock when the road crested the hill and Banks could see Edinburgh spread out in the distance in all its hazy glory: the stepped rows of tenements; the dark Gothic spire of the Sir Walter Scott Monument, like some alien space rocket; the hump of Arthur's Seat; the castle on its crag; the glimmer of sea beyond.

Apart from one or two brief police-related visits, it was years since Banks had spent any time there, he realized as he coasted down the hill, Van Morrison's 'Tupelo Honey' on the stereo. When he was a student, he used to drive up to see friends quite often for weekends and holidays. At one time he had a girlfriend, a raven-haired young beauty called Alison, who lived down on St Stephen Street. But as is the nature of such long-distance relationships, 'out of sight, out of mind' beats 'absence makes the heart grow fonder' any day of the week, and during one visit she simply turned up at the pub with someone else. Easy come, easy go. By then he had his eye on another woman, called Jo, anyway.

Banks tried to recollect if he had ever taken Jem up to Edinburgh with him, but for the life of him he couldn't remember even seeing Jem outside his room, though he must have gone out to buy food, records and dope, as well as to sign on the dole. Banks had never even seen him out in the hallway. He saw people come and go from time to time, strangers, sometimes at weird hours of the night, but Jem never mentioned any other friends.

Banks's Edinburgh days were all pre-*Trainspotting* and the place didn't look quite so romantic when he came down off the hill into the built-up streets of dark stone, the roundabouts and traffic lights, shopping centres and zebra crossings. He got through Dalkeith easily enough, but shortly afterwards he made one simple mistake and found himself heading towards Glasgow on a dual carriageway for about three miles before he found an exit.

Elizabeth Goodall lived just off Dalkeith Road, not far from the city centre. She had given him precise directions on the telephone the previous evening, and after only a couple more wrong turns, he found the narrow street of tall tenements.

Mrs Goodall lived on the ground floor. She answered Banks's ring promptly and led him into a high-ceilinged living room which smelled of lavender and peppermint. All the windows were shut fast, and not the slightest breeze stirred the warm, perfumed air. Only a little daylight managed to steal through. The wallpaper was patterned with sprigs of rosemary and thyme. Parsley and sage, too, for all Banks could tell. Mrs Goodall bade him sit in a sturdy damask armchair. Like all the other chairs in the room, its arms and back were covered by white lace antimacassars.

'So you found your way all right?' she asked.

'Yes,' Banks lied. 'Nothing to it.'

'I don't drive a motor-car myself,' she said, with a trace of her old Yorkshire accent. 'I have to rely on buses and

trains if I want to go anywhere, which is rare these days.'
She rubbed her small, wrinkled hands together. 'Well,
then, you're here. Tea?'

'Please.'

She disappeared into the kitchen. Banks surveyed the
room. It was a nondescript sort of place: clean and tidy,
but not much character. A few framed photographs stood
on the sideboard, but none of them showed Hobb's End.
One glass-fronted cabinet held a few knick-knacks, including trophies, silverware and crystal. That would be
tempting to burglars, Banks thought: old woman in a
ground-floor flat with a nice haul of silverware just there
for the taking. He hadn't noticed any signs of a security
system.

Mrs Goodall walked back into the room slowly, carrying a China tea-set on a silver tray. She set it down on a
doily on the low table in front of the sofa, then sat down,
knees together, and smoothed her skirt.

She was a short, stout woman, dressed in a grey tweed
skirt, white blouse and a navy-blue cardigan, despite the
heat. Her recently permed hair was almost white, and its
waves looked frozen, razor-sharp to the touch, Margaret
Thatcher style. Her forehead was high, and her glaucous,
watery eyes pink-rimmed. She had a prissy slit of a mouth
that seemed painted on with red lipstick.

'We'll just let it mash a few minutes, shall we?' she
said. 'Then we'll pour.'

'Fine,' said Banks, banishing the image of the two of
them holding the thin teapot handle and pouring.

'Now,' she said, hands clasped on her lap, 'let us begin.
You mentioned Hobb's End on the telephone, but that was
all you saw fit to tell me. What do you wish to know?'

Banks leaned forward and rested his forearms on his

thighs. A number of general questions came to mind, but he needed something more specific, something to take her memory right back, if possible. 'Do you remember Gloria Shackleton?' he asked. 'She lived in Bridge Cottage during the war.'

Mrs Goodall looked as if she had just swallowed a mouthful of vinegar. 'Of course I remember her,' she said. 'Dreadful girl.'

'Oh? In what way?'

'Not to put too fine a point on it, Chief Inspector, the girl was a brazen hussy. It was perfectly obvious. The flirtatious manner, the tilt of her head, the lascivious smile. I knew it the first moment I set eyes on her.'

'Where was that?'

'Where? Why, in church, of course. My father was the verger at St Bartholomew's. Though how such a . . . a painted strumpet would dare to show herself like that in the sight of the Lord is beyond me.'

'So you first met her in church?'

'I didn't say I *met* her, just that I *saw* her there first. She was still called Gloria Stringer then.'

'Was she religious?'

'No true Christian woman would go about flaunting herself the way she did.'

'Why did she go to church, then?'

'Because the Shackletons went, of course. She had her feet firmly under their kitchen table.'

'She was from London originally, wasn't she?'

'So she said.'

'Did she ever say anything about her background, about her family?'

'Not to me, though I vaguely remember someone told me her parents were killed in the Blitz.'

'She'd come to Hobb's End with the Women's Land Army, hadn't she?'

'Yes. A *land girl*. Tea?'

'Please.'

Mrs Goodall sat up, back erect, and poured. The tea-cups – with matching saucers – were tiny, fragile bone-china things with pink roses painted inside and out, a gold rim and a handle he couldn't possibly get a finger through. Not a drop stained the white lace doily. 'Milk? Sugar?'

'Just as it comes, thanks very much.'

She frowned, as if she didn't approve of that. Anything other than milk and two sugars was probably unpatriotic in her book. 'Of course,' she went on. 'One hoped that over time she would make attempts to fit in, to alter her manner and appearance according to the standards of village society, but—'

'She made no attempt?'

'She did not. None at all.'

'Did you know her well?'

'Chief Inspector, does she sound like the kind of person whose company I would cultivate?'

'It was a small village. You must have been about the same age.'

'I was one year older.'

'Even so.'

'Alice – that's Alice Pool – used to spend quite a bit of time with her. Against my advice, I might add. But then Alice always was a bit too free and easy.'

'Did you have any dealings with Gloria at all?'

Mrs Goodall paused, as if to bring to mind an unpleasant memory. Then she nodded. 'Indeed I did. It fell to me to advise her that her behaviour was unacceptable, as was the way she looked.'

'Looked?'

'Yes. The sort of clothes she wore, the way she sashayed about, the way she wore her hair, like some sort of cheap American film star. It was not ladylike. Not in the least. As if that weren't bad enough, *she smoked in the street.*'

'You say it *fell* to you? On what authority? Was there strong general feeling against her?'

'In my capacity as a member of the Church of England.'

'I see. Was everyone else in Hobb's End ladylike?'

She pursed her lips again and let him know with a quick dagger glance that she hadn't missed the insolence in his tone. 'I'm not saying that there weren't lower elements in the village, Chief Inspector. Don't get me wrong. Of course, there were. As there are in every village society. But even the lowly of birth can aspire to at least a certain level of good manners and decent behaviour. Wouldn't you agree?'

'How did Gloria react when you rebuked her?'

Mrs Goodall flushed at the memory. 'She laughed. I pointed out that it might do her much good, morally and socially, were she to become active in the Women's Institute and the Missionary Society.'

'What was her response to this?'

'She called me an interfering busybody and indicated that there was only one missionary position she was interested in, and it was *not* the Church's. Can you believe it? And she used such language as I would not expect from the mouth of the lowest mill girl. Despite her put-on speech, I think she showed her true colours then.'

'How did she speak?'

'Oh, she had her airs and graces. She spoke like someone on the wireless. Not the way they do these days, of course, but as they did back then, when people spoke properly on the wireless. But you could tell it was put on. She had clearly been practising the arts of imitation and deception.'

'She married Matthew Shackleton, didn't she?'

Mrs Goodall sucked in her breath with an audible hiss. 'Yes. I was at their wedding. And I must say that, although Matthew was only a shopkeeper's son, he married well beneath himself when he married the Stringer girl. Matthew was an exceptional boy. I expected far better of him than that.'

'Do you know anything about their relationship?'

'It wasn't long after they were married he was sent abroad. He went missing in action, poor Matthew. Missing, presumed dead.'

Banks frowned. 'When was this?'

'When he went missing?'

'Yes.'

'Sometime in 1943. He was in the Far East. Captured by the Japanese.' She gave a little shudder.

'What happened to him?'

'I have no idea. I presume he was dead.'

'You lost touch?'

She fiddled with her wedding ring. 'Yes. My husband, William, was engaged in top-secret work for the home front, and he was assigned to Scotland early in 1944. I accompanied him. My parents came to live with us, and we didn't have anything more to do with Hobb's End. I still keep in touch with Ruby Kettering and Alice Poole, but they are my only connections. It was all so long ago. We women don't dwell on the war the way the men do, with their legions and their regimental reunions.'

'Do you know if Gloria had affairs with anyone other than Matthew?'

Mrs Goodall sniffed. 'Almost certainly.'

'Who with?'

She paused a moment, as if to let him know that she shouldn't be telling him this, then she uttered just one word. 'Soldiers.'

'What soldiers?'

'This was wartime, Chief Inspector. Contrary to what you might imagine, not every man in the armed forces was over fighting the Hun or the Nip. Unfortunately. There were soldiers everywhere. Not all of them British, either.'

'What soldiers were these?'

For the first time in their conversation, Mrs Goodall let a small smile slip. It endeared her to Banks tremendously. 'Oversexed,' she said, 'overpaid and over here.'

'Americans?'

'Yes. The RAF handed Rowan Woods over to the American Air Force.'

'Did you see much of these Americans?'

'Oh, yes. They often used to come and drink in the village pubs, or attend our occasional dances at the church hall. Some even came to the Sunday services. They had their own on the base, of course, but St Bartholomew's was a beautiful old church. Such a pity it had to be knocked down.'

'Did Gloria have American boyfriends, then?'

'Several. And I needn't tell you about the opportunities for immorality and indiscretion that a wide area of wooded land like Rowan Woods has to offer, need I?'

Banks wondered if she would take a positive answer as an indication of personal experience. He decided not to risk it. 'Was there anyone in particular?' he asked.

'I have no first-hand knowledge. I kept my distance from them. According to Cynthia Garmen, she had more than one. Not that Cynthia was one to talk. No better than she ought to be, that one.'

'Why?'

'She married one of them, didn't she? Went off to live in Pennsylvania or some such place.'

'So there was no one serious for Gloria?'

'Oh, I've no doubt her liaisons were every bit as serious as a woman such as Gloria Shackleton was capable of. A *married* woman.'

'But you said she thought her husband was dead.'

'Missing, *presumed* dead. It's not quite the same. Besides, that's no excuse.' Mrs Goodall remained silent for a few moments, then said, 'May I ask *you* a question, Chief Inspector?'

'Go ahead.'

'Why are you asking me about the Shackleton girl after all these years?'

'Don't you watch the news?'

'I prefer to read historical biography.'

'Newspapers?'

'On occasion. But only the obituaries. What are you hinting at, Chief Inspector? Am I missing something?'

Banks told her about the reservoir drying up and the discovery of the body they believed to be Gloria's. Mrs Goodall paled and clutched at the silver crucifix around her neck. 'I don't like to speak ill of the dead,' she muttered. 'You should have told me sooner.'

'Would that have changed what you said?'

She paused a moment, then sighed and said, 'Probably not. I have always considered telling the truth to be an important virtue. All I can tell you, though, is that Gloria Shackleton was alive and well when William and I left Hobb's End in May 1944.'

'Thank you,' said Banks. 'That helps us narrow things down a bit. Do you know if she had any enemies?'

'Not what you'd call enemies. Nobody who would do what you have just described. Many people, like myself, disapproved of her. But that's quite a different thing. One would hardly murder a person for not joining the Women's Institute. Might I make a suggestion?'

'Please.'

'Given Gloria's wayward nature, don't you think you should be looking at this as a *crime passionnel*?'

'Perhaps.' Banks shifted in his chair and crossed his legs the other way. Mrs Goodall poured more tea. It was lukewarm. 'What about Michael Stanhope?' he asked.

She raised her eyebrows. 'There's another one.'

'Another what?'

'Debauched, perverted. I could go on. Birds of a feather, him and Gloria Shackleton. Have you *seen* any of his so-called paintings?'

Banks nodded. 'One of them seems to be a nude of Gloria. I wonder if you knew anything about that?'

'I can hardly say it surprises me, but no. Believe me, if such a painting exists, it was *not* public knowledge in Hobb's End. At least not while I was there.'

'Do you think Gloria might have had an affair with Michael Stanhope?'

'I can't say. Given that the two of them shared similar natures and views, I wouldn't rule it out. They did spend a lot of time together. *Drinking*. As I recollect, though, even Gloria's tastes weren't quite so exotic as to extend as far as a tortured, drunken, depraved artist.'

'Did Gloria and Matthew have any children?'

'Not that I ever knew of.'

'And you would have known?'

'I think so. It's hard to hide such things in a small village. Why do you ask?'

'There were certain indications in the post-mortem, that's all.' Banks scratched the tiny scar beside his right eye. 'But nobody seems to know anything about it.'

'She could have had a child after we left in 1944.'

'It's possible. Or perhaps she gave birth *before* she arrived in Hobb's End and married Matthew Shackleton. After all, she was nineteen when she came to the village. Perhaps she abandoned the baby and its father in London.'

'But . . . but that means . . .'

'Means what, Mrs Goodall?'

'Well, I never assumed that Matthew was her first conquest, not a woman like her. But a child . . .? Surely that would indicate she was already married, and that her marriage to Matthew was bigamous?'

'Just one more sin to add to her list,' said Banks. 'But it wasn't necessarily so. I imagine even back then, in the good old days, the odd child was born on the wrong side of the blanket.'

Mrs Goodall's lips tightened to a single red line for a moment, then she said, 'I don't appreciate your sarcasm, Chief Inspector, or your coarseness. Things *were* better back then. Simpler. Clearer. Ordered. And the wartime spirit brought people together. People of all classes. Say what you will.'

'I'm sorry, Mrs Goodall. I don't mean to be sarcastic, really, but I'm trying to get to the bottom of a particularly nasty murder here, one that I probably have hardly any chance of solving because it was committed so long ago. I believe the victim deserves my best efforts, no matter what you may think of her.'

'Of course she does. I stand corrected. Gloria Shackleton could not possibly have deserved what you say happened to her. But I'm sorry, I don't think I can help you any further.'

'Did you know Matthew's sister, Gwynneth?'

'Gwen? Oh, yes. Gwen was always rather the quiet one, head buried in a book. I imagined her becoming a teacher or something like that. Perhaps even a university professor. But she worked in the shop throughout the war, besides taking care of her mother and doing fire-watching at night. She was no shirker, wasn't Gwen.'

'Do you know what became of her? Is she still alive?'

'I'm afraid we lost touch when William and I went to Scotland. We weren't especially close, though she was a regular church-goer and wrote for the parish magazine.'

'Were she and Gloria close?'

'Well, they had to be, to some extent, being family. But they were different as chalk and cheese. There was some talk about Gloria leading Gwen astray. They were always off to dances together in Harkside, or to the pictures. Gwen had generally avoided social intercourse until Gloria arrived on the scene, preferring her own company, or that of books. Gwen was always a rather impressionable girl. Though she took Gloria under her wing at first, so to speak, it was soon quite clear who exactly was under whose wing.'

'What was their age difference?'

'Gwen was two or three years younger, perhaps. Believe me, though, it makes a vast difference at that age.'

'What did she look like?'

'Gwen? She was rather a plain girl, apart from her eyes. Remarkable eyes, almost oriental the way they slanted. And she was tall. Tall and awkward. A gangly sort of girl.'

'What about Matthew?'

'A dashing, handsome fellow. Very mature. Gifted with wisdom beyond his years.' Again, she allowed a little smile to flit across her hard-set features. 'If I hadn't met my William and the Stringer girl hadn't arrived on the scene, well . . . who knows? Anyway, she got her hands on him, and that was that.'

Banks let the silence stretch. He could hear a clock ticking in the background.

'If you'll excuse me, Chief Inspector,' she said after a few moments, 'I'm extremely tired. All those memories.'

Banks stood up. 'Yes, of course. I'm sorry for taking up so much of your time.'

'Not at all. It seems you've come a long way for nothing, or very little.'

Banks shrugged. 'Part of the job. Besides, you've been a great help.'

'If there's anything else I can help you with, please don't hesitate to telephone.'

'Thank you.' Banks looked at his watch. Going on for one. Time for a spot of lunch before the long drive home.

•

We took the night train from Leeds, where the platform was crowded with young soldiers. The train clanked and steamed into the station only an hour late, and we felt ourselves jostled and pushed along by the crowd like corks in a fast-flowing river. I was terrified that we were going to fall between the carriages and be run over by the huge iron wheels, but we clung on to each other for dear life amid all the shoving and heaving and hissing steam, and we finally managed to get ourselves more or less pushed on to seats in a cramped compartment that soon grew even more cramped.

Another hour passed before the engine groaned and shuddered out of the station.

I had loved train journeys ever since I was a little girl, loved the gentle rocking motion, the hypnotic clickety-click of the wheels on the lines and the way the landscape drifts by like images from a dream.

Not that time.

A lot of trains had been damaged and most of the railway workshops were being used for munitions production. As a result, many of the engines in use would have been good for nothing but scrap iron if it hadn't been for the war. The motion was jerky and we never really got going fast enough for a rhythmic clickety-click. Everyone was crushed far too closely together to make sleep possible. At least for me. I couldn't even read. The blinds were drawn tight and the whole compartment was lit by one ghostly blue pinpoint of light, so dim you could hardly make out the features of the person sitting opposite you. There wasn't even a restaurant car.

We talked for a while with two young soldiers, who offered us Woodbine after Woodbine. I think that was when I started to smoke, out of sheer boredom. Even when the first few puffs made me feel sick and dizzy, I persevered. It was something to do.

The soldiers sympathized and wished us luck when Gloria told them about Matthew. Then people started to fall silent, each drifting into his own world. For me it was a matter of gritting my teeth and enduring the long journey, the constant, unexplained delays, the jerking stops and starts.

Gloria managed to doze off after a while and her head slid slowly sideways until she was resting her cheek on my shoulder and I could feel her warm breath against my throat. I still couldn't sleep. I was left with nothing but my own gloomy thoughts and rasping snores from the soldiers. We stopped in the middle of nowhere for nearly two hours at one point. No explanation.

Because of the double summertime, it didn't get light as early as it used to, but even so we weren't more than six or seven hours into the journey before we were able to open the blinds on muted early morning sunlight slanting across the fields. People had put odd objects like old mangles and broken cars on some of the empty meadows to make obstacles for any enemy planes that might try to land there.

One field was scattered with country signposts stuck in the ground at strange angles. The signposts had been taken down at the start of the war, along with all the station nameplates, to confuse the enemy in case of invasion, but I was still surprised to see where some of them had ended up.

All in all, the journey took ten hours, and the last hour or two seemed to take us through the endless London suburbs. It was here that I caught my first sight of street after street of bombed-out terraces, shattered lamp-posts, powdered plaster, twisted girders and jagged walls. Rosebay willowherb and Oxford ragwort grew from the rubble, pushing between the cracks in the bombed masonry and brickwork.

Packs of children roved through the streets, playing among the derelict houses. One ingenious group had rigged up a rope from a lamp-post that seemed to be leaning at a precarious angle, like the Tower of Pisa, and they were proceeding to take it in turns to swing back and forth, playing at Tarzan the Ape Man.

Some houses were only half-destroyed, split open like a cross-section. You could see wallpaper, framed paintings and photographs on the walls, a bed half hanging over the jagged remains of the floor. Here and there, people had moved damaged items of furniture into the street: a doorless wardrobe, a cracked sideboard and a pram with buckled wheels. I felt like a voyeur at a disaster site, which is what I was, I suppose, but I couldn't stop looking. I'm not sure that I had any real grasp of the full extent of the war's devastation until then, despite seeing Leeds after that air raid.

It seemed that on every area of spare ground not taken up by allotments, a barrage balloon station had been set up to deter low-flying enemy planes. The fat silver balloons glinted in the sun and looked like whales trying to fly. In some of the green areas, rows of anti-aircraft guns pointed at the sky like steel arrows.

Of course, there were also plenty of buildings left standing and some of these were surrounded by sandbags, often to a height of about ten feet or more. I also noticed a lot of posters, on just about every available hoarding; they told us to grow our own food, save coal, buy war bonds, walk when we can and Lord knows what else.

I was so lost in the sights that I hardly noticed the time pass until King's Cross. It was after ten o'clock in the morning when we arrived at the station and I was starving. Gloria wanted to head straight for Whitehall, but I persuaded her to stop and we found a Lyons, where we managed to get a rasher of bacon and an egg.

After breakfast, we walked back into the street and I was at last able to take in where I was. My first sensation was of being a very small, tiny, insignificant little creature lost in an immense and sprawling city. People pressed in on me from all directions; tall buildings towered over me.

The whole place had a shabby, worn and slightly defeated air about it. Everybody looked pinched and pale, the kind of look you get after years of rationing, bombing and uncertainty. Even so, for a Yorkshire country girl, it might

as well have been another planet. I had never been anywhere bigger than Leeds before and I'm sure London would
have overwhelmed me even in peacetime.

It had started to drizzle, though the air was still warm, and
the damp sandbags gave off a musky smell. There were so
many people rushing about, most of them in uniform, that I
began to feel quite panicky and dizzy. I clutched at Gloria's
arm as she led me purposefully towards a bus stop. Often
people smiled or said hello as we passed. I saw my first
wounded soldiers, sad-looking men with bandaged heads,
missing limbs, eye patches, some on crutches or with their
arms in slings. All of them lucky ones; they were still alive.

Gloria was in her element. After only a few moments of
disorientation at first, something seemed to click, as if the
city actually made sense to her, which it certainly didn't to
me. She seemed to have only the slightest doubt over which
bus to catch, and a quick word with the clippie, who was
trying to look like Joan Crawford, soon set her right on that.
We went upstairs, where you could smoke, and then we
were off.

It was a whirlwind journey and more than once I feared
the bus would tip over turning a corner. In the east, I fancied
I could see the immense dome of St Paul's in the grey light
through the dirty, rain-streaked window. I was overwhelmed by the size of the buildings all around me. White
and grey stone darkened by rain; curving Georgian or
Edwardian façades five or six storeys high, with pediments,
gargoyles and pointed gables. Huge Ionic columns. Surely,
I thought, this must be a city built by giants.

At one point my heart jumped into my throat. I saw
broken glass and rubble on the pavement and, strewn among
it all, human body parts: a head, a leg, a torso. But when I
looked more closely, I could see no blood, and the limbs all

had a hard, unnatural look about them. I realized that a bomb must have hit a dress shop and blown all the mannequins into the street.

We passed Trafalgar Square, where Nelson's Column stood, much taller in reality than it had been even in my imagination. You could hardly see poor Lord Nelson up at the top. The base of the column was covered with hoardings asking us to buy National War Savings Bonds. Across the square, near the Insurance Office and the Canadian Pacific Building, was a huge billboard advertising Famel cough mixture.

There were a lot of soldiers milling about. I didn't recognize all the caps and uniforms, in just about every colour you could imagine, from black to bright blue and cherry-red. I also saw my first-ever Negro from that bus in Trafalgar Square. I knew they existed, of course – I had read about them – but I had never actually seen a black man before. I remember being rather disappointed that, apart from being black, he didn't look all that much different from anyone else.

Gloria nudged me gently and we got off on a broad street flanked with even more tall buildings.

And that was when our search began in earnest. I felt like a small child dragged along by its mother as Gloria took me from building to building. We asked policemen, knocked on doors, asked soldiers, strangers in the street, knocked on even more doors.

Finally, wet and weary and ready to give up, I rejoiced when Gloria found some sort of minor clerk who took pity on us. I don't honestly think he knew anything about Matthew or what had happened to him, but he did seem to know a little more about the war in the Far East than anyone else would admit to. And he seemed to take a shine to Gloria.

He was a tidy little man in a pinstripe suit, with grey hair parted at the centre and a neat, trim moustache. He glanced at his watch, pursed his lips and frowned before suggesting he might spare us ten minutes if we cared to accompany him to the tea house on the corner. He had a rather high-pitched, squeaky voice and spoke with a posh, educated accent. At that point I would have cheerfully murdered for a cup of tea. We dragged ourselves inside, bought tea at the counter, and Gloria started to pump the poor fellow for information before we had even had our first sip.

'What are the chances that Matthew might still be alive?' she asked.

This clearly wasn't the sort of question the man, who told us his name was Arthur Winchester, was trained to answer. He hemmed and hawed a bit, then measured his words as carefully as the sugar cubes in the bowl were rationed. 'I'm afraid I can't really answer that question,' he said. 'As I told you, I have no knowledge of the individual case to which you refer, merely a little general knowledge of the situation in the East.'

'All right,' Gloria went on, undaunted, 'tell me about what happened at Irridaddy, or whatever it is. That's if it's not classified.'

Arthur Winchester sniffed and granted us a little smile. 'Irrawaddy. It happened six months ago, so it's hardly classified,' he said. Then he paused, sipped some more tea and rubbed the bristly bottom of his moustache with the back of his hand. I glanced towards the window and saw the rain slanting down, distorting the shapes of the people passing by on Victoria Street.

'Burma,' he went on, 'as you probably know, stands between India and China, and it would be of inestimable value if our forces could reopen the Burma Road and clear the way to China, which could then be used as a direct base for operations against Japan. This, as I say, is general knowledge.'

'Not to me it isn't.' Gloria lit a Craven A. 'Go on,' she prompted, blowing out a long plume of smoke.

Arthur Winchester cleared his throat. 'To put things simply, since Burma fell, we have been trying to get it back. One of the offensives with this end in mind was the Chindit Operation, launched in February. They began east of the Irrawaddy, a river in central Burma. While they were there, the Japanese launched a major offensive on the Arakan Front and the British had to withdraw. Are you following me?'

We both nodded.

'Good.' Arthur Winchester finished his tea. 'Well, the Chindits were trapped behind the enemy lines, cut off, and they began to filter back in some disarray.' He looked at Gloria. 'This, no doubt, is why no one has been able to give you any specific information about your husband. He's an engineer, you said?'

'Yes.'

'Hmm.'

'What happened next?'

'Next? Oh, well the Chindits had suffered severe hardships. Most severe. Not long after, they were ordered to leave Burma.'

'But we're still trying to get Burma back?'

'Oh, yes. It's of great strategic importance.'

'So there's still a chance?'

'A chance of what?'

'That someone might find Matthew. When the British win back Burma.'

Arthur Winchester glanced out of the window. 'I wouldn't get your hopes up, my dear. A long time might pass before that happens.'

'Were the losses heavy?' I asked.

Arthur Winchester gazed at me for a moment, but he wasn't seeing me. 'What? Oh, yes. Rather worse than we had hoped for.'

'How do you know all this?' Gloria asked.

Arthur Winchester inclined his head modestly. 'I don't know very much, I'm afraid. But before the war, before this government work, I was a history teacher. The Far East has always interested me.'

'So you don't really have anything to tell us?' Gloria said.

'Well, any excuse to take tea with a pretty lady will do for me, if you don't mind my saying so.'

Gloria got to her feet in a fury and was about to storm out of the place, leaving even me behind, when Arthur Winchester blushed and grabbed hold of her sleeve meekly. 'I say, my dear, I'm sorry. Poor taste. I really didn't mean to offend you. A compliment, that's all. I meant no hint of any sort of prurient suggestion.'

If Gloria didn't know what *prurient* meant, she never let on. She merely sat down again, slowly, a hard, suspicious look in her eyes, and said, 'Can you tell us anything at all, Mr Winchester?'

'All I can tell you, my dear,' he went on gravely, 'is that during the retreat, many of the wounded had to be left behind enemy lines. They simply couldn't be transported. They were left with a little money and a weapon, of course, but what became of them, I can't say.'

Gloria had turned pale. I found myself twisting the fabric of my dress in my fist over my lap until my knuckles turned white. 'Are you saying this is what happened to Matthew?' she asked, her voice no louder than a whisper.

'I'm saying it may be what happened, if he is simply being described as missing, presumed dead.'

'And what if that was the case?'

Arthur Winchester paused and brushed an imaginary piece of lint from his lapel. 'Well,' he said, 'the Japanese don't like taking wounded prisoners. It would depend how badly wounded he was, of course, whether he could work, that sort of thing.'

'So you're saying they might have simply murdered him as he lay there wounded and defenceless?'

'I'm saying it's possible. Or . . .'

'Or what?'

He looked away. 'As I said, the wounded were left behind with a weapon.'

It took a second or two for what he was getting at to sink in. I think it was me who responded first. 'You mean Matthew might have committed suicide?'

'If capture was inevitable, and if he was badly hurt, then I'd say, yes, it's a possibility.' His tone brightened a little. 'But this is all pure conjecture, you understand. I know nothing at all of the circumstances. Maybe he was simply captured by the enemy, and he's going to while away the rest of the war in the relative safety of a prison camp. I mean, you've seen how well we take care of our Germans and Italians here, haven't you?'

It was true. The Italians in Yorkshire even worked on the farms at planting and harvest times. Gloria and I had talked to them on occasion and they seemed cheerful enough, for prisoners of war. They liked to sing opera while they worked, and some of them had beautiful voices.

'But you said the Japanese don't like taking prisoners.'

'It's true they despise the weak and the defeated. But if they capture fit men, they can put them to work on railways and bridges and suchlike. They're not fools. You *did* say your husband was an engineer, so he could be useful to them.'

'*If* he cooperated.'

'Yes. The main problem is that we don't know a lot about the Japanese, and our lines of communication are very poor, almost to the point of not existing at all. Even the Red Cross has great difficulties getting its parcels delivered and getting information out of them. The Japanese are notoriously difficult to deal with.'

'So he may be a prisoner of war and nobody has bothered to let anyone know? Is that what you're telling us?'

'That is a distinct possibility. Yes. There are probably hundreds, if not thousands, of others in that same position, too.'

'But you said you're a teacher. You know about the Japanese, don't you?'

Arthur Winchester laughed nervously. 'I know a little about their geography and history, but the Japanese have always been very insular. Comes from living on an island, perhaps.'

'We live on an island, too,' I reminded him.

'Yes, well, I mean insular more in that they've screened themselves off from the rest of the world, actively resisted contact with the West. We knew practically nothing at all about them until the turn of the century – their customs, beliefs – and even now we don't know a lot.'

'What *do* you know? What *can* you tell us?' Gloria asked.

He paused again. 'Well,' he said. 'I don't want to upset you, but you asked me to be honest with you. I'd say it's best to hope he's dead. It's best that way.' He paused. 'Look. It's wartime. Things are very different. You have to let go of the past. Your husband is probably dead. Or, if he isn't, he might as well be. Nothing will be the same when it's done.

All over the city people are living as if there's no tomorrow. How long are you staying in London?'

Gloria looked at him suspiciously. 'Until tonight. Why?'

'I know a place. Very nice. Very discreet. Perhaps I could—'

Gloria got to her feet so fast she bumped the table with her thighs and the remains of her tea spilled on to Arthur Winchester's lap. But he didn't stop around to mop it up. Instead, he bolted for the door saying, 'Good Lord, is that the time? I must dash.'

And with that, he was out of the door before Gloria could even pick up something to throw at him. She glared after him for a moment, then touched up her curls and sat down again. The serving girl frowned at us, then turned away. I thought we were lucky not to get thrown out.

We dawdled over our tea, Gloria calming down, smoking another cigarette and gazing out through the steamed-up window at the phantoms drifting by outside. In the café, soldiers came and went with their girls. I could smell the rain on their uniforms.

'What did he mean, it's best that way?' Gloria asked.

'I don't know,' I said. 'I suppose he meant to say that the Japanese don't treat their prisoners as well as we do.'

'What do they do? Torture them? Beat them? Starve them?'

'I don't know, Gloria,' I said, putting my hand over hers. 'I just don't know. All I can say is that it sounded to me as if he was saying Matthew would be better off dead.'

9

Annie parked in one of the hilly streets around St Mary's, at the back of the castle, and went looking for Alice Poole's cottage. The sky was bright blue, with only a few wisps of white cloud borne on the sea breeze. Pity she had to work. She could have brought her bucket and spade. As a child she had spent hours amusing herself on the beach. Some of her only memories of her mother took place on the beach at St Ives: building sandcastles together, burying one another in the sand so that only a head showed, or maybe a head and feet, running into the big waves and getting knocked over. In Annie's memory, her mother was a bright, mercurial figure, mischievous, devil-may-care, always laughing. Though her father, on the surface, was easygoing, bright, funny and caring, there was a darkness in his art that Annie felt excluded her; she didn't know where it came from or how he reconciled it with the rest of his life. Did he suffer terribly in private and simply put on a public face, even for his own daughter? She hardly knew him at all.

She found the cottage easily enough, according to directions she had received over the telephone. It was in a high, quiet part of town, away from the pubs and shopping centres crowded with holidaymakers from Leeds and Bradford. From the garden she could see a wedge of the North Sea far below, beyond Marine Drive, steely grey-blue today, dotted with small boats. Flocks of gulls gathered, squealing, above a shoal of fish.

The woman who answered the door was tall, with thin, wispy hair like candyfloss. She was wearing a long, loose purple dress with gold embroidery around the neck, hem and sleeves, and gold earrings of linked hoops that dangled almost as far as her shoulders. It reminded Annie of the sort of thing hippies used to wear. A pair of black horn-rimmed glasses hung on a chain around her neck.

'Come in, love.' She led the way into a bright, cluttered room. Dust motes spun in the rays of sunlight that lanced through the panes of the mullioned window. 'Can I offer you anything?' she asked, having settled Annie in an armchair so soft and deep she wondered how she'd ever get out of it. 'Only, I usually have elevenses around this time. Coffee and a Kit Kat. Instant coffee, mind you.'

Annie smiled. 'That'll be fine; thanks, Mrs Poole.'

'Alice. Call me Alice. And why don't you have a look through this while I see to things in the kitchen. Your call got me thinking about the old days and I realized I hadn't had it out in years.'

She handed Annie a thick leatherbound photograph album and headed for the kitchen. Most of the deckle-edged black-and-white photographs were family groups, what Annie took to be Alice and her parents, aunts, brothers and sisters, but several were village scenes: women stopping to chat in the street, baskets over their arms, scarves knotted on their heads; children fishing from the riverbanks. There were also a couple of pictures of the church, which was smaller and prettier than she had imagined from Stanhope's painting, with a squat, square tower, and of the dark, brooding flax mill, like a skull perched on its promontory.

Alice Poole came back holding a mug of coffee in each

hand and a Kit Kat, still in its wrapper, between her teeth. When she had freed her hands, she took the chocolate bar from her mouth and put it on a small coffee table beside her chair. 'A little indulgence of mine,' she said. 'Would you like one? I should have asked.'

'No,' said Annie. 'No, that's fine.' She accepted her coffee. It was milky and sweet, just the way she liked it.

'What do you think of the photos?'

'Very interesting.'

'You've come about poor Gloria, then?'

'You've heard?'

'Oh, yes. Your boss was on telly last night. I don't see very well, but there's nothing wrong with my ears. I don't watch a lot of television, but not much local news slips by me. Especially something like that. How horrible. Have you got any suspects yet?'

'Not really,' said Annie. 'We're still trying to find out as much as we can about Gloria. It's very difficult, what with it all being so long ago.'

'You don't say. I was seventy-five last birthday. Can you believe it?'

'Quite honestly, Mrs – sorry, Alice – I can't.' She really did seem remarkably spry for a woman of that age. Apart from a few liver spots on her hands and wrinkles on her face, the only real indication of the ravages of age was her sparse and lifeless hair, which Annie was now coming to believe had probably fallen victim to chemotherapy and not yet grown back properly.

'Look,' Alice pointed out, 'this is Gloria.' She turned to a photograph of four girls standing in front of a Jeep and pointed to the petite blonde with the long curls, the narrow waist and the provocative smile. Without a doubt it was the same girl from Stanhope's painting. Underneath, in tiny white letters, was written 'July 1944'. 'This one's Gwen, her sister-in-law.' Gwen was the tallest of them all. She wasn't smiling and had half turned away from the camera, as if shy about her looks. 'And this one here is Cynthia Garmen. The Four Musketeers, we were. Oh, that one's me.' Alice had been a svelte blonde, by the look of her. Also in the photograph, standing in the Jeep behind the girls, were four young men in uniform.

'Who are they?' Annie asked.

'Americans. That one's Charlie, and that's Brad. We saw quite a lot of them. I don't remember the names of the other two. They just happened to be there.'

'I'd like to make a copy of that photo, if you don't mind. We'll send it back to you.'

'Not at all.' Alice detached the photograph from its corners. 'Please take care of it, though.'

'I promise.' Annie slipped it in her briefcase. 'You knew Gloria well?' she went on.

'Quite well. She married Matthew Shackleton, as you probably know, and while he was away at war, Gloria and Gwen, Matthew's sister, became inseparable. But quite often the gang of us would do something together. Anyway, I wouldn't say we were the best of friends, but I did know her. And I liked her.'

'What was she like?'

'Gloria?' Alice unwrapped her Kit Kat and took a bite. When she had swallowed it, she said, 'Well, I'd say she was a good sort. Cheerful. Fun to be with. Kind. Generous. She'd give you the shirt off her back. Or make one for you.'

'Pardon?'

'Magic fingers. Gloria was such an expert sewer you could give her rags and she'd turn out a ball gown. Well, I might be exaggerating a little, but I'm sure you get my point. It was a skill in much demand back then, I can tell you. There wasn't a heck of a lot in the shops, and your clothing coupons didn't go very far.'

'She worked at Top Hill Farm, didn't she?'

'Yes. For Kilnsey. The lecherous old sod.'

'Do you think there was anything funny going on up there between him and Gloria?'

Alice laughed. 'Kilnsey and Gloria? In his wildest fantasies, maybe. Nellie, his wife, would have had his guts for garters if he'd so much as looked twice at another woman. And Gloria . . . well, she might have been generous in some ways, but she wasn't *that* generous. Old Kilnsey? No. You're barking up the wrong tree there, love. He was one of them serious religious types that always look like perverts to me. Probably need more religion than the rest of us just to keep their unnatural urges down.'

Annie made a note of the name. In her experience, that repressed type was more likely to lose control and kill than most. 'What kind of things did you do together?'

'The usual. Gloria was impulsive. She'd suggest a spur-of-the-moment picnic on Harksmere bank. Or a film at the Lyceum in Harkside. It's been converted to the KwikSave last time I saw it, but back then it was a popular place for lads and lasses to meet. Or walking in the fields at night during the blackout. And swimming.' She lowered her voice and leaned forward. 'Believe it or not, dearie, we once went swimming without costumes in Harksmere after dark. What a time we had of it! That was Gloria's idea, too. Spontaneous. She didn't like everything all planned out for her, but she always liked to have something to do or to look forward to doing.'

'Did she tell you anything about her past?'

'She never spoke much about that at all. From what

little I could gather, it must have been very painful for her, so I just thought if she doesn't want to talk about it, then that's all right with me. All she said was that she lost her family in the Blitz. She did sometimes seem very distracted. She had deep, quiet, sad moods that would just come on her out of nowhere, in the middle of a picnic, at a dance, whatever. But not often.'

'How did she fit into village life?'

'Well,' said Alice, 'I suppose that depends on your point of view. At first she wasn't around very much. Land girls worked very long hours. After she'd married Matthew and moved to Bridge Cottage we saw a bit more of her.'

'Did she have any enemies? Anyone who had reason to dislike her?'

'Quite a few people disapproved of her. Jealous, if you ask me. Gloria didn't care what people thought of her. She went in the pubs by herself, and she smoked in the street. I know that's nothing now, love, the street's the only place you *can* smoke in some places, but back then it was . . . well, to some people it meant you were nigh on being a prostitute. People had some funny ideas back then.' She shook her head slowly. 'They call them the good old days, but I'm not so sure. There was a lot of hypocrisy and intolerance. Snobbery, too. And Gloria was far too cheeky and flighty for some people.'

'Anyone in particular?'

'Betty Goodall could never take to her. Betty always was a bit of a snob, and a bit too High Church, too, if you ask me, but she's a good soul underneath it all, don't get me wrong. She has a good heart. She was always just a bit too quick with her moral judgments. I think she fancied Matthew Shackleton for herself, and I think it rather put her nose out of joint, Matthew marrying Gloria. Like I said,

Gloria was free and easy in her nature, besides being a real "stunna", as they say in the papers these days. I think a lot of women were just plain jealous of her.'

Annie smiled. From this description of Alice's, she could imagine what a time Banks would be having up in Edinburgh. 'Betty Goodall wasn't in the photograph,' she remarked.

'No. Betty and William had gone by then. He was some sort of dogsbody with the Home Guard, and they kept sending him from council to council. Not fit for real war work, apparently, and no one could quite figure out what to do with him.'

'Do you know if Gloria actually *did* anything to merit such disapproval, or was it simply because of her nature, her personality?'

'Oh dear. You want me to tell tales out of school?'

Annie laughed. 'Not if you don't want to. But it *is* a long time ago, and it might help us find her killer.'

'Oh, I know, love. I know.' Alice waved her hand. 'Just let me get my cigarettes. I usually have one after my elevenses, one after lunch and one after tea. And perhaps one with a nightcap before bed. But never more than five a day.' She got up and brought her purse over, fiddled for a packet of Dunhill and lit one with a slim gold lighter. 'Now then, dearie, where was I?'

'I wanted to know if Gloria had affairs, slept around.'

'Certainly no more than a lot of others did then, ones you'd generally consider "nice" girls. But people made a lot of assumptions about Gloria just because she was a free-thinking woman and spoke her mind. She definitely was a bit of a flirt, there's no denying that. But that doesn't mean anything, does it? It's just a bit of fun.'

'Depends on who you flirt with.'

'I suppose so. Anyway, I may have been naive, but I think there was more smoke than fire. Most of the time.'

'What did you think of Matthew?'

'Not very much, to tell you the truth. There was always something just a bit too smarmy and cocky about him for my taste. Oh, he was nice enough on the outside, handsome and charming, and one had to feel sorry for what happened to him later.'

'What happened?'

'Killed by the Japanese. Over in Burma. Anyway, Matthew was a big talker. I also heard he got more than one lass in the family way before Gloria came on the scene, while he was a student in Leeds. So he was no saint, wasn't Matthew Shackleton, though to hear some speak you'd think butter wouldn't melt in his mouth. Some folk said she only married him because he was a bright, handsome lad with a great future ahead of him – which seems to me like a very good reason to marry someone. I'm sure he made her all kinds of promises about how wonderful their future would be. He filled her head full of dreams of all the things he would build and all the far-off exotic lands they'd visit and all that rubbish. Underneath it all, Gloria was a romantic. I think she fell in love with this new world Matthew painted for her. All the bridges and cathedrals he was going to build, and her by his side. She was impatient for it all.'

'How did Gloria take his death?'

'She was heartbroken. Devastated. I was worried about her and I mentioned it to Gwen once or twice. Gwen said she'd be okay in a while, but then Gwen didn't look too good herself, either. Very close, they were, her and Matthew. Anyway, when Gloria started to go out again, she was more devil-may-care, you know, the way some people get when they feel they've nothing left to lose. A lot of people were like that then.' She paused and took another drag on her cigarette, then fiddled with the chain around her neck.

'So Gloria started going out again, to dances and things?'

'Yes, a few months later.'

'When did she form her relationship with Michael Stanhope, the artist?'

'Oh, he'd always been around. He was at their wedding. Gloria spent a lot of time with him. Used to drink with him in the Shoulder of Mutton. That's another reason those religious types disapproved of her.'

'Did you know Stanhope?'

'Just to say hello to. *Michael Stanhope.* I haven't thought of him in years. He was an eccentric. Always wearing that floppy hat of his. And the cane. Very affected. There was no mistaking that he was an *Artist*, if you know what I mean. I can't say I had much time for him, myself, but I think he was harmless enough. Anyway, he wouldn't have had anything to do with Gloria. It was all just a show.'

'What do you mean?'

'He was a homosexual, dearie. Queer as a three-pound note, as we used to say. Anyway, as you probably know, it was illegal back then.'

'I see. Would it surprise you to know that a painting of Gloria by Michael Stanhope *did* show up?' Annie asked.

'It did?'

'Yes. A nude. It's in Leeds Art Gallery.'

Alice put her hand to her mouth and laughed. 'Well, bless my soul. Is it really? A nude? Of Gloria? Still, I can't say it really surprises me. Gloria was never really shy about her body. I told you about the swimming party, didn't I? I'm not much of a one for art galleries, but I must go see it next time I'm in Leeds.'

'What *was* their relationship?'

'I think they genuinely liked one another. They were friends. Both of them were outsiders, free-thinkers. On some strange level, they *understood* one another. And I think she genuinely *liked* him and respected him as a painter. Not that she was an intellectual or anything, but she responded to his work. It touched her in some way.'

Annie could understand that. Over the years, her father had had many female friends who genuinely admired his art. No doubt he had also slept with some of them, but then Ray certainly wasn't homosexual, and it didn't mean the women hadn't respected him as a painter, too. 'Was she involved with anyone in particular after her husband's death?' she asked.

'She had a bit of a fling with a Yank from Rowan Woods called Billy Joe something or other. I never did like him. Wouldn't trust him and those bedroom eyes of his as far as I could throw him. She got a bit of a reputation for hanging around with American airmen, disappearing into the woods late at night, that sort of thing.' Alice winked. 'Not that she was the only one.'

'Do you think there was anything in it?'

'I'd be surprised if there wasn't. I think she was lonely. And she was also lovely. We met a lot of them, Betty, Cynthia, Gloria, Gwen and me. We'd go to dances, mostly at the base or in Harkside. There were a few in Hobb's End, at the church, but they were rather tame affairs. Betty Goodall tended to take charge, and I'm sure you can imagine there wasn't much fun to be had. Betty was a keen dancer – oh, did she *love* to dance! – but it was all waltzes and foxtrots, old-fashioned stuff. No jitterbugging. She was good, though. Her and Billy went in for ballroom dancing in a serious way after the war. Won trophies and all. Where was I?'

'Dances. Americans.'

'Oh, yes. Well, let's face it, most of the local lads were at war, except those unfit for service or in reserved occupations. And they just hung out in the Shoulder of Mutton and complained all the time. The Americans were different. They talked differently, spoke about places we'd only dreamed of or seen at the pictures. They were exotic. Exciting. They also had all sorts of things we hadn't been able to get because of rationing. You know – nylons, cigarettes and that stuff. We were friendly with PX, which was the nickname of the chap who ran their stores, sort of quartermaster, I suppose, and he used to get us all sorts of stuff. Gloria in particular. She was definitely his favourite. But she was everyone's favourite. Gloria was like a beautiful, exotic butterfly; she attracted every man who met her. There was something special about her. She sparkled and glowed. She radiated *it*.'

'This PX, what was his real name?'

'Sorry, love, I can't remember. Come to think of it, I don't know if I ever knew. We always just called him PX.'

'Was there anyone else in particular?'

'After Billy Joe, she developed a real soft spot for Brad, but after what happened to Matthew, she didn't want anything serious.'

'What about this Brad? What did he want?'

'He was a nice lad. No doubt about it, he was head over heels.'

'Do you remember his second name?'

'Sorry, love.'

'That's all right,' said Annie. 'How long did they go out together?'

'There you've got me. The best part of 1944, I think. At least they were still seeing each other when I left at Christmas.'

'Christmas 1944?'

'Yes.' She beamed. 'Best Christmas of my life. My Eric got wounded in the Battle of the Bulge, silly bugger. Nothing serious, but it got him an early discharge and he was home for Christmas. The doctor recommended a bit of sea air, so we came here, fell in love with the place and ended up staying. We left Hobb's End on Boxing Day 1944.'

'Where's Eric now?'

'Oh, he's out and about. Likes to go for his constitutional along the prom every morning, then he stops by the pub and plays dominoes with his mates.'

'Did Gloria ever mention anything about having a baby?'

Alice looked puzzled. 'No, not to me. And I never saw any evidence of children. I'm not even sure she liked them. Wait a minute, though . . .'

'What?'

'It was something I noticed when I was crossing the fairy bridge once. Something odd. A bloke turned up – a bloke in a soldier's uniform – with a little lad in tow, couldn't have been more than about six or seven, holding his hand. I'd never seen them before. They went in to see Gloria, talked for a while, then they left. I heard voices raised.'

'When was this?'

'Sorry, love, I can't remember. It was after Matthew had gone, though. I do know that.'

'And that's all that happened?'

'Yes.'

'Did you hear what was said?'

'No.'

'Who was he, do you know?'

'Sorry, dearie, I've no idea.'

'Did you ever ask Gloria about him?'

'Yes. She went all quiet on me. She did that sometimes. All she would say was that it was relations from down south. I thought maybe it was her brother and nephew or something. You don't think . . .?'

'I don't know,' said Annie. 'Did they ever come back, the man and the child?'

'Not that I ever heard of.'

'And what happened to Gwen and Gloria after you'd left?'

'I don't know. I sent Gloria a postcard, must have been March or April of 1945, telling her that Eric was better now and we were going to stay in Scarborough, and that she should come and visit us.'

'What happened?'

'Nothing. She never replied.'

'Didn't you think that odd?'

'Yes, I did, but there wasn't much I could do about it. Life goes on. I wrote again a few months later and still got no reply. After that, I gave up. You lose touch with a lot of people over the course of your life, I've found. It was the same with Gwen. I wouldn't say we were really *close* – she was a bit too quiet and bookish for that – but we did have some good times together. After we moved here, though, I never saw or heard of her again.'

'Did you ever go back to Hobb's End?'

'No reason to. After the war, it was like a new life –

except for the same old rationing. You just got on with it and tried not to dwell on the past. I'm sorry I never saw Gloria again – she was a breath of fresh air – but, as I said, when you get to my age you realize people lose touch all the time.'

Annie had found that true enough, even in her own short life. Schoolfriends, university colleagues, lovers, work partners, there were so many people she had completely lost touch with. They could be dead for all she knew. Like Rob.

She let the silence stretch for a few moments, then shifted in her armchair. 'Well, Alice,' she said, 'I think that's all for now. I'll make sure I get the photograph back to you within a couple of days. If I think of anything else, I'll get in touch with you.' She managed to get herself out of the deep, comfortable chair by pushing her hands down hard on the arms.

'Please do.' Alice got to her feet. 'It's been a great pleasure to me, though I can't see as it's done you much good, me rabbiting on like this about the past.'

'You've been very helpful.'

'Well, it's nice of you to say so, dearie. I must admit, I've enjoyed having a good chin-wag. It's been years since I thought about all that stuff. Hobb's End. Gloria. Gwen. Matthew. The war. I hope you find out who did this to her. Even if he's dead, I'd like to know he died as slow and painful a death as he deserved.'

•

We left the café saddened and dazed, with hours to kill before our train home. To tell the truth, I don't think either of us at that time had much hope that Matthew was still alive. I asked Gloria if she would take me to where she used to live, but she refused. That would have been simply too much for her to bear, she said, and I felt cruel for asking.

It stopped raining and the sun was trying to pierce its way through the ragged clouds. We walked through St James's Park, past the barrage-balloon station and the anti-aircraft guns, towards Oxford Street. Though our hearts weren't in it, we did some shopping. At least it took our minds off Matthew for a short while. On Charing Cross Road, I bought Graham Greene's new 'entertainment', *The Ministry of Fear*, as well as the last two issues of *Penguin New Writing*, the latest *Horizon* and some second-hand World's Classics copies of Trollope and Dickens for the lending library.

Gloria bought a black-red-and-white-checked Dorville dress at John Lewis's. It cost her three pounds fifteen shillings and eleven coupons. She persuaded me into buying a Utility design by Norman Hartnell in a shop nearby for only three pounds and nine coupons.

After fish and chips at a British Restaurant, we went to the Carlton in the Haymarket to see Gary Cooper and Ingrid Bergman in *For Whom the Bell Tolls*. It was one of the first films I ever saw in Technicolor, colour films not having made a real impact in Harkside by then. I hadn't read the Hemingway novel, so I couldn't judge how faithful the film version was.

It was getting dark when we walked out into the Haymarket, and Gloria suggested we catch the underground back to King's Cross.

It is hard to describe the London blackout, especially on a broad, busy street like the Haymarket. As it is never fully silent anywhere, so it is never fully dark, either. You can see the sharp edges and cornices of the buildings etched against the night sky in varying shades of darkness. If the half-moon slips out from behind the clouds, everything shimmers in its pale light for a few moments and then disappears again.

What I noticed most of all was the noise, the way blind people develop a more acute sense of hearing. Distant shouts and whistles, engines, laughter and singing from a public house, perhaps a dog howling in the distance or a cat miaowing down a ginnel – all these sounds seem to carry farther and echo longer in the darkness of the blackout. They all sound more sinister, too.

'Unnatural' is the word that comes to mind. But what could be more natural than darkness? Perhaps it is a matter of context. In the city, especially such a sprawling, busy city as London, darkness is unnatural.

In Piccadilly Circus, I could just make out the statue of Eros buttressed by sandbags. There was music coming from somewhere, too, a tune I later learned was Glenn Miller's 'Take the "A" Train'. There were soldiers all over the place, many of them drunk, and on more than one occasion men approached us and grabbed us or offered us money for sexual favours.

At one point, I heard some sounds down an alley and could just make out the silhouette of a man grunting as he thrust himself towards a woman, her back against a wall. It made me think of that icy Christmas of 1941, when I had seen Gloria and the Canadian airman, Mark, in exactly the same position.

The underground platforms, where people came to shelter during the air raids, were crowded, and I fancied I could smell sweat, unwashed clothes and urine mixed in with the sooty smell the trains made. Everything was grimy and run-down. The train soon came and we had to stand all the way. No one stood up to offer us seats.

I was glad our train for home left on time, and though I knew I would dream about the trip for weeks to come, I can't say I was sorry when, after a boring and uneventful journey of some seven hours, we caught the morning train from Leeds to Harrogate, thence to hook up with our little branch line back to Hobb's End.

•

It was after seven o'clock by the time Banks and Annie met up that evening. On his way back from Edinburgh, Banks got stuck in the mid-afternoon traffic around Newcastle, then he had to call in at the station to see if there had been any developments during his absence.

He had found about twenty telephone messages waiting for him in response to Monday evening's television news appearance. He spent an hour or so returning calls, but all he found out was that someone thought the Shackletons had moved to Leeds after VE day, and someone else remembered drinking with Matthew Shackleton in Hobb's End near the end of the war. Most people, though, simply wanted to relive wartime memories and had no useful information whatsoever.

There was also a message from John Webb, who said he had cleaned up the button Adam Kelly had taken from the skeleton. It was made of brass, probably about half an inch in diameter, and had a raised pattern on the front, possibly reminiscent of wings. The expert who had examined it suggested it might be some sort of bird. Clearly, he added, given the time period under consideration, the armed forces came to mind, perhaps the RAF.

When Banks had finished at the station, he phoned Annie and asked if she would mind coming up to Gratly, as he had been on the road most of the day. She said she didn't mind at all. Then he went home, took a long shower and tidied the place up. It didn't take long. Next he tried phoning Brian in Wimbledon again. Still no luck. What the hell was he supposed to do? It was nearly a week since their argument. He could go down there, he supposed, but not until the case was over. Anyway, he decided to try again the next day.

He thought of cooking something for Annie, then decided against it. Learning to cook might be his next project after fixing up the cottage, but he still had a long way to go. Besides, there was nothing in the fridge except a couple of cans of lager, half a tomato and a piece of mouldy Cheddar. He would take her out to the Dog and Gun in Helmthorpe for dinner and hope to God there was something vegetarian on the menu.

When Annie arrived, she first showed him the photograph of Gloria and her friends with the American airmen. Then, after a lightning tour of the house, which she described as 'very bijou', she agreed it was a perfect evening for a stroll. They left their cars parked in Banks's gravel laneway and headed for Helmthorpe in the hazy evening light, sharing the information each had learned that day as they walked.

Sheep grazed on the lynchets that descended towards the dried-up beck. Some of them had even managed to get through the gate at the back of the churchyard, where they grazed among the lichen-dappled tombstones.

'Have time for a walk on the prom in Scarborough?' Banks asked.

'Of course. Had to eat, didn't I? I can tell you, though, there's not much choice for a vegetarian in Scarborough. I ended up buying some chips – cooked in vegetable oil, or so the woman said – and sat on a bench by the harbour to eat them, watching a man painting his fishing boat. He tried to chat me up.'

'Oh?'

'He didn't get very far. I'm used to being chatted up by fishermen. It takes more than heroic tales of landing haddock or halibut to get into *my* knickers, I can tell you.'

Banks laughed. 'St Ives?'

'Right. Heard it all before. Got the T-shirt. Anyway, after that I went for a quick look at Anne Brontë's grave, then I came back to the station to write up the interview.'

'Do you like Anne Brontë's books?'

'I haven't read any. It's just the sort of thing you do, isn't it, when you're nearby. Go and see where famous people are buried. I saw *The Tenant of Wildfell Hall* on TV. It's all right if you like that sort of thing.'

'What sort of thing?'

'Governesses, bodices, tight corsets, all that repressed Victorian sexuality.'

'And you don't?'

Annie cocked her head. 'I didn't say that.'

It was early September now, and the nights were drawing in fast. When they got to the High Street, the sun was already low in the west, a red ball glowing like an ember through the gathering haze, and the shadows were lengthening. Sounds of laughter and music came from the open pub doors. Tourists, tired after the day out and a big meal, were getting in their cars and driving back to their cities.

Annie and Banks walked through the crowded bar and managed to find a table in the beer garden out back. Between the trees, the dying sunlight streaked the river shallows blood-orange and crimson. Annie sat down while Banks went to buy a couple of pints and order their food. Luckily, Annie said she wasn't very hungry and a cheese-and-pickle sandwich would do her fine. He was just in time; they were about to stop serving.

'It's nice out here,' Annie said when he came back with the drinks. 'Thanks.'

'Cheers.' Banks took a sip. Though there were a few other people sitting outside, conversations seemed hushed. 'So who have we got now, then?' he asked. 'Now we've discovered that Matthew was killed before Gloria was?'

Annie leaned back, stretched out her long legs and set them on the third white plastic chair at the table. 'What about the boyfriend?' she suggested. 'The American.'

'Brad? As her killer? Why?'

'Why not? Or one of his pals. She could have stirred them up, set them against one another. I get the impression that Gloria was the kind of woman who exerted an enormous power over men. Brad could have been hoping for more than he got. Alice said she thought he was more keen on Gloria than she was on him. Maybe she tried to shake him loose and he wouldn't go. Rowan Woods wasn't far away. It would have been easy for him to sneak in and out the back way, I should think.'

'We definitely need to find out more about the Americans in Hobb's End,' said Banks.

'How do we go about that?'

'You can start with the American Embassy. They might be able to point you in the right direction.'

'I notice the subtle pronoun usage there: "you". I don't suppose you're planning on spending a day on the phone?'

Banks laughed. 'Rank has its privileges. Besides, you're so good at it.'

Annie pulled a face and flicked some beer at him.

'If it makes you feel any better,' he added, 'I'll be trying to get more information on Matthew Shackleton from our own military authorities.'

Their food arrived, and they both ate in silence for a while. The river looked like an oil slick now. There were no clouds, but the air had turned more humid during the day, and the setting sun turned the western sky scarlet and purple. Clusters of small buzzing insects, gnats or midges, hovered over the still, shallow water.

'What about Michael Stanhope?' Banks suggested.

'What possible motive could he have? They were friends.'

'Inordinate desire? Drink? They can push a person beyond the normal limits, and it's likely Stanhope was a bit beyond them anyway to start with. If he was powerfully attracted to Gloria, if she wouldn't have anything to do with him sexually, then painting her in the nude might have inflamed him beyond all reason. Let's admit it, a man like Stanhope can't have been *entirely* dispassionate all the time he had a naked Gloria Shackleton in his studio.'

Annie raised her eyebrows. 'Can't he? Perhaps you mean *you* couldn't be. You'd be surprised how dispassionate an artist can be. Anyway, Alice Poole said she was sure they weren't lovers, and I believe her. The impression I get is that a lot of villagers – like the one you talked to – projected negative feelings on to Gloria. I think she was basically a decent woman and a devoted wife, but her good looks and her free and easy attitude gave her no end of problems, especially with men. Eventually someone went over the top.'

'You sound as if you know what you're talking about.'

Annie turned away and stared at the dark river. It had only been a teasing, offhand remark, but Banks felt as if he had trespassed on some private reserve, set her hackles up. They still had to be careful with one another, he realized. A couple of nights of passionate abandon and a sense of having something in common as mutual outsiders weren't enough to map the route through the emotional minefields that lay between them. *Tread carefully*, he warned himself.

After a pause, Annie went on, 'I think Gloria was one of the few people in Hobb's End who understood Michael Stanhope, who took him seriously. Besides, Alice also said he was gay.'

'She couldn't know that for certain. Or he could have been bisexual.'

'I think you're pushing it a bit, that's all.'

'You're probably right. Anyway, there's one obvious flaw with the Stanhope theory.'

'There is?'

Banks shoved his empty plate aside. 'Where do you think Gloria was killed?' he asked.

'In, or very close to, Bridge Cottage. I thought we'd already agreed on that because of where she was buried. By the way' – Annie consulted her notebook – 'I forgot to tell you before, but the blackout ended officially on the seventeenth of September, 1944. Not that it matters now we know Gloria was still alive that Christmas.'

'Every little bit helps.'

'Anyway, what's your point?'

'Most of the time Gloria visited Stanhope at his studio. That would certainly have been the case if he was painting her that autumn. If anything happened between them, it would be more likely to have happened there, that's all. That's where she was naked in front of him. If he killed her, I don't think he would have risked carrying the body all the way back to Bridge Cottage. He would have found some other way of disposing of her, some-where closer.'

'Unless they were having an affair, as you suggest. In which case he might well have visited her at her own home.'

'Would she risk that, with Gwen so close by?'

'Possibly. Gloria certainly sounds unconventional and unpredictable, from everything I've heard. Just going to his studio must have been scandalous enough, given his reputation in the village.'

'Good point. Elizabeth Goodall certainly seemed to think their relationship was a scandal. Another drink?'

'Better not,' Annie said, placing her hand over her glass. 'One's my limit when I'm driving.'

Banks paused a moment, his voice lost somewhere deep in his chest. 'You don't *have* to drive home,' he said finally, sure he was croaking.

Annie smiled and put her hand on his arm. Her touch set his pulse going faster. 'No, but I think I should, with it being a weeknight and all. I've got a busy day tomorrow. Besides, we agreed, didn't we?'

'Can't blame a bloke for trying. Mind if I have one?'

She laughed. 'Course not.'

Banks went inside. He hadn't expected Annie to rise to his offer, but he was disappointed that she hadn't. He knew they had agreed to stick to weekends, but surely there was room for a little spontaneity now and then? He wondered if he would ever be able to figure out this relationship business. It was easy when you were married; at least you didn't usually have to make appointments to see one another. On the other hand, he and Sandra hadn't seen all that much of each other, and they had been married over twenty years. Perhaps, if they had made more time for one another, they would still be together.

The dinner crowd had thinned out, leaving the lounge

half empty, mostly locals playing dominoes and darts in the public bar. A group of kids sat in one corner, and one of them put 'Concrete and Clay' on the jukebox. Christ Almighty, thought Banks. *Unit 4 + 2*. It had been recorded before they were born.

He bought himself another pint and went back outside. Annie wasn't much more than a silhouette now – and a beautiful one to his eyes, with her graceful neck and strong profile – staring at the river in that peculiarly relaxed and centred way she had.

He sat down and broke the spell. Annie stirred languidly. She still had half her drink left, which she swirled in her glass a few times before sipping.

'What about her family?' Banks asked.

'Family? Whose family?'

'Gloria Shackleton's.'

'Her family was killed in the Blitz.'

'All of them?'

'That's what she told Alice.'

'What about this mysterious stranger and the child who turned up looking for her? You said she told Alice that it was relations.'

'I know.' Annie shook her head slowly. 'That's what I don't understand. It does seem odd, doesn't it?'

'If she ran off and left a husband or boyfriend stuck with her kid, that might be someone else with reason to be angry with her. He could have tracked her down and killed her.'

'Yes, but maybe whoever it was didn't feel *stuck* with the kid. Maybe he loved the boy. Besides, men do that sort of thing all the time and women don't kill them for it.'

Banks wasn't going to jump at that one. 'The point is,' he said, 'did *this* particular man feel strongly enough to track down the wife or girlfriend who bore his child and deserted him? They did argue, according to what Alice Poole told you.'

'Gloria was still alive after he left.'

'He could have stewed for a while, gone back weeks, months later.'

'Possibly,' Annie admitted. 'I'd also like to know what happened to the sister-in-law, Gwynneth. Even with your appeals on the telly, no one's come forward with any useful leads.'

'Maybe she's dead?'

'Maybe she is.'

'Do you see her as a suspect?'

Annie frowned. 'She looked like a tall, strong woman in the photograph. Something could have happened between them.'

'Maybe DS Hatchley came up with something in London. We'll find out tomorrow. It's been a long day.'

A night bird called across the river in the silence. Then someone put an Oasis song on the jukebox. 'The kind of crime it was ought to be telling us something,' Annie said after a slight pause.

'What does it tell you that we haven't considered already?'

'Well, it was obviously violent, passionate. *Somebody* felt strongly enough about Gloria Shackleton to stab her so many times. *After* strangling her first.'

'You've said it yourself: Gloria was the kind of woman men felt passionately about, the sort to spark off strong feelings. But there are probably a lot of things we don't know about what happened.'

'Sorry, I don't follow.'

'It's an old crime scene, Annie. All we've got is bones

and a few odds and ends of corroded jewellery. We don't know whether she was raped or sexually interfered with in any way first. Or after. For all we know, this might be a sex crime, pure and simple.'

'The SOCOs haven't found any other victims buried in the area.'

'Not yet. Besides, sex crimes don't always mean multiple victims.'

'Usually they do. You can't tell me that someone raped and murdered Gloria Shackleton the way he did and never did it again before or after.'

'That's the point,' said Banks. 'Think about it. The body was buried in the outbuilding of Gloria and Matthew's cottage. The fact that we haven't found any other bodies in the vicinity doesn't mean there aren't any anywhere else. It *doesn't* mean that whoever did it didn't kill *elsewhere*, in exactly the same way.'

'A serial killer, then? A stranger to the area?'

'It's possible. DS Hatchley's already put out a request for information on crimes with similar MOs. It'll take time, though, and that's if anyone even bothers following it up. People can be pretty lazy, especially when what they want isn't on the computer. Let's face it, we're not exactly high on anyone's priority list with this one. Still, some curious or industrious PC might poke about and discover something. I'll have Jim send out a reminder.'

Annie paused. 'You realize we might never know who killed her, don't you?'

Banks finished his drink and nodded. 'If that's what it comes down to, we make out a final report based on all the evidence we've collected and point at the most likely solution.'

'How do you think you'll feel about that?'

'What do you mean?'

'It's become important to you, hasn't it? Oh, I'm not saying I don't care. I do. But for you it's something else. It goes deeper. You have a sort of compulsion.'

Banks lit a cigarette. As he did so, he realized how often he hid behind the smoke of his cigarettes. 'Somebody has to give a damn.'

'That sounds melodramatic. Besides, is it really as simple as that?'

'Nothing ever is, really, is it?'

'Meaning?'

Banks paused and tried to frame his nebulous thoughts. 'Gloria Shackleton. I know what she looked like. I've got some idea of her character and her ambitions, who her friends were, the things she liked to do to amuse and entertain herself.' He tapped the side of his head. 'She's real enough for me in there, where it counts. Somebody took all that away from her. Somebody strangled her, then stabbed her fifteen or sixteen times, wrapped her body in blackout curtains and buried it in an outbuilding.'

'But it happened years ago. The war's been over for ages now. Murders happen all the time. What's so different about this one?'

Banks shook his head. 'I don't know. Nothing, really. Partly, it's the war itself. I'm older than you. I grew up in its shadow, and it cast a long one for a long time after it was over. I was born with a ration book and a National Identity Card.' He laughed. 'It's funny, you know, the way people resist being named and counted these days, but I was proud of that card when I was a kid. It actually *gave* me an identity, told me who I was. Maybe I was already in training for my warrant card. Anyway, there were ruins all over the place in my hometown. I used to play in them just like Adam Kelly. And my dad had a collection of mementoes I used to sneak up to the attic and play with when he was out – an SS dagger, a Nazi armband. There were pictures I used to look at, photographs of the collaborators hanging from the balustrades in Brussels. It was another age, before my time, but in a way it wasn't; it was much closer than that. We used to play at being commandos. We even used to dig tunnels and pretend to escape from prison camps. I bought every book about fighter and bomber planes I could get my hands on. My childhood and early adolescence were saturated with the war. Somehow the idea of a vicious murder like this one being committed while all that carnage was going on in the world makes it seem even more of a travesty, if you see what I mean.'

'I think so. What else bothers you?'

'That's the simple part. As far as we can tell, nobody reported Gloria missing; there was no hue and cry. It looks as if nobody cared. I had a friend once . . . one day I'll tell you about him. Anyway, nobody cared then. Somebody has to. I seem to be good at it, overburdened with compassion, a natural.' Banks smiled. 'Am I still making sense?'

Annie brushed his sleeve with her fingers. 'I care, too,' she said. 'Maybe not for the same reasons or in the same way, but I do.'

Banks looked into her eyes. He could tell she meant what she was saying. He nodded. 'I know you do. Home?'

Annie stood up.

They walked out into the street, much quieter now night had fallen. The fish-and-chip shop was still serving, and two of the kids who had been in the pub were leaning against the wall eating from newspaper. A whiff of vinegar drifted by.

At the top of the ginnel that ran past the churchyard was a swing gate, and after that the narrow, flagged footpath curved around the steep banks of Gratly Beck about half a mile up the daleside to the village itself. Luckily, there was a moon, for there was no other illumination on the path. Sheep scampered out of the way and bleated. Again Banks thought of the blackout. His mother had told him a story of a friend of hers who made her way home from work at the munitions factory by touching 176 railings along the canalside before her left turn, then five lamp-posts down the street. It must have been in the early days, Banks thought, before Lord Beaverbrook ordered the collection of all railings for the war effort. His mother had also told him about the enormous mountain of pots and pans on the cricket pitch that were supposed to be turned into aircraft.

Once through the narrow stile at the other end, Banks and Annie turned left past the new houses. The pavement was broader there, and Annie slipped her arm through his. The small act of intimacy felt good. They crossed the stone bridge, walked along the lane and stood at Banks's front door.

'Coffee?' Banks asked.

Annie smiled. 'No, but I'll have a cold drink if you've got one. Non-alcoholic.'

He left her in the front room rummaging through his compact-disc collection while he went to the fridge. It was eerie how the kitchen always gave him that feeling of peace and belonging, even at night when the sun wasn't shining. He wondered if he would ever be able to tell Annie about it without feeling like an idiot.

He took out a carton of orange juice and poured them each a glass. An old Etta James CD started playing in the living room. Funky and fiery. He hadn't played it in years. Annie walked in, clearly pleased with her find.

'You've got a hell of a CD collection,' she said. 'It's a wonder you can ever decide what to play.'

'It *is* a problem sometimes. Depends on the mood.' He handed her the glass and they went through to the living room.

Soon Etta was belting out 'Jump Into My Fire' and 'Shakey Ground'.

'Sure you won't have a nightcap?' Banks asked when Annie had finished her orange juice.

'No. I told you, I've got to drive back. I don't want to get stopped by an overzealous country copper.'

'It's a pity,' said Banks. 'I was hoping you might change your mind.' His mouth felt dry.

'Come to Mama' was playing now, and the music's rhythmic, slow-moving sensuality was getting to him. He had to keep telling himself that Annie was a detective sergeant, someone he was working with on a case, and he shouldn't even be thinking like this. But the problem was that Annie Cabbot didn't seem like any detective sergeant he had ever come across before. And she was the first woman, apart from his daughter Tracy, to visit his new home.

'Well,' said Annie, smiling. 'I didn't say I had to go just yet, did I? You don't have to get me drunk to get me into bed, you know.' Then she stood up, crossed her arms in front of her and pulled her T-shirt slowly up over her head. She stood holding it in her hand, head tilted to one side, then smiled, held her hand out and said, 'Come to Mama.'

•

There are giant redwood trees in California, they say, that can grow another layer around the dead and blackened wood if they ever burn in a forest fire. Matthew's disappearance burned out my core like that and while, over time, I did grow another skin over it, a harder skin, there was part of me inside that was always black and dead. There still is, though over the years the new skin has grown so thick that most people take it for the real thing. I suppose, in a way, it is real, but it is not the *original*.

Of course, life went on. It always does. In time, we laughed and smiled again, stood on the fairy bridge and discussed the Italian campaign, lamented the shortages and complained about Lord Woolton Pie and the National Wholemeal Loaf.

Gloria threw herself into her work at the farm, making it clear that she was indispensable because the government was putting even more pressure on women to work in the aircraft and munitions factories, the idea of which terrified her. Rumour had it that there were spies from the Labour Exchange all over the place just looking for idle women. If there were, they left me alone, too, as I had enough work on my hands looking after an invalid mother and running the shop, as well as fire-watching and helping with the WVS, taking out pies and snacks to the field workers in the area.

In October, Gloria had her hair done like Veronica Lake, with a side parting, curling inwards over her shoulders. I had the new, short liberty cut because it was easy to manage and my hair just wouldn't do the things Gloria's did, even if I put sugar water on it.

That month also, *Gone With the Wind* finally came to Harkside, and Gloria and Mr Stanhope practically dragged me to see it. As it turned out, I enjoyed the film, and found it was made even more poignant by the death of Leslie

Howard, whose aeroplane had been shot down by Nazi fighters in June. Mr Stanhope, battered hat on his head, tapping with his snake-head-handled cane as we walked back, was enthusiastic about the use of colour and Gloria, needless to say, was potty about Clark Gable.

Autumn mists came to our shallow valley, often making it impossible for the aeroplanes to land or take off for days. In September we heard that the Rowan Woods Aerodrome had been closed and the RAF had gone somewhere else. It was hard to get a clear answer to any questions in those days, but one of the ground crew told me that the two-engined bombers they had been flying were old and were being phased out of operation. The runways at Rowan Woods had to be converted to be able to handle four-engined bombers. He didn't know whether his squadron would be back or not; things were so uncertain, people coming and going at a moment's notice.

Whatever the reason, the RAF moved out and a crew of labourers, mostly Irish, came in. Over the next couple of months, they brought in tons of cement, gravel and Tarmac to bring the runways up to standard. They also put up more Nissen huts.

Of course, the character of village life changed a little during this period: we had a few fights between the Irish and the soldiers at the Shoulder of Mutton, and we got used to the whiff of tar that would drift through the woods when the wind was blowing the right way.

Early in December the labourers finished their work and shortly before Christmas, Rowan Woods became the new home to the United States Eighth Air Force's 448th Bomber Group.

Just like that.

The Yanks had arrived.

•

Alone after Annie had left, Banks couldn't sleep, despite the lovemaking and the long day's drive. He lay in the dark for a while, his mind racing, images of the old days in Edinburgh, of Alison and Jo, keeping him awake. And Jem. And Annie. And Sandra. And Brian. The first night Banks had spent in the cottage, a bat flew in the open window and it took him half an hour to coax it out again. That was how his mind felt now, like a misshapen black rag flapping about wildly inside him. He felt an over-whelming sense of anxiety, not about anything specific, to such an extent that he began to sweat and his heart beat fast.

He put on his jeans and went downstairs to pour himself a small whisky. Ever since he had become worried about his drinking in the dark months after Sandra's departure, he had got into the habit of totting up his daily intake, as he did with cigarettes. A pint at lunchtime in Edinburgh, two pints with Annie at the Dog and Gun, and now one finger of Laphroaig close to midnight. Not bad. He had only smoked seven cigarettes, too, and he was especially proud of that.

He took the drink out to the wall and sat with his legs dangling over the dried-up falls. It was a warm night, but a slight breeze rustled through the leaves and cooled the sweat on his forehead a little. A small animal rustled through the undergrowth, probably a squirrel or a rabbit. Banks looked into the dark woods and remembered Robert Frost's words, which he had read recently in his anthology. 'And miles to go before I sleep.' It was the repetition of that line that made it so memorable, he thought, that sent that tingle up your spine. He didn't profess to understand it – at least he couldn't have stood up in class and described what it was *about* – but he got something from it.

He remembered what he had said to Annie earlier about *caring* and how he couldn't tell her it was partly because of Jem. Banks had found Jem's body himself on the bare dusty floor of the bedsit, the needle still in his arm, which was oddly discoloured here and there where the mice had nibbled.

He was sick, the same way he had been when Phil Simpkins spiralled slowly and inevitably down on to the spiked railings. But people had cared about Phil's accident; they even had a minute's silence in assembly and a morning off school for the funeral. Nobody had cared about Jem, though, the way no one seemed to have cared about Gloria's disappearance.

Over the years, Banks became inured to seeing corpses, like any other detective who investigates a fair number of murders. He developed a protective shell; he could crack jokes at the scene with someone's entrails spilling over his feet or brain matter sticking to the soles of his shoes. But no matter how hard his carapace, Banks had always felt *something*, no matter how low on the food chain the victim was. He always felt some connection with what had once been a living person.

After Jem's death, Banks had felt driven to find out more about him: who he was, where he came from, why no one seemed to care. He realized how little he knew, even though Jem had been his first and closest friend in a new and overpowering city. He was so innocent, he hadn't even suspected that Jem was a heroin addict. They had smoked hash and grass together on occasion, but that was all.

The police themselves hadn't been impressive, hardly

an advertisement for recruitment. They interviewed Banks, who described the man he had seen entering Jem's flat the previous evening, but they didn't seem interested. One of them, DC Carter, Banks remembered, played the concerned-parent role, feigning sadness at Jem's death, lecturing Banks on the drug subculture, while the other, DS Fallon, pockmarked face, a cynical smile on his thin, cruel lips, rifled through Banks's drawers and cupboards, looking for drugs.

Later, Banks found out that three junkies had died in Notting Hill that week because a shipment of unusually pure heroin hadn't been adequately cut. No arrests were made.

Disenchanted with both business and sixties navel-gazing, Banks joined the police force to change the system from within, despite Jem's advice, and when he found he couldn't do that, he settled for the adrenalin buzz of the investigation, the chase, the revelation, the strange bond with the murder victim, who couldn't speak for herself. And this bond was true no less in the case of Gloria Shackleton's cracked and filthy bones than it was with a corpse so fresh you could still see the flush on its cheek.

Finally, tired with remembering, Banks put out his cigarette, finished the whisky and went back inside. His bed still smelled of Annie, and he was grateful for that much, at least, as he tossed and turned and tried to get to sleep.

•

Ever since she had seen Gloria's image and heard her name on television, Vivian Elmsley had been expecting the police to come knocking at her door. It wasn't as if she had taken any great steps to cover her tracks. She had never consciously sought to hide her past and her identity, although she had certainly glossed over it. Perhaps, also, the life she had lived hinted at a certain amount of conscious escape. At every stage, she had had to reinvent herself: the selfless carer; the diplomat's wife; the ever so slightly 'with-it' young widow with the red sports car; the struggling writer; the public figure with the splinter of ice in her heart. Would that be the last? Which was the real one? She didn't know. She didn't even know if there *was* a real one.

Though the worry and fear gnawed away at her since the TV broadcast, Vivian tried to live a normal life: wandering up to Hampstead in the morning; reading the newspaper; sitting down in her study for the day, whether she wrote anything worth keeping or not; talking to her agent and publisher; answering correspondence. All the while waiting for that knock on the door, wondering what she would say, how she could convince them she knew nothing; or thinking that perhaps she should just tell them what she knew and let the chips fall where they would. Would it really make a difference, after all this time?

Yes, she decided; it would.

When it came, though, the shock came in a form she hadn't in the least expected.

That Tuesday night, the phone rang just as she was dropping off. When she picked up the receiver, all she heard was silence, or as much silence as you ever get on a telephone line.

'Who is it?' she asked, gripping the receiver more tightly. 'Please speak up.'

More silence.

She was just about to hang up when she heard what she thought was a sharp intake of breath. Then a voice she didn't recognize whispered, 'Gwen? Gwen Shackleton?'

'My name's Vivian Elmsley. There must be some mistake.'

'There's no mistake. I know who you are. Do you know who I am?'

'I don't know what you're talking about.'

'You will. Soon.'

Then the caller hung up.

10

Christmas 1943. It was a gloomy, chill and moonless night when the 448th held their first dance at Rowan Woods. Gloria, Cynthia, Alice and I walked there together along the narrow lane through the woods, our breaths misting in the air. We wore court shoes and carried our dance shoes because they were far too precious and flimsy to walk in. Luckily, the ground wasn't too muddy, because none of us would have been caught dead wearing wellies to a dance, even if we had to walk through Rowan Woods in a storm.

'How many of them do you think there are?' Cynthia asked.

'I don't know,' said Gloria. 'It's a big aerodrome, though. Probably hundreds. Thousands, even.'

Alice did a little dance. 'Ooh, just think of it, all those Yanks with money to throw away. They get paid much more than our boys, you know. Ellen Bairstow told me. She went out with a GI when she was working at that factory near Liverpool, and she'd never seen so much money.'

'Don't you try to tell yourself they won't want *something* in return, Alice Poole,' said Gloria. 'And don't you forget your poor Eric away fighting for his country.'

We were all a bit quiet after that. I don't know about the others, but I couldn't help thinking of Matthew. A fox or a badger suddenly flashed across the path and scared us, but the adrenalin at least broke the silence. We were still excited, and we giggled like silly schoolgirls the rest of the way.

Most villagers had already seen the newcomers around, and I had even served some of them in the shop, where they had looked puzzled at our meagre offerings and confused by the unfamiliar brand names. Some people disapproved of their arrival – especially Betty Goodall – thinking it would lower moral standards, but most of us quickly accepted them as part of the general scenery. I even helped the local WVS set up a Welcome Club for them in Harkside. Thus far, in my limited experience, Americans had always been friendly and polite, though I can't say I really warmed to the way they called me 'ma'am'. It made me feel so old.

They were certainly far more casual and confident in their manner than our lads, and they had much smarter uniforms. They even wore shoes rather than the great clodhopping boots the Ministry saw fit to issue to our poor armed forces. Of course, our view of Americans was still almost entirely formed by the glamour of Hollywood films, magazines and popular songs. To some, they were all cowboys and gangsters; to others, the men were handsome heroes and the women beautiful and rather vulgar molls.

That evening as we trudged through the forest, we had little real idea of what to expect. We had all fussed about what to wear for days, and we had taken special care with our appearance – even me, who was generally not overly concerned about such superficial matters. Under the overcoats we wore to keep out the chill, we all had on our best dresses. Gloria, of course, looked gorgeous in her black velvet V-neck dress with the puff sleeves and wide, padded shoulders. She had added a red felt rose at the neckline on the left side. I was a little more serviceable in the Utility dress I had bought in London.

One big problem was that we had all run out of fashion stockings and either we didn't have enough coupons to get new ones or we couldn't find any in the shops. When Gloria dropped by to meet me after I closed up shop, the first thing she told me to do was stand on a chair.

'Why?' I asked.

'Go on. You'll see.'

I could have said no, but I was curious, so I stood. The next thing I knew, Gloria was lifting up my skirt and applying some sort of cold greasy stuff to my legs.

I squirmed. 'What *is* that?'

'Shut up and keep still. It's Miner's Liquid Make-Up Foundation. Cost me two and sevenpence halfpenny, it did.'

I kept still. When the stuff she had slathered on my legs finally dried, Gloria had me stand on the chair again and she carefully drew a seam all the way down the backs of my legs with a special sort of pencil. It tickled and again she had to tell me to keep still.

'There.' She bit down on the corner of her lip and stepped back to admire her handiwork. I stood on the stool feeling like an idiot, holding my skirt up around my thighs. 'That'll do,' she pronounced at last. 'Me next.'

As I 'did' her, rubbing the foundation on her soft, pale skin, she started to laugh. 'Marvellous stuff, this,' she said. 'I was at my wits' end the summer before last, before Matthew . . . well, anyway, I was so desperate I tried a mixture of gravy powder and water.'

'What happened?'

'Bloody flies! Chased me all the way from here to Harkside, and the damn things even buzzed around my legs *inside* the hall. I felt like a piece of meat in a butcher's window.' She paused. 'Ooh, Gwen, do you remember what that looked like? All those lovely cuts of meat in the butcher's window?'

'Don't,' I said. 'You'll only make us miserable.'

We met the others by the fairy bridge. Cynthia Garmen was going for the Dorothy Lamour look. She had a black pageboy hairdo and wore a lot of makeup. She even had mascara on her eyes, which looked *really* strange, as women tended not to use a lot of eye makeup back then. It wasn't good-quality mascara. When she got hot from dancing later in the evening, it started to melt, and she looked as if she had been crying. She said she had bought it on the black market in Leeds, so she could hardly go back and complain.

Alice was in her Marlene Dietrich period: plucked eyebrows pencilled in a high arch, wavy blond hair parted in the centre, hanging down to her shoulders. She was wearing a Princess-style burgundy dress with long, tight sleeves and buttons all down the front. It came in at the waist to show how thin she was: almost as thin as Marlene Dietrich.

The dance was held in the mess. We could hear the music before we even got there. It was the song I remembered hearing in Piccadilly Circus a few months ago: 'Take the "A" Train'. We stood outside the door touching up our hair, checking our appearance one last time in our compact mirrors. Then we took off our coats – not wanting to walk in wearing bulky winter overcoats – stuffed our court shoes in the pockets and put on our dance shoes. Ready at last, we made our grand entrance.

The music didn't stop, though I swear it faltered for a moment the way records do sometimes when they become warped. It was a sextet, playing on a makeshift stage at the far end from the bar, and they all wore American air force uniforms. I suppose the odds are that when you gather so many disparate people together, you're bound to end up with enough musicians for a band.

Already the place was crowded with airmen and local girls, mostly from Harkside. The dance floor was busy and a knot of people stood laughing and drinking by the bar. Others sat at the rickety tables smoking and chatting. I had expected the large Nissen hut to be cold, but there was a peculiar-looking squat thing giving out heat in one corner, which I later discovered was called a 'pot-bellied stove' (a very apt description, I thought). Apparently, the air force had brought it all the way from America, having heard English winters were cold and wet, and so were the summers.

They hardly needed it tonight, though, as the press of bodies and the motion of dancing exuded all the heat we needed. The men had already covered the walls with photographs taken from magazines: landscapes of vast, snow-capped mountain ranges; long flat plains and prairie wheatfields; deserts dotted with huge, twisted cacti; and city streets that looked like scenes from Hollywood films. Little bits of America brought over to make them feel less far away from home. A Christmas tree stood in one corner, covered with tinsel and fairy lights, and paper trimmings hung around the ceiling.

'Take your coats, ladies?'

'Why, thank you,' said Gloria.

It was Gloria who had turned the heads, of course. Even with Dorothy Lamour and Marlene Dietrich for competition, she still stood way ahead of the field.

We handed our coats to the young airman, who was tall, slim and dark in complexion. He spoke with a lazy drawl and moved with agile, unhurried grace. He had brown eyes, short black hair and the whitest teeth I had ever seen.

'Over here.' He led us to the far wall, beside the bar, where everyone's coats hung. 'They'll be safe here, now don't you ladies worry.' When he turned his back, Gloria looked at me and raised an eyebrow in approval.

We followed him and held on to our handbags. It was always awkward not knowing what to do with your hand-bag when you danced. Usually, you left it under the table, but Cynthia once had hers stolen at a dance in Harkside.

'And now, ma'am,' he said, turning straightaway to Gloria, 'if I may have the pleasure of the first dance?'

Gloria inclined her head slightly, passed her handbag to me, took his hand and went off. It didn't take long before someone snapped up Cynthia, too, and I was holding three handbags. But, if I say so myself, a rather handsome young navigator from Hackensack, New Jersey, called Bernard – which he pronounced with the emphasis on the second syllable – asked me to dance even before his friend asked Alice. I passed the three handbags to her and left her standing there gawping in a way that Marlene Dietrich never gawped.

'First, you have to answer a question for me,' I said, before I let him lead, just to show I could be quite brave when I wanted to, though I was secretly scared to death of all these brash and handsome young men all around me.

Bernard scratched his head. 'What's that, ma'am?'

'What's an "A" train?'

'Huh?'

'The music that was playing when we came in. "Take the 'A' Train." What's an "A" train? I've always wondered. Is it better than a "B" train, for example?'

He grinned. 'Well, no, ma'am. I mean, it's just a subway train.'

'Subway? You mean the underground?'

'Yes, ma'am. In New York City. The "A" train's the subway that's the fastest way to Harlem.'

'Ah,' I said, the light finally dawning. 'Well, I never. Okay, then, let's dance.'

After 'Kalamazoo', 'Stardust' and 'April in Paris', we gathered at the bar and the tall airman who had taken our coats bought us all bourbon, which we took to the table. His name was Billy Joe Farrell. He hailed from Tennessee and worked on the ground crew. He introduced us to his friend, Edgar Konig, whom everyone called PX because on American bases PX meant the quartermaster's stores, which was exactly what he ran.

PX was a gangly young Iowan with a baby face and his fair hair shaved almost to his skull. He was tall, with Nordic cheekbones, pouting lips and the longest eyelashes over his cornflower-blue eyes. He was also very shy, far too shy to dance with any of us. He never quite made full eye contact with anyone. He was the sort of person who is always around but never really gets noticed, and I think the reason he was so generous to us all was simply that it made him feel needed.

When I look back on that evening now, over twenty-five years ago, especially considering all that has happened since, it seemed to go round in a whirl of dancing and talking and drinking, and it finished before it really began. I still remember the strange accents and the unfamiliar place names and phrases we heard; the young faces; the surprisingly soft feel of a uniform under my palm; the biting, yet sweet, taste of bourbon; the kisses; whispered plans to meet again.

As the four of us walked tipsily back through the woods, arms linked with our gallant escorts, little did we know how, before long, we'd be using words like 'lousy', 'bum' and 'creep' in our daily conversation, not to mention chewing gum and smoking Luckies. As we walked we sang 'Shenandoah' and after goodnight kisses agreed to meet them again in Harkside the following week.

•

It was the first time Banks had been to the Queen's Arms for lunch in some months. He had been trying to avoid boozing too much during the day, partly because it was sometimes hard to stop, and partly because it seemed too much a part of his old life.

It wasn't so much that he used to go there with Sandra frequently – though they often dropped in for a quick jar if they'd been in town together to see a film or a play – just that the Queen's Arms brought back memories of the days when his life and work were in harmony: the days before Jimmy Riddle; the days when he had enjoyed long brainstorming sessions with Gristhorpe, Hatchley, Phil Richmond and Susan Gay over a steak-and-kidney pud and a pint of Theakston's bitter; the days when Sandra had been happy with their marriage and with her work at the gallery.

Or so he had believed.

Like many things he had believed, it had all been an illusion, only true because he had been gullible enough to *believe* in it. In reality, it had all been as flimsy and fleeting as an optical illusion; it depended entirely on your point of view. In calendar time, perhaps, those days weren't so long ago, but in his memory they sometimes seemed as if they had been dreamed by another person in another century.

Even before he bought the cottage, in those days when he had been out on the booze in Eastvale nearly every night, he had avoided the Queen's Arms. Instead, he had sought out modern, anonymous pubs tucked away on the estates, places where the regulars enjoyed their quiz trivia nights and their karaoke and paid no attention to the sad figure in the corner who bumped against the table a little harder each time he went for a piss.

He got into a fight only once, with a paunchy loudmouth who thought Banks was eyeballing his girlfriend, a pasty-faced scrubber with bad hair. It didn't matter that Banks didn't think she was worth fighting over, her boyfriend was ready to rock and roll. Luckily, Banks was never so pissed that he forgot the rules of bar-room brawling: get in first and get in nasty. While the boyfriend was still building up steam verbally, Banks punched him in the stomach and brought up his knee to connect with his nose. Blood, snot and vomit spattered his trousers. Everyone went quiet, and no one tried to stop him leaving.

Banks had always had a violent streak; he knew that even when he used to talk about love and peace with Jem. That was one reason he could never fully give himself to the sixties scene in the first place, only hang around the fringes. The music was fine, the pot was okay, the girls were willing, but the turn-the-other-cheek philosophy sucked.

Today, he felt like indulging himself at the Queen's Arms. Cyril, the landlord, welcomed him back like a long-lost friend, not remarking on his absence, and Glenys, Cyril's wife, gave him her usual shy smile. He bought a pint and ordered a Yorkie filled with roast beef and onion gravy. The pub was busy with its usual lunchtime mix of tourists, local office workers and shopkeepers on their lunch breaks, but Banks managed to snag a small copper-topped table in the far corner, between the fireplace and the diamond-shaped amber and green window-panes.

He had brought with him the folder DS Hatchley had just dropped on his desk: information gleaned from the central registry of births, marriages and deaths. With any luck, it would answer a number of his questions. Already that morning, he had phoned army records and asked about Matthew Shackleton's service history. They said they would verify his identity and call him back. He knew from experience that the military didn't like people snooping into their affairs, even the police, but he didn't expect much trouble with this one; after all, Matthew Shackleton was long dead.

Hatchley's notes confirmed that Gloria was born on September 17, 1921, as she had correctly noted on the St Bartholomew's register. Instead of simply giving 'London' as her place of birth, the official record listed London Hospital, Mile End. Christ, Banks thought, that was in the thick of the East End, all right, and a real villains' thoroughfare these days. It would certainly have made her a Cockney, an accent she had worked hard to lose, if Elizabeth Goodall was to be believed.

Her father was Jack Stringer, whose illegible signature appeared in the 'Signature, Residence and Description of Informant' column along with the Mile End address. Her mother's name was Patricia McPhee. The father's rank or profession was listed as 'dock worker'. There was no column on the form to record the mother's.

Next, Hatchley had checked to see if Gloria's parents had, indeed, been killed in the Blitz, and had pulled death certificates for the two of them, dated September 15, 1940, listing the same Mile End address and 'injuries sustained during bombing' as the cause of death.

A series of black-and-white images passed through Banks's mind: vast stretches of rubble and craters; acrid smoke drifting through the night air; children's screams, flames licking soot-blackened walls, the screeching of the bombs before the shattering explosions; houses only half-destroyed, so you could see inside the rooms – the pathetic sticks of furniture, framed photographs askew on the walls, peeling wallpaper; families huddled together under blankets in underground stations, a few valued possessions with them.

The images came mostly from films and documentaries he had seen on the Blitz. His parents had actually lived through it, moving to Peterborough from Hammersmith only after the war. They never spoke about it much, as most people who had been through it didn't, but his mother had told him a comical story or two about the war days.

Some of the images of the war's devastation came from Banks's own experience, when he was a child, even that long after the war. As he had told Annie, wastelands of rubble and half-destroyed buildings remained in some areas for years. He remembered visiting London as a child and being surprised when his father told him that the acres of flattened streets in the East End were there because of the war.

Hatchley had been unable to find a death certificate for Gloria Kathleen Shackleton, but he did find one for Matthew, and the information on it caused Banks almost to choke on his beer.

According to the death certificate, Matthew Shackleton died at Leeds General Infirmary on 15 March, 1950, by his own hand. Cause of death was given as a 'self-inflicted gunshot wound'. At the time, he was thirty-one years of age, of no occupation, living at an address in Bramley, Leeds. The informant of his death was listed as Gwynneth Vivian Shackleton, of the same address. Banks checked again, but Hatchley had made no mistake.

He lit a cigarette and thought for a moment. Matthew

Shackleton was supposed to have died in Burma, but obviously he hadn't. Of the three survivors of the old Hobb's End days that Banks and Annie had talked to over the past few days, one had left the village in 1940, before Gloria's arrival there, the second had gone in May 1944, and the third at Christmas 1944. Neither Elizabeth Goodall nor Alice Poole had mentioned Matthew Shackleton's returning, so he must have come back after they had left.

Which made him a definite suspect in his wife's murder. Again.

What had he come home to?

And why had he killed himself five years later?

Banks flipped the sheet and carried on reading. A marriage certificate existed for Gwynneth Vivian Shackleton and Ronald Maurice Bingham. They were married at Christ Church, Hampstead, on 21 August, 1954. The groom's profession was listed as 'Civil Servant'. Ronald died of liver cancer at home on 18 July, 1967.

There was no death certificate for Gwynneth.

Hatchley had dug even deeper, and he had also discovered that there *was* a record of a child being born to Gloria Kathleen Stringer at her parents' home address in Mile End, London, on 5 November, 1937, shortly after her sixteenth birthday.

5 November. Guy Fawkes Night.

Banks imagined Gloria struggling to give birth as Catherine-wheels spun and jumping jacks and bangers exploded outside in the street, as volcanoes erupted dark red fire, changing to green, then white, and rockets burst into showers of bright colours in the darkness beyond the bedroom windows. Did she look out on the scene from her pain? Did the noise and colours take her mind off what she was going through?

The boy was christened Francis Paul Henderson, taking his father's surname. George Henderson, like Jack Stringer, was listed as 'dock worker'.

There was no trace of a wedding certificate.

So Gloria had given birth over three years before she turned up in Hobb's End. What had become of the child and its father? Had she turned over the boy's care completely to George Henderson? It looked that way. She had certainly indicated to none of her new friends that she had a son. Was George Henderson the man with the boy who had turned up at Bridge Cottage during the war? The one Gloria had argued with?

Glenys brought over Banks's Yorkie. He tucked into the huge stuffed Yorkshire pudding and washed each mouthful down with a sip of Theakston's.

According to Hatchley's final search, George Henderson had died of a heart attack just five months ago. There was no death or marriage certificate for his son Francis. That made three of them unaccounted for by death certificates. Gloria, in all likelihood, had been buried under the outbuilding, but that still left Gwynneth Shackleton and Francis Henderson. Why hadn't they come forward? One possibility was that they might both be dead, though Gwynneth would be in her early seventies and Francis only pushing sixty, hardly old in this day and age. Another possibility was that neither of them knew what was going on, which was too much of a coincidence for Banks to swallow. There again, maybe they had something to hide. But what?

Francis wouldn't be able to tell Banks much. Everything that happened in Hobb's End happened before he turned eight, so he was hardly a suspect in the murder of Gloria Shackleton. He would have been about sixteen when the village was flooded to make Thornfield Reservoir, and Banks doubted that the event would have meant anything to him.

Nonetheless, it would be interesting to know what had become of him. If nothing else, Francis Henderson's DNA could help determine beyond a shadow of a doubt whether the skeleton really was Gloria Shackleton's.

There was another issue, too: someone had to lay Gloria's body to rest, bury her properly, in a churchyard, this time. Two people who had been intimately involved with her were possibly still alive: her sister-in-law, Gwynneth Bingham, and her son, Francis Henderson. They should be the ones to do it, to bury their dead.

Banks sighed, put the files back in his briefcase and walked through the crowds across Market Street. He found a message waiting at the front desk from army personnel, informing him that Matthew Shackleton had been listed as 'Missing presumed dead' in 1943, and that was all they had on him. Curiouser and curiouser. Back in his office, Banks picked up the phone and called Detective Inspector Ken Blackstone at Millgarth Station, in Leeds.

'Alan,' said Blackstone. 'Long time no see.'

There was a coolness and distance in his voice. They hadn't been in touch often over the past year or so, and Banks realized he had probably alienated Ken along with just about everyone else who had tried to be his friend during the dark days. Ken had left a number of messages on his answering machine suggesting they get together and talk, but Banks had responded to none of them. He didn't feel like explaining how he just hadn't been able to handle people offering help and encouragement, feeling sorry for him, how he was managing to feel quite sorry enough for himself, thank you very much, and how he had preferred to seek anonymity among the crowds instead. 'You know how it is,' he said.

'Sure. So what can I do for you? Don't tell me this is just a social call.'

'Not exactly.'

'I thought not.' There was a slight pause, then Blackstone's tone softened a little. 'Any new developments between you and Sandra?'

'Nothing. Except I've heard she's seeing someone.'

'I'm sorry, Alan.'

'These things happen.'

'Tell me about it. I've been there.'

'Then you should understand.'

'I do. Want to get rat-arsed and talk about it sometime?'

Banks laughed. 'It'll be a pleasure.'

'Good. So, what can I do for you?'

'Well, if this little idea works out, we might have that piss-up quicker than you think. I'm looking for the details of a suicide. Leeds. Bramley. Gunshot wound. Name's Matthew Shackleton. Died the fifteenth of March, 1950. The local cop shop should have some sort of record, especially as there was a firearm involved.'

'Is there an explanation in here somewhere?'

'Long story, Ken. By the way, have you ever heard anything on the grapevine about a DS called Cabbot? Annie Cabbot?'

'Can't say as I have. But then I've not exactly been around the grapevine much for the past while. Why do you want to know? All right, I know, don't bother, another long story, right? Look, about this suicide. It could take a while.'

'You mean you're talking minutes instead of seconds?'

Blackstone laughed. 'Hours instead of minutes, more

like. I'll get DC Collins to make some phone calls – if I can drag him away from his paper. I'll call you back later.'

Banks heard a grunt and the rustle of a newspaper in the background. 'Thanks, Ken,' he said. 'Appreciate it.'

'You'd better. You owe me a curry.'

'You're on.'

'And, Alan . . .?'

'Yes.'

'I know some of what you've been going through, but don't be a stranger.'

'I know, I know. I told you; you're on. Curry and piss-up and talk about girls. Just like a couple of teenagers. Soon as you get the info.'

Blackstone chuckled. 'Okay. Talk to you later.'

•

Billy Joe and Gloria soon became a couple. Billy Joe was seen going alone to Bridge Cottage, and that got the village tongues wagging. Especially when PX was seen coming and going there the next day. He, too, seemed to have taken a shy sort of shine to Gloria, happy to be her slave and get for her whatever her heart desired. I suggested Gloria tell them to use the back door, where they couldn't be seen from High Street, but she just laughed and shrugged it off.

There was no real mystery to the visits. Gloria told me she wanted sex and she had chosen Billy Joe to supply it. She said he was good at it. I still didn't understand what *it* was all about. When I asked her if I had to be in love before I let men take liberties with me, she lapsed into one of her mysterious silences, then said, 'There's love, Gwen, and then there's sex. They don't have to be the same. Especially not these days. Not while there's a war on. Just try not to get them mixed up.' Then she smiled. 'But it's always nice to be a little bit in love.' After this, I was more confused than ever, but I let the subject drop.

Gloria also needed her Luckies, nylons, lipstick, rouge and scented soap. She drank too much, so she needed a source for whisky, too, and she also took to chewing gum, which she insisted on chewing in church, just to annoy Betty Goodall. And PX, of course, would get her all these things at the flutter of an eyelash. Whether she ever granted him any favours in exchange, I can't say for certain, but I doubt it. Whatever she was, Gloria was never a whore, and I couldn't imagine PX actually being *with* a woman in that way. He looked even younger and seemed even shyer and more awkward than me. There was some health reason that prevented him from serving in a more active branch of the forces – after all, he looked young and strong enough for combat – but he never told anyone exactly what it was.

PX did little favours for us all – for me, Cynthia, Alice, even Mother – especially when it came to nylons and makeup. One thing I soon started to wonder about was why the American forces, undoubtedly male as they were for the most part, had storage rooms full of women's underwear and cosmetics. It was either intended to endear them to the local women, or they had certain private proclivities that they managed to hide from the rest of the world.

Anyway, lucky for us, PX seemed willing and able to get hold of just about anything we needed. If we bemoaned the lack of decent meat, for example, he would mysteriously produce bacon, and on occasion, even a piece of beef. Once he even, miracle of miracles, came up with some oranges! I hadn't seen an orange in years.

I don't think his empire was limited to the contents of the Rowan Woods PX, either. Sometimes, when he got a weekend pass, he would disappear for the entire time. He never said where he went or why, but I suspected he had a few dealings with the Leeds black market. I think I rather liked him, even though he seemed so young, and I *might* have gone out with him if he had asked me. But he never did, and I was too shy to ask him. We were only together in a group. Besides, I know he preferred Gloria.

Billy Joe had other uses, too. He was essentially an aeroplane mechanic, but he could also fix anything on wheels. That came in useful when our little Morris van gave up the ghost. Billy Joe came down in the evening, with PX and a couple of others tagging along, fixed it in a jiffy, then the whole gang of us picked up Gloria and went to the Shoulder of Mutton for a drink. A curious incident occurred that night that coloured my view of Billy Joe for some time to come.

They were the only Americans in the pub and we were the only women. In addition to getting us plenty of suspicious and disapproving glances, even from people I had known for years and served in the shop, this also drew a few loud and pointed comments. Most of the men there were either too old to go to war or were excused because of health reasons. Some were in reserved occupations.

'Just think about it, Bert,' said one local as we bought our first drinks. 'Our lads are over there fighting the Nazis, and them damn Yanks are over here sniffing around our women like tomcats on heat.'

We ignored them, took a table in a quiet corner and kept to ourselves.

The next time we were ready for drinks, Billy Joe went to the bar. He was drinking pints of watery beer, and I had told him to hold on to his glass because there was a shortage. A lot of locals took their own, and some even used jam jars, but if you got one early in the evening you had to hold on to it for the night. As he was on his way back, one of the local strapping farm lads who hadn't been called up – something to do with an allergy to tinned food, I think – called out after him: 'Hey, Yank. Tha's ta'en me glass.'

Billy Joe tried to ignore him, but the man, Seth his name was, had drunk enough to make him feel brave. He lumbered over from the bar and stood right behind Billy Joe, back at the table. The place went quiet.

'I said that's *my* glass tha's got tha beer in, Yank.'

Billy Joe put the tray down on the table, glanced at the pint glass and shrugged. 'Same one I've had all evening, sir,' he said in that lazy Southern drawl.

'"Same one I've had all evening, sir."' Seth tried to mock him, but it didn't come out right. 'Well it's mine, sithee.'

Billy Joe picked up his glass of beer, turned to face Seth slowly and shook his head. 'I don't think so, sir.'

Seth thrust his chin forward. 'Well, I bloody do. Gimme it back.'

'You sure, sir?'

'Aye, Yank.'

Billy Joe nodded in that slow way of his, then he poured the beer all over Seth's feet and held out the glass to him. 'You can take the glass,' he said. 'But the beer was mine. I paid for it. And, by the way, sir, ah am not a Yankee.'

Even Seth's friends had started to laugh by now. It was that sort of fulcrum moment, when so much hangs in the balance, just the lightest touch the wrong way sends it all tumbling down. I could feel my heart beating hard and fast.

Seth made the wrong move. He stepped back and raised his fist. But he was slow. Billy Joe might have had that exaggerated sort of lazy grace, but his speed amazed me. Before anyone knew what had happened, there was the sound of breaking glass and Seth was on his knees, screaming, hands over his face, blood gushing out between his fingers.

'Ah am not a Yankee, sir,' Billy Joe repeated, then turned his back and sat down. The mood had soured, nobody wanted anything more to drink, and we all left shortly afterwards.

•

Vivian Elmsley got up at about one o'clock, turned on the bedside light and took a sleeping pill. She didn't like them, didn't like the way they made her feel woolly-minded the next morning, but this was getting ridiculous. They said old people didn't need as much sleep, but lying tossing and turning all night imagining someone scratching at the window or tapping at the door was exhausting. It was probably the wind, she told herself as she turned off the light and settled back on the pillows.

But there was no wind.

Slowly, the chemical Morpheus insinuated its way into her system. She felt sluggish, her blood heavy as lead, pushing her down into the mattress. Soon she hovered on the threshold between sleep and waking, where thoughts take on the aspect of dreams, and an image you conjure up consciously is suddenly snatched away for unconscious improvisations, like variations on a musical theme.

At first, she pictured Gloria's tilted head as she had appeared on the TV screen, the detail from Stanhope's painting, looking like a cartoon-Gloria.

Then the cartoon-Gloria started talking about a night in Rio de Janeiro when Vivian had had too much to drink and – the only time – succumbed to sexual advances at a cocktail party in a big hotel, remembered a whispered room number, waited until Ronald was fast asleep and slipped out into the corridor.

The cartoon-Gloria's monologue was cut with images of the night, which flicked past jerkily like the series of cards in an old 'What the Butler Saw' machine.

Vivian had always wondered what it would be like. They only did it once. Her lover was a gentle and sensitive woman from the French Embassy, conscious it was Vivian's first time, but ultimately frustrated at her lack of ability to respond. It wasn't for want of trying, Vivian thought. She couldn't lose herself in sex with a man, so she had hoped she could abandon herself to the caresses of another woman, enjoy the bliss that writers wrote about and people risked everything for.

But she couldn't. It wouldn't happen.

Finally, she put on her robe and hurried out, humiliated, back to her own room. Ronald was still snoring away. She lay on her own bed and stared at the dark ceiling, tears welling in her eyes, a dull ache in her loins.

As the cartoon-Gloria retold the story of Vivian's failed attempt at sex and infidelity, it was as if the TV camera started to move away from her, and the rest of Gloria came into view, showing more of her figure, and before long Vivian realized that Gloria wasn't wearing a red dress; she was covered in blood which oozed from cuts deep into the gristle of her flesh.

Yet she was still talking.

Talking about something that happened years after her death.

Vivian tried to stop it but she felt as if she were being held down by the weight of her own blood, an anchor hooked deep into the darkness and the horror. Too heavy.

She struggled to wake, and as she did, the telephone

rang. Her bonds were suddenly cut, and she shot up, gasping for air as if she had been drowning.

Without thinking, she picked up the receiver. A lifeline.

After a short pause, the monotone voice whispered, 'Gwen. Gwen Shackleton.'

'Go away,' she mumbled, her tongue thick and furred.

The voice laughed. 'Soon, Gwen,' the man said. 'Soon.'

11

Banks and Annie drove out to the estate from Millgarth police headquarters. When Annie asked Banks why he always wanted to do the driving himself, he didn't really know the answer. Being driven was one of the perks of his rank that he had never really capitalized on. Partly, he would always rather use his own car than sign one out because he didn't want to have to put up with other coppers' cigarette butts in the ashtrays, chocolate wrappers, used tissues and God knows what else all over the floor, not to mention the lingering germs and odours. Mostly, though, he needed to be in control, with *his* feet on the pedals, *his* hands on the steering wheel.

He also liked to control the music. It had always angered Sandra, the way he put on whatever CD *he* wanted to listen to, or turned on the television to a programme *he* wanted to watch. She claimed he was selfish. He said he always knew what he wanted to listen to or watch and she didn't; besides, why should he listen to music, or watch films he didn't like? Another stand-off.

Banks parked in front of a strip of shops set back from the main road near Bramley Town End, and he and Annie strolled down the hill towards the street where Gwen and Matthew Shackleton had lived. Both were dressed casually; neither looked like a police officer. Sometimes, feelings against all forms of authority ran high on these estates. People spotted strangers quickly enough as it was, and they were naturally suspicious of anyone in a suit. Which was hardly surprising: on an estate like this, if you saw someone you knew wearing a suit, you assumed he had a court appearance coming up; and if you saw a stranger wearing one, it was either the cops or the social.

Banks had grown up on a similar estate in Peterborough. More modern than this one, but basically the same mix of grim and grimy terrace houses alongside the newer red-brick maisonettes and tower blocks, all covered in graffiti. When he was a kid, the street was cobbled, and they would have bonfires there every Guy Fawkes Night. The whole estate would come out and share their fireworks and food. Potatoes baked in foil at the edges of the fire, and people passed around trays of homemade parkin and treacle toffee. Neighbours would seize the opportunity to chuck their old furniture on the fire – a practice Banks's mother said she thought was showing off. If Mrs Green at number 16 threw her battered armchair on the bonfire, it was tantamount to telling everyone she could afford a new one.

Eventually, the council Tarmacked the street and put an end to the celebrations. Afterwards, they had to have their bonfire on a large field half a mile away; strangers from other estates started muscling in, looking for trouble, and the older people began to stay at home and lock their doors.

'How are we going to approach this?' Annie asked.

'We'll play it by ear. I just want to get a look at the lie of the land.'

It was another hot day; people sat out on their doorsteps or had dragged striped deck-chairs on to postage-stamp lawns, where the grass was parched pale brown for lack of rain. Banks couldn't help but be aware of the suspicious eyes following their progress. From one garden, a couple of semi-naked teenage boys whistled at Annie and flexed the tattoos on their arms. Banks looked at her and saw her stick her hand behind her back and give them two fingers. They laughed.

They passed two girls, neither of whom looked older than fifteen. Each was pushing a pram with one hand and holding a cigarette with the other. One of them had short pink-and-white-dyed hair, green nail varnish, black lipstick and a nose-stud; the other had jet-black hair, a large butterfly tattoo on her shoulder, and a red dot in the centre of her forehead. Both wore high-heeled sandals, tight shorts and midriff-revealing tops; the one with the red dot also had a ring in her navel.

'Get *her*,' one of them sneered as Banks and Annie walked by. 'Little Miss Hoity-Toity.'

'I'm beginning to think this wasn't such a good idea, after all,' Annie said, when the girls had passed.

'Why not? What's wrong?'

'Easy for you to ask. Nobody's insulted *you* yet.'

'They're only jealous.'

'What of? My good looks?'

'No. Your designer jeans. Ah, here it is.'

The address turned out to be on one of the narrower side-streets. Most of the doors had scratched and weathered paintwork, and the whole street looked run-down. All the windows of the old Shackleton house were open, and loud music blasted from inside.

Next door, two men with huge beer bellies sat smoking and drinking Carlsberg Special Brew. An enormous woman sat on a tiny chair at an angle to them, hips and thighs flowing over the edge. She looked as if she might be their mother. Both men were stripped to the waist, skin white as lard despite the sun; the woman wore a bikini top and garish pink shorts. All three of them followed Banks and Annie with their narrowed piggy eyes, but nobody said anything.

Banks knocked on the door. A dog growled inside the house. The people next door laughed. Finally, the door jerked open and a young skinhead in a red T-shirt and torn jeans stuck his head out, holding the barking dog by its studded collar. It looked like a Rottweiler to Banks.

Banks swallowed and stepped back a couple of paces. He wasn't normally scared of dogs, but this one had wicked-looking teeth. Maybe Annie was right. What could they find out anyway, nearly fifty years after the fact?

'Who the fuck are you? What do you want?' the skinhead asked. The cords stood out on his neck. He couldn't have been older than eighteen or nineteen. Banks thought he could hear a baby crying somewhere beyond the music in the depths of the house.

'Your mum and dad in?' Banks asked.

He laughed. 'I should think so,' he said. 'They never go anywhere. Trouble is, you'll have a bloody long journey. They live in Nottingham.'

'So *you* live here?'

''Course I fucking do. Look, I haven't got all day.' The dog was still straining at its collar, drool dripping from its jowls, but it had turned quieter now and seemed to be settling down, just growling rather than barking and snapping.

'I'd like some information,' said Banks.

'About what?'

'Look, can we come in?'

'You must be fucking joking, mate. One step over this threshold and Gazza here'll have you singing soprano in the church choir before you know it.'

Banks looked at Gazza. He could believe it. He considered his options. Call Animal Control? The RSPCA? 'Fine,' he said. 'Then maybe you can tell us what we want to know out here?'

'Depends.'

'It's the house I'm interested in.'

The kid looked Annie up and down, then looked back at Banks. 'House-hunting are you, then? I'd've thought you two would be after something a bit more up-market than this fucking slum.'

'Not exactly house-hunting, no.'

'Who is it, Kev?' came a woman's voice from inside.

Kev turned round and yelled back. 'Mind yer own fucking business, yer stupid cunt! Or you'll be sucking yer meals through a straw for a week.'

Banks sensed Annie stiffen beside him. He touched her gently on the forearm. The trio next door howled with laughter. The kid stuck his head farther round the door, so they could see him, and grinned at them, pleased with himself. He gave them the thumbs-up sign.

'How long have you lived here?' Banks asked.

'Two years. What's it to you?'

'I'm interested in something that happened here fifty years ago. A suicide.'

'Suicide? Fifty years ago? What, fucking haunted, is it?' He stuck his head round the door again to talk to the people next door. 'Hear that, lads? This is a fucking haunted house, this is. Maybe we could start charging an entry fee like those fucking stately homes.'

They all laughed. Including Banks.

The kid seemed so thrilled with his audience response that he repeated the comment. He then let go of the dog, which glanced uninterestedly at Banks and Annie and slunk off deeper into the house, no doubt towards a bowl of food. Maybe it wasn't a Rottweiler after all. Banks was about as good on dogs as he was on wild flowers, constellations and trees. Most of nature, come to think of it. But he would get better now he had the cottage by the edge of the woods. He had already learned to identify some of the birds – nuthatches, dunnocks and blue tits – and he had often heard a woodpecker knocking away at an ash trunk.

'Do you know who lived here before you?' he asked.

'Haven't a clue, mate. But you can ask the wrinklies over the road. They've been here since the fucking ice age.' He pointed to the middle terrace house directly opposite. Mirror image. Banks could already see a figure peeking from behind moth-eaten curtains.

'Thanks,' he said. Annie followed him across the street.

'I smell pork,' said one of the doorstep trio as they went. The others laughed. Someone made a hawking sound and spat loudly.

After Banks and Annie had held their warrant cards up to the letter-box for inspection, the deadbolt and the chain came off and a hunched man, probably somewhere in his early seventies, opened the door. He had a hollow chest, deep-set eyes, a thin, lined face and sparse black-and-grey hair larded back with lashings of Brylcreem. That glint of self-pitying malice peculiar to those who have been knocked on their arses too many times by life had not been entirely extinguished from his rheumy eyes; a few watts of indignant outrage, at least, remained.

Making sure he'd locked up behind him, he led them into the house. The windows were all shut tight and most of the curtains were closed. The living room had the atmosphere of a hot and stuffy funeral parlour; it smelled of cigarette smoke and dirty socks.

'What's it all about, then?' The old man flopped down on a sagging brown corduroy settee.

'The past,' said Banks.

A woman walked through from the kitchen. About the same age as the man, she seemed a little better preserved. She certainly had a bit more flesh on her bones.

The old man reached for his cigarettes and lighter balanced on the threadbare arm of the settee, and he coughed when he lit up. What the future holds in store for us smokers if we don't stop, Banks thought glumly, deciding against joining him just at the moment.

'Police, Elsie,' the man said.

'Come to do something about those hooligans?' she asked.

'No,' said the man, a puzzled frown creasing his brow. 'They say it's about the past.'

'Aye, well, there's plenty of that about for everyone,' she said. 'Like a cuppa?'

'Please,' said Banks. Annie nodded.

'Sit yerselves down then. I'm Mrs Patterson, by the way. You can call me Elsie. And this is my Stanley.'

Stanley leaned forward and offered his hand. 'Call me Stan,' he said, with a wink. Elsie went to make the tea. 'I see you met that lot over the street?' Stan said with a jerk of his head.

'We did,' said Banks.

'He threatened to beat his wife,' Annie said. 'Have you ever seen any evidence of that, Mr Patterson? Any cuts or bruises?'

'Nay, lass,' said Stan. 'He's all wind and piss, is yon Kev. Colleen'd kill him like as not if he ever laid a finger on her. And she's not his wife, neither. Not that it seems to matter these days. It's not even his kid.' He took a drag on his cigarette, which Banks noticed was untipped, and launched into a coughing fit. When he recovered, his face was red and his chest was heaving. 'Sorry,' he said, thumping his chest. 'All them years grafting in that filthy factory. Ought to bloody sue, I did.'

'How long have you lived here?' Banks asked.

'For ever. Or so it seems,' Stan said. 'It were always a rough estate, even back then, but it weren't really such a bad place when we first moved in. Lucky to get it, we were.' He smoked and coughed again.

Elsie came back with the tea. A cold drink would probably have made more sense, Banks thought, but you take what you're offered.

'Stan was just saying you've lived here a long time,' Banks said to her.

She poured the tea into heavy white mugs. 'Since we got married,' she said. 'Well, we lived with Stan's mum and dad in Pontefract for a few months, didn't we, love, but this was our first home together.' She sat beside her husband.

'And our last, way things turned out,' Stan said.

'Well, whose fault were that?'

'Weren't mine, woman.'

'You knew I wanted to move to that new Raynville Estate when they built it, didn't you?'

'Aye,' said Stan. 'When were that? In 1963? And where is it now? They've had to knock the bloody place down now, things got so bad.'

'There were other places we could have moved. Poplars. Wythers.'

'*Wythers!* Wythers is worse than this.'

'What year was it?' Banks butted in. 'When you first came to live here?'

The Pattersons glared at one another for a moment, then Elsie stirred her tea. She sat up straight, knees pressed together, hands around the mug on her lap. In the distance, Banks could hear the music from the skinhead's house: tortured guitars, heavy bass, a testosterone-pumped voice snarling lust and hatred. Christ, he hoped Brian's band was better than that.

'In 1949,' Elsie said. 'October 1949. I remember because I were three months gone with Derek at the time. He was our first. Remember, Stan,' she said, 'you'd just got that job at Blakey's Castings?'

'Aye,' said Stan, turning to Banks. 'I were just twenty years old, and Elsie here were eighteen.'

Banks hadn't even been born then. The war had been over four years and the country was going through a lot of changes, setting up the Welfare State in the wake of the Beveridge Report, setting up the whole system that had given Banks far more opportunities and chances of self-improvement than previous generations had. And to his parents' dismay, he had become a copper instead of a business executive or managing director, the sort of position his father had always looked up to. Now, though, having felt very much like a business executive this past year, he was pleased to discover that he still thought he had made the right choice.

Banks tried to imagine the Pattersons as a young couple with hope in their hearts and a promising future before them crossing the threshold of their first home together. The image came in black and white, with a factory chimney in the background.

'Do you remember anything about your neighbours across the street?' Annie asked. 'Directly opposite, where Kev and his family live now.'

Elsie spoke first. 'Weren't that where those, you know, those . . . what's-their-names . . . lived, Stanley? A bit stuck up. There were some trouble.'

'A suicide,' Banks prompted her.

'Aye. That's right. Don't you remember, Stanley? Shot himself. That tall skinny young fellow, used to walk with a stick, never said a word to anyone. What were his name?'

'Matthew Shackleton.'

'That's right. We had police all over the place. They even came over and talked to us. By gum, that takes me back a bit. Matthew Shackleton. Don't you remember, Stanley?'

'Aye,' said Stan hesitantly. 'I think so.' He lit another cigarette and coughed. Then he glanced at his watch. Opening time.

'Did you know the Shackletons?' Banks asked.

'Not really,' Elsie said. 'Acted like they'd gone down in the world, fallen on hard times, like. From the country somewhere, though I found out she were nowt better than a shopkeeper's daughter. Not that there's owt wrong with that, mind you. I'm no snob. I tried to be friendly, you know, like you do, seeing as we were the newcomers and all that. But nobody bothered with them. The time or two I did talk to her, she didn't say owt about where they came from, except to mention that things had been different back in the village, like. Well, la-di-da, I thought.'

Well, Banks thought, from Hobb's End to this Leeds council estate would have been quite a frightening journey into purgatory for Gwen and Matthew, unless they were in a purgatory of their own making already.

'How many of them lived there?'

'Just the two,' Elsie said. 'I remember her saying her

mother used to live with them and all, but she died a year or so before we moved here.'

'Aye,' Stan chirped in. 'I remember them now. Just the two of them, weren't there? Him and his wife. Tall, gangly lass, herself.'

'Nay,' said Elsie, 'she were never his wife. He weren't right in his head.'

'Who were she, then?'

'I don't know, but she weren't his wife.'

'How do you know?' Banks asked Elsie.

'They didn't act like man and wife. I could tell.'

'Don't be so bloody daft, woman,' Stan said. Then he looked at Banks and rolled his eyes. 'She were his wife. Take it from me.'

'What was her name?' Banks asked.

'It's on the tip of my tongue,' Elsie said.

'Blodwyn,' said Stan. 'Summat Welsh, any road.'

'No, it weren't. Gwynneth, that were it. Gwynneth Shackleton.'

'What did she look like?'

'Ordinary, really, apart from them beautiful eyes of hers,' said Elsie. 'Like Stanley said, she were a bit taller than your average lass, and a bit clumsy, you know, the way some big people are. She were nearly as tall as Matthew.'

'How old, would you say?'

'She can't have been that old, but she had a hard-done-by look about her. I don't know how to say it, really. Old before her time. Tired, like.'

'Must've been from looking after her husband. He were an invalid. Battle fatigue. War wound.'

'He weren't her husband.'

Stan turned to face her. 'Did you ever see her stepping out with a young man?'

'Come to think on it, no, I don't recall as I did.'

'There you are then. Goes to show.'

'Show what?'

'You'd've thought if she weren't married she'd have had a boyfriend or two, girl like that, wouldn't you? I'll grant you she were no oil painting, but she were well enough shaped where it counts, and she were bonny enough.'

'Did they ever have many visitors?' Banks asked.

'Not as I noticed,' Elsie answered. 'But I'm not one of your nose-at-the-window types, you know.'

'How about an attractive young woman with blond hair?' Annie said, turning to Stanley. 'Might have looked like this.' She handed him the copy of Alice Poole's photograph and pointed to Gloria.

'No,' said Stan. 'Never seen anyone looked like her. And I think I'd remember.' He winked at Annie. 'I'm not that old, tha knows. But the other one's Gwynneth all right.' He pointed to the woman Alice had identified as Gwen Shackleton. 'I can't recall as they ever had *any* visitors, come to think on it.'

'Aye, you're right there, Stanley,' she said. 'They kept to themselves.'

'What happened after the suicide?' Banks asked.

'She went away.'

'Do you know where?'

'No. She never even said goodbye. One day she were there, the next she were gone. I'll tell you what, though.'

'What?' asked Banks.

A wicked smile twisted her features. 'I know who she is.'

'What do you mean?'

'Her. That Gwynneth Shackleton. That's not her name

now, of course, but it's her, right enough. Done right well for herself, she has.'

'Who is she?'

'I've seen her on telly, seen her picture in *Woman's Own*.'

'Yer barmy, woman,' Stan piped up.

'I'm telling you, Stanley: it's her. Those eyes. The height. The voice. I don't forget things like that. I'm surprised you can't see it for yourself.'

Banks was trying hard to remain patient and beginning to think he was fighting a losing battle. 'Mrs Patterson. Elsie,' he said finally. 'Do you think you could tell me *who* you think Gwen Shackleton is?'

'It's that woman writes those books, isn't it? Always being interviewed on telly. And she did that documentary about that little church in London, you know, like Alan Bennett did on Westminster Abbey. Used to live just down the road, did Alan Bennett. His dad were a butcher. Any road, you could see it were her, how tall she were. And those eyes.'

'What books?' Banks asked.

'Them detective books. Always on telly. With that good-looking what's-'is-name playing the inspector. Good they are, too. I've had her books out of the library. I must go through ten books a week. It's her, I'm telling you.'

'She's thinking of that Vivian Elmsley woman,' sighed Stan. 'Swore the first time she saw her interviewed by that bloke who talks through his nose.'

'Melvyn Bragg.'

'Aye, him. Swore blind it were Gwen Shackleton.'

'You don't agree?' Annie asked.

'Nay, I don't know, lass. I'm not good at faces, not the way our Elsie is. She's always telling me someone's baby looks like his mum or dad but I'm buggered if I can see it. They all look like Winston Churchill to me. Or Edward G. Robinson. There *is* a resemblance, but . . .' He shook his head. 'It's so long ago. People change. And things like that don't happen to people like us, do they, people from places like this? Someone across the street gets famous and writes books that get done on telly and all? I mean, life's not like that, is it? Not here. Not for the likes of us.'

'What about Alan Bennett?' Elsie argued. 'And she were well read. You could tell that about her.'

In the brief silence that followed, Banks heard more music and laughter from across the street.

'You hear what it's like?' Stan said. 'Never a moment's peace. Day and night, night and day, bloody racket. We keep our windows shut and curtains closed. You never know what's going to happen next. We had a murder last week. Bloke down the street playing cards with some bloody gyppos. Vinnie and Derek, our lads, they worry about us. They'd like us to go live in sheltered housing. We might just do it and all. Right now, I'd settle for three squares a day and a bit of peace and quiet.'

'Back to this woman,' said Banks, turning to Elsie. 'Gwen Shackleton.'

'Aye?'

'How long did she stay on the estate after the suicide?'

'Oh, not long. I'd say as long as it took to get him buried and get everything sorted out with the authorities.'

'Were the police suspicious about what happened?'

'Police are always suspicious, aren't they?' said Stan. 'It's their job.' He laughed and coughed. 'Nay, lad, you ought to know that.'

Banks smiled. 'Was Gwen in the house at the time of the suicide?' he asked.

Elsie paused and lowered her head. 'That's what they asked us back then,' she said. 'I've thought and thought about it to this day, and I still don't know. I *thought* I saw her get back from the shops – that was where she'd been, shopping up Town Street – *before* I heard the bang.' She frowned. 'But, you see, I were so close to having our Derek, and I weren't always seeing things right. I could have been wrong.'

'Did you tell the police this?'

'Yes. But nowt came of it. Or they'd have put her in gaol, wouldn't they?'

Now Banks *definitely* wanted to have a look at the Matthew Shackleton file. 'We might as well be off,' he said to Annie, then turned to Stan and Elsie. 'Thanks very much. You've been a great help.'

'Tell me summat,' said Stan. 'I know getting information out of you lot's like prising a penny from a Scotsman's arse, but I'm curious. This Gwen, were she his wife?'

Banks smiled. 'His sister. We think.'

Elsie nudged her husband hard in the ribs. He started coughing. 'See, Stanley. I told yer so, yer great lummox.'

Banks insisted they could find their own way out, and soon he and Annie walked gratefully in the fresh air. The people across the street were still enjoying their party, joined now by Kev and his dog, which was running wild across the tiny lawns, scratching on doors and ripping up what weeds had survived summer so far. Another woman, whom Banks assumed to be Colleen, was also there, holding her baby. She was a skinny girl, about seventeen, smiling, no bruises, but with a hard, defeated look about her.

As Banks and Annie neared the end of the street, an empty beer can skittered across the Tarmac behind them.

'What do you think about this Vivian Elmsley business?' Annie asked.

'I don't know. I'm surprised that neither Elizabeth nor Alice mentioned it.'

'Maybe they didn't know? Alice said she's got very poor eyesight, and Elizabeth Goodall didn't even know why you were visiting her, she pays so little attention to current affairs.'

'True,' said Banks. 'And Ruby Kettering left Hobb's End in 1940, when Gwen was only about fifteen. Definitely worth looking into.'

'So,' said Annie back in the car. 'What next?'

'The local nick. I want to see Matthew Shackleton's file.'

'I thought so. And then?'

'Back to Millgarth.'

'Have we time for a drink and a bite to eat later?'

'Sorry. I've got a date.'

She thumped him playfully. 'Seriously?'

'Seriously. With a detective inspector. A *male* detective inspector called Ken Blackstone. You met him briefly. He gave us the address.'

'I remember him. The snappy dresser. Cute.' If Annie was disappointed, she didn't show it. Banks explained his tenuous friendship with Ken and how he was in a mood for building bridges. Things seemed to be coming together for him – the cottage, an active investigation, Annie – and he realized that he had been neglecting his friends for too long.

'I see,' Annie said. 'A boys' night out, then?'

'I suppose so.'

She laughed. 'I wouldn't mind being a fly on the wall at *that* one.'

•

Billy Joe was confined to base for a few weeks. They said his punishment would have been far more severe had not all the witnesses, even Seth's friends, attested that he didn't start the fight. Seth was fine, too. At first, I thought Billy Joe had broken the glass in his face, but it had simply fallen off the edge of the table when he had tried to put it back there before preparing to defend himself. All Billy Joe had done was punch Seth in the nose, and everyone agreed it was well deserved.

Gloria never said as much, but I think the incident put her off Billy Joe. She hated violence. Some girls like being fought over. I'll never forget the primal blood lust in Cynthia Garmen's eyes when two soldiers fought over her favours at one of the Harkside dances. She didn't care who was hitting whom as long as someone was getting hit and blood was flowing. But Gloria wasn't like that. Violence upset her.

It was while Billy Joe was confined to base that we first met Brad and Charlie.

We were walking out of the Lyceum. It was a miserable February night in 1944, not snowing, but freezing cold, with icicles hanging from the cinema's eaves. We hadn't been out for a few days and Gloria was getting depressed with the cold and the hard working conditions at the farm. She needed cheering up.

We had been to see Bette Davis and Paul Henreid in *Now, Voyager*, and we were both humming the theme song as we put our coats back on in the foyer before going out into the bitter cold evening.

Before Gloria could dig out her own cigarettes, a young man in a fleece-lined leather jacket walked over, put two cigarettes in his mouth, lit them, then handed one to her. It was the same thing they had done in the film. We doubled over laughing.

'Brad,' said the young man. 'Brad Szikorski. And this is my pal Charlie Markleson.'

Gloria did a little mock curtsy. 'Charmed to meet you, I'm sure.'

'We're with the Four Hundred Forty-Eighth? Over at Rowan Woods?' Though they were statements, they sounded like questions. I had noticed this before with both Americans and Canadians. 'I don't mean to be forward,' said Brad, 'but would you ladies care to honour us by joining us for a drink?'

We exchanged glances. I could tell Gloria wanted to go. Brad was tall and handsome, with a twinkle in his eye and a little Clark Gable moustache. I looked at Charlie, who was probably destined to be my companion for the evening, and I had to admit I quite liked what I saw. About the same age as Brad, he had intelligent eyes, if a little puppy-dog, and a rather pale, thin face. His nose was too big, and it had a bump in the middle, but then mine was nothing to write home about, either. He also seemed reserved and serious. All in all, he'd do. At least for a drink.

We walked across to the Black Swan. The village green was deserted and the ice crackled under our feet. Icicles hung from the branches and twigs of the chestnut trees and frost covered the bark. If it hadn't been so cold, I could have imagined they were blossoms in May. Behind us, the illuminated sign over the Lyceum went off. Even in the blackout, cinemas, shops and a few other establishments were allowed a small measure of light, unless the air-raid siren went off. Ahead, St Jude's was partially lit, and close by stood the Black Swan, with its familiar timber-and-whitewash façade and sagging roof. We could hear the sounds of talking and laughter from inside, but heavy blackout curtains covered the mullioned windows.

The pub was crowded and we were lucky to get a table. Brad went to the bar for drinks while we took our coats off. A meagre fire burned in the hearth, but with all the warm bodies in there, it was enough. Also, in the Black Swan, Brad and Charlie weren't the only Americans; it seemed to be a popular place among the Rowan Woods crowd, and there were even some GIs from the army base near Otley. They were loud and they used hand gestures a lot; they also seemed to push and shove one another a lot, in a friendly way, as children do.

Brad came back bearing a tray of six drinks. We wondered who was going to join us. Gloria and I were both drinking gin, and when Brad and Charlie picked up their beer glasses, then poured the small measures of whisky into them, our unspoken question was answered. Nobody. Just another American peculiarity.

We toasted one another and drank, then Brad did the thing with the cigarettes again, and Charlie did it for me.

'What do you do?' Gloria asked.

'I'm a pilot,' said Brad, 'and Charlie here's my navigator.'

'A pilot! How exciting. Where are you from?'

'California.'

Gloria clapped her hands together. 'Hollywood!'

'Well, not exactly. A little place called Pasadena. You probably haven't heard of it.'

'But you must *know* Hollywood?'

Brad smiled, revealing straight white teeth. They must have wonderful dentists over in America, I thought, and people must have enough money to be able to afford them. 'As a matter of fact, yeah, I do,' he said. 'I did a little stunt flying there in the movies before I came over here.'

'You mean you've actually been in pictures?'

'Well, you can't really see it's me, but, I mean, yeah, I

guess so.' He named a couple of titles; we hadn't heard of either of them. 'That's what I want to do when all this is over,' he went on. 'Get back there and get in the movie business. My father's in oil and he wants me to join him. I know there's plenty of money there, but that's not what I want. I want a shot at being a stunt man.'

If Gloria was disappointed that Brad didn't want to be an oil millionaire or a movie star, she didn't show it. As they chatted away excitedly about films and Hollywood, Charlie and I started our own hesitant conversation.

The beer and whisky must have melted a little of his reserve, because he opened by asking me what I did. He regarded me seriously as I told him, his expression unchanging, nodding his head every now and then. Then he told me his father was a professor at Harvard, that he had completed his university degree in English just before the war, and when he went back he wanted to go to Harvard, too, to study law. He liked flying, he said, but he didn't see it as a career.

The more we talked, the more we found we had in common – Jane Austen and Thomas Hardy, for example, and the poetry of T. S. Eliot. And Robert Frost and Edward Thomas. He hadn't heard of many of our younger poets, so I offered to lend him some issues of *Penguin New Writing*, with poems by MacNeice, Auden and Day Lewis, and he said he would lend me Tate and Bishop's *American Harvest* anthology, if I took special care with it. I told him that I would no more damage a book than I would a living human being and that made him smile for the first time.

'Have you got a husband?' I overheard Brad ask Gloria. 'I mean, I don't mean to . . . you know . . .'

'It's all right. I did have. But he's dead. Killed in Burma. At least I hope to God he was.'

I turned from Charlie. It was true that we had tried to convince ourselves of Matthew's death, but there was still a lingering hope, at least in my mind, and I thought that was a terrible thing to say. I told her so.

She turned on me, eyes flashing. 'Well, you should know better than anyone that I'm right, Gwen. You're the one who reads the newspapers and listens to the news, aren't you?'

'Yes.'

'Look, I'm really sorry,' Brad cut in, but Gloria ignored him, kept staring at me.

'So you must know what they're saying about the Japanese, about the way they treat their prisoners?' she went on.

I had to admit that I had read one or two rather grim stories alleging that the Japanese beat and starved prisoners to death, and according to Anthony Eden, torture and decapitation were favourite pastimes in their POW camps. The *Daily Mail* called them 'monkey men', claimed that they were 'sub-human' and should be outlawed after they had been beaten back to their 'savage land'. I didn't know what to believe. If the stories were true, then I should probably agree with Gloria and hope to God Matthew was dead.

'I've got friends fighting in the Pacific,' said Charlie. 'I hear it's pretty rough out there. A lot of these stories are true.'

'Well, he's dead, anyway,' said Gloria. 'So nothing can hurt him now. Look, this is too depressing. Can we have another round of drinkies, please?'

Brad and Charlie drove us home in their Jeep. Charlie seemed a little embarrassed when Brad and Gloria started kissing passionately by the fairy bridge, but he managed to pluck up the courage to put his arm around me. We kissed dutifully and arranged to meet again soon to swap books. Brad told Charlie to drive on, that he'd walk back to the base alone later, and he followed Gloria into Bridge Cottage.

•

The Indian restaurant Ken Blackstone had chosen was a hole-in-the-wall on Burley Road with red tablecloths and a bead curtain in front of the kitchen. Every time the waiter walked through, the beads rattled. Sitar music droned from speakers high on the walls, and the aromas of cumin and coriander filled the air.

'Did you find what you were looking for in those incident reports?' Blackstone asked as they shared pop-padams, samosas and pakoras.

'I wasn't after anything in particular,' Banks said. 'Elsie Patterson was unsure as to whether she saw Gwen Shackleton enter the house with her shopping before or after she heard the shot. She even thought the shot might have been a car backfiring. And she was the only witness. Nobody else saw Gwen or Matthew that day. The other neighbours were at work, the local kids at school.'

'What did Gwen Shackleton say in her statement?'

Banks swallowed a mouthful of samosa. So far, the food was excellent, as Ken had promised; it was neither too greasy nor needlessly hot, the way many Indian restaurants made it, mistaking chili peppers and cayenne for creative spicing. Banks thought he might like to try his hand at Indian cooking, have Annie over for a vegetarian curry. 'She just said she found Matthew dead in the armchair when she got home from shopping.'

'Was there any real doubt? Was she ever a suspect?'

'I didn't get that impression. Matthew Shackleton had a

history of mental illness since the war. He was also an alcoholic. Functioning, more or less, but an alcoholic. According to the report, he had tried to kill himself once before, head in the gas oven that time. A neighbour smelled gas and saved him. The hospital suggested a period of psychiatric observation, which they carried out, then they sent him home again.'

'Why didn't he use the gun that time?'

'No idea.'

'But it was just a matter of time?'

'Seems that way.'

'You disagree?'

'No. Though I suppose there's always the possibility that he was helped on his way, that he had become an intolerable burden to his sister. Remember, Gwen had been taking care of both her mother *and* her brother. It's not much of a life for a young woman, is it? Anyway, if Elsie Patterson really did see Gwen Shackleton go into the house before the shot was fired, it's possible Gwen might have stood by and let him get on with it.'

'Still a crime.'

'Yes, but it happened over forty years ago, Ken. And we'd never prove it.'

'Not unless Gwen Shackleton confessed.'

'Why should she do that?'

'Years of accumulated guilt? The need to get it off her chest before her final confrontation with the Almighty? I don't know. Who knows why people confess? They do, though.'

Their main courses arrived: aloo gobi, rogan josh, and king prawns, with pilau rice, lime chutney and chapattis. They ordered more lager.

Banks looked at Blackstone. *Cute*, Annie had said. Cute

was the last thing that came to Banks's mind. Elegant, yes; donnish, even. But cute? No matter where Blackstone was – student hang-out, backstreet pub, five-star restaurant, cop shop – he was aways immaculately dressed in his Burton's best pinstripe or herringbone, monogrammed silk handkerchief poised over the edge of his top pocket, folds so aesthetic and delicate they might have been set by a Japanese flower arranger. Crisp white shirt, neat Windsor knot in his subdued tie. Thinning sandy hair curled around his ears and his wire-rimmed glasses balanced on the bridge of his straight nose.

'What about forensics?' Blackstone asked.

'Single shot in the mouth. Splattered his brains over the wall like blancmange. No evidence of a struggle. Empty whisky bottle by the chair. The angle of the wound was also consistent with the suicide theory.'

'Note?'

'Yes. The genuine article, according to forensics.'

'So what's bothering you?'

Banks ate some curry and washed it down before answering. Already a pleasant glow was spreading from his mouth and stomach throughout the rest of his body. The curry was just hot enough to produce a mild sweat, but not to burn his taste buds off. 'Nothing, really. Outside of normal curiosity, I'm not really interested in whether Gwen Shackleton helped her brother commit suicide or not. But I would like to know if he murdered Gloria Shackleton.'

'Perhaps he couldn't live with the guilt?'

'My first thought.'

'But now?'

'Oh, it's still the most likely explanation. The only person who can tell us is Gwen Shackleton.'

'What happened to her? Is she still alive?'

'That's another interesting thing. Elsie Patterson swears she's Vivian Elmsley.'

Blackstone whistled and raised his thin, arched eyebrows. 'The writer?'

'That's the one.'

'What do you think?'

'I don't know. It's possible, I suppose. The Pattersons said they could tell Gwen was well read, and everyone who remembers her said she always had her head stuck in a book. Annie's going to ask around, but there's only one way to find out for certain, isn't there? We'll have to talk to her. Like Gloria's son, if he's still alive, she certainly hasn't been in touch with us, and we've had calls out all over the country for information. It's hard to imagine that many people don't know the story.'

'Which may mean that, if it is her, she has a reason for not wanting to be found?'

'Exactly. A guilty secret.'

'Wasn't that the title of one of her books?'

Banks laughed. 'Was it? I can't say as I've read any.'

'I have,' said Blackstone. 'Seen them on telly, too. She's actually a very talented writer. Hasn't a clue about how we really operate, of course, but then none of them do.'

'It'd make for some pretty boring books if they did.'

'True enough.'

Blackstone ordered a couple more pints of lager. He looked at his watch. 'How about heading into town after this one?' he asked.

'Okay.'

'How are the kids?'

'Fine, I suppose. Well, at least Tracy is.'

'Brian?'

'Silly bugger's just cocked up his finals and come out with a third.'

Blackstone, who had a degree in art history, frowned. 'Any particular reason? You don't blame yourself, do you? The break-up? Stress?'

Banks shook his head. 'No, not really. I think he just sort of lost interest in the subject and found something he felt more passionate about.'

'The music?'

'Uh-huh. He's in a band. They're trying to make a go of it.'

'Good for him,' said Blackstone. 'I would have thought you'd approve.'

'That's the bloody problem, Ken, I do. Only when he first told me I said some things I regret. Now I can't get in touch with him to explain. They're out on the road somewhere.'

'Keep trying. That's about all you can do.'

'I sounded just like my own parents. It brought back a lot of stuff, things I hadn't really thought much about in years, like why I made some of the choices I did.'

'Any answers?'

Banks smiled. 'On a postcard, please.'

'Any great change in your circumstances tends to make you introspective. It's one of the stages you go through.'

'Been reading those self-help books again, Ken?'

Blackstone smiled. 'Fruits of experience, mate. This DS you were asking me about on the phone, the one who was with you at Millgarth. What's her name again?'

'Annie. Annie Cabbot.'

'Good-looking woman?'

'I suppose so.'

'You involved with her?'

Banks paused. If he told Ken Blackstone the truth, that would be *one* person too many who knew about them. But why keep it a secret? Why lie? Ken was a mate. He nodded briefly.

'Is it serious?'

'For crying out loud, Ken, I've only known her a week.'

Blackstone held his hand up. 'Okay, okay. Is she the first one since Sandra?'

'Yes. Well, apart from a mistake one night. Yes. Why?'

'Just be careful, that's all.'

'Come again?'

Blackstone leaned back in his chair. 'You're still vulnerable, that's what I'm talking about. It takes a long time to get over a relationship as long-lasting and as deep as yours and Sandra's.'

'I'm not sure how deep it went, Ken. I'm beginning to think I believed what I wanted to believe, missed the signposts to the real world.'

'Whatever. All I'm saying is that when someone goes through what you're going through, he either ends up angry at women for a long time or he misses what he had. Or both. If he's angry, then he probably just shags them and leaves them. But if he misses the relationship, then he looks for another one to replace it, and his judgment is not necessarily in the best of nick. If he's both, then he gets into another relationship and fucks it up royally all round and wonders why everyone ends up in tears.'

Banks pushed his chair back and stood up. 'Well, thanks for the amateur psychology, Ken, but if I'd wanted Claire fucking Rayner—'

Blackstone grabbed on to Banks's sleeve. 'Alan. Sit down. Please. I'm not suggesting you do anything except be aware of the pitfalls.' He smiled. 'Besides, you're bloody-minded enough to do what you want in any situation, I know that. All I'm saying is think about what you want and why you want it. Be aware of what's going on. That's all the wisdom I have to offer. You've always struck me as a bit of a romantic underneath it all.'

Banks hesitated, still half ready to leave and half ready to punch Blackstone. 'What do you mean?'

'The kind of detective who cares just a bit too much about every victim. The kind of bloke who falls a little bit in love with every woman he sleeps with.'

Banks glanced at Blackstone through narrowed eyes. 'I haven't slept with that many women,' he said. 'And as for—'

'Sit down, Alan. Please.'

Banks paused for a moment. When he felt the anger sluice away, he sat.

'What does she feel about it all?'

Banks reached for a cigarette. He felt uncomfortable, as if he were in the dentist's chair and Blackstone were probing a particularly sensitive nerve. He had never been good at talking about his feelings, even with Jenny Fuller, who *was* a psychologist. It was something he had in common with most of his male friends, and it gave him a special solidarity with Yorkshiremen. He should have remembered that Ken Blackstone was a bit artsy, read Freud and that sort of thing. 'I don't know,' he said. 'I haven't asked her. We haven't really talked about it.'

Blackstone paused. Banks lit his cigarette. On a night like this one was shaping up to be, he might go over his allowance. 'Alan,' Blackstone went on, 'ten months ago you thought you had a stable marriage of more than twenty years' standing, house, kids, the full Monty. Then, all of a sudden, the carpet's pulled out from under you and you find you've got nothing of the kind. The emotional fall-out from that sort of upset doesn't go away overnight, mate, I can tell you. And believe me, I speak from experience. It takes years to get it out of your system. Enjoy yourself. Just don't make it more than it is. You're not ready to deal with that yet. Don't confuse sex and love.' He slapped the table. 'Shit, now I *am* starting to sound like Claire Rayner. I didn't really want to get into this.'

'Why did you start it, then?'

Blackstone laughed. 'God knows. Because I've been there, maybe? Bit of personal therapy? Like anything, it's probably more about me than you. Maybe I'm just jealous. Maybe I wouldn't mind sleeping with an attractive young DS myself. Lord knows, it's been a bloody long time. Ignore me.'

Banks finished his pint and put the glass down slowly. 'Look, I take your point, Ken, really I do, but to be honest, it's the first time I've felt comfortable with a woman since Sandra left. Not comfortable, so much, that's not the right word. Annie's not a woman you necessarily feel comfortable with. She's a little weird. Bit of a free spirit. Very private. Hell, though, it's the first time I've really felt free enough to jump into something and say damn the consequences.'

Blackstone laughed and shook his head slowly. 'Sounds like you've got it bad.' He looked at his watch. 'What say we hit the fleshpots of Leeds and get irredeemably pissed?'

Banks smiled. 'Most sensible thing you've said all night. Let's do it.'

'And I've got a fine malt tucked away at home for afters.'

'Even better. Lead on.'

•

Winter finally gave way to a slow spring, with its snowdrops in Rowan Woods, then the bluebells, crocuses and daffodils. Brad and Charlie became our regular 'beaux' and we saw far less of Billy Joe, who became very sulky after he found he had lost Gloria to a pilot.

The Americans always seemed more casual about rank, unlike the English. I suppose it is because our class system instilled it in us from birth, while Americans were all created equal, or so they say. It must be nice for them; it would probably be confusing for *us*. But it's one thing for officers and enlisted men to eat, drink and billet together and quite another for a second lieutenant to steal a mere sergeant's girl.

I was worried that Billy Joe would start a fight, given his violent streak, but he soon found another girl and even started talking to us again when we met at dances and in pubs. He pestered Gloria on occasion to go back with him, or at least just to sleep with him again, but she was able to keep him at bay, even when she'd been drinking.

PX, of course, remained absolutely essential, so we made sure we still cultivated him. As none of us had actually gone out with him, anyway, we had no reason to think our new relationship with Brad and Charlie would have any effect on the friendship, and it didn't seem to.

I won't say that my affair with Charlie was a grand passion, but we became less awkward with the physical side of things as time went on, and he did become the first man I ever slept with. He was gentle, patient and sensitive, which was exactly what I needed, and I came to look forward to those times we spent in bed together at Bridge Cottage, courtesy of Gloria.

Our relationship remained more of an intellectual one;

we passed books back and forth with abandon: Forster, Proust, Dostoevsky. Charlie wasn't dull and dry, though; he loved to dance and was a great Humphrey Bogart fan. He took me to see *Casablanca* and *The Maltese Falcon*, even though he had seen them both before. He was also far more passionate about classical music than I was, and we sometimes went to concerts. Once, I remember, we went all the way to Huddersfield to see Benjamin Britten conduct his own *Hymn to St Cecilia.*

In all the excitement we were probably guilty of neglecting the people who had been good to us in the worst days after Matthew's disappearance, especially Michael Stanhope. We redeemed ourselves with him a little when he had an exhibition in Leeds. Charlie and I made a weekend of it and went to stay at the Metropole Hotel.

Charlie, who knew a lot more about painting than I did, praised the exhibition to the skies and I think Mr Stanhope was rather taken with him. Even Gloria went to see Mr Stanhope at his studio that summer and autumn far more often than she had before.

I tried not to dwell on the dangers inherent in Charlie's job, and for his part, he never seemed to want to talk about them. The war receded into the distance during those hours we spent together reading or making love, though it was difficult to ignore the rest of the time. The Americans were carrying out precision daylight bombing raids over Germany, often without fighter cover, and their casualties were appalling. Instead of listening to the drone of the planes taking off after dark, I now heard them in the mornings. The Flying Fortresses were much louder than the RAF planes that had been there before. They would warm up the engines at about five o'clock, which was the time I usually awoke anyway, and I would lie there stealing an extra few

minutes of warmth and imagine Charlie checking his maps
and preparing himself for another raid.

Charlie told me that up around twenty thousand feet
they were flying at temperatures of between minus 30 and
minus 50 degrees Fahrenheit. I couldn't imagine anything
that cold. He had to wear long woollen underwear and
electrically heated flying suits under his fleece-lined leather
jacket. I had to laugh when he said it would take him half an
hour to get undressed and into bed with me.

And so life went on. Books. Bed. Pictures. Dances.
Concerts. Talk. Double summertime began on the second
of April that year, giving us the long spring evenings to go
for walks to pick wild flowers in Rowan Woods or idle
down by the river. In May, when it was warmer, we would
often sit on the banks of Harksmere and read Coleridge and
Wordsworth out loud to one another. We had picnics of
Spam and potted-shrimp sandwiches on the terraces just off
The Edge.

Mother liked Charlie, I could tell, though she didn't say
much. She never did. Matthew's disappearance had taken
most of the wind out of her sails. But Charlie brought her
Lifesavers and Hershey bars, and she thanked him and ate
them all.

After the excitement of the Normandy landing, we soon
got back to reality: the summer of the doodlebugs. We only
experienced one V-1 rocket in Hobb's End, one which had
badly lost its way.

I was standing on the fairy bridge chatting with Cynthia
Garmen. It was a typical July day: muggy, with dark, leaden
clouds and the threat of storm. We were talking about the
Japanese defeat at Imphal, wishing Matthew could have
been there to experience it, when we heard the awful sound
in the sky, like a motorcycle without a silencer. All of a

sudden it spluttered to a stop. Then there was a dreadful silence. We could see it by then, a dark, pointed shape beginning the silent arc of its descent.

Fortunately, it fell in one of the fields between Hobb's End and Harkside without exploding, and by the time we had rushed down to see what was going on, the local ARP people already had the area cordoned off and were waiting for the UXB team to arrive.

The advance continued, and slowly things began to improve. The blackout was replaced by the 'dim-out' in September, but most of us left the curtains up anyway and didn't get round to taking them down until the following year. If by autumn, then, we were feeling flush with the possibility of victory, we had little idea of the grim winter to come.

•

By ten o'clock that night Annie was feeling so restless that even a large glass of wine didn't help settle her down.

She knew what part of the problem was: Banks. When he told her he was going out boozing with a mate instead of going to dinner with her, she *did* feel pissed off with him. She felt disappointed that he would rather go drinking with someone else than be with her, especially at such an early and delicate stage in their relationship. True, it was she who had suggested they limit their time together to weekends, but it was also she who had broken the rule the other night. Why couldn't he do the same tonight?

But at least she hadn't wasted *her* time that evening.

The long trail that had started on Wednesday, over the telephone, was beginning to bear fruit.

At first, she had come to the conclusion that it was easier finding a fully dressed woman in the *Sunday Sport* than getting information out of the American Embassy. People were polite – insufferably so – but she was shunted from one minion to another for the best part of an hour and came out with nothing but an earache and a growing distaste for condescending and suspicious American men who called her 'ma'am'.

By the end of the day, she had managed to discover that the personnel at Rowan Woods in late 1943 would have been members of the United States Eighth Air Force, and it was very unlikely that there would be any local records of who they were. One of the more helpful employees suggested that she try contacting the USAFE base in Ramstein and gave her the number.

When she got back from the Leeds council estate, even though it was early evening, she phoned Ramstein, where she discovered that all air force personnel records were kept at the National Personnel Records Center in St Louis, Missouri. She checked the time difference and found that St Louis was six hours behind Harkside. Which meant it would be afternoon there.

After a little more shunting around and a few abrupt requests to 'please hold', she was put through to a woman called Mattie, who just 'adored' her accent. They chatted about the differences in weather – it was raining hard in St Louis – and about other things for a short while, then Annie plucked up the courage to ask for what she wanted.

Expecting some sort of military smoke screen, she was pleasantly surprised when Mattie told her that there was no problem; the records were generally available to the public, and she would see what she could do. When Annie mentioned the initials 'PX', Mattie laughed and said that was the man who looked after the store. She also warned Annie that some of their records had been burned in a fire a few years ago, but if she still had Rowan Woods, she'd set the fax to send it out during the night. Annie should get it the next morning. Annie thanked her profusely and went home feeling absurdly pleased with herself.

But it didn't last.

Sometimes when she felt irritable and restless like this, she would go for a drive, and that was exactly what she did. Without making a conscious decision, she took the road west out of Harkside, and when she reached the turn-off for Thornfield Reservoir, she turned right.

By then she had realized that Banks wasn't the problem; *she* was. She was pissed off at herself for letting him get to her. She was behaving like some sort of silly love-struck schoolgirl. Vulnerable. Hurt. Let's face it, Annie, she told herself, life has been pretty simple, pretty much regimented for some time now. No real highs; no real lows. Only herself to think of. Manageable, but diminished.

She had been hiding from life in a remote corner of Yorkshire, protecting her emotions from the harsh world she had experienced 'out there'. Sometimes when you open yourself up to that life again, it can be confusing and painful, like when you open your eyes to bright light. Your emotions are tender and raw, more than usually sensitive to all its nuances, its little hurts and humiliations. So that was what was happening. Well, at least she knew that much. So much for cool, Annie, so much for detachment.

A misshapen harvest moon hung low in the western sky, bloated and flattened into a red sausage shape by the gathering haze. Otherwise the road was unlit, surrounded on both sides by tall dark trees. Her headlights caught dozens of rabbits.

She pulled into the car park and turned off the engine. Silence. As she got out and stood in the warm night air, she started to feel at peace. Her problems seemed to slip away; one way or another, she knew they would sort themselves out.

Annie loved being alone deep in the countryside at night, where you might hear only the very distant progress of a car, the rustles of small animals, see only the dark shapes of the trees and hills, perhaps a few pinpricks of light from farmhouses on distant hillsides. She loved the sea at night even more – the relentless rhythm of the waves, the hiss and suck, and the way the reflected moonlight sways and bends with the water's swell and catches the crests of the waves. But the sea was fifty miles away. She would have to make do with the woods for now. The appeal was still to the deep, primitive part of her.

She took the narrow footpath towards Hobb's End, walking carefully because of the gnarled tree roots that crossed it in places and the stones that thrust up out of the dirt. Hardly any moonlight penetrated the tree cover, but here and there she caught a slat or two of reddish-silver light between branches. She could smell the loamy, earthy smell of trees and shrubs. The slightest breeze butterfly-kissed the upper leaves.

When Annie reached the slope, she paused and looked down on the ruins of Hobb's End. It was easy to make out the dark, skeletal shape, the spine and ribs, but somehow tonight, with the slight curve of the High Street and the dry river-bed, the ruins looked more like the decayed stubs of teeth in a sneering mouth.

Annie skipped down the slope and walked towards the fairy bridge. From there, she looked along the river and saw the blood-red moonlight reflected in the few little puddles of water that remained on its muddy bed. She walked on past the outbuilding where Gloria's skeleton had been found, and the ruins of Bridge Cottage next to it. The ground around had all been dug up and was now taped off for safety. The SOCOs from headquarters had brought their own crime-scene tape. She headed down what was once the High Street.

As she went, Annie tried to visualize the scene from Michael Stanhope's painting: children laughing and splashing in the river shallows; knots of local women gossiping outside a shop; the butcher's boy in his blood-stained apron riding like the wind; the tall young woman arranging newspapers in a rack. *Gwynneth Shackleton*. That was who it was. Why hadn't she realized it before? Somehow, the revelation that Stanhope had also painted Gwen Shackleton into his scene thrilled her.

She looked at the ruins to her right and saw where once was a detached cottage with a little garden, once a row of terrace houses opening directly on to the pavement. This was where the ginnel led off to the tanner's yard; here was the Shackletons' newsagent's shop, here the butcher's, and a little farther down stood the Shoulder of Mutton, where the sign had swayed and creaked in the wind.

So real did it all seem as she walked towards the flax mill that she began to fancy she could even hear long-silent voices whispering secrets. She passed the street that led to the old church and stood at the western end of the village, on that stretch of empty ground where the houses ended and the land rose towards the mill.

As she stood and breathed in the air deeply, she realized how much she wanted to know what had happened here, every bit as much as Banks did. Without her wishing for it, or asking for it, Hobb's End and its history had imposed themselves on her, thrust themselves into her consciousness and become part of her life. It had happened at the same time that Banks had become part of her life, too. She knew that, whatever became of them, the two events would be united in her mind for ever.

When she had challenged him on *his* obsession with it the other night, she hadn't even attempted to explain hers. It wasn't because of the war, but because she identified with Gloria. This was a woman who had struggled and dared to be a little different in a time that didn't tolerate such behaviour. She had lost her parents, then had either abandoned or been cast out by the father of her child, had come to a remote place, taken on a hard job and fallen in love. Then she had lost her husband in the war, or so she must have believed. If Gloria had been still alive when Matthew came back, then she would have had to face a stranger, most likely. Whatever else happened, someone strangled her, stabbed her nearly twenty times and buried her under an outbuilding. And nobody had tried to find out what happened to her.

Suddenly, Annie noticed a movement and saw a figure scuttle across the fairy bridge towards the car parks. Her blood froze. At that moment, she became a little girl frightened of the dark, and she could believe that witches, demons and hobgoblins haunted Hobb's End. She was the whole length of the village away, so what she saw was nothing more than a fleeting silhouette.

Finding her voice, she called out. No answer came. The figure disappeared up the slope into the woods. Annie set off in pursuit. With every stride, the policewoman in her started to overcome the scared, superstitious girl.

Just when she had got back up the slope and was heading for the woods, she heard a car start ahead of her. There were two small car parks, separated by a high hedge, and whoever this was must have been parked in the other one, or Annie would have seen the car earlier.

She put on an extra burst of speed but could only get to the road in time to see the tail-lights disappearing. Even in the moonlight, all she could tell was that the car was dark in colour. She stood there leaning forward, hands resting on her knees, getting her breath back and wondering who the hell could be in such a hurry to escape discovery.

12

'He asked me to marry him,' Gloria repeated.

'I still don't believe you,' I said.

'Well, you can ask him yourself. It's true.'

It was early in the new year, 1945, and I had dropped by Bridge Cottage one evening to see how Gloria was coping. She had had a terrible cold over Christmas – had even missed Alice Poole's farewell party – and the doctor said she had almost caught pneumonia. Though she was weak and pale and had lost some weight, she seemed to be on the mend.

'You should have seen my nose when he asked me. It was red-raw.'

I laughed. It was good to laugh at something. Christmas that year had been a miserable affair not only because it was the coldest one I could remember, but because the advance that had seemed to be going so well earlier had bogged down in the Ardennes. It was all right for Alice. Her Eric had been wounded there and shipped home. But how long was this bloody war going to drag on? Couldn't everyone see we had all had enough? Sometimes I felt that I had never even known life during peacetime.

'What did you say?' I asked.

'I told him I'd think about it, but he'd have to wait until the war was over, until we could find out for certain about Matt.'

'Do you love him?'

'In a way. Not . . . Oh, I mean I don't really think I could ever love anyone like I loved Matt, but Brad and I get on well enough, in *and* out of bed. I like his company. And he's good to me. When the war's over, he wants to take me back to Hollywood with him.'

'It'll be a new lease of life, I suppose.'

'Yes.'

'And I'll have someone I can visit out there.'

'You will.'

'But?'

'What do you mean?'

'I still sense a "but". You only told him you'd think about it.'

'Oh, I don't know, Gwen. You know I can't even consider getting married again until the war's over, for a start. But I will think about it. Oh, look what PX brought me when I was ill. Isn't he sweet?'

It was a box of chocolates. A bloody *box* of chocolates! I hadn't even seen a single chocolate in years. Gloria held out the box. 'Please, take one. Take them all, in fact. They'll only make me fat.'

'What about me?' I asked, picking out the caramel.

'You could do with a bit of meat on your bones.'

I threw the screwed-up wrapper at her. 'Cheeky.'

'Well, you could. What about Charlie?'

'Oh, he's still depressed about Glenn Miller disappearing.'

'That's not what I mean, and you know it. Has he asked you yet?'

I'm sure I blushed. 'No,' I said. 'We haven't talked about marriage.'

'Books, that's all you two ever talk about.'

'It's not.'

She smiled. 'I'm teasing, Gwen. I'm glad you're happy. Honest, I am.'

'We still haven't talked about marriage.'

'Well, there's no hurry, I suppose. But you could do a lot worse. A lawyer! He'll be rich, just you wait and see.'

'Money isn't everything.'

'It certainly helps. Anyway, you can go to America, too, and be a rich lawyer's wife. We can see each other all the time. Have lunch together.'

'Gloria, Boston is miles away from Los Angeles.'

'Is it? Well, at least we'll be in the same country.'

And so we chatted on about love and marriage and what the future might offer us. Gloria soon recovered her health, and the round of dances, films and pub nights started all over again. February brought the prospect of victory closer and I actually began to believe that we were entering the last spring of the war.

Everything changed one grey afternoon in March, when a tall, gaunt stranger walked down the High Street towards me, struggling against the wind.

•

Banks really must have had a night on the tiles, Annie thought, pursing her lips and tapping her pen against the side of her thigh. It was after nine, and he wasn't in his office yet. Was he still in Leeds? Had he and his friend picked up some women?

She fought back the acid-burn of jealousy that curdled in her stomach. Jealousy and suspicion had ruined relationships for her before. Just before Rob got killed she had suspected he was seeing someone else and had consequently treated him badly. She thought she had conquered her feelings by now, thought she had learned detachment, but perhaps she had only put her insecurity in mothballs, along with everything else, since she had transferred to North Yorkshire. It was a frightening thought. Until she had met Banks, she had imagined she was in control, doing just fine.

Annie remembered she was supposed to check on the Gwen Shackleton/Vivian Elmsley link. First, she phoned Ruby Kettering, who said – as expected – that it was so long ago she couldn't even remember what Gwen looked or sounded like. Besides, Gwen would have only been fifteen then. Elizabeth Goodall told Annie that she had no idea who Vivian Elmsley was, and Alice Poole said that with her poor eyesight she couldn't be relied upon to tell Queen Elizabeth from Prince Charles.

Next, Annie phoned Millgarth and asked to speak to DI Blackstone. He told her Banks was on his way back to Eastvale. She could have sworn he was suppressing laughter as he said it. They had probably been talking about her; images of Banks telling all the steamy details to his pal after a few pints made her face burn and her throat constrict. All of a sudden, her pleasure in wanting to tell him about her success with USAFE evaporated.

Men, Annie thought. Never anything but bloody big kids when you got right down to it. And that was the most charitable view.

The fax machine hummed into action. Annie hurried over to see if it was the information from Mattie in St Louis. It was: a personnel breakdown of the 448th Bomber Group at Rowan Woods AAF base between 19 December, 1943, and 17 May, 1945, when they had left. There were a lot of names. Too many.

As she glanced over the list, Annie thought again about the Hobb's End incident last night. It had rattled her more than she realized at first, and she had had a difficult time getting to sleep. She didn't know why it should have affected her that way, apart from the misshapen red moon, the eerie atmosphere and the way the ruins had seduced her into believing in ghosts and goblins and things that go bump in the night. But ghosts and goblins don't run away and drive off in cars. Now, in the light of day, what bothered her most of all was *why* someone should hide from her in the first place, and then why take off like a bat out of hell when she gave chase?

There might be a simple explanation, of course. Whoever it was might have been more afraid of her than she was of him: a mischievous kid, perhaps. Given everything else they had discovered since Adam Kelly found the Hobb's End skeleton, however, Annie felt inclined to be more suspicious.

The answer still eluded her. There was nothing left at the site; the SOCOs had been over it thoroughly. Perhaps someone might *think* there was something there, though. Even so, how could anything buried there incriminate anyone living now? From what Annie had seen briefly of the figure last night, whoever it was hadn't been old enough to have murdered Gloria Shackleton over fifty years ago. People in their seventies or eighties don't usually move that fast.

So it remained a mystery. She wanted to talk to Banks about it, but he'd been off behaving like a silly kid getting pissed with his mates and telling tales about her sexual appetite and his ability to satisfy it. She hoped he had a hangover the size of China.

•

Debussy's chamber music for harp and wind instruments got Banks back to Gratly safe and sane via the slow back roads. He thought of stopping in at Harkside on his way to see how Annie was doing, but decided against it. He didn't want her to see him until he had at least managed a change of clothes. The ones he was wearing still stank of smoke and stale beer.

His head ached, despite the Paracetamol he had downed at Ken's flat that morning, and his mouth tasted like the bottom of a birdcage. When he had awoken and looked around Ken's living room, he had groaned at the detritus of a wild and foolish night: an empty bottle of Glenmorangie on the coffee table, alongside an empty bottle of claret and an overflowing ashtray. He didn't think the whisky bottle had been full when they got into it, but even a fifteen-year-old would have had more sense than to mix beer, wine and whisky that way.

Still, he had enjoyed what he remembered of their rambling talk about women, marriage, divorce, sex and loneliness. And there was wonderful music. Ken was an aficionado of female jazz singers – a vinyl-freak, too – and the LP sleeves scattered over the floor attested to this: Ella Fitzgerald, June Christy, Dinah Washington, Helen Forrest, Anita O'Day, Keely Smith, Peggy Lee.

The last thing Banks remembered was drifting off to late-period Billie Holiday singing 'Ill Wind', her smoked-honey voice beautifully mingling with Ben Webster's tenor sax. Then came oblivion.

He groaned and rubbed his stubbly face. All the hangover clichés ran through his mind, one after another: *You're getting too old for this sort of thing*; *Time you grew up*; and *I'll never touch another drop as long as I live*. It was a familiar litany of guilt and self-disgust. Last night would have to remain a one-off, a brief lapse, a necessary sacrifice to friendship.

As Banks emptied his pockets before dropping his jeans in the laundry basket – noticing how full it was getting – he found a slip of paper. On it was the name 'Maria' followed by a Leeds telephone number.

He racked his brains but he couldn't remember which one of the two girls they'd talked to in the Adelphi was Maria. Was it the petite blonde or the slender redhead with the freckles and the wide gap between her front teeth? He thought the blonde had been more interested in Ken, and he vaguely remembered them talking about the Pre-Raphaelites. If Maria was the redhead, she had a sort of Pre-Raphaelite look about her. Maybe that was how the subject had come up. No good. He couldn't remember. It had been that kind of night. He screwed up the slip of paper, aimed it at the waste-bin, then stopped, straightened it out and put it in the top drawer of his bedside table. You never know.

After a shave, a shower and a change of clothes, Banks drove to Eastvale and arrived at his office just after ten o'clock. He hardly had time to turn on his computer when his door opened and in strode Chief Constable Jeremiah 'Jimmy' Riddle himself, making one of his rare forays to Eastvale. Banks muttered a silent curse. Just what he needed, in his fragile state.

Banks looked up. 'Sir?'

'Banks, you look bloody awful,' said Riddle. 'What have you been doing, man? Drinking yourself silly?'

'Touch of flu, sir.'

'Flu, my arse. Anyway, that's your problem, you want to go on poisoning your liver.'

'What can I do for you, sir?'

'It's that skeleton case I gave you. Been all over the news lately. Attracting a lot of publicity. I hope you're on top of things?'

'Definitely, sir.'

'Good. I want you to bring me up-to-date. I've got to go to London today to tape an interview for "Panorama". They're putting together a special segment on the investigation of old cases, how DNA makes a difference, that sort of thing.' He brushed some imaginary fluff from the front of his uniform and glanced at his watch. 'I need an angle. And you'd better make it quick. My train leaves in an hour and a half.'

Well, be thankful for small mercies, Banks told himself. 'Where do you want me to begin, sir?' he asked.

'At the bloody beginning, man; where do you think?'

Banks told him what he and Annie had discovered so far from the SOCOs, from talking to Elizabeth Goodall and Alice Poole and from the visit to Leeds. When he had finished, Riddle ran his hand over his shiny bald scalp and said, 'It's not much to go on, is it? Memory of a couple of old biddies?'

'We're not likely to get much better,' said Banks. 'Not at this point. Too much time's gone by. I suppose you could make a point about how unreliable people's memories become over the years.'

Riddle nodded and made a note.

'Anyway, there's a lot we're still waiting on. We've got a report on Dr Williams's physical examination of the bones, but we're still waiting for the results of further tests both from him and our forensic odontologist. These things take time.'

'And cost money. It'd better be worth it, Banks. Don't think I'm not keeping my eye on the bottom line on this one.'

'We also found a button, possibly military, close to the body. She may have been holding it when she was killed. There's still a lot we don't know yet.'

Riddle rubbed his chin. 'Still,' he said, 'there's a good angle in what you've already told me. Nude paintings. Village scandals. Women playing around with Yanks. Yes. That's good stuff. That'll play. And give me a copy of the forensic anthropologist's report to read on my way. I want to sound as if I know what I'm talking about.'

You've been trying to do that for years without much success, Banks wanted to say, but he held his tongue and phoned the input clerk for a photocopy. Riddle could pick it up on his way out, seeing as he was in such a hurry. 'You mentioned DNA, sir,' he said. 'You might mention that we think her son is still alive and it would be a great help if he could get in touch with us. That way we could verify the identity of the remains once and for all.'

Riddle stood up. 'If I've got time, Banks. If I've got time.' He paused with his hand on the doorknob and half-turned. 'By the way,' he said. 'DS Cabbot. How's she working out?'

She. So he did know. 'Fine,' said Banks. 'She's a good detective. Wasted in a place like Harkside.'

A malicious smile flitted across Riddle's face. 'Ah, yes. Pity, really. I understand there was some trouble in her previous posting. Nice-looking girl, though, by all accounts?'

'Trouble, sir?'

'You should know all about that, Banks. Insubordination, failure to respect senior ranks.'

'I respect the rank, sir,' said Banks. 'But not always the person who fills it.'

Riddle stiffened. 'Well, I hope you're enjoying yourself

– for your sake, Banks – because this is about as good as it's going to get for you around here.'

With that he walked out and slammed the door.

Banks thought about what he had just heard. So Jimmy Riddle knew who Annie Cabbot was and had assigned him to work with her anyway. Why? Riddle already thought Banks was a rampant cocksman, making trysts with exotic Asians in Leeds during police time and basically shagging everything in a skirt. Riddle had also mentioned some trouble. What could all that be about?

Most of all, though, why would Riddle think that working with Annie Cabbot would be hell on earth for Banks? Because, if one thing was certain, hell on earth was all Riddle had in store for him.

On his way to the coffee machine, Banks bumped into DS Hatchley and asked him to find out what he could about Francis Henderson, Gloria's illegitimate child. It was probably a pointless exercise, but it was a loose end that nagged him.

Banks was still getting the hang of the station's new voicemail system, and was more often than not likely to forget about it or delete everything waiting for him, but that morning he got Annie's message loud and clear. The ice in her tone was enough to freeze his eardrum. There was also a message from a Major Gargrave, in military personnel. Banks phoned him first, building up the courage to call Annie later.

'It's about that query you made the other day,' said Major Gargrave. 'Matthew Shackleton.'

'Yes?'

'Well, it's all a bit embarrassing really.'

'He came back, didn't he? We found a death certificate dated 1950. I was going to ask you about it.'

'Yes, well, these things happen sometimes, you know. When my assistant was returning the file, he found some papers wedged down between two folders. It was because of the irregularity of it all, you see.'

'And a filing error.'

'Yes.'

'When did he return?' Banks asked.

'It was his sister who reported his return, actually. March 1945. Place called Hobb's End. Does that make any sense?'

'Yes,' said Banks. 'Go on.'

'I'm afraid there's not much more to tell, really. Sergeant Shackleton simply discharged himself from a London hospital and went home. The hospital said he'd been liberated from a Japanese POW camp in the Philippines and shipped home in pretty bad shape. No identification.'

'And that's all?'

'Yes. It would seem so. Very odd.'

'Okay,' said Banks, 'thanks very much for calling, Major.'

'No problem.'

After he hung up, Banks opened the window and let the sunshine in. He thought of lighting a cigarette but realized he didn't really feel like one. Too many last night. His throat and lungs still felt raw. There was something that didn't make sense in what the major had just told him; it was on the tip of his consciousness, but he couldn't quite force it out. Too many dead brain cells in the way.

Back at his desk, Banks steeled himself and picked up the phone. He was as ready as he would ever be for Annie now. She answered on the third ring.

'You're back, then,' was all she said.

'Yes.'

'Have a good time?'

'Pretty good, thanks.'

'Good. I'm glad.'

'I'd rather forget this morning, though.'

'You probably deserved it.'

'Probably.'

'I've got the info on the Rowan Woods personnel.'

'Wonderful.'

'It's a long list, though. It'll take a bit of whittling down. There was more than one person working in the PX, for a start.'

Banks sensed that her tone was softening a little. Should he tell her he had missed her last night? Or ask her what was wrong? Better hold off awhile. He ventured a tentative, 'Is there anything else?'

Annie told him about what happened at Hobb's End.

'What were you doing out there?' he asked.

'What does it matter? Maybe I just wanted to see what it looks like in the dark.'

'And?'

'It looks spooky.'

'It was probably just a kid.'

'I thought about that. It didn't look like a kid. And it drove away.'

'I've known ten-year-olds do that. Still, I take your point. There's not much we can do about it now, though, is there?'

'I just thought I'd let you know. For the record. It was interesting, that's all.'

'Sounds like it. Anything else?'

Annie told him about drawing a blank on trying to confirm Vivian Elmsley's identity through Ruby, Betty and Alice.

'We'd better track her down, anyway,' Banks said.

'I've already done that.'

'Now I'm *really* impressed.'

'So you should be. While you've been recovering from your self-inflicted damage, I've been on the phone.' Was there a hint of forgiveness there, perhaps? Depended how he played it: he needed to strike the right balance of remorse and praise, guilt and compliments.

'And?'

'Well, in her case it was easy. She's in the London telephone directory.'

'You didn't phone her, did you?'

'*Please*. Give me some credit. I'm not that gormless. But I've got her address. What do you want to do about it?'

'We should talk to her as soon as possible. If she really is the one we're looking for, she's holding something back. She might also know the names we want. There was another thing nagging at me a few minutes ago and I've just realized what it was.'

'Apart from the hangover?'

'Yes.'

'All right. What was it?'

Banks explained to her about the call from Major Gargrave. 'It's to do with the gun,' he said.

'What gun?'

'The one Matthew Shackleton's supposed to have shot himself with.'

'What about it? Handguns must have been common enough just after the war. You'd just had hundreds of thousands of *men* running around armed to the teeth killing one another, remember?'

'Yes, but why would Matthew have a gun?'

'I don't – wait a minute, I think I *do* see what you mean.'

'If he was a released POW, he'd hardly have his service revolver. I should imagine the Japanese confiscated the weapons off the people they captured, wouldn't you?'

'Unless his liberators gave him one?'

'I suppose that's remotely possible. Especially if they were Americans. Americans feel naked without guns.'

'But you don't think so?'

'I think it's highly unlikely,' said Banks. 'Why should they? And why would he still have it when he went back to Hobb's End from hospital? Anyway, it's a minor point, probably doesn't mean a thing.'

'If he did have a gun, though, why didn't he use that on Gloria instead of strangling her and stabbing her?'

'*If* it was Matthew who killed her.'

'Have you considered Gwen as a serious suspect?' Annie asked.

'Certainly. According to everything we've heard, she was very close to her brother. If Gloria was hurting him, running around with other men, Gwen might just have fought back on his behalf. At the very least she should be able to tell us more about Matthew's relationship with Gloria after he came back, assuming Gloria was still alive at the time. Fancy a trip to London tomorrow?'

'Who's driving?'

'We'll take the train. It's faster, and the London traffic's murder. If my memory serves me well, there's a train leaves York around a quarter to nine that'll have us at King's Cross by twenty to eleven. Can you manage that?'

'No problem. In the meantime I'll see if I can get any more information on the airmen.'

After Annie hung up, Banks walked over to the window

and looked out over the square, with its ancient market cross and square-towered church, grey-gold in the sunlight. He thought about Vivian Elmsley. Could she really be Gwen Shackleton? It seemed a preposterous idea, but stranger things had happened. He decided it wouldn't be a bad idea to have a go at one or two of Vivian Elmsley's books before he set off to interview her. Her writing might give him some insight into her character.

He tried dialling Brian's Wimbledon number again. Still nothing. Ken Blackstone was right, though; all he could do for the moment was keep on trying. If he was going to London tomorrow, he hoped he might be able to see Brian, have a talk, get things sorted. He didn't want Brian to keep on thinking his father was disappointed in him for what he was doing, the way Banks's own father always made clear his dismay at Banks's choice of career, even now, every time they met.

Banks went back to his desk. For about the third time since the case began, he spread out the objects found with Gloria Shackleton's body before him. Not much for the remnants of a life, or the detritus of a death: a locket whose original heart shape had been squashed and bent; a corroded wedding ring; clips from a brassière or suspenders; a pair of tiny, deformed leather shoes, which reminded him of the ones he had seen at the Brontë parsonage once; a few scraps of blackout cloth; and the button from Adam Kelly, greenish-blue with verdigris. Superintendent Gristhorpe might be able to tell him a bit about the button, he thought. Gristhorpe was a bit of an expert on military history, especially the Second World War.

Banks grabbed his jacket and was just about to leave the office when his phone rang.

'Hello, Alan.'

A woman's voice.

'Yes?'

'It's me. Jenny. Jenny Fuller. Don't you recognize my voice?'

'Jenny. It's been a long time. Where are you?'

'Home. Just got back yesterday. Look—'

'A bit early, aren't you?'

'It's a long story.'

'I'm glad you called. I need some advice.'

'If it's personal, I'm the last person to ask, believe me.'

'Professional?'

'I might be able to manage that. The reason I was phoning is, I know I shouldn't bother you at work and all, but I'm in town and I wondered if you've got time for lunch?'

Banks had intended to drive out to Lyndgarth to see Gristhorpe, who was taking his annual holidays at home, but that could wait until after. 'Queen's Arms, half-twelve?'

'Wonderful. I'll see you there.'

Banks smiled as he put down the receiver. He hadn't seen Jenny Fuller in almost a year, not since she'd decided to take a leave of absence from the University of York to teach in California. That was around the time he and Sandra had split up. He had received a couple of postcards asking how he was doing, but that was all.

Jenny was one of the two women his colleagues expected him to sleep with after Sandra left. Perhaps he would have slept with her if she had been around. But timing is everything. Jenny was spending most of her time in California these days, and there was a man at the bottom of that. The other friend, Pamela Jeffries, feeling restless and hemmed in, had taken off to play in an orchestra in Australia, of all places, and he hadn't seen her for months. Again, he got the occasional postcard from such exotic locales as Sydney, Melbourne, Adelaide and Perth. It made him want to travel more, too.

Now he and Jenny were having lunch in about an hour's time. Just enough time, in fact, to prepare his questions on Matthew Shackleton and nip over to Waterstone's for a couple of Vivian Elmsley's novels.

•

For some reason I was standing out in the street to check the window display (which was pretty meagre) when I glanced to my left and saw him coming across the fairy bridge. I had just heard the train arrive, so I assumed that he had come from the station. The wind howled around the chimneys, and clouds as black as a Nazi's heart besmirched the sky like grease stains. There was nobody else about. That was why I noticed him. That, and the fact that he was wearing only an over-large, baggy brown suit and carrying no luggage.

He was tall but stooped, as if suffering some affliction of the spine, and he walked with a sturdy stick. He moved slowly, almost like a figure in a dream, as if he knew where he was going, but felt no hurry to get there. His frame was thin to the point of emaciation. As he came closer, I realized that he wasn't as old as I had first thought, though his lank, lifeless hair was tinged here and there with grey, or white.

The wind tugged at my hair and clothes and chilled me to the marrow, but something about him compelled me to stand and watch, as if in a trance. When he got within a few feet of the shop, I saw his eyes. Deep, hollow, haunted eyes, turned completely inward, as if he was subjecting himself to a most intense and unflinching scrutiny.

He saw me, though, and he stopped.

I don't know when the truth dawned on me; it could have been seconds; it could have been minutes. But I started to shake like a leaf and it had nothing to do with the cold. I ran to him and threw my arms around him but his body felt stiff and unyielding as a tree. I caressed his cheek with my palm, noticing the puckered white scar that curved up from the side of his mouth in an ugly parody of a grin. Tears were pouring down my cheeks.

'Matthew!' I cried. 'Oh my God. Matthew!' And I took his arm and led him inside to Mother.

•

Banks walked into the Queen's Arms a couple of minutes before twelve-thirty carrying two of Vivian Elmsley's paperback mysteries in his Waterstone's bag. He bought a pint and sat down at a table near the empty fireplace. Jenny was always late, he remembered, opening the bag and looking at the books.

One was a suspense novel called *Guilty Secrets* – certainly an interesting title from Banks's point of view – which bore review quotes from the *Sunday Times*, *Scotland on Sunday*, the *Yorkshire Post* and the *Manchester Evening News*, all to the general effect that it was an 'amazing' and 'disturbing' achievement by one our best mystery writers, a true equal of P. D. James and Ruth Rendell.

The other was called *The Shadow of Death* and featured her regular series character, Detective Inspector Niven. In this one, he was called on to investigate the murder of an up-market Shepherd's Bush restaurateur. Banks didn't even know that such a creature existed. As far as he could remember, there weren't any up-market restaurants in

Shepherd's Bush. Still, it was a long time since he'd been there, so he gave her the benefit of the doubt. Anyway, the novel was praised for its 'compassionate realism in the portrayal of ordinary people' and its 'believable depictions of policemen's lives and police procedures'. Banks smiled. He'd see about that. On the cover was a picture of the handsome, craggy-faced young actor who, so the blurb informed Banks, played DI Niven in the television series. And got paid far more than a real copper did.

He was on page ten when Jenny dashed in, out of breath, tousled red hair flaming around her face as she looked this way and that. When she saw him she waved, patted her chest and hurried over. She bent and gave him a quick peck on the cheek. 'Sorry I'm late. My God, you look awful.'

Banks smiled and raised his glass. 'Hair of the dog.'

Jenny picked up the paperback he had set down on the table and turned up her nose. 'I didn't think this sort of thing was up your alley.'

'Work.'

'Aha.' She raised her eyebrows. The California tan looked good on her, Banks thought. The sun hadn't burned her, the way it did with most redheads, only darkened the natural creams and reds of her complexion and brought out her freckles, especially across her nose. Her figure looked as good as ever in tight black jeans and a loose jade silk top.

'So,' Banks said, when Jenny had settled herself down and deposited her oversized shoulder bag on the floor beside her. 'Can I get you a drink?'

'Campari and soda, please.'

'Food?'

'Scampi and chips. I've been craving scampi and chips for about a month now.'

'Scampi and chips it is.' Banks made his way to the bar, got them each a drink and ordered the food. There were a few more exotic dishes finding their way on to the menu these days, like fajitas and Thai noodles, but Banks finally settled for plaice and chips. It wasn't that he had anything against exotic food, but from experience he didn't trust the pub version of it. Besides, he could still taste the curry he had eaten in Leeds last night.

He carried the drinks back and found Jenny poring over *The Shadow of Death*, one hand holding her hair back from her eyes. When he approached she flashed him a quick smile and closed the book. 'I think I saw this on TV over there,' she said, touching the cover. 'On PBS. They interviewed her afterwards. Vivian Elmsley. She's very popular in the States, you know. Quite a striking woman.'

Banks told her briefly about the case so far, including the possibility of Vivian Elmsley's having a role in the affair. By the time he had finished, their food arrived.

'Is it as good as you remembered?' he asked after she had taken a couple of bites.

'Nothing ever is,' Jenny said. He noticed a new sadness and weariness in her eyes. 'It's good, though.'

'What happened over there?'

'What do you mean?' She glanced at him, then looked away quickly. Too quickly. He saw fear in her eyes.

He thought of the very first time he had met her in Gristhorpe's office, shortly after he had first arrived in Eastvale, how he had been struck by her sharp intelligence and her quick sense of humour, as well as her natural beauty, the flaming red hair, full lips and green eyes with their attractive laugh lines.

Jenny Fuller had been thirty-one then; she was nearly thirty-eight now. The lines had etched themselves a little deeper, and they weren't so easy to associate with laughter any more. His first impression had been that she was a knockout. He felt exactly the same today. They had come close to an affair, but Banks had backed off, unwilling to commit himself to infidelity. He had been different then, more confident, more certain of what his life was all about and where it was going. Life had been simpler for him then, or perhaps he had approached it on more absolute terms. It had *seemed* simple, at least: he loved Sandra and believed she loved him; therefore, he didn't want to do anything to jeopardize that, no matter how tempting. They had just moved up from London, where Banks felt he was quickly burning out, to a less hectic region, partly to save their marriage. And it had worked, up to a point. Seven years.

Against all odds, Banks and Jenny had remained friends. Jenny had become friends with Sandra, too, though Banks got the impression they had drifted apart over the past two or three years.

'Come on, Jenny,' he said. 'This sudden return wasn't on the agenda. I thought you'd become a California beach bunny for good.'

'*Beach bunny?*' Jenny laughed. 'I guess I just didn't quite make the grade, did I?'

'What do you mean?'

She sighed, looked away, tried to form some words, sighed again, then laughed. There were tears in her eyes. She seemed a lot more twitchy than he remembered, always moving her hands. 'It's all washed up, Alan. That's what I've been meaning to say.'

'What's all washed up?'

'All of it. The job. Randy. My life.' She cocked her head. 'I never did have much luck with men, did I? I should have listened to you years ago.'

There was no arguing with that. Banks remembered one or two of Jenny's disasters that he had been around to mop up after.

Jenny pushed her plate aside, scampi and chips unfinished, and took a long swig of Campari and soda. Her glass was almost empty; Banks still had the best part of his pint left. He didn't want any more. 'Another?' he asked.

'Am I becoming an alcoholic, too? No, don't answer that. I'll get it myself.' Before he could stop her, she stood up and headed for the ladies' loo.

Banks finished his plaice and chips and looked at the back cover of *The Shadow of Death* on the table beside him. 'A masterpiece.' 'Top-rate work.' 'A must read.' The critics obviously loved Vivian Elmsley. Or were the brief quotes cunningly edited from less flattering sentences? 'Whereas Dostoevsky wrote *a masterpiece*, Vivian Elmsley can be said to have written only a pot-boiler of the lowest kind.' Or 'Had this book shown even the slightest sign of literary talent or creative imagination, I would not have hesitated to declare it a *must read* and a piece of *top-rate work*, but as it possesses neither of these qualities, I have to say it's a dud.'

When Jenny came back, she had repaired what little damage the tears had caused to her makeup. She had also picked up another Campari and soda.

'You know,' she said, 'I've been imagining sitting here and talking this over with you like this all the way over on the plane. Picturing how it would be, just you and me here in the Queen's Arms, like old times. I don't know why I found it so difficult. I think I might still be jet-lagged.'

'Take it easy,' said Banks. 'Just tell me what you want to, at your own pace.'

She smiled and patted his arm. 'Thanks. You're sweet.' She snatched a cigarette from his packet and lit up.

'You don't smoke,' Banks said.

'I do now.' Jenny blew out a long plume. 'I've just about had it up to here with those nico-Nazis out there. You can't smoke anywhere. And to think California was a real hotbed of protest and innovation in the sixties. It's like a fucking kindergarten run by fascists now.'

He hadn't heard Jenny swear before. Something else new. Smoking, drinking, swearing. He noticed that she wasn't inhaling, and she stubbed the cigarette out halfway through. 'As I'm sure you've gathered already,' she went on, 'Randy, my main man, my paramour, my significant other, my reason for staying out there as long as I did, is no longer a part of my life. The little shit.'

'What happened?'

'Graduate students. Or, to put it more bluntly, blonde twenty-something bimbos with their brains between their legs.'

'I'm sorry, Jenny.'

She waved her hand. 'I should have seen it coming. Anyone else would have. Anyway, soon as I found out about what he was up to, there wasn't much to keep me there. After I confronted him with the evidence, my dear Randy made damn sure I wasn't going to be offered another year's visiting lectureship.'

'What are you going to do?'

'Well, thank God they're not all like that. I'll be going back to my old lecturing job at York. Start next month. If that doesn't work out, I'll hang up my sign next door to the cop shop and go into private practice. I'm quite the expert on deviants and criminal psychology, should you happen to have such a creature as a serial killer lurking in the general vicinity. I've even been on training courses with the FBI profilers.'

'I've heard that's all a load of bollocks,' said Banks. 'But I'm impressed. Sorry we don't have anything at the moment.'

'I know – don't call us . . . Story of my life.'

'I don't think you'll have any problem staying in work, Jenny, but if there's ever anything I can do . . .'

'Thanks. You're a pal.' She patted his hand.

'I do want to ask your advice on something.'

'Go ahead. I'm finished blubbering and moaning. And I didn't even ask about you. I haven't seen you since Sandra left. How are *you* doing?'

'I'm doing fine, thanks.'

'Seeing anyone?'

Banks paused a moment. 'Sort of.'

'Serious?'

'What kind of a question is that?'

'So it *is* serious. How about Sandra?'

'Do you mean is *she* seeing anyone? Yes, she is.'

'Oh.'

'It's okay. I'm fine, Jenny.'

'If you say so. What was it you wanted to ask me?'

'It's about Matthew Shackleton. Gwen's – possibly Vivian Elmsley's – brother. Apparently he was captured by the Japanese and spent a few years in one of their prison camps. By all accounts, he was pretty disturbed when he came home. Ended up committing suicide five years after the war. Thing is, all I can come up with in terms of psychiatric diagnoses are such vague terms as "shell shock".'

'I thought that went out with the First World War?'

'Apparently not, they just changed the name to "battle fatigue" or "combat fatigue". I was wondering what sort of diagnosis you'd come up with today.'

'That's a good one, Alan.' Jenny pointed her thumb at her chest. 'You want me, a *psychologist*, to come up with a *psychiatric* diagnosis of a dead man's mental problems? I like that, I really do. That takes the biscuit.'

Banks grinned. 'Oh, don't be such a nitpicker, Jenny.'

'This had better be between you and me.'

'Cross my heart.'

Jenny toyed with her beer mat, ripping off little pieces of damp cardboard. 'Well,' she said, 'I'm only guessing, you understand, but if your man had indeed been a prisoner of war under such terrible conditions, then he was probably suffering from some kind of post-traumatic stress disorder.'

Banks took his notebook from his inside pocket and jotted a few words down.

'Don't you dare quote me on this,' Jenny warned him. 'I told you, it's strictly between you and me.'

'Don't worry, you won't be called upon to testify in court. I realize this is pure speculation. Anyway, it all happened a long time ago. This condition would have been caused by his experiences in the war and the camp, right?'

'Right. Basically, PTSDs are caused by some event or series of events well beyond the normal range of human experience. Maybe we should redefine exactly what that means these days, given the state of the so-called normal world, but it generally refers to extreme experiences. Things that go way beyond marital breakdowns, broken love affairs, simple bereavement, chronic illness or bankruptcy. The things most of us suffer from on a daily basis.'

'That bad?'

Jenny nodded. 'Things like rape, assault, kidnapping, military combat, floods, earthquakes, fires, car crashes, bombing, torture, death camps. The list of divine and human atrocities goes on and on, but I'm sure you get the picture.'

'I get the picture. What are the symptoms?'

'Many and varied. Recurrent nightmares about the event are common. As is feeling that the event is recurring – things like flashbacks and hallucinations. Anything that reminds the person of the event is painful, too, such as an anniversary. Also things that were part of it. If a man was kept in a small cage for a long period, for example, then he would be likely to experience suffocating claustrophobia whenever those conditions were approximated. Maybe in a lift, for example.'

'What about amnesia?'

'Yes, there's psychological memory loss sometimes. Believe me, most of the people who suffer from this would find the memory loss preferable to the persistent nightmares. But the problem is that strong feelings of detachment, estrangement and separation come with it. You can't even enjoy your lack of recollection of the horror. People who suffer from PTSDs often find it difficult to feel or accept love, they become alienated from society, from their families and loved ones, and they have an extremely diminished sense of the future. Add to that insomnia, difficulty in concentrating, hypervigilance, depressive or panic disorders.'

'Sounds like me.'

'Much worse. Suicide is also not uncommon. He's a suspect, I assume?'

'Yes. That was another thing I wanted to ask you. Might he be likely to become violent?'

'That's a difficult one to answer. Anyone can become violent given the right stimulus. He would certainly be prone to irritability and outbursts of anger, but I'm not sure they'd necessarily lead him to murder.'

'I was thinking he might have killed his wife because he found out she'd been having an affair.'

'I suppose it's possible he got a bee in his bonnet about it,' Jenny said.

'But you don't think so?'

'I didn't say that. Let me just say I hold reservations. Don't forget the constraints you've got me working under.'

'I won't. Tell me about your reservations.'

'The outbursts of anger in PTSD are usually fairly irrational. By linking them to his wife's behaviour, you're making it all far more logical, do you see? Cause and effect.'

'Yes.'

'And the other thing is that if he did feel detached and was unable to love, then where does the hate come in? Or the jealousy?'

'So could he or couldn't he?'

'Oh, no, you're not trapping me like that. Of course he *could* have committed murder. People do all the time, often for no reason whatsoever. Yes, he could have heard about his wife having it off with some other bloke and as a result he could have, quite reasonably, come to hate her and to want rid of her. Or he could have just done it in an outburst of irrational rage, for no apparent reason.'

'Whoever did it probably strangled the woman, at least until she was unconscious, then stabbed her about fifteen or sixteen times.'

'Such rage. I don't know, Alan. From what you've told me about this man, and from what I know of PTSD, I'd say that most of his pain and anger would have been directed inward, not out at the world. While I wouldn't rule it out, I'd maybe hedge on the side of saying it's unlikely he would have killed that way for that reason. But it's hard to say anything about someone you've never met, never had the chance to talk to. Also, it's often too easy to pick on the mentally disturbed person as the most likely murderer. Most mentally ill people wouldn't harm a fly. I'm not saying all of them – there are some really sick puppies out there who manage to keep it well hidden – but most of the obvious ones are harmless. Sad and pathetic, perhaps, sometimes even a little scary, but rarely dangerous.'

'Thanks. You've given me a lot to think about.'

'Well, I'm just glad I can still be of some use to somebody.'

They both sat in silence, nursing what was left of their drinks. Banks thought about Matthew Shackleton's suffering and about what Jenny had said about his possible alienation, his estrangement from the world of normal human affairs. Maybe that could have made a killer out of him and maybe not. If you couldn't feel love for someone, why would you feel hate? When Banks first found out about Sandra and Sean, he had hated them both because he still loved Sandra. If he hadn't cared, he wouldn't have felt so passionate. Now, the feelings were receding into the distance. He wasn't sure if he loved Sandra any more. At least he was trying to make a life without her, reinventing and discovering himself. If she came and asked him to take her back tomorrow, he honestly didn't know what he would do.

'I fell apart, you know,' Jenny said suddenly, startling him out of his train of thought.

'You did what?'

She played with her hair. A number of expressions

battled for pride of place on her face. A sort of crooked grin won out. 'I had a breakdown. After all that with Randy. I suddenly found myself alone out there, completely cut off from everything and everyone I'd grown up with, alone in a foreign country. It's one of the scariest feelings I've ever had. I mean, they speak sort of the same language and all, but that only makes things worse, like a parody of all you've known. I'm not making myself clear . . . I felt like I was on another planet, a hostile one, and I couldn't get home. I fell to pieces.' She laughed. 'Do you know the song?'

'I've heard it,' said Banks, who tried to avoid country and western music the way he did a dose of clap.

'Well, I've done it.' She shook her head slowly. 'I even went to see a shrink.'

'Do any good?'

'Some. One of the things I realized was that I wanted to go home. I mean, that wasn't part of being ill. The desire was real and perfectly reasonable. It wasn't just Randy or not having the contract renewed, I could have got a teaching job somewhere else if I'd wanted. But I *missed* this place too much. Can you believe it? I actually missed overcooked scampi and chips. And, bloody hell, wouldn't you know it if I didn't miss winter too. It gets you down, all that sun, day in, day out, only the occasional flood, fire or earthquake for variety. Pretty soon you begin to feel like you're living in some kind of suspended animation, like everything's on hold. Or maybe you're not really living at all, you're in limbo. You keep telling yourself one day the snow's going to come, but it never does. Anyway, as soon as I realized what I really wanted to do, I gave myself the best therapy I could think of. I chucked my tranquillizers down the toilet and took the next flight home. Well,

almost the next flight. I had a few things to do first –
including, I'm almost ashamed to admit, a little act of
girlish revenge on poor, dear Randy.'

'What did you do?'

Jenny paused for a moment, then licked her lips and
flashed him a wicked grin. 'I planted one of those little
voice-activated tape recorders in his office and taped one
of his trysts. Then I retrieved the machine and sent the
tape to the dean.'

'In his *office*?'

'Yes. Over the desk. Don't be such a prude, Alan. It
happens all the time over there. What are offices for? Oh,
you should have heard them: "Give it to me, big boy. Fuck
me. Go on. Oh, yeah. Stick that big hard cock in me. Go
deep. Fuck me harder."'

Her voice had risen, and one or two tourist families
looked at her uncomfortably. 'Oops, sorry,' she said,
putting her hand over her mouth. 'Wash your mouth out,
Jenny Fuller. Anyway, there was no mistaking whose
voices they were.'

'What happened?'

'I don't know. I left before the shit hit the fan. So if I get
murdered, you know where to start looking. I should
imagine he got suspended. Maybe fired. Of course, it was
hardly evidence you could use at a tribunal, but they can
get quite stroppy about things like that over there. Fucking
your students is almost as bad as being caught smoking in
a restaurant.' She tossed back the rest of her drink and
looked at her watch. 'Look, I'm sorry, I'll have to go. The
university's been very good to me so far, but they won't
continue to be unless I get my courses prepared. It's great
seeing you again.'

She picked up her bag, paused and rested it on her lap.

Then she looked Banks in the eye, reached out and touched his hand softly and said, 'Why don't you give me a ring? We could . . . you know, have dinner or something together, if that's okay?'

Banks swallowed. 'I will. That would be great. And you've got to come out and see the cottage.'

'I'd love to.' She patted his hand, blew him a kiss and then she was gone in a whirl of red, jade and black, leaving a faint trace of Miss Dior behind in the smoky air. Banks looked down at his hand. It still tingled where she had touched him. Now that he had found the courage and desire to start a relationship with Annie, Jenny was a complication he didn't need. But she was a friend; he couldn't turn his back. And there was no reason at all why Annie should object to his having dinner with her. Even so, he felt more confused than he had half an hour earlier as he picked up his books and left the pub.

13

It took some time, but after I had run and fetched Gloria from the farm, I was finally able to piece together what had happened. Matthew himself wouldn't say a word. He looked at us as if he remembered knowing us once, as if some sort of deep homing instinct had brought him here, but our fussing didn't make much sense to him.

Gloria and Mother comforted him while I went down to the telephone and began the long round of calls. The Ministry was about as much help as usual, the Red Cross a little more forthcoming, but it was ultimately a doctor in one of the big London hospitals (for it was clear Matthew was ill and had probably discharged himself from hospital) who told me the most.

At first, he didn't know whom I was talking about, because they didn't know the name of the man who had walked out of the hospital yesterday. When I described Matthew, however, he was certain we were talking about the same person.

Matthew had been found, along with several other British and Indian soldiers, at a Japanese POW camp near Luzon, in the Philippines. All his identification was missing, and all anyone could tell about him, from the scraps of his uniform that remained, was that he was British. He hadn't spoken to any of the other prisoners and none of them had been captured in the same place or at the same time as he had. Consequently, nobody knew where he had come from or who he was.

When I asked the doctor why Matthew wouldn't speak and why he also refused, when offered pen and paper, to write anything down, he paused, then said, 'He's probably suffering from some form of combat fatigue. That's why he won't communicate. There may be other problems, but I'm afraid I can't be any more specific than that.'

'Is that why he refuses to talk?'

He paused again, longer this time, then went on slowly, 'I'm sorry to say, but when we gave him a thorough physical examination, one of the things we found was that his tongue had been cut out.'

I could think of nothing to say. I stood there, head spinning, clinging to the telephone as if it were all that was holding me to the earth.

'Miss Shackleton? Miss Shackleton? Are you there?'

'Yes . . . I'm sorry . . . Please go on.'

'I'm the one who should be sorry. It must have sounded so abrupt and callous to you. I didn't know how else to tell you. If you only knew . . . some of the lads we've got in here. Well . . . I apologize.'

'That's all right, Doctor. So Matthew is physically incapable of talking?'

'Yes.'

'But he could write if he wanted?'

'There's no reason why not. There's some damage to the fingers of his left hand, as if they have been broken and badly reset, but his right hand is fine, and as far as I can tell, he seems to be right-handed. Am I correct?'

'Yes, Matthew's right-handed.'

'All I can assume then is that he simply chooses not to communicate.'

'What should we do?'

'What do you mean?'

'Well, he ran away, didn't he? Should we send him back?'

'I can't see much point in doing that,' said the doctor. 'And, quite frankly, we need all the beds we can get. No, physically, there's nothing more we can do for him. There's some deformity of the spine, probably due to being forced into a cramped environment, like a box or a cage, for long periods of time. A pronounced limp in the left leg, caused by an improperly set fracture. He was also shot in the arm and the abdomen. The wounds are healed now, though by the looks of the scars the surgery was of a poor quality.'

I swallowed, trying not to think of all the suffering poor Matthew must have gone through. 'And mentally?'

'As I said, we don't really know what's wrong. He refuses to communicate. It's a good sign that he came home, though. He knew his way and he negotiated the journey with what little money he took.'

'Took?'

'Ah, yes. Please don't worry about it. We hadn't supplied him with any clothes or money. He took another patient's suit before he left.'

'Will there—'

'Don't worry. The other patient is most understanding. He knows something of what your brother has been through. Please don't worry about it any further.'

'But the money?'

'There wasn't much. Enough for his train fare and perhaps a bite to eat.'

'He doesn't look as if he's eaten in months. Is there any treatment? Will he get better?'

'It's impossible to say. There are treatments.'

'What sort of treatments?'

'Narcosynthesis is the most common.'

'And that is?'

'A drug-induced re-enactment of the traumatic episode, or episodes. It's used to assist the ego to accept what happened.'

'But if you don't know what the traumatic episode was . . .?'

'There are ways of getting at that. But I don't want to get your hopes up. The problem is, of course, that Matthew can't express himself vocally, and that could mean a severe limitation in the value of narcosynthesis.'

'What do you suggest?'

'I suggest you tell me where you live and I'll do my best to put you in touch with a doctor who knows about these things.'

I told him where I lived and where it was.

'It may mean visits to Leeds,' he said.

'That will be no problem.'

'I promise I'll get working on it. In the meantime, just take good care of him. I don't think I need to tell you that he has suffered appallingly.'

'No. Thank you, Doctor.' I put down the receiver and went back upstairs.

Matthew was sitting staring towards the window, though not through it, and Mother and Gloria seemed at their wits' end.

'I've tried to talk to him, Gwen,' Gloria said, voice quivering. 'I don't think he even knows me. I don't think he even knows where he is.'

I told her some of what the doctor had said. 'He came back here, didn't he?' I said, to comfort her. 'He made his way here by himself. It was the only place he knew to come. Home. Don't worry, he'll be fine now he's back with the people who love him.'

Gloria nodded, but she didn't seem convinced. I couldn't blame her; I wasn't convinced, either.

•

It was a long time since Banks had driven up the rutted driveway in front of Detective Superintendent Gristhorpe's squat stone house on the daleside above Lyndgarth.

As expected, he found Gristhorpe out back working on his dry-stone wall. Walling was a hobby the superintendent had taken up years ago. It was the ideal pointless activity; his wall went nowhere and fenced nothing in. He said he found it relaxing, like some form of meditation. You could just empty your mind and get in harmony with the natural world. So he said. Maybe the super and Annie would have a lot in common.

Gristhorpe was wearing a baggy pair of brown corduroy trousers held up by frayed red braces, and a checked shirt that might once have had a white background. He was holding a triangular lump of limestone in his hand and squinting at the wall. When Banks approached, he turned. His pockmarked face was redder than usual after the sun and exertion. He was also sweating, and his unruly mop of thatched hair lay plastered to his skull. Was it a trick of the light, Banks wondered, or was Gristhorpe suddenly looking old?

'Alan,' he said. It wasn't a greeting, or a question. Just a statement. Hard to tell anything much from the flat tone.

'Sir.'

Gristhorpe pointed towards the wall. 'They say a good waller doesn't put a stone aside once he's picked it up,' he said, then looked at the rock in his hand. 'I wish I could figure out where to put this bugger.' He paused for a moment, then he tossed the stone back on the pile, slapped his hands on his trousers to get rid of the dust and walked over. 'You'll have a glass of something?'

'Anything cold.'

'Coke, then. I've got some in the fridge. We'll sit out here.' Gristhorpe pointed to two fold-up chairs in the shade by the back wall of the old farmhouse.

Banks sat down. He thought he could see some tiny figures making their way along the limestone escarpment that ran along the top of Fremlington Hill.

Gristhorpe came out with two glasses of Coke, handed one to Banks and sat down beside him. At first, neither of them spoke.

Finally, Gristhorpe broke the silence. 'I hear Jimmy Riddle's given you a real case to work on.'

'Sort of. I'm sure he thinks of it as more of a dead end.'

Gristhorpe raised his bushy eyebrows. 'Is it?'

'I don't think so.' Banks told Gristhorpe what he and Annie Cabbot had discovered so far and handed him the button Adam Kelly had taken from the skeleton's hand. 'It's impossible to say,' he went on, 'but it *might* have been in the victim's hand. It was certainly buried with her, and it didn't walk there. She could have ripped it from her attacker's uniform when she was being strangled.'

Gristhorpe examined the button and took a sip of Coke. 'It looks like an American Army Air Force button,' he said. 'I could be wrong – it's so old and corroded it's hard to tell – but that design looks like the American eagle. It's not what the husband would have been wearing, even if he had been in uniform. Not from what you've told me. And it's very unlikely that he would have been in uniform if he had been liberated from a Japanese POW camp and repatriated.'

'So you think it's American?'

Gristhorpe weighed the metal in his palm. 'I wouldn't swear to it in court,' he said. 'The American armed forces were very casual dressers compared to our lot. Most of the time they wore "Ike jackets" with hidden front buttons, but this could have come from the collar. Usually it was worn on the right side. Officers wore them left or right, with the branch of service below. GIs not assigned to any specific service wore the eagle on both sides.'

'If she was being strangled,' said Banks, 'then it's quite likely she reached out to try to scratch her attacker's face and grab at his collar. Gloria and her friends went around with a group of American airmen from Rowan Woods.'

Gristhorpe handed back the button. 'It sounds like a reasonable theory to me.'

'There's another thing that puzzles me. Matthew Shackleton committed suicide in 1950. Shot himself. I'm wondering where he got the gun.'

'Anyone can get a gun if he wants one badly enough. Even today.'

'He was in no state to go out and buy one on the black market, even if he knew where to look.'

'So you're assuming he already had it?'

'Yes, but he wouldn't have had one in the prison camp, would he?'

'He could have got it from someone on his way home. Long journey, lots of opportunities.'

'I suppose so. All we know is that he went missing presumed dead in Burma in 1943, turned up at Hobb's End again in March 1945, then committed suicide in Leeds in 1950. It's a long gap.'

'What kind of gun was it?'

'A Colt forty-five automatic.'

'Really?'

'Yes. Why?'

'That was the gun the American military issued their servicemen. It raises interesting possibilities, doesn't it? American button in the wife's hand. American gun in the husband's mouth.'

Banks nodded. Though what the possibilities were, he hadn't a clue. The two events were separated by five years, more or less, and happened in different places. He sipped some more Coke.

'How's Sandra?' Gristhorpe asked.

'Fine, as far as I know.'

'I'm sorry about what happened, Alan.'

'Me, too.'

Gristhorpe gazed at a point in space somewhere above Fremlington Edge. 'This Annie Cabbot,' he said. 'What's she like?'

Banks felt himself blush. 'She's good,' he said.

'Too good for a God-forsaken outpost like Harksmere?'

'I think so.'

'Then what's she doing there?'

'I don't know.' Banks glanced sideways at Gristhorpe. 'Maybe she pissed somebody off, like I did.'

Gristhorpe narrowed his eyes. 'Alan,' he said, 'I don't approve of what you did last year, taking off like that without so much as a by-your-leave. You dropped me right in it. I can see why you did it. I might even have done it myself in your place. But I can't condone it. And while it pulled your chestnuts out of the fire in one sense, it's probably dropped them in it in another way.'

'What do you mean?'

'Jimmy Riddle already hated you. He also hates being proved wrong, especially *after* he's done his crowing to the press. Your maverick actions helped solve the case, but now he hates you even more. I can't do anything for you. You must be aware your grasp at Eastvale is pretty tenuous, to say the least.'

Banks stood up. 'I'm not asking for any favours.'

'Sit down, Alan. Hear me out.'

Banks sat and fumbled for a cigarette. 'I'd probably have looked for a transfer before now,' he said, 'but I've had a few other things on my mind.'

'Aye, I know. And I know you'd not ask for any favours, either. That's not your way. I might have a bit of good news for you, though, if you can promise to keep it to yourself.'

'Good news. That makes a change.'

'Between you and me and the stone wall, Jimmy Riddle might not be around much longer.'

Banks could hardly believe his ears. '*What*? Riddle's retiring? At his age?'

'A little bird tells me that the crooked finger of politics beckons. As you know, he can't enter into that as a copper, so you tell me what the logical solution is.'

'Politics?'

'Aye. His local Conservative member is practically gaga. Not that anyone would notice something like that much in the House. High-echelon rumour has it that Riddle has already had several interviews with the selection committee and they're pleased with him. Like I said, Alan, this is just between you and me.'

'Of course.'

'There's no guarantee he'll go. Or get elected, for that matter. Though the Conservative seat around here is so secure they could put Saddam Hussein up and he'd probably win it. Even if Riddle does go, he'll leave a bad smell around and swear it's yours. So I'm not saying there's no damage done. For a start, a lot depends on whether we get a CC who can tell the smell of shit from perfume.'

Banks began to feel a sort of warm glow deep inside. An interesting case. Annie Cabbot. Now this. Maybe there was a God, after all. Maybe his dry season really was coming to an end.

'Do you know,' he said, 'it might even be worth voting Conservative, just to make sure the bastard wins his seat.'

•

Charlie was killed on the nineteenth of March during a big raid over Berlin. Their Flying Fortress got badly shot up by a Messerschmitt. Brad managed to fly the burning aeroplane back across the Channel and land in an airfield in Sussex, only to find Charlie and two other members of his crew dead. Brad himself escaped with cuts and bruises and after a couple of days' observation in hospital, he returned to Rowan Woods.

Coming right after Matthew's return, this news was almost impossible for me to bear. Poor, gentle Charlie, with his poetry and his puppy-dog eyes. Gone.

When Brad got back from Sussex, he came over to the shop with a bottle of bourbon and told me the news in person. Though he had only known Charlie a couple of years, during that time they had become close friends. He tried to explain the kind of bond that is forged between pilot and navigator. I could tell he was devastated by what happened. He blamed himself and felt guilty about his own survival.

Gloria was busy taking care of Matthew and she had told Brad she couldn't see him again, that it would only upset her and would do them no good. Brad was angry and upset about her rejection, but there was nothing he could do except come to me and pour his heart out.

We sat in the small room above the shop after Mother had gone to bed, drank bourbon and smoked Luckies. We had the Home Service on the wireless and Vivien Leigh was reading poetry by Christina Rossetti and Elizabeth Barrett Browning. Neither of us said very much; there was nothing, really, *to* say. Charlie was gone, and there was an end to it. Poetry filled our periods of silence.

Not far down the High Street, Gloria – who adored Vivien Leigh, I remembered from our very first meeting – was devoting her time to caring for a man who couldn't speak, wouldn't communicate and probably didn't even know who she was. She was spoon-feeding him, bathing him, for all I knew, with no end in sight. That was what our lives had been reduced to by the war: the essence of misery and hopelessness.

The bottle lay empty; my head spun; the room reeked of cigarette smoke. "'How do I love thee? Let me count the ways,'" read Vivien Leigh. How Charlie hated such maudlin poetry. I let my head rest on Brad's shoulder and cried.

•

Banks went home early on Thursday evening. He didn't need to be in his office to prepare a list of questions for Vivian Elmsley, and he was far more comfortable at the pine table in his kitchen, a mug of strong tea beside him, Arvo Pärt's *Stabat Mater* on the stereo, and the early evening light, gold as autumn leaves, flooding through the window behind him.

When he had made a list of the essential things he

wanted to know, he went through to the living room and tried Brian's number yet again.

On the fifth ring, someone answered.

'Yeah?'

'Brian?'

'Andy. Who's calling?'

'His father.'

Pause. 'Just a sec.'

Banks heard muffled voices, then a few moments later, Brian came on the phone. 'Dad?'

'Where've you been? I've been trying to get in touch with you all week.'

'Playing holiday resorts in South Wales. We were doing some gigs with the Dancing Pigs. Look, Dad, I told you, we've got gigs coming out of our ears. We're busy. You weren't interested.'

Banks paused. He didn't want to blow it this time, but he was damned if he was going to grovel to his own son. 'That's not the point,' he said. 'I don't think it's out of line for a father to express some concern at his son's sudden change of plans, do you?'

'You know I'm into the band. You've always known I've loved music. Dad, it was *you* who bought me that guitar for my sixteenth birthday. Don't you remember?'

'Of course I do. All I'm saying is that you have to give it a little time to sink in. It's a shock, that's all. We were all expecting you to come out with a good degree and start working at a good firm somewhere. Music's a great hobby but a risky living.'

'So you keep saying. We're doing all right. Anyway, did you always do what your parents wanted you to?'

Low blow, Banks thought. *Almost never* would have been the truth, but he wasn't ready to admit to that. 'Not always,' he said. 'Look, I'm not saying you aren't old enough to make your own decisions. Just think about it, that's all.'

'I *have* thought about it. This is what I want to do.'

'Have you spoken to your mother?'

Banks swore he could almost hear the guilt in Brian's pause. 'She's always out when I call,' he said at last.

Bollocks, Banks thought. 'Well, keep trying.'

'I still think it would come better from you.'

'Brian, if it's your decision, you can take responsibility for it. Believe me, it *won't* come any better from me.'

'Yeah, yeah. Fine. All right. I'll try her again.'

'You do that. Anyway, the main reason I'm calling is that I'll be down in your neck of the woods tomorrow, so I wondered if we could get together and talk about things. Let me buy you a pint.'

'I don't know, Dad. We're really busy right now.'

'You can't be busy *all* the time.'

'There's rehearsals, you know . . .'

'Half an hour?'

Another pause followed. Banks heard Brian say something to Andrew, but he couldn't catch what it was. Then Brian came back on again. 'Look,' he said, 'tomorrow and Saturday we're playing at a pub in Bethnal Green. If you want to come and listen, we can have that pint during the break.'

Banks got the name of the pub and the time and said he'd do his best.

'It's all right,' said Brian. 'I'll understand if something else comes up and you can't make it. Wouldn't be the first time. One of the joys of being a copper's son.'

'I'll be there,' said Banks. 'Goodbye.'

It was almost dark by now. He took his cigarettes and

small whisky and went outside to sit on the wall. A few remaining streaks of crimson and purple shot the sky to the west and the waning moon shone like polished bone over the valley. The promise of a storm had dissipated and the air was clear and dry again.

Well, Banks thought, at least he had talked to Brian and would get to see him soon. He looked forward to hearing the band. He had heard Brian practising his guitar when he lived at home, of course, and had been impressed by the way he had picked it up so easily. Unlike Banks.

Way back in the Beatles days, when every kid tried to learn guitar, he had managed about three badly fingered chords before packing it in. He envied Brian his talent, perhaps in the same way he envied him his freedom. There had been a time when Banks had also contemplated the bohemian life. What he would actually have *done*, he didn't know; after all, he had no facility for music or writing or painting. He could have been a hanger-on, perhaps, a roadie, or just a real cool guy. It didn't seem to matter back then. But Jem's death soured the dream for him and he ended up joining the police. He was living with Sandra, too, by then, wildly in love and thinking seriously, for the first time in his life, of a real future together with someone. Kids. Mortgage. The lot. Besides, deep down, he knew he needed a career with some sort of disciplined structure, or God knew what would happen to him. He didn't really fancy the armed forces, and with images of the never-to-be-found Graham Marshall in his mind, that left the police. Mysteries to solve; bullies to send down.

Maybe he should have followed his original impulse and dropped out, he thought, looking back and considering all that had happened lately. But no. He wasn't going to fall into that trap. It would be far too easy. He had chosen the life and the job he had wanted – had two great kids and a slightly shop-soiled career to show for it – and he couldn't imagine himself doing anything else.

Nobody had ever promised him it was going to be a breeze. The dark moods, depressions that settled upon him like a flock of crows, would disappear eventually; the sense of futility, the feeling that the dark pit of his despair actually *had* no bottom would also dissipate over time. As Brian had said when Banks had first told him about the separation from Sandra, he just had to *hang in* there, hang in there and make the best of what he had: the cottage, Annie, a challenging case.

An agitated curlew screeched and shrieked way up the daleside. Some animal threatening its nest, perhaps. Banks heard his phone ring again. Quickly, he stubbed out the cigarette and went back inside.

'Sorry to disturb you at this time of night, sir,' said DS Hatchley, 'but I know you're off to London in the morning.'

'What is it?' Banks looked at his watch. Half past nine. 'It's not like you to be working so late, Jim.'

'I'm not. I mean, I wasn't. I was just over at the Queen's Arms with a couple of mates from the rugby club, so I thought I'd pop in the station, like, and see if I'd got any answers to my inquiries.'

'And?'

'Francis Henderson. Like I said, I know you're off down there tomorrow, so that's why I'm calling. I've got an address.'

'He lives in London?'

'Dulwich.' Hatchley read the address. 'What's interesting, why it came back so quick, is he's got form.'

Banks's ears pricked up. 'Go on.'

'According to Criminal Intelligence, Francis Henderson started working for one of the East End gangs in the sixties. Not the Krays, exactly, but that sort of thing. Mostly he dug up information for them, found people they were after, watched people they wanted watched. He developed a drug habit and started dealing to support it in the seventies. They say he's been retired and clean for years now, at least as far as they know.'

'Sure it's *our* Francis Henderson?'

'Yes, sir.'

'Okay. Thanks a lot for calling, Jim. Get yourself home now.'

'Don't worry, I will.'

'And give another push on that nationwide tomorrow if you can find time.'

'Will do. *Bon voyage.*'

14

Annie was waiting on the platform at York Station looking very businesslike in a navy mid-length skirt and silver-buttoned blazer over a white blouse. She had tied her hair back so tightly it made a V on her forehead and arched her dark eyebrows. For once, though, Banks didn't feel under-dressed. He wore a lightweight cotton summer suit and, with it, a red and grey tie, top shirt button undone.

'Good Lord,' she said, smiling, 'I feel like we're sneaking away for a dirty weekend.'

Banks laughed. 'If you play your cards right . . .'

The station smelled of diesel oil and ancient soot from the days of steam. Gouts of compressed air rushed out from under the trains with a deafening hiss, and pigeons flapped around the high ceiling. Announcements about late arrivals and departures echoed from the public address system.

The London train pulled out of the station only eleven minutes after the advertised departure time. Banks and Annie chatted for a while, lulled by the rattling and rocking rhythm, and Banks ascertained that whatever had been bothering Annie on the phone yesterday was no longer a problem. He had been forgiven.

Annie started reading the *Guardian* she had bought at the station news-stand and Banks went back to *Guilty Secrets*. In bed the previous evening, he had given up on *The Shadow of Death* when the erstwhile DI Niven arrested his first suspect, saying, 'You have the right to remain silent. If you don't have a lawyer, one will be provided for you.' So much for the realistic depiction of police procedures. Allowing that it was one of her early DI Niven books and feeling that she deserved a second chance, he started *Guilty Secrets*, her most recent non-series book, and had trouble putting it down to get to sleep.

The basic plot device was the kind of thing everyone has seen a dozen times on television. A man on holiday in a foreign country becomes involved in an altercation with another man in a crowded bar. He tries to calm the situation and eventually leaves, but the man pursues him outside and attacks him. Someone else, a stranger, comes to his aid, and together they get carried away and beat the attacker to death. They hide the body, then go their separate ways, and nothing more is heard of the incident.

Back in England, the first man becomes very successful in business and is poised at the edge of what promises to be an equally successful career in politics. Until the inevitable blackmailer turns up. What does he do? Pay up or kill again?

Despite the thinness of the plot, *Guilty Secrets* turned out to be a fascinating exploration of conscience and character. Because of the situation he finds himself in, the central character is forced to re-examine his entire life in relation to the crime he got away with, while at the same time agonizing over what to do to secure his future.

To complicate matters, killing does not come easy to this man; he is human, with a firm, if understated, belief in Christianity. At one point he considers letting it all come out so that he can pay the consequences he feels he should have paid years ago. But he also likes his life the way it is. Not without a streak of self-interest, he is ambitious, enjoys power and feels he can do the country some genuine good if he gets in the right position. He also has others to consider: family and employees who rely or depend on him for their livelihoods.

Chapter after chapter, with merciless compassion, Vivian Elmsley strips the man to his soul, lays bare his moral and spiritual dilemmas and tightens the net around him. In his time, Banks had arrested a number of men who had killed to protect their ill-gotten fame or fortune, or both, but rarely had he come across a character as complex as the one Vivian Elmsley had created here. Perhaps he just hadn't looked deeply enough into them. A police interview room was not the best place to get to know someone, and Banks had been far more concerned with obtaining a confession than with striking up a relationship. That was where real life and fiction parted ways, he thought; one is messy and incomplete, the other ordered and finished.

Banks finished the book just before Peterborough. Annie had closed her eyes by then and was either napping or meditating. He gazed out of the window at the uninspiring landscape of his childhood: a brick factory, a red-brick school, stretches of waste ground littered with weeds and rubbish. Even the spire of the beautiful Norman cathedral behind the shopping centre failed to inspire him. The train squealed to a halt.

Of course, it hadn't been so uninspiring back then; his imagination had imbued every miserable inch of the place with magical significance. The waste grounds were battle-fields where the local lads re-enacted the great battles of two world wars, using tree branches or sticks of wood for rifles, bayoneting opponents with great relish. Even when Banks was playing alone or fishing in the River Nene, it was easy enough for him to believe he was an Arthurian knight on a quest. Adam Kelly had been doing the same thing in Hobb's End when the world of his imagination had suddenly become real.

As the train left Peterborough Station, Banks thought of his parents, not more than a mile away. He looked at his watch. About now, he guessed, his mother would be drinking milky instant coffee and reading her latest women's magazine, and his father would be having his morning nap, snoring gently, feet up on the green velour pouffe, newspaper spread over his lap. Unchanging routine. It had been the same since his father was made redundant from his job as a steelworker in 1982, and his mother grew too old and tired to clean other people's houses any more. Banks thought of the disappointment and bitterness that had twisted their lives, problems that he had certainly contributed to, as well as Margaret Thatcher. But their disappointments had been visited on him, too, in turn. No matter how well he did, it was never good enough.

Even though Banks had 'bettered' himself – he had a secure job with a steady source of income and good opportunities for advancement – his parents didn't approve of his joining the police. His father never tired of pointing out the traditional opposition between the working classes and the police force. When the riot police on overtime taunted striking miners by waving rolls of five-pound notes at them in the '84 strike, he accused Banks of being 'the enemy' and tried to persuade him to resign. It didn't matter that Banks was working the drugs squad on the Met at the time and had nothing to do with the troubles up north. As far as his father was concerned, the police were merely Maggie's bully-boys, the enforcers of unpopular government policies, oppressors of the working man.

Banks's mother, for her part, took a more domestic view and relayed tales of police divorces she heard about over the grapevine. Being a policeman wasn't a good career choice for a family man, she never ceased to tell him. Never mind that it was over twenty years later when he and Sandra split up – most of that time relatively successful as modern marriages go – his mother took great satisfaction that she had finally been vindicated.

And there lay the main problem, Banks thought as he watched the city disappear behind him. He had never been able to do anything right. When bad things happened to other kids, parents usually took their side, but when bad things happened to Banks, it was his own fault. It had always been that way, ever since he started getting cuts and bruises in schoolyard fights, always him who must have started it, whether he did or not. As far as his parents were concerned, Banks thought, if he got killed on the job, *that* would probably be his own fault too. When it came to blame, they offered no quarter for family.

Still, he thought, in a way that was what made him good at his job. When he had been junior in rank, he had never blamed his bosses when things went wrong, and now he was DCI, he took the responsibility for his team, whether it consisted of Hatchley and Susan Gay or just Annie Cabbot. If the team failed, it was *his* failure. A burden, yes, but also a strength.

King's Cross was the usual madness. Banks and Annie negotiated their way through the crowds and the maze of tiled, echoing tunnels to the Northern Line and managed to cram into the first Edgware-bound train that came along.

A few minutes later, they came out of Belsize Park tube station, walked up Rosslyn Hill and turned into the side-street where Vivian Elmsley lived. Banks knew the area vaguely from his years in London, though after Notting Hill, he and Sandra had mostly lived south of the river, in Kennington. Keats used to live near here, Banks remembered; it was in one of these streets that the poor sod fell in love with his next-door neighbour, Fanny Brawne.

A woman's voice answered the intercom.

There was a long pause after Banks had stated his rank and his business, then a more resigned voice said, 'You'd better come up.' The lock buzzed and Banks pushed open the front door.

They walked up three flights of thickly carpeted stairs to the second-floor landing. That this was a well-maintained building was clear from the fresh lemon scent, the gleaming woodwork and freshly painted walls, decorated here and there with a still-life print or a seascape. Probably cost an arm and a leg, but then Vivian Elmsley could no doubt afford an arm and a leg.

The woman who opened the door was tall and slim, standing ramrod-straight, her grey hair fastened in a bun. She had high cheekbones, a straight, slightly hooked nose and a small, thin mouth. Crow's-feet spread around her remarkable deep blue eyes, slanted at an almost oriental angle. Banks could see what Elsie Patterson meant: if you were at all observant, there was no mistaking those eyes. She was dressed like a jogger, in baggy black exercise trousers and a white sweatshirt. Still, he supposed, it didn't matter what you wore if all you had to do was sit around and write all day. Some people have all the luck.

She looked tired. Bags puffed under her eyes, and broken blood vessels criss-crossed the whites. She also looked strained and edgy, as if she were running on reserves.

The flat was Spartan and modern in its furnishings, chrome and glass giving the small living room a generous sense of space. A framed print of one of Georgia O'Keeffe's huge yellow flowers hung on the wall over the mantelpiece.

'Please, sit down.' She gestured Banks and Annie towards two matching chrome-and-black-leather chairs, then sat down herself, clasping her hands on her lap. They looked older than her face, skeletal and liver-spotted. They were also unusually large for a woman's hands.

'I must admit, I'm quite used to talking to the police,' she said, 'but usually I'm the one questioning them. How can I help you?'

Banks remembered the police procedure in *The Shadow of Death* and bit his tongue. Maybe she hadn't known any police officers when she wrote that book. 'First of all,' he asked, 'are you Gwynneth Shackleton?'

'I was, though most people called me Gwen. Vivian is my middle name. Elmsley is a pseudonym. Actually, it's my mother's maiden name. It's all perfectly legal.'

'I'm sure it is. You grew up in Hobb's End?'

'Yes.'

'Did you kill Gloria Shackleton?'

Her hand went to her chest. 'Kill Gloria? Me? What a suggestion. I most certainly did not.'

'Could Matthew, your brother, have killed her?'

'No. Matthew loved her. She looked after him. He *needed* her. I'm afraid this is all rather overwhelming, Chief Inspector.'

'No doubt.' Banks glanced at Annie, who remained expressionless, notebook on her lap. 'May I ask why you haven't come forward in response to our requests for information?' he asked.

Vivian Elmsley paused before answering, as if composing her thoughts carefully, the way she might revise a page of manuscript. 'Chief Inspector,' she said, 'I admit that I have been following developments both in the newspapers and on television, but I honestly don't believe I can tell you anything of any value. I have also found it all very distressing. That's why I haven't come forward.'

'Oh, come off it,' said Banks. 'Not only did you live in Hobb's End throughout the war, and not only did you know the victim well, you were also her sister-in-law. You can't expect me to believe that you know nothing at all about what happened to her.'

'Believe what you will.'

'Were the two of you close?'

'I wouldn't say we were close, no.'

'Did you like her?'

'I can't honestly say I knew her very well.'

'You were about the same age. You must have had things in common besides your brother.'

'She was older than I. It does make a difference when you're young. I wouldn't say we had much in common. I was always a bookish sort of girl, whereas Gloria was the more flamboyant type. As with many extroverts, she was also a secretive person, very difficult to get to know.'

'Did you see a lot of her?'

'Quite a bit. We were in and out of one another's houses. Bridge Cottage wasn't far from the shop.'

'Yet you claim you didn't know her well?'

'I didn't. You probably have cousins or in-laws you hardly know at all, Chief Inspector.'

'Didn't you ever do things together?'

'Like what?'

'I don't know. Girl things.'

Annie shot him a glance that he felt even before he noticed it out of the corner of his eye. The hell with it, he thought, they *were* girls back then. He had been a boy once, too; he did boy things, and he didn't object to anyone saying so.

Vivian pursed her lips, then shrugged. 'Girl things? I suppose we did. The same sorts of things other people did during the war. We went to the pictures, to dances.'

'Dances with American airmen?'

'Sometimes, yes.'

'Was there anyone in particular?'

'I suppose we were quite friendly with several of them over the last year of the war.'

'Do you remember their names?'

'I think so. Why?'

'What about Brad? Ring a bell?'

'Brad? Yes, I think he was one of them.'

'What was his second name?'

'Szikorski. Brad Szikorski.'

Banks checked the list of Rowan Woods personnel he had brought with him. *Bradford J. Szikorski, Jr.* That had to be the one.

'And PX? Billy Joe?'

'Edgar Konig and Billy Joe Farrell.'

They were on the list, too.

'What about Charlie?'

Vivian Elmsley turned pale; a muscle by the side of her jaw began to twitch. 'Markleson,' she whispered. 'Charlie Markleson.'

Banks checked the sheet. 'Charles Christopher Markleson? That the one?'

'*Charlie*. He was always called *Charlie*.'

'Whatever.'

'How did you find out their names? I haven't heard them in so long.'

'It doesn't matter how we found out. We also discovered that Gloria was having an affair with Brad Szikorski. Was she still seeing him when Matthew came back? Is that what happened?'

'Not that I knew of. I don't know what you're getting at. You've been misinformed, Chief Inspector. Gloria was married to Matthew, whether he was there or not. Yes, we went to the pictures with those boys on occasion, perhaps to dances, but that's all there was to it. There was no question of romantic involvement.'

'Are you sure?'

'Of course I am.'

'How did Gloria behave during her husband's absence?'

'What do you mean?'

'When she thought he was dead. Obviously things would be different then, wouldn't they? It wasn't as if she were waiting for him any more. As far as she was concerned, she would never see him again. After a reasonable period of mourning, she could enter back into the spirit of the times, couldn't she? Surely an attractive woman like her must have had boyfriends?'

Vivian paused again. 'Gloria had a very gregarious side to her nature. She liked parties, group excursions, that sort of thing. She liked to keep things superficial. At a distance. Besides, we never gave Matthew up for dead completely. You must understand that, Chief Inspector; we never gave up hope. There was always *hope*, hope that he would return. And it proved well founded.'

'You haven't answered my question. Did Gloria have a

romantic affair with Brad Szikorski, or with anyone else?'

She looked away. 'Not that I knew about.'

'So she lived like a nun, even though she believed her husband was dead?'

'I didn't say that. I didn't spy on her. Whatever she got up to behind locked doors was none of my business.'

'So she *did* get up to something?'

'I told you: I didn't spy on her. You're twisting my words.'

'How did Brad take it when Matthew came back alive?'

'How should I know? Why would it matter to him?'

'It might have. If he fell in love with Gloria, and if she rejected him in favour of her husband. He might have been angry.'

'Are you suggesting that *Brad* killed Gloria?' Vivian sniffed. 'You're really clutching at straws now.'

Banks leaned forward. 'Somebody did, Ms Elmsley, and the most immediate suspects that come to mind are Matthew, one of the Americans, Michael Stanhope, or you.'

'Ridiculous. It must have been a stranger. We've got plenty of them in the village, you know.'

'What about Michael Stanhope?'

'It's been years since I've heard *his* name. They were friends. That's all.'

'Would it surprise you to hear that Gloria posed nude for a painting by Stanhope in 1944?'

'Yes, it would. Very much. I know that Gloria wasn't as fastidious about her body as some would have wished her to be, but I never saw any evidence of anything like that.'

'Next time you're in Leeds,' Banks said, 'drop by the art gallery and have a look. You're sure she never told you?'

'I would have remembered.'

'Was Gloria having an affair with Michael Stanhope?'

'I shouldn't think so. He was too old for her.'

'And homosexual?'

'I wouldn't know about that. As I said, I was very young. It certainly wasn't something people went around boasting about back then.'

'Did she ever tell you about her family in London? About her son Francis?'

'She did mention him to me once, yes. But she said she'd cut off all relations with him and his father.'

'Even so, they could have come to drag her back. Maybe they fought and he killed her?'

Vivian shook her head. 'I'm sure I would have known.'

'Was Matthew ever violent towards her?'

'Never. Matthew had always been a gentle person, and even his war experiences didn't change that.' Her voice had taken on a strained, wavering quality.

Banks paused and softened his tone. 'There is one thing that really puzzles me,' he said, 'and that's what you *did* think had happened to Gloria? Surely you can't have thought she had simply disappeared from the face of the earth?'

'It wasn't a mystery at the time. Not really. She left. That's what I had always thought until you found the remains. You *are* certain it's Gloria, aren't you?'

Banks felt a twinge of doubt, but he tried not to let it show. They still had no definite proof of the skeleton's identity. For that, they would need Francis Henderson so they could run DNA checks. 'We're sure,' he said. 'Why would she leave?'

'Because she couldn't stand it any more, taking care of Matthew, the way he was. After all, it wouldn't have been the first time she'd done that. She had clearly broken off all contact with whatever life she had had in London before coming to Hobb's End. I don't think Gloria was particularly strong when it came to emotional fortitude.'

True enough, Banks thought. If a person has bid one life goodbye, then it probably wouldn't be too difficult to do it again. But Gloria Shackleton hadn't bid Hobb's End goodbye, he reminded himself; she had been killed and buried there.

'When did she disappear?' he asked.

'Shortly after VE day. A week or so.'

'You must see how the discovery casts suspicion on your brother, most of all. Gloria was buried in an out-building adjoining Bridge Cottage. Matthew was living with her there at the time.'

'But he was never violent. I had never known him be violent. Never.'

'War can change a man.'

'Even so.'

'Did he go out much?'

'What do you mean?'

'After his return. Did he go out much? Was Gloria often alone in the house?'

'He went to the pub of an evening. The Shoulder of Mutton. Yes, she was alone there sometimes.'

'Did Gloria ever say anything to you about leaving?'

'She hinted at it once or twice, but I didn't take her seriously.'

'Why not?'

'Her manner. It was as if she was joking. You know, "Some day my prince will come. I'm going to leave all this behind and run off to untold wealth and riches." Gloria was a dreamer, Chief Inspector. I, on the other hand, have always been a realist.'

'I suppose that's debatable,' Banks said. 'Given what you do for a living.'

'Perhaps my dreams are very realistic.'

'Perhaps. Even though she hinted, you didn't believe Gloria would actually go?'

'No.'

'What were the circumstances surrounding her departure?' Banks asked. 'Did you see her go?'

'No. It happened on one of the days when I accompanied Matthew to his doctor in Leeds. When we got back that evening, she was gone.'

'*You* accompanied him? Why not Gloria? She was still his wife.'

'And he was still *my* brother. Anyway, she asked me to, on occasion. It was the only respite she got. She looked after him the rest of the time. I thought it only fair she got some time to herself once in a while.'

'Did she take anything with her when she left?'

'A few clothes, personal items. She didn't have much.'

'But she took her clothes?'

'Yes. A few.'

'That's interesting. What did she carry them in?'

'An old cardboard suitcase. The same one she arrived with.'

'Did she leave a note?'

'Not that I saw. If Matthew found one, he never indicated it to me.'

'Would he have?'

'Possibly not. He wasn't very communicative. In his condition, it's impossible to predict what he would have done.'

'Murder?'

'*No*. Not Matthew. I've already told you, he had a gentle

nature. Even his dreadful war experiences and his illness didn't change that about him, though they changed everything else.'

'But Gloria's belongings were definitely missing?'

'Yes.'

'And you and Matthew were in Leeds during the time she made her exit?'

'Yes.'

'So she never even said goodbye?'

'Sometimes it's easier that way.'

'So it is.' Banks remembered that Sandra, once she had made her mind up, had given him little time for protracted goodbyes. He paused for a moment. 'Ms Elmsley,' he asked, 'knowing what you know now, why do you think her clothes and suitcase were missing? Where do you think they got to?'

'I have no idea. I'm only telling you what I witnessed at the time, what I thought must have happened. Perhaps someone stole them? Perhaps she interrupted a burglar and he killed her?'

'Were they particularly fine clothes? Minks, a few diamond necklaces perhaps? A tiara or two?'

'Don't be absurd.'

'It's not me who's being absurd. You see, it's not often people get murdered for their clothes, especially if they're ordinary clothes.'

'Perhaps they were taken for some other reason.'

'Like what?'

'To make it *look* as if she had gone away.'

'Ah. Now *that* would be clever, wouldn't it? Who do you think would feel the need to risk taking time burying her body under the outbuilding floor?'

'I don't know.'

'Not a casual burglar, I don't think.'

'As I suggested, perhaps someone wanted to make it appear as if she had gone away.'

'But who would want to do that? And, perhaps more important: why?'

'To avoid suspicion.'

'Exactly. Which brings us back very close to home, doesn't it? Why try to avoid suspicion unless you have some reason to believe suspicion will fall on you?'

'Your rhetoric is too much for me, Chief Inspector.'

'But you write detective novels. I've read one of them. Don't play the fool with me. You know exactly what I'm talking about.'

'I'm very flattered that you have read my books, Chief Inspector, but I'm afraid you attribute to me a far more logical mind than I actually possess.'

Banks sighed. 'If someone took great pains to make it look as if Gloria had run away, I'd say that someone wasn't likely to be a stranger just passing through, or a burglar. It had to be someone who felt suspicion was likely to fall on him or her: Matthew, Brad Szikorski or *you*.'

'Well, it wasn't me. And I told you, Matthew never raised a finger to her.'

'Which leaves Brad Szikorski.'

'Perhaps. Though I doubt it. It doesn't matter, anyway.'

'Why not?'

She allowed him a thin smile. 'Because Brad Szikorski was killed in a flying stunt in the desert outside Los Angeles in 1952. Ironic, isn't it? During the war, Brad flew on bombing raids over Europe and survived, only to be killed in a stunt for a war film seven or eight years later.'

'What about Charles Markleson?'

'*Charlie*. He would have had no reason at all to harm Gloria. Besides, he was killed in the war.'

'Edgar Konig? Billy Joe Farrell?'

'I don't know what happened to them, Chief Inspector. It's all so long ago. I only know about Brad because it was in the newspapers at the time. I suppose you'll have to ask them yourself, won't you? That is, if you can find them.'

'Oh, I'll find them, if they're still alive. Had either of them reason to kill Gloria?'

'Not that I know of. They were simply part of a group we went around with. Though Billy Joe, I remember, did have a violent temper, and PX was rather smitten with Gloria.'

'Did she go out with him?'

'Not to my knowledge. You couldn't . . . he wasn't . . . I mean, he just seemed so *young* and so shy.'

'Did you notice any blood in Bridge Cottage after Gloria's disappearance?'

'No. Obviously, if I had done, I would have been suspicious and called the police. But then I can't say I was actually *looking* for blood.'

'Not one little spot? Nothing that might, in retrospect, have been blood?'

'Nothing. Anyway, what makes you think she was killed in Bridge Cottage?'

'It's a logical assumption.'

'She could have been killed outside, in the backyard, or even in the outbuilding where you found her remains.'

'Possibly,' Banks allowed. 'Even so, whoever did it was very thorough. What happened next?'

'Nothing. We just carried on. Actually, we only stayed on in the village a few weeks longer, then we got a council house in Leeds.'

'I know. I've seen it.'

'I can't imagine why you'd want to do that.'

'So you're saying you have absolutely no idea what happened to Gloria?'

'None at all. As I said, I simply thought she couldn't face life with Matthew any more – in his condition – so she ran off and started up elsewhere.'

'Did you think she might have run off with Brad Szikorski, arranged to meet him over in America or something? After all, the Four Hundred and Forty-Eighth Bomber Group moved out around the same time, didn't they?'

'I suppose it crossed my mind. It was always possible that she had ended up in America.'

'Did it not surprise you that she never got in touch?'

'It did. But there was nothing I could do about it if she wanted to disappear, sever all ties. As I said, she'd done it before.'

'Did you ever try to find her?'

'No.'

'Did anyone?'

'Not that I know of.'

'What about Matthew?'

'What about him?'

'Did you kill him?'

'I did not. He committed suicide.'

'Why?'

'It wasn't related to Gloria's disappearance. He was ill, confused, depressed, in pain. I did my best for him, but it was ultimately no use.'

'He shot himself, didn't he?'

'Yes.'

'With a Colt forty-five automatic.'

'Was it? I'm afraid I know nothing about guns.'

'Where did he get the gun?'

'The gun? I'm sorry, I don't follow.'

'Simple question, Ms Elmsley. Where did Matthew get the gun he shot himself with?'

'He always had it.'

'Always? Since when?'

'I don't know. Since he came back from the war, I suppose. I can't remember when I first saw it.'

'From the Japanese POW camp?'

'Yes.'

Banks got to his feet, shaking his head.

'What's wrong, Chief Inspector?' Vivian asked, hand plucking at the turkey flap at the base of her throat.

'Everything,' said Banks. 'None of it makes any sense. Think over what you've just told us, will you? You're telling us you believed that Gloria simply upped sticks and left without leaving a note, taking her clothes and a few personal belongings with her in a cardboard suitcase. If you're telling the truth, then whoever killed Gloria must have packed the suitcase and either taken it away with him or buried it somewhere to make it look as if she had run off. Then, five years later, your brother Matthew shot himself with an *American* service revolver he just happened to bring back from a Japanese POW camp. You write detective novels. Ask yourself if your Inspector Niven would believe it. Ask yourself if your readers would believe it.' He reached in his pocket. 'Here's my card. I want you to think seriously about our little talk. We'll be back. Soon. Don't bother yourself, we'll see ourselves out.'

Once they were out in the hot street again, Annie turned to Banks, whistled and said, 'What was all that about?'

'All what?'

'She was lying. Couldn't you tell?'

'Of course she was.' Banks looked at his watch. 'Want to grab a bite to eat?'

'Yes. I'm starving.'

They found a small café and sat outside. Annie had a Greek salad, and Banks went for the prosciutto, provolone and sliced red-onion sandwich.

'But why was she lying?' Annie asked when they had sat down with their food. 'I don't get it.'

Banks swatted a fly away from his sandwich. 'She's protecting herself. Or someone else.'

'After seeing her,' Annie said, 'I'd say she was probably big and strong enough to kill and bury Gloria. Fifty years ago, anyway. Did you notice her hands?'

'Yes. And Gloria Shackleton was petite.'

'So what do we do now?'

'Nothing,' said Banks. 'We'll leave her to stew overnight and then have another go at her tomorrow. I get the impression she has a lot on her conscience. There was a definite struggle going on inside her. If I'm right, she's near the end of her tether on this. It's amazing how guilt has a way of gnawing away at you through the small hours. She wants to tell the truth, but she still has a few things to weigh up, to settle with herself; she doesn't quite know how to go about it yet. It's like that character in her book.'

'The one you were reading on the train?'

'*Guilty Secrets*, yes.'

'And what did he do?'

Banks smiled and put his finger to his lips. 'That would be telling. I wouldn't want to spoil the ending for you.'

Annie thumped his arm. 'Bastard. And in the mean-time?'

'Vivian Elmsley's not going to do a runner. She's too old and too tired to run. She also has nowhere to go. First, we'll go see if we can find Francis Henderson.'

'And then?'

'If it's okay with you, I'd like to head out to Bethnal Green and see my son. His band's playing there. We've got a few things to talk over.'

'Of course. I understand. Maybe I'll go to the pictures. What about later?'

'Remember that naughty weekend you mentioned?'

Annie nodded.

'I don't know if you're still interested, but there's this discreet little hotel out Bloomsbury way. And it *is* Friday. Even CID get to work regular hours sometimes. We'll let Vivian Elmsley sleep on it. If she can.'

Annie blushed. 'But I didn't bring my toothbrush.'

Banks laughed. 'I'll buy you one.'

'Last of the big spenders.' She turned to him, the corner of her mouth twitching in a smile. 'I didn't bring my nightie, either.'

'Don't worry,' said Banks. 'You won't need your nightie.'

15

Over the next couple of weeks, as I continued to mourn Charlie, I noticed no improvement in Matthew's condition. He remained at Bridge Cottage with Gloria. I don't really think it mattered to him at that point *where* he was, if indeed he even *knew*, as long as his basic creature comforts were taken care of. There wasn't a day went by when I didn't spend time sitting with him, talking to him, though he never responded and hardly even acknowledged that he heard; he just stared off into space with that intense inward gaze of his, as if looking on horrors and agonies we could never even imagine in our wildest nightmares.

The London doctor was as good as his word and we soon got Matthew fixed up with Dr Jennings, a psychiatrist attached to the staff of the University of Leeds. He had his office in one of those big old houses in the streets behind the campus, houses where large families with servants used to live before the First War. Once a week, either I or Gloria would take him to his appointment, spend an hour or so looking around the shops, then collect him and take him home. Dr Jennings admitted to me privately on the third visit that he was having little success with straightforward methods and that he was considering narcosynthesis, despite the problems.

Matthew wasn't any trouble; he just wasn't there. He did, however, get into the habit of going to the Shoulder of Mutton every night and sitting alone in a corner drinking until closing time. Friends and neighbours who knew him would approach at first and ask how he was doing, but soon even those who remembered him most fondly left him alone. Once in a while he would have an angry outburst and smash a glass or kick a chair. But these were infrequent and soon passed over.

Gloria gave me a key, so I was able to pop in and out of Bridge Cottage whenever I could. She took as much time off from the farm as possible, of course, but she needed the income, and I don't think she could have borne the pain and the heartbreak of being with him twenty-four hours a day.

It was hard to believe that the war was almost over after all this time, even though you could smell victory in the air. The Americans had crossed the Rhine, and so had Monty's men. The Russians had Berlin surrounded. In April and May we started hearing the first rumours about concentration camps and human atrocities on a scale that had only been hinted at in the reports about Lublin the previous year. All the newspapers seemed at a loss as to how to describe what the liberating armies had found at places such as Belsen and Buchenwald. In addition to reading about Japanese cannibalism and the appalling tortures inflicted on prisoners like Matthew, I also read about the German camps where hundreds of thousands of people, or so we thought at the time, were shot, starved, beaten or made the subject of medical experiments.

Along with all our personal losses, such as Charlie, and Matthew's ruined health, it was impossible to take it all in. I don't think we even tried. We had suffered five years of fear and hardship and we were damned if we were going to be cheated out of the big party when it was all over.

•

Banks walked into the cavernous Victorian pub, all smoked and etched glass, brass fittings and mirrors. Somehow, it had survived the Blitz, as much of east London hadn't. Years of cigarette smoke had turned the high ceiling and the walls brown.

It wasn't far from Mile End, where Gloria Shackleton had been born. She may have even been here, Banks fancied, though he doubted it. People tended to stick very close to home, hardly venturing more than a street or two away except on emergencies or special occasions.

He and Annie had just been to Dulwich to see Francis Henderson, only to find him out. A neighbour told them she thought he had most likely gone on holiday, as he had cancelled his newspapers and milk. Banks slipped his card with a note through the letter-box and left it at that. What more could he do? As far as he was concerned, Francis Henderson wasn't guilty of any crime – or if he was, it was nothing to do with the Gloria Shackleton case. He wanted to meet Francis, mostly out of curiosity, to see what he was like and find out what he knew, if anything, but he could hardly justify the expense of a manhunt. The DNA would be helpful, but not essential.

It was half past five, and the band was due to start at six to draw in the after-work crowd. Not that anyone Banks could see in the audience looked as if they had been at work, unless they were all students or bicycle couriers. Brian stood on the low wooden stage along with the others, setting their equipment up. Maybe they were making money, but they clearly couldn't afford a crew of roadies yet. The mountain of speakers made Banks a little nervous. He loved music, and he knew that rock sometimes benefited from being played loud, but he feared deafness perhaps even more than blindness. Back in his

Notting Hill days, he had been to see just about all the major bands live – The Who, Led Zeppelin, Pink Floyd, Jimi Hendrix, The Doors – and more than once he had woken up the next day with ringing ears.

Brian waved him over. He looked a little nervous, but that was only to be expected; after all, he was with his mates and here was his old man coming to a gig. They would no doubt tease him about that. He introduced Banks to Andy, the keyboard player, Jamisse, the bassist, who was from Mozambique, and the percussionist, Ali. Banks didn't know if Brian had told them he was a detective. Probably not, he guessed. There might be a bit of pot around, and Brian wouldn't want to alienate himself from his friends.

'I've just got to tune up,' said Brian, 'then I'll come over. Okay?'

'Fine. Pint?'

'Sure.'

Banks bought a couple of pints at the bar and found an empty table about halfway down the room. Occasionally, feedback screeched from the amps, Ali hit a snare drum or Jamisse plucked at a bass string. It was a quarter to six when Brian, apparently satisfied with the sound, detached himself from the others and came over. Banks hadn't realized until now how much his son had changed. Brian wore threadbare jeans, trainers and a plain red T-shirt. His dark hair was long and straight, and he had a three or four days' growth around his chin. He was tall, maybe a couple of inches more than Banks's five foot nine and, being skinny, he looked even taller.

He sat down and scratched his cheek, avoiding Banks's eyes. Banks didn't want to launch right into the midst of things. The last thing he wanted was another row. 'I'm looking forward to this,' he said, nodding towards the stage. 'I haven't heard you play since you used to practise at home.'

Brian looked surprised. 'That was a long time ago, Dad. I hope I've got better since then.'

'Me, too.' Banks smiled. 'Cheers.' They clinked glasses, then Banks lit a cigarette.

'Still got that filthy habit, then?' said Brian.

Banks nodded. ''Fraid so. I've cut down a lot, though. What kind of music do you play?'

'You'll have to wait and hear it for yourself. I can't describe it.'

'Blues?'

'Not straight blues, no. That was the band I was with a couple of years ago. We broke up. Ego problems. Lead singer thought he was Robert Plant.'

'*Robert Plant*? I wouldn't have thought you'd have heard of him.'

'Why wouldn't I have? You were always playing "Stairway to Heaven" when you weren't playing bloody operas. The long version.' He smiled.

'I don't remember doing that,' Banks complained. 'Anyway, who writes the songs?'

'All of us, really. I do most of the lyrics, Jamisse does most of the music. Andy can read music, so he arranges and stuff. We do some cover versions, too.'

'Anything an old fogy like me would recognize?'

Brian grinned. 'You might be surprised. Got to go now. Will you be around after?'

'How long's the set?'

'Forty-five minutes, give or take.'

Banks looked at his watch. Six. Plenty of time. He was a short walk from the Central Line and it wouldn't take him more than an hour to get to Leicester Square. 'I don't have to leave until about eight,' he said.

'Great.'

Brian walked back up to the stage where the others looked ready to begin. The pub was filling up quickly now, and Banks was joined at his table by a young couple. The girl had jet-black hair, pale makeup and a stud in her upper lip. Was she a Goth? he wondered. But her boyfriend looked like a beatnik with his beret and goatee, and Brian's band didn't play Goth music.

Matching the fashions with the music used to be easy: parkas and motor-scooters with The Who and The Kinks; Brylcreem, leather and motorbikes with Eddie Cochran and Elvis; mop-tops and black polo-necks with The Beatles. And later, tie-dye and long hair with Pink Floyd and The Nice; skinheads, braces and bovver-boots with The Specials; torn clothes and spiky hair with The Sex Pistols and The Clash. These days, though, all the fashions seemed to coexist. Banks had seen kids with tie-dye *and* skinhead haircuts, leather jackets *and* long hair. He was definitely overdressed in his suit, even though he had put his tie in his pocket long ago, but he hadn't brought a change of clothes. Maybe he was just getting old.

The next thing he knew, the band had started. Brian was right; they played a blend of music difficult to pin down. There was blues underlying it, definitely, variations on the twelve-bar structure with a jazzy spring. Andy's ghostly keyboards floated around it all, and Brian's guitar cut through the rhythms clear as a bell. When he soloed, which he did very well, his sound reminded Banks of a cross between early Jerry Garcia and Eric Clapton. Not that he was as technically accomplished as either, but the echoes were present in his tone and phrasing, and he got the same sweet, tortured sounds out of his guitar. In each number, he did something a little different. The rhythm section was great; they kept the beat, of course, but both Jamisse and Ali were creative musicians who played off one another and liked to spring surprises. There was an improvisational, jazzy element to the music, but it was accessible, *popular*. For a few songs they were joined by a soprano saxophone player. Banks thought his tone was a bit too harsh and his style too staccato, but bringing the instrument in was a good idea, if only they could find a better player.

They paused between songs and Brian leaned into the microphone. 'This one's for an old geezer I know sitting in the audience,' he said, looking directly at Banks. The girl with the stud in her lip frowned at him and he felt himself blush. After all, he was the only old geezer in the place.

It took a few moments for Banks to recognize what the song was, so drastically had the group altered its rhythm and tempo, and so different was Brian's plaintive, reedy voice from the original, but what emerged from Banks's initial confusion was a cover version of one of his favourite Dylan songs, 'Love Minus Zero/No Limit'. This time it swung and swayed with interlaced Afro rhythms and a hint of reggae. Andy's organ imbued the whole piece, and Brian's guitar solo was subdued and lyrical, spinning little riffs and curlicues off the melody line.

Dylan's cryptic lyrics didn't really mesh with Brian's own songs, mostly straightforward numbers about teen-age angst, lust, alienation and the evils of society, but they resonated in Banks the same way they did the first time he heard them on the radio at home all those years ago.

Before the song was over, Banks got a lump in his throat and he felt his eyes prick with tears. He lit another cigarette, his fourth of the day. He wasn't feeling emotional only because his son was up there on a stage, giving something back, but the song also brought back memories of Jem.

After Jem's death, no one came to the bedsit to claim his belongings. The landlord, whose musical taste ran more towards skiffle than sixties rock, let Banks take the small box of LPs. Being more into Harold Robbins than Baba Ram Dass, he also let Banks take the books.

Banks and Jem had listened to *Bringing It All Back Home* a lot, and the first time he took it out to play in Jem's memory he found a letter stuffed inside the sleeve. It was addressed to Jeremy Hylton at an address in Cambridge-shire. At first, he wasn't going to read it, respecting Jem's privacy, but as it usually did, his curiosity got the better of him. According to the postmark, the letter was dated five years earlier. He had known Jem was older than him, but not by how much. The letter was very short.

Dear Jeremy,

I'm writing to your parents' address because I know you're going home for Whitsuntide, and I won't be here when you get back. I'm sorry, I've been trying to tell you that it just isn't working between us, but you won't listen to me. I know this is the coward's way out, and I know it's hurtful to you, but I don't want the baby, and it's my body, my lifelong burden. I have made arrangements with a good doctor, so you needn't worry about me. I've got the money, too, so I don't need anything from you. After that I'm going a long way away, so don't even try to look for me. I'm sorry, Jeremy, really I am, but things were going badly between us before the pregnancy, you must know that. I don't know how you could think that having a baby would bring us closer together. I'm sorry.

Clara

Banks remembered being puzzled and upset by what he read. Jem had never mentioned anyone named Clara, nor had he ever mentioned where his family lived or what they did. He looked at the address again: Croft Wynde. It sounded posh. He hadn't a clue what Jem's background was; his accent was neutral, really, and he never spoke about the world he had grown up in. He was clearly educated, well read, and he introduced Banks to a whole world of writing, from Kerouac and Ginsberg to Hesse and Sartre, but he never said anything about having been to university. Still, everyone was reading that kind of stuff then; you didn't need a university course to read On the *Road* or *Howl*.

When Banks had finished thinking about what he'd just read in the letter, he made a note of the address. He decided to drive out to see Jem's parents. The least he could do was offer his condolences. His time in London had been lonely, and would have been a lot more so if not for the shared conversations, music and warmth of Jem's tiny bedsit.

The song finished and the audience's applause brought Banks out of his reverie.

'That was weird,' the kid next to him said.

The black-haired girl nodded and gave Banks a mystified glance. 'I don't think they wrote it themselves.'

Banks smiled at her. 'Bob Dylan,' he said.

'Oh, yeah. Right. I knew that.'

After that, the band launched into one of Brian's songs, an upbeat rocker about race relations. Then the first set was over. The band acknowledged the applause, then Brian came over. Banks bought them both another pint. The couple at the table asked Banks if he would please save their seats, then they wandered off to talk with some friends across the room.

'That was great,' Banks said. 'I didn't know you liked Dylan.'

'I don't, really. I prefer The Wallflowers. It used to drive me crazy when I was a kid and you played him all the time. That whiny voice of his and the bloody awful harmonica. It's just a nice structure, that song, easy to deconstruct.'

Banks felt disappointed, but he didn't let it show. 'I liked the ones you wrote, too,' he said.

Brian glanced away. 'Thanks.'

There was no point putting it off any longer, Banks thought, taking a deep breath. Soon the band would be starting again, and he didn't know when he would get another chance to talk to his son. 'Look,' he said, 'about what we said on the phone the other day. I'm disappointed, of course I am, but it's your life. If you think you can really make a go of this, I'm certainly not going to stand in your way.'

Brian met Banks's gaze, and Banks thought he could see relief in his son's eyes. So his approval *did* matter, after all. He felt curiously light-headed.

'You mean it?'

Banks nodded.

'It was just so boring, Dad. You're right. I screwed it up, and I'm sorry if I caused you any grief. But it was only partly because of the band. I didn't do enough work last year because I was bored by the whole subject. I was lucky to get a third.'

Banks had felt exactly the same way about his business-studies course – bored – so he could hardly get on his moral high horse. Well, he could, but he managed to put a rein on his parents' voices this time. 'Have you told your mother yet?'

Brian looked away and shook his head.

'You'll have to tell her, you know.'

'I left a message on her machine. She's always out.'

'She has to work. Why don't you go over and pay her a visit? She's not far away.'

Brian said nothing for a while. He swirled the beer in his glass, pushed back his hair. The place was noisy and crowded around them. Banks managed to focus and cut out the laughter and shouted conversations. Just the two of them on a floodlit island, the rest of the world a buzz in the distance.

'Brian? Is there something wrong?'

'Nah, not really.'

'Come on.'

Brian sipped some beer and shrugged. 'It's nothing. It's just Sean, that's all.'

Banks felt a tingling at the back of his neck. 'What about him?'

'He's a creep. He treats me like a kid. Whenever I go over there he can't wait to get rid of me. He can't keep his hands off of Mum, either. Dad, why can't you two get back together? Why can't things be the way they were?' He looked at Banks, brow furrowed, tears of anger and pain in his eyes. Not the cool, accomplished young man any more but, for a moment, the scared little kid who has lost his parents and his only safe, reliable haven in the world.

Banks swallowed and reached for another cigarette. 'It's not that easy,' he said. 'Do you think I didn't want to?'

'*Didn't?*'

'A lot's changed.'

'You mean you've got a new girlfriend?'

If it were possible to inflect the word with more venom

than Brian did, Banks couldn't imagine how. 'That's not the point,' he said. 'Your mother has made it quite clear, over and over again, that she doesn't want to get back together. I've tried. I did have hopes at first, but . . . What more can I do?'

'Try harder.'

Banks shook his head. 'I don't know,' he said. 'It takes two to do that, and I'm getting no encouragement whatsoever from her quarter. I've sort of given up on it. I'm sorry about Sean. Sorry you don't get along.'

'He's a plonker.'

'Yeah, well . . . Look, when you get a bit of free time, why don't you come up to Gratly? You can help me work on the cottage. You haven't even seen it yet. We can go for long walks together. Remember the way we used to? Semerwater? Langstrothdale? Hardraw Force?'

'I don't know,' said Brian, pushing his hair back. 'We're gonna be really busy the next while.'

'Whenever. I'm not asking you to put a date to it. It's an open invitation. Okay?'

Brian looked up from his beer and smiled that slightly crooked smile that always reminded Banks so much of his own father. 'Okay,' he said. 'I'd like that. It's a deal. Soon as we get a few days' break I'll be knocking on your door.'

A bass note and drum roll cut through the buzz of conversation as if to echo what Brian had said. He looked up. 'Gotta go, Dad,' he said. 'Be around later?'

'I don't think so,' said Banks. 'I've got work to do. I'll stick around for part of the set, but I might be gone before you're through. It's been great seeing you. And don't be a stranger. Remember my offer. There's a bed there for you whenever you want, for as long as you want.'

'Thanks, Dad. What's it they say? "Home's the place

where they have to take you in." Wish I knew where mine was. Take care.'

Banks stuck out his hand and Brian shook it. Then, feeling guilty, he checked his watch. Time to hear a few more songs before slinking off to keep his date with Annie.

•

One day Gloria came to me and asked if I would mind closing the shop for an hour or so and walking with her. She looked pale and hadn't taken her usual pains with her appearance.

It was the beginning of May, I remember, and it was all over but the shouting. Hitler was dead, the Russians had Berlin, and all the German troops in Italy had surrendered. It could only be days from the end now.

I closed the shop, as she asked, and we walked into Rowan Woods, leaving the road behind and wandering in the filtered green light of the new leaves. The woodland flowers were all in bloom, clusters of bluebells here and there, wild roses, violets and primroses. Birds were singing and the air was pungent with the smell of wild garlic. Now and then, I could hear a cuckoo call in the distance.

'I don't know what to do with him, Gwen,' she said, wringing her hands as we walked, close to tears. 'Nothing I do to try to reach him does any good.'

'I know,' I said. 'We just have to be patient. Let the doctor do his job. Time will heal him.' Even as I spoke them, I felt the triteness and inadequacy of my words.

'It's all right for you. He's not your husband.'

'Gloria! He's my brother.'

She put her hand on my arm. 'Oh, I'm sorry, Gwen, that's not the way I meant it. I'm just too distraught. But it's not the same. He's taken to sleeping on the Chesterfield now when he gets in from the pub.'

'You don't . . . I mean, he doesn't . . .?'

'Not since he came back. It's not fair, Gwen. I know I'm being selfish, but this isn't the man I married. I'm living with a stranger. It's getting unbearable.'

'Are you going to leave him?'

'I don't know what to do. I don't think I can. Brad is still pestering me to run off back to America with him as soon as his new orders come in. He says he might have to go out to the Pacific first – the war's not over there yet – but he says he'll send for me. Just imagine it, Gwen: Hollywood! A new life in the sunshine under the palm trees in a faraway magical land. A young, healthy, handsome, vigorous man who dotes on me. Endless possibilities of riches and wealth. I could even become a movie star. Ordinary people like you and me can do that over there, you know.'

'But?'

She turned away, eyes downcast. 'A dream. That's all. I can't go. Silly, isn't it? A few years ago I did exactly that. Walked away from a life I didn't want and ended up here.'

'But you'd lost your whole family then. You had nothing to stay for. Anyone can understand your doing that.'

'Haven't I lost Matt now?'

'It's not the same.'

'You're right; it's not. Anyway, I'd walked away even before I lost them.'

'What do you mean?'

She paused and touched my arm again lightly. 'There are things you don't know about me, Gwen. I haven't been a good person. I've done terrible things. I've been selfish. I've hurt people terribly. But I want you to know one thing. This is important.'

'What?'

'Matt is the only man I have ever truly loved.'

'Not Brad?'

'Not Brad, not . . . Never mind.'

'What were you going to say?'

Gloria paused and looked away from me. 'I told you, I've done terrible things. If I tell you, you must promise never to tell anyone else.'

'I promise.'

She looked at me with those blue eyes of hers. I was shocked that I hadn't noticed the tragedy in them before. 'I won't ask you to forgive me,' she said. 'You might not be able to do that. But at least hear me out.'

I nodded. She leaned back against a tree.

'When I was sixteen,' she began, 'I had a baby. I didn't love the father, not really. Oh, I suppose I was infatuated. George was a few years older than me, good-looking, popular with all the girls. I was advanced for my age and flattered by his attentions. We . . . well, you know all about it. We only did it once, but I didn't know anything about . . . you know . . . then, and I got pregnant. Our families wanted us to get married. George would have done it like a shot – he said he loved me – but . . . I *knew*, I *knew* deep down that it would be the worst mistake of my life. I knew if I married George I would be unhappy. He loved me then, but how long would it last? He drank, like they all did down on the docks, and I really believed it was just a matter of time before he would start beating me, looking upon me as his slave. I'd seen it in my own home. My own father. I hated him. That was why I wanted so desperately to escape. I used to listen to the wireless for hours trying to learn to speak the way I thought real people spoke. If my dad caught me, he'd either laugh at me or beat me, depending on how much he'd had to drink. So I left them all.'

'Where did you go?'

'To a friend's house. Not far away. I didn't know anyone from outside the East End, except for my Uncle Jack in Southend, and he'd have just sent me right back home.'

'And you were with this friend when your parents were killed?'

'Yes. I was heartbroken about Joe, my little brother, but my father can rot in hell as far as I was concerned. And my mother . . . she was harmless, I suppose, but she did nothing to stop him. In a way she was better off dead. She didn't have much of a life. I don't remember ever seeing her smile.'

'But what about the baby?'

Again, Gloria paused, as if struggling for words. 'I hated being pregnant. I was sick all the time. After I had Francis I got very depressed and I didn't . . . I didn't feel what they said a normal mother should. I'm ashamed to say it, but I didn't like holding him. I felt revolted that such a thing could have come out of me. I hated my own baby, Gwen. That's why I could never be a real mother to him or to anyone else.'

She sobbed and fell forward into my arms. I held her and comforted her as best I could. I didn't understand; I had no idea that a mother could *not* love her child; I knew nothing about postnatal depression in those days. I'm not sure that anybody did. My heart felt hot and too big for my chest. Sniffling, dabbing her handkerchief to her eyes, Gloria went on, 'Francis is alive. George's sister Ivy can't have any children of her own. They live on the canal. Her husband John's a lock-keeper. I know he's teetotal and I've met Ivy once or twice. They're decent people, not like the others. They'd got away and bettered themselves. They said they would take care of Francis. I knew he would be better off with them.'

'What did George say?'

'He already knew that whatever there had been between us was over – though it never stopped him trying – but he couldn't understand it when I didn't object to giving up Francis to Ivy and John. George is a simple man. Traditional. He believes in family. He believes a mother should love her baby. Simple as that. Of course, he agreed. He could hardly bring up Francis on his own. He said I would still be the boy's mother no matter what happened, that a boy needed a real mother to love. When I agreed without any fuss and said I didn't mind if they kept him for ever, George refused to believe me. That's what he always did when I had one of my "funny turns", as he called them. Refused to believe me. He wasn't a bad man, Gwen, that's not what I'm saying. It's me who's bad. I think he loved his son more than I did. He wanted to be a father as much as he could. But he got called up, of course, like all the rest. Anyway, he always thought I would change my mind. He's stubborn, the way some men are. He's already been up to see me once with Francis. He said he still loves me, urged me to go back. I told him I was married and we had an argument. He went off. But he'll be back, Gwen. He won't give up that easily.'

'Are you afraid of him?'

'I don't know. Maybe. A little. He's got a temper, like his own father. Especially when he's been drinking.'

I didn't know what to say.

'Say you don't hate me, Gwen, please! I couldn't bear it if you hated me. You're my only real friend.'

'Of course I don't hate you. I just don't understand, that's all.'

'I don't know if I do, either, but don't you see that's exactly why I *can't* leave, no matter what life is like with Matt? Because of what I did before. Oh, I have plenty of excuses: I was too young; it was a mistake; I wasn't in love; I thought I was cut out for better things. But that's just what they are: excuses. When it came right down to it, I was selfish; I was a coward. I'm not going to be a coward again. This is my punishment, Gwen. Don't you see? Matt is my penance.'

'I think so,' I said.

She smiled through her tears. 'Good old Gwen. I'll bet there aren't many in Hobb's End would give me that much credit, don't you think? I've heard their tongues wagging already.' She imitated the local accent. '"She'll be off," they say. "Off with one of them Yanks before he's been back ten minutes, you just mark my words." Well, I won't, Gwen. Let them talk. But I *won't*.'

'Are you and Brad still . . .?'

'Sometimes. Don't be angry. I tried to stop seeing him when Matt first got back, I really did, but when I found out that he couldn't . . . I mean . . . Brad brings me comfort from time to time and as long as Matt doesn't know . . . To be honest, though, he's more trouble than he's worth right now. I just can't keep him off the subject of running away together. It's all getting to be too much of a strain. I told him if he didn't stop pushing me I'd run off and leave the whole lot of you behind, him included.'

I can't say that I approved of Gloria's seeing Brad after Matthew had returned, but I said nothing. I only felt that way because I was being protective towards Matthew; I wasn't a moral busybody like Betty Goodall. These were extraordinary times and Gloria was an extraordinary woman.

She laughed. 'You know, I don't know what I'd do without PX. It's funny, isn't it, but in times like this, when things are so grim, it's the little things that give you a moment's cheer. A piece of beef, a new shade of lipstick, a little whisky, a packet of cigarettes. New stockings. He's a gem.'

'What about Billy Joe? Have you had any more trouble from him?'

'No, not really. I saw him the other day. I got the impression he was secretly pleased that Matt had come back and spoiled things for me and Brad. He had that look in his eye, too, as if he thought he had a chance of getting me in bed again. I don't think he gives a damn about what it's all doing to *me*.'

'Well, he wouldn't, would he? I can't say I ever did really trust him. He's got a nasty, violent streak, you know.'

'Billy Joe? Oh, I can handle him. He's nothing but a big child, really.' She leaned back against the tree. 'But you're right, he can be violent. I don't like that in a man.' She paused, averting her eyes. 'Look, Gwen, I don't know if I should be telling you this, but I have to talk to someone. I've been having a few problems with Michael.'

'Michael? Good Lord. You don't mean he's—'

'Don't be a fool, Gwen. The man's only interested in boys. The younger, the better. No. Well, I suppose I'll have to tell you now, but you mustn't say a word to anyone. Promise?'

'What a day for secrets. All right, I promise.'

'Last summer and autumn, you might have noticed I spent quite a bit of time at his studio.'

'Yes.'

'Guess what?'

'He was painting you?'

'Oh. You guessed!'

'Well, it wasn't difficult. I mean, he is an artist. But that's wonderful, Gloria. Can I see it? Is it finished?'

'Yes. And it's very good.'

'So what's wrong?'

'It's a nude.'

I swallowed. 'You posed in the *nude* for Michael Stanhope?'

She laughed. 'Why not? There certainly wasn't much chance of him trying to put his hands on me, was there? Anyway, the point is, I went over to see him yesterday and begged him not to exhibit it, or even to sell it privately, as long as Matthew is alive. I know he just seems to sit there like a zombie between going to the pub and drinking himself to sleep, but I just don't know how it would affect him. Or if it would. The thing is, I don't want to take the chance. You know what this village is like. Matthew's health is hanging by a thread already. Who knows if seeing a nude painting of his wife, done while he was suffering in a Japanese POW camp, won't send him right over the edge?'

'That sounds reasonable,' I told her. 'What did Michael Stanhope have to say?'

'Oh, he agreed in the end. But he's not happy about it. Thinks it's one of the best things he's done, blah-blah-blah, opens up a new direction for him. Says his career needs a boost and this could give it one. He also argued that Matthew wouldn't be any the wiser and that even if he *did* see it he wouldn't recognize who it was. He's probably right. I'm being silly.'

'But he did agree?'

'He complained a lot, but, yes, he agreed in the end. He likes to play the miserable cynic, but he's pretty decent, deep down. He's got a good heart.'

And there she finished. We walked back to Hobb's End enjoying the sound of the breeze through the leaves and the songs of the birds in the high branches.

I didn't see Gloria again until a couple of days later, on

the afternoon of the seventh of May, and by then everyone knew Germany had surrendered. The war was over and everywhere people started putting up flags and closing up shop.

The last party had begun.

•

'Enjoy the film?' Banks asked, when he met Annie outside the Leicester Square Odeon at nine o'clock. She had been to see the latest megamillion special-effects extravaganza by one of those highly touted directors who used to make television adverts.

'Not much,' said Annie. 'I suppose it had its good points.'

'What?'

'*The End*, for one.'

Banks laughed. Leicester Square was crowded with tourists, as usual. Street kids, buskers, jugglers, clowns and sword swallowers were all working hard to prise a quid or two out of the punters' pockets, while the pickpockets took an easier route. The Hare Krishnas were back in force, too. Banks hadn't seen them in years.

'How were things with your son?' Annie asked.

'We mended a bridge or two.'

'And the band?'

'Pretty good, though I suppose I'm biased. We'll go see them if they ever play up north, and you can make your own mind up.'

'It's a date.'

Banks took Annie to a small bistro-style restaurant he knew just off Shaftesbury Avenue. The place was busy, but they managed to get a table for two after a short wait at the bar.

'I'm starving,' said Annie as she squeezed herself into the chair between the table and the wall, twisting around and setting her packages down behind her. 'But I can see that eating with you is going to become a serious problem.'

'What do you mean?'

'This kind of place hardly caters to the vegetarian eater,' she whispered. 'Just look at the menu.'

Banks looked. She was right: lamb, beef, chicken, fish, seafood, but little in the way of interesting vegetarian dishes, other than salads. Still, as far as Banks was concerned, 'interesting vegetarian dish' was up there with 'corporate ethics' as far as oxymorons went.

'Sorry,' he said. 'Do you want to try somewhere else?'

She put her hand on his arm. 'No, it doesn't matter. Next time, though, it's *my* choice.'

'Visions of tofu and seaweed are already dancing before my eyes.'

'Idiot. It doesn't have to be like that. Indian restaurants do great vegetarian dishes. So do Italian ones. You didn't complain about the meal I made last week, did you?'

'It was delicate timing. I didn't want to offend you just before I made a pass.'

Annie laughed. 'Well, there's something to be said for honesty, I suppose.'

'I wasn't being honest. I was being facetious. It was a great meal. Dessert wasn't bad, either.'

'There you go again.'

'Anyway, you're right. Next time, it's your choice. Okay?'

'Deal.'

'How about some wine?'

They chose a relatively inexpensive claret – relatively

being the key word – and Banks went for the roast leg of lamb with rosemary, while Annie, pulling a martyred expression, settled for a large green salad and some bread and cheese. The waiter, who must have been imported from France along with the decor and food style, grunted with disapproval and disappeared.

Their food arrived quicker than Banks expected, and they paused until the waiter had gone. The lamb was tender and succulent, still pink in the middle; Annie turned her nose up at it and said her salad was okay. There was a tape of romantic dinner music playing in the background, and beyond the bustling waiters, the hum of conversation, clinking of cutlery and glassware, Banks could hear strains of the *andante cantabile* from Tchaikovsky's String Quartet Number 1.

After his talk with Brian, he felt as if a burden had been lifted from his mind. There were still problems – Sean, for one – but Brian would just have to learn to live with the way things were. Banks had to admit that this Sean sounded like a real prick. Not for the first time, he speculated about going over there and kicking the shit out of him. Really mature way to deal with the problem, he told himself. A lot of good that would do everyone concerned. The important thing at the moment was that he and his son were talking again. And from what he had heard, the kid had talent; he might make it in the business yet. Banks tried to imagine being father to a famous rock star. When he was old and grey, would Brian buy him a mansion and a Mercedes?

The candlelight brought out the slight wine flush on Annie's cheeks and filled her dark eyes with mysterious shadows and reflections. She was still wearing the same business suit she had worn that morning, but she had loosened her hair so that it tumbled over her shoulders in sexy waves. It would probably just brush against the tattoo over her breast.

'What are you thinking about?' she asked, looking up and pushing some stray hair back behind one ear.

Perhaps this was the moment, Banks thought, emboldened by his buoyant mood, to take the plunge anyway. 'Annie, can I ask you a personal question?'

She arched her eyebrows and Banks sensed a part of her scurry back into the shadows. Too late now. 'Of course,' she said. 'But I can't promise to answer it.'

'Fair enough. What are you doing at Harkside?'

'What do you mean?'

'You know what I mean. It's a nowhere posting. It's the kind of place they send naughty boys and girls. You're bright. You're keen. You've got a future ahead of you if you want it, but you'll not get the job experience you need at Harkside.'

'I think that's rather insulting to Inspector Harmond and the others up there, don't you?'

'Oh, come on, Annie. You know as well as I do that's where they want to be. It's their choice. And it's not an insult that they choose the easy life.'

'Well, maybe it's what I've chosen, too.'

'Is it?'

'I didn't promise to answer your question.' Her mouth took on a sulky cast Banks hadn't seen before, the corners of her lips downturned; her fingers drummed on the tablecloth.

'No, you didn't,' Banks said, leaning towards her. 'But let me tell you something. Jimmy Riddle hates my guts. He isn't in the business of putting me in the way of anything I might find even remotely pleasant. Now, given that he

knows who you are, and given that what's happened
between us since could never in a million years fulfil his
idea of the circle of hell he thinks he's cast me into, I find
myself wondering why.'

'Or waiting for the punch line?'

'What?'

'Isn't that what you're saying? You think something's
wrong. You think there's some sort of a plot to get you.
You think I'm part of it.'

'That's not what I said,' said Banks, who realized
guiltily that the thought had crossed his mind.

Annie turned her head away. Her profile looked stern.

'Annie,' he said, after a few moments' silence, 'I'm not
saying I haven't been suspicious. But, believe me, the only
reason I'm asking you now is because I've come to . . .
Because I'm afraid you're being used, too.'

She glanced at him, not moving her head, eyes
narrowed. 'How?'

'I don't know. What else can I say? Riddle had to have
some reason for putting us together, something he thought
would be unpleasant for me. I hope you agree that it hasn't
turned out at all that way. Do you blame me for wondering
what's going on?'

Her expression softened a little. She tilted her head.
'Perhaps this is it?' she suggested. 'What he expected.'

'In what way?'

'That we'd get together somehow, break the rules and
get caught. That way he could be rid of both of us.'

'No, that's not enough. It's too easy. What we're doing
isn't . . . I mean, it's only the same kind of thing he thought
I was doing before. He has a far more sadistic mind than
that. And to be honest, I don't think he's as clever as that,
either. What is it the spies call it, a "honey trap"? Jimmy

Riddle feels no need to give me honey, only arsenic.'

'Jimmy Riddle didn't *give* you anything.'

'Okay. Sorry, you know what I mean.'

Annie shook her head slowly and the shadows danced through her hair. Dessert came, but she left it untouched for a while, then she seemed to come to some kind of decision. She picked up her spoon, tasted a mouthful, then looked at Banks. 'All right,' she said. 'I'll tell you, but only if you'll tell me something, too.'

•

Yorkshire weather has a very ironic sense of occasion. On the eighth of May, 1945, it poured down all morning, despite the fact that this was VE Day. By early afternoon, the rain was tapering off and we were left with clouds and light showers. I closed the shop at lunchtime and Gloria came down from the farm. That afternoon, leaving Mother and Matthew together, the two of us bicycled into Harkside and went to see a matinée of *Phantom of the Opera* at the Lyric.

All over Harkside we heard excited talk of parties and dances; people on the streets were hanging streamers and putting out flags. All the church bells were ringing. We bumped into some people we knew on the village green and they suggested we come back that evening to the celebration dance at the Mechanics Institute, to be followed by a street party. The Americans from Rowan Woods would be there, they assured us. We said we would try to come as soon as we had done some celebrating in Hobb's End first.

After tea, the sun lanced through the raggedy black clouds, sending shafts of light into Rowan Woods. Soon, all the clouds had gone and it was as beautiful a warm May evening as you could ever ask for, the grass green and moist from the rain.

Gloria gave me a pair of stockings she had got from PX, and helped me with my makeup. First, we spent an hour or so at the Hobb's End street party. People had brought little tables and put them together in a row all along High Street. It was a dull affair, though, as there were so few people left in the village, and the whole thing felt more like a wake than a celebration.

Mother sat at one of the tables with her friend, Joyce Maddingley, and she told us to behave ourselves when we slipped away to Harkside with Cynthia Garmen. Matthew refused to come out of the cottage at all; he wouldn't budge. Mother said not to worry, she would look in on him from time to time and make sure he was comfortable.

The three of us set off, taking the long way round on the roads so we wouldn't get our ankles and court shoes wet in the grass.

Harkside was much wilder than Hobb's End. Most of the soldiers and airmen from the nearby bases had come, so there were men in uniform all over the place. From the minute we got to the village green, we were swept into a mad whirl. It didn't take Gloria long to meet up with Brad. Billy Joe was there with his new girlfriend, and PX was tagging along, too. I felt a sudden pang of missing Charlie, then I tried to enter into the spirit of victory.

First we went to the dance. There was a big band playing Glenn Miller, Duke Ellington and Benny Goodman tunes, and people kept throwing coloured streamers across the dance floor.

Out in the streets, between songs, we could hear fire-works and people whooping with joy. At one point, when I was dancing a waltz with Billy Joe and trying to explain how Matthew took up so much of our time, I noticed Gloria and Brad slip outside. It was over an hour before I saw them again, and Gloria had retouched her makeup. She couldn't hide the ladder in one of her stockings, though. I resolved to say nothing. Since our talk a few days ago, I had thought a lot about Gloria and what she was sacrificing to care for Matthew, and I decided that she deserved her little pleasures, as long as she remained discreet about them.

The band was still playing when we piled out into the street. There was a huge bonfire on the village green and people were singing, dancing and setting off fireworks all around it, just like Guy Fawkes Night. The air was full of the acrid smell of smoke and the sky full of exploding colours. Someone had made up an effigy of Hitler and they were heaving it on top of the fire. Everyone was drunk. I don't know where Cynthia got to. I was with a group of people, and I could see Gloria and Brad through the flames having an argument. At least they looked as if they were shouting at one another, but I couldn't hear for all the singing and explosions.

At one point we went to someone's house and drank some whisky. It was a wild party. People were packed in like sardines and I felt hands all over my body as I pushed my way through the crowd to go to the toilet. The house was full of smoke and it stung my eyes. Gloria was dancing, but I couldn't see Brad. Someone fell down the stairs. At one point, I'm sure I saw a Negro dancing on the piano. PX was drunk, eyes closed almost to slits, and I saw him try to kiss a woman. She pushed him away and his face turned red. Then he stormed off. Cynthia reappeared with a sailor in tow. I don't know where she'd managed to find him, as we were at least fifty miles from the coast. It was almost one o'clock and we were back out on the street again when I told Cynthia and Gloria it was time for us to go.

The three of us were a little drunk. It was the emotion

and excitement as much as the alcohol, I think. We didn't even bother trying to cadge a lift but danced and laughed our way home instead. Hobb's End was quiet as a tomb.

Bridge Cottage was dark. I went in with Gloria to make sure everything was all right and we heard Matthew snoring on the Chesterfield as soon as we opened the door. Gloria put her finger to her lips and gestured me towards the kitchen. With the door shut, she poured us both another whisky, which was probably the last thing we needed. When she put her handbag down on the countertop, it slipped off and fell on the floor. I bent over to pick it up for her and noticed how heavy it was. Curious, I opened the clasp and nearly fainted when I saw a gun. Gloria turned with the bottle and glasses in time to see me.

'You weren't supposed to see that,' she said.

'But, Gloria, where did you get it?'

'From one of the Americans at the party. He was so drunk he won't miss it.'

'Not Brad?'

'No, not Brad. Nobody we know.'

'But whoever he was, he'll get into serious trouble.'

'I don't think so. Anyway, I don't care. It serves him right for being so careless, doesn't it? He was trying to put his hand up my skirt at the time.'

'What do you want a gun for?'

She shrugged. 'War souvenir.'

'Gloria!'

'All right!' She was whispering as loudly as she could, so as not to wake Matthew. 'Maybe I just feel a bit more comfortable knowing it's there, that's all.'

'But Matthew's harmless. He wouldn't hurt you.'

She looked at me as if I were the biggest fool she had ever met. 'Who said anything about Matthew?' she said, not even bothering to whisper, then she took the gun from me and put it in one of the kitchen cupboards behind the meagre supplies of tea and cocoa. 'Now will you have that drink?'

•

Vivian Elmsley was having a difficult time. Close to midnight she was sitting in her sparse living room, her third gin and tonic in her hand and some dreadful rubbish on television. Sleep refused to come. Her mysterious caller hadn't rung again, but she still regarded the telephone as an object of terror, ever on the verge of destroying what little peace of mind she had left. She wondered if she should have told the police about him. But what could they do? It was all so vague.

She had known the police would find out who she was and come for her eventually – she had known that the minute she knew Gloria's body had been dug up – but she hadn't been prepared for the effect that their visit would have on her. They knew she was lying; that was obvious. Chief Inspector Banks wasn't a fool; he knew that nobody who had been as close to the people involved as Vivian had could know so little as she had professed. And she wasn't a good liar.

Why *hadn't* she told them the truth? Fear for her own well-being? Partly. She didn't want to go to gaol. Not at her age. But would they really prosecute her after so long, no matter what the law books said? When they heard her full story, would they really go ahead and put her through the pain and humiliation of a trial and a gaol sentence? Were there not such things as mitigating circumstances?

She didn't know what they would do, and that was the problem. When it comes right down to it, we fear the unknown more than anything else.

On the other hand, if she didn't tell them, then they would never find out the truth about what happened that night. Nobody else knew. Living or dead. If she was careful, Vivian could take her secret to the grave with her.

Only one thing was certain: the police would be back; she had seen it in the chief inspector's eyes. Tonight she had to make her decision.

•

'You're right about one thing,' Annie began. 'I'm in Harkside because I was a naughty girl.'

'What happened?'

'Depends on your point of view. They called it an initiation rite. I called it attempted gang rape. Look, I'm not going to tell you where it was or who was involved. All I'm saying is it happened in a big city, and it wasn't in Yorkshire. Okay?'

'Okay. Go on.'

'This is hard.' Annie spooned down some more chocolate mousse. 'Harder than I ever thought.'

'You don't have to.'

She held up her hand. 'No. I've come this far.' The waiter drifted by and they both ordered coffee. He didn't give any indication that he had heard, but the coffee arrived in a matter of moments. Annie pushed aside her dessert bowl; it was empty. She played with the spoon.

'It was when I made DS,' she said. 'Nearly two years ago now. I'd done my stint in uniform there, and I wasn't sure where they were going to send me next. But I didn't care. I was happy just to be back in CID again after . . . well, you know what I mean.'

'Patrols? Shifts?'

'Exactly. Anyway, there was a celebration at the local

coppers' pub. The "private" room upstairs. I suppose I was dead chuffed with myself. I'd always wanted to be one of the boys. Naturally, we closed the place. It got down to just four of us left. One of them suggested we go back to his place and drink some more and we all agreed that was a good idea.'

She was speaking very quietly so that no one would hear. There wasn't much chance of that. The restaurant was packed now, full of laughter and loud voices. Banks had to strain to hear her, and somehow that made what he heard so much more affecting, that it was delivered in not much more than a whisper. He sipped some black coffee. Through the occasional hush in the background noise, he could hear the lush, romantic strains of Liszt's 'Liebestraum'.

'We were already three sheets to the wind,' Annie went on, 'and I was the only female. I didn't know the others well. Things were getting pretty wild. I suppose I should have known what was coming by the way the conversation was going in the taxi. You know. Flirting. Sexual innuendoes. Casual touches. That sort of thing. Call me naive. The other three kept making veiled references to initiation ceremonies, and there was a lot of nudging and winking going on, but I'd been drinking, too, and I didn't really think much of it until we'd been at the flat for a while and drunk some more. One of them grabbed my arm and suggested we go in the bedroom, said he could tell I'd been wanting it all night. I laughed and brushed him off. I thought he was joking. He got angry. Things got out of hand. The other two grabbed me and held me down over the back of the settee while he pulled up my skirt, tore off my underwear and raped me.'

Banks noticed that Annie was gripping the spoon

handle tightly in her fist. Her knuckles were white. She took a deep breath and went on. 'When he'd finished, they started rearranging positions, and I knew what was coming. It was like there were no individuals in the room any more; they were all caught up in this blind male lust and I was the object of it. It overwhelmed everything, conscience . . . decency. It's hard to describe. I was terrified, but I'd sobered up pretty damn quickly over the last few minutes. Soon as I got my chance, I slipped free from their grip, kicked the one who'd raped me hard as I could in the balls and caught another on the jaw with my elbow. I'd done some martial-arts training. I don't know, maybe if I hadn't been drinking, my reflexes would've been quicker, my coordination a bit more accurate. Anyway, I managed to put two of them out of action long enough to make it to the door. The third one caught me, and by then the one I'd hit with my elbow was up again. They were sweating, red in the face, and mad as hell. One of them punched me in the stomach and the other hit me hard in the chest. I went down. I think I was sick. I thought that was it again, that they were going to do what they'd intended, but they'd lost their bottle. It had all got too real for them. Suddenly they were individuals again, each looking out for number one, and they knew what they'd done. It was time to close ranks. They called me a lesbian bitch, told me to get out and if I knew what was good for me I wouldn't say a word. I left.'

'Did you report it? For crying out loud, Annie, you'd been *raped*.'

She laughed harshly. 'Isn't that so easy for a man to say? To sit in judgment over what a person in that position should or shouldn't do? To be *oh so* understanding about it?' She shook her head. 'You know what I did? I walked the city most of the night in a complete daze. People must have thought I was crazy. I wasn't drunk any more, I was plain cold sober, but I was drained, numb, I couldn't feel anything. I remember trying to feel some sort of emotion, thinking I ought to feel anger or pain. I was really angry at myself for not feeling angry. I know it sounds impossible, but that's the only way I can describe it. There was nothing. Just a deep cold numbness. When I finally found myself back at my flat, I had a long hot bath. Hours I must have lain there, just listening to the radio. News. Weather. Normal life. That was soothing somehow. And do you know what? I understand every one of those rape victims who never comes forward to report the crime.'

Banks could see tears glistening at the corners of her eyes, but as she noticed him looking, she seemed to draw them back in.

'What happened?' he asked.

'By morning I'd got a bit of nerve back. First thing, I went to see the chief super to tell him what they did. Know what?'

'What?'

'Two of the others had got there before me and queered the pitch. Pre-emptive strike. They told the super there'd been a spot of bother at a party last night, just an initiation rite that got a bit out of hand, nothing serious, like, but that I'd probably be coming to complain, making up all sorts of wild allegations. According to them I'd got totally rat-arsed and gone way over the top, telling them I'd take them all on and then backing down when it came to it.'

'And he believed them?'

'Their word against mine. Besides, they were all mates. People around the station already thought I was a bit weird. Some of them even used to call me the "Hippie

Cop" behind my back, or so they thought. You know, I did yoga and meditation and I didn't eat meat and watch sport on the telly and talk about sex all the time. That's enough to make you seem weird, for a start. I also had a reputation around the place for not being very interested in men, just because I didn't find any of the blokes I worked with particularly attractive. I'm sure they all thought I was gay. That hits a certain kind of male the wrong way. He thinks all a lesbian needs is a big hard cock in her and she'll soon come to her senses. And, of course, he's just the bloke to give it to her. As it happened, I did have a boyfriend at the time, nothing serious, but I kept my private life separate from the Job.'

'Did you tell the chief super what really happened?'

'Yes. Every detail.'

'What was his reaction?'

'He looked very embarrassed.'

'Didn't he initiate some sort of inquiry?'

'Like I said, their word against mine. And apart from a pair of torn knickers, I'd pretty much destroyed the evidence, hadn't I?'

'Even so . . . these days . . .'

'What about these days?'

'Annie, there are procedures to guard against these things.'

'Procedures? Hah. Tell that to the chief super. He also told me, by the way, that no one wants that sort of internal investigation going on. It hurts everyone, and it especially hurts the force. He said the officers involved would be disciplined for their excessive high spirits, but it would be best for all concerned if it went no further than his office. He told me to put the good of the force as a whole above my own selfish concerns.'

'You agreed to that?'

'What choice had I?'

'He should have been kicked off the force.'

'I'm glad you agree.'

'So all that happened was they got a slap on the wrist and you got shipped off to the middle of nowhere?'

'Not quite. Not immediately.' Annie looked down into her coffee cup. 'There were complications.'

'What complications?'

She wrapped a strand of hair around her forefinger and stared down into her cup for a few more seconds before looking up at Banks. 'Remember, I told you I kicked one of them in the balls?'

'Yes? What about it?'

'Something went wrong. They had to operate. He lost them. Both of them. The devil of it was that he was the youngest of the three and the most junior in rank. Just a DS himself and only married a year. Planning a family.'

'Jesus. I can imagine you were a popular woman around the station after that.'

'Exactly. For a while I thought of leaving the force altogether. But I'm stubborn. The chief super suggested it might be better for all concerned if I transferred somewhere else. He said he'd look into some possibilities, and they came up with Harkside. Millicent Cummings was immediately sympathetic, of course, and I think our ACC used to work with Chief Constable Riddle.'

'So Riddle knows all about what happened?'

'He knew my chief super's side of the story, yes.'

'Which means that to him you're a troublemaker? A ball-busting lesbian bitch?'

Annie mustered a crooked smile. 'Well, I've been called worse, but thanks for the compliment.'

'No wonder he put us together. Never was much of a judge of character, though, wasn't Jimmy Riddle. I'm surprised he got as far as he did. I'm sorry about what happened to you, Annie. Sorrier than I can say.'

'All water under the bridge.'

'I'm also amazed you would even consider getting involved with me, a DCI. I would have thought that what happened would have been enough to put you off your fellow coppers for life, especially senior CID ranks.'

'Oh, come on, Alan. You do yourself a disservice. Do you really think I'm that stupid? That's insulting to both of us. I've never, not for one moment, seen any similarity whatsoever between you and the men who assaulted me. I didn't even know you were a DCI when I first saw you, and I fancied you right away. The thing is, I thought I'd faced up to it and got on with my life.'

'Haven't you? You seem to be doing all right to me.'

'I've been in hiding. I shut myself away. I thought I was over it and that I'd simply chosen a quieter life. The celibate life of reflection and contemplation. There's a laugh. I thought that was my choice, but it was really a result of what happened, of not facing up. But I'd already practised meditation and yoga, had done for years, and I came from a small seaside town, so it seemed only natural to dig in my heels at Harkside.'

'You aren't happy there?'

'What's happiness? Something you measure in relation to unhappiness? I get by. I have my nice safe little life at the centre of the labyrinth, as you so astutely pointed out. I have few possessions. I go to work, I do my job, and then I come home. No social life, no friends. I certainly didn't dwell on what had happened to me. I didn't have recurring nightmares about it. I suppose I was lucky that way. And

I felt no guilt about what happened to that young DS. That might sound harsh, but I've probed myself deeply enough to know it's the case. He was egged on by his superiors, true, caught up in the spirit of drunken revelry. I suppose some people might excuse him by saying he was too weak to resist or he simply lost his rag, temporary insanity. But I was the one he raped. And I was the one who saw his face while he was doing it. He *deserved* all he got. The only real shame is that I didn't get the chance to do it to the other two as well.' She paused. 'But let's face it, I haven't even done any serious detective work in Harkside. I know I'm good at the job – I'm quick, I'm bright and I'm hard-working – but until this case came along it's all been break-ins, vandalism, the occasional runaway kid.'

'And now?'

She shrugged. 'Now I don't know. You're the first person I've told since it happened.'

'You didn't tell your father?'

'Ray? No. He'd be sympathetic, but he wouldn't under-stand. He didn't want me to join the police to start with.'

'A hippie artist? I shouldn't think he did.'

'He'd probably have led a protest march to New Scotland Yard.' She paused and played with her hair again. 'Now it's your turn. Remember, you promised to tell me something, too.'

'Did I?'

'Uh-huh.'

'What do you want to know?'

'Did you really punch Jimmy Riddle?'

Banks stubbed out his cigarette and slipped his credit card on the little tray the waiter had left. It was snatched up almost immediately. The theatres had come out now and people were queuing at the restaurant door.

'Yes,' he said. 'I did.'

She laughed. 'Bloody hell. I wish I'd been there.'

The waiter finished with the card in no time flat. Banks signed the receipt, Annie gathered her packages and they walked out into the busy West End evening. The streets were packed with people standing drinking outside the pubs. Four men blocked the pavement, all talking and laughing at once into a mobile phone. Banks and Annie skirted them. Across the street, Banks saw a drunken woman in a tartan schoolgirl mini, black thigh stockings and fuck-me shoes try to carry on an argument with her 'boyfriend' and walk at the same time. She failed, teetered at the edge of the pavement and went sprawling in the gutter, cursing all the way. Sirens blared in the distant city night.

'Don't laugh at this,' said Annie, 'but that time . . . you know, in the backyard, when you put your arm around me?'

'Yes.'

'Well, I was sort of expecting something might happen, and I didn't know if I was ready for it yet. I was going to tell you I was a lesbian. Just to let you down lightly, to make you think it wasn't anything personal, you know, that it wasn't that I didn't fancy you or anything, but that I just didn't go for men. I'd got it all worked out.'

'Why didn't you?'

'When the time came, I didn't want to. Believe me, I was probably just as surprised as you were about what happened. Just as scared. I know I invited you to my house and fed you drinks, but I really wasn't planning to seduce you.'

'I didn't think you were.'

'I was going to offer you the couch.'

'And I would have accepted gracefully.'

'But when it came to it, I wanted you. I was terrified. It was the first time since the night I've just told you about. But I wanted to do it as well. I suppose I wanted to overcome my fear. Sometimes it's the only way.'

They walked along Charing Cross Road, past all the closed bookshops, and crossed Oxford Street. As they turned on to Great Russell Street, Annie slipped her arm through Banks's. It was only the second time they had had any little intimate physical contact in public, and it felt good: the warmth, the gentle pressure. Annie leaned her head a little so it rested on his shoulder; her hair tickled his cheek.

Neither of them had been to the hotel yet; Banks had simply phoned earlier to book a room and said they would be arriving late. It was only a small place. He had stayed there twice before while on police business in London – both times alone – and had been impressed by the general cleanliness and level of service, not to mention the reasonable rates.

They passed the dark mass of the British Museum, set back behind its railings and courtyard, then crossed Russell Square. Conversation and laughter carried on the night air from a pub round the corner. A couple walked by, arms wrapped around one another.

'Here we are,' said Banks. 'Did you buy a toothbrush?'

'Yup.' Annie held up one of her bags. 'And a new pair of jeans, new shoes, a skirt and blouse, undies.'

'You really did go shopping, didn't you?'

'Hey. It's not often I get to the big city. I bought a nightie, too.'

'I thought I said you wouldn't need one.'

She laughed and moved closer. 'Oh, don't worry. It's

only a *little* nightie. I promise you'll like it.' And they walked up the stone steps to the hotel.

•

I couldn't stop thinking about the gun. Usually, the way the scene ran in my mind was that Gloria shot Matthew first and then herself. The images were so vivid I could even see the blood gush from their wounds. Finally, I determined I had to do something.

As I said, I had a key to Bridge Cottage. It wasn't that Matthew locked himself in, but he sometimes wouldn't bother getting up to answer the door. Most of the time he was in a sort of comatose state from alcohol anyway. When he wasn't at the pub he was sipping whisky at home. Whisky that Gloria got from PX.

So the next time it was Gloria's turn to take Matthew to see Dr Jennings in Leeds, I let myself in. Even if someone saw me, it wouldn't seem at all strange because I was in and out of Bridge Cottage all the time and everyone in the village knew about Matthew's condition.

I found the gun in the same place Gloria had left it: behind the cocoa and tea in the kitchen cupboard. I put it in the shopping bag I had brought with me, put the cupboard back in order and left. I didn't know how long it would take her to miss it, but the best I could hope for was that by the time she did she wouldn't feel the need for it any more and would realize what a favour I had done her.

We can be such fools for love, can't we?

16

It was about eleven o'clock on Saturday morning when Banks and Annie arrived back at Vivian Elmsley's building. Before Banks could even press the buzzer, the door opened and Vivian almost bumped into them.

'Going somewhere, Ms Elmsley?' asked Banks.

'You?' She put her hand to her heart. 'I didn't think . . . so soon . . . I was just . . . you'd better come in.'

They followed her upstairs to the flat. She was carrying a large buff envelope, which she dropped on the hall table as she entered the room. Banks glanced at it, saw his name and the Eastvale station address on it.

She turned to face them as they entered her living room. 'I suppose I should thank you for coming back,' she said. 'You've saved me the postage.'

'What were you sending me?' Banks asked. 'A confession?'

'Of sorts. Yes. I suppose you could call it that.'

'So you *were* lying yesterday?'

'Fiction's my trade. Sometimes I can't help it.'

'You should know the difference.'

'Between what?'

'Fiction and reality.'

'I've learned to leave that to the most arrogant among us. They're the only ones who seem to think they know everything.' She turned, walked back to the hall and picked up the envelope. 'Anyway,' she went on, handing

it to Banks, 'I'm sorry for being flippant. I've found this
whole thing extremely difficult. I tend to hide behind
language when I'm frightened. I'd like you to grant me the
favour of taking this away with you and reading it. I had a
copy made this morning. If you're worried about my
fleeing from justice, please don't. I'm not going to run
anywhere, I promise you.'

'Why the change of heart?'

'Conscience, would you believe? I thought I could live
with it, but I can't. The telephone calls didn't help, either.
In the early hours of the morning, I arrived at the end of
a long struggle, and I decided to tell the truth. What you
do with it once you know is up to you. I'd just rather do
things this way than answer a lot of questions at the
moment. I think it will help you understand. Of course,
you'll have questions eventually. I have to be in
Leeds next week to do some book signings, so you'll soon
have the opportunity. Will you allow me this much, at
least?'

It was an unusual request, and if Banks were to go by
the book, he wouldn't let a murder suspect hand him a
written 'confession', then go away and leave her to her
own devices. But it was time for a judgment call. This had
been an unusual case right from the start, and he believed
that Vivian Elmsley wasn't going anywhere. She was in
the public eye, and he didn't think she had anywhere to
run, even if she wanted to. The other possibility was
suicide. It was a risk, to be certain, but he decided to take
it. If Vivian Elmsley wanted to kill herself rather than
suffer through a criminal trial that cost the taxpayers
thousands and drew the media like blood draws leeches,
who was Banks to judge her? If Jimmy Riddle found out
about it, of course, Banks's career wouldn't be worth a

toss, but since when had he let thoughts of Jimmy Riddle get in his way?

'You mentioned telephone calls,' he said. 'What do you mean?'

'Anonymous calls. Sometimes he says things, others he just hangs up.'

'What kind of things does he say?'

'Nothing, really. He just sounds vaguely threatening. And he calls me Gwen Shackleton.'

'Have you any idea who it might be?'

'No. It wouldn't be too difficult for anyone to find out my real name, and my number's in the directory. But why?'

'What about the accent? Is it American?'

'No. But it's hard to say exactly what it is. The voice sounds muffled, as if he's speaking through a handkerchief or something.'

Banks thought for a moment. 'We can't really do anything about it. I wouldn't worry too much, though. In most cases people who make threatening phone calls don't confront their victims. That's why they use the phone in the first place. They're afraid of personal contact.'

Vivian shook her head. 'I don't know. He didn't sound like one of those heavy breathers or nutcases. It seemed more . . . personal.'

'Perhaps your line of work attracts one or two crackpot fans?' Banks suggested. 'Someone who thinks he's giving you an idea for a story, or helping you know what it's like to experience fear. I honestly wouldn't worry too much, but you should get in touch with your local police station as soon as possible. They'll be able to help. Do you have any contacts there?'

'Yes. There's Detective Superintendent Davidson. He helps me with my research.'

'Even better. Talk to him.' Banks held up the envelope. 'We'll do as you ask,' he said, 'but how do we know this is the truth and not just more fiction?'

'You don't. Actually, it's a bit of both, but the parts you'll be interested in are true. You'll just have to take my word for it, won't you?'

•

The day it happened began like any ordinary day; if any day could be deemed ordinary in those extraordinary times. I opened the shop, took in the ration coupons, apologized for shortages, made lunch and tea for Mother and settled down to an evening's reading and the wireless. The Americans were having a farewell party up at the base that night, as they had heard they would be moving out in a matter of days. We had been invited, but neither Gloria nor I had felt like going. Somehow, that part of our lives seemed over. Charlie was dead and Gloria had made it clear to Brad, after their last fling on VE Day, that she was sticking with Matthew and it would be best if they didn't see each other any more.

I'd like to say I felt some sort of premonition of disaster, some sense of foreboding, but I didn't. I was distracted and found it hard to concentrate on Trollope's *The Last Chronicle of Barset*, but I had a lot on my mind: Charlie's death, Matthew's illness, Gloria's problems, Mother.

I wouldn't normally have gone to Bridge Cottage so late in the evening except that Cynthia Garmen had dropped off some parachute silk on her way to Harkside. I hadn't seen Gloria for two or three days and I thought she might appreciate a small gift; she had been very drawn and depressed since VE Day and hadn't been taking care of herself at all. I can't say that I heard any small voice telling me to go; nor can I recollect any great feeling of apprehension, any involuntary shudder or burning of the ears. I couldn't concentrate on my book, and Gloria was on my mind; it was as simple as that.

This is where my diary stops, but however much I have tried over the years to expunge the events from my memory, I haven't been able to succeed.

It was just after ten o'clock and Mother had gone to bed. Distracted, I put my book aside and fingered the silky material. I thought the prospect of a new dress to make might cheer Gloria up. I was also feeling guilty over stealing the gun, I suppose, and I wanted to know whether she had noticed it missing yet. If she had, she certainly hadn't said anything.

I assumed Matthew would still be at the Shoulder of Mutton, so I thought I would call in there first and persuade him to walk home with me. Even though he didn't communicate, I believed that he knew who I was and knew that I loved him. I also think he felt comfortable being with me. As it turned out, he had been asked to leave a little earlier because he had had one of his little tantrums and broken a glass.

I walked down the dark, deserted High Street to Bridge Cottage. Over the river I could hear music and laughter from the Duke of Wellington, where, it seemed, the VE Day celebrations were still going on over a week after the day itself. Moonlight silvered the flowing water and made it look like some sort of sleek, slinking animal.

There was light showing between the curtains in Bridge Cottage. New curtains, I noticed, now we didn't have to worry about the blackout, or even the dim-out, any more. I knocked at the door but no one answered. I knocked again.

I didn't think Gloria would be out; she rarely went out

in the evenings except to the pictures with me. She certainly wouldn't go out and leave the lights on. Besides, Matthew should be there. Where else would he have gone after being ejected from the Shoulder of Mutton?

I knocked again.

Still nothing.

I put my key in the lock, turned it and entered, calling out Gloria's name.

There was no one in the living room but I noticed a strong smell of whisky. I called out Gloria's name again, then thought I heard a movement in the kitchen. Puzzled, I walked over and when I got to the doorway I saw her.

Gloria lay on the flagstone floor, legs and arms splayed at awkward angles like a rag doll a sulking child has tossed aside. One of her little fists was curled tight, as if she were about to hit someone, except for the little finger, which stuck out.

There wasn't a lot of blood; I remember being surprised at how little blood there was. She was wearing her royal-blue dress with the white lace collar, and the stains on the material looked like rust. They were all over the place: breast, stomach, ribs, loins. Everywhere the royal-blue dress was stained with blood, yet very little of it had flowed to the floor.

Not far from her body lay a broken whisky bottle, the source of the smell I had noticed earlier. Bourbon. An unopened carton of Lucky Strikes sat on the countertop. Above it, the cupboard was open and tea and cocoa had spilled all over the counter and the floor nearby, along with knives and forks from the cutlery drawer.

Beside her, holding a bloody kitchen knife, Matthew knelt in a small pool of blood. I went over to him, took the knife gently out of his hand and led him through to his armchair. He accompanied me as meekly as a weary, defeated soldier goes with his captors and flopped back in the chair like a man who hasn't slept for months.

'Matthew, what happened?' I asked him. 'What have you done? You've got to tell me. Why did you do it?'

I gave him pencil and paper, but he just drew in on himself and I could tell I would get nothing out of him. I put my hands on his shoulders and shook him lightly, but he seemed to shrink away, blood-stained thumb in his mouth. I noticed more blood on the cuffs of his white shirt.

I don't know how long I tried to get him to communicate something, but in the end I gave up and went back to the kitchen. I wasn't thinking clearly. I suppose if I assumed anything at all, it was that someone must have told him there was nasty gossip going around about what his wife got up to while he was out. I already knew that he had had a tantrum in the Shoulder of Mutton and I guessed that one way or the other, it had set off the explosion that had been building in him the way pressure builds in a boiler; now Gloria was dead and Matthew was empty of his rage.

As I stared down at poor Gloria's body, still half unable to believe what had happened, I knew I had to do something. If anyone found out about this, Matthew might be hanged, or, more likely, found insane and put in the lunatic asylum for the rest of his days. However difficult his life was right now, I knew he wouldn't be able to bear that; it would be purgatory for him. Or worse. I would have to care for him from now on.

As for Gloria, my heart wept for her; I had come to love her almost as much as I loved Matthew. But she was dead. There was nothing I could do for her. She had no other family; I was the only one who knew her story; it didn't matter now what happened to her. Or so I told myself.

I still had some vestiges of religion in me back then, though most of it had disappeared during the war, especially after Matthew's death and resurrection, which seemed to me a very cruel parody of Easter, but I didn't particularly give any thoughts to Gloria's immortal soul, a proper burial or things like that. The church didn't come into it. I didn't think of what I was doing in terms of right or wrong; nor did I really consider that I would be breaking the law. All I could think about was what to do to protect Matthew from all the prying policemen and doctors who would torment him if word of this got out.

Did I think of Matthew as a murderer? I don't think I did, though there was undoubted evidence of this at my feet. In a strange way, I also saw Gloria as my partner in wanting to protect Matthew from further cruelty and suffering. She wouldn't want him to go to gaol, I told myself; she wouldn't want him put away in a lunatic asylum. She had sacrificed so much to protect him. His comfort and ease were all she had lived for after his return; he was her penance, after all, and that was why she would never leave him; that was why she was dead. *Gloria wanted me to do this.*

I offer no more excuses. The blackout cloth was still rolled up below the windows in the living room, where it had been left after I helped Gloria take it down a couple of months ago. I carried it into the kitchen and gently rolled Gloria on to it, then I wrapped it around her as tightly as a shroud. Before I had finished I bent over, kissed her gently on the forehead and said, 'Goodbye, sweet Gloria. Goodbye, my love.' She was still warm.

Where could I hide her? The only place I could think of was the old outbuilding they never used. In the light of a small oil lamp I started to dig the hole. I wanted to make it deeper, but I couldn't manage more than about three or four feet before exhaustion overcame me. I went back to the house, where Matthew hadn't moved, and managed to find the energy to drag out the roll of blackout cloth and drop it in the hole. There was no one around. The cottage next door was empty and there was neither a light nor a sound out back. Only the black night sky with its uncaring stars.

With tears running down my cheeks, I shovelled back the earth. Some heavy stone slabs stood propped against the wall and I levered them down on top of the makeshift grave. It was the best I could do.

That left only the inside of the house. First, I swept up the broken glass, the spilled tea-leaves and cocoa powder, and put the tins back in the cupboard. As I said, there was very little blood and I managed to scrub that off the floor easily enough. There might have been minute traces left but nobody would be able to tell what they were. If things went according to plan, nobody would even look.

I say 'plan' now, but it was just something I had come up with while burying Gloria. I had to explain where she had gone.

After I had managed to lead Matthew upstairs and wash and undress him, I put him to bed. I packed his bloody shirt and trousers in a small suitcase and added as many of Gloria's favourite clothes as I could fit in. Then I went and picked up her personal odds and ends and put them in the suitcase too.

After checking the kitchen carefully to make sure that I had collected everything of importance and cleaned up to the best of my ability, I wrote a note on the same paper I had got out for Matthew earlier. Gloria's childlike handwriting and style were easy to imitate. After that, carrying the suitcase, I took the back way to the shop. I didn't want to leave Matthew, God knows, but what else could I do? Things had to appear more or less normal. He didn't seem aware of what was happening and I had no idea how he would face the next day, whether he would remember what he had done, feel remorse or guilt. Would he even notice she was gone?

Early the next day I went to Bridge Cottage, found Matthew still in bed, 'found' the note and proceeded to tell everyone we knew, including Mother, that Gloria had run away during the night because she couldn't bear her life with Matthew any more. She said she loved him, and she always would, but she couldn't be responsible for her actions if she stayed. Then I showed them the note, which said exactly that. She ended by saying that we shouldn't go looking for her because we would never be able to find her.

There was no reason to call in the police. Everyone believed the note without question. Hadn't Gloria already told me she had heard people predicting that she would run off with a Yank at the first opportunity? Of course, she hadn't gone off with a Yank, and Brad, for one, would know that, but I would cross that bridge when I came to it.

I gave up Bridge Cottage, sold the contents, including the radiogram and the records Gloria loved so much, and brought Matthew back to live with us above the shop.

One evening when Mother was at Joyce Maddingley's, I took Matthew's blood-stained clothes and Gloria's dresses and burned them in the grate. I cried as I watched all those beautiful dresses catch fire. The black-red-and-white-checked Dorville dress she had bought in London; the black velvet V-neck dress with the puff sleeves, wide, padded shoulders and red felt rose that she had worn to our first dance with the Americans at Rowan Woods; her fine underwear. I watched it all flare and twist, then collapse into ashes. I disposed of her trinkets in Leeds the next time I went there on shop business. I just stood on Leeds Bridge at the bottom of Briggate and dropped them one by one into the River Aire.

As I had expected, it was Brad who gave me the most trouble. On his last day at Rowan Woods, he came to the shop and pestered me with questions. He just couldn't believe that Gloria had simply left. If she wanted to go, he argued, then why didn't she go with him? He had asked her often enough. I told him I thought she wanted to escape from everyone; she needed a completely new start. He said she could have had that in California. Again, I argued that living with him in Los Angeles would always have felt tainted to her because of the circumstances in which it came about. No matter what, she would still have been Matthew's wife.

It hurt him deeply, which I hated to do, but he had to accept what I said in the end. After all, she had told him she didn't want to see him any more after VE Day. Absolutely no one suspected anything like the truth. The 448th Bomber Group moved out of Rowan Woods and I heard nothing more from Brad. It was all over.

Michael Stanhope expressed sorrow that such a beautiful spirit had left the community. He said something about Hobb's End having glimmered briefly, then turned dark again. He was free to sell the nude now, not that I ever saw or heard anything of it again. Perhaps it wasn't as good as he thought it was.

As for Matthew, he never really showed any sign that anything was different. He was a little more withdrawn, perhaps, but he went on with the same drinking and staring into space as before. I had to stop the visits to Dr Jennings, of course. Who knew what narcosynthesis might draw out of Matthew, should it work? Though the doctor protested, I think he was quite relieved. Doctors don't like failures and Dr Jennings had been getting nowhere with Matthew.

Soon, we were hearing rumours that the village was to be sold as a reservoir site, and when I looked around, it didn't surprise me.

Hobb's End had turned into a ghost village.

I hadn't noticed it happening because of other matters, but hardly anyone lived there any more. Those who had come back from the war had had a taste of more interesting locales or had been trained for jobs they could only get in the cities. Even the women, who had perhaps gained the most in terms of employment, were heading off for factory jobs in Leeds and Bradford. The mill closed. Buildings fell into disrepair. Old people died. Finally, there was nobody left.

A strange incident occurred before we left for Leeds, though Gloria had, in a way, predicted it. One day, a man in a brown demob suit came into the shop with a little boy of about eight or nine and asked to see Gloria. I knew immediately who they were, though I didn't want to admit it to them.

'Are you a relative?' I asked him.

'No,' he said. 'Nothing like that. Just an old friend, that's all. I was passing this way, so I thought I'd look her up.' He sounded rather sad, and I noticed he had a Cockney accent, just as Gloria did when she let her guard slip. And, of course, nobody just *passes* Hobb's End way.

I asked him more questions, to show interest and politeness, but I could get nothing more out of him. Most of all, I wanted him to be satisfied by my explanation of Gloria's disappearance; I certainly didn't want him to come back and pester Matthew and me.

I needn't have worried. When he left, he just said, 'If you do see her again, tell her George called, will you?' He looked down at the boy. 'Tell her George and little Frankie dropped by and send their love.'

I assured him I would. The little boy had said nothing at all, but I felt him staring at me the whole time, as if he were etching my features on to the tissue of his memory. On impulse, I gave him a quarter ounce of gumdrops, quite a rarity, as sweets were still rationed. He thanked me solemnly and then they left.

The following week, Matthew, Mother and I moved to Leeds and Hobb's End ceased to exist. Our life in Leeds was not without incident, but that's another story.

•

'If we go to the CPS with Vivian Elmsley's story,' Banks said to Annie, 'they'll laugh us out of the office.'

It was Sunday morning, and they were both lounging about Banks's cottage rereading Vivian Elmsley's manuscript and drinking coffee. It had been against Annie's better judgment to take up Banks's suggestion of spending the weekend together. What she had meant to do after getting in her car at York was drive straight home and spend the rest of the weekend in blissful, idle solitude. But next Friday, she was taking two weeks' holiday and was planning to go down to stay with her father at the colony. Best enjoy some time together now, she thought. She would have plenty of time for long, lonely coast walks when she got to St Ives.

So, on Sunday morning, she was lying back in Banks's front room, barefoot, wearing shorts, her feet dangling over the arm of the settee, reading about Gwen Shackleton's war.

'Why would they laugh?' she said. 'It's a confession of sorts, isn't it? She does admit to interfering with the body. That makes her an accessory.'

'I very much doubt that any judge would admit the manuscript as evidence. All she has to do is say it's fiction. The Crown knows that. It's a load of bollocks, Annie. Just as well the woman writes fiction and doesn't have to solve *real* crimes.'

'But she uses real names.'

'Doesn't matter. Any decent lawyer would make mince-meat of it as a confession to aiding and abetting. Look at what we've got. We've got a woman in her seventies who presented us with a manuscript she wrote nearly thirty years ago hinting that she covered up a murder she thinks her brother committed over twenty years before that in a village that no longer exists. Add to that she makes her living writing detective fiction.' He ran his hand across his head. 'Believe me, the CPS have enough of a backlog already. They can't even keep up with today's crimes, let alone put staff on prosecuting yesterday's on evidence so flimsy a puff of wind would blow it away.'

'So that's it? We go no further? She goes scot-free?'

'Do you *want* to see her in prison?'

'Not particularly. I'm just playing devil's advocate. To be honest, it looks as if the poor woman's suffered enough to me. What a blighted life.'

'I don't know. She's had a fair amount of success.'

'Sometimes that doesn't mean as much as those who don't have it seem to think it does.'

'Well,' Banks went on, 'we always knew the case might end nowhere. Matthew Shackleton is dead. I think Vivian Elmsley wanted to get what she did off her chest. She *wanted* us to know. Not for our sake, so we could solve the

mystery, but for hers, so she wouldn't have to bear
the burden alone any more. The discovery of Gloria
Shackleton's skeleton was a tremendous catalyst for her. It
pushed her towards some sort of catharsis, and when we
found out who she was it was just a matter of time. I
would imagine now it seems less important to her to
protect Matthew's memory than it did all those years ago.
He's in no position to hang or spend his days in a
psychiatric institution.'

'She still committed a crime, though.'

'Yes, but she's not the killer.'

'Unless she's lying in the story.'

'I don't think so. She did what she did to protect her
brother, who had already suffered terribly in the war. And
she kept the secret to protect herself and Matthew's name.
If she'd called the police at the time, it's almost certain he
would have been convicted of Gloria's murder. Unless . . .'

'Unless what?'

'Unless he didn't do it. There are a number of things in
Gwen's version that bother me. Look at the scenario.
Gwen walks into the cottage and sees Matthew bent over
Gloria's body, a kitchen knife in his hand. So far so good?'

Annie nodded.

'She also notices that Gloria's fist is clenched and the
little finger appears to be broken. Right?'

'Right.'

'And Gloria's body is still warm.'

'Yes.'

'Which means that the clenched fist wasn't caused
by rigor mortis; it was caused by a cadaveric spasm.
What if the killer, the *real* killer, had been trying to take
something out of Gloria's hand when he was disturbed
by Matthew coming home, chucked out of the pub early

for causing a ruckus? Something that might have incriminated him.'

'The button?'

'It makes sense, doesn't it?'

'It's certainly possible.'

Banks shook his head. 'But they'd still probably have arrested Matthew, depending on the copper in charge. Remember, most of the bright young detectives were at war. The crazy husband would have looked the most obvious suspect, and the button, even if they had found it, could have been explained away. From Vivian's point of view, if Matthew had even a scrap of sanity left before all hell broke loose, he wouldn't have had any by the time it was over. So she committed a crime. And a serious one at that. But not only would the CPS throw it out; if it ever got as far as a jury, *they* would chuck it out too. Think of the sympathy angle. Any decent barrister – and I'll bet you Vivian Elmsley can afford a more-than-decent barrister – would have the whole courtroom in tears.'

'So what do we do next?'

'We could hand the report to Jimmy Riddle and get on with our lives.'

'Or?'

'Or look into those one or two little inconsistencies I mentioned. For a start, I'm not convinced that—'

The doorbell rang.

Banks went to answer it. Curious, Annie let the manuscript drop on her lap. 'Maybe it's that hard-working DS Hatchley of yours?'

'On a Sunday morning? That'd be stretching credibility *too* far.'

Banks opened the door. Annie heard a woman's voice, then Banks stepped back slowly and in she walked.

Blonde hair, black eyebrows, attractive, good figure, nicely dressed in a pastel skirt and a white blouse.

She noticed Annie out of the corner of her eye and turned. For a moment, she seemed speechless, a slight flush suffusing her pale complexion, then she moved forward and said, 'Hello, I don't think we've been introduced.'

Feeling foolish, Annie took the manuscript off her stomach and stood up. 'Annie Cabbot,' she said. 'DS Cabbot.' She felt acutely aware of her bare legs and feet.

'Sandra Banks,' said the other. 'Pleased to meet you.'

Banks closed the door and stood behind them looking uncomfortable. 'DS Cabbot and I were just discussing the Thornfield Reservoir case,' he said. 'Maybe you've read about it?'

Sandra looked down at Annie's bare feet, then gave Banks a withering glance. 'Yes, of course,' she said. 'And on a Sunday morning, too. Such devotion to duty.' She started moving back towards the door.

Annie felt herself blush to her roots.

'Anyway,' Banks gibbered on, 'it's really nice to see you. Would you like some coffee or something?'

Sandra shook her head. 'No, I don't think so. I just came up to Eastvale to see to some things at the community centre. I'm staying with Harriet and David. While I was in the area, I thought I'd drop by to get some papers signed and talk to you about our son, but it'll do some other time. No hurry. Don't let me interrupt your brainstorming session.'

As she spoke she grasped the handle and opened the door. 'Nice meeting you, DS Cabbot,' she said over her shoulder, and with that she was gone.

Annie stood facing Banks in silence for a few moments,

aware only of her fast and loud heartbeat and burning skin. 'I didn't know what to say,' she said. 'I felt foolish, embarrassed.'

'Why should you?' said Banks. 'I've already told you, Sandra and I have been separated for almost a year.'

But you still love her, Annie thought. Where did that come from? She pushed the thought away. 'Yes, I know. It was just a shock, meeting her like that.'

Banks gave a nervous laugh. 'You can say that again. Look, let's have some more coffee and go sit outside, okay? Put Vivian Elmsley and her problems on the back burner for a while. It's a beautiful day, shame to waste it staying indoors. Maybe this afternoon we can go for a long walk? Fremlington Edge?'

'Okay.' Annie followed him outside, still feeling dazed. She sat on a striped deck-chair, feeling the warmth of the canvas against the backs of her bare thighs, the feeling that always reminded her of summers in St Ives. Banks was reading the *Sunday Times* book section, trying to pretend everything was just fine, but she knew he was rattled, too. Perhaps even more than she was. After all, he had been married to the woman for more than twenty years.

Annie stared into the distance at a straggling line of ramblers walking up Witch Fell, whose massive shape, like a truncated witch's hat, took up most of the western skyline. Crows wheeled over the heights.

'Are you okay?' Banks asked, looking up from his paper.

'Fine,' she said, mustering a smile. 'Fine.'

But she wasn't. She told herself she should have known how fleeting happiness was; how foolish it is to expect it at all, and what a mistake it is to allow oneself to get too close to anyone. Closeness like that stirs up all the old demons – the jealousy, the insecurity; all the things she thought she had mastered. The only possible outcome is pain. A shadow had blotted out her sun, just the way Witch Fell obscured the sky; a snake had crawled into her Eden. What, she wondered, would be the cost?

17

Vivian's manuscript haunted Banks long after he had read it. There were so many inconsistencies, so many branches in the road to Gloria's murder. On Wednesday, when they still hadn't found Gloria's son, he started thinking about the trip George and Francis Henderson had made to try to find Gloria after the war. Gwen had denied her, in a way, and that set Banks thinking about his visit to Jem's parents.

As vividly as if it were yesterday, he remembered the late May afternoon when he drove his ailing VW beetle to Cambridgeshire in search of Jem's parents. He didn't even know why he was making the journey, and more than once he thought of turning back. What could he say? What right had he to intrude on their grief? After all, he had hardly known Jem, knew nothing about his life. On the other hand, they had been friends, and now his friend was dead. The least he could do was offer his condolences and tell them they had a son they should be proud of, no matter how ignominious his death.

Besides, he was curious to see what sort of background Jem came from.

It was a fine day and Banks drove with his window down through the North London suburbs and into open countryside, the wind blowing through his hair, which at that time was well over his collar. He turned off the main road just south of Cambridge. A number of images of the drive came back: Tim Buckley on the radio singing 'Dolphins' just outside Saffron Walden; a whitewashed pub wall; a herd of cows blocking the road as they were moved, udders swinging, from field to field by a slow farmer, unconcerned about the minor traffic jam he was causing; the air smelling of warm straw and manure.

Banks stopped in the village newsagent's and asked for directions to the Hylton house. The shopkeeper looked suspicious, as if she thought he was out to rob the place, but she told him. The house – mansion, rather – stood at the end of an unpaved drive about half a mile from the village centre. It was originally Tudor, by the look of it, but was crusted with so many centuries of additions, like barnacles on the bottom of a boat – a conservatory here, a garage there, a dormer window – that it seemed on the verge of buckling under its own weight.

Banks sat in his car and stared for a moment, hardly able to take in that *this* was where Jem came from. He stubbed out his cigarette. The area was quiet, except for a few birds singing and the sound of someone talking on a radio deep inside the house. Surely they must have heard him arrive? Especially with the odd hiccuping sounds his beetle was making those days.

Banks got out of the car and looked around. Beyond a neatly trimmed croquet-size lawn the land dipped away, revealing a patchwork landscape of green and brown fields under a canopy of blue sky as far as the eye could see. A few small copses and a church steeple were all that broke the monotony. This was the *old* England, the place of order, of the labourer at work in the fields and the lord at ease in his manor. It was a far cry from Peterborough and Notting Hill. Banks had visited the countryside before, of course, but he had never been to a house so opulent, had never *known* anyone who came from such a house. The old class insecurities began to surface, and if he had been wearing one, he would probably have knocked on the door cap in hand. He felt self-conscious of his accent even before he opened his mouth.

A sweet-smelling honeysuckle bush stood beside the old oak door, and Banks could hear the bees droning around the blossoms. He banged the heavy knocker against the wood. The sound echoed through the country-side and sent a nearby flock of starlings flapping off into the sky.

It seemed for ever before Banks became aware of someone approaching the door, a creak of a floorboard perhaps, or swish of a skirt. When it opened a crack, he found himself looking at a dark-haired woman with high cheekbones and sunken brown eyes. She seemed old to him back then, when he had hardly turned twenty, but he realized that she was probably only in her early forties, about the same age he was now.

She raised an eyebrow. 'Yes? What is it?'

'Mrs Hylton?'

'I'm Mrs Hylton. What can I do for you?'

'I've come about Jem.'

She frowned. 'Who?'

'Jem. Sorry: Jeremy. Your son.'

A man appeared behind her, and she opened the door all the way. He had white hair, a red face, and watery pale blue eyes. 'What is it, darling?' he asked, putting his hand on the woman's shoulder and frowning at Banks. 'Who is he? What does he want?'

She turned to her husband with a puzzled expression on her face. 'Someone come about Jeremy.'

Banks introduced himself. 'I lived across the hall from

Jeremy in Notting Hill,' he said. 'We were friends. I just wanted to come and say I'm sorry about what happened.'

'I don't understand,' said the man. 'Our son died a long time ago. It's a bit late to be coming round with con- dolences, don't you think?'

'Jem? *Jeremy* Hylton? I am at the right house, aren't I?'

'Oh, yes,' said the woman. 'But the thing is, our Jeremy died *five years* ago.'

'But . . . but it was only about a month ago. I mean, I knew him. I *found* him. We *are* speaking about the same person, aren't we? Did Jeremy have a brother, perhaps?'

'We had only one son,' the man said. 'And he died five years ago. Now, if you don't mind, I think my wife has been disturbed enough, don't you? Good day.'

He started to close the door.

Banks made one last-ditch attempt. He stuck his foot in the door and said, 'Please, you don't understand. Jem died last month. I don't mean to upset you, but—'

Mr Hylton opened the door a fraction and Banks slipped his foot out. 'If you don't go away and get off our property immediately, I'm going to call the police,' he said. 'Is that clear?' And this time he slammed the door shut before Banks could move.

For a few moments, Banks stared at the weathered oak, his mind spinning. He saw a curtain move and assumed they were watching, ready to phone the police, so he got in his beetle, turned and drove away.

At the end of the drive, an elderly man wearing a cloth cap waved him down. Banks stopped, and the man leaned down to the open window. He had about five days' growth on his cheeks, and his breath smelled of beer. 'What you been bothering them there for, then?' he asked.

'I wasn't bothering them,' Banks said. 'I just came to

offer them my condolences on their son's death.'

The man scratched his cheek. 'And what did they say?'

Banks told him, all the time glancing in his mirror to see if the Hyltons had followed him down the drive.

'Well,' the man said, 'see, as far as they're concerned, their Jeremy died the day he dropped out of university and went off to London to be one of them drug-smoking hippies.' He scrutinized Banks for a moment, as if trying to make up his mind where *he* fitted in the scheme of things. 'I noticed they had the police round a while back and wondered what it were all about. Jeremy's *really* dead now, then?'

'Yes,' said Banks after another quick glance in the mirror.

'Drugs, were it?'

'Looks that way.'

'I'm sorry to hear it. I've known him since he were a babe in arms. Nice young lad he were till he went bad. He were going to be a doctor, like his dad. At Cambridge he was you know. I don't know what went wrong.' He pointed with his thumb back at the house. 'They never recovered. Don't talk to anyone. Don't have any visitors.' He shook his head slowly. 'Poor little Jeremy. They never even gave him a funeral service.' Then he wandered away along the road shaking his head and muttering to himself.

Banks was left alone at the intersection of the drive and the road, with only the birdsong and his own gloomy thoughts of estrangement and denial for company. He had a pretty good idea of what went wrong for Jem, having read Clara's letter, but it seemed that nobody wanted to know.

Horns blaring on Market Street broke into his reminiscences.

Now he had another denial on his mind. Jem's parents had convinced themselves their son had died five years before he really did, just because he had disappointed their expectations. Gwen Shackleton told George and Francis Henderson that Gloria had run away when she was well aware that Gloria was actually dead and buried out back. Somehow, the two denials seemed like curious mirror images to Banks.

A knock at the door interrupted this train of thought. Sergeant Hatchley walked in. 'Coffee break?'

Banks looked up and dragged himself back from a long distance. 'What? Oh, yes.'

'You all right, sir? You look a bit pale.'

'Fine. Just thinking, that's all.'

'Can be painful, thinking. That's why I try to avoid it.'

They walked across Market Street to the Golden Grill for toasted tea-cakes and coffee. Rain had finally come to the Dales, and the place was almost empty. Doris, the proprietor, claimed they were only the fourth and fifth customers to pass through her door that day.

'Does that put us in line for summat special, like?' Hatchley asked. 'Maybe a free cuppa?'

She slapped his arm and laughed. 'Get away with you.'

'Worth a try,' said Hatchley to Banks. 'Never ask, never get. I used to know a bloke years back who claimed he asked every girl he met if she'd go to bed with him. Said he only got slapped in the face nine times out of ten.'

Banks laughed, then he asked, 'Have you heard anything on that nationwide inquiry you put out yet?'

'Something came in this morning, as a matter of fact,' said Hatchley. 'That's what I wanted to talk to you about. Lass called Brenda Hamilton. Bit of a tart, by all accounts. Not a prossie by trade, but she wasn't averse to opening her legs for anyone who looked like he had a bob or two to spare. Anyway, she was found dead in a barn.'

'MO?'

'Strangled and stabbed. In that order.'

'It certainly *sounds* promising.'

Hatchley shook his head. 'Don't get your hopes up. There's a couple of problems.'

'What problems?'

'Location and time frame. It happened near Hadleigh, Suffolk, in August 1952. I only mentioned it because it was the same MO.'

Banks chewed on his tea-cake and thought it over. 'Any suspects?'

'Naturally, the farmer who owned the barn came in for a close look, but he had a watertight alibi. I'd have sent for more details, but . . . well, it's not likely to be connected with our business, is it?'

Banks shrugged. 'Wouldn't do any harm to ask a few more questions.'

'Maybe not. But that's seven years after Gloria Shackleton was killed. It's a long gap for the kind of killer we're looking at. It also happened in another part of the country.'

'There could be reasons for that.'

'And I doubt there'd be any American Air Force personnel around by then, would there? I mean the war was long over. Most of them went off to the Pacific after VE Day and the rest buggered off home as soon as they could.'

'You're probably right, Jim, but let's be thorough. Get on to East Anglia and ask them for more details. I'll ask DS Cabbot to contact the USAFE people again and see if she can find out anything.'

'Will do.'

Back in his office, Banks put off phoning Annie at Harkside, smoking a cigarette instead and staring out of the window. A warm slow rain fell on the market square, darkening the cobbles and the ancient market cross. It wasn't bringing much relief; the air was still sticky and humid. But slowly the clouds were gathering, the humidity increasing. One day soon it would break and the heavens would open. There were only a couple of cars parked in the square, and the few people in evidence ambled around under umbrellas looking gloomily at the shops. Radio Three was playing a programme of British light music, and Banks recognized the signature theme of 'Children's Favourites'.

The reason he was avoiding talking to Annie was that Sunday had gone badly after Sandra's visit. Both Banks and Annie had been on edge, conversation awkward, and she had eventually left just after lunch, forgoing the afternoon walk, claiming she had things to see to back in Harkside. They hadn't spoken to each other since.

At the time, Banks had not been sorry to see her go. He was more upset than he had let on by Sandra's visit, and it annoyed him that he felt that way. After all, *she* had a new boyfriend. *Sean*. Why did she have to turn up just then, when everything was going so well? What gave her the right to burst in and act so shocked that *he* was seeing someone, knocking everyone's feelings out of kilter? How would she like it if he just dropped in on her and Sean, without even phoning first? And he *had* wanted to talk to her, especially after his little heart-to-heart with Brian. Now God only knew when he would get the chance again.

He also realized that Sandra had been upset by what she saw, too. The withering coolness and sarcastic tone were her way of reacting to her own discomfort. He still had feelings for her. You can't just lose your feelings that quickly for someone you loved for so long. Love lost or rejected may first turn to hate, but only over time does it become indifference.

Finally, he plucked up the courage and picked up the phone. 'How's it going?' he asked.

'Fine.'

'You sound distracted.'

'No, I'm not. Just a bit busy. Really. It's fine.'

Banks took a deep breath. 'Look, if it's about Sunday, I'm sorry. I had no idea Sandra was going to turn up. I also didn't think it would have so much of an effect on you.'

'Well, you don't always know about these things till they happen, do you? As I said, I'm fine. Except I've got a lot on my plate right now. What's on your mind?'

'Okay, if that's how you want to play it. Get on to your military contacts again and see if you can find out anything about US Air Force presence in Suffolk in 1952.'

'What about it?'

'Find out if there were any bases left, for a start. And if there were, which was the nearest one to Hadleigh. If there was one, I'd also like a list of personnel.'

'Right.'

'Can you do it today?'

'I'll try. Tomorrow at the latest.'

'Annie?'

'What?'

'Can't we get together and talk about things?'

'There's nothing to talk about. Really. Look, you know I'm off home on holiday in a couple of days. I've got a lot to do before I go. Maybe when I get back. Okay? In the meantime, I'll get that information to you as soon as I can. Goodbye.'

Feeling more depressed than ever after that pointless conversation, Banks glanced at the pile of paper beside the computer on his desk: SOCO search results, post-mortem, forensic odontology. None of it contradicted what they had previously estimated; nor did any of it tell him anything more.

What would have happened if Gwen had done as she should and reported finding Gloria's body? A good copper might have asked around and not simply tried to pin the murder on Matthew. And maybe not. Too late for asking questions now; they were all dead except Vivian. Poor Gloria. She saw Matthew as her *penance*. Somehow that told Banks more about her than anything else.

And what if Vivian's ending was the real lie? The ultimate irony. What if Gwen herself had committed the murder?

•

Vivian Elmsley put her book down as the train pulled out of Wakefield Westgate on Thursday. It would only be a few more minutes to Leeds now, and built up the whole way: a typical Northern industrial landscape of shabby red-brick housing estates, low-rise office buildings, sparkling new shopping centres, factory yards full of stacked pallets wrapped in polythene, kids fishing in the canal, stripped to the waist. The only untypical thing was the sticky sunlight that seemed to encase everything like sugar water.

The publisher's rep was supposed to meet Vivian at the station and accompany her to the Metropole Hotel, where she would be staying until Sunday. She had book signings in Bradford, York and Harrogate, as well as in Leeds, but it made no sense to move everything lock, stock and barrel from one hotel to another every day. The cities were close enough together. The rep would drive her around.

Not that Vivian needed any help to find the hotel; the Metropole wasn't more than a couple of hundred yards from City Square, and she knew exactly where it was. She had stayed there with Charlie the time they went to Michael Stanhope's exhibition in 1944. What an evening they had made of it. After the show, they went to a classical concert and then to the 21 Club, where they had danced until late. That was why she had asked to stay there again this trip. For memory's sake.

She was nervous. It wasn't anything to do with this evening's reading at Armley Library, or the Radio Leeds interview tomorrow afternoon, but with meeting Chief Inspector Banks and his female sidekick again. She knew they would want to interview her after studying the manuscript; there was no doubt she was guilty of something. But what could she do? She was too old and too tired to run. She was also too old to go to gaol. The only way now was to face up to whatever charges might be brought and hope her lawyer would do a good job.

No one, she supposed, could stop the press finding out the details eventually, and there was no doubt that they would go to town on the scandal. She wasn't sure she could face public humiliation. Perhaps, if they didn't arrest her, she would leave the country again, the way she had done so many times with Ronald. Why not? She could work anywhere, and she had enough money to buy a little place somewhere warm: Bermuda, perhaps, or the British Virgin Islands.

Once again Vivian cast her mind back to the events of fifty years ago. Was there something she had missed? Had she got it all wrong? Had she been so ready to suspect

Matthew that she had overlooked the possibility of anyone else being guilty? Banks's questions about Michael Stanhope and about PX, Billy Joe, Charlie and Brad had shocked and surprised her at first. Now she was beginning to wonder. Could one of them have done it? Not Charlie, certainly – he was dead by then – but what about Brad? He and Gloria had been arguing a lot towards the end; she had even seen them arguing through the flames at the VE Day party. Perhaps the night she died he had gone to put his case forward one last time, and when she turned him down he went berserk? Vivian tried to remember whether Brad had been the kind to go berserk or not, but all she could conclude was that we all are, given the right circumstances.

Then there was PX. He had certainly lavished a lot of gifts on Gloria in that shy way of his. Perhaps he had hoped for something in return? Something she hadn't wanted to give? And while Billy Joe seemed to have moved on to other women quite happily, Vivian remembered his bitterness at being ditched for a pilot, the smouldering class resentment that came out as gibes and taunts.

People said they didn't have a class system in America, but Billy Joe had definitely been working-class, like the farm labourers in Yorkshire; Charlie was from a well-established Ivy League background; and Brad had come from new West Coast oil money. Vivian didn't think the Americans lacked class distinction so much as they lacked the tradition of inherited aristocratic titles and wealth – which was probably why they all went gaga over British royalty.

The train was nearing Leeds City Station now, wheels squealing as it negotiated the increasingly complicated system of signals and points. It had been a much faster and easier journey than the one Vivian had made to London and back with Gloria. She remembered the pinprick of blue light, the soldiers snoring, her first look at the desolation of war in the pale dawn light. She had slept most of the way back to Leeds, a six- or seven-hour journey then, and after she got back to Hobb's End, London had grown more and more distant and magical in her imagination until it might easily have been Mars or ancient Rome.

Looking back, she began to wonder if perhaps it was *all* just a story. As the years race inexorably on, and as all the people we know and love die, does the past turn into fiction, an act of the imagination populated by ghosts, scenes and images suspended for ever in water-glass?

Wearily, Vivian stood up and reached for her overnight bag. There was something else she had steeled herself to do while she was in Leeds, and she had set aside Friday afternoon, after the interview, for it. Before that, though, she would make time to call at the art gallery and see Michael Stanhope's painting.

•

When the phone rang on Thursday morning, Banks snatched the receiver from its cradle so hard he fumbled it and dropped it on the desk before getting a good grip.

'Alan, what's going on? You almost deafened me.'

'Oh, sorry.'

'It's Jenny.'

'I know. I recognized your voice. How are you?'

'Well, don't sound so excited to hear from me.'

'I'm sorry, Jenny, really. It's just that I'm expecting an important call.'

'Your girlfriend?'

'The case I'm working on.'

'That one you told me about? The war thing?'

'It's the only one I've got. Jimmy Riddle's made sure my cases have been thin on the ground lately.'

'Well, I won't take up much of your time. It just struck me that I was rather . . . well, emotional . . . on our last meeting. I want to apologize for dumping all over you, as they say in California.'

'What are friends for?'

'Anyway,' Jenny went on, 'by way of an apology, I'd like to invite you to dinner. If you think you can tolerate my cooking, that is?'

'It's bound to be better than mine.'

She laughed a little too quickly and a little too nervously. 'Don't count on it. I thought we could, you know, just talk about things over a meal and a bottle of wine. A lot's happened to both of us this past year.'

'When?'

'How about tomorrow, sevenish?'

'Sounds fine.'

'Are you sure it won't cause any problems?'

'Why should it?'

'I don't know . . . I just . . .' Then her voice brightened. 'That's great. I'll see you tomorrow about seven, then?'

'You're on. I'll pick up some wine.'

After he hung up, Banks sat back and thought about the invitation. Dinner with Jenny. At her place. That would be interesting. Then he thought about Annie, and that cast a shadow over him. She had basically cut him dead on the phone yesterday. After such quick and surprising intimacy, her coldness came as a shock. It was a long time since he had been given the cold shoulder by a girlfriend he had known for only a few days, and the whole thing brought back shades of adolescent gloom. Time to break out the sad songs again. Cry along with Leonard Cohen and learn how to get the best out of your suffering.

But he *was* anxious to hear from Annie about the East Anglia connection. She had said today at the latest, after all. He toyed with the idea of phoning her, but in the end decided against it. Whatever their personal problems, he knew she was a good enough copper to let him know the minute she got the information he'd asked for. Shortly before eleven, she did.

'I'm sorry for the delay,' she said. 'What with time differences and faulty fax machines, well, I'm sure you know . . .'

'That's all right. Just tell me what you've discovered.' Banks had already come to one or two conclusions of his own since his last talk with Annie, and he felt the tingling tremor of excitement that usually came as the pieces started to fall together; it was a feeling he hadn't experienced in quite a while.

'First off,' Annie said, 'there definitely *was* an American air base near Hadleigh in 1952.'

'What were they doing there?'

'Well, the US armed forces cleared out of England after the war, but a lot of them stayed on in Europe, especially Berlin and Vienna. The war hadn't solved the Russian problem. Anyway, the Americans came back to operate from British air bases in 1948, during the Berlin blockade and airlift. The first thing they did was deploy long-range B-29 bombers from four air bases in East Anglia. All this is from my contact in Ramstein. Apparently, there were so many bases by 1951 that they had to change their organizational structure to deal with them.'

'Any familiar names?'

'Just one. Guess who ran the PX?'

'Edgar Konig.'

'The very same. You don't sound so surprised.'

'Not really. What did you find out about him?'

'He left Rowan Woods in May 1945, with the rest of the Four Hundred and Forty-Eighth, and spent some time in Europe, then he returned to America. He was assigned to the base near Hadleigh in summer 1952.'

'He stayed in the air force all that time?'

'Seems that way. I suppose he had a pretty good job. Lots of perks. Tell me, why doesn't it surprise you? Why not one of the other Americans?'

'The whisky and the Luckies.'

'What?'

'In Vivian Elmsley's manuscript. She said there was a bottle of whisky smashed on the floor and an *unopened* carton of Lucky Strikes on the kitchen counter. It's hardly concrete evidence of anything, but I don't think a carton of Luckies would have stayed unopened for very long in wartime, do you?'

'Brad could have brought them.'

'Possible. But it was PX who had easiest access to the stores, PX who always supplied the goodies. The manuscript also mentioned a farewell party at Rowan Woods that night. PX must have got drunk and finally plucked up courage. He'd sneaked out of the base and brought the presents that night. One last-ditch attempt to buy what he yearned for. Gloria resisted and . . . Matthew only came in afterwards, the poor sod. Any idea where PX was between 1945 and 1952?'

'No. I can ask Mattie to check if it's important. You're thinking there might have been others?'

'Possibly. Do we know *anything* more about him?'

'No. Mattie said she'd try to find out what she can –

such as when and why he was discharged and if he's still alive, but she doesn't hold out a lot of hope. It's not their official position to give out such information, but Mattie's a mystery fan and it seems I've piqued her curiosity. She's become quite an ally.'

'Good. See what you can do. Let's see if we can link him to any other murders. How old will he be now if he's still alive?'

'According to Mattie's information, he'd be about seventy-five.'

'A possibility, then.'

'Could be. I'll talk to you later.'

When Annie had hung up, Banks felt restless. Sometimes waiting was the most difficult part; that was when he smoked too much and paced up and down, bad habits from his Met days he hadn't quite got rid of. There were a couple of things he could do in the meantime. First, he dialled Jenny Fuller's number.

'Alan,' she said. 'Don't tell me you want to cancel?'

'No, no. It's nothing like that. Actually, I need you to do a little favour for me.'

'Of course. If I can.'

'Didn't you say at lunch the other day that you trained with the FBI profilers?'

'At Quantico. Yes. And you said you thought profiling was a load of bollocks.'

'Forget that for now. Do you have any contacts there? Anyone close enough to ask a personal favour?'

Jenny paused a moment. 'Well, there is *one* fellow, yes. Why do you ask?'

Banks filled her in on the new developments, then said, 'This Edgar Konig, I'd like you to ask your friend to check his record. If he's the sort of man I think he is, the odds are that he'll have one. DS Cabbot's working with the military authorities, but any information they can supply us with is limited.'

'I'm sure Bill will be happy to oblige, if he can,' said Jenny. 'Just let me get a pencil, then you can tell me what you want to know.'

When Banks had finished giving Jenny the details, he asked DS Hatchley to call East Anglia and find out if a US airman called Edgar Konig had ever been questioned or suspected in connection with the Brenda Hamilton murder. After that, he sat back and told himself there was no rush. Nobody was running anywhere. Even if Konig did turn out to be the killer, even if he was still alive, there was no way he could know the North Yorkshire Police were on to him after all this time.

18

On Friday, the rep dropped Vivian back at her hotel a little later than she had expected. There had been a delay at the radio station when the sound technician discovered, halfway through the interview, that Vivian's microphone was faulty. She had to do the whole thing again. It was after four o'clock when she got out of the car, and the sky looked heavy and dark, the air crackling with pre-storm tension. In the distance, she could hear hesitant rumbles of thunder and see faint lightning flashes. Even the Metropole's façade, lovingly restored to its original orange terracotta, looked as black as it had when she had stayed there with Charlie all those years ago.

She would have liked nothing better than to rest in her room for an hour or so, perhaps take a long bath, but it would be fully dark before long. She supposed she could put off her trip and go another time. Tomorrow would be taken up with signings in York and Harrogate, but she could always catch a later train and make the visit on Sunday morning. No. She would not procrastinate. There was also something ironically appealing to the writer in her about visiting the place during a storm.

She called the concierge and asked him to arrange for a taxi, then she put on her raincoat and waterproof boots. The car was waiting downstairs, and she ducked in the back with her umbrella and gave the driver directions. The rain had started spotting now, making huge dark blobs on the pavement. The driver, a young Pakistani, tried to practise his English by making conversation about the weather, but he soon gave up and settled in to concentrate on his driving.

Woodhouse Road was busy with people leaving work early for the weekend, and the worsening weather made it a matter of stop and start. Beyond the city limits, though, things eased up.

As Vivian gazed out of the rain-streaked window, hypnotized by the slapping of the windscreen wipers, she thought about her visit to Leeds City Art Gallery yesterday. Seeing the nude painting of Gloria had evoked such a complex response in her that she still hadn't been able to sort out all the strands.

She had never seen Gloria naked before, had never accompanied her and Alice and the others on their skinny-dipping expeditions, out of shyness and out of shame at her body, so to see the smooth skin and the alluring curves as interpreted by Michael Stanhope's expert eye and hand came as a revelation.

What disturbed Vivian most of all was the pang of desire the painting engendered in her. She had thought herself long past such feelings, if she had ever, indeed, experienced them at all. True, she had loved Gloria, but she had never admitted to herself, had never even realized, that she might have loved her in *that* way. Now, as she remembered the innocent physical intimacies they had shared – painting one another's legs; the dancing lessons, when she had felt Gloria's body close to hers and breathed her perfume; the little kiss on her cheek after the wedding – she wasn't sure how innocent it had all been. The feelings, the urges, had been there, but Vivian had been ignorant of such things and had suppressed them. In the art gallery, she had felt like a pervert looking at pornography; not because there was anything pornographic about Stanhope's painting, but because of her own thoughts and feelings attached to it.

She thought of that moment when she had kissed Gloria's still-warm forehead before covering her with the blackout cloth. *'Goodbye, sweet Gloria. Goodbye, my love.'*

'Pardon me?' said the driver, turning his head.

'What? Oh, nothing. Nothing.'

Vivian shrank into her seat. Beyond Otley there was very little traffic. The roads were narrow, and they got stuck behind a lorry doing only about thirty for a while. It was after five o'clock when the driver pulled up in the car park near Thornfield Reservoir. The rain was coming down hard now, pattering against the leaves. At least, Vivian thought, in this weather she could be sure of having the place to herself. She told the driver she would only be about fifteen minutes and asked him to wait. He picked up a newspaper from the seat beside him.

A second car pulled up in the other car park, behind the high hedge, but Vivian was already walking through the woods, and she failed to notice it. The path was treacherous, as if the parched earth had been yearning for the chance to suck up every drop of rain that fell, and Vivian had to be really careful not to slip as she made her way slowly down the embankment, poking her umbrella in the ground ahead and using it as a sort of brake. God only knew how she would get back up again.

The ruined village lay spread out before her under the dark sky. Rain lashed the crumbled stones and every few seconds a flash of lightning lit the scene like a Stanhope painting.

Vivian paused to get her breath by the fairy bridge,

unfurled her umbrella, then walked forward and stood at the humped centre. She rested her free hand on the wet stone, hardly able to believe that this was the same bridge where she had stood and chatted with Gloria, Matthew, Alice, Cynthia, Betty and the others all those years ago. The last time she had been there, it had been under water.

The rain was already finding the old river's channel by the High Street, and a small stream had formed, heading towards Harksmere. Thunder hammered across the sky, and Vivian shuddered as she moved towards Bridge Cottage. There was nothing left of the place except the foundations, a dark stone outline two or three feet high, but she remembered where every room and cupboard had been, especially the kitchen at the back, where she had found Gloria's body.

The area around and inside the cottage had been dug up and was still surrounded by police signs warning that it might be dangerous. They had been looking for more bodies, Vivian supposed. Well, they would, wouldn't they? Inspector Niven would have done exactly the same thing.

Now she was standing there in the driving rain, which dripped off her umbrella and ran down inside her boots, she was beginning to wonder why she had come. There was nothing here for her now. At least when Hobb's End was under water she could imagine it, as she had done, as a place preserved in water-glass. Now it was nothing but a heap of rubble.

She ambled through the mud up what had been the High Street, past the Shoulder of Mutton, where Billy Joe had his fight with Seth, and where Matthew spent his evenings after his return from Luzon; past Halliwell the butcher's, where she had swapped Capstans for suet and pleaded for an extra piece of scrag-end; and past the newsagent's shop, where she had lived with Mother and sold her bits and pieces, built up her private lending library, met Gloria for the first time that blustery April day she came by in her new land-girl uniform asking for cigarettes.

It was no good; there was nothing of the place left but memories, and her memories were mostly painful. She hadn't known what to expect, had in mind only a simple sort of pilgrimage, an acknowledgment of some sort. Well, she had done that. Time to head back to the hotel for a hot bath and a change of clothes, or she would catch her death.

Lost in her thoughts, she hadn't noticed the gaunt, stringy-haired man who had followed her taxi all the way from Leeds. When she passed Bridge Cottage on her way back and turned towards the fairy bridge, he stepped from behind the outbuilding and held out a gun, then he moved forward quickly, grabbed her round the throat, and she felt the hard metal pushing at the side of her neck. Her umbrella went flying and landed upside down on High Street like a large black teacup.

Then his hand appeared in front of her, holding a dog-eared photograph creased with age. It took her a few moments to realize that it was Gloria. Her hair was darker and straighter, and it looked as if it had been taken perhaps a year or two before she had come to Hobb's End. Rain spattered the photograph and the hand that held it. Such a small hand. *Gloria's hand*, she thought, remembering that first meeting, when she had shaken hands and Vivian had felt heavy and awkward holding that tiny, moist leaf.

What was he doing with hands like Gloria's?

●

By six o'clock on Friday evening, Banks was starting to get nervous about his dinner date with Jenny. The thunder and lightning and driving rain that buffeted his tiny cottage didn't help. He had already showered and shaved, agonizing over whether to put on any aftershave and finally deciding against it, not wanting to smell like a tart's window-box. Now he was surveying his wardrobe, what little there was of it, trying to decide which version of casual he should put on tonight. It was a decision made a lot easier by the overflowing laundry basket: the Marks & Sparks chinos and the light blue denim shirt.

Almost ready at last, Banks stood in front of the mirror and ran his hand over his closely cropped hair. Nothing to write home about, he thought, but it was the best he could do with what nature had given him. He wasn't a vain man, but today he seemed to take longer than a woman getting ready to go out. He remembered how he had always had to wait for Sandra, no matter how much time he gave her. It had got so bad that when they had to be somewhere for seven-thirty, he told her seven o'clock, just to get an edge.

He thought of Annie. Did he owe her fidelity, or were all bets off after the way she had cut him? He didn't know. At the very least, he owed her an explanation of the case, given all the hard work she had put in. Late that afternoon, Bill Gilchrist of the FBI had sent him, at Jenny's request, a six-page fax on Edgar 'PX' Konig, and Banks had been gob-smacked by its contents. DS Hatchley had also determined that Konig *had* been questioned in connection with the Brenda Hamilton murder. He wasn't a serious suspect, but the two had been friendly. Rationing was in force until 1954, so PX still had his uses among the locals as late as 1952.

Annie wasn't at the section station when he phoned

her. He had tried her at home, too, but either she had already left for St Ives, or she wasn't answering her phone. Next he dialled her mobile number but still got no answer. Maybe she didn't want to talk to him.

Banks went downstairs and lit a cigarette. Miles Davis's *Bitches Brew* was playing on the stereo, bringing back more memories of Jem.

During one of those periods when the Met had brought in a new broom, and corruption charges were flying right, left and centre, Banks again saw the man he had first seen walking up the stairs on the night of Jem's death. A dealer. His name was Malcolm, and he had been brought in to give evidence against a certain DS Fallon, who was charged with extorting heroin from importers he busted instead of arresting them. Fallon then set up his own distribution network, which included Malcolm. In Banks's eyes, that made Malcolm partly responsible for Jem's death, and when he saw DS Fallon, he recognized immediately the pockmarked face and cynical smile of the cop who had rifled his bedsit after he'd reported Jem's death. No wonder no charges had ever been laid.

Fallon was arrested and sentenced. He hadn't been more than eighteen months in Wormwood Scrubs before a lifer who recognized him stabbed him through the ear with a filed-down length of metal. *Karma.* After five years or more it was hardly instant, but it was karma nonetheless. Jem would have liked that sense of symmetry.

Banks stubbed out his cigarette and was just heading into the bathroom to brush his teeth when the telephone rang. The sound startled him. He hoped it wasn't Jenny phoning to cancel. With Annie going all cold on him, he had been entertaining some pleasant fantasies about the forthcoming dinner. As soon as he heard the voice, though, he realized there could be much worse things in the world than Jenny phoning to cancel dinner.

'Why is it, Banks,' growled Chief Constable Riddle, 'that you manage to make a pig's arse out of everything you do?'

'Sir?'

'You heard me.'

'Sir, it's after six on a Fri—'

'I don't give a monkey's toss what bloody time it is, or what day it is. I give you a perfectly simple case to work on. Nothing too urgent. Nothing too exacting. Out of the goodness of my heart. And what happens? All my good intentions blow up in our faces, that's what happens.'

'Sir, I don't know what you're talking about.'

'You might not, but the rest of the bloody country does. Don't you watch the news?'

'No, sir. I've been getting ready to go out.'

'Then you'd better cancel. I'm sure she'll forgive you. Not that I care about your sex life. Do you know where I'm calling from?'

'No, sir.'

'I'm calling from Thornfield Reservoir. Listen carefully and you'll hear the rain. And the thunder. Let me fill you in. Shortly over an hour ago, a woman was taken hostage. She had taken a taxi out here and told the driver to wait while she went to look at something. When he thought he'd waited long enough, he went to look for her and saw her standing with a man who appeared to be holding a gun to her head. The man fired a shot in the air and shouted his demand, and the taxi driver ran back to his car and phoned the police. The woman's name is Vivian Elmsley. Ring any bells?'

Banks's heart lurched. 'Vivian Elmsley? Yes, she's—'

'I know damn well who she is, Banks. What I don't
know is why some maniac is holding a gun to her head and
demanding to talk to the detective in charge of the Gloria
Shackleton investigation. Because that's what he demanded
the taxi driver report. Can you fill me in on that?'

'No, sir.'

'"No, sir." Is that all you can say?'

Banks fought back the urge to say, 'Yes, sir.' Instead he
asked, 'What's his name?'

'He hasn't said. We, however, have gone into full
bloody Hollywood production mode out here, with a big
enough budget to bankrupt us well into the millennium.
Are you still listening to me, Banks?'

'Yes, sir.'

'A hostage negotiator has spoken with him briefly from
a distance, and all he says is that he wants to see justice
done. He won't say any more until we get you to the scene.
There's an Armed Response Unit here already, and they're
getting itchy fingers. Apparently one of their marksmen
said he can get a clear shot.'

'For crying out loud—'

'Get yourself down here, man. Now! And this time you
really will need your wellies. It's pissing down cats and
dogs.'

When Riddle hung up, Banks reached for his raincoat
and shot out the door. He had a damn good idea who
Vivian Elmsley's captor might be, and why he was holding
her. Behind him, Miles's mournful trumpet echoed in the
empty cottage.

●

Annie had managed to get away from the station early,
before the shit hit the fan, and by six o'clock she was

approaching Blackburn on the M65, shuttling from lane to lane to pass the convoys of enormous lorries that seemed to cluster together at regular intervals. It was Friday rush hour, the sky dark with storm clouds that gushed torrential rain over the whole of the North. Lightning forked and flickered over the humped Pennines, and thunder rumbled and crashed like a mad percussionist in the distance. Annie counted the gaps between the lightning and thunder, wondering if that really *did* tell you how far away the storm was.

What was the gap between her and Banks now? Could it be counted, like that between the thunder and the lightning? She knew she was being a coward, running away, but a little time and distance would give her a clearer perspective and a chance to sort out her feelings.

It was all getting to be too much: first, there was the annoyance she had felt when he went out boozing with his mate in Leeds instead of going to dinner with her; then the time in London he had gone to Bethnal Green to meet his son and made it clear she wasn't welcome; and then the last straw, Sandra's appearance at the cottage on Sunday morning. She had made Annie feel about an inch high. And Banks still loved her, that was obvious enough to anyone.

It wasn't Banks's fault; it wasn't because of him she was running, but because of herself. If every little thing like that was going to rub up against her raw nerve ends, then where would she find any peace? She couldn't blame Banks for making time for friends and family, but nor could she allow herself to be drawn so deeply into his life, tangled up in his past. All she wanted was a simple, no-strings relationship, but there were already too many complications.

If she stayed with him, she would have to meet his son eventually and audition for the Dad's-new-girlfriend test. There was a daughter, too, and she would probably be even harder to win over. She would no doubt also meet the redoubtable Sandra again. Even though no one needed a co-respondent in divorce cases these days, Annie was beginning to feel like one. And there would be the divorce, something else they'd have to go through.

She didn't think she could face all the emotional detritus of someone else's life impinging on her own. She had enough to deal with as it was. No, she should cut her losses and get out now; it was time to go back home, regroup, recuperate, then return to her labyrinth, her meditation and yoga. With any luck, in a couple of weeks Banks would have let her go from his thoughts and found someone else.

Annie had the electronic gizmo in the car stereo set so that no matter what programme she was listening to, the nearest local station would cut in with its weather and travel updates. She hadn't a clue how this worked – some sort of electronic signal, she assumed – but sometimes the interruption continued beyond the traffic and weather into the local news bulletin. Just as she was overtaking a convoy of lorries churning up so much water she could hardly see, the weather cut in, and she also caught the beginning of a news bulletin about a hostage situation at Thornfield Reservoir.

Unfortunately, the same gizmo that caused the bulletins to cut in also cut them off at the most inappropriate times, and this happened halfway through the item. All she had discovered was that the detective writer Vivian Elmsley was being held by an armed man at Thornfield Reservoir.

Annie turned off the tape and jabbed at the search

buttons, sending the LCD lights into a digital frenzy. She got country and western, a gardening programme and a classical concert, but the scanner couldn't find the damn newsbreak. She swore and thumped the wheel, swerving dangerously, then tried again, searching manually this time. When she finally did get the right frequency, all she heard were the final words, '. . . bizarre twist in the affair, it seems the hostage-taker has asked to talk to the detective in charge of the so-called Hobb's End skeleton case, believed to be Detective Chief Inspector Banks of the Eastvale CID. We'll give you more details as they come in.'

Well, Annie thought on the outskirts of Blackburn, there was nothing else for it; she would have to go back. She negotiated her way carefully across the lanes of traffic, took the next exit, crossed the overpass, then followed the signs heading east. In this weather, it would take her about an hour, she calculated, and these were no conditions for impatient driving. She hoped she wouldn't be too late to find out what the hell was going on.

•

Banks arrived at Thornfield car park, put on his wellington boots and hurried through the short stretch of woods to the scene. Riddle hadn't been far wrong when he compared it to a Hollywood production. It probably cost as much as *Waterworld*. Though the patrol cars, Armed Response Vehicles and Technical Support Unit vans couldn't drive right to the rim of the reservoir because of the trees, some of them had forced their way through as far as they could, and long, thick wires and cables trailed the rest of the way. The local media people were there, too. The entire bowl of Hobb's End was floodlit, and the occasional lightning flash gave everything a split-second blue cast. At the centre of it all, two small, pathetic figures were cruelly illuminated just beyond the fairy bridge.

Riddle stood by the phalanx of TV cameras and microphones clustered well behind the police tape. Banks ignored him and went straight over to the hostage negotiator. He looked young. Banks guessed he had a psychology degree and this was his first real-life situation. Officially, the local superintendent was in charge of the scene, but as a rule the negotiator called the shots. Banks couldn't see any police sharpshooters, but he knew they were around somewhere.

'I'm DCI Banks,' he said.

'Sergeant Whitkirk,' said the negotiator.

Banks nodded towards the two figures. 'Let me go and talk to him.'

'You're not going down there,' Whitkirk said. 'That's against the rules. Do your talking on this.' He held a loud-hailer out. Banks didn't take it. Instead, he lit a cigarette and gazed out over the eerie scene, a set from a horror film, perhaps the same film that began with the skeletal hand scratching at the edge of a tombstone. He turned to Sergeant Whitkirk. 'How old are you, sonny?'

'What's that got—'

'You're clearly not old enough to realize that not all wisdom comes out of books. What's it called, this rule book of yours? *The Handy Pocket Guide to Hostage Negotiation*?'

'Now, you listen to me—'

'No. *You* listen to *me*.' Banks pointed to the two figures. 'I don't know how many scenes like this you've handled successfully, but I do know this situation. I know what it's all about, and I think I've got a hell of a lot better chance than you or anyone else of making sure no one gets hurt.'

Whitkirk thrust his chin out. There was an angry red spot in the cleft. 'You can't guarantee that. Leave it to the professionals. He's obviously a fucking madman.'

'He's not a fucking madman. What do you professionals intend to do? Shoot him?'

Whitkirk snorted. 'We could've done that an hour ago, if that's what we wanted. We're containing the situation.'

'Bully for you.'

'How do you know he's not a madman?'

Banks sighed. 'Because I know who he is and what he wants.'

'How can you know that? He hasn't communicated any demands yet.'

'Except to talk to me.'

'That's right. And our first rule is that we don't comply.'

'He hasn't done anything yet, has he?'

'No.'

'Why not, do you think?'

'How would I know? All I know is he's a fucking nutter and he's unpredictable. We can't give in to him, and you can't just go walking into the situation. Look at it this way. He asked for you. Maybe you're the one he really wants to kill.'

'I'll take my chances.'

'No, you won't. I'm in charge of the scene here and you're not going in.'

'What do we do, then?'

'We play for time.'

Banks felt like laughing, but he held it back. 'And in time, what's your plan?'

'First we do all we can to turn an imprecise situation into a precise one.'

'Oh, stop quoting the fucking textbook at me,' Banks said. 'How long have you been here already? An hour? Hour and a half? Have you turned your imprecise situation into a precise one yet?'

'We've established communication.'

Banks looked down at the loud-hailer. 'Yes. Great communicators, those.'

Whitkirk glared at him. 'We offered to send down a phone but he refused.'

'Look,' said Banks, 'he's asked for me. We might not know what he wants, but he must have something to tell me, and you and I both know there's only one way to find out. I think I can talk him out of doing any harm. Can't you give me a bit of leeway?'

Whitkirk chewed on his lip for a moment. 'Securing the scene's my responsibility,' he said.

'Let me go in.' Banks pointed over to the chief constable. 'Believe me, there's a bloke over there will give you a medal if I get shot.'

Whitkirk managed a thin smile. 'One condition,' he said.

'What is it?'

'You wear a bullet-proof vest.'

'All right.'

Whitkirk sent someone to pick up the vest from the Armed Response Vehicle, then he told the hostage taker over his loud-hailer what he was planning.

'Send him in,' the man shouted back.

Whitkirk stood aside and Banks, kitted out with his bulletproof vest, trod his cigarette in the mud and set off down the side of the reservoir. He heard Whitkirk whisper, 'Good luck', as he went. About halfway down, he slipped and went the rest of the distance on his backside. Not very dignified. Though it probably did more harm to his pride than to his clothing, it also reminded him that he had put on his best trousers for dinner with Jenny, a dinner he was very unlikely to be having now, especially as he had forgotten his mobile in all the excitement and hadn't been able to phone her and cancel.

When he got to the bottom of the embankment, he heard a curse behind him and turned to see Annie Cabbot come sliding down after him, also on her bum, feet in the air. At the bottom, she got to her feet and flashed him a grin. 'Sorry. It was the only way I could give them the slip.'

'I take it you don't have a bullet-proof vest?'

'No.'

'I could be gallant and give you mine, but we're a little too close to the scene now. Just stay back, behind me. We don't want to scare him.'

They approached the fairy bridge. Banks told the man who he was. He indicated that it was okay and told the two of them to stop at the far side. They faced one another over the bridge. Vivian Elmsley looked frightened but otherwise unhurt as far as Banks could see. The gun looked like a .32 automatic.

'This is DS Cabbot,' Banks said. 'She's been working on the case with me. Is it okay for her to be here?'

The man looked at Annie and nodded. 'I know who she is,' he said. 'I saw her on television the day you found the skeleton, then down here that night a week or so ago.'

'So it was you,' Annie said. 'What were you doing? Surely you weren't looking for anything after all this time?'

'Perhaps I was. Not the sort of thing you mean. But perhaps I was looking for something. I've been here a lot at night. Thinking.'

'Why did you run?'

'I recognized you from the television. You walked right past me and didn't even see me. But I saw you. I couldn't risk being caught, having to explain myself, before I'd finished what I had to do.'

Banks decided it was time to take charge. He held his hands up and gestured for Annie to do the same. Rain dripped down the back of his neck. 'We're not armed, Francis,' he said. 'We don't want to hurt you. We just want to talk. Let Ms Elmsley go.'

'So you know who I am?'

'Francis Henderson.'

'Clever. But my name's Stringer now. Frank Stringer.' He licked his lips. So he had adopted his mother's maiden name. Strange. That told Banks something about the situation they were dealing with. Frank looked twitchy, and Banks wondered if he had been drinking or if he was on drugs again. If it's hard to make an imprecise situation precise, he thought, then it's a bloody sight harder to make a hallucinatory situation real.

'Anyway,' Frank went on, 'I'm not ready to let anyone go yet. I want to hear it all first. I want to hear her confess to you, then I'll decide whether to kill her or not. It makes no odds to me.'

'Okay, Frank. What do you want to hear?'

'She killed my mother. I want to hear her say so, and I want to know why.'

'She didn't kill anyone, Frank.'

'What are you talking about? You're lying. You're trying to protect her.'

His grip tightened on Vivian. Banks caught her sudden intake of breath and saw the gun barrel pushed into the flesh under her ear.

'Listen to me, Frank,' he said. 'It's important you listen

to me. You asked for me to come here. You want the truth, don't you?'

'I already know the truth. I want to hear it from your mouth. I want to hear her confess in front of you. I want to hear what she did to my mother.'

'It didn't happen the way you think it did, Frank. It didn't happen the way any of us thought it did. We were all wrong.'

'My mother was murdered.'

'Yes, she was murdered.'

'And this . . . this bitch here lied to my father and me when we went and asked about her.'

'No,' said Banks. 'She didn't lie. She thought she was telling you the truth.' He noticed the look of confusion in Vivian's eyes.

'All those years,' Frank went on, as if he hadn't heard. 'Do you know he worshipped her, my father? Even though she left us. He said she was a dreamer, a free spirit, a beautiful butterfly who just had to spread her wings and fly away. But I hated her for leaving us. For depriving us of all that beauty. Why couldn't she share it with us? Why couldn't *we* be part of her dreams? We were never good enough for her. I hated her and I loved her. All my life dominated and blighted by a mother I never even knew. What do you think Mr Freud would make of that? Don't you think that's funny?'

Banks looked away. He didn't want to tell Frank the truth, that his mother had turned her back on him at birth. All those years, George had fed him on illusions. Gloria certainly had been wrong about the father of her child; he hadn't turned out so bad after all. 'No,' he said. 'I don't think it's funny at all, Frank.'

'My father used to tell me how she always wanted to be

one of those Hollywood actresses. Used to spend hours in front of the mirror practising her makeup and the way they talked. Even before I was born it was no-go for them. She was too young, he said. Made just one mistake, that's all. *Me*. It was enough.'

'She *was* very young, Frank. When she got pregnant, she was frightened. She didn't know what to do.'

'So she had to run away and leave us?'

'For some people it seems like the only solution. She obviously wanted the child, *you*, to live. She didn't have an abortion. She must have told your father where she was going? Did she keep in touch?'

He sniffed. 'A postcard every now and then, telling him she was doing fine and not to worry. When my dad came home on leave once, he took me up to Hobb's End to see her. It was the only time I . . . the only time I really remember seeing her, being with her, hearing her voice. She told me I was a fine-looking boy. I loved her then. She was a magical creature to me. Dazzling. Like someone from a dream. She seemed to move in a haze of light. So beautiful and so tender. But they argued. He couldn't help asking her to come back when he saw her, but she wouldn't. She told him she was married now and had a new life and we should leave her alone if we wanted her to be happy.'

'What did your father do?'

'What she asked. He was devastated. I think he'd always hoped that one day, perhaps, she would come back. We tried once more, when it was all over.' He turned so he was speaking into Vivian's ear. 'But this lying bitch here told us she had run away and she didn't know where. All my life I believed that, believed my mother had run away and abandoned us for ever. I tried to find her. I'm good at finding people, but I got nowhere. Now I find out she was dead all the time. Murdered and buried right here.'

'Let her go, Frank!' Banks shouted over a peal of thunder. 'She didn't know.'

'What do you mean, she didn't know? She must have known.' Frank tore his attention away from Vivian and glared at Banks. His eyes were wild, his lank hair was plastered to his skull and rain dripped from his eyes like tears. 'I want to hear it all. I want to hear her admit it to you. I want the truth.'

'You've got it all wrong, Frank. Vivian didn't kill Gloria. Listen to me.'

'Even if she didn't do the actual killing, she was involved. She covered for somebody. Who was it?'

'Nobody.'

'What do you take me for?'

'Vivian had nothing to do with your mother's death.' As he spoke, Banks noticed Vivian's eyes fill with curiosity, despite the gun at her neck. Annie stood beside him now, and Frank didn't seem to care about her presence. Banks was aware of the activity in the background, but he didn't think anyone would make a move yet. Thunder rumbled and lightning flashed. His raincoat and trousers stuck to his skin and rain stung his eyes.

'What do you mean, she had nothing to do with it?' Frank said. 'She told my father that my mother had gone away, when all the while she was buried up here. She lied. Why would she do that unless she'd killed her, or knew who had?'

'As far as she was concerned,' Banks said, 'your mother *had* gone away. She had spoken about running away often since Matthew got back from the war. He'd been badly hurt by the Japanese. He wasn't the man she had married. Life was miserable for her. It seemed only natural to everyone who knew her that she'd go, just like she left you and your father in the first place.'

'No!'

Frank's grip tightened on Vivian's throat and she gasped. Banks felt his heart lurch. He held his hands out, palms towards Frank.

'Okay, Frank,' he went on. 'Calm down. Please. Calm down and listen to me.'

They waited a moment, the four of them, all silent but for the pattering of the rain and the storm disappearing into the distance, the occasional crackle of a police radio from the rim.

Then Banks felt things relax, the same way as when you undo a tight button. 'Matthew drove her away,' he went on. 'It was only natural for Gwen to assume that was what happened. Your mother's suitcase was gone. Her things were gone.'

Frank didn't say anything for at least a minute. Banks could see him processing information, trying to shore up his defences. The storm passed into the distance now and the rain eased off, leaving the four of them soaked to the skin.

'If it wasn't her, who was it?' Frank said eventually. 'I'll bet you can't tell me that, can you?'

'I can, Frank.' Annie stepped forward and spoke. Frank turned to her and blinked the rain out of his eyes.

'Who?' Frank asked. 'And don't you lie to me.'

'His name was Edgar Konig,' Annie said. 'He ran the PX at Rowan Woods USAAF base, about a mile from here.'

'PX?' Vivian gasped.

'I don't believe you,' said Frank.

'It's true,' said Banks, picking up the thread. He realized that Annie didn't have the full story yet. 'Konig killed your mother. He also killed at least one other woman over here the same way, down in East Anglia. There were others, too, in Europe and America.'

Frank shook his head slowly.

'Listen to me, Frank. Edgar Konig knew your mother and her friends from the dances they went to. He was attracted to her from the start, but he had serious problems with women. He was always tongue-tied around them. He brought her presents, but even then she didn't offer herself to him, she wouldn't help him overcome his shyness. She went out with other men. He watched and waited. All the time the pressure was building up in him.'

'You say he killed other women?'

'Yes.'

'How do you know it was him?'

'We found a collar button from an American airman's uniform. We think your mother must have torn it off as they struggled. Then we looked into the unsolved murder in Suffolk and found he had been questioned in connection with that, too. Are you listening, Frank?'

'I'm listening.'

Frank's grip around Vivian's throat had loosened a little, and Banks could tell that he had relaxed the hand holding the gun. 'Edgar Konig went to Bridge Cottage that night to collect what he thought your mother owed him while her husband Matthew was at the pub as usual. The bomber group was due to move out in a couple of days and that had pushed him to the brink. He didn't have much time. He'd been torturing himself for over a year. He'd been drinking that night, getting more and more lustful, and he thought he had plucked up the courage, thought he could overcome his inadequacies. Something short-circuited, though. She must have rejected him, maybe laughed at him, and the next thing he knew he'd killed her in a rage. Do you understand what I'm saying, Frank? There was something wrong with him.'

'A psycho?'

'No. Not technically. Not at first, anyway. He became a sex murderer. The two things – sex and murder – became tangled up in his mind. The one demanded the other.'

'If that's how it happened, why did no one know about it?'

Slowly, Banks reached for his cigarettes and offered Frank one. 'Gave them up years back,' he said. 'Thanks for the offer, though.'

Banks lit up. Definite progress. Frank seemed less tightly wound, more willing to listen to reason. And he didn't appear to be drunk or on drugs. Better not cock it up now.

'No one knew about it,' Banks went on, 'because Edgar Konig realized what he'd done. That sobered him up fast. He covered his tracks well.' Banks looked at Vivian Elmsley as he spoke. She averted her eyes. 'He cleaned up the mess and he buried the body in the outbuilding. Then he packed a few of her clothes and belongings in a suitcase to make it look as though she had run off. He even faked a note. It was wartime. People went missing all the time. Everyone in the village knew Gloria wasn't happy with Matthew, what a burden she had to bear. Why should they question that she'd just done a moonlight?'

Frank spoke in Vivian's ear. 'Is that right, what he's saying?'

Banks couldn't hear her, but he saw her mouth form the word 'Yes.'

'Frank,' Banks pressed on, playing his advantage. 'The gun. I know you don't want to hurt anyone, but it's dangerous. It's easy to make a wrong move. Nobody's been hurt yet. No harm's been done.'

Frank looked at the gun as if he were seeing it for the first time.

Banks stepped on to the fairy bridge and moved forward slowly, holding his hand out. He knew there were probably two or three trained marksmen aiming in his direction, and the thought made his stomach churn. 'Give the gun to me, Frank. It's all over. Vivian didn't kill your mother. She had nothing to do with it. She loved Gloria like a sister. It was Edgar Konig.'

Frank let his gun hand drop and released his grip on Vivian Elmsley's throat. She staggered aside and slipped down one of the muddy holes the SOCOs had dug in the Bridge Cottage floor. Annie ran to help her. Frank handed the gun to Banks. It weighed heavy in his hand. 'What happened to him?' Frank asked. 'This Konig. Did he ever get caught?'

'I'll tell you all about that later, Frank,' said Banks, taking Frank by the elbow. 'Just for now, though, we're all a bit tired and wet. Okay? I think we should leave here, go somewhere to dry off and get some clean clothes, don't you?'

Frank hung his head. Banks draped an arm across his shoulder. As he did so, he noticed something on the ground, partially covered by mud. He bent and picked it up. It was a photograph of a sixteen-year-old Gloria Shackleton, her beautiful, determined, defiant face staring out at the camera. It was damaged by the water, but still salvageable.

Several police officers had already come dashing and

sliding down the embankment. Two went to help Annie get Vivian out of the pit, and two of them grabbed Frank roughly and started handcuffing him.

'There's no need to be so rough with him,' said Banks.

'Leave this to us, sir,' said one of the officers.

Bank sighed and handed over the gun, then he held up the photograph of Gloria. 'I'll get this cleaned up for you, if you want, Frank,' he said.

Frank nodded. 'Please,' he said. 'And don't worry about me. I'll be all right. It's not the first time I've had the cuffs on.'

Banks nodded. 'I know.'

They hustled Frank Stringer away, practically dragging him up the muddy slope, and Banks turned to see Annie and the other policemen helping Vivian Elmsley stumble over the fairy bridge.

Vivian stopped in front of him, covered in mud, while the others went on ahead. 'Thank you,' she said. 'You saved my life.'

'I lied for you,' said Banks. 'I also sullied Gloria's loyalty to Matthew.'

She paled and whispered, 'I know. I appreciate what you did. I'm sorry.'

'There was a chance, you know. Maybe just a small chance, but a chance. If you'd come forward after you found Gloria dead, if you hadn't destroyed all the evidence, if you'd gone to the police . . .' Banks held his anger in check; this was neither the time nor the place for it. 'Ah, to hell with it. Too late now.'

Vivian bowed her head. 'Believe me, I know what I've done.'

Banks turned and slogged on alone through the mud. It was difficult, but he made it up the edge without falling down. At the top, he was aware of Annie standing beside him. Before he could say anything, Jimmy Riddle came running over and grabbed his arm. 'I'm glad you've salvaged at least something out of this situation, Banks,' he hissed, 'but you're bloody incompetent. I don't want incompetent officers under my command. I'll be talking to you first thing Monday morning.' Then he turned to Annie. 'As for you, DS Cabbot, you disobeyed a direct order. I don't like insubordinate officers, either. I'll be talking to you, too.'

Banks shook his arm free, turned on his heel and walked back towards his car. All he wanted was a long hot bath, a large Laphroaig and a change of clothes.

And Annie.

She was already leaning against her car, arms folded.

'Are you all right?' Banks asked.

'I'm fine. Fine as anyone can be who's spent the last half-hour standing in the rain wondering if someone was going to get her head blown off.'

'Frank Stringer wasn't going to hurt anyone.'

'Easy for you to say. I respect what you did out there, by the way.'

'What do you mean?'

'You lied to protect Frank Stringer's feelings. I told you, my mother died when I was six. I like to remember her as a beautiful, dazzling creature moving in a haze of light, the same way he remembers Gloria. And I wouldn't want anyone to spoil that illusion for me, no matter what the truth.'

'I lied to get us all out of there alive.'

Annie smiled. 'Whatever. It worked both ways.'

'What next?'

Annie stretched, arching her back and reaching her

arms towards the sky. 'Onward to St Ives. After I've stopped off at home for some dry clothes. I was already on my way when I heard. I couldn't just leave it.'

'Of course not. Thanks for being here.'

'You?'

'Home, I suppose.' Banks remembered dinner with Jenny. Too late now, especially the state his clothes were in, but he could at least borrow a mobile from someone and phone her, apologize.

Annie nodded. 'Look, I'll be gone for two weeks. Right now I'm still a bit mixed up about my feelings. Why don't you phone me when I get back? Maybe we can have that talk?'

'Okay.'

She grinned at him crookedly. 'If there weren't so many policemen about I'd kiss you goodbye.'

'Not a good idea.'

'No. See you, then.'

And with that she opened the car door and got in. Banks ignored his cutting-down programme and lit another cigarette, aware that his hands were shaking. Without looking back, Annie started her car. Banks watched the red tail-lights disappear down the muddy track.

EPILOGUE

After a long, rainy winter and overdue repairs by York-shire Water, Thornfield Reservoir filled up again and Hobb's End once more disappeared. On 27 July of the year after the Gloria Shackleton murder had entered and left the public's imagination, Vivian Elmsley lay on a king-size bed in her Florida hotel room, propped up with pillows, and watched the local news channel.

Vivian was in the midst of a national book tour, seven-teen cities, and while Gainesville wasn't on the itinerary, she had enough clout with her publishers for this brief diversion. She would have come anyway, tour or no tour. Yesterday she had been in Baltimore, Bethesda and Washington, DC, tomorrow she was going to Dallas, but tonight she was in Gainesville.

For tonight was the night that Edgar Konig had his appointment with Old Sparky, and after everything she had been through, Vivian desperately needed *some* sense of an ending.

It was a sultry, mosquito-ridden night, but that didn't seem to deter the crowds that gathered outside the gates of Starke Prison, about twenty-five miles away. One or two were quietly carrying placards that asked for an end to capital punishment, but by far the majority were chanting, 'Fry Konig! Fry Konig!' Bumper stickers echoed the same sentiments, and the crowd had created what the com-mentator called a tailgate-party atmosphere. It wasn't big enough to attract any of the national networks – after all, executions in Florida were as common as muggings – but the Konig case had caught a lot of local interest.

Frank Stringer would have come, too – and Vivian would have willingly paid his way – but he was in gaol. English gun laws are far stricter than they are in Florida. Besides, no matter how good his reasons for taking Vivian hostage at Thornfield the past September, he had committed a serious crime and occasioned a hugely expensive and highly publicized police operation. Vivian had visited him several times in gaol and told him she would help him get back on his feet when he came out. It was the least she could do for Gloria's memory.

In his turn, Frank had told her how his father's sister Ivy and her husband John had taken good care of him during the war and how he had thought of them as his parents. When his real father came home on leave, they would spend time together. That was when they had made the first journey north, in 1943, and he had seen his mother.

After the war, his father married and took him away from Ivy and John. Frank's stepmother turned out to be a drunk and a shrew who had no time for her husband's bastard son. Increasingly isolated and neglected, he got involved with crooks and gangs, and one thing led to another. The only constant was that he had always worshipped his true mother's memory.

Frank also told Vivian how the death of his father that spring and the re-emergence of Hobb's End from Thornfield Reservoir had caused his obsession with the past to escalate. His father had been the first to recognize Gwen Shackleton as Vivian Elmsley on television, but Frank had confirmed it; he had memorized her eyes and her voice all those years ago, when he was eight, the same way he had also memorized his mother's face.

He couldn't explain why he had taken the trouble to find out where Vivian lived and why he had followed her and approached her at the bookshop; it was just that she was the only one left, the only one who had known Gloria. He said that he meant no harm at first, that he might even have found the courage to approach her eventually.

Then the skeleton was discovered, and he knew she must have lied all those years ago. He hated her after that; he telephoned to scare her, to make her suffer. He could have taken her anytime, but he enjoyed the anticipation. After all, once he had confronted her, it would be all over. So he followed her, watched her. When she got the taxi outside her hotel, he knew where she was going, and he felt it was fitting that things should end there, where they began.

But tonight, Vivian was alone in Gainesville with her memories, the television, a bottle of gin, ice and tonic water. And an execution.

They had already shown a fairly recent photograph of Edgar Konig. Vivian hadn't been able to recognize the gangly, baby-faced young airman with the shy eyes and the blond brush cut. His hair was gone, his cheeks had sagged and wrinkled, his brow was creased, and his eyes were deep, dark pits in which slimy monsters squirmed.

As she watched the coverage, Vivian imagined the officials carrying out the preliminary steps of state-sanctioned murder with swift and impersonal efficiency, much like dentists or doctors.

First they would settle the patient in the heavy oak chair and buckle thick leather straps round his arms and legs. Then they would place the bit between his teeth and attach electrodes to his body as if they were carrying out an ECG.

She wondered if the leather straps smelled, if they were sour with the sweat and fear of previous victims. How many hands and legs had they strapped down before? Or were they replaced after every execution? What about the chair itself? How many bladders and bowels had emptied there?

Then they would clamp the metal skullcap on.

Vivian shook her head to clear the images. She felt dizzy, and she realized she was already a bit drunk. If anyone deserved this sort of end, she told herself, ambivalent as she was about the idea of capital punishment, it was probably Edgar Konig.

Vivian had been shocked when Banks told her the day after Frank's arrest that Gloria's murderer was not dead, but on death row in a Florida prison.

Did he think of Gloria now, Vivian wondered, now the end was so close? Did he spare a thought for a beautiful young woman all those years ago in a village that no longer existed, in a war long since won? And what about the others? How many had there been? Even Banks hadn't been able to give her a definite number. Did he think about them?

If he was like most such killers she had read about in the course of her research, he probably felt nothing but self-pity and spent his last moments cursing the bad luck that resulted in his capture. What Banks had told her a few days after the scene at Hobb's End did nothing to dispel that idea.

Banks's FBI contact had interviewed Konig last December and sent in a report. Konig said he remembered the first one he did was in England during the war. He couldn't remember her name or the circumstances, but he thought maybe she was a blonde. He *did* remember that he had been giving her stockings and gum and cigarettes and bourbon for more than a year and when he came to collect she didn't show a scrap of gratitude. He'd been drinking. He remembered the way the pressure had been building and building in him all that time until he'd had too much that night and the dam finally burst. She wouldn't have anything to do with *him*, a lowly PX grunt. Oh, no. She was fucking a *pilot*.

It was always the drink, he said. If it hadn't been for the drink he would never have done any of them. But booze made something deep inside him just snap, and the next thing he knew, they were dead at his feet. Then he was angry at them for dying and he used the knife. It was like that with the second one. Berlin, 1946. When he didn't get found out the first time, when he realized there wasn't even going to be an investigation, he thought he must be leading a charmed life.

It was all her fault. If she hadn't stopped to straighten her stockings as he was driving by, hiking her skirt up and showing those long, white legs in his headlights, then he would never have done her. If he hadn't been drunk, too, which he wouldn't normally have been while driving if he hadn't known the lonely road like the back of his hand. *If. If. If.* His life was a tragedy of cruel *ifs*.

She was willing enough to go into the field with him. He hadn't planned to hurt her; he had only seen her flashing her legs for him on the road back there and wanted a piece, like any normal guy would. But she had shown no patience with him and his little problem – it happened sometimes when he'd been drinking – and she had asked him for money. That made him see red.

Literally see red. The knife? Yes, he usually carried a knife with him. A habit from the farm days back in Iowa when he used to whittle pieces of wood.

The third woman, back Stateside in 1949, he didn't really remember at all, and of the second one in England, all he remembered was something red happening in a barn. Again, it was the drink. Konig's daddy had been a vicious alcoholic who regularly beat poor Edgar to within an inch of his life; his mother was a drunken whore who'd do it with anyone for a dime. All his life the drink had caused his problems; it made him do these evil things, and then he had the bad luck to be caught on that highway in California.

So went Edgar Konig's story.

The drink. Vivian looked at her glass, then, with a shaking hand, she poured herself another tumbler of gin and grasped a fistful of ice cubes from the bucket on the bedside table, tossing them in the glass carelessly, so a little gin splashed on the table. An American habit she had picked up, that, ice in her drink.

It was almost time.

Edgar Konig, just turned seventy-six, was finally getting what he deserved. Vivian still felt a twinge of guilt when she realized that Banks was right, that she *might* have helped put an end to his killing all those years ago, after Gloria, the very first victim. She was partly responsible for Konig's feeling that he led a charmed life of murder without consequence.

She had tried to rationalize it to herself so many times since Banks told her what had happened and turned his back in scorn that evening when the storm broke at Hobb's End. Even if she had reported what happened, she told herself, they would have still probably arrested

Matthew. He wasn't well enough to face that sort of treatment. Though Banks was a little easier on her when they spoke the next day, she could still feel his censure, and it stung.

But what could she have told the police that would have pointed them specifically towards Edgar Konig? The whisky and Lucky Strikes on the kitchen counter? They were hardly evidence. Gloria could have got them anywhere, and they could have been lying there on the counter for a couple of days. She and Gloria had known plenty of American air force officers in the area, and she had no reason at the time to suspect any of them of murder. It was all very well for Banks to say in retrospect that *she* was responsible for all those deaths, that *she* could somehow have stopped all this had she acted differently, but it wasn't fair. Twenty-twenty hindsight. And who wouldn't, given the chance, go back and change *something*?

Time.

The first shock would boil his brain and turn all the nerve cells to jelly; the second or third shock would stop his heart. His body would jerk and arch against the straps; his muscles would contract sharply, and a few small bones would probably snap. Most likely the fingers, the fingers he had used to strangle Gloria.

If he didn't have a leather band strapped across his eyes, the heat would cause his eyeballs to explode. The death chamber would be filled with the smell of burning hair and flesh. Steam and smoke would puff out from under the hood. The hood itself might catch fire. When it was over, someone would have to turn on an air vent to get rid of the stench. Then a doctor would come, pronounce him dead, and the public would be informed.

Besides, Vivian told herself as she watched the people chanting outside the prison gates, others could have stopped him, too, if the system had worked properly. It wasn't only her fault. She had acted only from the purest of motives: love of her brother. These past few weeks, she had read all the articles on Edgar Konig and his impending doom. There had been plenty of them.

Konig had finally been caught in California in the late sixties, when he was about forty-five, attacking a young female hitch-hiker by the side of a lonely road. Fortunately for her, another motorist had happened along. Even more fortunate, this man wasn't the kind who scared easily or who didn't want to get involved. He was an ex-serviceman, and he was armed. When he saw a woman in trouble, he stopped and managed to disarm and disable Konig before calling the police. Already the girl was unconscious from strangulation. She had five stab wounds, but she survived.

Konig served nine years of a fourteen-year sentence. He was released early because of good behaviour and prison overcrowding. A lot of people in the know opposed his release, regarding him as extremely dangerous and suspecting – but never being able to prove – his involvement in at least four murders. The prison officials said there wasn't much else they could do at the time but let him go.

After his release in the late seventies, for years Konig was driven from one community to another as people found out what he was, trying to get work as a store clerk, more often than not failing and going on welfare. Just a few years ago he had finally settled in the small Florida town where it all came to a messy and predictable end.

His neighbours had already started protesting, and one local business had even offered him money to up sticks and move elsewhere. But Konig stayed on. Then, one day, a couple of Jehovah's Witnesses came to call and saw, through the screen door, Konig with a knife in his hand standing over the body of a woman, who turned out to be a local prostitute. They called the police on their mobile phone. Konig was drunk; he offered no resistance. After that, of course, came the obligatory years of waiting for trial, for sentencing, the failed appeals, death row.

And it was all over now. A cheer went up from the crowd outside the prison. News had come out. Edgar Konig was dead.

Why was it that Vivian felt no relief, felt nothing but the stirrings of a bad headache? She closed her eyes and pressed her fingers to the lids. *All over. All over.* She was so tired. Konig's statement to the FBI had been bald and unembellished, but with her morbid imagination, Vivian was able to fill in the nuances and the emotions.

She saw Gloria run into the kitchen as she became frightened by PX's erratic behaviour, behaviour she had witnessed in embryo at the VE Day party – saw her frantically pulling tins of tea and cocoa out of the kitchen cupboard, looking for the gun, shocked and scared to find that it wasn't there. Did she realize in the last moments of her life that Gwen must have taken it?

Next, Vivian saw PX grab Gloria, put his hands round her throat, felt the breath going out of her. Then she saw him pick up the kitchen knife from the counter, felt one sharp pain, then another, another, everything starting to slip away from her.

Vivian put her hand to her throat.

The gun.

She was the one who had taken the gun, the one thing

that *might* have saved Gloria's life if she had got to it in time. And Brenda Hamilton's life. And all the others.

Then, for all those terrible years, she had cared for Matthew in his fallen state, believing he was a murderer. Poor, gentle Matthew, who wouldn't harm a soul, who couldn't even kill himself, no more than her husband Ronald could, despite the pain. Vivian had helped them both: Ronald with an extra dose of morphine, and Matthew, all those years ago . . .

Before she started crying, she had a vivid memory of that afternoon in Leeds when she came back from the shops and saw Matthew sitting in the chair with the gun in his mouth, the gun she had taken from Gloria, kept and brought all the way from Hobb's End. He was trying to find the courage, willing himself to pull the trigger.

But he couldn't do it. Just like all the other times he had tried and failed. He had such a forlorn expression on his face, such a hopelessness about him. His eyes pleaded with her, and this time, almost without thinking, she walked over to him, tenderly wrapped her hand around his, kissed his forehead and pressed his finger on the trigger.

Outside Starke Prison the crowd was dancing and chanting, shaking up bottles and spraying beer at each other. In the hotel room, Vivian Elmsley let her tears flow freely for the first time in over fifty years and reached again for her gin.

ACKNOWLEDGMENTS

Many people helped, both directly and indirectly, with this book. On the writing side, I would particularly like to thank my wife Sheila Halladay for her perceptive first reading and my agent Dominick Abel for his encouragement and hard work. Special thanks to my editor at Avon Books, Patricia Lande Grader, for her faith and for pushing me to the limit, and to Cynthia Good at Penguin for keeping me on track, as ever. I would also like to thank Robert Barnard for reading and commenting on the manuscript, and copy-editors Mary Adachi and Erika Schmid for spotting those important details the rest of us overlooked.

Then there are those who helped me reconstruct the past. Thanks to my father, Clifford Robinson, for sharing his wartime memories of Yorkshire; to Jimmy Williamson for informing me about the war in Burma; to Dan Harrington, USAFE History Officer, for patiently answering my e-mail messages; to Jack McFadyen for tracking down the uniforms and buttons, and to Dr Aaron Elkins for his help with the forensic anthropology.

A number of police officers also answered my questions, and if I got any of it wrong, it's not their fault. Thanks to Detective Sergeant Keith Wright, as ever, and to the crowd who drink in The Whale: Sergeant Claire Stevens, Chief Inspector Phil Gormley and Detective Inspector Alan Young. Particular thanks to Alan for the tour of the police station and the pint in the police bar afterwards.

Last but not least, thanks to John Halladay, of the Law Faculty at the University of Buckingham, and to Judith Rhodes, of the Leeds Library Services, for answering a variety of questions.

DRY BONES THAT DREAM

For Sheila

ACKNOWLEDGMENTS

My thanks are long overdue to Cynthia Good, my editor from the beginning of the series. I must also thank my agent, Dominick Abel, for his advice and encouragement. This book in particular could not have been completed without the help of many people, all generous with their time and expertise. My thanks go especially to Keith Wright of Nottingham CID, both detective and novelist; Douglas Lucas, Director of the Centre for Forensic Sciences, Toronto; Mario Possamai for his book *Money on the Run*; Ken McFarland, Chartered Accountant; John Picton, journalist; and to Rick Blechta for putting me right about viola players. Any errors are entirely my own and were made purely in the interests of dramatic fiction.

Dry bones that dream are bitter.
They dream and darken our sun.

W. B. Yeats
The Dreaming of the Bones

1

ONE

The uniformed constable lifted the tape and waved Detective Chief Inspector Banks through the gate at two forty-seven in the morning.

Banks's headlights danced over the scene as he drove into the bumpy farmyard and came to a halt. To his left stood the squat, solid house itself, with its walls of thick limestone and mossy, flagstone roof. Lights shone in both the upstairs and downstairs windows. To his right, a high stone wall buttressed a copse that straggled up the dale-side, where the trees became lost in darkness. Straight ahead stood the barn.

A group of officers had gathered around the open doors, inside which a ball of light seemed to be moving. They looked like the cast of a fifties sci-fi film gazing in awe on an alien spaceship or lifeform.

When Banks arrived, they parted in silence to let him through. As he entered, he noticed one young PC leaning against the outside wall dribbling vomit on his size twelves. Inside, the scene looked like a film set.

Peter Darby, the police photographer, was busy video-taping, and the source of the light was attached to the top of his camera. It created an eerie chiaroscuro and sudden, sickening illuminations as it swept around the barn's interior. All he needed, Banks thought, was for someone to yell 'Action!' and the place would suddenly be full of sound and motion.

But no amount of yelling would breathe life back into the grotesque shape on the floor, by which a whey-faced young police surgeon, Dr Burns, squatted with a black notebook in his hand.

At first, the position of the body reminded Banks of a parody of Moslem prayer: the kneeling man bent forward from the waist, arms stretched out in front, bum in the air, forehead touching the ground, perhaps facing Mecca. His fists were clenched in the dirt, and Banks noticed the glint of a gold cufflink, initialled 'KAR', as Darby's light flashed on it.

But there was no forehead to touch the ground. Above the charcoal suit jacket, the bloodsoaked collar of the man's shirt protruded about an inch, and after that came nothing but a dark, coagulated mass of bone and tissue spread out on the dirt like an oil stain: a shotgun wound, by the look of it. Patches of blood, bone and brain matter stuck to the whitewashed stone walls in abstract-expressionist patterns. Darby's roving light caught what looked like a fragment of skull sprouting a tuft of fair hair beside a rusty hoe.

Banks felt the bile rise in his throat. He could still smell the gunpowder, reminiscent of a childhood bonfire night, mixed with the stink of urine and faeces and the rancid raw meat smell of sudden violent death.

'What time did the call come in?' he asked the PC beside him.

'One thirty-eight, sir. PC Carstairs from Relton was first on the scene. He's still puking up out front.'

Banks nodded. 'Do we know who the victim was?'

'DC Gay checked his wallet, sir. Name's Keith Rothwell. That's the name of the bloke who lived here, all right.' He pointed over to the house. 'Arkbeck Farm, it's called.'

'A farmer?'

'Nay, sir. Accountant. Some sort of businessman, any road.' One of the constables found a light switch and turned on the bare bulb, which became a foundation for the brighter light of Darby's video camera. Most regions didn't use video because it was hard to get good enough quality, but Peter Darby was a hardware junkie, forever experimenting.

Banks turned his attention back to the scene. The place looked as if it had once been a large stone Yorkshire barn, with double doors and a hayloft, called a 'field house' in those parts. Originally, it would have been used to keep the cows inside between November and May, and to store fodder, but Rothwell seemed to have converted it into a garage.

To Banks's right, a silver-grey BMW, parked at a slight angle, took up about half the space. Beyond the car, against the far wall, a number of metal shelf units held all the tools and potions one would associate with car care: anti-freeze, wax polish, oily rags, screwdrivers, spanners. Rothwell had retained the rural look in the other half of the garage. He had even hung old farm implements on the whitewashed stone wall: a mucking rake, a hay knife, a draining scoop and a Tom spade, among others, all suitably rusted.

As he stood there, Banks tried to picture what might have happened. The victim had clearly been kneeling, perhaps praying or pleading for his life. It certainly didn't look as if he had tried to escape. Why had he submitted so easily? Not much choice, probably, Banks thought. You usually don't argue when someone is pointing a shotgun at you. But still . . . would a man simply kneel there, brace himself and wait for his executioner to pull the trigger?

Banks turned and left the barn. Outside, he met Detective Sergeant Philip Richmond and Detective Constable Susan Gay coming from around the back.

'Nothing there, sir, far as I can tell,' said Richmond, a large torch in his hand. Susan, beside him, looked pale in the glow from the barn entrance.

'All right?' Banks asked her.

'I'm okay now, sir. I was sick, though.'

Richmond looked the same as ever. His sang-froid was legendary around the place, so much so that Banks sometimes wondered if he had any feelings at all or whether he had come to resemble one of those computers he spent most of his time with.

'Anyone know what happened?' Banks asked.

'PC Carstairs had a quick word with the victim's wife when he first got here,' said Susan. 'All she could tell him was that a couple of men were waiting when she got home and they took her husband outside and shot him.' She shrugged. 'Then she became hysterical. I believe she's under sedation now, sir. I fished his wallet from his pocket, anyway,' she went on, holding up a plastic bag. 'Says his name's—'

'Yes, I know,' said Banks. 'Have we got an Exhibits Officer yet?'

'No, sir,' Susan answered, then both she and Phil Richmond looked away. Exhibits Officer was one of the least popular jobs in an investigation. It meant keeping track of every piece of possible evidence and preserving a record of continuity. It usually went to whoever was in the doghouse at the time.

'Get young Farnley on the job, then,' Banks said. PC

Farnley hadn't offended anyone or cocked up a case, but he lacked imagination and had a general reputation around the station as a crashing golf bore.

Clearly relieved, Richmond and Susan wandered off towards the Scene of Crime team, who had just pulled into the farmyard in a large van. As they piled out in their white boiler suits, they looked like a team of government scientists sent to examine the alien landing spot. Pretty soon, Banks thought, if they weren't all careful, there would be a giant spider or a huge gooey blob rolling around the Yorkshire Dales gobbling up everyone in sight.

The night was cool and still, the air moist, tinged with a hint of manure. Banks still felt half asleep, despite the shock of what he had seen in the garage. Maybe he was dreaming. No. He thought of Sandra, warm at home in bed, and sighed.

Detective Superintendent Gristhorpe's arrival at about three-thirty brought him out of his reverie. Gristhorpe limped over from his car. He wore an old donkey-jacket over his shirt, and he clearly hadn't bothered to shave or comb his unruly thatch of grey hair.

'Bloody hell, Alan,' he said by way of greeting, 'tha looks like Columbo.'

There's the pot calling the kettle black, Banks thought. Still, the super was right. He had thrown on an old rain-coat over his shirt and trousers because he knew the night would be chilly.

After Banks had explained what he had found out so far, Gristhorpe took a quick look in the barn, questioned PC Carstairs, the first officer at the scene, then rejoined Banks, his usually ruddy, pockmarked face a little paler. 'Let's go in the house, shall we, Alan?' he said. 'I hear PC

Weaver's brewing up. He should be able to give us some background.'

They walked across the dirt yard. Above them, the stars shone cold and bright like chips of ice on black velvet.

The farmhouse was cosy and warm inside, a welcome change from the cool night and the gruesome scene in the barn. It had been renovated according to the yuppie idea of the real rustic look, with exposed beams and rough stone walls in an open, split-level living room, all earthy browns and greens. The remains of a log fire glowed in the stone hearth, and beside it stood a pair of antique andirons and a matching rack holding poker and tongs.

In front of the fire, Banks noticed two hardbacked chairs facing one another. One of them had fallen over, or had been pushed on its side. Beside both of them lay coils of rope. One of the chair seats looked wet.

Banks and Gristhorpe walked through into the ultramodern kitchen, which looked like something from a colour supplement, where PC Weaver was pouring boiling water into a large red teapot.

'Nearly ready, sir,' he said when he saw the CID officers. 'I'll just let it mash a couple of minutes.'

The kitchen walls were done in bright red and white patterned tiles, and every available inch of space had been used to wedge fitted microwave, oven, fridge, dishwasher, cupboards and the like. It also boasted a central island unit, complete with tall pine stools. Banks and Gristhorpe sat down.

'How's his wife?' Gristhorpe asked.

'There's a wife and daughter here, sir,' said Weaver. 'The doctor's seen them. They're both unharmed, but they're suffering from shock. Hardly surprising when you consider they found the body. They're upstairs with WPC

Smithies. Apparently there's also a son rambling around America somewhere.'

'Who was this Rothwell bloke?' Banks asked. 'He must have had a bob or two. Anything missing?'

'We don't know yet, sir,' Weaver said. He looked around the bright kitchen. 'But I see what you mean. He was some sort of financial whizz-kid, I think. These new-fangled kitchens don't come cheap, I can tell you. The wife's got in the habit of leaving the *Mail on Sunday* supplement open at some design or another. Her way of dropping hints, like, and about as subtle as a blow on the head with a hammer. The price of them makes me cringe. I tell her the one we've got is perfectly all right, but she—'

As he talked, Weaver began to pour the tea into the row of cups and mugs he had arranged. But after filling the second one, he stopped and stared at the door. Banks and Gristhorpe followed his gaze and saw a young girl standing there, her slight figure framed in the doorway. She rubbed her eyes and stretched.

'Hello,' she said. 'Are you the detectives? I'd like to talk to you. My name's Alison Rothwell and someone just killed my father.'

TWO

She was about fifteen, Banks guessed, but she made no attempt to make herself look older, as many teenagers do. She wore a baggy, grey sweatshirt advertising an American football team, and a blue tracksuit bottom with a white stripe down each side. Apart from the bruiselike pouches under her light blue eyes, her complexion was pale. Her mousy blonde hair was parted in the centre and hung in uncombed strands over her shoulders. Her mouth, with its pale, thin lips, was too small for her oval face.

'Can I have some tea, please?' she asked. Banks noticed she had a slight lisp.

PC Weaver looked for direction. 'Go ahead, lad,' Gristhorpe told him. 'Give the lass some tea.' Then he turned to Alison Rothwell. 'Are you sure you wouldn't rather be upstairs with your mum, love?'

Alison shook her head. 'Mum'll be all right. She's asleep and there's a policewoman sitting by her. I can't sleep. It keeps going round in my mind, what happened. I want to tell you about it now. Can I?'

'Of course.' Gristhorpe asked PC Weaver to stay and take notes. He introduced Banks and himself, then pulled out a stool for her. Alison gave them a sad, shy smile and sat down, holding the mug of tea to her chest with both hands as if she needed its heat. Gristhorpe indicated subtly that Banks should do the questioning.

'Are you sure you feel up to this?' Banks asked her first.

Alison nodded. 'I think so.'

'Would you like to tell us what happened, then?'

Alison took a deep breath. Her eyes focused on something Banks couldn't see.

'It was just after dark,' she began. 'About ten o'clock, quarter past or thereabouts. I was reading. I thought I heard a sound out in the yard.'

'What kind of sound?' Banks asked.

'I . . . I don't know. Just as if someone was out there. A thud, like someone bumping into something or something falling on the ground.'

'Carry on.'

Alison hugged her cup even closer. 'At first I didn't pay

it any mind. I carried on reading, then I heard another sound, a sort of scraping, maybe ten minutes later.'

'Then what did you do?' Banks asked.

'I turned the yard light on and looked out of the window, but I couldn't see anything.'

'Did you have the television on, some music?'

'No. That's why I could hear the sounds outside so clearly. Usually it's so quiet and peaceful up here. All you can hear at night is the wind through the trees, and sometimes a lost sheep baa-ing, or a curlew up on the moors.'

'Weren't you scared being by yourself?'

'No. I like it. Even when I heard the noise I just thought it might be a stray dog or a sheep or something.'

'Where were your parents at this time?'

'They were out. It's their wedding anniversary. Their twenty-first. They went out to dinner in Eastvale.'

'You didn't want to go with them?'

'No. Well . . . I mean, it was *their* anniversary, wasn't it?' She turned up her nose. 'Besides, I don't like fancy restaurants. And I don't like Italian food. Anyway, it's not as if it was *Home Alone* or something. I *am* nearly sixteen, you know. And it was my choice. I'd rather stay home and read. I don't mind being by myself.'

Perhaps, Banks guessed, they hadn't invited her. 'Carry on,' he said. 'After you turned the yard light on, what did you do?'

'When I couldn't see anything, I just sort of brushed it off. Then I heard another noise, like a stone or something, hitting the wall. I was fed up of being disturbed by then, so I decided to go out and see what it was.'

'You still weren't frightened?'

'A bit, maybe, by then. But not *really* scared. I still

thought it was probably an animal or something like that, maybe a fox. We get them sometimes.'

'Then what happened?'

'I opened the front door, and as soon as I stepped out, someone grabbed me and dragged me back inside and tied me to the chair. Then they put a rag in my mouth and put tape over it. I couldn't swallow properly. It was all dry and it tasted of salt and oil.'

Banks noticed her knuckles had turned white around the mug. He worried she would crush it. 'How many of them were there, Alison?' he asked.

'Two.'

'Do you remember anything about them?'

She shook her head. 'They were both dressed all in black, except one of them had white trainers on. The other had some sort of suede slip-ons, brown I think.'

'You didn't see their faces?'

Alison hooked her feet over the crossbar. 'No, they had balaclavas on, black ones. But they weren't like the ones you'd buy to keep you warm. They were just made of cotton or some other thin material. They had little slits for the eyes and slits just under the nose so they could breathe.'

Banks noticed that she had turned paler. 'Are you all right, Alison?' he asked. 'Do you want to stop now and rest?'

Alison shook her head. Her teeth were clenched. 'No. I'll be all right. Just let me . . .' She sipped some tea and seemed to relax a little.

'How tall were they?' Banks asked.

'One was about as big as you.' She looked at Banks, who at only five foot nine was quite small for a policeman – just over regulation height, in fact. 'But he was fatter. Not really fat, but just not, you know, wiry . . . like you. The other was a few inches taller, maybe six foot, and quite thin.'

'You're doing really well, Alison,' Banks said. 'Was there anything else about them?'

'No. I can't remember.'

'Did either of them speak?'

'When he dragged me back inside, the smaller one said, "Keep quiet and do as you're told and we won't hurt you."'

'Did you notice his accent?'

'Not really. It sounded ordinary. I mean, not foreign or anything.'

'Local?'

'Yorkshire, yes. But not Dales. Maybe Leeds or something. You know how it sounds different, more citified?'

'Good. You're doing just fine. What happened next?'

'They tied me to the chair with some rope and just sat and watched television. First the news was on, then some horrible American film about a psycho slashing women. They seemed to like that. One of them kept laughing when a woman got killed, as if it was funny.'

'You heard them laugh?'

'Just one of them, the tall one. The other one told him to shut up. He sounded like he was in charge.'

'The smaller one?'

'Yes.'

'That's all he said: "Shut up"?'

'Yes.'

'Was there anything unusual about the taller man's laugh?'

'I . . . I don't . . . I can't remember.' Alison wiped a tear from her eye with the sleeve of her sweatshirt. 'It was just a laugh, that's all.'

'It's all right. Don't worry about it. Did they harm you in any way?'

Alison reddened and looked down into her half-empty

mug. 'The smaller one came over to me when I was tied up, and he put his hand on my breast. But the other one made him stop. It was the only time he said anything.'

'How did he make him stop? What did he do?'

'He just said not to, that it wasn't part of the deal.'

'Did he use those exact words, Alison? Did he say, "It's not part of the deal"?'

'Yes. I think so. I mean, I'm not completely sure, but it was something like that. The smaller man didn't seem to like it, being told what to do by the other, but he left me alone after that.'

'Did you see any kind of weapon?' Banks asked.

'Yes. The kind of gun that farmers have, with two barrels. A shotgun.'

'Who had it?'

'The smaller man, the one in charge.'

'Did you hear a car at any time?'

'No. Only when Mum and Dad came home. I mean, I heard cars go by on the road sometimes, you know, the one that goes through Relton and right over the moors into the next dale. But I didn't hear anyone coming or going along our driveway.'

'What happened when your parents came home?'

Alison paused and swirled the tea in the bottom of her mug as if she were trying to see into her future. 'It must have been about half past eleven or later. The men waited behind the door and the tall one grabbed Mum while the other put his gun to Dad's neck. I tried to scream and warn them, honest I did, but the rag in my mouth . . . I just couldn't make a sound . . .' She ran her sleeve across her eyes again and sniffled. Banks gestured to PC Weaver, who found a box of tissues on the window-sill and brought them over.

'Thank you,' Alison said. 'I'm sorry.'

'You don't have to go on if you don't want,' Banks said. 'It can wait till tomorrow.'

'No. I've started. I want to. Besides, there's not much more to tell. They tied Mum up the same as me and we sat there facing each other. Then they went outside with Dad. Then we heard the bang.'

'How long between the time they went out and the shot?'

Alison shook her head dreamily. She held the mug up close to her throat. The sleeves of her sweatshirt had slipped down, and Banks could see the raw, red lines where the rope had cut into her flesh. 'I don't know. It seemed like a long time. But all I can remember is we just sat looking at each other, Mum and me, and we didn't know what was happening. I remember a night-bird calling somewhere. Not a curlew. I don't know what it was. And it seemed like forever, like time just stretched out and Mum and I got really scared now looking at one another not knowing what was going on. Then we heard the explosion and . . . and it was like it all snapped and I saw something die in Mum's eyes, it was so, so . . .' Alison dropped the mug, which clipped the corner of the table then fell and spilled without breaking on the floor. The sobs seemed to start deep inside her, then she began to shake and wail.

Banks went over and put his arms around her, and she clung on to him for dear life, sobbing against his chest.

THREE

'It looks like his office,' Banks said, when Gristhorpe turned on the light in the last upstairs room.

Two large desks formed an L-shape. On one of them stood a computer and a laser printer, and on a small table next to them stood a fax machine with a basket attached at the front for collecting the cut-off sheets. At the back of the computer desk, a hutch stood against the wall. The compartments were full of boxes of disks and software manuals, mostly for word processing, spreadsheets and accounting programmes, along with some for standard utilities.

The other desk stood in front of the window, which framed a view of the farmyard. Scene of Crime officers were still going about their business down there: taking samples of just about everything in sight, measuring distances, trying to get casts of footprints, sifting soil. In the barn, their bright arc lamps had replaced Darby's roving light.

This was the desk where Rothwell dealt with handwritten correspondence and phone calls, Banks guessed. There was a blotter, which looked new – no handy wrong-way-around clues scrawled there – a jam jar full of pens and pencils, a blank scratch-pad, an electronic adding machine of the kind that produces a printed tape of its calculations and an appointment calendar open at the day of the murder, 12 May.

The only things written there were 'Dr Hunter' beside the 10:00 a.m. slot, 'Make dinner reservation: Mario's, 8:30 p.m.' Below that, and written in capitals all across the afternoon, 'FLOWERS?' Banks had noticed a vase full of fresh flowers in the living room. An anniversary present? Sad when touching gestures like that outlive the giver. He thought of Sandra again, and suddenly he wanted very much to be near her, to bridge the distance that had grown between them, to hold her and feel her warmth. He shivered.

'All right, Alan?' Gristhorpe asked.

'Fine. Someone just walked over my grave.'

'Look at all this.' Gristhorpe pointed to the two metal filing cabinets and the heavy-duty shelves that took up the room's only long, unbroken wall. 'Business records, by the looks of it. Someone's going to have to sift through it.' He looked towards the computer and grimaced. 'We'd better get Phil to have a look at this lot tomorrow,' he said. 'I wouldn't trust myself to turn the bloody thing on without blowing it up.'

Banks grinned. He was aware of Gristhorpe's Luddite attitude towards computers. He quite liked them, himself. Of course, he had only the most rudimentary skills and never seemed to be able to do anything right, but Phil Richmond, 'Phil the Hacker' as he was known around the station, ought to be able to tell them a thing or two about Rothwell's system.

Finding nothing else of immediate interest in the office, they walked out to the rear of the house, which faced north, and stood in the back garden, the hems of their trousers damp with dew. It was after five now, close to dawn. A pale sun was slowly rising in the east behind a veil of thin cloud that had appeared over the last couple of hours, mauve on the horizon, but giving the rest of the sky a light grey wash and the landscape the look of a water-colour. A few birds sang, and occasionally the sound of a farm vehicle starting up broke the silence. The air smelled moist and fresh.

It was certainly a *garden* they stood in, and not just a backyard. Someone – Rothwell? His wife? – had planted rows of vegetables – beans, cabbage, lettuce, all neatly marked – a small area of herbs and a strawberry patch. At the far end, beyond a dry-stone wall, the land fell away steeply to a beck that coursed down the daleside until it fed into the River Swain at Fortford.

The village of Fortford, about a mile down the hillside, was just waking up. Below the exposed foundations of the Roman fort on its knoll to the east, the cottages with their flagstone roofs huddled around the green and the square-towered church. Already, smoke drifted from some of the chimneys as farm labourers and shopkeepers prepared themselves for the coming day. Country folk were early risers.

The whitewashed front of the sixteenth-century Rose and Crown glowed pink in the early light. Even in there, someone would soon be in the kitchen, making bacon and eggs for the paying guests, especially for the ramblers, who liked to be off early. At the thought of food, his stomach rumbled. He knew Ian Falkland, the landlord of the Rose and Crown, and thought it might not be a bad idea to have a chat with him about Keith Rothwell. Though he was an expatriate Londoner, like Banks, Ian knew most of the local dalesfolk, and, given his line of work, he picked up a fair amount of gossip.

Finally, Banks turned to Gristhorpe and broke the silence. 'They certainly seemed to know what was what, didn't they?' he said. 'I don't imagine it was a lucky guess that the girl was in the house alone.'

'You're thinking along the same lines as I am, aren't you, Alan?' said Gristhorpe. 'An execution. A hit. Call it what you will.'

Banks nodded. 'I can't see any other lines to think along yet. Everything points to it. The way they came in and waited, the position of the body, the coolness, the professionalism of it all. Even the way one of them said touching the girl wasn't part of the deal. It was all planned. Yes, I think it was an execution. It certainly wasn't a robbery or a random killing. They hadn't been through the house, as far as we could tell. Everything seems in order. And if it was a robbery, they'd no need to kill him, especially that way. The question is why? Why should anyone want to execute an accountant?'

'Hmm,' said Gristhorpe. 'Unhappy client, maybe? Someone he turned in to the Inland Revenue?' Nearby, a peewit sensed their closeness to its ground nest and started buzzing them, piping its high-pitched call. 'One of the things we have to do is find out how *honest* an accountant our Mr Rothwell was,' Gristhorpe went on. 'But let's not speculate too much yet, Alan. We don't know if there's anything missing, for a start. Rothwell might have had a million in gold bullion hidden away in his garage for all we know. But you're right about the execution angle. And that means we could be dealing with something very big, big enough to contract a murder for.'

'Sir?'

At that moment, one of the SOC officers came into the garden through the back door.

Gristhorpe turned. 'Yes?'

'We've found something, sir. In the garage. I think you'd both better come and have a look for yourselves.'

FOUR

They followed the officer back to the brightly lit garage. Rothwell's body had, mercifully, been taken to the morgue, where Dr Glendenning, the Home Office pathologist, would get to work on it as soon as he could. Two men from the SOC team stood by the barn door. One was holding something with a pair of tweezers and the other was peering at it closely.

'What is it?' Banks asked.

'It's wadding, sir. From the shotgun,' said the SOCO with the tweezers. 'You see, sir, you can buy commercially made shotgun cartridges, but you can also reload the shells at home. Plenty of farmers and recreational shooters do it. Saves money.'

'Is that what this bloke did?' Banks asked.

'Looks like it, sir.'

'To save money? Typical Yorkshireman. Like a Scotsman stripped of his generosity.'

'Cheeky southern bastard,' said Gristhorpe, then turned to the SOCO. 'Go on, lad.'

'Well, sir, I don't know how much you know about shotguns, but they take cartridges, not bullets.'

Banks knew that much, at least, and he suspected that Gristhorpe, from Dales farming stock, knew a heck of a lot more. But they usually found it best to let the SOCOs show off a bit.

'We're listening,' said Gristhorpe.

Emboldened by that, the officer went on. 'A shotgun shell's made up of a primer, a charge of gunpowder and the pellets, or shot. There's no slug and there's no rifling in the barrel, so you can't get any characteristic markings to trace back to the weapon. Except from the shell, of course, which bears the imprint of the firing and loading mechanisms. But we don't have a shell. What we do have is this.' He held up the wadding. 'Commercial wadding is usually made of either paper or plastic, and you can sometimes trace the shell's manufacturer through it. But this isn't commercial.'

'What exactly is it?' asked Banks, reaching out.

The SOCO passed him the tweezers and said, 'Don't know for certain yet, but it looks like something from a colour magazine. And luckily, it's not too badly burned inside, only charred around the edges. It's tightly packed, but we'll get it unfolded and straightened out when we get it to the lab, then maybe we'll be able to tell you the name, date and page number.'

'Then all we'll have to do is check the list of sub-scribers,' said Banks, 'and it'll lead us straight to our killer. Dream on.'

The SOCO laughed. 'We're not miracle workers, sir.'

'Has anyone got a magnifying glass?' Banks asked the assembly at large. 'And I don't want any bloody cracks about Sherlock Holmes.'

One of the SOCOs passed him a glass, the rectangular kind that came with the tiny-print, two-volume edition of the *Oxford English Dictionary*. Banks held up the wadding and examined it through the glass.

What he saw was an irregularly shaped wad of crumpled paper, no more than about an inch across at its widest point. At first he couldn't make out anything but the blackened edge of the wadded paper, but it certainly looked as if it were from some kind of magazine. He looked more closely, turning the wadding this way and that, holding it closer and farther, then finally the dis-embodied shapes coalesced into something recognizable. 'Bloody hell,' he muttered, letting his arm fall slowly to his side.

'What is it, Alan?' Gristhorpe asked.

Banks handed him the glass. 'You'd better have a look for yourself,' he said. 'You won't believe me.'

Banks stood back and watched Gristhorpe scrutinize

the wadding, knowing that it would be only a matter of moments before he noticed, as Banks had done, part of a pink tongue licking a dribble of semen from the tip of an erect penis.

2

ONE

Traditional police wisdom has it that if a case doesn't yield leads in the first twenty-four hours, then everyone is in for a long, tough haul. In practice, of course, the period doesn't always turn out to be twenty-four hours; it can be twenty-three, nine, fourteen, or even forty-eight. That's the problem: when do you scale down your efforts? The answer, Banks reminded himself as he dragged his weary bones into the 'Boardroom' of Eastvale Divisional Police Headquarters at ten o'clock that morning, is that you don't.

The Suzy Lamplugh case was a good example. It started as a missing-persons report. One lunch-time, a young woman left the estate agent's office in Fulham, where she worked, and disappeared. Only after over a year's intensive detective work, which resulted in more than six hundred sworn statements, thousands of interviews, 26,000 index cards and nobody knew how many man-hours, was the investigation wound down. Suzy Lamplugh was never found, either alive or dead.

By the time Banks arrived at the station, Superintendent Gristhorpe had appointed Phil Richmond Office Manager and asked him to set up the Murder Room, where all information regarding the Keith Rothwell case would be carefully indexed, cross-referenced and filed. At first,

Gristhorpe thought it should be established in Fortford or Relton, close to the scene, but later decided that they had better facilities at the Eastvale station. It was only about seven miles from Fortford, anyway.

Richmond was also the only one among them who had training in the use of the HOLMES computer system – acronym for the Home Office Major Enquiry System, with a superfluous 'L' for effect. HOLMES wasn't without its problems, especially as not all the country's police forces used the same computer languages. Still, if no developments occurred before long, Richmond's skill might prove useful.

Gristhorpe had also given a brief press conference first thing in the morning. The sooner photographs of Keith Rothwell and descriptions of the killers, balaclavas and all, were sitting beside the public's breakfast plates or flashing on their TV screens, the sooner information would start to come in. The news was too late for that morning's papers, but it would make local radio and television, the *Yorkshire Evening Post* and tomorrow's national dailies.

Of course, Gristhorpe had given hardly any details about the murder itself. At first, he had even resisted the idea of releasing Rothwell's name. After all, there had been no formal identification, and they didn't have his fingerprints on file for comparison. On the other hand, there was little doubt as to what had happened, and they were hardly going to drag Alison or her mother along to the mortuary to identify the remains.

Gristhorpe had also been in touch with the anti-terrorist squad at Scotland Yard. Yorkshire was far from a stranger to IRA action. People still remembered the M62 bomb in 1974, when a coach carrying British servicemen and their families was blown up, killing eleven and wounding fourteen. Many even claimed to have heard the explosion from as far away as Leeds and Bradford. More recently, two policemen had been shot by IRA members during a routine traffic check on the A1.

The anti-terrorist squad would be able to tell Gristhorpe whether Rothwell had any connections, however tenuous, that would make him a target. As an accountant, he could, for example, have been handling money for a terrorist group. In addition, forensic information and details of the *modus operandi* would be made known to the squad, who would see if the information matched anything on file.

While Gristhorpe handled the news media and Richmond set up the Murder Room, Banks and Susan Gay had conducted a breakfast-time house-to-house of Relton and Fortford – including a visit to the Rose and Crown and a generous breakfast from Ian Falkland – trying to find out a bit about Rothwell, and whether anyone had seen or heard anything unusual on the night of the murder.

Gristhorpe, Richmond and Susan Gay were already in the room when Banks arrived and poured himself a large black coffee. The conference room was nicknamed the 'Boardroom' because of its well-polished, heavy oval table and ten stiff-backed chairs, not to mention the coarse-textured burgundy wallpaper, which gave the room a constant aura of semi-darkness, and the large oil painting (in ornate gilt frame) of one of Eastvale's most successful nineteenth-century wool merchants, looking decidedly sober and stiff in his tight-fitting suit and starched collar.

'Right,' said Gristhorpe, 'time to get up to date. Alan?'

Banks slipped a few sheets of paper from his briefcase and rubbed his eyes. 'Not much so far, I'm afraid. Rothwell was trained as an accountant. At least we've got that much confirmed. Some of the locals in Relton and Fortford knew him, but not well. Apparently, he was a quiet sort of bloke. Kept himself to himself.'

'Who did he work for?'

'Self-employed. We got this from Ian Falkland, landlord of the Rose and Crown in Fortford. He said Rothwell used to drop by now and then for a quick jar before dinner. Never had more than a couple of halves. Well-liked, quiet, decent sort of chap. Anyway, he used to work for Hatchard and Pratt, the Eastvale firm, until he started his own business. Falkland used him for the pub's accounts. I gather Rothwell saved him a bob or two from the Inland Revenue.' Banks scratched the small scar by his right eye. 'There's a bit more to it than that, though,' he went on. 'Falkland got the impression that Rothwell owned a few businesses as well, and that accountancy was becoming more of a sideline for him. We couldn't get any more than that, but we'll be having a close look at his office today.'

Gristhorpe nodded.

'And that's about it,' Banks said. 'The Rothwell family had been living at Arkbeck Farm for almost five years. They used to live in Eastvale.' He looked at his watch. 'I'm going out to Arkbeck Farm again after this meeting. I'm hoping Mrs Rothwell will have recovered enough to tell us something about what happened.'

'Good. Any leads on the two men?'

'Not yet, but Susan spoke to someone who thinks he saw a car.'

Gristhorpe looked at Susan.

'That's right, sir,' she said. 'It was around sunset last night, before it got completely dark. A retired school-teacher from Fortford was coming back home after visiting his daughter in Pateley Bridge. He said he liked to take the lonely roads over the moors.'

'Where did he see this car?'

'At the edge of the moors above Relton, sir. It was parked in a turn-off, just a dip by the side of the road. I think it used to be an old drovers' track, but it's not used any more, and only the bit by the road is clear. The rest has been taken over by moorland. Anyway, sir, the thing is that the way the road curves in a wide semicircle around the farm, this spot would only be about a quarter of a mile away on foot. Remember that copse opposite the farmhouse? Well, it's the same one that straggles up the daleside as far as this turn-off. It would provide excellent cover if someone wanted to get to the farm without being seen, and Alison wouldn't have heard the car approaching if it had been parked way up on the road.'

'Sounds promising,' said Gristhorpe. 'Did the witness notice anything about the car?'

'Yes, sir. He said it looked like an old Escort. It was a light colour. For some reason he thought pale blue. And there was either rust or mud or grass around the lower chassis.'

'It's hardly the bloody stretch-limousine you associate with hit men, is it?' Gristhorpe said.

'More of a Yorkshire version,' said Banks.

Gristhorpe laughed. 'Aye. Better follow it up, then, Susan. Get a description of the car out. I don't suppose your retired schoolteacher happened to see two men dressed in black carrying a shotgun, did he?'

Susan grinned. 'No, sir.'

'Rothwell didn't do any farming himself, did he?' Gristhorpe asked Banks.

'No. Only that vegetable patch we saw at the back. He rented out the rest of his land to neighbouring farmers. There's a fellow I know farms up near Relton I want to talk to. Pat Clifford. He should know if there were any problems in that area.'

'Good,' said Gristhorpe. 'As you know, a lot of locals don't like newcomers buying up empty farms and not using them properly.'

Gristhorpe, Banks knew, had lived in the farmhouse above Lyndgarth all his life. Perhaps he had even been born there. He had sold off most of the land after his parents died and kept only enough for a small garden and for his chief off-duty indulgence, a dry-stone wall he worked on periodically, which went nowhere and fenced nothing in.

'Anyway,' Gristhorpe went on, 'there's been some bad feeling. I can't see a local farmer hiring a couple of killers – people like to take care of their own around these parts – but stranger things have happened. And remember: shotguns are common as cow-clap around farms. Anything on that wadding yet?'

Banks shook his head. 'The lab's still working on it. I've already asked West Yorkshire to make a few inquiries at the kind of places that sell that sort of magazine. I talked to Ken Blackstone at Milltgarth in Leeds. He's a DI there and an old mate.'

'Good,' said Gristhorpe, then turned to Richmond. 'Phil, why don't you go up to Arkbeck Farm with Alan and have a look at Rothwell's computer before you get bogged down managing the office?'

'Yes, sir. Do you think we should have it brought in after I've had a quick look?'

Gristhorpe nodded. 'Aye, good idea.' He scratched his pockmarked cheek. 'Look, Phil, I know you're supposed to be leaving us for the Yard at the end of the week, but—'

'It's all right, sir,' Richmond said. 'I understand. I'll stick around as long as you need me.'

'Good lad. Susan, did you find anything interesting in the appointment book?'

Susan Gay shook her head. 'Not yet, sir. He had a doctor's appointment for yesterday morning with Dr Hunter. I called the office and it appears he kept it. Routine physical. No problems. I'm working my way through. He didn't write much down – or maybe he kept it on computer – but there's a few names to check out, mostly local businesses. I must say, though, sir, he didn't exactly have a full appointment book. There are plenty of empty days.'

'Maybe he didn't need the money. Maybe he could afford to pick and choose. Have a word with someone at his old firm, Hatchard and Pratt. They're just on Market Street. They might be able to tell us something about his background.' Gristhorpe looked at his watch. 'Okay, we've all got plenty to do, better get to it.'

TWO

'I'm afraid my mother's still in bed,' Alison told Banks at Arkbeck Farm. 'I told her you were here . . .' She shrugged.

That was odd, Banks thought. Surely a mother would want to comfort her daughter and protect her from prying policemen? 'Have you remembered anything else?' he asked.

Alison Rothwell looked worn out and worried to death. She wore her hair, unwashed and a little greasy, tied back, emphasizing her broad forehead, a plain white T-shirt and stonewashed designer jeans. She sat with her legs tucked under her, and as she talked, she fiddled with a ring on the little finger of her right hand. 'I don't know,' she said. The lisp made her sound like a little girl.

They sat in a small, cheerful room at the back of the house with ivory-painted walls and Wedgwood blue upholstery. A bookcase stood against one wall, mostly full of paperbacks, their spines a riot of orange, green and black. Against the wall opposite stood an upright piano with a highly lacquered cherry-wood finish. On top of it stood an untidy pile of sheet music. WPC Smithies, who had stayed with the Rothwells, sat discreetly in a corner, notebook open. Phil Richmond was upstairs in Keith Rothwell's study, clicking away on the computer.

The large bay window, open about a foot to let in the birdsongs and fresh air, looked out over Fortford and the dale beyond. It was a familiar enough view to Banks. He had seen it from 'Maggie's Farm' on the other side of Relton, and from the house of a man called Adam Harkness on the valley bottom. The sight never failed to impress, though, even on a dull day like today, with the grey-brown ruins of Devraulx Abbey poking through the trees of its grounds, the village of Lyndgarth clustered around its lopsided green and, towering over the patchwork of pale green fields and dry-stone walls that rose steeply to the heights, the forbidding line of Aldington Edge, a long limestone scar streaked with fissures from top to bottom like gleaming skeleton's teeth.

'I know it's painful to remember,' Banks went on, 'but we need all the help we can get if we're to catch these men.'

'I know. I'm sorry.'

'Do you remember hearing any sounds between the time they went outside and when you heard the bang?'

Alison frowned. 'I don't think so.'

'No sounds of a struggle, or screaming?'

'No. It was all so quiet. That's what I remember.'

'No talking?'

'I didn't hear any.'

'And you don't know how long they were out there before the explosion?'

'No. I was scared and I was worried. Mum was sitting facing me. I could see how frightened she was, but I couldn't do anything. I just felt so powerless.'

'When it was all over, did you hear any sounds then?'

'I don't think so.'

'Try to remember. Did you hear what direction they went off in?'

'No.'

'Any sounds of a car?'

She paused. 'I think I heard a car door shut, but I can't be sure. I mean, I didn't hear it drive away, but I think I kept sort of drifting in and out. I think I heard a sound like the slam of a car door in the distance.'

'Do you know which direction it came from?'

'Farther up the daleside, I think. Relton way.'

'Good. Now, can you remember anything else about the men?'

'One of them, the one who touched me. I've been thinking about it. He had big brown eyes, a sort of light hazel colour, and watery. There's a word for it. Like a dog.'

'Spaniel?'

'Yes. That's it. Spaniel eyes. Or puppy dog. He had puppy-dog eyes. But they're usually . . . you know, they usually make you feel sorry for the person, but these didn't. They were cruel.'

'Did either of the men say anything else?'

'No.'

'Did they go anywhere else in the house? Any other rooms?'

'No.'

'Did you see them take anything at all?'

Alison shook her head.

'When your father saw them and later went outside with them, how did he seem?'

'What do you mean?'

'Was he surprised?'

'When he first came in and they grabbed him, yes.'

'But after?'

'I . . . I don't know. He didn't do anything or say anything. He just stood there.'

'Do you think he recognized the men?'

'How could he? They were all covered up.'

'Did he seem surprised after the immediate shock had worn off?'

'I don't think he did, no. Just . . . resigned.'

'Was he expecting them?'

'I . . . I don't know. I don't think so.'

'Do you think he knew them, knew why they were there?'

'How could he?'

She spoke with such disbelief that Banks wondered if she had noticed that her father really *wasn't* so shocked or surprised and it confused her. 'Do you think he knew what was happening?' he pressed. 'Why it was happening?'

'Maybe. No. I don't know. He couldn't possibly, could he?' She screwed up her eyes. 'I can't see it that clearly. I don't want to see it clearly.'

'All right, Alison. It's all right. I'm sorry, but I have to ask.'

'I know. I don't mean to be a cry-baby.' She rubbed her bare arm over her eyes.

'You're being very brave. Just one more question

about what happened and then we'll move on. Okay?'

'Okay.'

'Did your father go quietly or did they have to force him?'

'No, he just walked out with them. He didn't say anything.'

'Did he look frightened?'

'He didn't look anything.' She reddened. 'And he didn't *do* anything. He just left Mum and me all tied up and let them take him and . . . and kill him like an animal.'

'All right, Alison, calm down. How did you get free from the chair after they'd gone?'

Alison sniffled and blew her nose. 'It was a long time,' she said finally. 'Hours maybe. Some of the time I just sat there, but not really there, if you know what I mean. I think Mum had fainted. They'd really tied us tight and I couldn't feel my hands properly.'

As she spoke, she rubbed at her wrists, still ringed by the burn marks. 'In the end, I tipped my chair and crawled over near the table where my mother's sewing basket was. I knew there were scissors in there. I had to rub my hands for a long time, so they could feel properly, and I don't know how . . . but in the end I cut the rope, then I untied Mum.' She shifted her position. 'I'm worried about Mum. She's not herself. She doesn't want to eat. What's going to happen to her?'

'I'm all right, Alison, dear. There's no need to worry.'

The voice came from the doorway, and Banks turned for his first glance of Mrs Rothwell. She was a tall woman with short grey hair and fine-boned, angular features, the small nose perhaps just a little too sharply chiselled. There seemed an unusually wide space, Banks thought, between her nose and her thin upper lip, which gave her tilted head a haughty, imperious aspect. Banks could see where Alison got her small mouth from.

Her chestnut-brown eyes looked dull. Tranquillizers prescribed by Dr Burns, Banks guessed. They would help to explain her listless movements, too. Her skin was pale, as if drained of blood, though Banks could tell she had put some make-up on. In fact, she had made a great effort to look her best. She wore black silk slacks over her thin, boyish hips, and a cable-knit jumper in a rainbow pattern, which looked to Banks's untutored eye like an exclusive design. At least he had never seen one like it before. Even in her sedated grief, there was something controlled, commanding and attention-demanding about her, a kind of tightly reined-in power.

She sat down in the other armchair, crossed her legs and clasped her hands on her lap. Banks noticed the chunky rings on her fingers: diamond clusters, a large ruby and a broad gold wedding band.

Banks introduced himself and expressed his condolences. She inclined her head slightly in acceptance.

'I'm afraid I have some difficult questions for you, Mrs Rothwell,' he said.

'Not about last night,' she said, one bejewelled hand going to her throat. 'I can't talk about it. I feel faint, my voice goes and I just can't talk.'

'Mummy,' said Alison. 'I've told him about . . . about that. Haven't I?' And she looked at Banks as if daring him to disagree.

'Yes,' he said. 'Actually, it wasn't that I wanted to ask about specifically. It's just that we need more information on your husband's movements and activities. Can you help?'

She nodded. 'I'm sorry, Chief Inspector. I'm not usually

such a mess.' She touched her hair. 'I must look dreadful.'

Banks murmured a compliment. 'Did your husband have any enemies that you knew of?' he asked.

'No. None at all. But then he didn't bore me with the details of his business. I really had no idea what kind of people he dealt with.' Her accent, Banks noticed, was Eastvale filtered through elocution lessons. *Elocution lessons*. He hadn't thought people took those in this day and age.

'So he never brought his business home, so to speak?'

'No.'

'Did he travel much?'

'Do you mean abroad?'

'Anywhere.'

'Well, he did go abroad now and then, on business, and of course, we'd holiday in Mexico, Hawaii or Bermuda. He also travelled a lot locally in the course of business. He was away a lot.'

'Where did he go?'

'Oh, all over. Leeds, Manchester, Liverpool, Birmingham, Bristol. Sometimes to London, Europe. He had a very important job. He was a brilliant financial analyst, much in demand. He could pick and choose his clients, could Keith, he didn't have to take just any old thing that came along.'

'You mentioned financial analysis. What exactly did he do?'

She picked at the wool on her sleeve with long, bony fingers. 'As I said, he didn't tell me much about work, not about the details, anyway. He qualified as a chartered accountant, of course, but that was only part of it. He had a genius for figures. He advised people what to do with their money, helped businesses out of difficulties. I suppose he was a kind of troubleshooter, if you like. A very exclusive one. He didn't need any new clients and people only found out about him by word of mouth.'

That all sounded sufficiently vague to be suspicious to Banks. On the other hand, what did *he* do? Investigate crimes, yes. But to do so, he chatted with locals over a pint, interviewed bereaved relatives, pored over fingerprints and blood samples. It would all sound rather nebulous and aimless to an outsider.

'And you never met any of his business associates?'

'We had people for dinner occasionally, but we never talked business.'

'Maybe, if you have a moment later, you could make a list of those you entertained most frequently?'

She raised her eyebrows. 'If you want.'

'Now, Mrs Rothwell,' Banks said, wishing he could have a cigarette in what was obviously a non-smoking household, 'this next question may strike you as rather indelicate, but were there any problems in the family?'

'Of course not. We're a happy family. Aren't we, Alison?'

Alison looked at Banks. 'Yes, Mother,' she said.

Banks turned back to Mrs Rothwell. 'Had your husband been behaving at all unusually recently?' he asked. 'Had you noticed any changes in him?'

She frowned. 'He *had* been a bit edgy, tense, a bit more preoccupied and secretive than usual. I mean, he was always quiet, but he'd been even more so.'

'For how long?'

She shrugged. 'Two or three weeks.'

'But he never told you what was wrong?'

'No.'

'Did you ask?'

'My husband didn't appreciate people prying into his private business affairs, Chief Inspector.'

'Not even his wife?'

'I assumed that if and when he wanted to tell me, he would do so.'

'What did you talk about over dinner yesterday?'

She shrugged. 'Just the usual things. The children, the house extension we wanted to have done . . . I don't know, really. What do *you* talk about when you're out for dinner with *your* wife?'

Good question, Banks thought. It had been so long since he and Sandra had gone out to dinner together that he couldn't remember what they talked about. 'Did you have any idea what he might have been worried about?' he asked.

'No. I suppose it was one of the usual business problems. Keith really cared about his clients.'

'What business problems? I thought he didn't talk to you about business.'

'He didn't, Chief Inspector. Please don't twist what I say. He just made the occasional offhand comment. You know, maybe he'd read something in the *Financial Times* or something and make a comment. I never understood what he meant. Anyway, I think one of the companies he was trying to help was sinking fast. Things like that always upset him.'

'Do you know which company?'

'No. It'll be on his computer. He put everything on that computer.' Suddenly, Mrs Rothwell put the back of one ringed hand to her forehead in what seemed to Banks a gesture from a nineteenth-century melodrama. Her forehead looked clammy. 'I'm afraid I can't talk any more,' she whispered. 'I feel a bit faint and dizzy. I . . . Alison.'

Alison helped her up and they left the room. Banks glanced over at WPC Smithies. 'Have you picked up anything at all from them?' he asked.

'Sorry, sir,' she said. 'Nothing. I'll tell you one thing, though, they're a weird pair. It's an odd family. I think they're both retreating from reality, in their own ways, trying to deny what happened, or *how* it happened. But you can see that for yourself.'

'Yes.'

Banks listened to a clock tick on the mantelpiece. It was one of those timepieces with all its brass and silver innards showing inside a glass dome.

A couple of minutes later, Alison came back. 'I'm sorry,' she said. 'Mummy's still weak and in shock. The doctor gave her some pills.'

'That's understandable, Alison,' said Banks. 'I'd almost finished, anyway. Just one last question. Do you know where your brother is? We'll have to get in touch with him.'

Alison picked up a postcard from the top of the piano, gave it to Banks and sat down again.

The card showed the San Francisco Golden Gate Bridge, which looked orange to Banks. He flipped it over. Postmarked two weeks ago, it read,

Dear Ali,

Love California, and San Francisco is a *great* city, but it's time to move on. I'm even getting used to driving on the wrong side of the road! This sightseeing's a tiring business so I'm off to Florida for a couple of weeks just lying in the sun. Ah, what bliss! Also to check out the motion picture conservatory in Sarasota. I'm driving down the coast highway and flying to Tampa from LA on Sunday. More news when I get there. Love to Mum,

Tom

'How long has he been gone?'

'Six weeks. Just over. He left on the thirty-first of March.'

'What does he do? What was that about a motion picture conservatory?'

Alison gave a brief smile. 'He wants to work in films. He worked in a video shop and saved up. He's hoping to go to film college in America and learn how to become a director.'

'How old is he?'

'Twenty-one.'

Banks stood up. 'All right, Alison,' he said. 'Thanks very much for all your help. WPC Smithies will be staying here for a while, so if you need anyone . . . And I'll ask the doctor to pay your mother another visit.'

'Thank you. Please don't worry about us.'

Banks looked in on Richmond, who sat bathed in the bluish glow of Rothwell's monitor, oblivious to the world, then went out to his car and lit a cigarette. He rolled the window down and listened to the birds as he smoked. Birds aside, it was bloody quiet up here. How, he wondered, could a teenager like Alison stand the isolation? As WPC Smithies had said, the Rothwells were an odd family.

As he drove along the bumpy track to the Relton road, he slipped in a tape of Dr John playing solo New Orleans piano music. He had developed a craving for piano music – *any* kind of piano music – recently. He was even thinking of taking piano lessons; he wanted to learn how to play *everything* – classical, jazz, blues. The only thing that held him back was that he felt too old to embark on such a venture. His forty-first birthday was coming up in a couple of weeks.

In Relton, a couple of old ladies holding shopping

baskets stood chatting outside the butcher's shop, probably about the murder.

Banks thought again about Alison Rothwell and her mother as he pulled up outside the Black Sheep. What were they holding back? And what was it that bothered him? No matter what Mrs Rothwell and Alison had said, there was something wrong in that family, and he had a hunch that Tom Rothwell might know what it was. The sooner they contacted him the better.

THREE

Laurence Pratt delved deep in his bottom drawer and pulled out a bottle of Courvoisier VSOP and two snifters.

'I'm sorry,' he apologized to DC Susan Gay, who sat opposite him at the broad teak desk. 'It's not that I'm a secret tippler. I keep it for emergencies, and I'm afraid what you've just told me most definitely constitutes one. You'll join me?'

'No, thank you.'

'Not on duty?'

'Sometimes,' Susan said. 'But not today.'

'Very well.' He poured himself a generous measure, swirled it and took a sip. A little colour came back to his cheeks. 'Ah . . . that's better.'

'If we could get back to Mr Rothwell, sir?'

'Yes. Yes, of course. But you must understand Miss, Miss . . .?'

'Gay, sir. DC Gay.'

She saw the inadvertent smile flash across his face. People often smiled like that when she introduced herself. 'Gay' had been a perfectly good name when she was a kid

– her nickname for a while had been 'Happy' Gay – but now its meaning was no longer the same. One clever bugger had actually asked, 'Did you say AC or DC Gay?' She comforted herself with the thought that he was doing three to five in Strangeways, thanks largely to her court evidence.

'Yes,' he went on, a frown quickly displacing the smile. 'I'd heard about Keith's death, of course, on the radio this lunchtime, but they didn't say *how* it happened. That's a bit of a shock, to be honest. You see, I knew Keith quite well. I'm only about three years older than he, and we worked here together for some years.'

'He left the firm five years ago, is that right?'

'About right. A big move like that takes quite a bit of planning, quite a bit of organizing. There were client files to be transferred, that sort of thing. And he had the house to think of, too.'

'He was a partner?'

'Yes. My father, Jeremiah Pratt, was one of the founders of the firm. He's retired now.'

'I understand the family used to live in Eastvale, is that right?'

'Yes. Quite a nice house out towards the York round-about. Catterick Street.'

'Why did they move?'

'Mary always fancied living in the country. I don't know why. She wasn't any kind of nature girl. I think perhaps she wanted to play Lady of the Manor.'

'Oh? Why's that?'

Pratt shrugged. 'Just her nature.'

'What about her husband?'

'Keith didn't mind. I should imagine he liked the solitude. I don't mean he was exactly antisocial, but he was never a great mixer, not lately, anyway. He travelled a lot, too.'

Pratt was in his mid-forties, Susan guessed, which did indeed make him just a few years older than Keith Rothwell. Quite good-looking, with a strong jaw and grey eyes, he wore his white shirt with the sleeves rolled up and his mauve and green tie clipped with what looked like a silver American dollar sign. His hairline was receding and what hair remained was grey at the temples. He wore black-framed glasses, which sat about halfway down his nose.

'Did you ever visit him there?'

'Yes. My wife and I dined with the Rothwells on several occasions.'

'Were you friends?'

Pratt took another sip of cognac, put his hand out and waggled it from side to side. 'Hmm. Somewhere between friends and colleagues, I'd say.'

'Why did he leave Hatchard and Pratt?'

Pratt broke eye contact and looked into the liquid he swirled in his snifter. 'Ambition, maybe? Straightforward accountancy bored him. He was fond of abstractions, very good with figures. He certainly had a flair for financial management. Very creative.'

'Does that imply fraudulent?'

Pratt looked up at her. She couldn't read his expression. 'I resent that implication,' he said.

'Was there any bad feeling?'

'I don't know what you mean.'

'When he left the firm. Had there been any arguments, any problems?'

'Good lord, this was five years ago!'

'Even so.'

Pratt adopted a stiffer tone. 'No, of course there hadn't.

Everything was perfectly amicable. We were sorry to lose him, of course, but . . .'

'He wasn't fired or anything?'

'No.'

'Did he take any clients with him?'

Pratt shuffled in his chair. 'There will always be clients who feel they owe their loyalty to an individual member of the firm rather than to the firm as a whole.'

'Are you sure this didn't cause bad feeling?'

'No, of course not. While it's unprofessional to solicit clients and woo them away, most firms *do* accept that they will lose some business whenever a popular member leaves to set up on his own. Say, for example, you visit a particular dentist in a group practice. You feel comfortable with him. He understands how you feel about dentists, you feel safe with him. If he left and set up on his own, would you go with him or stay and take your chances?'

Susan smiled. 'I see what you mean. Do you think you could provide me with a list of names of the clients he took?'

Pratt chewed his lower lip for a moment, as if debating the ethics of such a request, then said, 'I don't see why not. You could find out from his records anyway.'

'Thank you. He must have made a fair bit of money somehow,' Susan said. 'How did he do it?'

Pratt, who if truth be told, Susan thought, suppressing a giggle, might not be entirely happy about *his* name, either, made a steeple of his hairy hands. 'The same way we all do, I assume,' he said. 'Hard work. Good investments. Excellent service. Arkbeck Farm was in pretty poor shape when they bought it, you know. It didn't cost a fortune, and he'd no trouble arranging a fair mortgage. He put a lot into that house over the years.'

Susan looked at her notes and frowned as if she were having trouble reading or understanding them. 'I understand Mr Rothwell actually owned a number of businesses. Do you know anything about this?'

Pratt shook his head. 'Not really. I understand he was interested in property development. As I said, Keith was an astute businessman.'

'Did Mrs Rothwell work?'

'Mary? Good heavens, no! Well, not in the sense that she went out and made money. Mary was a housewife all the way. Well, perhaps "house manager" or "lady of leisure" would be a more appropriate term, as she didn't actually do the work herself. Except for the garden. You must have seen Arkbeck, how clean it is, how well appointed?'

'I'm afraid I had other things on my mind when I was there, sir,' Susan said, 'but I know what you mean.'

Pratt nodded. 'For Mary,' he went on, 'everything centred around the home, the family and the immediate community. Everything had to be just so, to look just right, and it had to be *seen* to look that way. I imagine she was a hard taskmaster, or should that be taskmistress? Of course, she didn't spend *all* her time in the house. There were the Women's Institute, the Church committees, the good works and the charities. Mary kept very busy, I can assure you.'

'Good works? Charities?' There was something positively Victorian about this. Susan pictured an earnest woman striding from hovel to hovel in a flurry of garments, long dress trailing in the mud, distributing alms to the peasants and preaching self-improvement.

'Yes. She collected for a number of good causes. You know, the RSPCA, NSPCC, cancer, heart foundation and the like. Nothing political – I mean, no ban the bomb or anything – and nothing controversial, like AIDS research. Just the basics. She was the boss's daughter, after all. She had certain Conservative standards to keep up.'

'The boss's daughter?'

'Yes, didn't you know? Her maiden name was Mary Hatchard. She was old man Hatchard's daughter. He's dead now, of course.'

'So Keith Rothwell married the boss's daughter,' Susan mused aloud. 'I don't suppose that did his career any harm?'

'No, it didn't. But that was more good luck than good management, if you ask me. Keith didn't just marry the boss's daughter, he got her pregnant first, with Tom, as it turns out, *then* he married her.'

'How did that go over?'

Pratt paused and picked up a paperclip. 'Not very well at first. Old man Hatchard was mad as hell. He kept the lid on it pretty well, of course, and after he'd had time to consider it, I think he was glad to get her off his hands. He could hardly have her married to a mere junior, though, so Keith came up pretty quickly through the ranks to full partner.'

Pratt twisted the paperclip. He seemed to be enjoying this game, Susan thought. He was holding back, toying with her. She had a sense that if she didn't ask exactly the right questions, she wouldn't get the answers she needed. The problem was, she didn't know what the right questions were.

They sat in his office over Winston's Tobacconists, looking out on north Market Street, and Susan could hear the muted traffic sounds through the double-glazing. 'Look,' Pratt went on, 'I realize I'm the one being questioned, but could you tell me how Mary is? And Alison? I do regard myself as something of a friend of the family, and if there's anything I can do . . .'

'Thank you, sir. I'll make sure they know. Can you think of any reason anyone might have for killing Mr Rothwell?'

'No, I can't. Not in the way you described.'

'What do you mean?'

'Well, I suppose I could imagine a burglar, say, perhaps killing someone who got in the way. You read about it in the papers, especially these days. Or an accident, some kids joyriding. But this . . .? It sounds like an assassination to me.'

'When was the last time you saw him?'

'About a month ago. No, earlier. In March, I think. Shortly after St Patrick's Day. The wife and I went for dinner. Mary's a splendid cook.'

'Did they entertain frequently?'

'Not that I know of. They had occasional small dinner parties, maximum six people. Keith didn't like socializing much, but Mary loved to show off the house, especially if she'd acquired a new piece of furniture or something. So they compromised. Last time it was the kitchen we had to admire. They used to have a country-style one, Aga and all, but someone started poking fun at "Aga-louts" in the papers, so Mary got annoyed and went for the modern look.'

'I see. What about the son, Tom? What do you know of him?'

'Tom? He's travelling in America, I understand. Good for him. Nothing like travel when you're young, before you get too tied down. Tom was always a cheerful and polite kid as far as I was concerned.'

'No trouble?'

'Not in any real sense, no. I mean, he wasn't into drugs or any of that weird stuff. At worst I'd say he was a bit uncertain about what he wanted to do with his life, and his father was perhaps just a little impatient.'

'In what way?'

'He wanted Tom to go into business or law. Something solid and respectable like that.'

'And Tom?'

'Tom's the artsy type. But he's a bright lad. With his personality he could go almost anywhere. He just doesn't know where yet. After he left school, he drifted a bit. Still is doing, it seems.'

'Would you say there was friction between them?'

'You can't be suggesting—'

'I'm not suggesting anything.' Susan leaned back in the chair. 'Look, Mr Pratt, as far as we know Tom Rothwell is somewhere in the USA. We're trying to find him, but it could take time. The reason I'm asking you all these questions is because we need to know *everything* about Keith Rothwell.'

'Yes, of course. I'm sorry. But what with the shock of Keith's death and you asking about Tom . . .'

Susan leaned forward again. 'Is there any reason,' she asked, 'why you should think I was putting forward Tom as a suspect?'

'Stop trying to read between the lines. There's nothing written there. It was just the way you were asking about him, that's all. Tom and his father had the usual father–son arguments, but nothing more.'

'Where did Tom get the money for a trip to America?'

'What? I don't know. Saved up, I suppose.'

'You say you last saw Keith Rothwell in March?'

'Yes.'

'Have you spoken with him at all since then?'

'No.'

'Did he seem in any way different from usual then? Worried about anything? Nervous?'

'No, not that I can remember. It was a perfectly normal evening. Mary cooked duck à l'orange. Tom dropped in briefly, all excited about his trip. Alison stayed in her room.'

'Did she usually do that?'

'Alison's a sweet child, but she's a real loner, very secretive. Takes after her father. She's a bit of a bookworm, too.'

'What did you talk about that evening?'

'Oh, I can't remember. The usual stuff. Politics. Europe. The economy. Holiday plans.'

'Who else was there?'

'Just us, this time.'

'And Mr Rothwell said nothing that caused you any concern?'

'No. He was quiet.'

'Unusually so?'

'He was usually quiet.'

'Secretive?'

Pratt swivelled his chair and gazed out of the window at the upper storey of the Victorian community centre. Susan followed his gaze. She was surprised to see a number of gargoyles there she had never noticed before.

When he spoke again, Pratt still didn't look at Susan. She could see him only in profile. 'I've always felt that about him, yes,' he said. 'That's why I hesitated to call him a *close* friend. There was always something in reserve.' He turned to face Susan again and placed his hands, palms down, on the desk. 'Oh, years ago we'd let loose once in a while, go get blind drunk and not give a damn. Sometimes we'd go fishing together. But over time, Keith sort of reined himself in, cut himself off. I don't really know how to explain this. It was just a feeling. Keith was a very private person . . . well, lots of people are . . . But the thing was, I had no idea what he lived for.'

'Did he suffer from depression? Did you think—'

Pratt waved a hand. 'No. No, you're getting me wrong. He wasn't suicidal. That's not what I meant.'

'Can you try and explain?'

'I'll try. It's hard, though. I mean, I'd be hard pushed to say what I live for, too. There's the wife and kids, of course, my pride and joy. And we like to go hang-gliding over Semerwater on suitable weekends. I collect antiques, I love cricket and we like to explore new places on our holidays. See what I mean? None of that's what I actually *live for*, but it's all part of it.' He took off his glasses and rubbed the back of his hand over his eyes and the bridge of his nose, then put them back on again. 'I know, I'm getting too philosophical. But I told you it was hard to explain.'

Susan smiled. 'I'm still listening.'

'Well, all those are just *things*, aren't they? Possessions or activities. Things we do, things we care about. But there's something behind them all that ties them all together into *my* life, who I am, what I am. With Keith, you never knew. He was a cipher. For example, I'm sure he loved his family, but he never really showed it or spoke much about it. I don't know what really *mattered* to him. He never talked about hobbies or anything like that. I don't know what he did in his spare time. It's more than being private or secretive, it's as if there was a dimension *missing*, a man with a hole in the middle.' He scratched his temple. 'This is ridiculous. Please forgive me. Keith was a perfectly nice bloke. Wouldn't hurt a fly. But you never really knew what gripped him about life, what his *dream* was. I mean, mine's a villa in Portugal, but a dream doesn't have to be a thing, does it? I don't know . . . maybe he valued abstractions too much.'

He paused, as if he had run out of breath and ideas. Susan didn't really know what to jot down, but she finally settled for 'dimension missing . . . interests and concerns elusive'. It would do. She had a good memory for conversations and could recount verbatim most of what Pratt had said, if Banks wished to hear it.

'Let's get back to Mr Rothwell's work with your firm. Is there anything you can tell me about his . . . style . . . shall we say, his business practices?'

'You want to know if Keith was a crook, don't you?'

She did, of course, though that wasn't why she was asking. Still, she thought, never look a gift-horse in the mouth. She gave him a 'you caught me at it' smile. 'Well, was he?'

'Of course not.'

'Oh, come on, Mr Pratt. Surely in your business you must sail a little close to the wind at times?'

'I resent that remark, especially coming from a policeman.'

Susan let that one slip by. '*Touché*,' she said. Pratt seemed pleased enough with himself. Let him feel he's winning, she thought, then he'll tell you anyway, just to show he holds the power to do so. She was still sure he was holding something back. 'But seriously, Mr Pratt,' she went on, 'I'm not just playing games, bandying insults. If there was anything at all unusual in Mr Rothwell's business dealings, I hardly need tell you it could have a bearing on his murder.'

'Hmm.' Pratt swirled the rest of the brandy and tossed it back. He put the snifter in his 'Out' tray, no doubt for the secretary to take and wash. 'I stand by what I said,' he went on. 'Keith Rothwell never did anything truly *illegal* that I knew of. Certainly nothing that could be relevant to his death.'

'But . . .?'

He sighed. 'Well, maybe I wasn't *entirely* truthful earlier. I suppose I'd better tell you about it, hadn't I? You're bound to find out somehow.'

Susan turned her page. 'I'm listening,' she said.

3

ONE

The Black Sheep was the closest Swainsdale had to a well
kept secret. Most tourists were put off by the pub's exter-
nal shabbiness. Those who prided themselves on not
judging a book by its cover would, more often than not,
pop their heads around the door, see the even shabbier
interior and leave.

The renowned surliness of the landlord, Larry Grafton,
kept them away in droves, too. There was a rumour that
Larry had once refused to serve an American tourist with
a Glenmorangie and ginger, objecting to the utter lack of
taste that led her to ask for such a concoction. Banks
believed it.

Larry was Dales born and bred, not one of the new
landlords up from London. So many were recent immi-
grants these days, like Ian Falkland in the Rose and
Crown. That was a tourist pub if ever there was one,
Banks thought, probably selling more lager and lime,
pork scratchings and microwaved curries than anything
else.

The Black Sheep didn't advertise its pub grub, but anyone who knew about it could get as thick and fresh a ham
and piccalilli sandwich as ever they'd want from Elsie,
Larry's wife. And on some days, if her arthritis hadn't
been bothering her too much and she felt like cooking, she

could do you a fry-up so good you could feel your arteries hardening as you ate.

As usual, the public bar was empty apart from one table of old men playing dominoes and a couple of young farm-hands reading the sports news in the *Daily Mirror*.

As Banks had expected, Pat Clifford also stood propping up the bar. Pat was a hard, stout man with a round head, stubble for hair and a rough, red face burned by the sun and whipped by the wind and rain for fifty years.

'Hello, stranger,' said Pat, as Banks stood next to him. 'Long time, no see.'

Banks apologized for his absence and brought up the subject of Keith Rothwell.

'So tha only comes when tha wants summat, is that it?' Pat said. But he said it with a smile, and over the years Banks had learned that Yorkshire folk often take the sting out of their criticisms that way. They put a sting *in* their compliments, too, on those rare occasions they get around to giving any.

In this case, Banks guessed that Pat wasn't mortally offended at his protracted absence; he only wanted to make a point of it, let Banks know his feelings, and then get on with things. Banks acknowledged his culpability with a mild protest about the pressures of work, as expected, then listened to a minute or so of Pat's complaining about how the elderly and isolated were neglected by all and sundry.

When Pat's glass was empty, an event which occurred with alarming immediacy at the end of the diatribe, Banks's offer to buy him another was grudgingly accepted. Pat took a couple of sips, put the glass down on the bar and wiped his lips with the back of his grimy hand.

'He came in once or twice, did Mr Rothwell. Local, like. Nobody objected.'

'How often?'

'Once a week, mebbe. Sometimes twice. Larry—?' And he asked the landlord the same question. Larry, who hardly had a charabanc full of thirsty customers to serve, came over and stood with them. He still treated Banks with a certain amount of disdain – after all, Banks was a southerner *and* a copper – but he showed respect, too.

Banks had never tried *too* hard to fit in, to pretend he was one of the crowd like some of the other incomers. He knew there was nothing annoyed a Dalesman so much as pretentiousness, airs and graces, and that there was nothing more contemptible or condescending than a southerner appropriating Dales speech and ways, playing the expert on a place he had only just come to. Banks kept his distance, kept his counsel, and in return he was accorded that particular Yorkshire brand of grudging acceptance.

'Just at lunchtimes, like,' Larry said. 'Never saw him of an evening. He'd come in for one of Elsie's sandwiches and always drink half a pint. Just one half, mind you.'

'Did he talk much?'

Larry drifted off to dry some glasses and Pat picked up the threads. 'Nay. He weren't much of chatterbox, weren't Mr Rothwell. Bit of a dry stick, if you ask me.'

'What do you mean? Was he stuck-up?'

'No-o. Just had nowt to talk abaht, that's all.' He tapped the side of his nose. 'If you listen as much as I do,' he said, 'you soon find out what interests people. There's not much when it comes down to it, tha knows.' He started counting on the stubby fingers that stuck out of his cut-off gloves. 'Telly, that's number one. Sport – number two. And sex. That's number three. After that there's nobbut money and weather left.'

Banks smiled. 'What about politics?' he asked.

Pat pulled a face. 'Only when them daft buggers in t'Common Market 'ave been up to summat with their Common Agricultural Policy.' Then he grinned, showing stained, crooked teeth. 'Aye, I suppose that's often enough these days,' he admitted, counting it off. 'Politics. Number four.'

'And what did Mr Rothwell talk about when he was here?' Banks asked.

'Nowt. That's what I'm telling thee, lad. Oh, I s'pose seeing as he was an accountant, he was interested in money, but he kept that to himself. He'd be standing there, all right, just where you are, munching on his sandwich, supping his half-pint, and nodding in all the right places, but he never had owt to say. It seemed to me as if he were really somewhere else. And he didn't know *Neighbours* from *Coronation Street*, if you ask me – or Leeds United from Northampton.'

'There's not a lot of difference as far as their performances go over the last few weeks, if you ask me, Pat.'

Pat grunted.

'So you didn't really know Keith Rothwell?' Banks asked.

'No. Nobody did.'

'That's right, Mr Banks,' added Larry as he stood by them to pull a pint. 'He said he came for the company, what with working alone at home and all that, but I reckon as he came to get away from that there wife of his.' Then he was gone, bearing the pint.

Banks turned to Pat. 'What did he mean?'

'Ah, take no notice of him,' Pat said with a dismissive wave in Grafton's direction. 'Mebbe he was a bit henpecked, at that. It must be hard working at home when the wife's around all the time. Never get a minute's peace, you wouldn't. But Larry's lass, Cathy, did for Mrs Rothwell now and again, like, and she says she were a bit of an interfering mistress, if you know what I mean. Standing over young Cathy while she worked and saying that weren't done right, or that needed a bit more elbow grease. I nobbut met Mrs Rothwell once or twice, but my Grace speaks well of her, and that's enough for me.'

Banks thought he might have a word with Larry's lass, Cathy. He noticed Pat's empty glass. 'Another?'

'Oh, aye. Thank you very much.' Banks bought him a pint, but decided to forgo a second himself, much as the idea appealed. 'There were one time, when I comes to think on it,' Pat said, 'that Mr Rothwell seemed a bit odd.'

'When was this?'

'Abaht two or three weeks ago. He came in one lunchtime, as usual, like, but he must have had a couple of pints, not 'alves. Anyroad, he got quite chatty, told a couple of jokes and we all had a good chuckle, didn't we, Larry?'

'Aye,' shouted Larry from down the bar.

That sounded odd to Banks. According to Mrs Rothwell, her husband had been tense and edgy over the past three weeks. If he could chat and laugh at the Black Sheep, then maybe the problem had been at home. 'Is that all?' he asked.

'*All*? Well, it were summat for us to see him enjoying himself for once. I'd say that were enough, wouldn't you?'

'Did he say anything unusual?'

'No. He just acted like an ordinary person. An ordinary *happy* person.'

'As if he'd received some good news or something?'

'He didn't say owt about that.'

Banks gave up and moved on. 'I know there's been a bit of ill feeling among the hill-farmers about incomers lately,' he said. 'Did any of it spill over to Mr Rothwell?'

Pat sniffed. 'You wouldn't understand, Mr Banks,' he said softly, offering an unfiltered cigarette. Banks refused it and lit a Silk Cut. 'It's not that there's any ill feeling, as such. We just don't know where we stand, how to plan for the future. One day the government says this, the next day it's something else. Agricultural Policy . . . Europe . . . grugh.' He spat on the floor to show his feelings. Either nobody noticed or the practice was perfectly welcome in the Black Sheep, another reason why people stayed away. 'It needs years of experience to do it right, does hill-farming,' Pat went on. 'Continuity, passed on from father to son. When too many farms fall to weekenders and holiday-makers, pasture gets abused, walls get neglected. Live and let live, that's what I say. But we want some respect and some understanding. And right now we're not getting any.'

'But what about the incomers?'

'Aye, hold thy horses, lad, I'm getting to them. We're not bloody park keepers, tha knows. We don't graft for hours on end in all t'weather God sends keeping stone walls in good repair because we think they look picturesque, tha knows. They're to keep old Harry Cobb's sheep off my pasture and to make sure there's no hanky-panky between his breed and mine.'

Banks nodded. 'Fair enough, Pat. But how deep did the feeling go? Keith Rothwell bought that farm five years ago, or thereabouts. I've seen what he's done to it, and it's not a farm any more.'

'Aye, well at least Mr Rothwell's a Swainsdale lad, even if he did come from Eastvale. Nay, there were no problems.

He sold off his land – I got some of it, and so did Frank Rowbottom. If you're thinking me or Frank did it, then . . .'

'No, nothing like that,' Banks said. 'I just wanted to get a sense of how Rothwell fitted in with the local scene, if he did.'

'Well, he did and he didn't,' said Pat. 'He was here and he wasn't, and that's all I can tell thee. He could tell a joke well enough when he put his mind to it, though.' Pat chuckled at the memory.

As puzzled as he was before, Banks said goodbye and went outside. On the way back, he slipped in a cassette of Busoni's Bach transcriptions. The precise, ordered music had no influence on the chaos of his thoughts.

TWO

Back in his office, Banks first glanced at Dr Glendenning's post-mortem notes. Generally, there was no such thing as a preliminary post-mortem report, but Dr Glendenning usually condescended to send over the main points in layman's language as quickly as possible. He also liked to appear at the scene, but this time he had been staying overnight with friends in Harrogate.

There was nothing in the notes that Banks hadn't expected. Rothwell hadn't been poisoned before he was shot; the stomach contents revealed only pasta and red wine. Dr Glendenning gave cause of death as a shotgun wound to the occipital region, the back of the head, most likely a contact wound given the massive damage to bone and tissue. He also noted that it was lucky they already knew who the victim was, as there wasn't enough connected bone or tissue left to reconstruct the face, and though the tooth fragments could probably be collected and analysed, it would take a bloody long time. The blood group was 'O', which matched that supplied by Rothwell's doctor, as well as that of about half the population.

Rothwell had most likely been killed in the place and position they found him, Dr Glendenning pointed out, because what blood remained had collected as purplish hypostasis around the upper chest and the ragged edges of the neck. He estimated time of death between eleven and one the previous night.

A cadaveric spasm had caused Rothwell to grab and hold on to a handful of dust at the moment of death, and Banks thought of the T. S. Eliot quotation, 'I will show you fear in a handful of dust', which he had come across as the title of an Evelyn Waugh novel.

Rothwell had been in generally good shape, Dr Glendenning said, and the only evidence of any ill health was an appendix scar. Rothwell's doctor, Dr Hunter, was able to verify that Rothwell had had his appendix removed just over three years ago.

When Banks had finished, he phoned Sandra to say he didn't know when he would be home. She said that didn't surprise her. Then he went over to the window and looked down on the cobbled market square, most of which was covered by parked cars. The gold hands against the blue face of the church clock stood at a quarter to four.

Banks lit a cigarette and watched the local merchants taking deliveries and the tourists snapping pictures of the ancient market cross and the Norman church front. It was fine enough weather out there, sports-jacket warm, but the grey wash that had come at dawn still obscured the sunshine. On Banks's *Dalesman* calendar, the May photograph showed a field of brilliant pink and purple flowers below Great Shunner Fell in Swaledale. So far, the real May had been struggling against showers and cool temperatures.

Sitting at his rattly metal desk, Banks next opened the envelope of Rothwell's pocket contents and spread them out in front of him.

There were a few business cards in a leather slipcase, describing Rothwell as a 'Financial Consultant'. In his wallet were three credit cards, including an American Express Gold; the receipt from Mario's on the night of his anniversary dinner; receipts from Austick's bookshop, a computer supplies shop and two restaurants, all from Leeds, and all dated the previous week; and photos of Alison and Mary Rothwell. Happy families indeed. In cash, Rothwell had a hundred and five pounds in his wallet, in new twenties and one crumpled old fiver.

Other pockets revealed a handkerchief, good quality silk and monogrammed 'KAR', like the cufflinks on the body, BMW keys, house keys, a small pack of Rennies, two buttons, a gold Cross fountain pen, an empty leather-bound notebook and – horror of horrors – a packet of ten Benson and Hedges, six of which had been smoked.

Banks felt a surge of respect for the late Keith Rothwell. But perhaps the cigarettes helped to explain something, too. Banks was certain that Mary Rothwell would never have permitted her husband to pollute the house with his filthy habit. Smoking, then, could be the main reason he liked to sneak off to the Black Sheep or the Rose and Crown every now and then. It certainly wasn't drinking. A secret smoker, then? Or did she know? He found no gold lighter, only a sulphurous old box of Pilot matches; and Rothwell was the kind of person who put his spent matches back in the box facing the opposite direction from the live ones.

It was almost six when the phone rang: Vic Manson

calling from the forensic lab. Vic spent almost as much time with the Scene of Crime team from North Yorkshire Headquarters, in Northallerton, as he did at the lab, and though Banks knew Vic was a fingerprints expert, he sometimes wasn't sure exactly what he did or where he really worked.

'What have you got for us?' Banks asked.

'Hold your horses.'

'Social call, is it, then?'

'Not exactly.'

'Then what?'

'The wadding, for a start.'

'What about it?'

'We managed to get some more of the paper unfolded. It wasn't too badly burned inside. Anyway, the document analysts say it's good magazine quality, probably German. No prints. Nothing but blurs. It's not your common-or-garden girlie magazine, but it's not hardcore perversion either. The fullest picture we could get seemed to be a shaved vagina with a finger touching the clitoris. Bright red nail varnish. The fingernail, that is.'

'That must be the other side of what I saw,' said Banks. 'Does it help?'

'It might do. Apparently there are people who have a fetish about shaved vaginas. It's something to go on, anyway.'

Banks sighed. 'Or maybe our killer's just got a warped sense of humour. We can check with the PNC, anyway, see if there's been any similar incidents. What about the weapon?'

'Twelve-gauge, double-barrel. Judging by the amount of shot we've collected, the bastard who did it must have used both of them.'

'Anything from the house?'

'No prints, if that's what you mean. They wore gloves. And there was nothing special about the rope they used to tie up the wife and daughter, either. By the way, remember one of the chairs was wet, the one overturned by the table?'

'Yes.'

'It was urine. The poor lass must have been so scared she pissed herself.'

Banks swallowed. That was Alison's chair. She was the one who had eventually made her way to the sewing basket and toppled her chair. 'Any footprints?' he asked.

'We're still working on it, but don't hold your breath. The ground had pretty much dried out after last week's rain.'

'Okay, Vic, thanks for calling. Keep at it and keep me informed, okay?'

'Will do.'

After he had hung up, Banks lit another cigarette and walked over to the window again. Most of the tourists were getting in their cars, removing the crook-locks and driving home. The cobbles, cross and church front looked slate grey in the dull afternoon light. At the far side of the square, the El Toro coffee bar and Joplin's newsagent's seemed to be doing good business.

Banks thought of Alison, who had shown so much courage in telling them about what had happened at Arkbeck Farm. Someone had scared her so much she had sat in her own urine, probably for hours. The idea of her indignity and humiliation made him angry. He vowed he would find whoever was responsible for doing that to her and make damn sure they suffered.

THREE

The Queen's Arms was always busy at six o'clock on a Friday, and it was only through good luck and quick reflexes that Banks and Susan Gay managed to grab a copper-topped table by the window when a party of cashiers from the NatWest Bank gathered their things and left.

As happened so often in the Dales, the weather had changed dramatically over a very short period. A light breeze had sprung up and blown away the clouds. Now, the early evening sunlight glowed through the red and amber panes and shot bright rays through the clear ones, lighting on a foaming glass of ale and highlighting the smoke swirling in the air.

The sunlight and smoke reminded Banks of the effect the projection camera created at the cinema when smoking was allowed there. As kids, he and his friends used to put their money together for a packet of five Woodbines, then go to the morning matinee at the Palace: a Three Stooges short, a Buck Rogers or Flash Gordon serial and a black-and-white Western, maybe a Hopalong Cassidy. Slumped down in their seats, they would smoke 'wild woodies' until they felt sick. He smiled at the memory and reached for a Silk Cut.

Conversation and laughter ebbed and flowed all around them, and the general mood was ebullient. After all, it was the weekend. For most people in the pub, there would be no work until Monday morning. They could go off shopping to York or Leeds, wallpaper the bedroom, visit Aunt Maisie in Skipton or just lounge around and watch football or racing on telly. It was Cup Final day tomorrow, Banks remembered. Fat chance he'd get of watching it.

The best he could hope was that he would get home before too late tonight and spend some time with Sandra. It was the ideal opportunity for a bit of bridge-building. Tracy was away in France on a school exchange, and Brian was at Portsmouth Polytechnic, so they had the house to themselves for once. He would be too late for a shared dinner, but maybe a nice bottle of claret, a few Chopin 'Nocturnes', candlelight . . . then, who knew what might follow?

It was a nice fantasy. But right now he was waiting for Gristhorpe and Richmond, here to combine the pleasure of a pint and a steak-and-kidney pud with the business of swapping notes and fishing for leads at an informal meeting.

Once in a while, through the laughter and the arguments, Banks heard the Rothwell case mentioned. 'Did you hear about that terrible murder up near Relton . . .?' 'Hear about that bloke got shot out in the dale? I heard they blew his head right off his shoulders . . .' By now, of course, everyone had had a chance to read the *Yorkshire Evening Post*, and people were only too willing to embroider on the scant details the newspaper gave. Rumour and fantasy were rife. What Gristhorpe hadn't told the media so far was that Rothwell had been executed 'gangland' style, and that the weapon used was a shotgun.

The best the press could manage so far was 'LOCAL BUSINESSMAN MURDERED . . . Not more than a mile above the peaceful Swainsdale village of Fortford, a mild-mannered accountant was shot to death in his own garage in the early hours of this morning . . .' There followed an appeal for information about 'two men in black' and a photograph of Keith Rothwell, looking exactly like a mild-mannered accountant, with his thinning fair hair combed back, showing the slight widow's peak, his high forehead, slightly prissy lips and the wire-rimmed glasses. The glasses, Banks knew, had been found shattered to pieces along with the other wreckage of Rothwell's skull.

Banks waved to Gristhorpe and Richmond, who nudged their way through the crowd to join them at the table. While he was on his feet, Richmond went to get a round of drinks and put in the food orders.

'At least we don't have to worry about civilians over-hearing classified information,' Gristhorpe said as he sat down and scraped his stool forward along the worn stone flagging. 'I can hardly even hear myself think.'

When Richmond got back with the tray of drinks, Gristhorpe said, 'Right, Phil, tell us what you found.'

They huddled close around the table. Richmond took a sip of his St Clements. 'There are several items that have been either encrypted or assigned passwords,' he said. 'Some are complete directories, and one's just a document file in a directory. He's called it "LETTER".'

'Can you get access?' Gristhorpe asked.

'Not easily, no, sir. Not unless you type the password at the prompt. Believe me, I've tried every trick and all I've got for my pains is gibberish.'

'All right.' Gristhorpe coughed and waved away Banks's smoke with an exaggerated gesture. 'Let's assume he had some special reason for keeping these items secret. That means we're definitely interested. You said you couldn't gain access easily, but is there a way?'

Richmond cleared his throat. 'Well, yes there is. Actually, there are two ways.'

'Come on, then, lad. Don't keep us in suspense.'

'We could bring in an expert. I mean a *real* expert, like someone who writes the programmes.'

'Aye, and the other option?'

'Well, it's not much known, for obvious reasons, but I went to a seminar once and the lecturer told me something that struck me as very odd.'

'What?'

'Well, there's a company that sells bypass programmes for various software security systems.'

'That would probably be cheaper and quicker, wouldn't it?' said Gristhorpe. 'Can you get hold of a copy?'

'Yes, sir. But it's not cheap. Actually, it's quite expensive.'

'How much?'

'About two hundred quid.'

Gristhorpe whistled between his teeth, then he said, 'We don't have a lot of choice, do we? Go ahead, order one.'

'I already have done, sir.'

'And?'

'They're based in Akron, Ohio, but they told me there's a distributor in Taunton, Devon, who has some in stock. It could take a while to get it up here.'

'Tell the buggers to send it by courier, then. We might as well be hung for a sheep as a lamb. Lord knows what the DCC will have to say come accounting time.'

'Maybe if it helps us solve the case,' Banks chipped in, 'he'll increase our budget.'

Gristhorpe laughed. 'In a pig's arse, he will. Go on, Phil.'

'That's all, really,' said Richmond. 'In the meantime, I'll keep trying and see what I can do. People sometimes write their passwords down in case they forget them. If Rothwell did, the only problem is finding out *where* and in what form.'

'Interesting,' Banks said. 'I've got one of those plastic cards, the ones you use to get money at the hole in the wall. I keep the number written in my address book disguised as part of a telephone number in case I forget it.'

'Exactly,' said Richmond.

'Short of trying every name and number in Rothwell's address book,' Gristhorpe said, 'is there any quick way of doing this?'

'I don't think so, sir,' Richmond said. 'But often the password is a name the user has strong affinities with.'

'"Rosebud"?' Banks suggested.

'Right,' said Richmond. 'That sort of thing. Maybe something from his childhood.'

'"Woodbines",' said Banks. 'Sorry, Phil, just thinking out loud.'

'But it could be anything. The name of a family member, for example. Or a random arrangement of letters, spaces, numbers and punctuation marks. It doesn't have to make any sense at all.'

'Bloody hell.' Gristhorpe ran his hand through his unruly thatch of grey hair.

'All I can say is leave it with me, sir. I'll do what I can. And I'll ask the software distributor to put a rush on it.'

'All right. Susan? Anything from Hatchard and Pratt?'

Susan leaned forward to make herself heard. Just as she was about to start, Cyril called out their food number, and Richmond and Banks went through to bring back the trays. After a few mouthfuls, Susan started again. 'Yes,' she said, dabbing at the side of her mouth with a napkin. 'As it turns out, Rothwell was asked to leave the firm.'

'Asked to leave?' Gristhorpe echoed. 'Does that mean fired?'

'Not exactly, sir. He was a partner. You can't just fire

partners. He was also married to the boss's daughter. Mary Rothwell's maiden name is Hatchard. He was asked to resign. They didn't want a fuss.'

'Interesting,' said Gristhorpe. 'What was it all about, then?'

Susan ate another mouthful of her Cornish pasty, then washed it down with a sip of Britvic orange and pushed her plate aside. 'Laurence Pratt was reluctant to tell me about it,' she said, 'but I think he knew he'd be in more trouble if we found out some other way. It seems Rothwell was caught padding the time sheets. It's not a rare fiddle, according to Pratt. And he doesn't regard it as strictly illegal, but it *is* unethical, and it's bad luck for anyone who gets caught. Rothwell got off lucky.'

'What happened?' asked Gristhorpe.

'This was about five years ago. Rothwell was doing a lot of work for a large company. Pratt wouldn't tell me who it was, but I don't think that really matters. The point is that Pratt's father was looking over the billings and noticed that Rothwell had doubled up on his hours here and there, at times he couldn't have been working on their account because he'd been on another job, or out of town.'

'What did he do? Isn't there some regulatory board he should have been reported to?'

'Yes, sir, there is. But, remember, Rothwell was married to Hatchard's daughter, Mary. They'd been together nearly sixteen years by then, had two kids. Old man Hatchard would hardly want his son-in-law struck off and his family name dragged through the mud, which is probably what would have happened if Rothwell had been reported. I also got the impression that it might have been Mary's demands that set Rothwell padding his accounts in the first place. Nothing was directly stated, you understand, sir, just hinted. Imagine the headlines: "Accountant fired for padding books to keep boss's daughter in the manner to which she was accustomed." Hardly bears thinking about, does it? Anyway, Laurence Pratt and Rothwell were quite close friends then, so Pratt interceded and stuck up for him. Rothwell was lucky. He had a lot going for him. And there's another reason they didn't want a hue and cry.'

'Which is?'

'Confidence and confidentiality, sir. If it got out to the large company that Rothwell was fiddling, then it would put the partnership in an awkward position. Much better they don't find out and Rothwell simply decides to move on. Keep it in the family. They'd never question the bills, or miss the money.'

'I see.' Gristhorpe rubbed his whiskery chin.

'It's something that could have led to a motive, isn't it, sir? Greed, dishonesty.'

'Aye,' said Gristhorpe. 'It is that. Which makes me think even more that these secret files might prove interesting reading.' He tapped the tabletop. 'Good work, Susan. Let's make Rothwell's business affairs a major line of inquiry. I'll get in touch with the Fraud Squad. I've heard from the anti-terrorist squad, by the way, and they've come up with nothing so far. They want to be kept up to date, of course, but I think we can rule out Rothwell dealing arms or money to the IRA. Anything to add, Alan?'

'I think we should follow up on the wadding. There could be a porn connection.'

'Rothwell in the porn business?'

'It's possible. After all, he had plenty of money, didn't he? He must have got it from somewhere. I'm not suggesting he was a front player, one who got his hands dirty.

Maybe he just made some investments or handled finances. Take the lid off that can of worms – video nasties, prostitution and the like – and it wouldn't surprise me to find murder. Perhaps the wadding was a kind of signature, a symbol.'

'It sounds a bit too fanciful to me,' said Gristhorpe, 'but I take your point. It's all tied together, anyway, isn't it? If he was in the porn business, then that makes porn part of his business affairs. We'll follow up on it.'

'DS Hatchley's coming back on Monday,' said Banks. 'I think he'd be a good man for the job. Remember he spent a while working on the Vice Squad for West Yorkshire? Besides, he'd enjoy it.'

Gristhorpe snorted. 'I suppose he would. But keep him on a tight leash. He's like a bloody bull in a china shop.'

Banks grinned. He knew that Gristhorpe and Hatchley didn't get along. Jim Hatchley was a big, bluff, burly, boozy, roast-beef sort of Yorkshireman, a rugby prop forward until cigarettes and drink took their toll. More at home playing darts in the public bar than chatting in the lounge, he was the kind of person everyone under-estimated, and that often worked to the advantage of the Eastvale CID. And he also had a valuable, countywide network of lowlife, quasi-criminal informers that nobody had been able to penetrate.

'The Rothwells are an interesting family,' Banks went on after a sip of Theakston's. 'Mrs Rothwell assured me everything was fine and dandy on the domestic front, but methought the lady did protest too much. I wonder how much communication there really was between them all. It's nothing I can put my finger on, but there's something bothering me. I think the son, Tom, might have something to do with it.'

'I got that impression, too,' said Susan. 'It all looks fine on the surface, but I'd like to know what life at Arkbeck Farm was like. After I'd talked to Laurence Pratt, I got to thinking that if Tom was the reason Keith and Mary Rothwell had to get married, and Rothwell was unhappy in his marriage, then he might blame Tom. Irrational, of course, but things happen like that.'

'I'd leave the psychology to Jenny Fuller,' said Gristhorpe.

Susan reddened.

'Susan's right,' said Banks. 'The sooner we find Tom Rothwell, the better.'

Gristhorpe shrugged. 'It's up to the Florida police now. We've passed on all the information we've got. Come on, Alan, surely you don't think the wife and daughter had anything to do with it?'

'It would be hard to believe, wouldn't it? On the other hand, we've only *their* word for what happened. Nobody else saw the two men in black. What if Alison and her mother *did* want rid of Rothwell for some reason?'

'Next you'll be telling me the wife and daughter were making porno films for Rothwell. You talked to Alison. You could see the lass was upset.'

'Alison might not have had anything to do with it.'

'You mean Mrs Rothwell? Wasn't she in shock?'

'So I'm told. I didn't get to see her until late this morning. That gave her plenty of time to compose herself, work up an act.'

'But the SOC team went through the place as thoroughly as they usually do, hayloft and all. They couldn't find any traces of a weapon.'

'I'm not saying she shot him.'

'What then? She hired a couple of killers to do it for her?'

'I don't know. She could certainly afford it. I suppose I'm playing devil's advocate, trying to look at it from all angles. I still maintain they're an odd family. Alison was genuinely terrified, I know that. But there's something not quite right about them all, and I'd like to know what that is. I knew when I drove away from Arkbeck Farm that something I'd seen there was bothering me, nagging away, but I didn't know what it was until a short while ago.'

'And?' asked Gristhorpe.

'It was Tom's postcard from California. It was addressed to Alison – he called her Ali – and at the end he wrote, "Love to Mum". There was no mention of his father.'

'Hmm,' said Gristhorpe. 'It doesn't have to mean anything.'

'Maybe not. But that's not all. When I looked through Rothwell's wallet a while back, I found photos of Mary and Alison, but none of Tom. Not one.'

4

ONE

A good night's sleep is supposed to refresh you, not make you feel as if you're recovering from a bloody anaesthetic, thought Banks miserably on Saturday morning. Never a morning person at the best of times, he sat over his second cup of black coffee and a slice of wholewheat toast and Seville marmalade, newspaper propped up in front of him, trying to muster enough energy to get going. As a background to the radio traffic reports, he could hear Sandra having a shower upstairs. Banks hated the contraption – he always seemed to get a lukewarm dribble rather than a hot shower – but Sandra and Tracy swore by it. Banks preferred a long, hot bath with a little quiet background music and a good book.

After catching up with paperwork, he hadn't got home until almost eleven the previous night. He wished Sandra had been angry that they'd had to miss the claret, the Chopin and the candlelight, but she hadn't seemed to care. He didn't know whether she was pretending or she *really* didn't care. In fact, she said she'd just got back from a reception at the community centre herself. It was getting to be par for the course. They had seen so little of one another lately that they were fast becoming strangers. It seemed to Banks that what had been a strength in their relationship – their natural independence – was quickly becoming a threat.

And while Sandra had slept like a log, Banks had tossed and turned all night beside her, worried about the Rothwell case, with only brief, fitful periods of sleep full of shifting images: the pornographic wadding, the headless corpse. Now it was eight-thirty the next morning, and his eyes felt like sandpaper, his brain stuffed with cotton wool.

The national dailies and radio news carried stories on the Keith Rothwell killing – sandwiched between a blood-thirsty put-down of riots on a Caribbean island, where another dictator was nearing the end of his reign of terror, and a male Member of Parliament caught *in flagrante delicto* with a sixteen-year-old rentboy on Clapham Common. It probably wouldn't have even made the papers if it had happened somewhere a bit more up-market, like Hampstead Heath, Banks thought.

The Rothwell murder would be on television too, no doubt, amidst all the speculation on that afternoon's Cup Final, but Banks had never been able to bring himself to turn the thing on during daylight hours.

Now, hints were appearing in the media that the killing was more than a run-of-the-mill domestic disagreement or a burglary gone wrong. According to the radio, Scotland Yard, Interpol and the FBI had been called in. That, Banks reflected, was a slight exaggeration. The Americans had been asked to help trace Tom Rothwell, though as far as Banks knew it was the Florida State Police, not the FBI. Interpol was something the reporters always threw in for good measure, these days, and Scotland Yard was an outright lie.

Banks scanned the *Yorkshire Post* and the *Independent* reports to see if either newspaper knew more than the police. Sometimes they did, and it could be damned embarrassing all round. Not this time, though. To them,

Rothwell was as much the 'quiet, unassuming local accountant and businessman' as he was to the rest of the world.

'More coffee?'

Banks looked up to see Sandra standing at the machine in her navy-blue bathrobe, wet hair hanging over the terry-cloth at her shoulders. He hadn't heard her come down.

'Please.' He held his cup out.

Sandra poured, then put some bread in the toaster and picked up the *Yorkshire Post*. After she had read about Rothwell, she whistled. 'Is this what kept you out so late last night?'

'Hmm,' murmured Banks.

The toast popped up. Sandra put the paper down and went to see to it. 'I've met her a couple of times, you know,' she said over her shoulder, buttering toast.

Banks folded the *Independent* and looked at Sandra's profile. When it was wet, her hair looked darker, of course, but one of the things Banks found attractive about her was the contrast between her blonde hair and black eyebrows. This time, when he looked at her, he felt an ache deep inside. 'Who?' he asked.

'Mrs Rothwell. Mary Rothwell.'

'How on earth did you come across her?'

'At the gallery.'

Sandra ran the local gallery in the Eastvale community centre, where she organized art and photography exhibitions.

'I didn't know she was the artistic type.'

'She's not really. I think for her it was just the thing to do. Women's Institute sort of stuff, you know, organize cultural outings.' Sandra sat down with her toast and wrinkled her nose.

Banks laughed, sensing a definite thaw in the cold war. 'Snob.'

'What! Me?' She hit him lightly with the folded news-paper.

'Anyway,' Banks said, 'the poor woman's on tranquil-lizers. Both she and her daughter saw Rothwell's body before they called us, and you can take my word for it, that's enough to give anyone the heebie-jeebies.'

'How's the daughter?'

'Alison? Not quite so bad, at least not on the surface.' Banks shrugged. 'More resilient, maybe, or she could just be repressing it more. Tina Smithies says she's worried they're both losing touch.' He looked at his watch. 'I'd better go.'

Sandra followed him to the door and leaned against the banister. She nibbled her toast as she watched him put on his light grey sports jacket and pick up his briefcase. 'I can't say I know her well enough to get any kind of impression,' she said, holding her dressing gown at the collar when Banks opened the door, 'but I did sense that she's the kind who . . . well, she puts on a few airs and graces. Not so much as to be a complete pseud, but you can tell there's a touch of the Lady Muck about her. Imperious. And she likes people to know she's not short of a bob or two. You know, she flashes her rings, jewellery, stuff like that. She also struck me as being a very *cold* woman, I don't know why. All sharp edges, like a drawer full of kitchen knives.'

Banks leaned against the door jamb. 'It's a bloody strange family altogether,' he said.

Sandra shrugged. 'Just thought I'd put in my two penn'orth. I don't suppose you know when you'll be back?'

'No. Sorry, got to dash.' Banks risked a quick kiss on the lips. They tasted of strawberry jam.

'Can you leave me the car, today?' Sandra called after him. 'There's a watercolour exhibition I want to see in Ripon. One of our locals is exhibiting. I don't know when I'll be back, either.'

'Okay,' said Banks, wincing at the barb. He could always sign a car out of the pool if he needed one. It wouldn't have a cassette deck, but then this was hardly the best of all possible worlds, was it? At least it should have a radio. He set off determined, after a miserable night, not to let things get him down.

It was a beautiful morning. Calendar weather. May, as he knew it, had finally arrived. The sky was a cloudless blue, apart from a few high milky swirls, and even this early in the morning the temperature seemed to have risen a few notches since yesterday. Banks wouldn't be surprised if it were shirt-sleeves weather before the day was out.

As he walked, he plugged in his earphones and switched on the Walkman in his briefcase. The tape started at the jazzy 'Forlane' section of Ravel's *Le Tombeau de Couperin*. Not bad for a walk to work on a fine spring morning.

It was only about a mile to the station along Market Street, and Banks liked the way the townscape changed almost yard by yard as he walked. At his end of town, the road was broad, and the area was much like the outer part of any town centre: the main road with its garage, supermarket, school, zebra crossings and roundabouts, surrounded by residential streets of tall Victorian houses, most of them converted to student flats, all with names like Mafeking Avenue, Sebastopol Terrace, Crimea Close and Waterloo Road, and a strong smell of petrol and diesel fumes pervading the air.

But the closer Market Street got to the actual market-place, the more it narrowed and turned into a tourist attraction with its overhanging first-floor bays, where people could almost shake hands with someone across the street; the magnifying-glass windows of twee souvenir shops; an expensive walkers' gear shop with orange Goretex clothing hanging by the doorway and a stand of walking sticks out on the pavement; a Waterstone's bookshop, the street's most recent addition; the mingled aromas from Hambleton's Tea and Coffee Emporium and Farleigh's bakery across the street; an Oddbins wine shop; the Golden Grill café; and a newsagent's with a rack of newspapers out front, some of them folded over at Roth-well's grainy photograph, and a display of local guides and Ordnance Survey maps in the window. This narrow part of Market Street was always jammed with honking traffic too – mostly visitors and delivery vans.

Halfway through the 'Menuet' section, Banks arrived at the station, a three-storey, Tudor-fronted building facing the market square. First he called in at the Murder Room and talked to Phil Richmond. The Florida State Police had tracked down the car rental company Tom Rothwell had used at Tampa airport. At least it was a start. Now the police had a licence number to look for among the millions of cars parked at the thousands of Florida hotels, motels and beach clubs.

The PNC reported nothing doing on the use of porno-graphic wadding at other crime scenes.

Gristhorpe was in a meeting with Inspector Macmillan of the Fraud Squad, and Susan Gay was in her hutch phoning around the list of Rothwell's clients Laurence Pratt had given her. Banks poured a coffee and went to his office.

He opened his window and sniffed the air, then lit a cigarette and stood looking down on the early tourists in their bright anoraks and cagoules milling about the cobbled square. It was ten past nine on a Saturday morning, market-day in Eastvale, and the vendors at their canvas-covered stalls, like the old wild-west wagon trains, hawked everything from flat caps and multi-pocketed fishing jackets to burglar alarms, spark plugs and non-stick oven-ware. The cheese van was there, as usual, and Banks thought he might nip out and buy a wedge of Coverdale or Wensleydale Blue if he got the chance. If.

Banks mulled over what Sandra had told him about Mary Rothwell. So far, he had an impression of her as an ostentatious and overbearing woman who put too much value on appearances, and of Keith Rothwell as an unassuming, yet sly and greedy, man, easily prey to temptation. Greed, as Susan Gay had remarked, is often a way of making dangerous enemies, and a habit of secrecy is a damn good way of making things difficult for the police. But did the greed originate in Rothwell himself, or had he felt pushed into it by the demands of his wife?

There had certainly been hints in what both Ian Falkland and Larry Grafton had said that Rothwell had been something of a henpecked husband, escaping to the pub for a half-pint and a quiet smoke whenever he could.

In Banks's experience, such people often developed rich and secret fantasy lives, which sometimes imposed on reality with messy and unpredictable results. Keith Rothwell had supplied his wife and children with all the conveniences and many of the luxuries they wanted. What did he get out of it? What did he have going for himself? Nobody seemed to know or care what made him tick.

Banks moved away from the window and stubbed out

his cigarette. There was at least one thing he could do right now, he thought, reaching for a pen and notepad. 'WANTED,' he wrote, 'male Caucasian, about five feet nine, slight paunch, large wet brown eyes, commonly described as "spaniel" or "puppy dog" eyes, fondness for shotguns, can't keep his hands off young girls and probably has a taste for pornography of the shaved pussy variety.' He could just imagine the laughter and the nudge-nudges in police stations around the country as that went out over the PNC.

Just as he was about to start working on a revised version, the phone rang and Sergeant Rowe put him through to a distraught woman asking for the ubiquitous 'someone in charge'.

'Can I help you?' Banks asked her.

'They said they'd put me through to someone in charge. Are you in charge?'

'Depends what you mean,' said Banks. 'In charge of what? What's it about?'

'The man in the paper this morning, the one who was killed.'

Suddenly Banks pricked up his ears. Was he mistaken, or was she sobbing as she spoke? 'Yes,' he said. 'Go on.'

'I knew him.'

'You knew Keith Rothwell?'

'No, no—' She sobbed again then came back on the line. 'You've got it wrong. That's not his name. His name is Robert. Robert Calvert. That's who he is. You've got it all wrong. Is Robert really dead?'

The back of his neck tingling, Banks gripped his pen tight between his fingers. 'I think we'd better have a talk, love,' he said. 'The sooner, the better. Would you like to give me your name and address?'

TWO

Susan Gay drove the unmarked police Fiesta to Leeds, with Banks beside her tapping his fingers on his knees. It wasn't because of her driving. Ordinarily, he would enjoy such a trip and take his time if there were no rush, but today he was anxious to interview the woman who had phoned, Pamela Jeffreys.

He wasn't smoking, either, and that also made him jittery. He refrained in deference to Susan, though she magnanimously said it was okay if he opened the windows. There wasn't much worse, in his experience, than trying to enjoy a cigarette in a car next to a non-smoker with a force nine gale blowing all around you, no matter how good the weather.

As Banks had hoped, though the car had no cassette player, it did have a radio, and he was able to lose himself in a Poulenc chamber concert on Radio Three as he considered the implications of what he had just heard.

'How are we going to play this, sir?' Susan asked as she turned on to the Inner Ring Road and went into the yellow-lit tunnel.

Banks dragged himself out of a passage in the 'Sextet' where a sense of sadness seemed to pervade the levity of the woodwinds. 'By ear,' he said.

They had already called DI Ken Blackstone, out of courtesy for intruding on his patch, and Ken had found nothing on Pamela Jeffreys in records. Hardly surprising, Banks thought, as there was no reason to suppose she was a criminal. He glanced out of the window and saw they were crossing the bridge over the River Aire and the Leeds–Liverpool Canal. The dirty, sluggish water looked especially vile in the bright sunlight.

'Do we tell her anything?' Susan asked.

'If she's read the papers, she'll know almost as much about Keith Rothwell's life as we do. Whether she'll believe it or not is another matter.'

'What do you think it's all about?'

'I haven't a clue. We'll soon find out.'

Susan negotiated the large roundabout on Wellington Road. Above them, the dark, medieval fortress of Armley Jail loomed on its hill. Susan veered right at the junction with Tong Road, passed the disused Crown bingo hall, the medical centre and the New Wortley Cemetery and headed towards Armley. It was an area of waste ground and boarded-up shopfronts, with the high black spire of St Bartholomew's visible above the decay. She slowed to look at the street names, found Wesley Road, turned right, then right again and looked for the address Pamela Jeffreys had given.

'This is it, sir,' she said finally, pulling into a street of terraced back-to-backs, nicely done up, each with a postage-stamp lawn behind a privet hedge, some with new frosted-glass or wood-panel doors and dormer windows. 'Number twenty, twenty-four . . . Here it is.' She pulled up outside number twenty-eight.

The row of houses stood across the street from some allotments behind a low stone wall, where a number of retired or unemployed men worked their patches, stopping now and then to chat. Someone had rested a transistor radio on the wall, and Banks could hear the preamble to the Cup Final commentary. Not far down the street was an old chapel which, according to the sign, had been converted into a Sikh temple. They walked down the path to number twenty-eight and rang the doorbell.

The woman who opened the door had clearly been

crying, but it didn't mar her looks one bit, Banks thought. Perhaps the whites of her almond eyes were a little too red and the glossy blue-black hair could have done with a good brushing, but there was no denying that she was a woman of exceptional beauty.

Northern Indian, Banks guessed, or perhaps from Bangladesh or Pakistan, she had skin the colour of burnished gold, with high cheekbones, full, finely drawn lips and a figure that wouldn't be out of place in *Playboy*, revealed to great advantage by skin-tight ice-blue jeans and a jade-green T-shirt tucked in at her narrow waist. Around her neck, she wore a necklace of many-coloured glass beads. She also wore a gold stud in her left nostril. She looked to be in her mid-twenties.

Her fingers, Banks noticed as she raised her hand to push the door shut, were long and tapered, with clear nails cut very short. A spiral gold bracelet slipped down her slim wrist over her forearm. On the other wrist, she wore a simple Timex with a black plastic strap. She had only one ring, and that was a gold band on the middle finger of her right hand. Light down covered her bare brown arms.

The living room was arranged for comfort. A small three-piece suite with burgundy velour upholstery formed a semicircle around a thick glass coffee table in front of the fireplace, which may once have housed a real coal fire but now was given over to an electric one with three elements and a fake flaming-coals effect. On the coffee table, the new Mary Wesley paperback lay open, face down beside a copy of the *Radio Times* and an earthenware mug half full of milky tea.

A few family photographs in gilt frames stood on the mantelpiece. On the wall above the fire hung a print of Ganesh, the elephant god, in a brightly coloured, primitive style. In the corner by the front window stood a television with a video on a shelf underneath. The only other furniture in the room was a mini stereo system and several racks of compact discs, a glass-fronted cabinet of crystalware and a small bookcase mostly full of modern fiction and books about music.

But it was the far end of the room that caught Banks's interest, for there stood a music stand, with some sheet music on it, and beside that, on a chair, lay what he first took to be an oversized violin, but quickly recognized as a viola.

The woman sat on the sofa, curling her legs up beside her, and Banks and Susàn took the armchairs.

'Are you a musician?' Banks asked.

'Yes,' she said.

'Professional?'

'Uh-huh. I'm with the Northern Philharmonia, and I do a bit of chamber work on the side. Why?'

'Just curious.' Banks was impressed. The English Northern Philharmonia played for Opera North, among other things, and was widely regarded as one of the best opera orchestras in the country. He had been to see Opera North's superb production of *La Bohème* recently and must have heard Pamela Jeffreys play.

'Ms Jeffreys,' he began, after a brief silence. 'I must admit that your phone call has us a bit confused.'

'Not half as much as that rubbish in the newspaper has *me* confused.' She had no Indian accent at all, just West Yorkshire with a cultured, university edge.

Banks slipped a recent good-quality photograph of Keith Rothwell from his briefcase and passed it to her. 'Is this the man we're talking about?'

'Yes. I think this is Robert, though he looks a bit stiff

here.' She handed it back. 'There's a mistake, isn't there?
It must be someone who looks just like him, that's it.'

'What exactly was your relationship?'

She fiddled with her necklace. 'We're friends. Maybe
we were more than that, at one time, but now we're just
friends.'

'Were you lovers?'

'Yes. For a while.'

'For how long?'

'Three or four months.'

'Until when?'

'Six months ago.'

'So you've known him for about ten months
altogether?'

'Yes.'

'How did you meet?'

'In a pub. The Boulevard, on Westgate, actually. I was
with some friends. Robert was by himself. We just got
talking, like you do.'

'Have you seen him since you stopped being lovers?'

'Yes. I told you. We remained friends. We don't see
each other as often, of course, but we still go out every
now and then, purely platonic. I like Robert. He's good fun
to be with, even when we stopped being lovers. Look,
what's all this in—'

'When did you last see him, Ms Jeffreys?'

'Pamela. Please call me Pamela. Let me see . . . it must
have been a month or more ago. Look, is this some
mistake, or what?'

'We don't know yet, Pamela,' Susan Gay said. 'We
really don't, love. You'll help us best get it sorted out if you
answer Chief Inspector Banks's questions.'

Pamela nodded.

'Was there anything unusual about Mr . . . about Robert the last time you saw him?' Banks asked.

'No.'

'He didn't say anything, tell you about anything that was worrying him?'

'No. Robert never seemed to worry about anything. Except he hated being called Bob.'

'So there was nothing at all different about him?'

'Well, I wouldn't say that.'

'Oh?'

'It's just a guess, like.'

'What was it?'

'I think he'd met someone else. Another woman. I think he was in love.'

Banks swallowed, hardly able to believe what he was hearing. This couldn't be dull, dry, mild-mannered Keith Rothwell. Surely Rothwell wasn't the kind of man to have a wife and children in Swainsdale and a beautiful girl-friend like Pamela Jeffreys in Leeds, whom he could simply dump for yet *another* woman?

'Don't get me wrong,' Pamela went on. 'I'm not bitter or anything. We had a good time, and it was never anything more. We didn't lie to each other. Neither of us wanted to get too involved. And one thing Robert doesn't do is mess you around. That's why we can still be friends. But he made it clear it was over between us – at least in *that* way – and I got the impression it was because he'd found someone else.'

'Did you ever see this woman?'

'No.'

'Did he ever speak of her?'

'No. I just *knew*. A woman can tell about these things, that's all.'

'Did you ask him about her?'

'I broached the subject once or twice.'

'What happened?'

'He changed it.' She smiled. 'He has a way.'

'How often did you see each other?'

'When we were going out?'

'Yes.'

'Just once or twice a week. Mostly late in the week, weekends sometimes. He travels a lot on business. Anyway, he's usually at home every week at some time, at least for a day or two.'

'What's his business?'

'Dunno. That's another thing he never said much about. I can't say I was really that interested, either. I mean, it's boring, isn't it, talking about business. I liked going out with Robert because he was fun. He could leave his work at home.'

'Did he smoke?'

'What an odd question. Yes, as a matter of fact. Not much, though.'

'What brand?'

'Benson and Hedges. I don't mind people smoking.'

Encouraged, Banks slipped his Silk Cut out of his pocket. Pamela smiled and brought him a glass ashtray. 'What was he like?' Banks asked. 'What kind of things did you used to do together?'

Pamela looked at Banks with a glint of naughty humour in her eyes and raised her eyebrows. Banks felt himself flush. 'I mean where did you used to go?' he said quickly.

'Yeah, I know. Hmmm . . . Well, we'd go out for dinner about once a week. Brasserie 44 – you know, down by the river – or La Grillade, until it moved. He likes good food. Let's see . . . sometimes we'd go to concerts at the Town

Hall, if I wasn't playing, of course, but he's not very fond of classical music, to be honest. Prefers that dreadful trad jazz. And sometimes we'd just stay in, order a pizza or a curry and watch telly if there was something good on. Or rent a video. He likes oldies. *Casablanca*, *The Maltese Falcon*, that kind of thing. So do I. Let me see . . . we'd go to Napoleon's every once in a while—'

'Napoleon's?'

'Yeah. You know, the casino. And he took me to the races a couple of times – once at Pontefract and once at Doncaster. That's about it, really. Oh, and we went dancing now and then. Quite fleet on his feet is Robert.'

Banks coughed and stubbed out his cigarette. 'Dancing? The casino?'

'Yes. He loves a flutter, does Robert. It worried me sometimes the way he'd go through a hundred or more some nights.' She shrugged. 'But it wasn't my place to say, was it? I mean it wasn't as if we were *married* or anything, or even living together. And he seemed to have plenty of money. Not that that's what interested me about him.' She pulled at her necklace again. 'Can't you tell me what's going on, Chief Inspector? It's not the same person that was murdered, is it? I was so upset when I saw the paper this morning. Tell me it's a case of mistaken identity.'

Banks shook his head. 'I don't know. Maybe he had a double. Did he ever say anything about being married?'

'No, never.'

'Did he have an appendix scar?'

This time, Pamela blushed. 'Yes,' she said. 'Yes, he did. But so do lots of other people. I had mine out when I was sixteen.'

'When you spent time together,' Banks said, 'did he

always come here, to your house? Didn't you ever visit him at his hotel?'

She frowned. 'Hotel? What hotel?'

'The one he stayed at when he was in town, I assume. Did you always meet here?'

'Of course not. Sometimes he came here, certainly. I've nothing to be ashamed of, and I don't care what the neighbours say. Bloody racists, some of them. You know, my mum and dad came over to Shipley to work in the woollen mills in 1952. *Nineteen fifty-two*. They even changed their name from Jaffrey to Jeffreys because it sounded more English. Can you believe it? I was born here, brought up here, went to school and university here and some of them still call me a bleeding Paki.' She shrugged. 'What can you do? Anyway, you were saying?'

'I was asking why you never saw him at his hotel.'

'Oh, that's easy. I don't know what you're talking about. You see, it *can't* be the same person, can it? That proves it.' She leaned forward quickly and clapped her hands. The bracelet spiralled. 'You see, Robert didn't stay at any hotel. Sometimes he came here, yes, but not always. Other times I went to his place. His flat. He's got a flat in Headingley.'

THREE

Banks turned the Yale key in the lock and the three of them stood on the threshold of Robert Calvert's Headingley flat. It was in the nice part of Headingley, more West Park, Banks noted, not the scruffy part around Hyde Park that was honeycombed with student bedsits.

It hadn't been easy getting in. Pamela Jeffreys didn't

have a key, so they had to ask one of the tenants in the building to direct them to the agency that handled rentals. Naturally, it was closed at four o'clock on a Saturday afternoon, so then they had to get hold of one of the staff at home and arrange for her to come in, grumbling all the way, open up the office and give them a spare key.

And no, she told them, she had never met Robert Calvert. The man was a model tenant; he paid his rent on time, and that was all that mattered. One of the secretaries probably handed him the key, but he'd had the place about eighteen months and turnover in secretaries was pretty high. However, if Banks wanted to come back on Monday morning . . . Still, Banks reflected as they stood at the front door, all in all it had taken only about an hour and a half from the first time they had heard of the place, so that wasn't bad going.

'Better not touch anything,' Banks said as they stood in the hallway. 'Which is the living room?' he asked Pamela.

'That one, on the left.'

The door was ajar and Banks nudged it open with his elbow. The bottom of the door rubbed over the fitted beige carpet. Susan Gay and Pamela walked in behind him.

'There's only this room, a bedroom, kitchen and bathroom,' Pamela said. 'It's not very big, but it's cosy.'

The living room was certainly not the kind of place Banks could imagine Mary Rothwell caring much for. Equipped with all the usual stuff – TV, video, stereo, a few jazz compact discs, books, armchairs, gas fireplace – it smelled of stale smoke and had that comfortable, lived-in feel Banks had never sensed at Arkbeck Farm. Perhaps it was something to do with the old magazines – mostly jazz and racing – strewn over the scratched coffee table, the overflowing ashtray, the worn upholstery on the armchair by the fire or the framed photographs of a younger-looking Rothwell on the mantelpiece. On the wall hung a framed print of Monet's *Waterloo Bridge, Grey Day*.

They went into the bedroom and found the same mess. The bed was unmade, and discarded socks, underpants and shirts lay on the floor beside it.

There was also a small desk against one wall, on which stood a jar of pens and pencils, a roll of Sellotape and a stapler, in addition to several sheets of paper, some of them scrawled all over with numbers. 'Is this the kind of thing you're looking for?' Pamela asked.

Carefully, Banks opened the drawer and found a wallet. Without disturbing anything, he could see, through the transparent plastic holder inside, credit cards in the name of Robert Calvert. He put it back.

A couple of suits hung in the wardrobe, along with shirts, ties, casual jackets and trousers. Banks felt in the pockets and found nothing but pennies, sales slips, a couple of felt-tip pens, matches, betting slips and some fluff.

As wood doesn't usually yield fingerprints, he didn't have to be too careful opening cupboards and drawers. Calvert's dresser contained the usual jumble of jeans, jumpers, socks and underwear. A packet of condoms lay forlornly next to a passport and a selection of Dutch, French, Greek and Swiss small change in the drawer of the bedside table. The passport was in the name of Robert Calvert. There were no entry or exit stamps, but then there wouldn't be if he did most of his travelling in Europe, as the coins seemed to indicate. On the bedside table was a shaded reading lamp and a copy of the *Economist*.

The kitchen was certainly compact, and by the sparsity of the fridge's contents, it looked as if Calvert did most of his eating out. A small wine rack stood on the counter. Banks checked the contents: a white Burgundy, Veuve Clicquot Champagne, a Rioja.

Calvert's bathroom was clean and tidy. His medicine cabinet revealed only the barest of essentials: paracetamol tablets, Aspro, Milk of Magnesia, Alka Seltzer, Fisherman's Friend, Elastoplast, cotton swabs, hydrogen peroxide, Old Spice deodorant and shaving cream, a packet of orange disposable razors, toothbrush and a half-used tube of Colgate. Calvert had squeezed it in the middle, Banks noticed, not from bottom to top. Could this be the same man who returned his used matches to the box?

'Come on,' Banks said. 'We'd better use a call-box. I don't want to risk smudging any prints there may be on the telephone.'

'What's going on?' Pamela asked as they walked down the street.

'I'm sorry,' Susan said to her. 'We really don't know. We're not just putting you off. We're as confused as you are. If we can find some of Robert's fingerprints in the flat, then we can check them against our files and find out once and for all if it's the same man.'

'But it just *can't* be,' Pamela said. 'I'm sure of it.'

A pub on the main road advertised a beer garden at the back, and as they were all thirsty, Banks suggested he might as well make the call from there.

He phoned the station and Phil Richmond said he would arrange to get Vic Manson to the flat as soon as possible.

That done, he ordered the drinks and discovered from the barman that Arsenal had won the FA Cup. Good for them, Banks thought. When he had lived in London, he had been an Arsenal supporter, though he always had a soft spot for Peterborough United, his home-town team, struggling as they were near the bottom of the First Division.

The beer garden was quiet. They sat at a heavy wooden bench beside a bowling green and sipped their drinks. Two old men in white were playing on the green, and occasionally the clack of the bowls disturbed the silence. Banks and Susan shared salted roast peanuts and cheese-and-onion crisps, as neither had eaten since breakfast. The sun felt warm on the back of Banks's neck.

'You can go home whenever you want,' Banks told Pamela as she took off the tan suede jacket she had put on to go out. 'We have to stay here, but we'll pay for a taxi. I'm sorry we had to ruin your day for you.'

Pamela squinted in the sun, reached into her bag and pulled out a pair of large pink-rimmed sunglasses. 'It's all right,' she said, picking up her gin and tonic. 'I know it wasn't Robert they were talking about in the paper. Who was this man, this Keith Rothwell?'

'He was an accountant who got murdered,' Banks told her. 'We can't really say much more than that. Did you ever hear the name before?'

Pamela shook her head. 'The papers said he was married.'

'Yes.'

'Robert didn't act like a married man.'

'What do you mean?'

'Guilt. Secrecy. Fleeting visits. Furtive phone calls. The usual stuff. There was none of that with Robert. We went about quite openly. He wasn't tied down. He was a dreamer. Besides, you just *know*.' She took her glasses off and squinted at Banks. 'I'll bet you're married, aren't you?'

'Yes,' said Banks, and saw, he hoped, a hint of disappointment in her eyes.

'Told you.' She put her sunglasses on again.

Banks noticed Susan grinning behind her glass of lemonade. He gave her a dirty look. A clack of bowls came from the green and one of the old men did a little dance of victory.

'So, you see,' Pamela went on. 'It can't be the same man. If I'm sure of one thing, it's that Robert Calvert definitely wasn't a married man with a family.'

Banks picked up his pint and raised it in a toast. 'I hope you're right,' he said, looking at her brave smile and remembering the scene in Rothwell's garage only two nights ago. 'I sincerely hope you're right.'

5

ONE

There was always something sad about an empty farmyard, Banks thought as he got out of the car in front of
Arkbeck Farm again. There should be chickens squawking
all over the place, the occasional wandering cow, maybe a
barking sheepdog or two.

He thought of the nest egg he had held at his Uncle
Len's farm in Gloucestershire on childhood family visits.
They used it to encourage hens to lay, he remembered,
and when his Aunt Chloe had handed it to him in the coop,
it had still felt warm. Banks also remembered the smells of
hay and cow dung, the shiny metal milk churns sitting by
the roadside waiting to be picked up.

As he rang the doorbell, he doubted that the Rothwells
felt the same way about empty farmyards. The place
seemed to suit Alison's introspective nature; her father
had no doubt appreciated the seclusion and the protection
from prying eyes and questions it offered; and Mary Rothwell . . . well, Banks could hardly imagine her mucking
out the byre or feeding the pigs. He couldn't imagine her
handing a child a warm porcelain egg, either.

'Do come in,' Mary Rothwell said, opening the door.
Banks followed her to the split-level living room. Today
she wore a white shirt that buttoned on the 'man's' side
and a loose grey skirt that reached her ankles. Alison lay
sprawled on the sofa reading.

On the way to Arkbeck Farm, he had considered what to say to them regarding his talk with Pamela Jeffreys in Leeds, but he hadn't come up with any clear plan. Vic Manson hadn't got back to him yet about the prints, so he still couldn't be absolutely certain that Robert Calvert and Keith Rothwell were the same person. Best play it by ear, he decided.

'How are you doing?' he asked Mary Rothwell.

'Could be worse,' she replied. He noticed her eyes were baggy under the make-up. 'I haven't been sleeping well, despite the pills, and I'm a mass of nerves, but if I keep myself busy, time passes. I have the funeral to organize. Please, sit down.'

Banks had come partly to explain that a van was on its way to pick up Keith Rothwell's computer disks and business files and spirit them off to the Fraud Squad's head-quarters in Northallerton, where a team of suits would pore over them for months, maybe years, costing the taxpayers millions. He didn't put it like that, of course. Just as he had finished explaining, he heard the van pull up out front.

He went to the front door and directed the men to Roth-well's office, then returned to the living room, shutting the door firmly behind him. It was dark in the room, and a little chilly, despite the fine weather outside. 'They shouldn't bother us,' he said. 'Perhaps a little music?'

Mary Rothwell nodded and turned on the radio. Engelbert Humperdinck came on, singing 'Release Me'. Banks often regretted that humans hadn't been born with the capacity to close their ears as they did their eyes. He did his best, anyway, and reflected that it was all in a good cause, blanking out the sounds of Keith Rothwell's office being dismantled and carried away.

'Have you found Tom?' Mary Rothwell said, sitting

down. She sat at the edge of the armchair, Banks noticed, and twisted her hands in her lap, a mass of gold and precious stones. She seemed so stiff he wished someone would give her a massage. Her skin, he felt, would be brittle as lacquered hair to the touch.

Banks explained that they had tracked down the car rental agency he had used and that it wouldn't be long before someone spotted the car.

'He should be home,' she said. 'We need him. There's the funeral . . . all the arrangements . . .'

'We're doing our best, Mrs Rothwell.'

'Of course. I didn't mean to imply anything.'

'It's all right. Are you up to answering a few more questions?'

'I suppose so. As long as you don't want to talk about what I went through the other night. I couldn't bear that.' Her eyes moved in the direction of the garage and Banks could see the fear and horror flood into them.

'No, not that.' She would have to talk about it some-time, Banks almost told her, but not now, not yet. 'It's Mr Rothwell I want to talk about. We need a better idea of how he spent his time.'

'Well, it's hard to say, really,' she began. 'When he was here, he was up in his office most of the time. I could hear him clicking away on the computer.'

'Did you ever hear him on the phone?'

'He had his own line up there. I didn't listen in, if that's what you mean.'

'No, I didn't mean that. But sometimes you just can't help overhearing something, anything.'

'No. He always kept the door shut. I could hear his voice, like I could hear the keyboard, but it was muffled, even if I was passing by the office.'

'So you never knew who he was talking to or what he was saying?'

'No.'

'Did he have many calls in the days leading up to his death?'

'Not so much as I noticed. No more than usual. I could always hear it ring, you see, even from downstairs.' She stood up. 'Would you like a cup of tea? I can—'

'Not at the moment, thank you,' Banks said. He didn't want her crossing the path of the removal team. For one thing, it would upset and distract her, and for another she would start telling them off about trailing dirt in and out.

She walked over to the fireplace, straightened a porcelain figurine, then came and sat down in the same position. Alison went on reading her book. It was *Villette*, by Charlotte Brontë, Banks noticed. Surely a bit heavy for a fifteen-year-old?

'I understand your husband would drop in at the Black Sheep or the Rose and Crown now and then?' Banks asked.

'Yes. He wasn't much of a drinker, but he liked to get out of the house for an hour or so. You do when you work at home, don't you? You get to feel all cooped up. He'd usually walk there and back. It was good exercise. Businessmen often don't exercise enough, do they, living such sedentary lives, but Keith believed in keeping in good shape. He swam regularly, too, in Eastvale, and he would sometimes go for long runs.' She started picking pieces of imaginary lint from her skirt. Banks heard a thud from the staircase, and this time he couldn't stop her from dashing to the door and yanking it open.

'Watch what you're doing, you clumsy little man!' she said. 'Just look at this. You've gouged a hole in my wall.

The plaster's fallen off. You'll have to pay for that, you know. I'll be talking to your superior.' She popped her head back around the door and said, 'I'll make that tea now, shall I?' then disappeared into the kitchen.

Banks, still sitting, noticed Alison look up and raise her eyes. 'She's been like this since yesterday,' she said. 'Can't sit still. It's even worse than usual.'

'She's upset,' Banks said. 'It's her way of dealing with it.'

'Or *not* dealing with it. I saw him too, you know. Do you think I can forget so easily?'

'You've got to talk to each other,' Banks said. He noticed the book was shaking in her hands and she was making an effort to keep it still.

'If Tom doesn't come home soon, I'm going to run away,' she said. 'I can't stand it any longer. She's always going on about something or other and running about like a headless chi—' She put her hand to her mouth. 'My God, what a thing to say. I'm awful, aren't I? Oh, I hope Tom comes back soon. He must or I'll go mad. We'll both go mad.'

A bit melodramatic, Banks thought, but perhaps to be expected from a young girl on a steady diet of Charlotte Brontë.

Mary Rothwell came in bearing a tea tray and wearing a brave smile. Alison picked up her book again and lapsed into moody silence while her mother poured the tea into delicate china cups with hand-painted roses on the sides and gold around the rims. Banks always felt clumsy and nervous drinking from such fine china; he was afraid he would drop the cup or break off the flimsy handle while lifting it to his mouth.

'Why are they taking all Keith's files anyway?' Mary Rothwell asked.

'We're beginning to think that your husband might have been involved in some shady financial dealings,' Banks explained. 'And they could have something to do with his murder.'

'Shady?' She said it as Lady Bracknell said, 'A handbag?'

'He might not have known what he was involved in,' Banks lied. 'It's just a line of inquiry we have to follow.'

'I can assure you that my husband was as honest as the day is long.'

'Mrs Rothwell, can you tell me *anything* about what your husband did when he was travelling on business?'

'How would I know? I wasn't there.'

'Which hotels did he stay in? You must have phoned him.'

'No. He phoned me occasionally. He told me it was better that way for his tax expenses.' She shrugged. 'Well, *he* was the businessman. I've already told you he travelled all over the place.'

'You never went with him?'

'No, of course not. I have an aversion to lengthy car rides. Besides, they were business trips. One doesn't take one's spouse on business trips.'

'So you've no idea what he got up to in Leeds or wherever?'

She put down her cup. 'Are you implying something, Chief Inspector? Keith didn't "get up to" anything.'

Banks was dying for a cigarette. He finished the weak tea and put his cup and saucer down gently on the coffee table. 'Do you know if your husband was much of a gambler?' he asked.

'Gambler?' She laughed. 'Good heavens, no. Keith never even bet on the Grand National, and most people do that, don't they? No, money for my husband was too hard earned to be frittered away like that. Keith had a poor childhood, you know, and one learns the value of money quite early on.'

'What sort of childhood?'

'His father was a small shopkeeper, and they suffered terribly when the supermarkets started to become popular. He eventually went bankrupt. Keith didn't like to talk about it.'

Banks remembered the cigarettes he had found among the contents of Rothwell's pockets. 'Did you know that your husband smoked?' he asked.

'One minor weakness,' Mary Rothwell said, turning up her nose. 'It's a smelly and unpleasant habit, as well as a possibly fatal one. I certainly wouldn't let him do it in the house, and I was always trying to persuade him to stop.'

I'll bet you were, Banks thought. 'Have you ever heard of a woman called Pamela Jeffreys?' he asked.

Mary Rothwell frowned. For the first time, she sat back in the chair and gripped its arms with both hands. 'No. Why?' Banks saw suspicion and apprehension in her eyes.

Outside, the van door closed and the engine revved up. Banks noticed Mrs Rothwell glance towards the window. 'They're finished,' he said. 'What about Robert Calvert? Does the name mean anything to you?'

She shook her head. 'No, nothing. Look, what's this all about? Are these the people you think killed Keith? Are these the ones who got him involved in this criminal scheme you were talking about?'

Banks sighed. 'I don't know,' he said. 'Maybe, but I don't know.'

'Why don't you go and arrest *them* instead of bothering us?'

Banks didn't think he was likely to get anything else out of Mary Rothwell, or out of Alison. He stood up. 'I'm sorry we had to bother you,' he said. 'We'll be in touch as soon as we track down your son. And please let us know if you hear from him first. Don't worry, I'll see myself out.' And he left.

Maybe she hadn't heard of Pamela Jeffreys, he thought as he got in the car, but he was certain that she suspected her husband might have been seeing another woman. It was there in her eyes, in the whiteness of her knuckles.

He slipped a Thelonious Monk tape in the deck and set off for his next appointment. As the edgy, repetitive figure at the opening of 'Raise Four' almost pushed his ears to the limits of endurance, he wondered how long Mary Rothwell would be able to maintain her thinly lacquered surface before the cracks started to show.

TWO

'Well, now, if it ain't Mr Banks again,' said Larry Grafton when Banks walked into the Black Sheep that lunchtime with the *Sunday Times* folded under his arm. 'Twice in one week. We are honoured. What can we do for you this time?'

'You could start with a pint of best bitter and follow it with a plate of your Elsie's delightful roast beef and York-shire pud. And you could cut the bloody sarcasm.'

Grafton laughed and started pulling. Elsie's Sunday lunches were another well-kept secret, and only a privileged few got to taste them. Banks didn't fool himself that he was an accepted member of the élite; he knew damn well that publicans liked to keep on the good side of the law.

'And,' he said, when Larry handed him his pint, 'I'd like a word with your Cathy, if I might.'

'About the Rothwells, is it?'

'Yes.'

'Aye. Well she's just having her dinner. I'll send her through when she's done.'

'Thanks.'

Banks took his drink and sat by the tiled fireplace. Before he sat, he glanced at the collection of butterflies pinned to a board in a glass case on the wall. The pub wasn't as busy as most on a Sunday lunchtime. Of course, there was no sandwich board outside advertising 'Traditional Sunday Lunch'.

Bank's roast beef and Yorkshires came, as good as ever. Not for the first time, he reflected that Elsie's was the only roast beef in Yorkshire, apart from Sandra's, that was pink in the middle. As he ate, he propped the paper against a bottle of HP sauce and began to read an analysis of the growing political unrest on an obscure Caribbean island, feeling an irrational rage grow in him as he read. Christ, how he loathed these tinpot dictators, the ones who stuffed their maws with the best of everything while their subjects starved, who tortured and murdered anyone who dared to complain.

Just as he had picked up the books supplement, he noticed a tourist couple walk in and look around. They went to the bar and the man asked Larry Grafton what food he offered.

'Nowt,' said Grafton. 'We don't do food.'

The man looked towards Banks. 'But he's got some.'

'Last plate.'

The man looked at his watch. 'But it's only twelve-thirty.'

Grafton shrugged.

'Besides, you said you don't do food. You're contra-dicting yourself. You heard him, didn't you, darling?'

His wife said nothing; she just stood there looking embarrassed. He had the kind of upper-class accent that expects immediate subservience, but he obviously didn't know there could be nothing more calculated to get right up a Yorkshireman's nose.

'Look,' said Grafton, 'does tha want a drink or doesn't tha?'

'We want food,' the man said.

His wife tugged at his sleeve. 'Come on, darling,' she whispered just in Banks's range of hearing. 'Don't cause a fuss. Let's go. There are plenty of other pubs.'

'But I—' The man glared petulantly at Grafton, who stared back stone-faced, then followed his wife's advice.

'Really,' Banks heard him say on his way out, 'you'd think these people didn't want to make an honest living. They're supposed to be in the service industry.'

Larry Grafton winked at Banks and ambled off to serve one of the locals. Banks reflected that maybe the tourist was right. What the hell was wrong with Larry Grafton? Nowt so queer as folk, he decided, and went back to his roast beef. A couple of minutes later, when he had just finished, Cathy Grafton came from the back and joined him. He folded up his newspaper, pushed his empty plate aside and lit a cigarette.

Cathy was a plump girl of about sixteen with a fringe and a blotchy complexion, as if she had been sitting too close to the fire too long. She also had the longest, curliest and most beautiful eyelashes Banks had ever seen.

'Dad says you want to talk to me,' she said, wedging herself into a chair. Her accent was thick, and Banks had to listen closely to understand everything she said, even though he had been in Swainsdale for four years.

'You helped Mary Rothwell do the housework at Arkbeck Farm, didn't you?'

'Aye. I do for a few folk around here. I know I should be paying more mind to school, like, but Mum says we need t'money.'

Banks smiled. Not surprising, given the way Grafton scared business away. 'What was it like, working at Arkbeck?' he asked.

Cathy frowned. 'What do you mean?'

'Did you like working there?'

'It were all reet.'

'How about Mary Rothwell? Did you get along well with her?'

Cathy wouldn't meet his eyes. She shifted in her chair and looked down at the scored table.

'Cathy?'

'I heard. It's just I was always told not to speak ill.'

'Of the dead? Mary Rothwell isn't dead.'

'No. Of me employer.'

'Am I to take it that you *didn't* get along, then?'

'Take it as you will, Mr Banks.'

'Cathy, this could be very important. Mr Rothwell was killed, you know.'

'Aye, I know. It's got nowt to do with *her*, though, does it?'

'We still need to know all we can about the family.'

Cathy contemplated the table for a while longer. More locals came in. One or two looked in Banks's direction, nudged their friends and raised their eyebrows.

'She were just bossy, that's all,' Cathy said at last.

'Mary Rothwell was?'

'Aye. She'd stand over you while you were working, with her arms folded, like this, and tell you you'd missed a bit or you weren't polishing hard enough. I used to hate doing for her. Will I still have to, do you think?'

'I don't know,' Banks said. 'What about Alison?'

'What about her?'

'You're about the same age, surely you must have had things in common, things to talk about. Pop stars and the like.'

Cathy emitted a loud snort. 'Little Miss La-di-da,' she sneered, then shook her head. 'No, I can't say as we did. She always had her nose stuck in a book.'

'You never chatted with her?'

'No. Every time she saw me she turned up her nose. Stuck-up little madam.'

'How did the family members get along with one another?'

'I weren't there often enough to notice. Not when they was all together, like.'

'But you must have some idea, from your observations?'

'They didn't say much. It were a quiet house. He were in his office, when he were at home, like, and I were never allowed up there.'

'Who cleaned it?'

'Dunno. Maybe he did it himself. I know he didn't like people to go in. Look, Mr Banks, I've got to get back and help me mum. Is there anything else?'

'Did you notice any changes in the family recently? Did they behave any differently?'

'Not so far as I could tell.'

'What about Tom, the son? Did you know him?'

'He were t'best of the lot,' Cathy said without hesita-

tion. 'Always had a smile and a good-morning for you.'
She blushed.

'He's been away for a while now. Did you notice any
changes before he left?'

'They used to argue.'

'Who did?'

'Him and his father.'

'What about?'

'How would I know? I didn't listen. Sometimes you
couldn't help but hear.'

'Hear what?'

'Just their voices, when they were shouting, like.'

'Did you ever hear what they were arguing about?'

'Once t'door were open a bit, and I heard his dad
mention a name then say something like, "I'm disappointed in you." He said "shame", too.'

'What was a shame?'

'No. Just the word. I just heard the word "shame",
that's all. I could tell Mr Rothwell were very angry, but he
sounded cold, you know.'

'Did he say why he was disappointed?'

She shook her head.

'What was the name he mentioned?'

'Sounded like Aston or Afton or summat like that.'

'Did you hear what Tom said back?'

'He said, "You're a right one to talk about being
disappointed in *me*."'

'Did you hear anything more?'

'No.' The chair scraped along the stone flags as she
stood up. 'I've got to go, really. Me mum'll kill me.' And
she hurried back behind the bar with surprising agility.

THREE

'Vic Manson matched prints from the Calvert flat with the ones from the body,' Gristhorpe explained back at the station later that afternoon. 'There were a couple of other sets, too, mostly smudged, not on file.'

It was hot, and Banks was standing by the open window of his office. Gristhorpe sat with his feet up on the desk.

'So Rothwell was Calvert and Calvert was Rothwell,' Banks said.

'It certainly looks that way, aye.'

Banks leaned against the window frame and shook his head. 'I still can't believe it. All right, so we know Rothwell had a secretive side to his nature, and he was greedy, or desperate for cash, to the point of dishonesty once. But this Calvert sounds to me like some sort of playboy. If you could have heard Pamela Jeffreys. Casinos, races, dancing . . . bloody hell. And you should have seen her, the one he chucked over.'

'So you've told me already, two or three times at least,' Gristhorpe said with a smile. 'A proper bobby-dazzler by the sound of her. I'll take your word for it.'

'Well, she dazzled this bobby, anyway,' said Banks, sitting opposite Gristhorpe. He sighed. 'I suppose we just have to accept it: Rothwell led a double life. Like Alec Guinness in that film about the ship's captain.'

'*The Captain's Paradise?*'

'That's the one. The question we have to ask ourselves now is what, if anything, does that fact have to do with his murder?'

'Has the girlfriend dazzled you so much you haven't considered she might have a part to play?'

'The thought's crossed my mind once or twice, yes. I just can't see how. Apparently Roth . . . Calvert found *another* woman five or six months ago. Pamela Jeffreys seemed to think he'd fallen in love. It's her we need to find, but she hasn't come forward yet.'

'There's always jealousy as a motive, then.'

'I don't think so. It's *possible*, though. Maybe Mary Rothwell found out about him and arranged a hit.'

'I was thinking more about this Pamela Jeffreys.'

'Couldn't afford it. She's a classical musician. Besides, she didn't really strike me as the jealous type. She said Calvert was just fun to be with. They never made any commitments.'

'She could be lying.'

'I suppose so.'

'And don't forget the possible porn connection. If Rothwell was mixed up with beautiful women, even under another identity, who knows?'

Banks couldn't believe it, but he didn't bother protesting to Gristhorpe. 'I'll have to talk to her again anyway,' he said.

'Poor you.'

'What did the Fraud Squad have to say?'

Gristhorpe scratched his hooked nose. 'Funny lot, aren't they?' he said. 'I spent a good part of this morning with DI Macmillan. Used to be in banking. Boring little bugger, but you should have seen his eyes light up when he heard about the locked files. Anyway, they've had a quick look at the stuff from Arkbeck Farm, and Macmillan and I had another chat about an hour ago. They haven't much to go on, yet, of course, and they're as anxious as young Phil for that bypass software, but Macmillan's even more excited now.'

'Where has the software got to, by the way?'

'On its way, according to Phil. Apparently they were out of stock but they managed to scrounge around.'

'Sorry. What did Macmillan have to say?'

'Well, he said he won't know anything for certain until they manage to open some of those locked directories. He thinks that's where the really interesting stuff is. But even some of the written documents in the filing cabinets gave him enough to suspect Rothwell was heavily into money-laundering or betting-tax evasion. Apparently, there was a fair bit of cryptic correspondence with foreign banks: Lichtenstein, Netherlands, Antilles, Jersey, Switzerland, the Cayman Islands, among others. Dead giveaway, Macmillan said.'

'Tax havens,' said Banks. 'Isn't that what they are?'

Gristhorpe held up a finger. 'Aha! That was my first thought, too. But they're only tax havens because they have strict secrecy policies and a very flexible attitude towards whom they take on as their clients.'

'In other words,' offered Banks, 'if you want to deposit a lot of money with them, they'll take it, no questions asked?'

'That's about it, aye. Within the law, of course. They do insist that they verify the money's source is legal. When it comes down to it, though, banks are basically run on greed, aren't they?'

'I won't argue with that. So Keith Rothwell was putting a lot of money in foreign banks?'

'Macmillan thought he might have been acting for a third party. He could hardly have made that much money himself. It's a very complicated business. As I said, either he was involved in aiding and abetting some pretty serious tax evasion, or he was part of a money-laundering scheme. There are still more questions than answers.'

'Did Macmillan tell you how this money-laundering business works?' Banks asked.

'Aye, a bit. According to him, it's basically simple. It's only in the application it gets complicated. What happens is that somebody gets hold of a lot of money illegally, and he wants it to look legal so he can live off it without raising any suspicions.' Gristhorpe paused.

'Go on,' Banks urged.

Gristhorpe ran his hand through his hair. 'Well, that's about it, really. I told you it was basically simple. Macmillan said it would take forever to explain all the technicalities of doing it. As far as legal money is concerned, he said, you can either earn it, borrow it or receive it as a gift. When you've laundered your dirty money, it has to look like it came to you one of those ways.'

'I assume we're talking about drug money here,' Banks said. 'Or the profits from some sort of organized crime – prostitution, pornography, loan sharks?'

Gristhorpe nodded. 'You know as well as I do, Alan, that the top cats in the drug trade pull in enormous wads of cash every day. You can't just walk into a showroom and buy a Rolls in cash without raising a few eyebrows, and the last thing you want is any attention from the police or the Inland Revenue.'

Banks walked over to the window again and lit a cigarette. Most of the cars were gone from the cobbled square now and the hush of an early Sunday evening had fallen over the town. A young woman in jeans and a red T-shirt struck a pose by the ancient market cross as her male companion took a photograph, then they got into a blue Nissan Micra and drove off.

'What's in it for the launderer?' Banks asked.

'According to Macmillan, he'd get maybe four per cent for laundering the safer sort of funds and up to ten per cent for seriously dirty money.'

'Per cent of what?'

'Depends,' said Gristhorpe. 'On a cursory glance, Macmillan estimated about between four and six million quid. He said that was conservative.'

'Over how long?'

'That's four to six a year, Alan.'

'Jesus Christ!'

'Money worth murdering for, isn't it? In addition to Rothwell's legitimate earnings as a financial consultant, if he were in this money-laundering racket he also stood to earn, let's say five per cent of five million a year, to make it easy. How much is that?'

'Quarter of a million quid.'

'Aye, my arithmetic was never among the best. Well, no wonder the bugger could afford a BMW and a new kitchen.' He rubbed his hands together. 'And that's about it. Macmillan said they'll start putting a financial profile together first thing in the morning: bank accounts, credit cards, building societies, Inland Revenue, loans, investments, the lot. He said they shouldn't have any trouble getting a warrant from the judge, given the circumstances. He's also getting in touch with the Yard. This is big, Alan.'

'What about Calvert?' Banks asked.

'Well, they'll have to cover him too, now, won't they?'

A sharp knock at the door was immediately followed by Phil Richmond holding a small package. 'I've got it,' he said, an excited light in his eyes. 'The bypass software. Give me a few minutes to study the manual and we'll see what we can do.'

They all followed him to the computer room, once a

cupboard for storing cleaning materials, and stood around
tensely in the cramped space while he booted up and
consulted the instructions. All Rothwell's computer gear
and records were with the Fraud Squad, but Richmond
had made back-up disks of the relevant files.

Susan Gay popped her head around the door and,
finding no room left inside, stood in the doorway. Banks
watched as Richmond went through a series of com-
mands. Dialogue boxes appeared and disappeared; drive
lights flashed on and off; the machine buzzed and
hummed. Banks noticed Gristhorpe chewing on his
thumbnail.

'Got it,' Richmond said. Then a locked file called
SUMMARY.924 came to the screen:

Halcyon Props.	16/9/92	82062	C.I.	Ibk.	GCA
Mercury Exps.	18/9/92	49876	Jsy.Cbk	PA	
Jupiter Pds.	23/9/92	47650	Lst.	Zbk	SA
Marryat Dvpts.	4/10/92	76980	N.A.Kbk	PA	
(end 1st shpt)					
Neptune Hlds	6/11/92	65734	Jsy. Cbk	SPA	
City Ents	13/11/92	32450	Sw.	Nbk	LRA
Harbour Trst.	21/11/92	23443	BVI. Hbk	DTFA	
Sunland Props	29/11/92	85443	B.	Gbk	RDA

'What the hell is all that about?' Banks asked.

'It looks like financial records for the last quarter of
1992,' Gristhorpe said. 'Companies, banks, dates, maybe
numbered accounts. Keep going, Phil. Try that "LETTER"
file you mentioned.'

Richmond highlighted the locked file, tapped at the keyboard again, and the file appeared unscrambled, for all to
see.

It was a letter, dated 1 May and addressed to a Mr

Daniel Clegg, Solicitor, of Park Square, Leeds, and on first glance, it seemed innocuous enough:

Dear Mr Clegg,

In the light of certain information that has recently come to my attention, I regret that we must terminate our association.

Yours faithfully,
Keith Rothwell

'That's it?' Gristhorpe asked. 'Are you sure you didn't lose anything?'

Richmond returned to the keyboard to check, then shook his head. 'No, sir. That's it.'

Banks backed towards the door. 'Interesting,' he said. 'I wonder what "information" that was?' He looked at Gristhorpe, who said, 'Get it printed out, will you, Phil, before it disappears into the bloody ether.'

6

ONE

In Park Square on that fine Monday morning in May, with the pink and white blossom still on the trees, Banks could easily have imagined himself a Regency dandy out for a stroll while composing a satire upon the Prince's latest folly.

Opposite the Town Hall and the Court Centre, but hidden behind Westgate, Park Square is one of the few examples of elegant, late eighteenth-century Leeds remaining. Unlike most of the fashionable West End squares, it survived Benjamin Gott's Bean Ing Mills, an enormous steam-powered woollen factory which literally smoked out the middle classes and sent them scurrying north to the fresher air of Headingley, Chapel Allerton and Round-hay, away from the soot and smoke carried over the town on the prevailing westerly winds.

Banks faced the terrace of nicely restored two- and three-storey Georgian houses, built of red brick and yellow sandstone, with their black iron railings, Queen Anne pediments and classical-style doorways with columns and entablatures. Very impressive, he thought, finding the right house. As expected, it was just the kind of place to have several polished brass nameplates beside the door, one of which read 'Daniel Clegg, Solicitor'.

A list on the wall inside the open front door told him

that the office he wanted was on the first floor. He walked up, saw the name on the frosted-glass door, then knocked and entered.

He found himself in a dim anteroom that smelled vaguely of paint, where a woman sat behind a desk sorting through a stack of letters. When he came in, he noticed a look of fear flash through her eyes, quickly replaced by one of suspicion. 'Can I help you?' she asked, as if she didn't really want to.

She was about thirty, Banks guessed, with curly brown hair, a thin, olive-complexioned face and a rather long nose. Her pale green eyes were pink around the rims. She wore a loose fawn cardigan over her white blouse, despite the heat. Banks introduced himself and showed his card. 'I'd like to see Mr Clegg,' he said. 'Is he around?'

'He's not here.'

'Do you know when he'll be back?'

'No.' It sounded like 'dough.'

'Do you know where he is?'

'No.'

'What's your name?'

'Elizabeth. Elizabeth Moorhead. I'm Mr Clegg's secretary. Everyone calls me Betty.' She took a crumpled paper tissue from the sleeve of her cardigan and blew her nose. 'Cold,' she said. 'Godda cold. In May. Can you believe it? I hate summer colds.'

'I'd like to see Mr Clegg, Betty,' Banks said again. 'Is there a problem?'

'I should say so.'

'Can I help?'

She drew back a bit, as if still deciding whether to trust him. 'What do you want him for?'

Banks hesitated for a moment, then told her. At least he

would get some kind of reaction. 'I wanted to ask a few questions about Keith Rothwell.'

Her brow wrinkled in a frown. 'Mr Rothwell? Yes, of course. Poor Mr Rothwell. He and Mr Clegg had some business together now and then. I read about him in the papers. It was terrible what happened.'

'Did you know him well?'

'Mr Rothwell? No, not at all, not really. But he'd been here, in this office. I mean, I knew him to say hello to.'

'When did you see him last?'

'Just last week, it was. Tuesday or Wednesday, I think. He was standing right there where you are now. Isn't it terrible?'

Banks agreed that it was. 'Can you try and remember which day it was? It could be important.'

She muttered to herself about appointments and flipped through a heavy book on her desk. Finally, she said, 'It was Wednesday, just before I finished for the day at five. Mr Rothwell didn't have an appointment, but I remember because it was just after Mr Hoskins left, a client. Mr Rothwell had to wait out here a few moments and we chatted about how lovely the gardens are at this time of year.'

'That's all you talked about?'

'Yes.'

'Then what?'

'Then Mr Clegg came out and they went off.'

'Do you know where?'

'No, but I think they went for a drink. They had business to discuss.'

So Rothwell had visited Clegg in Leeds the day before his murder, almost two weeks after the letter ending their association. Why? It certainly hadn't been noted in his appointment book. 'How did Mr Rothwell seem?' he asked.

'No different from usual.'

'And Mr Clegg?'

'Fine. Why are you asking?'

'Did you notice any tension between them?'

'No.'

'Has anything odd been happening around here lately? Has Mr Clegg received any strange messages, for example?'

'No-o.' Some hesitation there. He would get back to it later.

Banks glanced around the small, tidy anteroom. 'Does everything go through you? Mail, phone calls?'

'Most things, yes. But Mr Clegg has a private line, too.'

'I see. How did he react to the news of Mr Rothwell's death?'

She studied Banks closely, then appeared to decide to trust him. She sighed and rested her hands on the desk, palms down. 'That's just the problem,' she said. 'I don't know. I haven't seen him since. He's not here. I mean, he's not just out of the office right now, but he's disappeared. Into thin air.'

'Disappeared? Have you told the local police?'

She shook her head. 'I wouldn't want to look a fool.'

'Has he done anything like this before?'

'No. Never. But if he *has* just gone off . . . you know. With a woman or something . . . I mean he *could* have, couldn't he?'

'When did you last see him?'

'Last Thursday. He left the office about half past five and that was the last I saw of him. He didn't come in to work on Friday morning.'

'Have you tried to call him at home?'

'Yes, but all I got was the answering machine.'

'Did he say anything about a business trip?' Banks asked.

'No. And he usually tells me if he's going to be away for any length of time.'

'Do you know what kind of business relationship Mr Clegg had with Keith Rothwell?'

'No. I'm only his secretary. Mr Clegg didn't take me into his confidence. All I know is that Mr Rothwell came to the office now and then and sometimes they'd go out to lunch together, or for drinks after work. I knew Mr Rothwell was an accountant, so I supposed it would be something to do with tax. Mr Clegg specializes in tax law, you see. I'm sorry I can't be of more help.'

'Maybe you can be. It seems a bit of a coincidence, doesn't it, Mr Rothwell getting killed and Mr Clegg disappearing around the same time?'

She shrugged. 'I didn't hear about Mr Rothwell's death until Saturday. I just never thought . . .'

'Have you ever heard of someone called Robert Calvert?'

'No.'

'Are you sure? Did Mr Clegg never mention the name?'

'No. He wasn't a client. I'm sure I'd remember.'

'Why didn't you get in touch with the police when you realized Mr Clegg had disappeared and you heard about Mr Rothwell's murder?'

'Why should I? Mr Clegg had a lot of clients. He knew a lot of businessmen.'

'But they don't usually get murdered.'

She sneezed. 'No. As I said, it's tragic what happened, but I don't see how as it connects with Mr Clegg.'

'Maybe it does, and maybe it doesn't,' Banks said. 'But don't you think that's for us to decide?'

'I don't know what you mean.' She reached for the tissue again. This time it disintegrated when she blew her nose. She dropped it in the waste-paper bin and took a fresh one from the box on her desk.

Banks regarded her closely. He didn't think she was lying or evading the issue; she simply didn't understand what he was getting at. He sometimes expected everyone to view the world with the same suspicious mind and jaundiced eye as he did. Besides, she didn't know about the letter Rothwell had left in the locked file.

He sat on the edge of the desk. 'Right, Betty, let's go back a bit. When I came in, you were frightened. Why?'

She paused for a moment, then said, 'I thought you might be one of them again.'

'One of whom?'

'On Saturday morning I was here doing some filing and two men came in and started asking questions about Mr Clegg. They weren't very nice.'

'Is that what you were thinking of when I asked you earlier if anything odd had been going on?'

'Yes.'

'Why didn't you tell me then?'

'It . . . I . . . I didn't connect it. You've got me all confused.'

'All right, Betty, take it easy. Did they hurt you?'

'Of course not. Or I certainly *would* have called the police. You see, sometimes in this business you get people who are . . . well, less than polite. They get upset about money and sometimes they don't care who they take it out on.'

'And these men were just rude?'

'Yes. Well, just a bit brusque, really. Nothing unusual.

I mean, I'm only a secretary, right? I'm not important. They can afford to be short with me.'

'So what bothered you? Why does it stick in your mind? Why were you frightened? Did they threaten you?'

'Not in so many words. But I got the impression that they were testing me to see what I knew. I think they realized early on that I didn't know anything. If they'd thought differently, I'm sure they would have hurt me. Don't ask me how I know. I could just feel it. There was something about them, some sort of coldness in their eyes, as if they'd done terrible things, or witnessed terrible things.' She shivered. 'I don't know. I can't explain. They were the kind of people you look away from when they make eye contact.'

'What did they want to know about?'

'Where Mr Clegg was.'

'That's all?'

'Yes. I asked them why they wanted to know, but they just said they had important business with him. I'd never seen them before, and I'm sure I'd know if they were new clients.'

'Did they leave their names?'

'No.'

'What did they look like?'

'Just ordinary businessmen, really. One was black and the other white. They both wore dark suits, white shirts, ties. I can't remember what colours.'

'What about their height?'

'Both about the same. Around six foot, I'd say. But the white one was burly. You know, he had thick shoulders and a round chest, like a wrestler or something. He had very fair hair, but he was going bald on top. He tried to disguise it by growing the hair at the side longer and combing it right over, but I just think that looks silly, don't you? The black man was thin and fit-looking. More like a runner than a wrestler. He did most of the talking.'

Banks got her to describe them in as much detail as she could and took notes. They certainly didn't match Alison Rothwell's description of the two men in black who had tied her up and killed her father. 'What about their accents?' he asked.

'Not local. The black one sounded a bit cultured, well educated, and the other didn't speak much. I think he had a slight foreign accent, though I couldn't swear to it and I can't tell you where from.'

'You've done fine, Betty.'

'I have?'

Banks nodded.

'There's something else,' she said. 'When I came in this morning, I got the impression that someone had been in the place since then. Again, I can't say why, and I certainly couldn't prove it, but in this job you develop a feel for the way things should be – you know, files, documents, that sort of thing – and you can just tell if something's out of place without knowing what it really is, if you follow my drift.'

'Were there any signs of forced entry?'

'No. Nothing obvious, nothing like that. Not that it would be difficult to get in here. It's hardly the Tower of London. I locked myself out once when Mr Clegg was away on business and I just slipped my Visa card in the door and opened it.' She put her hand to her mouth. 'Oops. I don't suppose I should be telling you that, should I?'

Banks smiled. 'It's all right, Betty. I've had to get into my car with a coat-hanger more than once. Was anything missing?'

'Not so far as I can tell. It's pretty secure inside. There's a good, strong safe and it doesn't look as if anyone tried to tamper with it.'

'Could it have been Mr Clegg?'

'I suppose so. He sometimes comes in on a Sunday if there's something important in progress.' Then she shook her head. 'But no. If it had been Mr Clegg I'd have known. Things would have looked different. They looked the same, but not quite the same, if you know what I mean.'

'As if someone had messed things up and tried to restore them to the way they were originally?'

'Yes.'

'Do you employ a cleaning lady?'

'Yes, but she comes Thursday evenings. It can't have been her.'

'Did she arrive as usual last Thursday?'

'Yes.'

'May I have a look in the office?'

Betty got up, took a key from her drawer and opened Clegg's door for him. He stood on the threshold and saw a small office with shelves of law books, box files and filing cabinets. Clegg also had a computer and stacks of disks on a desk at right angles to the one on which he did his other paperwork. The window, closed and locked, Banks noticed, looked out over the central square with its neatly cut grass, shady trees and people sitting on benches. The office was hot and stuffy.

Certainly nothing *looked* out of the ordinary. Banks was careful not to disturb anything. Soon, the Fraud Squad would be here to pore over the books and look for whatever the link was between Rothwell and Clegg.

'Better keep it locked,' he told Betty on his way out.

'There'll be more police here this afternoon, most likely. May I use the phone?'

Betty nodded.

Banks phoned Ken Blackstone at Millgarth and told him briefly what the situation was. Ken said he'd send a car over right away. Next he phoned Superintendent Gristhorpe in Eastvale and reported his findings. Gristhorpe said he'd get in touch with the Fraud Squad and see if they could co-ordinate with West Yorkshire.

He turned back to Betty. 'You'll be all right here,' he said. 'I'll wait until the locals arrive. They'll need you to answer more questions. Just tell them everything you told me. What's your address, in case I need to get in touch?'

She gave him the address of her flat in Burmantofts. 'What do you think has happened?' she asked, reaching for her tissue again.

Banks shook his head.

'You don't think anything's happened to him, do you?'

'It's probably nothing,' Banks said, without conviction. 'Don't worry, we'll get to the bottom of it.'

'It's just that Melissa will be so upset.'

'Who's Melissa?'

'Oh, didn't you know? It's Mrs Clegg. His wife.'

TWO

After a hurried bowl of vegetable soup in the Golden Grill, Susan Gay walked out into the street, with its familiar smells and noises: petrol fumes, of course; car horns; fresh coffee; bread from the bakery; a busker playing a flute by the church doors.

In the cobbled market square, she noticed an impromptu

evangelist set up his soapbox and start rabbiting on about judgment and sin. It made her feel vaguely guilty just hearing him, and as she went into the station, she contemplated asking one of the uniforms to go out and move him on. There must be a law against it somewhere on the books. Disturbing the peace of an overworked DC?

Charity prevailed, and she went up to her office. It faced the car park out back, so she wouldn't have to listen to him there.

First, she took out the blue file cards she liked to make notes on and pinned them to the cork-board over her desk. It was the same board, she remembered, that Sergeant Hatchley had used for his pin-ups of page-three girls with vacuous smiles and enormous breasts. Now Hatchley was due back any moment. What a thought.

Then, after she had made another appointment to talk to Laurence Pratt, she luxuriated in the empty office, stretching like a cat, feeling as if she were in a deep, warm bubble-bath. Out of the window she could see the maintenance men with their shirtsleeves rolled up washing the patrol cars in the large car park. Sun glinted on their rings and watch-straps and on the shiny chrome they polished; it spread rainbows of oily sheen on the bright windscreens.

One of the men, in particular, caught her eye: well-muscled, but not overbearingly so, with a lock of blond hair that slipped over his eye and bounced as he rubbed the bonnet in long, slow strokes. The telephone broke into her fantasy. She picked it up. 'Hello. Eastvale CID. Can I help you?'

'To whom am I speaking?'

'Detective Constable Susan Gay.'

'Is the superintendent there?'

'I'm afraid not.'

'And Chief Inspector Banks?'

'Out of the office. Can I help you? What's this about?'

'I suppose you'll have to do. My name is Mary Rothwell. I've just had a call from my son, Tom.'

'You have? Where is he?'

'He's still in Florida. A hotel in Lido Key, wherever that is. Apparently the British newspapers are a couple of days late over there, and he's just read about his father's murder. It's only eight in the morning there. He can't get a flight back until this evening. Anyway, he said he should get into Manchester at about seven o'clock tomorrow morning. I'm going to meet him at the airport and bring him home.'

'That's good news, Mrs Rothwell,' Susan said. 'You do know we'd like to talk to him?'

'Yes. Though I can't imagine why. You'll pass the message on to the Chief Inspector, will you?'

'Yes.'

'Good. And by the way, I've made funeral arrangements for Wednesday. That *is* still all right, isn't it?'

'Of course.'

'Very well.'

'Is there anything else, Mrs Rothwell?'

'No.'

'Goodbye, then. We'll be in touch.'

Susan hung up and stared into space for a moment, thinking what an odd woman Mary Rothwell was. Imperious, highly strung and businesslike. Probably a real Tartar to live with. But was she a murderess?

Though it would take the Fraud Squad a long time to work out exactly how much Rothwell was worth – and to separate the legal from the illegal money – it was bound to be a fortune. Money worth killing for. The problem was, though Susan could imagine Mary Rothwell being cold-blooded enough to have her husband killed, she could not imagine her having it done in such a bloody, dramatic way.

The image of the kneeling, headless corpse came back to her and she tasted the vegetable soup rise in her throat. No, she thought, if the wife were responsible, Rothwell would have been disposed of in a neat, sanitary way – poison, perhaps – and he certainly wouldn't have made such a mess on the garage floor. What was the phrase? *You don't shit on your own doorstep.* It was too close to home for Mary; it would probably taint Arkbeck Farm for her for ever.

Still, there was a lot of money involved. Susan had seen Rothwell's solicitor that morning, and, according to him, Rothwell had owned, or part-owned, about fifteen businesses, from a shipping company registered in the Bahamas to a dry cleaner's in Wigan, not to mention various properties dotted around England, Spain, Portugal and France. Of course, the solicitor assured her, they were all legitimate. She suspected, however, that some had served as fronts for Rothwell's illegal activities.

As Susan was wondering if Robert Calvert's money would now simply get lumped in with Keith Rothwell's, she became aware of a large shadow cast over her desk by a figure in the doorway.

She looked up, startled, right into the smiling face of Detective Sergeant Jim Hatchley. So soon? she thought, with a sinking feeling in the pit of her stomach. Now she knew there really was no God.

'Hello, love,' said Hatchley, lighting a cigarette. 'I see you've taken my pin-ups down. We'll have to do some-thing about that now I'm back to stay.'

THREE

At one-thirty, the hot, smoky pub was still packed with local clerks and shopkeepers on their lunch break. When Banks had phoned Pamela Jeffreys before leaving for Leeds that morning, she had suggested they meet in the pub across from the hall in West Leeds, where she was rehearsing with a string quartet. There was no beer garden, she said, but the curry of the day was usually excellent. Though he had to admit to feeling excitement at the thought of seeing Pamela again, this wasn't a meeting Banks was looking forward to.

She hadn't arrived yet, so Banks got himself a pint of shandy at the bar – just the thing for a hot day – and managed to grab a small table in the corner by the dartboard, fortunately not in use. There, he mulled over Daniel Clegg's disappearance and the mysterious goons Betty Moorhead had seen.

There was no end of trouble a lawyer could get himself into, Banks speculated. Especially if he were a bit crooked to start with. So maybe there was no connection between Clegg's disappearance and Rothwell's murder. But there were too many coincidences – the letter, the timing, the shady accounts – and Banks didn't like coincidences. Which meant that there were two sets of goons on the loose: the ones who killed Rothwell, and the ones who scared Clegg's secretary. But did they work for the same person?

He was saved from bashing his head against a brick wall any longer by the arrival of Pamela Jeffreys, looking gorgeous in black leggings and a long white T-shirt with the Opera North logo on front. She had her hair tied back and wore black-rimmed glasses. As she sat down, she smiled at him. 'The professional musician's look,' she said. 'Keeps my hair out of my eyes so I can read the music.'

'Would you like a drink?' Banks asked.

'Just a grapefruit juice with an ice-cube, please, if they've got any. I have to play through "Death and the Maiden" again this afternoon.'

While he was at the bar, Banks also ordered two curries of the day.

'What's been happening?' Pamela asked when he got back.

'Plenty,' said Banks, hoping to avoid the issue of Calvert's identity for as long as possible. 'But I've no idea how it all adds up. First off, have you ever heard of a man called Daniel Clegg?'

She shook her head. 'No, I can't say as I have.'

'He's a solicitor.'

'He's not mine. Actually, I don't have one.'

'Are you sure Robert never mentioned him?'

'No, and I think I'd remember. But I already told you, he never talked about his work, and I never asked. What do I know or care about business?' She looked at him over the top of her glass as she sipped her grapefruit juice, thin black eyebrows raised.

'Did you ever introduce Robert to any of your friends?'

'No. He never seemed really interested in going to parties or having dinner with people or anything, so I never pushed it. They probably wouldn't have got on very well anyway. Most of my friends are young and artsy. Robert's more mature. Why?'

'Did you ever meet anyone he knew when you were out together, say in a restaurant or at the casino?'

'No, not that I can recall.'

'So you didn't have much of a social life together?'

'No, we didn't. Just a bit of gambling, the occasional day at the races, then it was mostly concerts or a video and a pizza. That was a bit of a problem, really. Robert was a lot of fun, but he didn't like crowds. I'm a bit more of a social butterfly, myself.'

'I don't mean to embarrass you,' Banks said slowly, 'but did Robert show any interest in pornography? Did he like to take photographs, make videos? Anything like that?'

She looked at him open-mouthed, then burst out laughing. 'Sorry, sorry,' she said, patting her chest. 'You know, most girls might be insulted if you suggested they moonlighted in video nasties, but it's so absurd I can't help but laugh.'

'So the answer's no?'

'Don't look so embarrassed. Of course it's no, you silly man. The very thought of it . . .' She laughed again and Banks felt himself blush.

Their curries came and they tucked in. They were, as Pamela had said, delicious: delicately spiced rather than hot, with plenty of chunks of tender beef. They exchanged small talk over the food, edging away from the embarrassing topic Banks had brought up earlier. When they had finished, Pamela went for more drinks and Banks lit a cigarette. Was she going to ask now, he wondered, or was he going to have to bring it up? Maybe she was avoiding the moment, too.

Finally, she asked. 'Did you find out anything? You know, about Robert and this Rothwell fellow.' Very casual, but Banks could sense the apprehension in her voice.

He scraped the end of his cigarette on the rim of the red

metal ashtray and avoided her eyes. A group at the next table burst into laughter at a joke one of them had told.

'Well?'

He looked up. 'It looks very much as if Robert Calvert and Keith Rothwell were the same person,' he said. 'We found fingerprints that matched. I'm sorry.'

For a while she said nothing. Banks could see her beautiful almond eyes fill slowly with tears. 'Shit,' she said, shaking her head and reaching in her bag for a tissue. 'Sorry, this is stupid of me. I don't know why I'm crying. We were just friends really. Can we . . . I mean . . .' She gestured around.

'Of course.' Banks took her arm and they left the pub. Fifty yards along the main road was a park. Pamela looked at her watch and said, 'I've still got a while yet, if you don't mind walking a bit.'

'Not at all.'

They walked past a playground where children screamed with delight as the swings went higher and higher and the roundabout spun faster and faster. A small wading-pool had been filled with water because of the warm weather and more children played there, splashing one another, squealing and shouting, all under their mother's or father's watchful eyes. Nobody let their kids play out alone these days, as they used to do when he was a child, Banks noticed. Being in his job, knowing what he knew, he didn't blame them.

Pamela seemed lost in her silent grief, head bowed, walking slowly. 'It's crazy,' she said at last. 'I hardly knew Robert and things had cooled off between us anyway, and here I am behaving like this.'

Banks could think of nothing to say. He was aware of the warmth of her arm in his and of her scent: jasmine, he thought. What the hell did he think he was doing, walking arm in arm in the park with a beautiful suspect? What if someone saw him? But what could he do? The contact seemed to form an important link between Pamela and something real, something she could hold on to while the rest of her world shifted under her feet like fine sand. And he couldn't deny that the touch of her skin meant something to him, too.

'I was wrong about him, wasn't I?' she went on. 'Dead wrong. He was married, you say? Kids?'

'A son and a daughter.'

'I should know. I read it in the paper but it didn't sink in because I was so *sure* it couldn't have been him. Robert seemed so . . . such a free spirit.'

'Maybe he was.'

She glanced sideways at him. 'What do you mean?'

They stopped at an ice-cream van and Banks bought two cornets. 'It was a different life he lived with you,' he said. 'I can't begin to understand a man like that. It's not that he had a split personality or anything, just that he was capable of existing in very different ways.'

'What ways?' Pamela stuck out her pink tongue and licked the ice-cream.

'The people in Swainsdale knew him as a quiet, unassuming sort of bloke. Bit of a dry stick really.'

'Robert?' she gasped. 'A dry stick?'

'Not Robert. Keith Rothwell. The hard-working, clean-living accountant. The man who put his spent matches back in the box in the opposite direction to the unused ones.'

'But Robert was so alive. He was fun to be with. We laughed a lot. We dreamed. We danced.'

Banks smiled sadly. 'There you are, then. Keith Rothwell probably had two left feet.'

'Are you saying it *wasn't* the same man?'

'I don't know what I'm saying. Just that your memories of Robert Calvert won't change, shouldn't change. He's who he was to you, what he meant to you. Don't let this poison it for you. On the other hand, I need to know who killed Keith Rothwell, and it looks as if there might be a connection.'

She put her arm in his again and they walked on. There was hardly any breeze at all, but they passed a boy trying to fly a red-and-green kite. He couldn't seem to get it more than about twenty feet off the ground before it came flopping down again.

'What do you mean, a connection?' Pamela asked, shifting her gaze from the kite back to Banks.

'Maybe something in his life as Robert Calvert spilled over into his life as Keith Rothwell. Are you sure you didn't know he was married, you didn't suspect it?'

She shook her head. 'No. I've been a right bloody fool, haven't I? Muggins again.'

'But you were sure he'd found a new girlfriend?'

'Ninety-nine per cent certain, yes.'

'How did you feel about that?'

'What?'

'His new girlfriend. How did you feel about her? On the one hand you tell me you shouldn't be so upset, you hardly knew Robert Calvert, and your relationship had cooled off anyway. On the other hand, it seems to me from what you say and the way you behave that you were extremely fond of him. Maybe in love with him. What's the truth? How did you really feel when someone else came along and stole him from you? Surely you must have felt hurt, angry, jealous?'

Pamela pulled back her arm and stepped aside from

him, an expression of pain and anger shadowing her face. She dropped her ice-cream. It splattered on the Tarmac path. 'What's that got to do with anything? What are you saying? What are you getting at? First you imply that I'm some kind of porn actress, and now you're implying that I killed Robert out of jealousy?'

'No,' said Banks quickly. 'No, nothing like that.'

But she was already backing away from him, hands held up, palms out, as if to ward him off.

'Yes, you are. How could you even . . .? I thought you . . .'

Banks stepped towards her. 'That's not what I mean, Pamela. I'm just—'

But she turned and started to run away.

'Wait!' Banks called after her. 'Please, stop.'

One or two people gave him suspicious looks. As he set off walking quickly after her, a child's coloured ball rolled in front of him, and he had to pull up sharply to avoid knocking into its diminutive owner, whose large father, fast approaching from the nearest bench, didn't seem at all happy about things.

Pamela reached the park exit and dashed across the road, dodging her way through the traffic, back towards the hall. Banks stood there looking after her, the sweat beading on his brow. The remains of his ice-cream had started to melt and drip over the flesh between his thumb and first finger.

'Shit,' he cursed under his breath. Then louder, 'Shit!'

The little boy looked up, puzzled, and his father loomed closer.

7

ONE

The Merrion Centre was one of the first indoor shopping malls in Britain. Built on the northern edge of Leeds city centre in 1964, it now seems something of an antique, a monument to the heady sixties days of slum clearance, tower blocks and council estates.

Covered on top, but open to the wind at the sides, it also suffers competition from a number of more recent, fully enclosed, central shopping centres, such as the St John's Centre, directly across Merrion Street, and the plush dark green and brass luxury of the Schofields Centre, right on The Headrow.

Still, the Merrion Centre does have a large Morrison's supermarket, Le Phonographique discothèque – the longest-surviving disco in Leeds – a number of small speciality shops, a couple of pubs, a flea market and the Classical Record Shop, which is how Banks had come to know the place quite well. And on a warm, windless May afternoon it can be pleasant enough.

Banks found Clegg's Wines and Spirits easily enough. He had phoned Melissa Clegg an hour or so earlier, still smarting over his acrimonious parting with Pamela Jeffreys in the park, and she had told him she could spare a little time to talk. It was odd, he thought, that she hadn't seemed overly curious about his call. He had said that it concerned her husband, yet she had asked for no details.

He opened the door and found himself in a small shop cluttered with bottles and cases. There were a couple of bins of specials on the floor by the door – mostly Bulgarian, Romanian and South African varietals, and some yellow 'marked down' cards on a few of the racks that lined the walls to his right and left, including a Rioja, a Côtes du Rhône and a claret.

Banks looked at the racks and thought he might take something home for dinner, assuming that he and Sandra ever got the chance to sit down to dinner together again, and assuming that she wanted to. Perhaps they could have that wine, candlelight and Chopin evening he had had to cancel when the Rothwell inquiry got in the way.

Behind the counter ranged the bottles of single malt Scotch: Knockando, Blair Athol, Talisker, Glendronach. Evocative names, but he mustn't look too closely. He had a weakness for single malt that Sandra said hit them too hard in the pocket. Besides, he still had a drop of Laphroaig left at home.

The spotty young man behind the counter smiled. 'Can I help you, sir?' He wore a candy-striped shirt with the sleeves rolled up and his tie loose at the neck, the way Banks always wore his own when he could get away with it. His black hair had so much gel or mousse on that it looked like an oil slick.

'Boss around?' Banks asked, showing his card.

'In the back.' He lifted up the counter flap and Banks went through. Stepping over and around cases of wine, he walked along a narrow corridor, then saw on his left a tiny office with the door open. A woman sat at the desk talking on the phone. It sounded to Banks as if she were complaining over non-delivery of several cases of Hungarian Pinot Noir.

When she saw him, she waved him in and pointed to a chair piled high with papers. Banks moved them to the edge of the desk and she grinned at him over the mouthpiece. There were no windows, and it was stuffy in the back room, despite the whirring fan. The office smelled of freshly cut wood. Banks took his jacket off and hung it over the back of the chair. He could feel the steady draught of the fan on the left side of his face.

Finally, she put the phone down and rolled her eyes. 'Some suppliers . . .'

She was wearing a yellow sun-dress with thin straps that left most of her nicely tanned and freckled shoulders and throat bare. About forty, Banks guessed, she looked as if she watched what she ate and exercised regularly, tennis probably. Her straight blonde hair, parted in the middle, hung just above her shoulders, framing a heart-shaped face with high cheek-bones. It was a cheerful face, one to which a smile was no stranger, and the youthful, uneven fringe suited her. But Banks also noticed marks of stress and strain in the wrinkles under her blue-grey eyes and around her slightly puckered mouth. A pair of no-nonsense glasses with tortoiseshell frames dangled on a cord around her neck.

'Your phone call piqued my curiosity,' she said, leaning back in her chair and linking her hands behind her head. Banks noticed the shadow of stubble under her arms. 'What has Danny-boy been up to now?'

'I'm sorry?' said Banks. 'I don't follow.'

'Didn't Betty tell you?'

'Tell me what?'

'Oh, God, that woman. Gormless. About Danny and

me. We're separated. Have been for about two years now. It was all perfectly amicable, of course.'

Of course, Banks thought. How often had he heard that? If it was all so bloody amicable, he wondered, then why aren't you still together? 'I didn't know,' he said.

'Then I'm sorry you're probably on a wild goose chase.' She changed her position, resting her hands on the desk and playing with a rubber band. There were no rings on her fingers. 'Anyway, I'm still intrigued,' she said. 'I *am* still fond of Danny. I would be concerned if I thought anything had happened to him. It hasn't, has it?'

'Do you still see one another?'

'From time to time.'

'When did you last see him?'

'Hmm . . .' She pursed her lips and thought. 'A couple of months ago. We had lunch together at Whitelocks.'

'How did he seem?'

'Fine.' She stretched the rubber band tight. 'Look, you've got me worried. All this interest in Danny all of a sudden. First those clients of his. Now you.'

Banks pricked up his ears. 'What clients?'

'On Saturday. Saturday afternoon. Just a couple of businessmen wondering if I knew where he was.'

'Did they know you were separated?'

'Yes. They said it was a long shot and they were sorry to bother me but they'd had an appointment scheduled with him that morning and he hadn't shown up. He'd mentioned me and the shop at some time or other, of course. He often does, by way of sending me business. What a sweetheart. Anyway, they asked if I had any idea where he was, if he'd suddenly decided to go away for the weekend. As if I'd know. It all seemed innocent enough. Is something wrong?'

'What did they look like?'

She described the same two men who had visited Betty Moorhead. It wouldn't have been difficult for them to find out about Melissa's shop – perhaps even Betty had told them – and if they were looking for Clegg, it was reasonable to assume that his ex-wife might know where he was. She must have convinced them quickly that she neither knew nor cared.

The rubber band snapped. 'Look,' she said, 'I've a right to know if something's happened to Danny, haven't I?'

'We don't know if anything has happened to him,' Banks said. 'He's just gone missing.'

She breathed a sigh of relief. 'So that's all.'

Banks frowned. 'His secretary seems worried enough. She says it's unusual.'

'Oh, Betty's a nice enough girl, but she is a bit of an alarmist. Danny always did have an eye for the ladies. That's one reason we're no longer together. I should imagine if he's gone missing, then something came up, so to speak.' She grinned, showing slightly overlapping front teeth.

'Wouldn't he at least let his secretary know where he was?'

'I'll admit that is a bit unusual. While Danny was never exactly tied to his desk, he didn't like to be too far from the action. You know the type, always on his car phone to the office. Who knows? Maybe he's having a mid-life crisis. Maybe he and his bit of crumpet have gone somewhere where there are no telephones. He's such a romantic, is Danny.'

The phone rang and Mrs Clegg excused herself for a moment. Banks caught her half of the conversation about an order of *méthode champenoise*. A couple of minutes later she put the phone down. 'Sorry. Where were we?'

'Mrs Clegg, we think your husband might have been mixed up in some shady dealings and that might have had something to do with his disappearance.'

She laughed. 'Shady dealings? That hardly surprises me.'

'Do you know anything about his business activities?'

'No. But dishonest in love . . .' She let the thought trail, then shrugged. 'Danny never was one of the most ethical, or faithful, of people. Careful, usually, yes, but hardly ethical.'

'Would you say he was the type to get mixed up in something illegal?'

She thought for a moment, frowning, then answered. 'Yes. Yes, I think so. If he thought the returns were high enough.'

'Is he a greedy man?'

'No-o. Not in so many words, no. I wouldn't call him greedy. He just likes to get what he wants. Women. Money. Whatever. It's more a matter of power, manipulation. He just likes to win.'

'What about the risk?'

She tipped her head to one side. 'There's always *some* risk, isn't there, Chief Inspector? If something's worth having. Danny's not a coward, if that's what you mean.'

'Did you know Keith Rothwell?'

'Yes. Not well, but I had met him. Poor man. I read about him in the paper. Terrible. You're not suggesting there's any link between his murder and Danny's disappearance, are you?'

She's quicker on the ball than Betty Moorhead, Banks thought. 'We don't know. I don't suppose you'd be in a position to enlighten us about their business dealings?'

'Sorry. No. I haven't seen Keith since Danny and I split up. Even then I'd just bump into him at the office now and then, or when he helped with my taxes.'

'So you've no idea what kinds of dealings they were involved in?'

'No. As I said, Keith Rothwell did my accounts a couple of times – you know, the wine business – when Dan and I were together, before things became awkward and our personal life got in the way. He was a damn good accountant. He saved me a lot of money from the Inland Revenue – all above board. Now, it doesn't take a Sherlock Holmes to figure out that if the two of them were in business together it probably involved tax havens of one kind or another, and that they both probably did quite well from it.'

'Have you ever heard of a man called Robert Calvert?'

'Calvert? No. I can't say I have. Should I have? Look, I'm really sorry I can't help you, Chief Inspector. And I certainly didn't mean to sound callous at all. But knowing Danny, I'm sure he's popped off to Paris for the weekend with some floozie or other and just got too overexcited to remember to let anyone know. He'll turn up.'

Banks stood up. 'I hope you're right, Mrs Clegg. And if he gets in touch, please let us know.' He gave her his card. She stood up as he left the office. He turned in the doorway and smiled. 'One more thing.'

'Yes.'

'Could you recommend a decent claret for dinner, not too pricey?'

'Of course. If you're not absolutely stuck on Bordeaux, try a bottle of the Château de la Liquière. It's from Faugères, in Languedoc. Very popular region these days.

Lots of character.' She smiled. 'And you can even afford it on a policeman's salary.'

After Banks thanked her, he made his way back down the corridor, dodging the wine cases, and bought the bottle she had suggested. Not an entirely wasted visit, he thought. At least he'd got a decent bottle of wine out of it. And then there was the Classical Record Shop just around the corner. He couldn't pass so closely without going in. Besides, he needed balm for his wounds. He was still feeling annoyed with himself after the way he had messed things up with Pamela Jeffreys. The new CD of the Khachaturian Piano Concerto, if they had it, might just help make him feel better.

As he walked outside with his bottle of wine, he felt a large hand clap down on his shoulder.

'Well, if it isn't my old mate, Banksy,' a voice said in his ear.

Banks spun round and saw the source of the voice: Detective Superintendent Richard 'Dirty Dick' Burgess, from Scotland Yard. What the hell was he doing here?

'I hope you haven't been accepting bribes,' Burgess said, pointing to the wine. Then he put his arm around Banks's shoulders. 'Come on,' he said. 'We need to go somewhere and have a little chat.'

TWO

Laurence Pratt was waiting in his office, again with his shirtsleeves rolled up, black-framed glasses about halfway down his nose, fingers forming a steeple on the neat desk in front of him. His white shirt was more dazzling than any Susan had seen in a detergent advert. Susan felt stifled. The temperature outside was in the twenties, and the window was closed.

Pratt seemed less easy in his manner this time, Susan observed, and she guessed it was because he had given too much away on her last visit. This was going to be a tough one, she thought, taking her notebook and pen out of her handbag. They had discovered a lot more about Keith Rothwell since Friday, and this time, *she* didn't want to give too much away.

Susan opened her notebook, resisting the impulse to fan her face with it, and unclipped her pen. 'The last time I talked to you, Mr Pratt,' she began, 'you told me you saw the Rothwells for the last time in March.'

'That's right. Carla and I were out to Arkbeck for dinner. Duck *à l'orange*, if I remember correctly.'

'And the new kitchen.'

'Ah, yes. We all admired the new kitchen.'

'Can you be a bit more precise about the date?'

Pratt frowned and pulled at his lower lip. 'Not exactly. It was just after St Patrick's Day, I think. Hang on a sec.' He fished in his briefcase by the side of the desk and pulled out a Filofax. 'Be lost without it,' he grinned. 'Even in the computer age. I mean, you don't want to turn the computer on every time you need an address, do you?' As he talked, he flipped through the pages. 'Ah, there it is.' He held up the open page for Susan to see. '19 March. Dinner with Keith and Mary.'

'And you said Tom dropped in to talk about his trip?'

'Yes.'

'From where?'

'What? Oh, I see. From his room, I suppose. At least I think he'd been up there. He just came in to say hello while we were having cocktails. Is he back from America, by the way?'

No harm in telling a family friend that, Susan thought. 'He's on his way,' she said. 'What was the atmosphere like between Tom and his father that night?'

'They didn't talk, as I remember.'

'Did you notice any antagonism or tension between them?'

'I wouldn't say that, no. I told you before that their relationship was strained because Tom drifted off the course his father had set for him.'

'Was anything said about that on the night you were there?'

'No, I'm certain of it. They didn't talk to one another at all. Tom was excited about going to America. I think he'd been upstairs poring over a map, planning his route.'

'And Keith Rothwell said nothing during your little chat?'

'No. He just sat there rather po-faced. Now you mention it, that *was* a bit odd. I mean, you'd hardly call old Keith a live wire these days, but he'd usually take a bit more interest than he did that night. Especially as his son was off on a big adventure.'

'So his behaviour *was* strange?'

'A little unusual, on reflection, yes.'

'What about Tom? Did he say anything to or about his father?'

Pratt shook his head slowly. Susan noticed a few beads of sweat around his temples where his hairline was receding. She could feel her own sweat tickling her ribs as it slid down her side. So much for the expensive extra-dry, long-lasting anti-perspirant she had put on after her morning shower. This didn't happen to the high-powered women executives and airline pilots in the television adverts. On the other hand, *they* didn't have to deal with the return of Sergeant Hatchley. It had taken her a good five minutes to stop shaking after he had left the office.

She asked Pratt to open the window. He complied, but it didn't do much good. The air outside was still and hot. Even the gargoyles on the upper walls of the community centre looked grumpy and sweaty.

'Did Mr Rothwell ever express any interest in pornography?'

Pratt raised his eyebrows. 'Good lord. How do you mean? As a business venture or for personal consumption?'

'Either.'

'Not in my presence. As I said, I don't know about the extent of his business interests, but he always struck me as rather . . . say . . . sexless. When we were younger, of course, we'd chase the lasses, but since his marriage . . .'

'Have you ever met a solicitor called Daniel Clegg?'

'No. The name doesn't sound familiar. Are you sure he practises in Eastvale?'

'You've never met him?'

'I told you, I've never even heard of him. Why do you ask? Is there some—'

'Did Mr Rothwell ever mention him?'

'Is there some connection?'

'Did Mr Rothwell ever mention him?'

Pratt stared at Susan for about fifteen long seconds, then said, 'No, not that I recall.'

Susan ran the back of her hand across her moist brow. She was beginning to feel a little dizzy. 'What about Robert Calvert?'

'Never heard of him, either. Is this another business

colleague of Keith's? I told you we never talked about his business. He played his cards close to his chest.'

'Did he ever mention a woman called Pamela Jeffreys?'

Pratt raised an eyebrow. 'A woman? Keith? Another woman? Good lord, no. I told you he didn't strike me as the type. Not these days, anyway. Besides, Mary would have killed him. Oh, my God . . .'

'It's all right, Mr Pratt,' Susan said. 'Slip of the tongue. Jealous type, is she?'

He pushed his glasses back up to the bridge of his nose. 'Mary? Well, I'd guess so, yes.'

'But you don't know for certain?'

'No. It's just the impression she gives. How everything centred around Keith, the house, the family. If anything came along to jeopardize that, threaten it, then she'd be a formidable enemy. Possessive, selfish, I'd say, definitely. Is that the same thing?'

Susan closed her notebook and stood up. 'Thank you, Mr Pratt. Thank you very much. Again, you've been most helpful.' Then she hurried out of the hot, stuffy office before she fainted.

THREE

They walked down to Stumps, under the museum, and made their way to the bar, where Burgess ordered a pint of McEwan's lager and Banks a pint of bitter. It wasn't Theakston's, but it would have to do.

As it was a warm day, they took their drinks outside and found a free table. There was a broad, tiled area between the museum-library complex and the buses roaring by on The Headrow, and pedestrians hurried back and forth, some heading for the Court Centre or the Town Hall and some taking short-cuts to Calverley Street and the Civic Hall. A group of people stood playing chess with oversize figures on a board drawn on the tiles. Scaffolding covered the front of one of the nineteenth-century buildings across The Headrow, Banks noticed. Another renovation.

Banks felt both puzzled and apprehensive at Burgess's arrival on the scene. The last time they had locked horns was over the killing of a policeman at an anti-government demonstration in Eastvale back in the Thatcher era.

Burgess had fitted in just fine back then. An East Ender, son of a barrow boy, he had fought his way up from the bottom with a fierce mixture of ego, ambition, cunning and a total disregard for the rules most people played by. He also felt no sympathy for those who had been unable to do likewise. Now, at about Banks's age, he was a Detective Superintendent working for a Scotland Yard department that was not quite Special Branch and not quite M15, but close enough to both to give Banks the willies.

In a period when a fully functioning human heart was regarded as a severe disability, he had been one of the new, golden breed of working-class Conservatives, up there in the firmament of the new Britain alongside the bright young things in the City, the insider traders and their like. Cops and criminals: it didn't seem to make a lot of difference, as long as you were successful. But then, it never did to some people.

Nobody could gainsay Burgess's abilities – intelligence and physical courage being foremost among them – but 'The end justifies the means' could have been written just for him. The 'end' was some vague sort of loyalty to whatever the people in power wanted done for the preservation of order, as long as the people in power weren't liberals or socialists, of course; and as for the 'means', the sky was the limit.

Maybe he had changed, Banks wondered. After all the recent inquiries and commissions, a policeman could surely no longer walk into a pub, pick up the first group of Irish people he saw and throw them in jail as terrorists, could he? Or walk down the Brixton Road and arrest the first black person he saw running? According to the public-relations people, today's policeman was a cross between Santa Claus and a hotel manager.

On the other hand, perhaps that was only according to the PR people: truth in advertising, *caveat emptor* and the rest. Besides, if there was one thing not likely to make the slightest impression on Burgess's obsidian conscious-ness, it was political correctness.

Banks lit a cigarette and held out his lighter as Burgess fired up one of his Tom Thumb cigars. He was still in good shape, though filling out a bit around the belly. He had a square jaw and slightly crooked teeth. His black, slicked-back hair was turning silver at the temples and sideboards, and the bags under his seen-it-all grey eyes looked as if they had taken on a bit more weight since Banks had last seen him. About six feet tall, casually dressed in a black leather jacket, open-neck shirt and grey cords, he was still handsome enough to turn the heads of a few thirtyish women, and had a reputation as something of a rake. It wasn't entirely unfounded, Banks had discovered the last time they worked together.

Banks reached for his pint. 'To what do I owe the honour?' he asked. He had never dignified Burgess with the 'sir' his rank demanded, and he was damned if he was about to start now.

Burgess swigged some lager, swished it around his mouth and swallowed.

'Well?' said Banks. 'Enough bloody theatrics, for Christ's sake.'

'I don't suppose you'd believe me if I said I'd missed you?'

'Get on with it.'

'Right. Thought not. Ever heard of a place called St Corona?'

'Of course. It's a Caribbean island, been in the news a bit lately.'

'Clever boy. That's the one. Population about four point eight million. Area about seven thousand square miles. Chief resources: bauxite, limestone, aluminium, sugar cane, plus various fruits and spices, fish and a bit of gold, silver and nickel. A lot of tourism, too, or there used to be.'

'So you've been studying *Whitaker's Almanack*,' said Banks. 'Now what the bloody hell is this all about?'

A tipsy youth bumped into the table and spilled some of Burgess's lager. The youth stopped to apologize, but the look Burgess gave him sent him stumbling off into the bright afternoon sunlight before he could get the words out.

'Fucking lager lout,' Burgess muttered, wiping the beer off the table-top with a handkerchief. 'Gone to the dogs, this country. Where was I? Oh, yes. St Corona. Imports just about everything you need to live, including the machinery to make it. Lots of television sets, radios, fridges, washing machines.' He paused and whistled between his teeth as a young redhead in a mini-skirt walked by. 'Now *that's* not bad,' he said. 'Which reminds me, have you rogered that young redhead in Eastvale yet?

You know, the psychologist.' He flicked the stub of his cigar towards the gutter; it hit the wall just above with a shower of sparks.

Burgess meant Jenny Fuller, as he knew damn well. Banks managed a smile, remembering what happened the last time those two met. 'St Corona,' he said. 'You were saying?'

Burgess pouted. 'You're no fun. Know who the president is?'

'What is this, bloody *Mastermind*? Martin Churchill. Now, if you've got something to tell me, get it off your chest and let me go home. It's been a long day.'

'Back to that lovely wife of yours, eh? Sandra, isn't it? All right, all right. St Corona is a republic, and you're right, Martin Churchill is president for life. Good name for the job, don't you think?'

'I've read about him.'

'Yes, well, the poor sod's a bit beleaguered these days, what with the opposition parties raking up the muck and the independence and liberation movements going from strength to strength.' He sighed. 'I don't know. It seems people just don't believe in a good old benevolent dictatorship any more.'

'Benevolent, my arse,' said Banks. 'He's been bleeding the country dry for ten years and now they're closing in on him. What am I supposed to do, cry?'

Burgess glared at Banks through squinting eyes. 'Still the bloody pinko, huh? Still the limp-wristed, knee-jerking liberal?' He sighed. 'Somehow, Banks, I hadn't expected you to change. That's partly why I'm here. Anyway, whatever you or I might think about it, the powers that be decided it was a good idea to have a stable government in that part of the world, someone we could trust. Of course, it doesn't seem quite so important now, with the Russkies swapping their rusty old atomic warheads for turnips, but other threats exist. Anyway, Britain, France, Canada, the States and a few others pumped millions into St Corona over the years, so you can estimate how important it is to us.'

Banks listened intently. There could be no rushing Burgess; he would get where he was going in his own sweet time.

'Churchill's finished,' Burgess went on with a sweeping hand gesture. 'It's just a matter of time. Weeks . . . months. He knows it. We know it. The only thing now is for him to get out alive with his family while he still can and take up life in exile.'

'And he wants to come here?'

Burgess looked around at the chess players and The Headrow. 'Well, I don't think he's got the north of England in mind specifically, but you're on the right track. Maybe a nice little retirement villa in Devon or Cornwall, the English Riviera. Somewhere where the weather's nice. Cultivate his herbaceous borders. Live out his days in the contemplation of nature. Prepare himself for the life hereafter. Make his peace with the Almighty. That kind of thing. Somewhere he won't do any more harm.'

Burgess lit another little cigar and spat out a flake of loose tobacco. 'The Yanks have said no, but then they've got a good record of turning their backs on their mates. The French are dithering and jabbering and waving their arms about, as usual. They'd probably sneak him in the back door like the good little hypocrites they are, if they had any real incentive left. And the Canadians . . . well, they're just too fucking moral for their own good. The bottom line, Banks, is that there's a lot of pressure on our government to take him in, as quietly as possible, of course.'

'Sneak him in the back door, you mean, like the hypocritical French?'

'If you like.'

'His human rights record is appalling,' Banks said. 'The infant mortality rate in St Corona is over fifteen per cent, for a start. Life expectancy isn't much more than fifty for a man and sixty for a woman.'

'Oh, dear, dear. You've been reading the *Guardian* again, haven't you, Banks?'

'And other papers. The story's the same.'

'Well, you should know better than to believe all you read in the papers, shouldn't you?' Burgess looked around conspiratorially and lowered his voice. Nobody seemed in the least bit interested in them. Laughter and fragments of conversation filled the air. 'Have you ever wondered,' he said, 'why women always seem to have a higher life expectancy rate than men? Don't they have as many bad habits as we do? Maybe they just don't work as hard, don't suffer as much stress? Maybe it's all that slimming and aerobics, eh? Maybe there's something in it.

'Anyway, back to Mr Churchill's predicament. And this is classified, by the way. There are some people in power who want him here, who feel we owe him, and there are some who don't, who feel he's a lowlife scumbag and deserves to die as slowly and painfully as possible.' As usual, Burgess liked to show off his American slang. He went to the States often, on 'courses'.

'Oh, come off it,' said Banks. 'If they want him here it's not out of any sense of duty, it's because he's got something they want, or because he's got something on them.'

Burgess scratched his cheek. 'Cynic,' he said. 'But you're partly right. He's not a nice man. As far as I can gather he's a glutton, a boor, a murderer and a rapist, sodomy preferred. But that's not the issue at all. The problem is that we educated him, made him what he is. Eton and Cambridge. He read law there. Did you know that? He went through school and university with a lot of important people, Banks. Cabinet ministers, bankers, power brokers, backroom boys. You know how people can behave indiscreetly when they're young? Do things they wouldn't want to come back and haunt them when they're in the public eye? And we're talking about people who have the power to loosen the government purse strings now and then, whenever St Corona asks for more aid. And rumour has it that he's also got quite a nice little savings account that won't do our economy any harm at all.'

'Let me guess,' said Banks. 'Laundered money?'

Burgess raised his eyebrows. 'Well, of course. Which brings me to the murder of Keith Rothwell. You are senior field investigator, I understand?'

'Yes.'

'That's why I thought I'd better deal with you in person. I know you, Banks. You're still a pinko liberal, as you've proved time and time again. In fact, as soon as they told me you were on the case, I thought, "Oh, fuck, we're in trouble." You've no respect for the venerable institutions of government, or for the necessity of secrecy in some of their workings. You've got no respect for tradition and you don't give a toss about preserving the natural order of things. You probably don't even stand up for "God Save the Queen". In short, you're a bloody bolshie trouble-maker and a menace to national security.'

Banks smiled. 'Thanks for the compliment,' he said. 'But I wouldn't go quite *that* far.'

Burgess grinned. 'Maybe I exaggerate. But you get my point?'

'Loud and clear.'

'Good. That's why I'm going to tell you something very, very important and very, very secret, and I'm going to trust you with it. We've been keeping an eye on the St Corona situation, and anything that could possibly have to do with Martin Churchill gets flagged. Now, we just got a report from your Fraud Squad late yesterday evening that they found something on Keith Rothwell's computer that indicates he may have been laundering money for Martin Churchill. Lots of trips to the Channel Islands and the Caribbean. Some very dodgy bank accounts. Some very dodgy banks, too, for that matter. Anyway, there's a pattern and a time period that matches exactly the sort of thing we've been looking for. We've known this was going on for some time, but until now we hadn't a clue who was doing it. There's no proof it was Rothwell, yet – the Fraud Squad still has a lot of work to do, chasing down transactions and what have you – but if I'm right, then we're talking about a lot of money. Something in the region of thirty or forty million pounds over three or four years. Mostly money that was originally provided as aid by leading western nations. It's the same kind of thing Baby Doc did in Haiti.'

'And you think this might have something to do with Rothwell's murder?'

Burgess shook his head. 'I don't really know, but the odds are that there's some kind of connection, don't you think? Especially considering the way he was killed. I mean, it was hardly a domestic, was it?'

'Possibly,' Banks agreed. 'Do you have any leads on the killers?'

'No more than you. I'm only *suggesting* that Churchill might be behind them.'

'And if he is?'

'Watch your back.'

Banks thought about that for a moment. He wasn't sure who constituted the greatest threat to his exposed back, Churchill or Burgess. 'I must say this is pretty quick work on your part,' he said.

Burgess shrugged. 'Like I said, orders to flag. When I called your station, Superintendent Gristhorpe told me where you were. I missed you at the solicitor's office, but the secretary told me you were coming here.'

'What's Daniel Clegg's connection with all this?'

'We don't know yet. We don't even know if there is one. I only just found out about his disappearance. It's early days yet.'

'Two other men have been looking for him, too. One black, one white. Are they your lot?'

Burgess frowned. 'No, they're nothing to do with me.'

'Know anything about them?'

'No.'

He was lying, Banks was certain. 'So why are you here?' he asked. 'What do you want me to do?'

'Nothing. Just carry on as normal. I simply wanted to warn you to tread very carefully, that's all, that things might be more complicated than they appear on the surface. And to let you know there's help available if you want it, of course. Naturally, if you get close to uncovering the killers' identities, I'd be interested in talking to them.'

'Why?'

'Because I'm interested in everything to do with Martin

Churchill, as I told you.' Burgess looked at his watch. 'Good lord, is that the time already?' he said, then knocked back the rest of his pint, winked and stood up. 'Got to be off now. Be seeing you.' And he strutted off over the square towards Park Row.

Banks lit a cigarette and brooded over the meeting as he finished his pint, wondering what the hell the bastard was up to. He didn't trust Burgess as far as he could throw him, and he was convinced that all that stuff about offering help and giving a friendly warning was rubbish. Burgess was up to something.

At a guess, he wanted to be one of the first to get to the killers so he could find a way of hushing them up. The last thing he would want was a big story about Churchill hiring assassins to murder a Yorkshire accountant splashed all over the press. Churchill might well be up to much worse things on St Corona, but this was England, after all.

Still, no matter what Burgess suspected, and whether or not Martin Churchill was behind it all, Banks still had two killers to find, locals by the sound of them, and he wasn't going to do that by sitting around in Stumps fretting about Dirty Dick Burgess.

FOUR

Banks didn't expect to find anything new in Calvert's Headingley flat, but for some reason he felt the need to revisit the place after he had picked up the Khachaturian compact disc.

West Yorkshire police had talked to the other tenants, who all said they knew nothing about Mr Calvert or Keith Rothwell: they never really saw much of him; he was out a lot; and, yes, now you mention it, there was a resemblance, but it was only a newspaper photo and Mr Calvert didn't look quite the same; besides, Calvert wasn't an Eastvale accountant, was he? He lived in Leeds. Couldn't argue with that. Banks headed upstairs.

The only immediate difference he noticed was the thin layer of fingerprint powder on surfaces of metal or glass: around the gas fireplace, on the glass-topped coffee table and the TV set.

This time, Banks examined the books more closely. There weren't many, and most of them were the usual bestseller list paperbacks: Tom Clancy, Clive Cussler, Ken Follett, Robert Ludlum. There was also some espionage fiction – Len Deighton, John le Carré, Adam Hall, Ian Fleming – plus a couple of Agatha Christies and an oddly out-of-place copy of *Middlemarch*, which looked unread. Hardly surprising, Banks thought, having given up on even the television adaptation. The only other books were Palgrave's *Golden Treasury*, the first part of William Manchester's Churchill biography and a *Concise Oxford Dictionary*.

The small compact disc collection concentrated entirely on jazz, mostly Kenny Ball, Acker Bilk and a few collections of big-band music. Banks noticed some decent stuff: Louis, Bix, Johnny Dodds, Bud Powell. On the whole, though, judging from the Monet print over the fireplace, the Palgrave and the music, Robert Calvert had agreed with Philip Larkin about the evils of Parker, Pound and Picasso.

In the bedroom, all the papers had been removed from the desk, as had the wallet with the Calvert identification and credit card. The Fraud Squad would be working already on Calvert's financial profile, now they knew that he and Rothwell were one and the same. The magazines and coins were still there, the bed still unmade.

Why had Rothwell *needed* Calvert? Banks wondered. Simple escapism? According to what everyone said, he was a different person altogether at Arkbeck Farm and in the wider community of Swainsdale. Most people there spoke of him as a rather dull chap, maybe a bit henpecked.

Then there was Robert Calvert, the dancing, gambling, laughing, fun-loving Lothario and dreamer. The man who had attracted and bedded the beautiful Pamela Jeffreys. The man who squeezed his toothpaste tube in the middle.

So which was the real Keith Rothwell? Both or neither? In a sense, Banks guessed, he needed both worlds. Did that make him a Jekyll and Hyde figure? Did it mean he was mad? Banks didn't think so.

He remembered Susan's account of her interview with Laurence Pratt, in which Pratt had indicated that Rothwell had changed over the years, cut himself off, penned himself in. Perhaps he had once been the kind of person who liked gambling, dancing and drinking. Then he had been pushed into marriage with the boss's daughter, and marriage had changed him. It happened often enough; people settled down. But, for some reason, Rothwell had felt the need for an outlet, one that would not interfere with his family life, or with his local image as a respectable, decent citizen.

Banks could think of one good reason why it was important for Rothwell to maintain this fiction: Rothwell was a crook. He certainly didn't want to draw attention to himself by high living. As Calvert, he could relive his youth as much as he wished and enjoy the proceeds of his money-laundering. Perfect.

Did Mary Rothwell know about her husband's other life? She had probably suspected something was wrong time and time again over the last few years, but denied and repressed the suspicions in order to maintain the illusion of happy, affluent family values in the community. She probably needed to believe in the lies as much as her husband needed to live them.

But you can only maintain an illusion for so long, Banks thought, then cracks appear and the truth seeps in. You can ignore that for a long time, too, but ultimately the wound begins to fester and infect everything. That's when the bad things start to happen. Did Alison know? Or Tom? It would be interesting to meet the lad.

He looked through the wardrobe and dresser drawers again. Most of Calvert's clothes were still there, though the condoms had gone. Genuine scientific testing, Banks wondered, or a Scene of Crime officer with a hot date and no time to get to the chemist's?

He looked under chairs, under the bed, on top of the wardrobe, in the cistern, and in all the usual hiding places before he realized that Vic Manson and his lads had probably already done most of that, even though the flat wasn't a crime scene *per se*, and that he didn't know what he was looking for anyway. He paused by the front window, which looked out onto a tree-lined side street off Otley Road.

Fool, he told himself. He had been looking for Keith Rothwell in Robert Calvert's flat. But he wasn't there. He wasn't anywhere; he was just a slab of chilled meat waiting for a man with his collar on the wrong way around to chant a few meaningless words that might just ease the living's fear of death until the next time it touched too close to home for comfort.

As he glanced out of the window, he glimpsed two men in suits across the street looking up at him. They were partially obscured by trees, but he could see that one was black, the other white.

He hurried down to the street. When he got there, nobody was about except a young man washing his car three houses down.

Banks approached him and showed his identification. The man wiped the sweat off his brow and looked up at Banks, shielding his eyes from the glare. Sunlight winked on the bubbles in his bucket of soapy water.

'Did you see a couple of blokes in business suits pass by a few minutes ago?' Banks asked.

'Yeah,' said the man. 'Yeah, I did. I thought it was a bit odd the way they stopped and looked up at that house. To be honest, though, the way they were dressed I thought they were probably coppers.'

Banks thanked him and went back to the car. So he wasn't getting paranoid. How did the saying go? Just because you think they're out there following you, it doesn't mean they aren't.

8

ONE

Tom Rothwell resembled his father more than his mother, Banks thought, sitting opposite him in the split-level living room at Arkbeck Farm the following morning. Though his hair was darker and longer, he had the same thin oval face and slightly curved nose and the same grey eyes as Banks had seen in the photograph. His sulky mouth, though, owed more to early Elvis Presley, and was no doubt more a result of artifice than nature.

His light brown hair fell charmingly over one eye and hung in natural waves over his ears and the collar of his blue denim shirt. Both knees of his jeans were torn, and the unlaced white trainers on his feet were scuffed and dirty.

The best of the lot, Cathy Grafton had said, and it wasn't hard to guess why a rather plain girl like her would value a smile and a kind word from a handsome lad like Tom.

But right from the start Banks sensed something else about him, an aura of affected arrogance, as if he were condescending from a great intellectual and moral height to answer such stupid questions as those relating to his father's murder.

It was rebellious youth, in part, and Banks certainly understood that. Also, Tom seemed to exhibit that mix of vanity and overconfidence that Banks had often encountered in the wealthy. In addition there was a hell of a lot of the wariness and subterfuge that he usually associated with someone hiding a guilty secret. Tom's body language said it all: long legs stretched out, crossed at the ankles, arms folded high on his chest, eyes anywhere but on the questioner. Susan Gay sat in the background to take notes. Banks wondered what she thought about Tom.

'Did you have any problems getting a flight?' Banks asked.

'No. But I had to change at some dreary place in Carolina, and then again in New York.'

'I know you must be tired. I remember from my trip to Toronto, the jet lag's much worse flying home.'

'I'm all right. I slept a little on the plane.'

'I can never seem to manage that.'

Tom said nothing. Banks wished that Alison and Mary Rothwell weren't flanking Tom on the sofa. And again the room felt dark and cold around him. Though it had windows, they were set or angled in such a way that they didn't let in much natural light. And they were all closed.

'I imagine you're upset about your father, too,' he said.

'Naturally.'

'We wanted to talk to you so soon,' Banks said, 'because we hoped you might be able to tell us something about your father, something that might help lead us to his killers.'

'How would I know anything? I've been out of the country since the end of March.'

'It's possible,' Banks said, weighing his words carefully, 'that the roots of the crime lie farther back than that.'

'That's ridiculous. You lot have far too much imagination for your own good.'

'Oh? What do *you* think happened?'

Tom curled his lip and looked at the carpet. 'It was clearly a robbery gone wrong. Or a kidnap attempt. Dad *was* quite well off, you know.'

Banks scratched the scar beside his right eye. 'Kidnapping, eh? We'd never thought of that. Can you explain?'

'Well, that's your job, isn't it? But it's hardly difficult to see how it could have been a kidnap attempt gone wrong. My father obviously wouldn't co-operate, so they had to kill him.'

'Why not just knock him out and take him away?'

Tom shrugged. 'Perhaps the gun went off by accident.'

'Then why not take the body and pretend he was still alive till they got the money?'

'How would I know? You're supposed to be the professionals. I only said that's what it *might* have been. I also suggested a bungled robbery.'

'Look, Tom, this is a pointless game we're playing. Believe me, we've covered all the possibilities, and it wasn't a kidnap attempt or a bungled burglary. I realize how difficult it is for the family to accept that a member may have been involved in something illegal, but all the evidence points that way.'

'Absurd,' spat Mary Rothwell. 'Keith was an honest businessman, a good person. And if you persist in spreading these vicious rumours, we'll have to contact our solicitor.'

'Mrs Rothwell,' Banks said, 'I'm trying to talk to your son. I'd appreciate it if you would keep quiet.' More than once he had thought about breaking the news that her husband led another existence as Robert Calvert, but he held back. In the first place, it would be cruel, and in the second, Gristhorpe said the Chief Constable wanted it kept from the press and family, if possible, at least until they developed a few more leads on the case.

Mary Rothwell glared at him, lips pressed so tight they were white around the edges.

Banks turned back to Tom. 'Were you close to your father?'

'Close enough. He wasn't . . .' Tom turned up his nose. 'He wasn't a clinging, emotional sort of person.'

'But you were on good terms?'

'Yes, of course.'

'Then you might know something that could help us.'

'I still don't see how, but if I can be of any use . . . Ask away.'

'Did he ever mention a man called Martin Churchill?'

'Churchill? No.'

'Do you know who he is?'

'That chap in the Caribbean?'

'Yes.'

'Are you serious?' Tom looked puzzled. 'You are, aren't you? The answer's no, of course he didn't. Why would he?'

'Did you ever see your father with two well-dressed men, both about six feet tall, one black, one white?'

Tom frowned. 'No. Look, I'm sorry but I don't know what you're talking about.'

'Did he ever talk to you about business?'

'No.'

'Did you ever meet any of his business associates?'

'Only if they came over to dinner. And even then, I wasn't generally invited.' Tom looked at his mother. 'I had to find something else to do for the evening. Which usually wasn't much trouble.' He glanced over at Susan, and Banks sensed a softening in his expression as he did so. He seemed interested in her presence, curious about her.

The radio had been playing a request programme quietly in the background, and Banks suddenly picked out the haunting chorus of Delibes' '*Viens, Mallika . . . Dôme épais*', popularized as the 'Flower Duet' by a television advert. Even trivialization couldn't mar its beauty and clarity. After pausing for a moment, he went on.

'When did you leave for your holiday?'

'March,' he said. 'The thirty-first. But I don't see—'

'What about your job?'

'What job?'

'The one in the video shop in Eastvale.'

'Oh, that. I packed it in.'

'What kind of videos did they deal in?'

'All sorts. Why?'

'Under-the-counter stuff?'

'Oh, come off it, Chief Inspector. Suddenly my father's a crook and I'm a porn merchant? You should be writing for television.' Alison looked up from her book and giggled. Tom smiled at her, obviously pleased with his insolence. 'It was called Monster Videos, that place in the arcade by the bus station. Ask them if you don't believe me.'

'Why did you leave?' Banks pressed on.

'Not that it's any of your business, but it was hardly a fast track to a career.'

'Is that what you want?'

'I'm going to film school in the States.'

'I see.'

'I want to be a movie director.'

'Was that what your father wanted?'

'I don't see that what *he* wanted has anything to do with it.'

It was there, the rancour, Banks thought. Time to push a little harder. 'It's just that I understood you had a falling out over your career choice. I gather he wanted you to become an accountant or a lawyer but he thought you preferred to be an idle, shiftless sod.'

'How dare you?' Mary Rothwell jumped to her feet.

'It's all right, Mother,' Tom sneered. 'Sit down. It's all part of their game. They only say things like that to needle you into saying something you'll regret. Just ignore it.' He looked at Susan again, as if expecting her to defend Banks, but she said nothing. He seemed disappointed.

Mary Rothwell sat down again slowly. Alison, at the other side of Tom, glanced up from *Villette* again for a couple of seconds, raised the corners of her lips in what passed for a smile, then went back to her book.

'Well?' said Banks.

'Well what?'

'What is it that I might needle you into regretting you said?'

'Clever. It was just a figure of speech.'

'All right. Did you and your father have such an argument?'

'You must know as well as I do,' Tom said, 'that fathers and sons have their disagreements. Sure, Dad wanted me to follow in his footsteps, but I had my own ideas. He's not big on the arts, isn't Dad, except when it's good for business to get tickets for the opera or the theatre or something to impress his clients.'

'Where did you travel in America?'

'All over. New York. Chicago. Los Angeles. San Francisco. Miami. Tampa.'

'How did you get around?'

'Plane and car rental. Where is this—'

'Did you visit the Caribbean? St Corona?'

'No, I didn't.'

'How did you finance the trip?'

'What?'

'You heard me. You were over there a month and a half, and you'd still be there now if it weren't for your father's death. All that travelling costs money. You can't have earned that much working in a video shop, especially one that only deals in legal stuff. How could you afford a lengthy trip to America?'

Tom shifted uncomfortably. 'My parents helped me out.'

Banks noticed a confused look flit across Mary Roth-well's face.

'Did you?' Banks asked her.

'Why, yes, of course.'

He could tell from the hesitation that she knew nothing about it. 'Do you mean your father helped you?' he asked Tom.

'He was the one with all the money, wasn't he?'

'So your father financed your trip. How?'

'What do you mean?'

'How did he finance it? Cash? Cheque?'

'He got me the ticket, some travellers' cheques and a supplementary card on his American Express Gold account. You can check the records, if you haven't done already.'

Banks whistled between his teeth. 'American Express Gold, eh? Not bad.' Judging by the look on Mary Roth-well's face, it was news to her. Alison didn't seem to care. She turned a page without looking up. 'Why would he do that?' Banks asked.

'I'm his son. It's the kind of thing parents do, isn't it? Why not?'

Banks had never spent so much on Brian and Tracy, but

then he had never been able to afford it. 'Was he usually so generous?' he asked.

'He was never mean.'

Banks paused. When the silence had made Tom restless, he went on. 'Just before you went away, you had an argument with your father in which he expressed great disappointment in you. Now, I know why that is. You've just told me you didn't want to follow the career he set out for you. But you also expressed disappointment in him. Why did you do that?'

'I don't remember any argument.'

'Come on, Tom. You can do better than that.'

Tom looked at Susan again, and Banks noticed a plea for help in his eyes. He looked left and right for support, too, but found none. His mother seemed lost in thought and Alison was still deep in her Charlotte Brontë.

'I'm telling you,' Tom said, 'I don't know what you're talking about.'

'Why were you disappointed in your father, Tom?'

Tom reddened. 'I wasn't. I don't know what you mean.'

'Did you find out something incriminating about his business dealings?'

'Is *that* what you think?'

'You'd better tell me, Tom. It could help us a lot. What was he up to?'

Tom seemed to relax. 'Nothing. *I* don't know. You're way off beam.'

'Does the name Aston or Afton mean anything to you?'

Banks was sure he saw a flicker of recognition behind Tom's eyes. Recognition and fear. 'No,' Tom said. 'Never heard of him.'

Banks decided they would get nothing more out of this situation, not with the whole family closing ranks. It would be best to leave it for now. No doubt, when Banks and Susan left, the Rothwells would fall into an argument, for Mary Rothwell wasn't looking at all pleased with the return of her prodigal son. Tom could stew over whatever it was that confused him. Plenty of time.

It was a gorgeous morning in the dale. Banks put a Bill Evans solo piano tape in the cassette player as he drove through Fortford, gold and green in the soft, slanting light. To their left, the lush fields of the Leas were full of buttercups, and here and there the fishermen sat, still as statues, lines arcing down into the River Swain.

'What do you think?' he asked Susan.

'He's lying, sir.'

'That's obvious enough. But why? What about?'

'I don't know. Everything. I just got a strange feeling.'

'Me, too. Next time, I think it might be a good idea if you talked to him alone.'

'Maybe I can catch him after the funeral?'

'You were thinking of going? Damn!'

Half a mile before the road widened at the outskirts of Eastvale, a farmer was moving his sheep across from one pasture to another. There was nothing to be done. They simply had to stop until the sheep had gone.

'Stupid creatures,' Banks said.

'I think they're rather cute, in a silly way,' Susan said. 'Anyway, I thought I might go. You never know, the murderers might turn up to pay their respects, like they do in books.'

Banks laughed. 'Do you know that actually happened to me once?' he said.

'What?'

'It did. Honest. Down in London. There was a feud between two families, the Kinghorns and the Franklins –

none of them exactly intellectual giants – been going on for years. Anyway, old man Franklin gets shot in broad daylight, and there's half a dozen witnesses say they saw Billy Kinghorn, the eldest son, do it. Only trouble is, Billy does a bunk. Until the funeral, that is. Then there he is, young Billy, black tie, armband and all, face as long as a wet Sunday, come to pay his last respects.'

'What happened?'

'We nabbed him.'

Susan laughed. The sheep kept wandering all over the road, despite the ministrations of an inept collie, which looked a bit too long in the tooth for such exacting work.

'I thought there had to be a reason for going,' Susan said. 'Anyway, I quite like funerals. My Auntie Mavis died when I was six and my mum and dad took me to the funeral. It was very impressive, the hymns, the readings. I couldn't understand a word of it at that age, of course, but it certainly sounded important. Anyway, when we got outside I asked my mum where Auntie Mavis was and she sniffled a bit then said, "In Heaven." I asked her where that was and she pointed up at the sky. It was a beautiful blue sky, a bit like today, and there was only one cloud in it, a fluffy white one that looked like a teddy bear. From then on I always thought when people died they became clouds in a perfect blue sky. I don't know . . . it made me feel happy, somehow. I mean, I know funerals are solemn occasions, but I don't seem to mind them so much after that.'

The last sheep finally found the gate and scrambled through. The farmer held up his hand in thanks, as if Banks had had any option but to wait, and closed the gate behind him. Banks set off.

'Rather you than me,' he said. 'I can't stand them. Anyway, see if you can take young Tom aside, take him for a drink or something. I've a feeling he really wants to tell us what he knows. Did you notice the way he kept looking at you?'

'Yes.'

'Think he fancies you?'

'No,' Susan said, after a pause for thought. 'No. Somehow, I don't think it was that at all.'

TWO

Banks crunched the last pickled onion of his ploughman's lunch and swilled it down with a mouthful of Theakston's bitter, then he lit a cigarette. He would have to resort to a Polo mint if he found himself interviewing anyone in the afternoon. Superintendent Gristhorpe sat opposite him in the Queen's Arms, cradling a half-pint. It was the first time they had been able to get together since Banks had met Burgess.

'So,' Gristhorpe said, 'according to Burgess, Rothwell was laundering money for Martin Churchill?'

'Looks that way,' said Banks. 'He said he couldn't be certain but I don't think he'd come all the way up here if he wasn't, do you?'

'Knowing how little Burgess thinks of the north, no. But I still don't think we should overlook the possibility of Rothwell's involvement in some other kind of organized crime, most likely drugs, prostitution or porn. Even if he were laundering money for Churchill, he could have been into something else dirty too. We can't assume it was the Churchill link that got him killed until we know a hell of a lot more.'

'I agree,' said Banks.

'Better do as Burgess says and watch your back, though.'

'Don't worry, sir, I will.'

'Anyway,' Gristhorpe went on, 'I've just had a meeting with Inspector Macmillan, and he tells me that Daniel Clegg acted as Robert Calvert's reference for his bank account and his credit card in Leeds. The account has about twenty thousand in it. Interesting, isn't it?'

'Play money,' Banks said.

'Aye. I wouldn't mind that much to play with, myself. Anyway, according to Inspector Macmillan, the bank employees didn't recognize Rothwell's picture as Calvert because they hardly saw him. He used a busy branch in the city centre, and the only person who did make the connection when Macmillan pushed it said Calvert looked and dressed so differently she wouldn't have known.'

'Thank the lord for Pamela Jeffreys, then.'

'Aye, or we might never have known. What does his family have to say?'

Banks sighed and put the edge of his hand to his throat. 'I've had it up to here with the bloody Rothwells,' he said. 'They give a whole new meaning to "dysfunctional". There's the victim laundering illegal money and leading a double life just for a hobby. There's the daughter, who'd rather bury her face in a book than face reality now that the shock and the tiredness have worn off. There's the son with more than a few guilty secrets hidden away. And then, watching over them all, there's the Queen Bee, who just wants to keep up the usual upper-middle-class appearances and swears the sun shone out of her husband's arse.'

'What do you expect her to do, Alan? Her world's fallen apart. She must be having a hell of a job just holding things together. Have a bit more bloody compassion, lad.'

Banks took a drag at his cigarette, and blew the smoke out slowly. 'You're right,' he said. 'I'm sorry. I've just had it with the bloody Rothwells, that's all. What do they know? It's hard to tell. I think the wife suspects something weird was going on, but she doesn't know what and she doesn't want to know. She denies it, especially to herself.'

'Could they have any involvement?'

'I've thought about it,' Banks said, 'and I've discussed it with Susan. In the final analysis, I don't really think so. Mary Rothwell might well hit out at anything that threatens her comfortable world, and if she thought her husband were profiting from porn, for example, I can't just see her sitting still and accepting it.' He shook his head. 'But not this way. This brings her exactly the kind of attention she *doesn't* want. I don't know how she'd deal with him – Susan guessed poison, maybe, or an accident – but it wouldn't be like this.'

'Hmm. Try this for size,' said Gristhorpe. 'One: let's assume that Rothwell and Clegg are in the money-laundering business together, for Martin Churchill or whoever.'

Banks nodded. 'It makes sense, Clegg being a tax specialist and all.'

'And we'll leave Robert Calvert out of it, as, say, just a personal aberration on Rothwell's part, at least for the moment. A red herring, right?'

'Okay.'

'Something goes wrong. Rothwell finds out something that makes him want to get out of it, so he writes to Clegg ending their association.'

'And,' said Banks, 'Churchill, or whoever it is they're working for, doesn't like this at all.'

'Makes sense, doesn't it?'

'So far. Keep going.'

'Rothwell gets scared. Either he's been cheating on his masters, and they've found out, or they're afraid he's getting nervous and is going to blow the whistle. So what do they do?'

'Take out a contract.'

'Right. And that's the end of Rothwell.'

Gristhorpe paused as a couple of office-workers on a lunch break brushed past them and sat down at the next table. Cyril's cash register rang up another sale.

'He could have been cheating on them to finance his life as Calvert,' said Banks. 'I know we were going to leave him out of the equation, but it fits. He had twenty grand in the bank, you say, and he liked to gamble, according to Pamela Jeffreys.'

'True, but let's stick to the simple line. What's important is that Rothwell has become a liability, or a threat, and his masters want him dead. They've got enough money to be able to pay for the privilege without getting their own hands dirty. Which brings us to Mr Daniel Clegg. The killers had a fair bit of information about Rothwell. They seemed to know that he and his wife would be out celebrating their wedding anniversary, for example. Clegg could probably have told them that. They knew Rothwell had a daughter, too, and that she would be at home. She wasn't "part of the deal", remember? And they knew where he lived, the layout, everything.'

'Clegg?'

Gristhorpe nodded. 'Let's put it this way. If Rothwell were laundering money for someone, there'd be little, if any, contact between him and his masters, wouldn't there?'

'That would seem to be one point of a laundering operation,' Banks agreed. 'Certainly Tom Rothwell seemed genuinely puzzled when I brought up Martin Churchill.'

'Right. And Clegg was the only other person we suspect was involved, and he had information about Rothwell's personal life.'

'So you reckon Clegg was behind it?'

'It's a theory, isn't it? They weren't exactly friends, Alan. Not according to what you've told me. They were business colleagues. Different thing. It was a matter of you scratch my back, I'll scratch yours. Strange bedfellows, maybe. And crooked too. It's an odd thing is a professional gone bad. They talk about bent coppers, but what about bent lawyers, bent accountants, bent doctors? If push came to shove, would you expect one crooked business-man to stick up for another?'

'So you think Clegg was not just involved in the laundering business but in Rothwell's murder, too?'

'Aye. He could be our link.'

'And his disappearance?'

'Scarpered. He knew what was coming, knew when. Maybe they paid him well. It doesn't matter whether he was scared of us or them, the result was the same. He took his money and ran, collected two hundred pounds when he passed go, didn't go to jail. Then his bosses couldn't get in touch with him, so they sent their two goons to find him. The timing's right.'

'What about this scenario,' Banks offered. 'Maybe Churchill had Clegg killed, too. With Rothwell gone, Clegg might just be a nuisance who knew too much, a loose cannon on the deck. If Churchill is planning on coming here, maybe he wanted a clean break.'

Gristhorpe took a sip of his beer. 'Possible, I'll grant you.'

'You know, it's just struck me,' said Banks, 'but do we know if Clegg ever practised criminal law?'

'Seems to be the only kind he practised,' replied Gristhorpe, then held up his hand and grinned as Banks groaned. 'All right, all right, Alan. I promise. No more bad lawyer jokes. As far as we know he didn't. He's a solicitor, not a barrister, so he didn't represent clients in court. But people might have come to him, and he could have referred them. Why?'

'I was just wondering where a man like Clegg might meet a killer for hire.'

'Local Conservative Club, probably,' said Gristhorpe. 'But I see what you mean. It's a loose end we've got to pursue. If we assume Clegg was involved in arranging for Rothwell's murder, then we can look through his contacts and his activities to find a link with a couple of likely assassins. We've got that and the wadding. Not very much, is it?'

'No,' said Banks. 'What if Clegg's dead?'

'Nothing changes. West Yorkshire police keep looking for a body and we keep nosing around asking questions. We could get in touch with Interpol, see if he's holed up somewhere in Spain.' He looked at his watch. 'Look, Alan, I'd better get finished and be off. I've got another meeting with the Chief Constable this afternoon.'

'Okay. I'll be over in a minute.'

Gristhorpe nodded and left, but no sooner had Banks started to let his imagination work on Clegg meeting two hired guns in a smoky saloon than the superintendent poked his head around the door again. 'They think they've found the killers' car,' he said. 'Abandoned near Leeds city centre. Ken Blackstone asks if you want to go and have a look.'

Banks nodded. 'All roads lead to Leeds,' he sighed. 'I might as well bloody move there.' And he followed Gristhorpe out.

9

ONE

A tape of Satie's piano music, especially the 'Trois Gymnopédies', kept Banks calm on his way to Leeds, even though the A1 was busy with juggernauts and commercial travellers driving too fast. He found the car park without too much difficulty; it was an old school playground surrounded by the rubble of demolished buildings just north of the city centre.

'Cheers, Alan,' said Detective Inspector Ken Blackstone. 'You look like a bloody villain with those sunglasses on. How's it going?'

'Can't complain.' Banks shook his hand and took off the dark glasses. He had met Blackstone at a number of courses and functions, and the two of them had always got along well enough. 'And how's West Yorkshire CID?'

'Overworked, as usual. Bit of a bugger, isn't it?' said Blackstone. 'The weather, I mean.'

Banks scratched the scar beside his right eye. Sometimes when it itched, it was trying to tell him something; other times, like this, it was just the heat. 'I remember an American once told me that all we English do is complain about the weather,' he said. 'It's either too hot or too cold for us, too wet or too dry.'

Blackstone laughed. 'True. Still, the station could do with a few of those air-conditioner thingies the Yanks use.

It's hotter indoors than out. Sends the crime figures up, you know, a heat wave. Natives get restless.'

A light breeze had sprung up from the west, but it did nothing to quell the warmth of the sun. Banks took off his sports jacket and slung it over his shoulder as they walked across the soft tarmac to the abandoned car. His tie hung askew, as usual, and his top shirt button was open so he could breathe easily. He could feel the sweat sticking his white cotton shirt to his back. This weather was following a pattern he recognized; it would get hotter and hazier until it ended in a storm.

'What have you got?' he asked.

'You'll see in a minute.' Despite the weather, Ken Blackstone looked cool as usual. He wore a lightweight navy-blue suit with a grey herringbone pattern, a crisp white shirt with a stiff collar and a garish silk tie, secured by a gold tie-clip in the shape of a pair of handcuffs. Banks was willing to bet that his top button was fastened.

Blackstone was tall and slim with light brown hair, thin on top but curly over the ears, and a pale complexion, definitely not the sun-worshipping kind. His Cupid's bow lips and wire-rimmed glasses made him look about thirty, when he was, in fact, closer to Banks's age. He had a long, dour sort of face and spoke with a local accent tempered by three years at Bath University, where he had studied art history.

Blackstone had, in fact, become something of an expert on art fraud after his degree, and he often found himself called in to help out when something of that nature happened. In addition, he was a fair landscape artist himself, and his work had been exhibited several times. Banks remembered Blackstone and Sandra getting into a long conversation about the Pre-Raphaelites at a colleague's

wedding once, and remembered the stirrings of jealousy
he had felt. Though he was eager to learn, read, look and
listen as much as his time allowed, Banks was always
aware of his working-class background and his lack of a
true formal education.

They arrived at a car guarded by two hot-looking
uniformed constables and Banks stood back to survey it.
Ancient, but not old enough to attract attention as an
antique, the light blue Ford Escort was rusted around the
bottom of the chassis and had spider-leg cracks on the passenger side of the windscreen. It matched the description,
as far as that went.

'How long's it been here?' Banks asked.

'Don't know,' said Blackstone. 'Our lads didn't notice it
until last night. When they ran the number they found it
was stolen.'

Banks knelt by the front tyre. Flat. There was plenty of
soil and gravel lodged in the grooves. They could have it
analysed and at least discover if it came from around
Arkbeck Farm. He looked through the grimy window. The
beige upholstery was dirty, cracked and split. A McDonald's
coffee cup lay crushed on the floor at the driver's side, but
apart from that he could see nothing else inside.

'We've looked in the boot,' said Blackstone. 'Nothing.
Not even a jack or a spare tyre. I've arranged for it to be
taken to our police garage for a thorough forensic examination, but I thought you'd like a look at it *in situ* first.'

'Thanks,' said Banks. 'I don't expect we'll get any
prints, if they were pros, but you never know. Who's the
lucky owner?'

'Bloke called Ronald Hamilton.'

'When did he report it missing?'

Blackstone paused before answering. 'Friday morning.

Said he left it in the street as usual after he got in about five or six in the evening and it was gone when he went out at ten the next morning. Thought it was maybe kids joyriding. There's been a lot of it on the estate lately. It's not the safest place in the city. He lives on the Raynville estate in Bramley. Ring any bells?'

Banks shook his head. Pamela Jeffreys lived in Armley, which wasn't far away, and Daniel Clegg lived in Chapel Allerton, a fair distance in both miles and manners. Most likely the killers had picked it at random a good distance from where they lived. 'That's four days ago, Ken,' said Banks. 'And nobody spotted it before last night?'

Again, Blackstone hesitated. 'Hamilton's an unemployed labourer,' he said finally. 'He's got at least one wife and three kids that we know of, and lately he's been having a few problems with the social. He's also got a record. Dealing. Aggravated assault.'

'You thought he'd arranged to have it nicked for the insurance?'

Blackstone smiled. 'Something like that. I wasn't involved personally. I don't know what you lot do, but here in the big city we don't send detective inspectors out on routine traffic incidents.'

Banks ignored the sarcasm. It was just Blackstone's manner. 'So your lads didn't exactly put a rush on it?'

'That's right.' Blackstone glanced towards the horizon and sighed. 'Any idea, Alan, how many car crimes we've got in the city now? You yokels wouldn't believe it. So when some scurvy knave comes on with a story about a beat-up old Escort, you think he'd have to pay somebody to steal that piece of shit. So let the fucking insurance company pay. They can afford it. In the meantime we've got joyriding kids, real villains and organized gangs of car thieves to deal with. I'm not making excuses, Alan.'

'Yeah, I know.' Banks leaned against a red Orion. The metal burned through his shirt, so he stood up straight again.

'Didn't you once tell me you came up from the Met for a peaceful time in rural Yorkshire?' Blackstone asked.

Banks smiled. 'I did.'

'Getting it?'

'I can only suppose it's got proportionately worse down there.'

Blackstone laughed. 'Indeed. Business is booming.'

'Have you talked to Hamilton?'

'Yes. This morning. He knows nothing. Believe me, he's so scared of the police he'd sell his own mother down the tubes if he thought we were after her.' Blackstone made an expression of distaste. 'You know the type, Alan, belligerent one minute, yelling that you're picking on him because he's black, then arse-licking the next. Makes you want to puke.'

'Where's he from?'

'Jamaica. He's legit; we checked. Been here ten years.'

'What's his story?'

'Saw nothing, heard nothing, knows nothing. To tell you the truth, I got the impression he'd driven back from the pub after a skinful then settled in front of the telly with a few cans of lager while his wife fed the kiddies and put them to bed. After that he probably passed out. Whole bloody place smelled of shitty nappies and roll-ups and worse. We could probably do him for possession if it was worth our while. At ten the next morning he staggers out to go and sign on, finds his car missing and, bob's your uncle, does the outraged citizen routine on the local bobby, who's got more sense, thank the lord.'

Blackstone stood, slightly hunched, with his hands in his pockets, and kicked at small stones on the tarmac. You could see your face in his shoes.

'Do me a favour, Ken, and have another go at him. You said he was done for dealing?'

'Uh-huh. Small stuff. Mostly cannabis, a little coke.'

'It's probably just a coincidence that the car used belongs to a drug dealer, but pull his record and have another go at him all the same. Find out who his suppliers are. And see if he has any connections with St Corona. Friends, family, whatever. There might be a drug connection or a Caribbean connection in Rothwell's murder, and it's a remote possibility that Mr Hamilton might have done some work for the organization behind it, whoever they are.'

'You mean he might have *loaned* his car?'

'It's possible. I doubt it. I think we're dealing with cleverer crooks than that, but we'd look like the rear end of a pantomime horse if we didn't check it out.'

'Will do.'

'Have you questioned the neighbours?'

'We're doing a house-to-house. Nothing so far. Nobody sees anything on these estates.'

'So that's that?'

'Looks like it. For the moment, anyway.'

'No car-park attendant?'

'No.' Blackstone pointed to the rubble. 'As you can see, it's just an old schoolyard with weeds growing through the tarmac. The school was knocked down months ago.'

Banks looked around. To the south-west he could see the large dome of the Town Hall and the built-up city centre; to the west stood the high white obelisk of the university's Brotherton Library, and the rest of the horizon seemed circled with blocks of flats and crooked terraces of back-to-backs poking through the surrounding rubble like charred vertebrae. 'I could use a break on this, Ken,' Banks said.

'Aye. We'll give it our best. Hey up, the lads have come to pick up the car.'

Banks watched the police tow-team tie a line to the Escort. 'I'd better be off,' he said. 'You'll let me know?'

'Just a minute,' said Blackstone. 'What are your plans?'

'I'm checking into the Holiday Inn. For tonight, at least. There's a couple of people I want to talk to again in connection with Clegg and Rothwell – Clegg's secretary and his ex-wife, for a start. I'd like to get a clearer idea of their relationship now we've got a bit more to go on.'

'Holiday Inn? Well, la-di-da. Isn't that a bit posh for a humble copper?'

Banks laughed. 'I could do with a bit of luxury. Maybe they'll give me the sack when they see my expenses. These days we can't even afford to do half the forensic tests we need.'

'Tell me about it. Anyway, if you're going to be sticking around, I'd appreciate it if we could have a chat. There seems to be a lot going on here I don't know about.'

'There's a lot I don't know about, too.'

'Still . . . I'd appreciate it if you would fill me in.'

'No problem.'

Blackstone hesitated and shifted from foot to foot. 'Look,' he said, 'I'd like to invite you over for a bit of home-cooking but Connie left a couple of months ago.'

'I'm sorry to hear that,' said Banks. 'I didn't know.'

'Yeah, well, it happens, right? Comes with the territory. Still taking care of that lovely wife of yours?'

'You wouldn't think so by the amount of time we've spent together lately.'

'I know what you mean. That was one of the problems. She said we were living such separate lives we might as well make it official. Anyway, I'm not much of a cook myself. Besides, Connie got the house and I'm in a rather small bachelor flat for the moment. But there's a decent Indian restaurant on Eastgate, near the station, if you fancy it? It's called the Shabab. About half past six, seven o'clock? We might have something on Hamilton and the car by then, too.'

'All right,' said Banks. 'You're on. Make it seven o'clock.'

'And, Alan,' said Blackstone as Banks walked away, 'you watch yourself. Hotels give married men strange ideas sometimes. I suppose it's the anonymity and the distance from home, if you know what I mean. Anyway, there's some seem to act as if the normal vows of marriage don't apply in hotels.'

Banks knew what Blackstone meant, and he felt guilty as an image of Pamela Jeffreys flashed unbidden through his mind.

TWO

Susan Gay heard Sergeant Hatchley burp before she had even opened the office door after more fruitless interviews with Rothwell's legitimate clients. She felt apprehension churn in her stomach like a badly digested meal. She could not work with Hatchley; she just couldn't.

Hatchley sat at his desk, smoking. The small, stifling room stank of stale beer and pickled onions. The warped window was open about as far as it would go, but that didn't help much. If this oppressive weather didn't end soon, Susan felt she would scream.

And, by God, he's repulsive, she thought. There was his sheer bulk, for a start – a rugby prop forward gone to fat. Then there was his face: brick-red complexion, white eyelashes and piggy eyes; straw hair, thinning a bit at the top; a smattering of freckles over a broad-bridged nose; fleshy lips; tobacco-stained teeth. To cap it all, he wore a shiny, wrinkled blue suit, and his red neck bulged over his tight shirt collar.

From the corner of her eye, Susan noticed the coloured picture on the cork-board: long blonde hair, exposed skin. Without even stopping to think, she walked over and pulled it down so hard the drawing-pin shot right across the room.

'Oy!' said Hatchley. 'What the hell do you think you're playing at?'

'I'm not playing at anything,' Susan said, waving the picture at him. 'With all respect, sir, I don't care if you are my senior officer, I won't bloody well have it!'

A hint of a smile came to Hatchley's eyes. 'Calm down, lass,' he said. 'You've got steam coming out of your ears. Maybe you're being a bit hasty?'

'No, I'm not. It's offensive. I don't see why I should have to work with this kind of thing stuck to the walls. You might think it's funny, but I don't. *Sir.*'

'Susan. Look at it.'

'No. Why—'

'Susan!'

Slowly, Susan turned the picture over and looked at it. There, in all her maternal innocence, Carol Hatchley, with her long blonde hair hanging over her shoulders, held her naked, newborn baby to her breast, which was covered well beyond the point of modesty by a flesh-tone T-shirt. Susan felt herself blush. All she had seen were the woman's face, hair and a lot of skin colour. 'I . . . I thought . . .' She could think of nothing else to say.

'I know what you thought,' said Hatchley. 'You thought my daughter's head was a tit. You *could* apologize.'

Susan felt such a fool she couldn't even bring herself to do that.

'All right,' Hatchley said, putting his feet up on the desk, 'then you can listen to me. Now, nobody's ever going to convince me that looking at a nice pair of knockers is wrong. Since time immemorial, since our ancestors scratched images on cave walls, men have enjoyed looking at women's tits. They're beautiful things, nothing dirty or pornographic about them at all.'

'But they're private,' Susan blurted out. 'Don't you understand? They're a woman's private parts. You don't see pictures of men's privates all over the place, do you? You wouldn't like people staring at yours, would you?'

'Susan, love, if I thought it would make you happy I'd drop my trousers right now. But that's not the point. What I'm saying is it's my opinion that there's nowt wrong in admiring a nice pair of bristols. A lot of people agree with me, too. But you don't like it.' He held up his large hand. 'All right, now I might not be the most sensitive bloke in Christendom, and I certainly reserve my right to disagree with you, but I'm not that much of a monster that I'd use my rank to expose you to something you feel offends you day in, day out, however wrongheaded I think you are. I respect your opinion. I don't agree with you, and I never will, but I respect it. I can live without.

'And another thing. I know you're a bugger about smoking. I'll try and cut down on the cigarettes in the office, too. But don't expect miracles, and don't expect it's going to be all bloody give and no take on my part. You don't like my smoke. I don't like your perfume. It makes my nose itch and it's probably rotting my lungs as we speak. But for better or for worse, lass, we've got to work together, and we've got to do it in the same damn little cubby-hole for the time being. Mebbe one day we'll have separate offices. Myself, I can hardly wait. But for now, let's just keep the window open and make a bit of an effort to get along, all right?'

Susan nodded. She felt all the wind go out of her sails. She swallowed. 'All right. Sorry, sir.'

Hatchley swung his legs to the floor and rubbed his hands together. 'We'll say no more, then. Now, about that wadding?'

'Yes, sir?'

Hatchley burped again and put his hamlike hand to his mouth. 'Shaved pussies. Smooth and shiny as a baby's bottom.'

'Yes, sir.' Susan felt herself blush again and hated herself for it. Hatchley smiled at her. He seemed to be enjoying himself. Her spirits sank. She had thought for a moment that he might be getting serious about the case, but here he was simply creating another opportunity to embarrass her.

'Aye. Now, I know that's not a lot to go on, but at least we know it's not kiddie porn or the bum brigade. And we've got penetration and a clear image of "a penis in an excited state", as it says in the book, so this is definitely under-the-counter stuff.'

'True, sir.'

'And as far as I can tell,' he went on, 'there's no sign of dogs or cats, either.'

'Sir, can you get to the point?' Susan couldn't keep the impatience out of her voice.

'Hold your horses, lass.' He started to laugh. 'Get that? No animals. Hold your horses? Never mind. The point is, shaved pussies aren't exactly ten a penny, though if we'd come up with something *really* kinky it would have made my job a lot easier. I mean, there aren't many people sell photos of Rottweilers bonking thirteen-year-old girls that we don't know about.'

'I still don't see what you're getting at, sir,' said Susan, a little calmer. She should have known that, if anyone was, Hatchley would be an expert on pornography. 'Surely most of that stuff is sent through the mail from abroad, or from London?'

'Not all of it. There's a fair chance it was bought under the counter somewhere. When I did my stint on Vice with West Yorkshire a few years back, I made one or two useful contacts. Now, if we're assuming these lads were at all local, the odds are they're from the city, as there aren't that many killers-for-hire living in rural areas. Too exposed. That means Leeds, Bradford, Manchester, maybe Newcastle or Liverpool at a stretch. Now if the boss thinks this Clegg chap from Leeds was involved, then Leeds is as good a choice as any, agreed?'

Susan nodded. 'Yes. The daughter, Alison, thought the man had a Leeds accent. She could be wrong about that, of course. Not everyone's accurate on voices. I don't reckon I could tell the difference. But it looks like they've found the car used for the job there. Anyway, as I've already told you, West Yorkshire's got some men asking around. Have had for days.'

'Well, you know how I hate sitting idle,' Hatchley said. 'Guess where I've been this lunchtime.'

'The Queen's Arms, sir?'

Hatchley smiled. 'Not far off. We'll make a detective of

you yet, lass. I've been having drinks with an old informer of mine in The Oak, that's what.' He touched the side of his nose. 'Lives in Eastvale now, but he used to live in Leeds. Gone straight. See, I thought I probably remembered a few purveyors of this kind of porn – if they're still around, that is – and it's odds on that some wet-behind-the-ears young pansy DC fresh from university doesn't even know they exist. There aren't as many as you think, you know, at least not selling shaved pussy porn. It *is* something of a specialist taste. Anyway, there's still plenty prefer the friendly old corner shop to the impersonal supermarket, if you get my drift. I'm not talking about sex shops – I imagine they've all been checked already – just regular newsagents that sell a bit of imported stuff from under the counter along with their *Woman's Weekly*s and gardening magazines. Harmless enough. Hardly any reason for our lads to be interested, really. So I asked my old friend.'

'And?'

'Yes. They're still in business, still selling the same kind of stuff to the same old customers. Some of them, anyway. A couple have retired, some have moved on, and one's dead. Heart attack. Not business-related. The point is, I knew these blokes were a bit bent, but I left them alone. In exchange, they'd pass on the odd tip if anyone came hawking really serious stuff, like kiddie porn or snuff films. Live and let live. Now, what I propose is that you and me go to Leeds and ask a few questions of our own.' He looked at his watch. 'Tomorrow, of course. Don't worry, I'll arrange permission from the super and from West Yorkshire CID. Are you game?'

Susan was aware of her jaw dropping. He made sense, all right, and that was the problem. She was about to go on a porn hunt with Sergeant Hatchley, she could feel it in her bones. But it could pay off. If it led to the owner of the wadding, that would be feathers in both their caps. She swallowed.

'It's a hell of a long shot,' she said.

Hatchley shrugged. 'Nothing ventured, nothing gained. What do you say?'

Susan thought for a moment. 'All right,' she said. 'But *you*'ve got to convince Superintendent Gristhorpe.'

'Right, lass,' Hatchley beamed, rubbing his hands together. 'You're on.'

Oh my God, thought Susan, with that sinking feeling. *A porn hunt.* What have I let myself in for?

THREE

By the looks of it, the heat had drawn one or two refugees from the Magistrates Court over to Park Square. Two skinheads, stripped to the waist, dozed on the grass under a tree. One, lying on his back, had tattoos up and down his arms and scars criss-crossing his abdomen, old knife wounds by the look of them; the other, on his stomach, boasted a giant butterfly tattoo between his shoulder-blades.

In Clegg's office, Betty Moorhead was still holding the fort and fighting off her cold.

'Oh, Mr Banks,' she said when he entered the ante-room. 'It's nice to see a friendly face. There's been nothing but police coming and going since you were last here, and nobody will tell me anything.'

Had she forgotten he was a policeman, too? he wondered. Or was it just that he had been the first to arrive and she had somehow latched on to him as a lifeline?

'Some men in suits took most of his papers,' she went on, 'and there's been others asking questions all day. They've got someone keeping an eye on the building as well, in case those two men come back. Then there was that man from Scotland Yard. I don't know what's what. They all had identification cards, of course, but I don't know whether I'm coming or going.'

Banks smiled. 'Don't worry, Betty,' he said. 'I know it sounds complicated, but we're all working together.'

She nodded and pulled a tissue from the box in front of her and blew her nose; it looked red-raw from rubbing. 'Is there any news of Mr Clegg?' she asked.

'Nothing yet. We're still looking.'

'Did you talk to Melissa?'

'Yes.'

'How is she?'

Banks didn't really know what to say. He wasn't used to giving out information, just digging it up, but Betty Moorhead was obviously concerned. 'She didn't seem unduly worried,' he said. 'She's sure he'll turn up.'

Betty's expression brightened. 'Well, then,' she said. 'There you are.'

'Do you mind if I ask a few more questions?'

'Oh, no. I'd be happy to be of help.'

'Good.' Banks perched at the edge of her desk and looked around the room. 'Sitting here,' he said, 'you'd see everyone who called on Mr Clegg, wouldn't you? Everyone who came in and out of his office.'

'Yes.'

'And if people phoned, you'd speak to them first?'

'Well, yes. But I did tell you Mr Clegg has a private line.'

'Did he receive many calls on it?'

'I can't say, really. I heard it ring once in a while, but I was usually too busy to pay attention. I'm certain he didn't give the number out to just anyone.'

'So you didn't unintentionally overhear any of the conversations?'

'I know what you're getting at,' she said, 'and you can stop right there. I'm not that sort of a secretary.'

'What sort?'

'The sort that listens in on her boss's conversations. Besides,' she added with a smile, 'the walls are too thick. These are old houses, solidly built. You can't hear what's being said in Mr Clegg's office with the door shut.'

'Even if two people are having a conversation in there?'

'Even then.'

'Or arguing?'

'Not that it happened often, but you can only hear the raised voices, not what they're saying.'

'Did you ever hear Mr Clegg arguing with Mr Rothwell?'

'I don't remember. I don't think so. I mean if they ever did, it would certainly have been a rarity. Normally they were all cordial and businesslike.'

'Mr Clegg specializes in tax law, doesn't he?'

'Yes.'

'How many clients does he have?'

'That's very hard to say. I mean, there are regular clients, and then people you just do a bit of work for now and then.'

'Roughly? Fifty? A hundred?'

'Closer to a hundred, I'd say.'

'Any new ones?'

'He's been too busy to take on much new work this year.'

'So there's been no new clients in, say, the past three months?'

'Not really, no. He's done a bit of extra work for friends of friends here and there, but nothing major.'

'What I'm getting at,' Banks said, leaning forward, 'is whether there's been anyone new visiting him often or phoning in the past two or three months.'

'Not visiting, no. There's been a few funny phone calls, though.'

'What do you mean, funny?'

'Well, abrupt. I mean, I know I told you people are sometimes rude and brusque, but usually they at least tell you what they want. Since you were here last, I've been thinking, trying to remember, you know, if there was anything odd. My head's so stuffed up I can hardly think straight, but I remembered the phone calls. I told the other policeman, too.'

'That's okay. Tell me. What did this brusque caller say?'

'I don't know if it was the same person each time, and it only happened two or three times. It was about a month ago.'

'Over what time period?'

'What? Oh, just a couple of days.'

'What did he say? I assume it was a *he*?'

'Yes. He'd just say, "Clegg?" And if I said Mr Clegg was out or busy, he'd hang up.'

'I see what you mean. What kind of voice did he have?'

'I couldn't say. That's all I ever heard him say. It just sounded ordinary, but clipped, impatient, in a hurry.'

'And this happened two or three times over a couple of days?'

'Yes.'

'You never heard the voice again?'

'I never had that sort of call again, if that's what you mean.'

'Nobody visited the office who sounded like the man?'

She sneezed, then blew her nose. 'No. But I told you, I don't think I would recognize it.'

'It wasn't anything like one of the men who came around asking questions?'

'I don't know. I don't think so. I'm sorry.'

'That's all right.'

'What's going on?'

'We don't know,' Banks lied. He was testing Gris-thorpe's theory about Clegg's involvement in Rothwell's murder, but he didn't want Betty Moorhead to realize he suspected her boss of such a crime. Certainly the odd phone calls *could* have been from someone giving him orders, or from the people he hired to do the job. The timing was about right. 'Do you think Mr Clegg might have given this caller his private number?'

She nodded. 'That's what must have happened. The first two times, Mr Clegg was out or with a client. The third time, I put the caller through, and he never called me again.'

'And you're sure you never put a face to the voice?'

'No.'

Banks stood up and walked around the small room. Well-tended potted plants stood on the shelf by the small window at the back that looked out on to narrow Park Cross Street. Clegg had obviously been careful where Betty Moorhead was concerned. If he had been mixed up with hired killers and Caribbean dictators, he had been careful to keep them at arm's length. He turned back to Betty. 'Is there anything else you can tell me about Mr Clegg?'

'I don't know what you mean.'

'How would you describe him as a person?'

'Well, I wouldn't know.'

'You never socialized?'

She blushed. 'Certainly not.'

'Had he been depressed lately?'

'No.'

'Did Mr Clegg have many women calling on him?'

'Not as far as I know. What are you suggesting?'

'Did you ever see or hear mention of a woman called Pamela Jeffreys? An Asian woman.'

She looked puzzled. 'No. She wasn't a client.'

'Did he have a girlfriend?'

'I wouldn't know. He kept his private life private.'

Banks decided to give up. Melissa Clegg might know a bit more about her husband's conquests, or Ken Blackstone's men would question his colleagues and perhaps come up with something. It was after five and he was tired of running around in circles. Betty Moorhead clearly didn't know anything else, or if she did she didn't realize its importance. Getting at information like that was like target practice in the dark.

Why not just accept Gristhorpe's theory that Clegg had arranged for Rothwell to be killed, and that they hadn't a hope in hell of finding either Clegg or the killers? And what could they do to Martin Churchill, if indeed he was behind it all? Banks didn't like the feeling of impotence this case was beginning to engender.

On the walk back to his hotel, Banks picked up a half-bottle of Bell's. It would be cheaper than using the minibar in his room. As he threaded his way among the office workers leaving the British Telecom Building for their bus stops on Wellington Street, Banks wished he could just go home and forget about the whole Clegg-Rothwell-Calvert mess.

After leaving Blackstone at the car park, he had phoned Pamela Jeffreys at home, half hoping she might be free for a drink that evening, but he had only got her answering machine. She was probably playing with the orchestra or something. He had left a message anyway, telling her which hotel he was staying at, and now he was feeling guilty. He remembered Blackstone's warning about hotels.

On the surface, he wanted to apologize for their mis-understanding yesterday, but if truth be told, he had let himself get a bit too carried away with his fantasies. Would he do anything if he had the chance? If she agreed to come back to his hotel room for a nightcap, would he try to seduce her? Would he make love to her if she were willing? He didn't know.

He remembered his attraction to Jenny Fuller, a professor of psychology who occasionally helped with cases, and wondered what his life would be like now if he had given in to his desires then. Would he have told Sandra? Would they still be together? Would he and Jenny still be friends? No answer came.

Rather glumly, he recalled the bit at the beginning of the Trollope biography he was reading, where Trollope considers the dreary sermons persuading people to turn their backs on worldly pleasure in the hope of heaven to come and asks, if such is really the case, then 'Why are women so lovely?' That set him thinking again about Pamela's shapely, golden body, her bright personality and her passion for music. Well, at least he had a curry with Ken Blackstone to look forward to, and time for a shower and a rest before that. He thought he might even check out the hotel's Health and Leisure Club, maybe have a swim, take a sauna or a whirlpool.

There were no messages. Banks went straight up to his room, took off his shoes and flopped on the bed. He phoned Sandra, who wasn't in, then called the Eastvale station again and spoke to Susan Gay. Nothing new, except that she sounded depressed.

•

After a brisk shower, much better than the tepid dribble at home, he poured himself a small Scotch and put the television on while he dried off and dressed. He caught the end of the international news and heard that the St Corona riots had been put down swiftly and brutally by Martin Churchill's forces. And Burgess wanted to give the man a retirement villa in Cornwall?

After that, he was only half paying attention to the local news, but at one point, he saw a house he recognized and heard the reporter say, '. . . when she failed to report for rehearsals today. Police are still at the scene and so far have refused to comment . . .'

It was Pamela Jeffreys's house, and outside it stood two patrol cars and an ambulance. Stunned, Banks sat on the side of the bed and tossed back his Scotch, then he got his jacket out of the cupboard and left the room so fast he forgot to turn off the television.

10

ONE

It was hard to imagine that anything terrible could happen on such a fine spring evening, but the activity around the little terrace house in Armley indicated that evil made no allowances for the weather.

Three police cars were parked at angles in front of the house. Beyond the line of white tape, reporters badgered the PCs on guard duty, one of whom jotted down Banks's name and rank before he let him through. Neighbours stood on their doorsteps or by privet hedges and gazed in silence, arms folded, faces grim, and the people working their allotments stopped to watch the spectacle. A small crowd also stood gawping from the steps of the Sikh Temple down the street.

Banks stood on the threshold of the living room. Whatever had happened here, it had been extremely violent: the glass coffee table had been smashed in two; the three-piece suite had been slashed and the stuffing ripped out; books lay torn all over the carpet, pages reduced to confetti; the glass front of the cocktail cabinet was shattered and the crystal-ware itself lay in bright shards; the music stand lay on the floor with the splintered pieces and broken bow of Pamela's viola beside it; even the print of Ganesh over the fireplace had been taken from its frame and torn up. Worst of all, though, was the broad dark stain on the cream carpet. Blood.

One of the officers cracked a racist joke about Ganesh and another laughed. The elephant god was supposed to be the god of good beginnings, Banks remembered. Upstairs, someone was whistling 'Lara's Theme' from *Doctor Zhivago*.

'Who the hell are you?'

Banks turned to face the plain-clothes man coming out of the wreckage of the kitchen.

'Press?' he went on before Banks had time to answer. 'You're not allowed in. You ought to bloody well know that. Bugger off.' He grabbed Banks's arm and steered him towards the door. 'What does that fucking useless PC think he's up to, letting you in? I'll have his bloody balls for Christmas tree decorations.'

'Hang on.' Banks finally managed to get a word in and jerk his arm free of the man's grasp. He showed his card. The man relaxed.

'Oh. Sorry, sir,' he said. 'Detective Sergeant Waltham. I wasn't to know.' Then he frowned. 'What's North Yorkshire want with this one, if you don't mind my asking?'

He was in his early thirties, perhaps a few pounds overweight, about three inches taller than Banks, with curly ginger hair. He had a prominent chin, a ruddy complexion and curious catlike green eyes. He wore a dark brown suit, white shirt and plain green tie. Behind him stood a scruffy-looking youth in a leather jacket. Probably his DC, Banks guessed.

'First things first,' said Banks. 'What happened to the woman who lives here?'

'Pamela Jeffreys. Know her?'

'What happened to her? Is she still alive?'

'Oh, aye, sir. Just. Someone worked her over a treat.

Broken ribs, broken nose, broken fingers. Multiple lacerations, contusions. In fact, multiple just about everything. And it looks as if she broke her leg when she fell. She was in a coma when we found her. First officer on the scene thought she was dead.'

Banks felt a wave of fear and anger surge through his stomach, bringing the bile to his throat. 'When did it happen?' he asked.

'We're not sure, sir. There's a clock upstairs was smashed at twenty past nine, but that doesn't necessarily mean anything. A bit too Agatha Christie, if you ask me. Doc thinks last night, but we're still interviewing the neighbours.'

'So you think she lay there for nearly twenty-four hours?'

'Could be, sir. The doctor said she'd have bled to death if she hadn't been a good clotter.'

Banks swallowed. 'Raped?'

Waltham shook his head. 'Doc says no signs of sexual assault. When we found her she was fully clothed, no signs of interference. Some consolation, eh?'

'Who found her?'

'One of her musician friends got worried when she didn't show up for rehearsals this morning. Some sort of string quartet or something. Apparently she'd been a bit upset lately. He said she was usually reliable and had never missed a day before. He phoned the house several times during the day and only got her answering machine. After work he drove by and knocked. Still no answer. Then he had a butcher's through the window. After that, he phoned the local police. He's in the clear.'

Banks said nothing. DS Waltham leaned against the banister. The scruffy DC squeezed by them and went upstairs. In the front room, someone laughed out loud again.

Waltham coughed behind his hand. 'Er, look, sir, is there something we should know? There'll have to be questions, of course, but we can be as discreet as anyone if we have to be. What with you showing up here and . . .'

'And what, Sergeant?'

'Well, I recognize your voice from her answering machine. It *was* you, wasn't it?'

Banks sighed. 'Yes, yes it was. But no, there's nothing you need to be discreet about. There is probably a lot you should know. Shit.' He looked at his watch. Almost seven. 'Look, Sergeant, I'd clean forgot I'm supposed to be meeting DI Blackstone for dinner.'

'*Our* DI Blackstone, sir?'

'Yes. Know him?'

'Yes, sir.'

'Do you think you can get one of the PCs to page him or track him down? It's the Shabab on Eastgate.'

Waltham smiled. 'I know it. Very popular with the lads at Millgarth. I'll see to it, sir.'

He went to the door and spoke to one of the uniformed constables, then came back. 'He's on his way. Look, sir, PC O'Brien there just told me there's an old geezer across the street thinks he might have seen something. Want to come over?'

'Yes. Very much.' Banks followed him down the path and through the small crowd. One or two reporters shouted for comments, but Waltham just waved them aside. PC O'Brien stood by the low, dark stone wall that ran by the allotments, talking to a painfully thin old man wearing a grubby, collarless shirt. Behind them, other allotment workers stood in a semicircle, watching, some of them leaning on shovels or rakes. Very Yorkshire Gothic, Banks thought.

'Mr Judd, sir,' O'Brien said, introducing Waltham, who, in turn, introduced Banks. 'He was working his allotment last night just before dark.' Waltham nodded and O'Brien walked off. 'Keep those bloody reporters at bay, will you, please, O'Brien?' Waltham called after him.

Banks sat on the wall and took out his cigarettes. He offered them around. Waltham declined, but Mr Judd accepted one. 'Might as well, lad,' he croaked, tapping his chest. 'Too late to worry about my health now.'

He did look ill, Banks thought. Sallow flesh hung off the bones of his face above his scrawny neck with its turkey-flaps and puckered skin, like a surgery scar, around his Adam's apple. The whites of his eyes had a yellow cast, but the dark blue pupils glinted with intelligence. Mr Judd, Banks decided, was a man whose observations he could trust. He sat by and let Waltham do the questioning.

'What time were you out here?' Waltham asked.

'From seven o'clock till about half past nine,' said Judd. 'This time of year I always come out of an evening after tea for a bit of peace, weather permitting. The wife likes to watch telly, but I've no patience with it, myself. Nowt but daft buggers acting like daft buggers.' He took a deep draw on the cigarette. Banks noticed him flinch with pain.

'Were you the only one working here?' Waltham asked.

'Aye. T'others had all gone home by then.'

'Can you tell us what you saw?'

'Aye, well it must have been close to knocking-off time. It were getting dark, I remember that. And this car pulled up outside Miss Jeffreys's house. Dark and shiny, it were. Black.'

'Do you know what make?'

'No, sorry, lad. I wouldn't know a Mini from an Aston Martin these days, to tell you the truth, especially since we've been getting all these foreign cars. It weren't a big one, though.'

Waltham smiled. 'Okay. Go on.'

'Well, two men gets out and walks up the path.'

'What did they look like?'

'Hard to say, really. They were both wearing suits. And one of them was a darkie, but that's nowt to write home about these days, is it?'

'One of the men was black?'

'Aye.'

'What happened next?'

Judd went through a minor coughing fit and spat a ball of red-green phlegm on the earth beside him. 'I packed up and went home. The wife needs a bit of help getting up the apples and pears to bed these days. She can't walk as well as she used to.'

'Did you see Miss Jeffreys open the door and let the men in?'

'I can't say I was watching that closely. One minute they were on the doorstep, next they were gone. But the car was still there.'

'Did you hear anything?'

'No. Too far away.' He shrugged. 'I thought nothing of it. Insurance men, most like. That's what they looked like. Or maybe those religious folks, Jehovah's Witnesses.'

'So you didn't see them leave?'

'No. I'd gone home by then.'

'Where do you live?'

Judd pointed across the street. 'Over there. Number fourteen.' It was five houses down from Pamela Jeffreys's. 'Been there forty years or more, now. A right dump it was when we first moved in. Damp walls, no indoor toilets, no bathroom. Had it done up over the years, though, bit by bit.'

Waltham paused and looked at Banks, who indicated he would like to ask one or two questions. Waltham, Banks noted, had been a patient interviewer, not pushy, rude and condescending towards the old, like some. Maybe it was because he had a DCI watching over his shoulder. And maybe that was being uncharitable.

'Did you know Miss Jeffreys at all?' Banks asked.

Judd shook his head. 'Can't say as I did.'

'But you knew her to say hello to?'

'Oh, aye. She was a right nice lass, if you ask me. And a bonny one, too.' He winked. 'Always said hello if she passed me in the street. Always carrying that violin case. I used to ask her if she were in t'mafia and had a machine-gun in it, just joking, like.'

'But you never stopped and chatted?'

'Not apart from that and the odd comment about the weather. What would an old codger like me have to say to a young lass like her? Besides, people round here tend to keep themselves to themselves these days.' He coughed and spat again. 'It didn't used to be that way, tha knows. When Eunice and I first came here there used to be a community. We'd have bloody great big bonfires out in the street on Guy Fawkes night – it were still just cobbles, then, none of this Tarmac – and everyone came out. Eunice would make parkin and treacle-toffee. We'd wrap taties in foil and put 'em in t'fire to bake. But it's all changed. People died, moved away. See that there Sikh Temple?' He pointed down the street. 'It used to be a Congregationalist Chapel. Everyone went there on a Sunday morning. They had Monday whist drives, too, and a youth club, Boys'

Brigade and Girl Guides for the young uns. Pantos at Christmas.

'Oh, aye, it's all changed. People coming and going. We've got indoor toilets now, but nobody talks to anyone. Not that I've owt against Pakis, like. As I said, she was a nice lass. I saw them taking her out on that stretcher an hour or so back.' He shook his head slowly. 'Nowadays you keep your door locked tight. Will she be all right?'

'We don't know,' Banks said. 'We're keeping our fingers crossed. Did she have many visitors?'

'I didn't keep a lookout. I suppose you mean boy-friends?'

'Anyone. Male or female.'

'I never saw any women call, not by themselves. Her mum and dad came now and then. At least, I assumed it was her mum and dad. And there was one bloke used to visit quite regularly a few months back. Used to park outside our house sometimes. And don't ask me what kind of car he drove. I can't even remember the colour. But he stopped coming. Hasn't been anyone since, not that I've noticed.'

'What did this man look like?'

'Ordinary really. Fair hair, glasses, a bit taller than thee.'

Keith Rothwell – or Robert Calvert, Banks thought. 'Anyone else?'

Judd shook his head then smiled. 'Only you and that young woman, t'other day.'

Banks felt Waltham turn and stare at him. If Judd had seen Banks and Susan visit Pamela Jeffreys on Saturday, then he obviously didn't miss much – morning, afternoon or evening. Banks thanked him.

'We'll get someone to take a statement soon, Mr Judd,' said Waltham.

'All right, son,' said the old man, turning back to his allotment. 'I won't be going anywhere except my final resting place, and that'll be a few months off, God willing. I only wish I could have been more help.'

'You did fine,' said Banks.

'What the bloody hell was all that about, sir?' Waltham asked as they walked away. 'You didn't tell me you'd been here before.'

Banks noticed Ken Blackstone getting out of a dark blue Peugeot opposite the Sikh Temple. 'Didn't have time,' he said to Waltham, moving away. 'Later, Sergeant. I'll explain it all later.'

TWO

Banks and Blackstone sat in an Indian restaurant near Woodhouse Moor, a short drive across the Aire valley from Pamela Jeffreys's house, drinking lager and nibbling at pakoras and onion bhajis as they waited for their main courses. Being close to the university, the place was full of students. The aroma was tantalizing – cumin, coriander, cloves, cinnamon, mingled with other spices Banks couldn't put a name to. 'Not exactly the Shabab,' Blackstone had said, 'but not bad.' A Yorkshire compliment.

In the brief time they had been there, Banks had explained as succinctly as he could what the hell was going on – at least to the extent that he understood it himself.

'So why do you think they beat up the girl?' Blackstone asked.

'They must have thought she knew where Daniel Clegg was, or that she was hiding something for him. They ripped her place up pretty thoroughly.'

'And you think they're working for Martin Churchill?'

'Burgess thinks so. It's possible.'

'Do you think it was the same two who visited Clegg's secretary and his ex-wife?'

'Yes. I'm certain of it.'

'But they didn't beat up either of them, or search their places. Why not?'

'I don't know. Maybe they were getting desperate by the time they got to Pamela. Let's face it, they'd found out nothing so far. They must have been frustrated. They felt they'd done enough pussyfooting around and it was time for business. Either that or they phoned their boss and he told them to push harder. They also probably thought she was lying or holding out on them for some reason, maybe something in her manner. I don't know. Perhaps they're just racists.'

Banks shook his head, feeling a sudden ache and rage. He couldn't seem to banish the image of Pamela Jeffreys at the hands of her torturers: her terror, her agony, the smashed viola. And would her broken fingers ever heal enough for her to play again? But he didn't know Blackstone well enough to talk openly about his feelings. 'They'd been polite but pushy earlier,' he said. 'Maybe they just ran out of patience.'

The main course arrived: a plate of steaming chapatis, chicken bhuna and goat vindaloo, along with a selection of chutneys and raita. They shared out the dishes and started to eat, using the chapatis to shovel mouthfuls of food and mop up the sauce. Blackstone ordered a couple more lagers and a jug of ice-water.

'There is another explanation,' Blackstone said between mouthfuls.

'What?'

'That she *did* know something. That she was involved in the double-cross, or whatever it was. From the quick look I got at her house, I'd agree there's no doubt they were looking for something. DS Waltham suggested the same thing.'

'Don't think I haven't considered it,' Banks said, carefully piling a heap of the hot vindaloo on a scrap of chapati. 'But I'm sure she didn't even know Clegg.'

'That's only what she told you, remember.'

'Nobody else contradicted her, Ken. Not Melissa Clegg, not the secretary, not even Mr Judd.'

'Oh, come on, Alan. The old man can't have seen everything. Nor could the secretary or the ex-wife have *known* everything. Maybe Clegg never visited her at her home. They could have had some clandestine relationship, met in secret.'

'Why the need for secrecy? Neither of them was married.'

'Perhaps because they were involved in some funny business – not necessarily of a sexual nature – and it wouldn't be good to be seen together. Maybe she was involved in whatever scam Clegg and Rothwell had going?'

Banks shook his head. 'Clegg was a lawyer, Rothwell a financial whizz-kid and Pamela Jeffreys is a classical musician. It just doesn't fit.'

'They *could* have had business interests in common, though.'

'True. Anything's possible. But remember, Pamela Jeffreys knew *Robert Calvert*. She told me they met by chance in a pub. She'd never heard of Keith Rothwell until after his murder, when his photo appeared in the papers. She had no reason to lie. She was even putting herself in an awkward situation by calling us. She needn't have done so. We hadn't heard of Robert Calvert and might never have done if it weren't for her. Usually people want to stay as far away from a murder investigation as they can get. You know that, Ken. Until we find out differently, we have to assume that Calvert was a persona invented by Rothwell, with Clegg's help, solely for pleasure.'

Blackstone swallowed a mouthful of bhuna. 'I sometimes think I could do with one of those myself,' he said.

Banks laughed. 'Calvert helped Rothwell express another side of his nature, a side he couldn't indulge at home. Or perhaps it helped him be the way he used to be, relive something he'd lost. As Calvert, he'd have fun gambling and womanizing, and probably subsidizing himself with his illicit earnings from the money-laundering. And Pamela Jeffreys wasn't his only conquest, you know. There were no doubt others before her, and she was convinced that he'd met someone else, someone he'd really fallen for.'

'That would upset the apple-cart, wouldn't it?' said Blackstone.

Banks stopped chewing for a moment.

'Alan?' Blackstone said. 'Alan, are you all right? I know the curry's hot, but . . .'

'What? Oh, yes. It was just something you said, that's all. I'm surprised I never thought of it before.'

'What?'

'If *Calvert* really did do it, you know, fall in love, the real thing, with all the bells and whistles, then what would happen to Rothwell?'

'I don't get you. It's the same person, isn't it?'

'Yes and no. What I mean is, how could he go on living his Rothwell life, the one we assumed was his *real* life, at Arkbeck Farm with Mary, Alison and Tom? Forgive me, I'm just thinking out loud, going nowhere. It doesn't matter.'

'I do see what you mean,' said Blackstone. 'It would bugger up everything, wouldn't it?'

'Hmm.' Banks finished his meal and washed away some of the spicy heat with a swig of watery lager. His lips still burned, though, and he felt prickles of sweat on his scalp. The signs of a good curry.

'Did the suspects in the Jeffreys beating know about Rothwell?' Blackstone asked.

Banks shook his head. 'Don't know. They haven't been seen locally, and they certainly don't match the daughter's description of his killers.'

'How old is she?'

'Alison? Fifteen.'

'She didn't see their faces. Could she be wrong?'

'It's possible, but not that wrong, I don't think. Nothing matches.'

'Just a thought. I mean, if Rothwell and Clegg were in the laundering business together, and whoever they were working for sent a couple of goons to find Clegg and whatever money he's made off with, you'd think they'd start with Rothwell's family, wouldn't you?'

'Perhaps. But we've been keeping too close a watch. They wouldn't dare show up within twenty miles of Arkbeck Farm.'

'And another thing: if they killed Rothwell, why did they use different people to chase down Clegg? It seems a bit excessive, doesn't it?'

'Again,' said Banks, 'I can only guess. I think some of what's been happening took them by surprise. It's possible that they asked Clegg to get rid of Rothwell and he hired his own men. As you know, we're looking into what connections he might have had with criminal types.'

Blackstone nodded. 'I see,' he said. 'Then Clegg became a problem and they had to send their own men?'

'Something like that.'

'Makes sense. Clegg was a bit of a ladies' man, you know, according to my DC who talked to his colleagues,' Blackstone said.

'Yes. His estranged wife, Melissa, suggested as much. Did he have a girlfriend?'

'Yes. Apparently nothing serious since he split up with his wife. Prefers to play the field. Recently he's been seeing a receptionist from Norwich Insurance. Name of Marci Lapwing, if you can believe that. Aspiring actress. DC Gaitskill had a word with her this morning. Says she's a bit of a bimbo with obvious attractions. But he's a bit of an arsehole himself, is Gaitskill, so I'd take it with a pinch of salt. Anyway, they saw each other the Saturday before Clegg's disappearance. They went for dinner, then to a nightclub in Harehills. She spent the night with him and he took her home – that's Seacroft – after a pub lunch out at the Red Lion in Burnsall on Sunday afternoon. She hasn't seen or heard from him since.'

'Is she telling the truth?'

'Gaitskill says so. I'd trust him on that.'

'Okay. Thanks, Ken.'

'Clegg had a reserved parking space at the back of the Court Centre. According to what we could find out, he used to eat at a little trattoria on The Headrow after work on Thursdays. The waiters there remember him, all right. Nothing odd about his behaviour. He left about six-thirty or a quarter to seven last Thursday, heading west, towards where his car was parked, and that's the last sighting we have.'

'The car?'

'Red Jag. Gone. We've put it out over the PNC along with this.' Blackstone took a photograph from his briefcase and slid it over the tablecloth. It showed the head and shoulders of a man in his early forties, with determined blue eyes, a slightly crooked nose, fair hair and a mouth that had a cruel twist to its left side.

'Clegg?'

Blackstone nodded and put the photograph back in his briefcase. 'We've also been through Clegg's house in Chapel Allerton. Nothing. Whatever he was up to, he kept it at the office.'

'Anything on Hamilton and the other car?'

'The boffins are still working on the car. I pulled Hamilton's record myself and we had another chat with him at the station this afternoon.' He shook his head. 'I can't see it, Alan. The man's as thick as two short planks. I don't think he's even *heard* of St Corona, and he's strictly small fry on the drugs scene. By the time he gets his stuff to sell, it's been stepped on by just about every dealer in the city.'

'It was just a thought. Thanks for giving it a try.'

'No problem. We'll have another shot in a day or two, just in case. And we'll keep a discreet eye on him. Look, back to what I was saying before. How do you think the goons knew about Pamela Jeffreys if she wasn't involved?'

Banks felt the anger flare up inside him again, but he held it in check. 'That's all too easy,' he said. 'Remember, they were also following me around yesterday. I think they started at Clegg's office first thing yesterday morning and one, or both of them, stayed on my tail until I spotted them outside Calvert's flat that evening. They didn't know who the hell I was, and the only other person I met that they hadn't talked to already was Pamela Jeffreys. They must have thought we were in it together. I met her near the hall where she was rehearsing, and either one of them hung around to follow her home, or they found out some other way who she was and where she lived.

'She must have looked like their best lead so far. They thought she had some connection with Clegg and that she knew where he was or was holding something for him. Clegg has obviously got something they want. Most likely money. If he was laundering for their boss, then it looks like he might have skipped with a bundle. Either that or he's got some sort of evidence for blackmail – books, bank account records. And that's probably what they were looking for when they tore her place apart. Back to square one. The goons worked Pamela over because they thought she knew something, or had something of theirs. She didn't. And I blame myself. I should have bloody well known I was putting her at risk.'

'Come off it, Alan. How could you know?'

Banks shrugged and tapped out a cigarette. He was the only smoker in the entire restaurant and had to ask the waiter specially for an ashtray. It was getting like that these days, he noted glumly. He'd have to stop sometime soon; he knew he was only postponing the inevitable. He had thought about getting a nicotine patch, then quickly dismissed the idea. It was the feel of the cigarette between his fingers he wanted, the sharp intake of tobacco smoke into the lungs, not some slow oozing of poison through his skin into his blood. Pity about the health problems.

He felt rather like St Augustine must have felt when he wrote in his *Confessions*: 'Give me chastity and continency – but not yet!'

'You know what really pisses me off?' Banks said after he had lit the cigarette. 'Dirty Dick Burgess was following me around that day, too, and it wouldn't surprise me at all if he'd seen them outside Melissa Clegg's shop.'

'How would he know who they are?'

'Oh, I think he knows them, all right.'

'Even so, what could he have done? They hadn't broken any laws.'

Banks shrugged. 'I suppose not. It's too bloody late now, anyway,' he said. 'Let's just hope they don't go back to see Betty Moorhead and Melissa Clegg.'

'Don't worry. Charlie Waltham will have them both covered by now. He's a good bloke, Alan. And he'll have descriptions of Mutt and Jeff out, too. They won't get far.'

'I hope not,' said Banks. 'I bloody hope not. I'd like a few minutes alone with them in a quiet cell.'

THREE

Back at the hotel, Banks felt caged. Anger burned inside him like the hot Indian spices, but it would take more than Rennies to quell it. What a bloody fool he'd been to do nothing when he realized he had been followed. He had practically signed Pamela Jeffreys's death warrant, and it was through no virtue of his that she had survived her ordeal. So far.

He poured himself a shot of Bell's and turned to the television. Nothing but a nature programme, a silly comedy, an interview with a has-been politician and an old Dirty Harry movie. He watched Clint Eastwood for a while. He had never much enjoyed cop films or cop programmes on television, but watching right here and now, he could identify with Dirty Harry tracking down the villains and dealing with them in his own way. He had meant what he said to Blackstone. A few minutes alone with Pamela Jeffreys's attackers and they would know what police brutality was all about.

But he hated himself when he felt that way. Luckily, it was rare. After all, policemen are only human, he reminded himself. They have their loyalties, their lusts, their prejudices, their agonies, their tempers. The problem was that they have to keep these emotions in check to do their jobs properly.

'You go home and puke in your own time if you want to get anywhere in this job, lad,' one of his early mentors had told him at a grisly crime scene. 'You don't do it all over the corpse. And you go home and punch holes in your own wall, not in the child molester's face.'

Unable to concentrate, even on Dirty Harry, he turned off the television. He couldn't stand up, couldn't sit down, didn't know what he wanted to do. And all the time, the anger and pain churned inside him, and he couldn't find a way to get them out.

He picked up the phone and dialled the code for Eastvale, then put it down before he started dialling his own number. He wanted to talk to Sandra, but he didn't think he could explain his feelings to her right now, especially the way they'd been drifting apart of late. God knew, under normal circumstances she was an understanding wife, but this would be pushing it a bit far: a woman he had lusted after, fantasized about, gets beaten within a hair's breadth of her life, and he's whipping himself over it. No, he couldn't explain that to Sandra.

And it wasn't just a fantasy. Had things turned out differently, he would have phoned Pamela Jeffreys again and would probably be having dinner or drinks with her right now, plucking up the courage to ask her up to his hotel room, Bell's at the ready. Well, he would never know the outcome now; his virtue hadn't even been put to the test. Hadn't St Augustine said something about that, too, or was that someone else?

He phoned the hospital, and after a bit of officious rank-pulling, actually got a doctor on the line. Yes, Ms Jeffreys was stable but still in intensive care . . . no, she was still unconscious . . . there was no way of telling when or if she would come round . . . no idea yet if there was any permanent damage. He didn't feel any better when he hung up.

It was just after nine-thirty. He knocked back the rest of the glass of Scotch, grabbed his sports jacket and went out. Maybe a walk would help, or the anonymous comfort of a crowded pub, not that he expected Leeds city centre on a Tuesday evening to be the West End.

He walked along Wellington Street past the National Express coach station and the tall Royal Mail Building to City Square, which was deserted except for the silent nymphs, who stood bearing their torches around the central statue of the Black Prince on his horse. From somewhere along Boar Lane, a drunk shouted in the night; a bottle smashed and a woman laughed loudly.

Banks crossed City Square. He walked fast, trying to burn off some of his rage, and soon found himself in the empty Bond Street Centre with only his reflection in the shop windows he passed.

His memories of Leeds's city centre were vague, but he was sure that somewhere among the jungle of refurbished Victorian arcades and modern shopping centres there were a number of pubs down the dingy back alleys that riddled the heart of the old city centre.

And he was right.

The first one he found was an old brass, mirrors and dark wood Tetley's house with a fair-sized crowd and a jukebox at tolerable volume. He ordered a pint and stood sideways at the bar, just watching people chat and laugh. It was mostly a young crowd. Only kids seemed to venture into the city centres at night these days. Perhaps that was why their parents and grandparents stayed away. The pubs in Armley and Bramley, in Headingley and Kirkstall, would be full of locals of all age groups mixed together.

As he leaned against the bar, drinking and smoking, nobody paid him any attention. Banks had always been pleased that he didn't stand out as an obvious policeman. There'd be no mistaking Hatchley or Ken Blackstone no matter how 'off duty' they were, but Banks could fit in almost anywhere without attracting too much attention. Over the years, he had found it a useful quality. It wasn't only that he didn't look like a copper, whatever that meant, but for some reason his presence didn't set off the usual warning bells. At the same time, he didn't like to sit or stand with his back to the door, and he didn't miss much.

He finished his pint quickly and ordered another one, lighting up again. He was smoking too much, he realized, and he would feel it in the morning. But that was the morning. In the meantime, it gave him something to do with his hands, which, left to their own devices, curled and hardened into fists.

His second pint went down easily, too. The ebb and flow of conversation washed over him. Loudest was a group of two middle-aged couples sitting behind the engraved smoked glass and dark wood at the side of the door. The only people over twenty-five, apart from Banks and the bar staff, they had all had a bit too much to drink. The men were on pints of bitter, and the women on oddly coloured concoctions with umbrellas sticking out of them and bits of fruit floating around. By the sound of things, they were celebrating the engagement of one couple's daughter, who wasn't present, and this brought forth all the old, blue jokes Banks had ever heard in his life.

'There's these three women,' said one of the men. 'The prostitute, the nymphomaniac and the wife. After sex, the prostitute says, "That's it, then," all businesslike. The nympho says, "That's *it*?" And the wife says, "Beige. I think the ceiling should be beige."'

They howled with laughter. One of the women, a rather blowsy peroxide blonde, like a late-period Diana Dors, with too much make-up and unfocused eyes, looked over and winked at Banks. He winked back and she nudged her friend. They both started to laugh. A man Banks assumed to be her husband popped his head around the divide and said, 'Tha's welcome to her, lad, but I'll warn thee, she'll have thee worn out in a week. Bloody insatiable, she is.' She hit him playfully and they all laughed so much they had tears in their eyes. Banks laughed with them, then turned away. The barmaid raised her eyebrows and drew a finger across her throat. Banks drank up and moved on.

Outside, he noticed that the evening had turned a little cooler and dark clouds were fast covering the stars. There was an electric edge to the air that presaged a storm. As if he didn't feel tense and wound up enough already without the bloody weather conspiring against him, too.

The next pub, down another alley off Briggate, was busier. Groups of young people stood about outside, leaning against the wall or sitting on the wooden benches. The place danced with long shadows like something out of an old Orson Welles film. Banks took his pint out into the narrow, whitewashed alley and rested it on a ledge at elbow level, like a bar.

He thought of his last meeting with Pamela Jeffreys. She had run off in tears and he had stood there like an idiot in the park watching his ice-cream melt. He had wanted to apologize for treating her feelings so shoddily, but at the same time another part of him, the professional side, knew he had had to ask, and knew an apology would never be completely genuine. Still, he was only human; susceptible to beauty, he found her attractive, and he liked her warm, open personality, her enthusiasm for life and her sense of humour. Her connection with music also excited him. How much of that would she have left when she came out of hospital? If she came out.

Now, slurping his ale in a back alley in Leeds, he considered again what Blackstone had suggested about her involvement in the affair, but he didn't think Pamela Jeffreys was that good an actress. She had liked Calvert; they had had simple fun together, with no demands, no strings attached, no deep commitment. And what was wrong with that? She may have felt hurt when he found someone else – after all, nobody likes rejection – but she had liked him enough to swallow her pride and remain friends. She was young; she had energy enough to deal with a few hard knocks. If she had been jealous enough for murder, she would have killed Robert Calvert, probably in his Leeds flat, and if she had been involved in the laundering operation with Rothwell and Clegg, she wouldn't have phoned the Eastvale station and told them about Calvert.

It was close to eleven; most of the people had gone home. Banks ordered one more for the road, as he would be walking beside it, not driving on it. He was glad he had taken a little time out. The drink had helped douse his anger, or at least dampen it for a while. He was also rational enough to know that tomorrow he would be the professional again and nobody would ever know about his complex, knotted feelings of lust and guilt for Pamela Jeffreys.

He drained his glass, put his cigarettes back in his jacket pocket and set off down the alley. It was long and narrow, rough whitewashed stone on both sides, and lit only by a single high bulb behind wire mesh. When he was a couple of yards from the end, two men walked in from the street and blocked the exit. One of them asked Banks for a light.

Contrary to what one sees on television, detectives rarely find themselves in situations where immediate physical violence is threatened. Banks couldn't remember the last time he had been in a fight, but he didn't stop to try to remember. A number of thoughts flashed through his mind at once, but so quickly that an observer would not have seen him hesitate for a second.

First, he knew that they underestimated him; he was neither as drunk nor as unfit as they probably believed. Secondly, he had learned an important lesson from school-yard fights: you go in first, fast, dirty and hard. Real violence doesn't take place in slow motion, like a Sam Peckinpah film; it's usually over before anyone realizes it has begun.

Before they could make their move, Banks took a step closer, pretended to fumble for matches, then grabbed the nearest one by his shirt-front and nutted him hard on the bridge of the nose. The man put his hands over his face and went down on his knees groaning as blood dripped down his shirt-front.

The other hesitated a moment to glance down at his

friend. Mistake. Banks grabbed him by the arm, whirled him around and slammed him into the wall. Before the man could get his breath back, Banks punched him in the stomach, and as he bent forward in pain, brought his knee up into the man's face. He felt cheekbone or teeth smash against his kneecap. The man fell, putting his hands to his mouth to stem the flow of blood and vomit.

His mate had clambered to his feet by now and he threw himself at Banks, knocking him hard into the wall and banging the side of his head against the rough stone. He got in a couple of close body punches, but before he could gain any further advantage, Banks pushed him back far enough to start throwing quick jabs at his already broken nose. In the sickly light of the alley, Banks could see blood smeared over his attacker's face, almost closing one eye and dripping down his chin. The man backed off and slumped against the wall.

By this time, the other was back wobbling on his feet, and Banks went for him. He aimed one sharp blow to the head after the other, splitting an eyebrow, a lip, jarring a tooth loose. The other stumbled away towards the exit. There was no fight left in either of them, but Banks couldn't stop. He kept slugging away at the man in front of him, feeling the anger in him explode and pour out. When the man tried to protect his face with his hands, Banks pummelled his exposed stomach and ribs.

The man backed away, begging Banks to stop hitting him. His friend, swaying at the alley's exit now, yelled, 'Come on, Kev, run for it! He's a fucking maniac! He'll fucking kill us both!' And they both staggered off towards Commercial Street.

Banks watched them go. There was no one else around, thank God. The whole debacle couldn't have taken more than a couple of minutes. When they were out of sight, Banks fell back against the whitewashed wall, shaking, sweating, panting. He took several deep breaths, smoothed his clothes and headed back to the hotel.

11

ONE

The storm broke in the middle of the night. Banks lay in the dark in his strange hotel bed tossing and turning as lightning flashed and thunder first rumbled in the distance then cracked so loudly overhead that the windows rattled.

Once unbound, the shape of his rage was fluid; it could be as easily warped and twisted into fanciful images by sleep as it had been channelled into violence earlier. He kept waking from one nightmare and drifting back into another. Rain lashed against the windows, and in the background something hissed constantly, the way something always hisses in hotel rooms.

In the worst nightmare, the one he remembered the most clearly, he was talking on the telephone to a woman who had dialled his number by mistake. She sounded disoriented, and the longer she spoke the longer the spaces stretched between her words. Finally, silence took over completely. Banks called hello a few times, then hung up. As soon as he had done so, he was stricken by panic. The woman was committing suicide. He knew it. She had taken an overdose of pills and fallen into a coma while she was still on the line. He didn't know her name or her telephone number. If he had kept the line open and not hung up, he would have been able to trace her and save her life.

He awoke feeling guilty and depressed. And it wasn't only his soul that hurt. His head pounded from too much whisky and from the 'Glasgow handshake' he had given one of his attackers, his chest felt tight from smoking, his knuckles ached and his side felt sore where he had been slammed into the wall. His mouth tasted as dry as the bottom of a budgie's cage and as sour as month-old milk. When he got up to go to the toilet, he felt a stabbing pain shoot through his kneecap and found himself limping. He felt about ninety. He took three extra-strength Panadols from his traveller's survival kit and washed them down with two glasses of cold water.

It was four twenty-three a.m. by the red square numbers of the digital clock. Cars hissed by through the puddles in the road. Around the edges of the curtains, he could see the sickly amber glow of the street-lights and the occasional flash of distant lightning as the storm passed over to the north.

He didn't want to be awake, but he couldn't seem to get back to sleep. All he could do was lie there feeling sorry for himself, remembering what a bloody fool he had been. What had started as a simple bit of childish self-indulgence, drowning his sorrows in drink, had turned into a full-blown exhibition of idiocy, and both his skinned knuckles and the empty Scotch bottle on the bedside table were evidence enough of that.

After the fracas, he had dashed back to the hotel and hurried straight up to his room before anyone could notice his bloody knuckles or torn jacket. Once safe inside, he had poured himself a stiff drink to stop the shakes. Lying on the bed watching television until the programmes ended for the night, he had poured another, then another. Soon, the half-bottle was empty and he had fallen asleep.

Now it was time to pay. He had heard once that guilt and shame contributed to the pain of hangovers, and at four thirty-two that morning, he certainly believed it.

Christ, it was so bloody easy to slide down one's thoughts into the pit of misery and self-recrimination at four thirty-two a.m. At four thirty-two, if you feel ill, you just *know* you have cancer; at four thirty-two, if you feel depressed, suicide seems the only way out. Four thirty-two is the perfect time for fear and self-loathing, the time of the dark night of the soul.

But it wouldn't do, he told himself. Feeling sorry for himself just wouldn't bloody well do. So he wasn't perfect. He had contemplated committing adultery. So what? He wasn't the first and he wouldn't be the last. He felt responsible for Pamela Jeffreys's injuries. Maybe, just *maybe*, he should have acted differently when he knew he was being followed – put a guard on everyone he had talked to – but it was a big maybe. He wasn't God almighty; he couldn't anticipate everything.

Most detective work was pissing about in the dark, anyway, waiting for the light to grow slowly, as it was doing now outside. On rare occasions, the truth hit you quick as a lightning flash. But they were very rare occasions indeed. Even then, before the lightning hit you, you had spent months looking for the right place to stand.

So last night, in the alley, he had lost it. So what? Two yobbos had tried to mug him and he had gone wild on them, plastered them all over the walls. Most of it was a blur now, but he remembered enough to embarrass him.

They had just been kids, really, early twenties at most, out looking for aggro. But one had been black and one white, like the men who had put Pamela Jeffreys in hospital. Banks knew in his mind that they weren't the same ones, but when the bubble of his anger burst and the fury unleashed itself, when the blood started to flow, they were the ones he was lashing out at. No wonder they ran away shitting bricks. There was nothing rational about it; blinded by rage, he had thought he was hurting the people he really wanted to hurt. He had taken out his anger on two unwary substitutes. They had simply been in the wrong place at the wrong time.

Still, he told himself, they bloody well deserved it, bleeding amateurs. At least he might have discouraged two apprentice muggers from their chosen career. And nobody would ever know what happened. *They* certainly wouldn't say anything. After all, he *hadn't* killed them; they had managed to run away and lick their wounds. They would survive to fight again another day, if they got back the bottle. It wasn't the worst thing he had ever done. And soon, surely, that feeling of being a total fucking idiot would go away and he could get on with his life.

He dozed briefly and woke again at five forty-one. Not quite as bad as four thirty-two, he thought, at first glance. He got up and looked outside at the grey morning. The road and pavement were still awash with puddles. Green double-decker buses were already running people to work, splashing up the water where it had collected in the gutters. Banks was on the fifth floor, and he could see the grey sky streaked with blood and milk behind the majestic dome of the Town Hall. Already, dim shadows were shuffling out of the Salvation Army shelter opposite.

Banks made a cup of instant coffee with the electric kettle and sachet provided and took it back to bed with him. He turned on the bedside light and picked up the copy of Evelyn Waugh's *Sword of Honour* trilogy he had brought with him. Guy Crouchback's misadventures should cheer him up a bit. At least he didn't have that much misfortune.

He would put last night behind him, he decided, sipping the weak Nescafé. A man was allowed his mistakes; he had just better not cling to them or they would drag him down to the bottom of the abyss.

TWO

At nine o'clock that morning, Susan Gay sat alone on the second pew from the back of the small nondenominational chapel at Eastvale Crematorium. It was cool inside, thanks to a large fan below the western stained-glass window, and the lighting was suitably dimmed. The place smelled of shoe polish, not the usual musty hymn books she associated with chapels.

The service went briskly enough. The rent-a-vicar said a few words about Keith Rothwell's devotion to his family and his dedication to hard work, then he read Psalm 51. Susan thought it particularly apt, all that guff about being cleansed of sin. 'Bloodguiltiness' was a word she hadn't heard before, and it made her give a little shudder without knowing why. The mention of 'burnt offering' brought the unwelcome image of Rothwell's corpse, the head a black mess, as if it had indeed been burned, but 'Wash me; and I shall be whiter than snow' almost made her laugh out loud. It brought to mind an old television advert for detergent, then Rothwell's money-laundering.

After the vicar read a bit from Revelation about a new heaven and a new earth and all sorrow, pain and death disappearing, it was all over.

The Rothwells, all suitably dressed in shades of black

for the occasion, sat in the front row. Throughout the ceremony, Mary sat stiffly, Alison kept glancing around her at the stained-glass and the font and Tom sat hunched over. As far as Susan could tell from behind, nobody reached for a handkerchief.

When she watched them walk out into the sunlight, she could tell she was right: dry eyes; not a tear in sight; Mary Rothwell doing her stiff-upper-lip routine, bearing her loss and grief with dignity.

Everyone ignored Susan except Tom, who approached her and said, 'You're the detective who was at our house when I got back from the States, aren't you?'

'Yes. DC Susan Gay, in case you've forgotten.'

'I hadn't forgotten. What are you doing here?'

'I'd like a word with you, if you can spare a few minutes.'

Tom took a silver pocket-watch from his waistcoat and looked at it. Susan saw it was attached by a chain to one of his belt loops. Somehow, it seemed like a very affected gesture in one so young. Maybe it had impressed the Americans. He slipped it back in his pocket. 'All right,' he said. 'But I can't come just now. Everyone's going back to Mr Pratt's for coffee and cake. I'll have to show up.'

'Of course. How about an hour?'

'Okay.'

'Look, it's a fine morning,' Susan said. 'How about that café by the river, the one near the pre-Roman site?'

'I know it.'

Susan busied herself with paperwork back at the station for three quarters of an hour, then set off to keep her appointment.

The River Swain was flowing swiftly, still high after the spring thaw. On the grass by the bank, the owner of the small café had stuck a couple of rickety white tables and chairs. Susan bought a can of Coke for Tom and a pot of tea for herself and they sat by the water. Two weeping willows framed the rolling farmland beyond. Right across, in the centre of the view, was a field of bright yellow rape.

Flies buzzed around her head, and Susan kept fanning them away. 'How was it?' she asked.

Tom shrugged. 'I hate those kinds of social gatherings,' he said. 'And Laurence Pratt gets on my nerves.'

Susan smiled. At least they had something in common. She let the silence stretch as she looked closely at the youth sitting opposite her. Wavy brown hair fell over his ears about halfway down his neck. He was tanned, slender, handsome and he looked as good now in his mourning suit as he had in torn jeans and a denim shirt. The more she let herself simply feel his presence, the more she was sure she was right about him.

He shifted in his chair. 'Look,' he said, 'I'm sorry about the other day. I was rude, I know. But I was tired, upset.'

'I understand,' Susan said. 'It's just that I got the impression there was something you wanted to tell me.'

Tom looked away over the river. His face was scrunched up in a frown, or maybe the sun was in his eyes. 'You know, don't you?' he asked. 'You can tell.'

'That you're homosexual? I have a strong suspicion, yes.'

'Am I that obvious?'

Susan laughed. 'Maybe not to everyone. Remember, I'm a detective.'

Tom managed a weak smile. 'Funny thing, that, isn't it?' he said. 'You'd think it would be men who'd guess.'

'I don't know. Women are used to responding to men in certain ways. They can tell when something's . . .'

'Wrong?'

'I was going to say missing, but even that's not right.'

'Different, then?'

'That'll do. Look, I'm not judging you, Tom. You mustn't think that. It's really none of my business, unless your sexual preference connects somehow with your father's murder.'

'I can't see how it does.'

'You're probably right. Tell me about this Aston, or Afton, then. When Chief Inspector Banks mentioned the name, you assumed it was a man. Why?'

'Because I didn't assume. I know damn well who he is. His name's Ashton. Bloody Clive Ashton. How could I forget?'

'Who is he?'

'He's the son of one of my father's clients – Lionel Ashton. We were at a party together once. I made a mistake.'

'You made advances towards him?'

'Yes.'

'And they weren't welcome?'

Tom gave a dry laugh. 'Obviously not. He told his father.'

'And?'

'And his father told my father. And my father told me I was disgusting, sick, *queer*, and that I should see about getting myself cured. That's the exact word he used, *cured*. He said it would kill Mum if she ever found out.'

'And he suggested you take off to America for a while, at his expense?'

'Yes. But that came a bit later. First we let it lie while we figured out what was best.'

'What did you do in the meantime?'

Tom looked at her, tilted his can back and finished his Coke. His Adam's apple bobbed up and down. Susan turned away and watched a family of ducks drift by on the Swain. Tom wiped his lips with the back of his hand, then said, 'I followed him.'

She turned back towards him. 'You followed your father? Why?'

'Because I thought he was up to something. He was away so often. He was always so remote, like he wasn't really with us even when he was at home. I thought he was doing damage to the family.'

'He wasn't always like that?'

Tom shook his head. 'No. Believe it or not, Dad used to have a bit of life about him. I'm sorry, I didn't intend to make a bad joke.'

'I know. How long had he been behaving this way?'

'Hard to say. It was gradual, like. But this past couple of years it was getting worse. You could hardly talk to him.' He shrugged.

'Was that the only reason you followed him, because you thought he was up to something?'

'I don't know. Maybe I wanted to get something on *him*. Revenge, I don't know. Find out what *his* guilty secret was.'

'And did you?'

Tom took a deep breath, held it for a moment, then let it out loudly with a nervous laugh. 'This is harder than I thought. Okay. Here goes. Yes. I saw my father with another woman.' He said it fast, staccato-style. 'There, that's it. I said it.'

Susan paused a moment to take the information in, then asked, 'When?'

'Sometime in February.'

'Where?'

'Leeds. In a pub. They were sitting together at a table in the Guildford, on The Headrow. They were holding hands. Christ.' His eyes were glassy with gathering tears. He rubbed the backs of his hands over them and collected himself. 'Do you know what that feels like?' he asked. 'Seeing your old man with another woman. No, of course you don't. It was like a kick in the balls. Sorry.'

'That's all right. Did your father see you?'

'No. I kept myself well enough hidden. Not that they had eyes for anyone but each other.'

'What happened next?'

'Nothing. I left. I was so upset I just got in the van and drove around the countryside for a while. I remember stopping somewhere and walking by a river. It was very cold.'

'Was the woman dark-skinned? Indian or Pakistani?'

Tom looked surprised. 'No.'

Susan took her notepad and pen out. 'What did she look like?'

Tom closed his eyes. 'I can see her now,' he said, 'just as clearly as I could then. She was young, much younger than Dad. Probably in her mid-twenties, I'd guess. Not much older than me. She was sitting down, so I couldn't really see her figure properly, but I'd say it was good. I mean, she didn't look fat or anything. She looked nicely proportioned. She was wearing a blouse made of some shiny white material and a scarf sort of thing, more like a shawl, really, over her shoulders, all in blues, whites and reds. It looked like one of those Liberty patterns. She had long fingers. I noticed them for some reason. Am I going too fast?'

'No,' said Susan. 'I've got my own kind of shorthand. Carry on.'

'Long, tapered fingers. No nail varnish, but her nails looked well kept, not bitten or anything. She had blonde hair. No, that's not quite accurate. It was a kind of reddish blonde. It was piled and twisted on top with some strands falling loose over her cheeks and shoulders. You know the kind of look? Sort of messy but ordered.'

Susan nodded. Hairstyles like that cost a fortune.

'She was extraordinarily good-looking,' Tom went on. 'Very fine, pale skin. A flawless complexion, like marble, sort of translucent. The kind where you can just about see the blue veins underneath. And her features could have been cut by a fine sculptor. High cheekbones, small, straight nose. Her eyes were an unusual shade of blue. They may have been contact lenses, but they were sort of light but very bright blue. Cobalt, I guess. Is that it?'

'It'll do. Go on.'

'That's about all really. No beauty spots or anything. She was wearing long dangly earrings, too. Lapis lazuli. No rings, I don't think.'

'That's a very good description, Tom. Do you think you could work with a police artist on this? I think we'd like to have a talk with this woman, and your description might help us find her.'

Tom nodded. 'No problem. I could paint her myself from memory if I had the talent.'

'Good. We'll arrange something, then. Maybe this evening.'

Tom took his watch out again. 'I suppose I'd better be going home. Mum and Alison need my support.'

'Did you ever challenge your father about what you saw?' Susan asked.

Tom shook his head. 'I came close once, when he kept going on about how disappointed he was in me, how sick

I was. I told him I was disappointed in him, too, but I wouldn't tell him why.'

'What did he say?'

'Nothing. Just carried on as if I hadn't spoken.'

'Does your mother know?'

He shook his head. 'No. She doesn't know. I'm sure of it.'

'Do you think she suspects?'

'Maybe. Who knows? She's been living in a bit of a dream world. I'm worried about her, actually. Sometimes I get the feeling that underneath all the lies she knows the truth but she just won't admit it to herself. Do you know what I mean?'

'Yes. What about Alison?'

'Alison's a sweet thing really, but she hasn't got a clue. Lives in her books. She's Brontë mad, is Alison, you know. Reads nothing but. And she's got notebooks full of her own stories, all in tiny handwriting like the Brontës did when they were kids. Made up her own world. I keep thinking she'll grow out of it, but . . . I don't know . . . she seems even worse since . . . since Dad . . .' He shook his head slowly. 'No, she doesn't know. I wouldn't confide in her. I kept it all to myself. Can you imagine that? I still do. You're the first person I've told.' He stood up. 'Look, I really must be off.'

'We'll be in touch about the artist, then.'

'Yes. Okay. And . . .'

'Yes?'

'Thanks,' he said, then turned abruptly and hurried off.

Susan watched him go down the path, hands in pockets, shoulders slumped. She poured herself another cup of tea, stewed though it was, and looked out at the river. A beautiful insect with iridescent wings hovered a few feet above the water. Suddenly, a chaffinch shot out from one of the trees and took the insect in its beak in mid-air. Susan left her lukewarm tea and headed off to meet Sergeant Hatchley. The porn hunt awaited.

THREE

After Banks had gone for a swim in the hotel pool, taken a long sauna, and put away three cups of freshly brewed coffee and a plateful of bacon and eggs, courtesy of room service, he was feeling much better.

As he made a few phone calls, he tried to remember something that had been nagging away at him since the early hours, something he should do, but he failed miserably. At about the same time that Susan Gay was talking to Tom Rothwell, he went out for his first appointment, with Melissa Clegg.

The morning sun had burned off most of the rain, and the pavements had absorbed the rest, leaving them the colour of sandstone, with small puddles catching the light here and there. As wind ruffled the water's surface, golden light danced inside the puddles.

It wasn't as warm as it had been, Banks noticed. He had left his torn sports jacket at the hotel. All he wore on top was a light blue, open-neck shirt. He carried his notebook, wallet, keys and cigarettes in his briefcase.

A cool wind whispered through the streets, and there were plenty of dark, heavy clouds now lurking on the northern horizon behind their town hall. It looked like the region was in for some 'changeable' weather, as the forecasters called it: sunny with cloudy periods, or cloudy with sunny periods.

He could drive to his appointment, he knew, but the one-way system was a nightmare. Besides, the city centre wasn't all that big, and the fresh air would help blow away the cobwebs that still clung to his brain.

Banks had grown quite fond of Leeds since he had been living in Yorkshire. It had an honest, slightly shabby charm about it that appealed to him, despite the new 'Leeds-look' architecture – redbrick revival with royal blue trim – that had sprouted up everywhere, and despite the modern shopping centres and the yuppie developments down by the River Aire. Leeds was a scruff by nature; it wouldn't look comfortable in fancy dress, no matter what the price. And then there was Opera North, of course.

Avoiding City Square and the scene of the previous evening's debacle, he cut up King Street instead, walked past the recently restored Metropole Hotel, all redbrick and gold sandstone masonry, and along East Parade through the business section of banks and insurance buildings in all their jumbled glory. Here, Victorian Gothic rubbed shoulders with Georgian classicism and sixties concrete and glass. As in many cities, you had to look up, above eye level, to see the interesting details on the tops of the buildings: surprising gables where pigeons nested, gargoyles, balconies, caryatids.

As he walked along The Headrow past Stumps and the art gallery, he became aware again of the sharp pain in his knee, with which he had probably chipped a cheekbone or broken a jaw the previous evening.

He arrived at the Merrion Centre a couple of minutes early. Melissa Clegg had told him on the phone that she had a very busy day planned. She was expecting a number of important deliveries and had appointments with her suppliers. She could, however, allow him half an hour.

There was a quiet coffee bar with outside tables, she told him, on the second level, up the steps over the entrance to Le Phonographique. She would meet him there at half past ten.

Banks found the coffee bar, and an empty table, with no trouble. At that time on a Wednesday morning, the Merrion Centre was practically deserted: especially the upper level, which seemed to have nothing but small offices and hairdressers.

Melissa Clegg arrived on time with all the flurry of the busy executive. When she sat down, she tucked her hair behind her ears. Today, she wore a pink dress cut square at her throat and shoulders.

The last thing on earth Banks felt he needed was another cup of coffee, but he took an espresso just to have something in front of him. Also, by the feel of his chest, he didn't need a cigarette, either, but he lit one nonetheless. The first few drags made him a bit dizzy, then it tasted fine.

'You look a bit the worse for wear,' Melissa observed.

'You should have seen the other two,' Banks said. He could tell by the way she laughed that she didn't believe him, just as he had expected. But he had also noticed the angry contusion high on his left cheek, just to the side of his eye, when he shaved that morning. Another result of his crash into the alley wall. He tried to keep his skinned knuckles out of sight, which made drinking coffee difficult.

'What can I do for you this time, Inspector, or Chief Inspector, is it?'

'Chief Inspector. I don't suppose you've heard anything from your husband?'

'Ex. Well, near as. No, I haven't. But he's hardly likely

to get in touch with me. I still don't know why you're so worried. I'm sure he'll turn up.'

'I don't think so, Mrs Clegg. Remember last time we met I asked you if you knew a Robert Calvert?'

'Yes. I said I didn't and I still don't.'

'I'd appreciate it if you would keep this quiet for the moment, but we believe that Robert Calvert was also Keith Rothwell.'

'I don't understand. Do you mean he had a false name, an alias?'

'Something like that. More, actually. He lived in Leeds, had a flat in the name of Robert Calvert. A whole other life. Mary Rothwell doesn't know, so—'

'Don't worry, I won't say anything. You've got me puzzled.'

'We were, too. But the reason I'm telling you this is that your husband acted as a reference for Robert Calvert in the matter of his bank account and credit card. Also, ironically enough, Calvert listed his employer as Keith Rothwell.'

'Curiouser and curiouser,' said Melissa. 'Daniel must have known about this double life, then?'

'It looks that way.'

'Well, I certainly knew nothing about it. As I told you before, I haven't seen Keith Rothwell since Danny and I split up two years ago.' She frowned. 'I must say it surprises me that Daniel would risk doing something so obviously dishonest as that. Not that dishonesty is beneath him, but it seems too much of a risk for no return.'

'We don't know what the returns were,' Banks said. 'How close are you and Daniel?'

'What do you mean?'

'Did he ever mention a woman called Marci Lapwing to you?'

'God, what a name. No. Who is she? His girlfriend?'

'Someone he's been seeing lately.'

'Well, he wouldn't tell me about her, would he?'

'Why not?'

She shrugged. 'He never does. Maybe he thinks I'd be jealous.'

'Would you?'

'Look, I don't see what it has to do with anything, but no. It's over. O.V.E.R. We made our choices.'

'Is there someone else?'

She blushed a little but met his gaze with steady eyes as she fingered the top of her dress over her freckled collarbone. 'As a matter of fact there is. But I won't tell you anything more. I don't want him dragged into this. It's none of your business, anyway. Danny's probably run off with his bimbo.'

'No. Marci Lapwing is still around. Never mind. Let's move on. How do you explain the two men who visited you?'

'I don't know. Perhaps her husband sent them?'

'Whose husband?'

'The bimbo's. Marci whatever-her-name-is.'

'She's not married. Since we last talked,' Banks said, lowering his voice, 'things have taken several turns for the worse. We're talking about very serious matters indeed. It looks as if your husband might be implicated in murder, money-laundering, theft and fraud, and that he may be partly responsible for the savage beating of a young woman.'

'My God . . . I . . .'

'I know. You didn't take all this seriously. Nor did you want to. Now will you?'

She began to fidget with her coffee-spoon. 'Yes. Yes, of

course. I assume you're talking about Keith Rothwell's murder?'

'Yes.'

'And who has been beaten?'

'A friend of Mr Rothwell's. The way it looks, both Keith Rothwell and your husband were laundering money for a Mr X. We think we know his identity, but I'm afraid I can't reveal it to you. Rothwell was either stealing or threatening to talk, or both, and Mr X asked your husband to get rid of him.'

She shook her head. 'Danny? No. I don't believe it. He couldn't kill anyone.'

'Hear me out, Mrs Clegg. He did as he was asked. Maybe his own life was threatened, we don't know. Immediately after he arranged to get rid of Keith Rothwell, he either became a threat himself, or he made off with a lot of illegal money, so Mr X sent two goons to track him down. Maybe he'd seen it coming and anticipated what they would do. At this point, there's a lot we can only speculate about.'

'And that explains the two men?'

'Yes.' Banks leaned forward and rested his arms on the table. 'They visited your ex-husband's office, they visited you, then they visited a girl they saw me talking to. She was the one they beat up. Now tell me again, Mrs Clegg, have you ever seen or heard of a woman called Pamela Jeffreys? She was born here in Yorkshire, but her family came originally from Pakistan. She's about five foot four, slender figure, with almond eyes and long black hair that she sometimes wears tied back. She has a smooth, dark gold complexion and a gold stud through her left nostril. She's a classical musician, a viola player with the Northern Philharmonia.'

Banks watched Melissa's face as he described Pamela Jeffreys. When he had finished, she shook her head. 'Honestly,' she said, 'I've never seen her, and Danny never mentioned anyone like that. She sounds impressive, but he doesn't go for that type.'

'What type?'

'Bright women. Career women. It scared him to death when I started to make a success of the wine business. At first he could just look down on it as my little hobby. You said she was a classical musician?'

'Yes.'

'He doesn't like classical music. All he likes is that bloody awful trad jazz. A woman like the one you describe would bore Danny to death. Besides, she sounds so gorgeous, I'm sure I'd remember her.'

A gentle gust of wind blew through the centre, carrying the smells of espresso and fried bacon from the café. 'Two more things,' Banks said. 'First, in the time you lived with your husband, did you ever come across any acquaintances, say, or clients of his whom you'd describe as shady?'

She laughed. 'Oh, a tax lawyer has plenty of shady clients, Chief Inspector. That's what keeps him in business. But I assume you mean something other than that?'

'Yes. If Daniel did have anything to do with Keith Rothwell's death, he certainly didn't commit the murder himself, as you pointed out.'

'That's true. The Daniel I know wouldn't have had the stomach for it.'

'So he must have hired someone. You don't usually just walk into your local and say, "Look chaps, I need a couple of killers. Do you think you could help me out?"'

Melissa smiled. 'You might try it at a Law Society

banquet. I'm sure you'd get a few takers. But I see what you mean.'

'So he might have known someone who would consider the task, and it might have been someone he met through his practice. I doubt very much that the two of you socialized with hitmen, but there might be someone who struck you as dangerous, perhaps?'

'Who knows who we socialized with?' Melissa said. 'Who knows anything about anyone, when it comes right down to it? No one immediately springs to mind, but I'll think about it, if I may.'

'Okay.' Banks passed on Alison Rothwell's vague description of the two men, especially the one with the puppy-dog eyes, the only distinguishing feature. 'I'll be at the Holiday Inn here for the next day or so, or you can leave a message with Detective Inspector Blackstone at Millgarth.'

'Is he the one who came over last night with my bodyguard?'

'No, that's Detective Sergeant Waltham. I don't honestly believe you're in any danger, Mrs Clegg – I think they're probably miles from here by now – but it's best to be on the safe side. Are you happy with the arrangement?'

'I didn't really understand all the fuss at first, but after what you've just told me I'll sleep easier tonight for knowing there's someone out there watching over me.' She looked at her watch. 'Sorry, Mr Banks. Time's pressing. You said you had two things to ask.'

'Yes. The other is a bit more personal.'

Melissa raised her eyebrows. 'Yes?'

'I mean personal in the true sense, not necessarily embarrassing.'

She frowned, still looking at him. It was a strong,

attractive face with its reddish tan and freckles over the nose and upper cheeks; every little wrinkle around her grey-blue eyes looked as if it had been earned.

'We think Daniel Clegg has probably done a bunk with a lot of money,' Banks began. 'Enough to set him up for life, otherwise these goons wouldn't be so keen on finding him. But it's a bloody big world if you don't know where to look. The two of you shared your dreams at one stage, I suppose, like most married couples. Where do you think he would go? Where did he dream of living?'

Melissa continued to frown. 'I see what you mean,' she murmured. 'That's an interesting question. Where's Danny's Shangri-la, his Eldorado?'

'Yes. We all have one, don't we?'

'Well, Danny wasn't much of a dreamer, to tell you the truth. He didn't have a lot of imagination. But whenever he talked of winning the pools and packing it all in, it was always Tahiti.'

'Tahiti?'

'Yes. He was a big fan of *Mutiny on the Bounty*. Had every version on video. I think he liked the idea of those bare-breasted native girls serving him long, cool drinks in coconut shells.' She laughed and looked at her watch again. 'Look, Mr Banks, I'm sorry, but I really *do* have to go now. I've got a hell of a day ahead.' She pushed her chair back and stood up.

Banks stood with her. 'Of course,' he said, shaking her hand.

'But if I can be any more help, I'll get in touch. I mean it. I never thought Danny was capable of real evil, but if what you say is true . . .' She shrugged. 'Anyway, I'll give what you said some thought. I . . . just a minute.'

Her brow furrowed and she turned her eyes up, as if

inspecting her eyelashes. She looked at her watch again, bit her lip, then perched on the edge of the chair, knees together, clutching her briefcase to her chest. 'There *was* someone. I really can't stay. I'm going to be late. I can't think of the name, but I might be able to remember if you give me a bit of time. He did have those sort of sad eyes, like a puppy, now I think of it.'

Banks sat forward. 'What were the circumstances?'

'I told you Danny doesn't do criminal work, but he is a solicitor, and apparently he was the only one this chap knew. According to Danny, they met in a pub, had a few drinks, got talking. You know how it is. This chap had been in the army or something, over in Northern Ireland. When he got himself arrested, Danny was the only one he knew to call on.'

'What happened?'

'Danny referred him to someone else. I only remember because he came round to the house once. He wasn't too happy about the solicitor Danny passed him on to for some reason. I think it might have been the fee or something like that. They argued a bit, then Danny managed to calm him down. They had a drink, then the man left. I never saw or heard of him again. I'm sorry, I didn't really hear what was going on. Not that I'd remember now.'

'How long ago was it?'

'A little over two years. Shortly before we separated.'

'And you remember nothing more about this man?'

'No. Not off-hand.'

'What pub did they meet in?'

'I can't remember. Isn't that odd? You mentioning about meeting a killer in a pub? What if it was him?'

'What was he arrested for?'

'It was something to do with assault, I think. A fight. I

know it wasn't really serious. Certainly not murder or anything. Look, I really must go. I'll try and remember more, I promise.'

'Just one thing,' Banks said. 'Can you remember the name of the solicitor your husband referred him to? We might be able to trace him through our records.'

She compressed her lips in thought for a moment, then said, 'Atkins. Of course, it would have been Harvey Atkins. He and Danny are good friends, and Harvey does a fair bit of criminal work.'

'Thank you,' Banks said, but she was already dashing away.

'I'll be in touch,' she called over her shoulder.

Banks headed for the staircase. While he had been talking with Melissa Clegg, he had remembered what it was that had been nagging at him all morning. He decided to satisfy his curiosity before meeting Ken Blackstone. Things were moving fast.

12

ONE

'**Take the scenic route,**' said Sergeant Hatchley. 'We're not in a hurry.'

Instead of going east to the A1 at the roundabout by the Red Lion Hotel, Susan headed south-west along the edge of the Dales through Masham, Ripon and Harrogate.

Hatchley didn't smoke at all during the journey, though he insisted she stop once at a café in Harrogate for a cup of coffee, during which he chain-smoked three cigarettes. It was very different from travelling with Banks. For a start, Banks liked to drive, and with him there was always music, sometimes tolerable, sometimes execrable. Hatchley preferred to sit with his arms crossed and look out of the window at the passing scenery, no doubt with visions of bare breasts flashing through what passed for his mind.

She wished she didn't have to work with men all the time. One crying jag or sharp response, and it was PMT; a day off for any reason meant it was 'that time of the month'. She had to put up with it without complaint, just take it all in her stride.

Maybe she was being unfair, though. Hatchley aside, the men she worked with were mostly okay. Phil Richmond, with whom she spent the most time, was a sweetheart. But Phil was leaving soon.

Superintendent Gristhorpe frightened her a little, perhaps because he made her think of her father, and she always felt like a silly little girl when he was around.

Banks, though, was like an older brother. And, like a brother, he teased her too much, especially about music when they were in the car. She was sure he played some terrible things just to make her uncomfortable. Right now, though, as she approached the busy Leeds Ring Road, she would have welcomed something soothing to listen to.

Susan was building up a nice collection of classical music. Every month, she bought a magazine that gave away a free CD of bits and pieces of the works reviewed. It provided a breakdown of what to listen for at what points of time – like '6:25: The warm and sunny feeling of the spring day returns', or '4:57: Second theme emerges from interplay of brass and woodwinds'. Susan found it very helpful, and if she liked the part she heard, she would buy the complete work, unless it was a lengthy and expensive opera. At the moment her favourite piece was Beethoven's Pastoral Symphony. She knew Banks would approve, but she was too embarrassed to tell him.

Susan went on to think about her talk with Tom Rothwell by the river, and about the agonies he must be going through. It was hard enough being homosexual anywhere, she imagined, but it would be especially tough in Yorkshire, where men prided themselves on their masculinity and women were supposed to know their place and stick to it.

There was a prime example of Yorkshire manhood sitting right next to her, she thought, all Rugby League, roast beef and pints of bitter. And she couldn't imagine what he could find offensive about her perfume. It certainly smelled pleasant enough to her, and she used it sparingly.

The traffic snarled up on the Ring Road, and Hatchley sat there with the tattered Leeds and Bradford *A to Z* on his lap squinting at signs. He was the kind of navigator who shouted, 'Turn here!' just as you passed by the turning. After several misdirections and a couple of hair-raising U-turns, they pulled up outside candidate number one, a newsagent's shop at the edge of a rundown council estate in Gipton.

Two scruffy kids swaggered out as Susan and Hatchley went in. The girl behind the counter couldn't have been more than fifteen or sixteen. She was pale as a ghost and skinny as a rake. Her hair, brown streaked with silver, red and green, teetered untidily on top of her head, and unruly strands snaked down over her white neck and face, partly covering one over-mascaraed eye.

She looked as if she had a small, pretty mouth underneath the full and pouting one she had superimposed with brownish-purple lipstick. Susan also noticed a pungent scent, which she immediately classified as cheap, not at all like her own. The girl rested her ring-laden fingers with the long crimson nails on the counter and slanted her bony shoulders towards them, head tilted to one side. She wore a baggy white T-shirt with SCREW YOU written in black across her flat chest.

'Mr Drake around, love?' Hatchley asked.

She moved her head a fraction; the hair danced like Medusa's snakes. 'In the back,' she said, without breaking the rhythm of her chewing.

He moved towards the counter and lifted the flap.

'Hey!' she said. 'You can't just walk through like that.'

'Can't I, love? Do you mean I have to be announced all formally, like?' Hatchley took out his identification and held it close to her eyes. She squinted as she read. 'Maybe you'd like to get out your salver?' he went on. 'Then I can put my calling card on it and you can take it through to Mr Drake and inform him that a gentleman wishes to call on him?'

'Sod off, clever arse,' she said, slouching aside to let them pass. 'You're no fucking gentleman. And don't call me love.'

'Who have we got here, then?' Hatchley stopped and said, 'Glenda Slagg, feminist?'

'Piss off.'

They went through without further ceremony into the back room, an office of sorts, and Susan saw Mr Drake sitting at his desk.

Below the greasy black hair was the lumpiest face Susan had ever seen. He had a bulbous forehead, a potato nose and a carbuncular chin, over all of which his oily, red skin, pitted with blackheads, stretched tight, and out of which looked a pair of beady black eyes, darting about like tiny fish in an aquarium. His belly was so big he could hardly get close enough to the desk to write. A smell of burned bacon hung in the stale air, and Susan noticed a hotplate with a frying-pan on it in one corner.

When they walked in, he pushed his chair back and grunted, 'Who let you in? What do you want?'

'Remember me, Jack?' said Hatchley.

Drake screwed up his eyes. They disappeared into folds of fat. 'Is it . . .? Well, bugger me if it isn't Jim Hatchley.'

He floundered to his feet and stuck out his hand, first wiping it on the side of his trousers. Hatchley leaned forward and shook it.

'Who's the crumpet?' Drake asked, nodding towards Susan.

'The "crumpet", as you so crudely put it, Jack, is Detective Constable Susan Gay. And show a bit of respect.'

'Sorry, lass,' said Drake, executing a little bow for Susan. She found it hard to hold back her laughter. She knew that old-fashioned sexism was alive and well and living in Yorkshire, but it felt strange to have Sergeant Hatchley defending her honour. Drake turned back to Hatchley. 'Now what is it you want, Jim? You're not still working these parts, are you?'

'I am today.'

Drake held his hands out, palms open. 'Well, I've done nowt to be ashamed of.'

'Jack, old lad,' said Hatchley heavily, 'you ought to be ashamed of being born, but we'll leave that aside for now. Girlie magazines.'

'Eh? What about 'em?'

'Still in business?'

Drake shifted from one foot to the other and cast a beady eye on Susan, guilty as the day is long. 'You know I don't go in for owt illegal, Jim.'

'Believe it or not, at the moment I couldn't care less. It's not you I'm after. And it's *Sergeant* Hatchley to you.'

'Sorry. What's up, then?'

Hatchley asked him about the masked killer with the puppy-dog eyes. Drake was shaking his head before he had finished.

'Sure?' Hatchley asked.

'Aye. Swear on my mother's grave.'

Hatchley laughed. 'You'd swear night was day on your mother's grave if you thought it would get me off your back, wouldn't you, Jack? Nonetheless, I'll believe you, this time. Any ideas where we might try?'

'What have you got?'

'Shaved pussies, excited penises. Right up your alley, I'd've thought.'

Drake turned up his misshapen nose in disgust. 'Shaved pussies? Why, that's pretty much straight stuff. Nay, Jim, times have changed. They're all into the arse-bandit stuff or whips and chains these days.'

'I'm not just talking about the local MPs, Jack.'

'Ha ha. Very funny. Even so.'

Hatchley sighed. 'Benny still in business?'

Drake nodded. 'Far as I know. But he deals mostly in body-piercing now. Very specialized taste.' He looked at Susan. 'You know, love – pierced nipples, labia, foreskins, that kind of thing.'

Susan repressed a shudder.

'Bert Oldham?' Hatchley went on. 'Mario Nelson? Henry Talbot?'

'Aye. But you can practically sell the stuff over the counter, these days, Ji – Sergeant.'

'It's the "practically" that interests me, Jack. You know what the law says: no penetration, no oral sex and no hardons. Anyroad, if you get a whiff of him, phone this number.' He handed Drake a card.

'I'll do that,' said Drake, dropping back into his chair again. Susan thought the legs would break, but, miraculously, they held.

The girl didn't look up from her magazine as they went out. 'Better give that reading a rest, love,' said Hatchley. 'It must be hell on your lips.'

'Fuck off,' she said, chewing gum at the same time.

Shit, thought Susan, it's going to be one of those days.

TWO

Banks was right, he saw, as he stood on the threshold of Robert Calvert's flat and surveyed the wreckage. The only difference between this and Pamela Jeffreys's flat was that there had been no human being hurt and no prized possessions utterly destroyed. Stuffing from the sofa lay strewn over the carpet, which had been partly rolled up to expose the bare floorboards. In places, wallpaper had been ripped down, and the television screen had been shattered.

So they had come back. It supported his theory. They obviously didn't know that Banks was a policeman, didn't know that Calvert's flat had already been thoroughly searched by professionals. If they had known, they would never have come here.

It was as he had suspected. They had started following him when he left Clegg's Park Square office on Monday morning. They must have seen the police arrive first, but from their point of view, the police arrived sometime *after* Banks, and he left alone, so there was no reason to make a connection, certainly none to suspect that *he* was a policeman. For all they knew, he could have been a friend of Betty Moorhead's, or a colleague of Clegg's.

Still looking for clues to Clegg's whereabouts, they had trailed him on his lunch date with Pamela and noted where she was rehearsing. One of them must have found out where she lived. They didn't know about the Calvert flat until Banks led them there, and they must have thought the place had something to do with Clegg. Finally, when Banks saw them from the window, they ran off, only to come back later and search the place when the coast was clear.

Where were they now? Already, their descriptions had been sent to other police forces, to the airports and ports. If the men had any sense, they would lie low for a while before trying to leave the country. But criminals don't always have sense, Banks knew. In fact, more often than not, they were plain stupid.

And what about Rothwell's killers? If the man Melissa Clegg remembered was involved – and it was a big if – then he was local. Was he the kind to stay put or run? And what about his partner?

No one else was at home in the building, and there was no point looking over the rest of the flat. From the box at the corner of the street, Banks went through the motions of calling the local police to report the break-in, but he knew there was nothing they could do. He had no doubts as to *who* had done it; he just had to find them. Dirty Dick Burgess knew something, Banks believed, but he would talk only when he wanted and tell only as little as he needed.

When Banks had finished the call, he took a bus to Millgarth at the bottom of Eastgate. Over the road, on the site of the demolished Quarry Hill flats, stood the new West Yorkshire Playhouse with its 'City of Drama' sign. It seemed uncannily appropriate, Banks thought, given the events of the past couple of days. Beyond the theatre, high on a hill, was Quarry House, new home of the Department of Health and Social Security, and already nicknamed 'The Kremlin' by locals.

Ken Blackstone was in his office bent over a stack of paperwork. He pushed the pile aside and gestured for Banks to sit opposite him.

'No earth-shattering developments to report, before you get your hopes up,' he said. 'We're still no closer to finding Clegg or Rothwell's killers, but there's a couple of interesting points. First off, you might like to know that the lab boys say the dirt and gravel on the tyres of Ronald Hamilton's Escort match that around Arkbeck Farm. They said a lot of other things about phosphates and sulphides or whatever, which I didn't understand, but it looks like the car the killers used. Rest of it was clean as a whistle. And airport security at Heathrow have found Clegg's red Jag in the long-stay car park.'

'Surprise, surprise,' said Banks.

'Indeed. Coffee?'

Banks's stomach was already grumbling from too much caffeine, so he declined. Blackstone went and poured himself a mug from a machine in the open-plan office and returned to his screened-off corner. There was a buzz of constant noise around them – telephones, computer printers, fax machines, doors opening and closing and the general banter of a section CID department – but Blackstone seemed to have carved himself a small corner of reasonably quiet calm.

Banks told him about Calvert's flat.

'Interesting,' said Blackstone. 'When do you think that happened?'

'I'd say before they went to Pamela's,' Banks said. 'Finding nothing there would put them in a fine mood for hurting someone. Is there any news from the hospital?'

Blackstone shook his head. 'No change. She's stable, at least.' He frowned at Banks and touched the side of his own cheek. 'What about you? And I noticed you limping a bit when you came in.'

'Slipped in the shower. Look, Ken, I might have a lead on one of Rothwell's killers.' He went on quickly to tell Blackstone what Melissa Clegg had said about the mysteri-

ous client with the puppy-dog eyes that Clegg had passed
on to Harvey Atkins.

Blackstone put the tip of a yellow pencil to his lower lip.
'Hmm . . .' he said. 'We're already running a check on all
Clegg's contacts and clients. We can certainly check the
court records. At least we've got the brief's name, which
helps a bit. Harvey Atkins is certainly no stranger around
here. He's not a bad bloke, as lawyers go. It's a bit vague,
though, isn't it? About two years ago, she says, something
to do with assault, maybe? Do we know if the bloke was
convicted?'

Banks shook his head. 'I'm afraid we'll have to depend
on the kindness of microchips.'

Blackstone scowled. 'Hang on a minute.' He made
a quick phone call and set the inquiry in motion.
'They say it could take a while,' he said. 'It might be a
long list.'

Banks nodded. 'What do you know about Tahiti?' he
asked.

'Tahiti? That's where Captain Bligh's men deserted in
the film. It's part of French Polynesia now, isn't it?'

'I think so. It's in the South Pacific at any rate. And
Gauguin painted there.'

'Why are you interested?'

Banks told him what Melissa Clegg had said.

'Hmm,' said Blackstone. 'It wouldn't do any harm to
put a few inquiries in motion, check on flights, would it?
Especially now we've found the car at Heathrow. A relative
newcomer might stand out there. I'll see what I can do.'

'Thanks. Anything else?'

'We finished the house-to-house in Pamela Jeffreys's
street. Nothing really, except I think we've fixed the time.
One neighbour remembered hearing some noise at about

nine-fifteen Monday evening, which fits with what the doc said, and with Mr Judd's statement.'

Banks nodded.

'The people on the other side were out.'

'These neighbours,' said Banks, 'they said they just heard *some noise*?'

'Yes.'

'Ken, imagine how much noise it must have made when they smashed that stuff. Imagine how Pamela Jeffreys must have screamed for help when she realized what was happening.'

'I know, I know.' Blackstone shook his head and sighed. 'I suppose they would have gagged her.'

'Still . . .'

'Look, Alan, according to DC Hyatt, who talked to them, they said they thought it was the television at first. He asked them if she usually played her television set so loud, and they said no. Then they said they thought she was having a fight with her boyfriend. He asked them if that was a regular occurrence, too, and again they said no. Then they said, or implied, that dark-skinned people have odd forms of entertaining themselves and that we white folks had best leave them to it.'

'They really said that?'

Blackstone nodded. 'Words to that effect. They're the sort of people who wouldn't cross the street to piss on an Asian if she was on fire. And they don't want to get involved.'

'And that's it?'

'Afraid so.' Blackstone looked at his watch. 'I don't know about you, but I'm a bit peckish. What do you say about lunch, on me?'

Banks didn't feel especially hungry, but he knew he

ought to try to eat something if he were to keep going all day. 'All right, you're on,' he said. 'But no curries.'

THREE

The other shops were not much different from the first: usually with the windows barred or covered in mesh, and usually close to dilapidated, graffiti-scarred corporation estates or surviving pre-war terraces of back-to-backs in areas like Hunslet, Holbeck, Beeston and Kirkstall. One moment the sun was out, the next it looked like rain. Around and around they drove, Hatchley flipping through the *A to Z*, which had now become so well thumbed that the pages were falling out, missing turnings, looking for obscure streets. It was all depressing enough to Susan, and a far cry from the nice big semi at the top of the hill in Sheffield where she grew up.

But Hatchley, she noticed, seemed to relish the task, even though after another three visits they had got nowhere. His reputation for laziness, she was beginning to realize, might be unfounded. He certainly didn't like to waste energy, and usually took the line of least resistance, but he was hardly alone in that.

Susan had known truly lazy policemen – some of them had even made detective sergeant – but none of them were like Hatchley. They simply put in the time until the end of their shift, generally trying to stay out of the way of any situation that might generate paperwork. Hatchley was determined. When he was after something, he didn't let go until he got it.

The fifth shop was larger and more modern than the others, a kind of mini-market cum off-licence that sold milk, tinned foods, bread and all sorts of odds and ends as well as booze, newspapers and magazines. It was on Beeston Road, not far from Elland Road, where Leeds United played, and it was run, Hatchley said, by a man called Mario Nelson, who, as his name suggested, had an Italian mother and an English father.

It was immediately clear to Susan that Mario took after his father. She knew there were blond-haired Italians in the north of the country, but they didn't look as downright Nordic as Mario. Tall, slim, wearing a white smock, he looked far too elegant to be running a shop. In his early fifties, Susan guessed, he was handsome in a Robert Redford sort of way, and he looked as if he would be more comfortable being interviewed on a film set than unpacking a box of mushroom soup, which is what he was doing when they entered. When he saw Hatchley, a look of caution came to his ice-blue eyes. There was nobody else in the shop.

'Mario, old mate,' said Hatchley. 'Long time no see.'

'Not long enough for me,' muttered Mario, putting the box aside. 'What can I do for you?'

'No need to be so surly. How's business?' Hatchley took out a cigarette and lit up.

'There's no smoking in here.'

Hatchley ignored him. 'I asked how's business?'

Mario stared at him for a moment, then broke off eye contact. 'Fair to middling.'

'Doing much special trade?'

'Don't know what you mean. Look, if you've just come to chat, I'm a busy man.'

Hatchley looked exaggeratedly around the shop. 'Doesn't look that way to me, Mario.'

'There's more to running a shop than serving customers.'

'Well, soon as you've answered our questions, you can get back to it.' He described the man in the balaclava. 'Ever seen anyone like that in here? Is he on your list?'

'It's a bit of a vague description.'

'True, but concentrate on the eyes. They'd just about come up to your chin. Poor misguided bloke has an appetite for shaved pussy magazines, and I know you supply them.'

'You've never proved that.'

'Come off it! The only reason you're still in business is that you've done me a few favours over the years. Remember that. You're a filth-peddler. You know I don't like filth-peddlers, Mario. You know I rank them a bit below a dollop of dog-shit on my shoe.'

Hatchley made some very interesting distinctions, Susan thought, some delicate moral judgments. Simple display of naked flesh was fine with him, obviously, but anything more was pornographic. Bit of a puritan, really, when it came down to it.

She watched Mario shift from foot to foot, and she saw something in his eyes other than wariness; she saw that he recognized Hatchley's description, or thought he did. Hatchley noticed it, too. And she saw fear.

Hatchley dropped his cigarette on the floor and ground it out. 'Susan,' he said, 'would you go put up the "Closed" sign, please?'

'You can't do that,' said Mario, coming out from behind the counter and moving to stop Susan. Hatchley got in the way. He was about the same height and two stones heavier. Mario stopped. Susan went to the door and turned the sign over.

'Might as well drop the latch and pull the blinds down, too,' said Hatchley, 'seeing as it's such a quiet time.'

Susan did as he said.

'Right.' Hatchley turned to face Mario. 'What's his name?'

'Whose name? I don't know what you're on about.'

'We're not gormless, Susan and I. We're detectives. That means we detect. And I detect that you're lying. What's his name?'

Mario looked pale. Beads of sweat formed on his brow. Susan almost felt sorry for him. Almost. 'Honest, Mr Hatchley, I don't know what you mean,' he said. 'I run an honest business here. I—'

But before he could finish, Hatchley had grabbed him by the lapels of his shop-coat and pushed him against the shelves. A jar of instant coffee fell to the floor and smashed; tins dropped and rolled all over; a packet of spaghetti noodles burst open.

'Watch what you're doing!' Mario cried. 'That stuff costs money.'

Hatchley pushed him up harder against the shelving, twisting the lapels. Mario's face turned red. Susan was worried he was going to have a heart attack or something. She wished she hadn't become part of this. Gristhorpe would find out, she knew, and she would be thrown off the force in shame. Outside, she heard somebody rattle the door. Do something, her inner voice screamed. 'Sir,' she said levelly. 'Maybe Mr Nelson wants to tell us something, and he's having difficulty speaking.'

Hatchley looked at Nelson and relaxed his grasp. 'Is that so, Mario?'

Mario nodded as best he could under the circumstances. Hatchley let him go. A jar of pickled onions rolled off the shelf and smashed, infusing the air with the acrid smell of vinegar.

'Who is he?' asked Hatchley.

Mario massaged his throat and gasped for breath. 'You
. . . shouldn't . . . have done . . .' he wheezed. 'Could have
k-k-killed me. Weak heart. I c-c-could report you.'

'But we both know you won't, don't we? Imagine trying
to run an honest business with the local police breathing
down your neck day and night. Come on, give us the
name, Mario.'

'I . . . I don't know his name. J-just that he's been in
occasionally.'

'For your under-the-counter stuff? Shaved pussies?'

Mario nodded.

Hatchley shook his head. 'I wouldn't believe it if I hadn't
seen it with my own eyes,' he said, 'but you're lying again.
After all this.' He reached out for Mario's lapels.

'No!' Mario jumped back, dislodging a few more tins
from the shelf. A bottle of gin fell and smashed. He put his
hands out. 'No!'

'Come on, then,' said Hatchley. 'Give.'

'Jameson. Mr Jameson. That's all I know,' said Mario,
still rubbing his throat.

'I want his address, too. He's on one of your paper
routes, isn't he? I'll bet one of your lads delivers his
papers, maybe with a special colour supplement on
Sundays, eh? Come on.'

'No. I don't know.'

'Be reasonable, Mario. It's no skin off your nose, is it?
And it'll put you in good stead with the local bobbies.
What's his address?'

Mario paused a moment, then went behind the counter
and looked in the ledger where he kept the addresses for
newspaper deliveries. 'Forty-seven Bridgeport Road,' he
said. 'But you won't find him there.'

'Oh?'

'Cancelled his papers.'

'How long for?'

'Three weeks.'

'Since when?'

'Last Friday.'

'Where's he gone?'

'I've no idea, have I? Off on his holidays, maybe.'

'Don't come the clever bugger with me.'

'I'm not. Honest.'

'Is that all you know?' Hatchley moved forward and Mario backed off.

'I swear it. We're not mates or anything. He's just a customer. And do me a favour – when you do find him, don't tell him you found out from me.'

'Scared of him?'

'He's got a bit of a reputation for scrapping, that's all. When he's had a few, like. I don't think he'd take kindly.'

'Aye, all right, then,' said Hatchley. 'Susan, would you do the honours?'

Susan went over and unlocked the door. A red-faced old woman bustled in. 'What's going on here? I've been waiting five minutes. My poor Marmaduke is going to starve to death if you—' She stopped talking, looked at the mess on the floor, then back at the three of them.

'Slight accident, Mrs Bagshot,' said Mario, straightening his tie and smiling. 'Nothing serious.'

Hatchley bent down and grabbed a pickled onion. After a cursory check to make sure there was no broken glass clinging to it, he popped it in his mouth, smiled at Mrs Bagshot and left.

FOUR

After a light lunch in the police canteen with Ken Blackstone – a toasted cheese sandwich and a plastic container
of orange juice – Banks set off back to the hotel. The
weather was the same, fast-moving cloud on the wind, sun
in and out casting shadows over the streets and buildings.
He would have to do something about his jacket, he
realized, as he walked past the Corn Exchange. Maybe
he could get it fixed this afternoon. The hotel should be
able to help. Or maybe he should buy a new one.

He wasn't looking forward to explaining his adventures
to Sandra, either. He hadn't phoned her last night, and she
would probably be out until this evening. He could phone
the gallery, he knew, but she would be busy. Besides, it
would only worry her if he told her about the fight over the
telephone. He might get his jacket fixed, but there would
be no hiding the skinned knuckles and bruised cheekbone
from Sandra, let alone the bruises that would soon show
up on his side.

All he had to say was that two kids had tried to mug
him, simple as that. It might not be the complete truth, but
it certainly wasn't a lie. On the other hand, he wondered
who he was trying to fool. If he couldn't talk to Sandra
about what had happened, who could he talk to? Right
now, he just didn't know.

A local train must have just come in, judging from the
hordes issuing from the station and heading for the bus
stops around City Square and Boar Lane. Banks picked up
a *Yorkshire Evening Post* from the aged vendor, who was
shouting out a headline that sounded like 'TURKLE AN
HONEST LIAR' but which, on reading, turned out to be

'TWO KILLED IN HUNSLET FIRE.' Banks refused the free packet of Old El Paso Taco Shells he was offered with his newspaper.

At the hotel, he found three messages: one to call Melissa Clegg at the wine shop; one to meet Sergeant Hatchley and Susan Gay at The Victoria, behind the Town Hall, as soon as possible; and one to call Ken Blackstone at Millgarth. First, he went to his room and phoned Melissa Clegg.

'Oh, Mr Banks,' she said. 'I didn't want to get your hopes up, but I've remembered his name, the man Daniel met in the pub.'

'Yes?'

'Well, I knew there was something funny about it. After I left you I just couldn't get it out of my mind. Then I was filling some orders and I saw it written down. It came to me, just like that.'

'Yes?'

'Irish whiskey. Funny how the mind works, isn't it?'

'Irish whiskey?'

'His name. It was Jameson. I'm sure of it.'

Banks thanked her and called Ken Blackstone.

'Alan, we've got some names for you,' Blackstone said. 'Quite a lot, I'm afraid.'

'Never mind,' said Banks. 'Is Jameson among them?'

Banks heard Blackstone muttering to himself as he went through the list. 'Yes. Yes, there he is. Bloke called Arthur Jameson. Alan, what—'

'I can't talk now, Ken. Can you pull his file and meet me at The Victoria in about fifteen minutes? I assume you know where it is?'

'The Vic? Sure. But—'

'Fifteen minutes, then.' Banks hung up.

13

ONE

It was foolish, Susan knew, but she couldn't help feeling butterflies in her stomach as she turned the corner where Courtney Terrace intersected Bridgeport Road at number thirty-five. It was mid-afternoon; there was no one about. She felt completely alone, and the click of her heels, which seemed to echo from every building, was the only sound breaking the blanket of silence. Her instructions were simple: find out what you can about Arthur Jameson and his whereabouts.

In her blue jacket and matching skirt, carrying a brief-case and clipboard, she looked like a market researcher. A light breeze ruffled her tight blonde curls and a sudden burst of sun through the clouds dazzled her. She could smell rain in the air.

We know he's not at home, she repeated to herself. He has cancelled his papers for three weeks and gone on a long holiday on the proceeds earned from killing Keith Rothwell. He doesn't answer his telephone, and the two men observing the house over the past hour or so have seen no signs of occupation. So there's nothing to worry about.

But still she worried. She remembered Keith Rothwell kneeling there on the garage floor in his suit, his head blown to a pulp. She remembered the tattered pieces of the girlie magazine, ripped images of women's bodies, as if the killer had intended some kind of sick joke.

And she remembered what Ken Blackstone had told her about Jameson at the makeshift briefing in The Victoria. He had been kicked out of the army for rushing half-cocked, against orders, into an ambush that had killed two innocent teenage girls as well as one suspected IRA trigger-man. After that, he had drifted around Africa and South America as a mercenary. Then, back home, he had beaten an Irishman senseless in a pub because the man's Belfast accent hit a raw nerve. Since the GBH, he hadn't done much except work on building sites and, perhaps, the occasional hit, though there was no evidence of this. He had four A-levels and an incomplete degree in Engineering from the University of Birmingham.

Susan looked around her as she walked. Bridgeport Road was a drab street of dirty terrace houses with no front gardens. From each house, two small steps led right on to the worn pavement, and the tarmac road surface was in poor repair. At the back, she knew, each house had a small bricked-in backyard, complete with privy, full of weeds, and each row faced an identical row across an alley. A peculiar smell hung in the air, a mix of raw sewage and brewery malt, Susan thought, wrinkling her nose.

Outside one or two houses, lines of washing propped up by high poles hung out to dry right across the street. A woman came out of her house with a bucket and knelt on the pavement to scour her front steps. She glanced at Susan without much interest, then started scrubbing. If Jameson really is our man, Susan thought, he'll probably be looking for somewhere a bit more upmarket to live after he has laid low for a while.

There was nobody at home in the first two houses; the timid woman at number thirty-nine said she knew nothing about anyone else in the street; the man at number forty-one didn't speak English; the West Indian couple at number forty-three had just moved into the area and didn't know anyone. Number forty-five was out. Susan felt her heart beat faster as she lifted the brass lion's head knocker of number forty-seven, Jameson's house. She was sure the whole street could hear her heart and the knocker thumping in concert, echoing from the walls.

She had it all rehearsed. If the man with the puppy-dog eyes answered the door, she was going to lift up her clipboard and tell him she was doing market research on neighbourhood shopping habits: how often did he use the local supermarket, that kind of thing. Under no circumstances, Banks had said, was she to enter the house. As if she would. As her mother used to say, she wasn't as green as she was cabbage-looking.

But the heavy knocks just echoed in the silence. She listened. Nothing stirred inside. All her instincts told her the house was empty. She relaxed and moved on to number forty-nine.

'Yes?' An old lady with dry, wrinkled skin opened the door, but kept it on the chain.

Susan kept her voice down, even though she was sure Jameson wasn't home. She showed her card. 'DC Susan Gay, North Yorkshire Police. I'd like to talk to you about your neighbour Mr Jameson, if I may.'

'He's not at home.'

'I know. Do you know where he is?'

The face looked at Susan for some time. She couldn't help but be reminded of reptile skin with slit lizard eyes peeping out of the dry folds.

The door shut, the chain rattled, and the door opened again. 'Come in,' the woman said.

Susan walked straight into the small living room, which smelled of mothballs and peppermint tea. Everything was in shades of dark brown: the wallpaper, the wood around the fireplace, the three-piece suite. And in the fireplace stood an electric fire with fake coals lit by red bulbs. All three elements blazed away. There might be a chilly breeze outside, but the temperature was still in the mid-teens. The room was stifling, worse than Pratt's office. As the door closed, Susan suddenly felt claustrophobic panic, though she had never suffered from claustrophobia in her life. A heavy brown curtain hung from a brass rail at the top of the door; it swept along the floor with a long hissing sound as the door closed.

'What's Arthur been up to now?' the woman asked.

'Will you tell me your name first?'

'Gardiner. Martha Gardiner. What's he been up to? Here, sit down. Can I get you a cup of tea?'

Susan remained by the door. 'No, thank you,' she said. 'I can't stop. It's very important we find out where Mr Jameson is.'

'He's gone on his holidays, that's where. Has he done anything wrong?'

'Why do you keep asking me that, Mrs Gardiner? Would it surprise you?'

She chuckled. 'Surprise me? Nowt much surprises me these days, lass. That one especially. But he's a good enough neighbour. When my lumbago plays me up he'll go to the shops for me. He keeps an eye on me, too, just in case I drop dead one of these days. It happens with us old folk, you know.' She grabbed Susan's arm with a scrawny talon and hissed in her ear, 'But I know he's been in jail. And I saw him with a gun once.'

'A gun?'

'Oh, aye. A shotgun.' She let go. 'I know a shotgun when I see one, young lady. My Eric used to have one when we lived in the country, bless his soul. Young Arthur doesn't think I know about it, but I saw him cleaning it through the back window once. Still, he's always polite to me. Gives me the odd pint of milk and never asks for owt. Who am I to judge? If he likes to go off shooting God's innocent creatures, then he's no worse than many a gentleman, is he? Ducks, grouse, whatever. Even though he says he's one of that *green* lot.'

'How long ago did you see him with the shotgun?'

'Couldn't say for certain. Time has a funny way of moving when you're my age. Couple of months, perhaps. Are you going to arrest him? What are you going to arrest him for? Who'll do my shopping?'

'Mrs Gardiner, first we've got to find him. Have you any idea where he went?'

'How would I know? On his holidays, that's what he said.'

'Abroad?'

She snorted. 'Shouldn't think so. Doesn't like foreigners, doesn't Arthur. You should hear him go on about the way this country's gone downhill since the war, all because of foreigners taking our jobs, imposing their ways. No, he's been abroad, he said, and had enough of foreigners to last him a lifetime. Hates 'em all. "Foreigners begin at Calais, Mrs Gardiner, just you remember that." That's what he says. As if I needed reminding. My Eric was in the war. In Burma. Never the same, after. England for the English, that's what Mr Jameson always says, and I can't say I disagree.'

Susan gritted her teeth. 'And all he told you was that he was going on holiday?'

'Aye, that's what he told me. Likes to drive around the English countryside. At least that's what he's done before. Sent me a postcard from the Lake District once. He wished me well and asked me to keep an eye on his place. You know, in case somebody broke in. There's a lot of that these days.' She snorted. 'Foreigners again, if you ask me.'

'I don't suppose he left you a key, did he?'

She shook her head. 'Just asked me to keep an eye out. You know, check the windows, try the door every now and then, make sure it's still locked.'

'When did he leave?'

'Late Thursday afternoon.'

'When did you last see him?'

'Just before he went. About four o'clock.'

'Was he driving?'

'Of course he was.'

'What kind of car does he drive?'

'A grey one.'

'Did he take his shotgun with him?'

'I didn't see it, but he might have. I don't know. I imagine he'd want to shoot a few animals if he's on holiday, wouldn't he?'

Susan could feel the sweat itching behind her ears and under her arms. Her breathing was becoming shallow. She couldn't take much more of Mrs Gardiner's hothouse atmosphere. But there were other things she needed to know.

'What make was the car?'

'A Ford Granada. I know because he told me when he bought it.'

'I don't suppose you know the number?'

'No. It's new, though. He only got it last year.'

That would make it an 'M' registration, Susan noted. 'How was he dressed?' she asked.

'Dressed? Just casual. Jeans. A short-sleeved shirt. Green, I think it was. Or blue. I've always been a bit colour blind. One of those anoraks – red or orange, I think it was.'

'And he drove off at about four o'clock on Thursday.'

'Yes, I told you.'

'Was he alone?'

'Aye.'

'Do you have any idea where he was heading first?'

'He didn't say.'

Susan needed to know about any friends Jameson might have entertained, but she knew if she stayed in the house a moment longer she would faint. She opened the door. The welcome draught of fresh air almost made her dizzy. Banks would want to question Mrs Gardiner further, anyway. They would need an official statement. Any other questions could wait. They had enough.

'Thank you, Mrs Gardiner,' she said, edging out of the door. 'Thank you very much. Someone else will be along to see you soon to take a statement.'

And she hurried off down the street, heels clicking in the silence, to where Banks and the rest waited in their cars in the Tesco car park off the main road.

TWO

It took the locksmith all of forty-five seconds to open Arthur Jameson's door for Banks and Blackstone to get in. As it wasn't often that four detectives and two patrol cars appeared in Bridgeport Road, and as it was still a nice enough day, despite the occasional clouds, everyone who happened to be home at the time stood out watching, gathered on doorsteps, swapping explanations. The consensus of opinion very quickly became that Mr Jameson was a child molester, and it just went to show you should never trust anyone with eyes like a dog. And, some added, this kind of thing wouldn't happen if the authorities kept them locked up where they belonged, or fed them bromide with their cornflakes or, better still, castrated them.

Like Mrs Gardiner's, Jameson's front door opened directly into the living room. But unlike the gloomy number forty-nine, this room had cream wallpaper patterned with poppies and cornflowers twined around a trellis. Banks opened the curtains and the daylight gave the place a cheery enough aspect. It smelled a little musty, but that was to be expected of a house that had been empty for almost six days.

Jameson's mug shot and a description of his car had already gone out to police all over the country. They had got the Granada's number quickly enough from the central Driver and Vehicle Licensing Centre in Swansea. Local police were warned *not* to approach him under any circumstances, simply to observe and report.

Hatchley and Susan Gay were taking a statement from the woman next door, whom they had managed to persuade, at Susan's insistence, to accompany them to the local station. Mrs Gardiner had, in fact, been quite thrilled to be asked to 'come down to the station', just like on television, and had managed a regal wave to all the neighbours, who had whistled and whooped their encouragement as she got in the car. Things were on the move.

In the living room, Banks and Blackstone examined a small bookcase filled with books on nature, the English heritage and the environment: rain forests, ozone layers, whaling, oil spills, seal-clubbing, the whole green spectrum. Jameson had a healthy selection on birds, flowers and wildlife in general, including Gilbert White's *Natural History of Selborne* and Kilvert's diaries. There were also a few large picture books on stately homes and listed buildings.

Blackstone whistled. 'Probably a member of Greenpeace and the National Trust, as well,' he said. 'There'll be trouble if we arrest this one, Alan. Loves Britain's heritage, likes furry little animals and wants to save the seals. They'll be calling him the Green Killer, just you wait and see.'

Banks laughed. 'It's not every murderer you meet has a social conscience, is it?' he said. 'I suppose we should take it as an encouraging sign. Loves animals and plants but has no regard for human life.' He pulled a girlie magazine from down the side of a battered armchair. 'Yes, it looks like we've got a real nature boy here.'

After the living room, they went into the kitchen. Everything was clean, neat and tidy: dishes washed, dried and put away, surfaces scrubbed clean of grease. The only sign of neglect was a piece of cheddar, well past its sell-by date, going green in the fridge. The six cans of Tetleys Bitter on the shelf above it would last for a long time yet.

As he looked in the oven, Banks remembered a story he had heard from Superintendent Gristhorpe's nephew in Toronto about a Texan who hid his loaded handgun in the oven when he went to Canada to visit his daughter and son-in-law, Canadian gun laws being much stricter than those in the USA. He forgot about it when he got back, until his wife started to heat up the oven for dinner the first night. After that, he always kept it in the fridge. Jameson didn't keep his shotgun in the oven or the fridge.

The first bedroom was practically empty except for a few cardboard boxes of small household appliances: an electric kettle, a Teasmade, a clock radio. They looked too old and well used to be stolen property. More likely things that had broken, things he hadn't got around to fixing or tossing out. There were also an ironing board and a yellow plastic laundry basket.

The other bedroom, clearly the one Jameson slept in, was untidy but basically clean. The sheets lay twisted on the bed, and a pile of clothes lay on the floor under the window. A small television stood on top of the dresser-drawers opposite the bed. All the cupboard held was clothes and shoes. Perhaps the soil expert might be able to find something on the shoes linking Jameson to Arkbeck Farm and its immediate area. After all, he had succeeded with the car. The only reading material on his bedside table was a British National Party pamphlet.

There was a small attic, reached through a hatch in the landing ceiling. Banks stood on a chair and looked around. He saw nothing but rafters and beams; it hadn't been converted for use at all.

Next, they opened the cistern and managed to get the side of the bath off, but Jameson had avoided those common hiding places.

Which left the cellar.

Banks never had liked cellars very much, or any underground places, for that matter. He always expected to find something gruesome in them, and he often had when he worked in London. At their very best, they were dark, dank, dirty and smelly places, and this one was no exception. The chill air gripped them as soon as they got down the winding steps and Banks smelled mould and damp coaldust. It must have been there for years, he thought, because the area was a smoke-free zone now, like most of the country. Thank the lord there was an electric light.

The first thing they saw was a bicycle lying in parts on the floor next to a workbench and a number of planks of wood leaning against the wall. Next to them hung a World War II gas mask and helmet.

Dark, stained brick walls enclosed a number of smaller storage areas, like the ones used for coal in the old days. Now they were empty. The only thing of interest was Jameson's workbench, complete with vice and expensive tool-box. On the bench lay a box of loose shot and a ripped and crumpled page from a magazine. When Banks rubbed his latex-covered index finger over the rough surface wood, he could feel grains of powder. He lifted up the finger and sniffed. Gunpowder.

There was a drawer under the bench and Banks pulled it open. Inside, among a random collection of screws, nails, electrical tape, fuse wire and used sandpaper, he found a half-empty box of ammunition for a 9mm handgun.

'Right, Ken,' he said. 'I think we've got the bastard, National Trust or not. Time to call in the SOCOs.'

THREE

Banks cadged a lift with Blackstone back to Millgarth, where Susan and Hatchley were just about to take Mrs Gardiner home before returning to Eastvale. They had found out nothing more from her, Hatchley said as they stood at the doors ready to leave. It seemed that Jameson was a bit of a loner. He had had no frequent visitors, male or female, and she had seen no one answering the vague description of his partner. Neither had the other neighbours, according to the results of the house-to-house.

Banks asked about Pamela Jeffreys's condition and was told there had been some improvement but that she was still in intensive care.

Christ, Banks thought, as he sat opposite Blackstone, it had been a long day. He felt shagged out, especially given his previous night's folly, which seemed light years ago now. He looked at his watch: ten to six. He wanted to go home, but knew he might not be able to make it tonight, depending on the developments of the next few hours. At least he could go back to the hotel and have a long bath, phone Sandra, listen to Classic FM and read the army and probation officer's reports on Jameson while he waited around. If nothing happened by, say, eight o'clock, then he would perhaps go back to Eastvale for the night.

He slipped the reports into his briefcase and again decided to walk back to the hotel. It was that twilight hour between the evening rush-hour and going-out-on-the-town time. The city centre was practically deserted; the shops had closed, workers had gone home, and only a few people lingered in the few cafés and restaurants still open in the arcades and pedestrian precincts off Vicar Lane and Briggate. The sun had at last won its day-long battle with cloud; it lay in proud gold pools on the dusty streets and pavements, where last night's rain was a dim memory; it cast black shadows that crept slowly up the sides of buildings; it reflected harshly in shop windows and glittered on the specks of quartz embedded in stone surfaces.

Back at the hotel, he picked up his jacket, which he had handed over to be mended before leaving for The Vic. There was one message for him: 'Please come to Room 408 as soon as you get back, where you will find out some useful information.' It wasn't signed.

That was odd. Informers didn't usually operate this

way. They certainly didn't book rooms in hotels to pass along their information.

'Who's staying in room 408?' Banks asked, slipping his jacket on. After the obligatory refusal to give out such information on the part of the clerk, and the showing of a warrant card on the part of Banks, he discovered that the occupant of said room was a Mr Wilson. Very odd indeed. It was a common enough name, but Banks couldn't remember, offhand, any Mr Wilson.

He was tempted to ignore the message and carry on with what he planned, but curiosity got the better of him, as it always did.

When the lift stopped at the fourth floor, he poked his head through the doors first to see if there was anyone in the corridor. It was empty. He followed the arrow to room 408, took a deep breath and knocked. He debated whether to stand aside, but decided it was only in American films that people shot holes through hotel doors. Still, he found himself edging away a little, so he couldn't be seen through the peep-hole.

The door opened abruptly. Banks tensed, then let out his breath. Before him stood Dirty Dick Burgess.

'You again? What the hell?' Banks gasped. But before he could even enter the room Burgess had put on a leather jacket and taken him by the elbow.

'About bloody time, Banks,' he said. 'I'm sick of being cooped up in here. There's been developments. Come on, let's go get a drink.'

14

ONE

Despite Burgess's protest that it would be full of commercial travellers and visiting rugby teams, Banks insisted on their drinking in the Holiday Inn's idea of a traditional English pub, the Wig and Pen. He did this because his car was nearby and he still held hopes of getting back to Eastvale that evening. As it turned out, Burgess seemed to take a shine to the place.

He sat at the table opposite Banks with his pint of McEwan's lager, lit a Tom Thumb and looked around the quiet pub. 'Not bad,' he said, tapping his cigar on the rim of the ashtray. 'Not bad at all. I never did like those places with beams across the ceiling and bedpans on the walls.'

'Bed warmers,' Banks corrected him.

'Whatever. Anyway, what do you think of those two over there as a couple of potential bed warmers? Do you think they fancy us?'

Banks looked over and saw two attractive women in their late twenties or early thirties who, judging by their clothes, had dropped by for a drink after working late at one of the many Wellington Street office buildings. There was no doubt about it, the one with the short black hair and the good legs did give Burgess the eye and whisper something in her friend's ear.

'I think they do,' said Burgess.

'Didn't you say something about developments?'

'What? Oh, yes.' Burgess looked away from the women and leaned forward, lowering his voice. 'For a start, Fraud Squad think they've found definite evidence in Daniel Clegg's books and records that Clegg and Rothwell were laundering money for Martin Churchill.'

'That hardly counts as a development,' Banks said. 'We were already working on that assumption.'

'Ah, but now it's more than an assumption, isn't it? You've got to hand it to those Fraud Squad boys, boring little fuckers that they are, they've been burning the candle at both ends on this one.'

'Have you any idea why Churchill would use a couple of provincials like Rothwell and Clegg?'

'Good point,' said Burgess. 'As it happens, yes, I do know. Daniel Clegg and Martin Churchill were at Cambridge together, reading law. Simple as that. The old boy network. I'd reckon the one knew the other was crooked right from the start.'

'Did they keep in touch over the years?'

'Obviously. Remember, Clegg's a tax lawyer. He's been using St Corona as a tax shelter for his clients for years. It must have seemed a natural step to call on him when Churchill needed expert help. You can launder money from just about anywhere, you know. Baby Doc used a Swiss lawyer and did a lot of his business in Canada. You can take it out or bring it into Heathrow or Gatwick by the suitcase-load, using couriers, or you can run it through foreign exchange wire services, whatever. Governments keep coming up with new restrictive measures, but it's like plugging holes in a sieve. It's easy if you know how, and a tax lawyer and a financial consultant with a strong background in accounting certainly knew how.'

'What made Clegg choose Rothwell as his partner?'

'How would I know? You can't expect me to do your job for you, Banks, now can you? But they clearly knew one another somehow. Clegg must have known that Rothwell was exceptionally good with finances and none too concerned about their source. Takes one to know one, as they say.'

Burgess looked over at the two women, who had got another round of drinks, and smiled. The black-haired one crossed her long legs and smiled back shyly; the other put her hand over her mouth and giggled.

'My lucky night, I think,' Burgess said, clapping his hands and showering cigar ash over his stomach. He had a disconcerting habit of sitting still for ages then making a sudden, jerky movement. 'I'll say one thing for the north,' he went on, 'you've got some damned accommodating women up here. *Damned* accommodating. Look, why don't you get a couple more pints in, then I'll tell you something else that might interest you? And mine's lager, remember, not that pissy real ale stuff.'

Banks thought about it. Two pints. Yes, he would be fine for driving back to Eastvale, if he got the chance. 'All right,' he said, and went to the bar.

'Okay,' said Burgess, after his first sip. 'The two men, the white one and the darkie who were following you around?'

Banks lit a cigarette. 'You know who they are?'

'I've got to admit, I wasn't entirely truthful with you last time we met.'

'When have you ever been?'

'Unfair.'

'So you knew who they were last time we talked?'

'Suspected. Now we've got confirmation. They're

Mickey Lanois and Gregory Jackson, two of Churchill's top enforcers. They came into Heathrow last Friday. The way it looks is that Churchill asked Clegg to get rid of Rothwell, and after he did it he took off with a lot of money, probably figuring that he might be next. Churchill heard about Clegg's scarpering pretty quickly and sent his goons to do some damage control. You know what their favourite torture is, Banks?'

Banks shook his head. He didn't want to know, but he knew Burgess would tell him anyway.

'They get a handful of those little glass tubes the doctors use to keep liquid in. What do you call them, phials, right? Really thin glass, anyway. And they put them in the victim's mouth, lots of them. Then they tape the mouth shut securely and beat him a bit about the face. Or her. Churchill himself thought that up. He likes to watch. Think about it.'

Banks thought, swallowed and felt his throat constrict. 'Been letting you practise it at the Yard, have they?' he asked.

Burgess laughed. 'No, not yet. They're still running tests in Belfast. Anyway, the point is that we know who they are.'

'No, that's not entirely the point,' said Banks. 'The point is where are they now and what are you going to do about them?'

Burgess shook his head. 'That's a whole different ball game. We're talking about international politics here, politically sensitive issues. It's out of your hands, Banks. Accept that. All you need to know is that we know who they are and we're keeping tabs.'

'Don't give me that politically sensitive crap,' said Banks, stabbing out his cigarette so hard that sparks flew out of the ashtray. 'These two men damn near killed a woman here a few days ago. You say they like to go around stuffing people's mouths full of glass, then you tell me to trust you, you're keeping tabs. Well, bollocks, that's what I say.'

Burgess sighed. 'Somehow, I knew you were going to be difficult, Banks, I just knew it. Can't you leave it be? They won't get away with it, don't worry.'

'Do you know where they are now?'

'They won't get away with it,' Burgess repeated.

Banks took a sip of his beer and held back his rage. There was something in Burgess's tone that hinted he had something up his sleeve. 'What are you telling me?' Banks asked.

'That we'll get them. Or somebody will. But they'll go down quietly, no fuss, no publicity.'

Banks thought for a moment. He still didn't trust Burgess. 'Can I talk to them?' he asked, aware he was speaking through clenched teeth, still keeping his anger in check.

Burgess narrowed his eyes. 'Got to you, did it? What they did to the girl? I've seen pictures of her, before and after. Nasty. I'll bet you fancied her, didn't you, Banks? Nice dusky piece of crumpet, touch of the tarbrush, probably knew a lot of those *Kama Sutra* tricks. Just your type. Tasty.'

Banks felt his hand tighten on the pint glass. Why did he always let Burgess get to him this way? The bastard had a knack of touching on exactly the right raw nerve. Did it every time. 'I'd just like to be there when you question them, that's all,' he said quietly.

Burgess shrugged. 'No problem. If it's possible, I'll arrange it. All I'm saying is no publicity on the Churchill matter, okay? Let your liberal humanist sentiments fuck this one up and you'll be in deep doo-doo, Banks, very deep doo-doo indeed.'

'What about the press?'

'They can be dealt with. Have you ever considered that for every scandal you read about there are many that you don't? Do you think it's all left to chance? Don't be so bloody naïve.'

'Come off it. You might be able to tape a few mouths shut, but even you can't guarantee that no hotshot investigative reporters aren't going to be all over this one like flies around shit.'

Burgess shrugged. 'Maybe they'll hear Churchill's been killed in a coup. Maybe they'll even see the body.'

'Maybe it'd be best for everyone if he did get killed in a coup. Less embarrassing all round.'

Burgess remained silent for a moment, glass in hand. Then he said, slowly, 'And maybe he's got life insurance.'

'Well, I suppose you'd know. Let's hope there's a good plastic surgeon on St Corona.'

'Look,' Burgess said, 'let's stop pissing around. What I want from you is a promise that you won't talk to the press about the Churchill angle.'

Banks lit another cigarette. What could he do? If Burgess were telling the truth, Mickey Lanois and Gregory Jackson would be caught and punished for their crimes. He could live with that. He would have to. Burgess certainly had a better chance of catching them than Banks did, by the sound of things. Perhaps they were even in custody already.

Also, with luck, Arthur Jameson and his accomplice would go down for the murder of Keith Rothwell. But was Burgess telling the full truth? Banks didn't know. All he knew was that he couldn't trust the bastard. It all sounded too easy. But what choice did he have?

'All right,' he said.

Burgess reached over and patted his arm. 'Good,' he said. 'Good. I knew I could depend on you to keep mum when it counts.'

Banks jerked his arm away. 'Don't push it. And if I find out you've been buggering me around on this one, my promise is null and void, okay?'

Burgess held up his hands in mock surrender. 'Okay, okay.'

'There is another thing.'

'What's that?'

'Rothwell's killers. Lanois and Jackson didn't do that.'

Burgess shook his head. 'I'm not interested in them. They're not in my brief.'

'So what happens when we catch Jameson, if we catch him?'

'Jameson?'

'Arthur Jameson. One of Rothwell's killers.'

'I don't give a monkey's toss. That's up to you. I'm not interested. It's unlikely that this Jameson, whoever he is, knows anything about Churchill's part in the matter. He was probably just a hired killer working for Clegg, who has conveniently disappeared with a shitload of cash.'

'Any ideas where?'

Burgess shook his head then jabbed his finger in the air close to Banks's chest. 'But I can tell you one thing. Wherever he is, he won't be there for long. Churchill has the memory of an elephant, the reach of a giraffe and the tenacity of a bloody pit bull. He didn't get to bleed an entire country dry for nothing. It takes a special talent. Don't underestimate the man just because he's a butcher.'

'So we write off Clegg?'

'I think he's already written himself off by double-crossing Churchill.'

'And Jameson?'

'*If* he goes to trial, and *if* he talks – both big ifs, by the way – all he can say is that Clegg hired him to kill Rothwell. I doubt that Clegg would tell him the real reason. He might be a crooked lawyer, but I'm sure he still knows the value of confidentiality. He wouldn't want to let his hired killers know exactly how much money was involved, would he? It would make him too vulnerable by half. Anyway, I trust you'll have enough physical evidence to prosecute this Jameson when the time comes. If not, maybe we can fabricate some for you. Always happy to oblige.' He held his hand up. 'Only kidding. My little joke.'

Burgess glanced over at the two women, who had got yet another round of drinks and seemed to be laughing quite tipsily. 'Look,' he said, 'if I don't strike soon they'll be past it. Are you sure you won't join me? It'll be a laugh, and the wife need never know.'

'No,' said Banks. 'No, thanks. I'm going home.'

'Suit yourself.' Burgess stretched back his shoulders and sucked in his gut. 'Anything to liven up a miserable evening in Leeds,' he said. 'Once more unto the breach.' And with that, he strutted over to their table, smiling, pint in hand. Banks watched them make room for him, then shook his head, drank up and left.

TWO

'What on earth happened to you?' asked Sandra when Banks walked into the living room at about ten o'clock that evening.

'I had a slight disagreement with a couple of would-be muggers,' Banks said. 'Don't worry, I'm okay.' And he left it at that. Sandra raised her dark eyebrows but didn't pursue it. He knew she wouldn't. She wasn't the mothering type, and she rarely gave him much sympathy when he whimpered through flu or moaned through a bad cold.

Banks walked over to the cocktail cabinet and poured a stiff shot of Laphroaig single malt whisky. Sandra said she'd have a Drambuie. A good sign. After that, he put on his new CD of Khachaturian's piano concerto and flopped on to the sofa.

As he listened to the music, he looked at Sandra's framed photograph over the fireplace: a misty sunset in Hawes, taken from the daleside above the town, all subdued grey and orange with a couple of thin streaks of vermilion. The unusual church tower, square with a turret attached to one corner, dominated the grey slate roofs, and smoke curled up from some of the chimneys. Banks sipped the peaty malt whisky and smacked his lips.

Sandra sat beside him. 'What are you thinking?' she asked.

Banks told her about his meetings with Dirty Dick Burgess. 'There's always some sort of hidden agenda with him,' he said. 'I'm not sure what he's up to this time, but there's not a hell of a lot I can do about it except wait and see. That's about all we can do now, wait.'

'They also serve . . .'

'I was thinking about the Rothwells on the drive home, too. How could a man lead an entire other life, away from his family, under another name?'

'Is that what happened?'

'Yes.' Banks explained about Robert Calvert and his flat in Leeds, his fondness for gambling, women and dancing.

'And Pamela Jeffreys said she was sure he wasn't a married man. She said she'd have been able to tell.'

'Did she? Who's Pamela Jeffreys?'

'His girlfriend. It doesn't matter.'

Sandra sipped her drink and thought it over. 'It's probably not as difficult as you think for two people who live together on the surface to lead completely separate lives, one unknown to the other. Lord knows, so many couples have drifted so far apart anyway that they don't communicate any more.'

Banks felt his chest tighten. 'Are you talking about us?' he asked, remembering what Ken Blackstone had said about *his* marriage.

'Is that what you think?'

'I don't know.'

Sandra shrugged. 'I don't know, either. It was just a comment. But if the cap fits . . . Think about it, Alan. The amount we see each other, talk to each other, we could both be living other lives. Mostly, we just meet in passing. Let's face it, you could be up to anything most of the time. How would I know?'

'Most of the time I'm working.'

'Just like this Rothwell was?'

'That's different. He was away a lot.'

'What about the last couple of nights? You didn't phone, did you?'

Banks sat forward. 'Oh, come on! I tried. You weren't home.'

'You could have left a message on the machine.'

'You know how I hate those things. Anyway, it's not as if you didn't know where I was. You could easily have checked up on me. And it's not that often I'm away from home for a night or more.'

'Secret lives don't always have to be lived at night.'

'This is ridiculous.'

'Is it? Probably. All I'm saying is we don't talk enough to know.'

Banks slumped back and sipped his drink. 'I suppose so,' he said. 'Is it my fault? You always seemed to handle my absences so well before. You understand the *job* better than any other copper's wife I've met.'

'I don't know,' Sandra said. 'Maybe it just took longer for the strain to work its way through. Or maybe it's just worse because *I'm* busy a lot now, too.'

He put his arm around her. 'I don't know what's been happening to us lately, either,' he said, 'but maybe we'll go away when this is all over.'

He felt Sandra stiffen beside him. 'Promises,' she said. 'You've been saying that for years.'

'Have I?'

'You know you have. We haven't had a bloody holiday since we moved to Eastvale.'

'Well, dust off your camera. I've got a bit of leave due and I might just surprise you this time.'

'How long do you think the case will last?'

'Hard to say.'

'There you are, then.'

He stroked her shoulder. 'Tell me you'll think about it.'

'I'll think about it. Tracy comes back on Sunday.'

'I know.'

'Won't you be pleased to see her? Will you even be around to meet her at the airport?'

'Of course I will.'

Sandra relaxed a little and moved closer. A very good sign. The Drambuie was clearly working. 'You'd better,' she said. '*She* phoned earlier tonight. She sends her love.'

'How's she getting on?'

Sandra laughed. 'She said it's not quite like *A Year in Provence* down there, but she likes it anyway. She hasn't bumped into John Thaw yet.'

'Who?'

'John Thaw. You know, the actor who was in *A Year in Provence* on television? I liked him better as Morse.'

'Who?'

She elbowed him in the ribs. 'You know quite well who I'm talking about. I know you liked Morse. He used to be in *The Sweeney*, too, years ago, and you used to watch that down in London. Remember, in your old macho days? Didn't you even go drinking with him once?'

'What do you mean, "old"?' Banks flexed his biceps.

Sandra laughed and moved closer. 'I don't want to fight,' she said. 'Honest, I don't. Not since we've seen so little of one another.'

'Me neither,' said Banks.

'I just think we've got a few problems to deal with, that's all. We need to communicate better.'

'And we will. How about a truce?' He tightened his arm around her shoulder.

'Mmm. All right.'

'I'll have to call the station and see if there's been any developments,' he said.

But he didn't move. He felt too comfortable. His limbs felt pleasantly heavy and weary, and the warmth of the malt whisky flowed through his veins. The slow second movement started in its haunting, erotic way. Soon, the eerie flexatone entered and sent shivers up and down his spine. A cheap effect, perhaps, but sometimes effective if you happened to be in the right mood.

Banks drained his glass and put it on the table by the

sofa. Sandra let her head rest between his shoulder and chest. Definitely a good sign. 'Remember that silly film we saw on TV a while back?' he said. 'The one where the couple has sex listening to Ravel's *Bolero*?'

'Hmm. It's called *10*. Dudley Moore and Bo Derek. And I don't think they were really listening. More like using it as background music.'

'Well, I've never really liked *Bolero*. It's far too ordered and mechanical. It's got a kind of inevitability about it that's too predictable for my taste. I've always thought this Khachaturian piece would be a lot better to make love to. Much better. Wanders all over the place. You never really know where it's going next. Slow and dreamy at the start, with plenty of great climaxes later on.'

'Sounds good to me. Have you ever tried it?'

'No.'

Sandra moved her head up until she was facing him, her lips about two inches away. He swept back a strand of hair from her cheek and let his fingers rest on her cool skin. 'I thought you had to call the station?' she said.

'Later,' he said, stroking her cheek. 'Later. Are the curtains closed?'

THREE

Boredom. They never told you about that down at the recruitment drives, thought PC Grant Everett as he rolled down the window of the patrol car and lit a cigarette. His partner, PC Barry Miller, was good about the smoking. He didn't indulge, himself, but he understood Grant's need to light up every now and then, especially on a quiet night like this one.

They were parked in a lay-by between Princes Risborough and High Wycombe. To the south, through the rear-view mirror, Grant could see the faint glow of the nearest town, while to the north only isolated lights twinkled from scattered farms and cottages. All around them spread the dark, rolling landscape of the Chilterns. It was an attractive spot on a nice day, especially in spring with the bluebells and cherry blossom out, but in the dark it seemed somehow forbidding, inhospitable.

A light breeze swirled the smoke out of the car. Grant inhaled deeply. It had just stopped raining and he loved the way the scent of rain seemed to blend with the tobacco and make it taste so much better. It was at moments like this when he understood why he smoked, despite all the health warnings. On the other hand, he never quite understood it when he got up after a night's chain-smoking in the pub and coughed his guts up for half an hour.

Next to him, Barry was munching on a Mars bar. Grant smiled to himself. Six foot two and sixteen stone already and the silly bugger still needed to feed his face with chocolate bars. Who am I to talk? Grant thought, sucking on his cigarette again. To each his own poison.

Grant felt sleepy and the cigarette helped keep him awake. He had never got used to shift work; his biological rhythms, or whatever they were, had never adapted. When he lay down his head in the morning as the neighbour's kids were going to school, the postman was doing his rounds and everyone else was off to work, he could never get to sleep. Especially if the sun were shining. And then there was Janet, bless her soul, doing her best, trying hard to be as quiet as she could around the house, and Sarah, only six months, crying for feeding and nappy-changing. And the bills to pay, and . . . Christ, he wasn't going to think about that. At least the job got him out of the house, away from all that for a while.

A lorry rumbled by. Grant flicked the stub of his cigarette out of the window and heard it sizzle as it hit a puddle. Occasionally, voices cut through the static on the police radio, but the messages weren't for them.

'Shall we belt up and bugger off, then?' said Barry. He screwed up the wrapper of his Mars bar and put it in his pocket. Ever the careful one, Grant thought, with an affectionate smile. Wouldn't even be caught littering, wouldn't Barry.

'Might as well.' Grant reached for his belt. Then they heard the squealing sound of rubber on wet tarmac. 'What the fuck was that?'

On the main road, a northbound car skidded as it turned the bend too fast, then righted itself.

'Shall we?' said Barry.

'My pleasure.'

Grant loved it when the lights were flashing and the siren screaming. First he was pushed back in the seat by the force when he put his foot down, and then he felt as if he were taking off, seeming somehow to be magically freed from all the restraints of the road: not just the man-made rules, but the laws of nature. Sometimes, Grant even felt as if they were really taking off, wheels no longer on the ground.

But there was no chase to be had here; it was over before it began. The car was about two hundred yards ahead of them when its driver seemed to realize they meant business. He slowed down as they caught up and pulled over to the side of the road, spraying up water from the hedgerow. His number plate was too muddy to read.

Grant pulled up behind him, and Barry got out to approach the car.

It wasn't likely to be much, Grant thought as he sniffed the fresh night air through the open window – maybe a drunk, maybe a few outstanding parking tickets – but at least it was *something* to relieve the boredom for a few minutes.

He could hear perfectly clearly when Barry asked the driver to turn off his ignition and present his driving documents. The driver did as he was told. Barry looked at the papers and passed them back. Next, he asked the man if he had been drinking. Grant couldn't hear the man's reply, but it seemed to satisfy Barry. Grant knew he would be listening for slurred words and sniffing for booze on the driver's breath.

After that, Barry asked the man where he had been and where he was going. Grant thought he heard the man mention Princes Risborough.

No other cars passed. The night was quiet and Grant caught a whiff of beech leaves and cherry wood on the damp air. He thought he heard some cows low in the distance and, farther still, a nightingale.

Then Barry asked the man to get out of the car and clean off his number plate. Grant heard him explain patiently that it was an offence to drive with a number plate that is 'not easily distinguishable' and smiled to himself at the stilted, textbook phrase. But the man would get off with a caution this time; Barry seemed satisfied with his behaviour.

The man got back in the car and Grant heard Barry speak over his personal radio.

'465 to Control.'

'465 go ahead.'

'Ten nine vehicle check please.'

The voices crackled unnaturally over the country night air.

'Pass your number.'

'Mike four, three, seven, Tango Zulu Delta.'

'Stand by.'

Grant knew it would take three or four minutes for the operator to check the number on the computer, then, all being well, they could be on their way.

Barry and the driver seemed to be chatting amiably enough as they waited. Grant looked at the newly cleaned number plate and reached idly for the briefing-sheet beside him. There seemed to be *something* familiar about it, something he ought to remember.

He ran his finger down the list of stolen cars. No, not there. He wouldn't remember any of those numbers; there were always too many of them. It had to be something more important: a vehicle used in a robbery, perhaps? Then he found it: M437 TZD, grey Granada.

Suddenly, he felt cold. The owner was wanted in connection with a murder in North Yorkshire. Possibly armed and dangerous. Shit. All of a sudden, Barry seemed to be taking a hell of a long time out there.

A number of thoughts passed quickly through Grant's mind, the first of which was regret that they didn't do things the American way. Get the guy out of the vehicle, hands stretched on the roof, legs apart, pat him down. 'Assume the position, asshole!' Why pretend they were still living in a peaceful society where the local bobby was your best friend? Christ, how Grant wished he had a gun.

Should he go out and try to get Barry to the car, use some excuse? He could say they'd been called to an emergency. Could he trust himself to walk without stumbling, to speak without stuttering? His legs felt like jelly and his throat was tight. But he felt so impotent, just watching. All he could hope was that the radio operator would understand Barry's predicament and give the guy a clean bill of health. According to the information on the sheet, the man, Arthur Jameson, didn't even *know* he was wanted.

The radio crackled back into life.

'Control to 465.'

'Go ahead, over.'

'Er . . . Mike four, three, seven, Tango Zulu Delta . . . No reports stolen. Er . . . Do you require keeper details over?'

'Affirmative.'

More static. Grant tensed in his seat, hand on the door-handle. Too many pauses.

'Keeper is Arthur Jameson, 47 Bridgeport Avenue, Leeds. Er . . . is keeper with you, over?'

'Affirmative. Any problem?'

She was blowing it, Grant sensed. Someone, probably the super, was standing over her trying to help her calmly get Barry back to the car and the driver on his way, but she was nervous, halting. It was all taking far too long, and if the suspect couldn't sense there was something wrong over the radio, then he was an idiot.

'No reports stolen.'

'You already told me that, love,' said Barry. 'Is something wrong?'

'Sorry . . . er . . . 465 . . . Stand by.'

Grant tightened his grip on the door-handle. This was it. He wasn't going to stand around and let his partner, who had probably dozed off at the briefing and to whom the number obviously meant bugger-all, just stand there and take it.

But before he got the door half open, he saw Barry, all sixteen stone and six foot two of him, drop to the wet road clutching the side of his neck, from which a dark spray of blood fountained high and arced to the ground. Then he heard the shots, two dull cracks echoing through the dark countryside.

Left foot still in the car, right foot on the road, Grant hesitated. Mistake. His last thought was that it was so bloody unfair and pointless and miserable to die like this by a roadside outside High Wycombe. Then a bullet shattered the windscreen and took him full in the face, scattering blood, teeth and bone fragments all over the car. After its echo had faded, the Granada revved up and sped off into the night, and the nightingale sang again into the vacuum of silence the car left behind.

15

ONE

The sky was a sheet of grey shale, smeared here and there by dirty rags of cloud fluttering over the wooded hillsides on a cool wind. Rooks and crows gathered noisily in the roadside trees like shards of darkness refusing to dispel. Even the green of the dense beech forests looked black.

Banks and Sergeant Hatchley, who had driven through the night at breakneck speed from Eastvale, stood and looked in silence at the patrol car with the shattered windscreen and at the outline of the body on the tarmac about six or seven feet ahead, near which dark blood had coagulated in shallow puddles on the road surface. Close by, Detective Superintendent Jarrell from the Thames Valley Police paced up and down, shabby beige raincoat flapping around his legs.

The road had been cordoned off, and several patrol cars, lights circling like demented lighthouses, guarded the edges of the scene, where the SOCOs still worked. Local traffic had been diverted.

'It was a cock-up,' Superintendent Jarrell growled, glaring at the two men from Yorkshire the minute they got out of Banks's Cortina and walked over to him. 'A monumental cock-up.'

Jarrell was clearly looking for somewhere to place the blame, and it irritated the hell out of him that no matter how hard he tried, it fell squarely on his own shoulders. The two PCs might have made a mistake in not tattooing the Granada's number on their memories, and the radio operator had certainly screwed up royally, but in the police force, as in other hierarchical structures, when an underling screws up, the responsibility goes to the top. You don't blame the foot-soldiers, you blame the general, and *everybody* gets a good bollocking, from the top down.

Banks knew that Ken Blackstone at West Yorkshire had followed correct procedure in getting a photograph, description and details about Arthur Jameson out to all divisions. And the point he had most emphasized was, 'May be armed. Observe only. UNDER NO CIRCUMSTANCES ATTEMPT TO APPREHEND.'

Jarrell's was one of those unfortunate faces in which the individual features fail to harmonize: long nose, small, beady eyes, bushy brows, a thin slit of a mouth, prominent cheekbones, receding chin, mottled complexion. Somehow, though, it didn't dissolve into total chaos; there was an underlying unity about the man himself that, like a magnetic field, drew it all together.

'Any update on the injured officer, sir?' Banks asked.

'What? Oh.' Jarrell stopped pacing for a moment and faced Banks. He had an erect, military bearing. Suddenly the fury seemed to bleed out of him like air from a tyre. 'Miller was killed outright, as you know.' He gestured at the outline and the surrounding, stained tarmac with his whole arm, as if indicating a cornucopia. 'There's about seven pints of his blood here. Everett's still hanging on. Just. The bullet went in through his upper lip, just under the nose, and it seems to have been slowed down or deflected by cartilage and bone. Anyway, it didn't get a chance to do serious brain damage, so the doc says he's got a good chance. Bloody fool.'

'If you don't mind my saying so, sir,' Banks said, 'it looks like they got into a situation they couldn't get out of. We had no reason to think Jameson knew we were on to him. Nor had we any reason to think he was a likely spree killer. We want him for a job he was hired to do cold-bloodedly. He must have panicked. I know it doesn't help the situation, sir, but the men *were* inexperienced. I doubt they'd handled much but traffic duty, had they?'

Jarrell ran his hand through his hair. 'You're right, of course. They pulled him over on a routine traffic check. When Miller called in the vehicle number, the radio operator called the senior officer on the shift. He tried to talk her through it calmly, but . . . Hell, she was new to the job. She was scared to death. It wasn't her fault.'

Banks nodded and rubbed his eyes. Beside him, Hatchley's gaze seemed fixed on the bloody tarmac. When Banks had got the call close to two a.m. – his first night at home in days – he had first thought of taking Susan Gay, then, not without malice entirely, though affectionate malice, he had decided that it was time Sergeant Hatchley got his feet wet. He knew how Hatchley loved his sleep. Consequently, they hadn't said much on the way down. Banks had played Mitsuko Uchida's live versions of the Mozart piano sonatas, and Hatchley had seemed content to doze in the passenger seat, snoring occasionally.

Most chief inspectors, Banks knew, would have had someone else drive, but he was using his own car, the old Cortina, no longer produced now and practically an antique. And, damn it, he *liked* driving it himself.

'Seen enough here?' Jarrell asked.

'I think so.'

'Me, too. Let's go.'

Jarrell drove them down the road. 'Believe it or not,' he said, 'this is very pretty countryside under the right circumstances.'

About a mile along the road, towards Princes Risborough, Jarrell turned left on to a muddy farm track and bumped along until they got to a gate on the right, where he pulled up. A hedgerow interspersed with hawthorns shielded the field and its fence from view. Cows mooed in the next field.

The gate stood open, and as Banks and Hatchley followed Jarrell through, they both sank almost to their ankles in mud. Too late, Banks realized, he hadn't brought the right gear. He should have known to bring the wellingtons he always carried in the boot of his car. Like most policemen, he took pride in keeping his shoes well polished; now they were covered in mud and probably worse, judging by the prevalence of cows. He cursed and Jarrell laughed. Hatchley stood holding on to the gatepost trying to wipe most of it off on the few tufts of grass there. Banks looked at the muddy field dotted with cowpats and didn't bother. They'd only get dirty again.

In the field, a group of men in white boiler suits and black wellington boots worked around a car that stood bogged down in the mud with its doors open. The air was sharp with the tang of cow-clap.

One of the men had propped a radio on a stone by the hedgerow, and it was tuned to the local breakfast show, at the moment featuring a golden oldie: Cilla Black singing 'Anyone Who Had a Heart'. One of the SOCOs sang along with it as he worked. The cows mooed even louder, demonstrating remarkably good taste, Banks thought. They weren't so far away after all. They were, in fact, all lying down in a group just across the field. Cows lying down. That meant it was going to rain, his mother always said. But it had rained already. Did that mean they'd been in the same position for hours? That it was going to rain again?

Giving up on folk wisdom, Banks turned instead to look at the abandoned Granada, the bottom of its chassis streaked with mud and cow-shit. It had been found, Jarrell said, just over an hour ago, while Banks and Hatchley had been in transit.

'Anything?' Jarrell shouted over to the team.

One of the men in white shook his head. 'Nothing but the usual rubbish, sir,' he said. 'Sweet wrappers, old road maps, that sort of thing. He must have taken everything of use or value. No sign of any weapons.'

Jarrell grunted and turned away.

'He'd hardly have left his guns, would he?' said Banks. 'Not now he's officially on the run. I'd guess he probably had a rucksack or something with him in the car. Look, sir, you know the landscape around here better than I do. If you were him, where would you go?'

Jarrell looked up at the louring sky for a moment, as if for inspiration, then rubbed at the inside corner of his right eye with his index finger. 'He has a couple of choices,' he said. 'Either head immediately for the nearest town, get to London and take the first boat or plane out of the country, or simply lie low.' He pointed towards the hills. 'A man could hide himself there for a good while, if he knew how to survive.'

'We'd better cover both possibilities,' Banks said. 'He's spent time in the army, so he's probably been on survival courses. And if he heads for London, he'll likely know someone who can help him.'

'Whatever he does, I'd say he'll most likely go across country first,' said Jarrell. 'He'd be smart enough to know that stealing a car or walking by the roadside would be too risky.' He looked at his watch. 'The shooting occurred at about half past twelve. It's half past six now. That gives him a six-hour start.'

'How far could he get, do you reckon?'

'I'd give him about three miles an hour in this terrain, under these conditions,' Jarrell went on. 'Maybe a bit less.'

'Where's the nearest station?'

'That's the problem,' said Jarrell slowly. 'This is close to prime commuter country. There's Princes Risborough, Saunderton and High Wycombe on the Chiltern Line, all nearby. If he heads east, he can get to the Northampton Line at Tring, Berkhamsted or Hemel Hempstead. If he heads for Amersham, he can even get on the underground, the Metropolitan Line. Unfortunately for us, there's no shortage of trains to London around here, and they start running early.'

'Let's say he's managed about sixteen or seventeen miles,' said Banks. 'What's his best bet?'

'Probably the Chiltern Line. Plenty of trains and an easy connection with the underground. He could even be in London by now.'

They started walking back to the car. 'I can tell you one thing,' said Banks. 'Wherever he is, his shoes will be bloody muddy.'

TWO

If. If. If. Such were Banks's thoughts as he followed Superintendent Jarrell into Jameson's rented cottage an hour or so later. *If* Everett and Miller hadn't stopped Jameson last night. *If* Jameson hadn't panicked and shot them. *If.*

In an ideal world, they would have tracked Jameson to this cottage through a cheque stub or a circled address in an accommodation guide. Quietly, they would have surrounded the place when they were certain Jameson was inside, then arrested him, perhaps as he walked out to his car, unsuspecting, without a shot being fired. For he *hadn't known.* That was the stinger; he hadn't known they were after him. Now, though, things were different. Now he was a dangerous man on the run.

As it turned out, they discovered that Jameson was renting a cottage just to the east of Princes Risborough through an Aylesbury estate agent shortly after the office opened at eight-thirty that Friday morning. Policemen were showing Jameson's photograph around and asking the same questions in every estate agent's, hotel and bed-and-breakfast establishment in Buckinghamshire, and the pair of DCs given the Aylesbury estate agents just happened to get lucky. Like Everett and Miller got unlucky. Swings and roundabouts. That was often the way things happened.

Jameson had simply driven off from Leeds on his holidays. Being a lover of nature, he had headed for the countryside. Why the Chilterns? It was anyone's guess. It could just as easily have been the Cotswolds or the Malverns, Banks supposed.

According to the estate agent, the man had simply

dropped in one afternoon and asked after rental cottages in the area. He had paid a cash deposit and moved in. There was no need for subterfuge or secrecy. Arthur Jameson had nothing to fear from anyone. Or he wouldn't have had, were it not for a weakness for pornography, a fleeting contact with Daniel Clegg's estranged wife, Melissa, and Sergeant Hatchley's network of informers. He had either been careless about the wadding, or he thought it was a joke; they didn't know which yet. It hadn't shown up as a trademark in any other jobs over the past few years.

Last night he had probably gone into High Wycombe for a bite to eat, lingered over his dessert and coffee, maybe celebrated his new-found wealth with a large cognac, then headed back for the rented cottage, taking the bend a little too fast.

The cottage was certainly isolated. It stood just off a winding lane about two miles long, opposite a small, perfectly rounded tor. The lane carried on, passed another farmhouse about a mile further on, then meandered back to the main road.

From the mud on the floor, it looked very much as if Jameson had been there after the shooting. A bit of a risk, maybe, but the cottage wasn't far from his abandoned car. In the kitchen, yesterday's lunch dishes soaked in cold water, and breadcrumbs, cheese shavings and tiny florets of yellowed broccoli dotted the counter.

In the living room, Jameson had left the contents of his suitcase strewn around, including a number of local wildlife guides beside a girlie magazine on the table. Hatchley picked up the magazine and flipped through it quickly, tilting the centrefold to get a better look. Then they all followed the mud trail upstairs.

At the bottom of the wardrobe, hardly hidden at all by the spare blankets Jameson had obviously used to cover them, lay a twelve-gauge shotgun wrapped in an oil-stained cloth, and a small canvas bag. Carefully, Banks leaned forward and opened the flap of the bag with the tip of a Biro. It was empty, but on the floor by the blankets lay a few used ten-pound notes. Banks visualized the hunted man hurriedly stuffing the notes into his pockets until they spilled over on the floor. The shotgun was obviously too big and awkward for him to take with him, but he was still armed with the handgun.

Banks pointed to the shotgun and the canvas bag. 'Can we get this stuff to your lab?' he asked Jarrell. 'That shotgun's probably evidence in a murder case.'

Jarrell nodded. 'No problem.'

As Hatchley bent to pick up the shotgun, careful to handle only the material it was wrapped in, and as Banks reached for the canvas bag, a message for Jarrell crackled through on his personal radio.

'Jarrell here. Over.'

'HQ, sir. Subject, Arthur Jameson, spotted at Aylesbury railway station at nine fifty-three a.m. Subject bought London ticket. Now standing on platform. Locals await instructions. Over.'

'Has he spotted them?'

'They say not, sir.'

'Tell them to keep their distance.' Jarrell looked at his watch. It was ten o'clock. 'When's the next train?' he asked.

'Twelve minutes past ten, sir.'

'Which route?'

'Marylebone via Amersham.'

'Thank you. Stand by.' Jarrell turned to Banks and

Hatchley. 'We can pick up that train at Great Missenden or Amersham if you want,' he said.

Banks looked first at Hatchley, then back at Jarrell. 'Come on, then,' he said. 'Let's do it.'

THREE

Banks and Hatchley boarded the train separately at Amersham at ten thirty-two. Reluctantly, Superintendent Jarrell, being the local man, had agreed to stay behind and co-ordinate the Thames Valley end of the operation.

Neither Banks nor Hatchley looked much like a policeman that morning. Waking miserably to the middle-of-the-night phone call, Banks had put on jeans, a light cotton shirt and a tan sports jacket. Over this, he had thrown on his Columbo raincoat. Even though he had done his best to clean the mud off his shoes with a damp rag, it still showed.

Sergeant Hatchley wore his shiny blue suit, white shirt and no tie; he looked as if he had been dragged through a hedge backwards, but there was nothing unusual in that.

They had been told by the Transport Police, who had spotted Jameson, that the suspect still resembled his photograph except that he had about two days' growth around his chin and cheeks. He looked like a rambler. He was wearing grey trousers of some light material tucked into walking boots at the ankles, a green open-neck shirt and an orange anorak. Nice of him, Banks thought, dressing so easy to spot. He was also carrying a heavy rucksack, which no doubt held his gun and money, amongst other things.

The train rattled out of the station. Banks managed to

find a seat next to a young woman who smiled at him briefly as he sat down, then went back to reading her copy of *PC Magazine*. Banks had his battered brown leather briefcase with him, and its chief contents were his omnibus paperback copy of Waugh's *Sword of Honour* and his Walkman. He opened the book at the marker and started to read, but every so often he glanced at the man in the green short-sleeve shirt who sat about four seats down, over to his left. The rucksack and the orange anorak lay on the luggage rack above.

The train moved in a comforting rhythm, but Banks couldn't help feeling tense. He left the Walkman in his briefcase because he was too distracted to listen to music.

They could probably take Jameson right now, he thought. He and Jim Hatchley. Just approach quietly from behind like anyone going to the toilet and grab an arm each. The gun, surely, was up in the rucksack on the luggage rack.

But it wasn't worth the risk. Something could go wrong. Jameson could hold the entire coach hostage. It didn't bear thinking about. This way was far safer and would, with a little patience, skill and luck, guarantee success.

Banks and Hatchley had got on the train simply to keep an eye on Jameson. At the station, Superintendent Jarrell had talked to the Yard, who promised that there would be a number of plain-clothes officers waiting at Marylebone, mixed in with the crowds. These men were experts at surveillance, and they would keep Jameson in sight, no matter how he travelled, without being spotted, until he arrived at his final destination, be it hotel or house.

Some were posing as taxi-drivers, and, with luck, Jameson would get into one of their cabs. Banks had every intention of trying to keep up with the chase, but it was comforting to know that if he lost sight of Jameson, someone else would have him. There were plain-clothes officers at all the stops on the way, too, in case he got off, but Jameson had bought a ticket for London and it was almost certain that was where he was heading. Given his past, he would likely know someone there who could help get him out of the country. What Banks hoped – and this was one of the main reasons for letting their quarry go to ground – was that Jameson would lead them to his accomplice in the Rothwell murder.

As the train rattled out of Rickmansworth, Jameson got up and walked past Banks on his way to the toilet. Banks looked down at his book, not registering the words his eyes passed over. While Jameson was gone, he stared at the khaki rucksack and held himself back. How easy it would be, he thought, just to take it, then grab Jameson when he came back. But he had to keep thinking like a policeman, not give in to the maverick instinct, however strong. This way, with a little patience, the catch might be bigger.

And there was another reason. The gun might not be in the rucksack. Jameson's trousers were of the bulky, many-pocketed kind favoured by ramblers. Banks had glanced quickly as he went by and hadn't been able to discern the weight or outline of a gun, but it *could* be there, and there were too many civilians present to make the risk worth-while. Best wait. He thought of how much money there might be in the rucksack and smiled at how ironic it would be if someone snatched it while Jameson was having a piss.

Jameson came back. They passed Harrow and entered a landscape of factory yards, piles of tyres and orange oil drums, pallets, warehouses, school yards full of screaming kids, bleak housing estates, concrete overpasses. Before long, the people in the carriage were standing up to get their jackets and bags as the train rumbled slowly into Marylebone station, all anxious to be first off.

Banks spotted Hatchley ahead of him, his head above most people in the crowd that shuffled through the ticket gate. Jameson had his anorak on now and was easy to keep in sight. Banks noticed him look around and lick his lips every now and then, sad, cruel puppy-dog eyes scanning the station forecourt.

But there was nothing to see. Nothing out of the ordinary. The uniformed Transport Police went about their business as usual, people leafed through magazines at the bookstall or headed for the buffet, checked the schedule displays, ran for trains. Carts of luggage and mail threaded in and out of the crowds, announcements about forthcoming departures came over the public-address system in the usual monotone echoing from the roof, where pigeons nested. To Banks, the station smelled of diesel oil and soot, though the age of steam was long gone.

Jameson made his way through the exit and managed to get a taxi. That was their first stroke of good fortune. If things went according to plan, the driver would be a DC; if not, then a taxi crawling through London traffic was easy enough for even a one-legged septuagenarian on foot to follow.

Banks opened the door of the next taxi, Hatchley beside him now. Banks was dying to jump in and say, 'Follow that taxi!' but the driver didn't want to let them in. He leaned over and tried to pull the door shut, holding up a police ID card. 'Sorry, mate,' he said. 'Police business. There's another one behind.' Just in time, Banks managed to get his own card out. 'Snap,' he said. 'Now open the fucking door.'

'Sorry, sir,' said the driver, eyes on the road, following

Jameson's cab through the thick traffic on Marylebone Road. 'I wasn't to know. They never said to expect a DCI jumping in the cab.'

'Forget it,' said Banks. 'I'm assuming it's one of your men driving in the taxi ahead?'

'Yes, sir. DC Formby. He's a good bloke. Don't worry, we're not going to lose the bastard.'

With excruciating slowness, the taxis edged their way south towards Kensington, along the busy High Street and down a side street of five- or six-storey white buildings with black metal railings at the front. Jameson's taxi stopped outside one that announced itself a HOTEL on the smoked glass over the huge shiny black doors. Across the street came the sound of drilling where workmen stood on scaffolding renovating the building opposite. The air was dry with drifting stone dust and thick with exhaust fumes. Jameson got out, looked around quickly and went into the hotel. His taxi drove off.

'Right,' said Banks. 'Looks like we've run the bastard to earth. Now we wait for the reinforcements.'

FOUR

For grey, the hotel manager could have given John Major a good run for his money. His suit was grey; his hair was grey; his voice was grey. He also had one of those faces – receding chin, goofy teeth, stick-out ears – that attract such abusive and bullying attention at school. At the moment, his face was grey, too.

He reminded Banks of Parkinson, a rather unpleasant large-nosed boy who had been the butt of ridicule and recipient of the occasional thump in the fourth form.

Banks had always felt sorry for Parkinson – had even defended him once or twice – until he had met him later in life, fully transformed into a self-serving, arrogant and humourless Labour MP. Then he felt Parkinson probably hadn't been thumped enough.

The manager had obviously never seen so many rough-looking, badly dressed coppers gathered in one place since they stopped showing repeats of *The Sweeney*. Jeans abounded, as did leather jackets, anoraks, blousons, T-shirts and grubby trainers. There wasn't a uniform, a tie or a well-polished shoe in sight, and the only suit was Sergeant Hatchley's blue polyester one, which was so shiny you could see your face in it.

It was also obvious that a number of the officers were armed and that two of them wore bullet-proof vests over their T-shirts.

Short of the SAS, Police Support Units or half a dozen Armed Response Vehicles, none of which the police authorities wanted the public to see mounting a major offensive on a quiet Kensington hotel on a Thursday lunchtime, these two were probably the best you could get. Vest One, the tallest, was called Spike, probably because of his hair, and his smaller, more hirsute associate was called Shandy. Spike was doing all the talking.

'See, squire,' he said to the wide-eyed hotel manager, 'our boss tells us we don't want a lot of fuss about this. None of this evacuating the area bollocks you see on telly. We go in, we disarm him nice and quiet, then bob's your uncle, we're out of your hair for good. Okay? No problems for us and no bad publicity for the hotel.'

The manager, clearly not used to being called 'squire', swallowed, bobbing an oversize Adam's apple, and nodded.

'But what we do need to do,' Spike went on, 'is to clear the floor. Now, is there anyone else up there apart from this Jameson?'

The manager looked at the keys. 'Only room 316,' he said. 'It's lunchtime. People usually go out for lunch.'

'What about the chambermaids?'

'Finished.'

'Good,' said Spike, then turned to one of the others in trainers, jeans and leather jacket. 'Smiffy, go get number 316 out quietly, okay?'

'Right, boss,' said Smiffy, and headed for the stairs.

Spike tapped his long fingers on the desk and turned to Banks. 'You know this bloke, this Jameson, right, sir?' he said.

Banks was surprised he had remembered the honorific. 'Not personally,' he said, and filled Spike in.

'He's shot a policeman, right?'

'Yes. Two of them. One's dead and the other's still in the operating room waiting to find out if he's got a brain left.'

Spike slipped a stick of Wrigley's spearmint gum from its wrapper and popped it in his mouth. 'What do you suggest?' he asked between chews.

Banks didn't know if Spike was being polite or deferential in asking an opinion, but he didn't get a chance to find out. As Smiffy came down the stairs with a rather dazed old dear clutching a pink dressing gown around her throat, the phone rang at the desk. The manager answered it, turned even more grey as he listened, then said, 'Yes, sir. Of course, sir. At once, sir.'

'Well?' Spike asked when the manager had put the phone down. 'What's put the wind up you?'

'It was *him*. The man in room 324.'

'What's he want?'

'He wants a roast beef sandwich and a bottle of beer sent up to his room.'

'How'd he sound?'

'Sound?'

'Yeah. You know, did he seem suspicious, nervous?'

'Oh. No, just ordinary.'

'Right on,' said Spike, grinning at Banks. 'Opportunity knocks.' He turned back to the manager. 'Do the doors up there have those peep-hole things, so you can see who's knocking?'

'No.'

'Chains?'

'Yes.'

'No problem. Right,' said Spike. 'Come with me, Shandy. The rest of you stay here and make sure no one gets in or out. We got the back covered?'

'Yes, sir,' one of the blousons answered.

'Fire escape?'

'That, too, sir.'

'Good.' Spike looked at Banks. 'I don't suppose you're armed?'

Banks shook his head. 'No time.'

Spike frowned. 'Better stay down here then, sir. Sorry, but I can't take the responsibility. You probably know the rules better than I do.'

Banks nodded. He gave Spike and Shandy a floor's start, then turned to Sergeant Hatchley. 'Stay here, Jim,' he said. 'I don't want to lead you astray.'

Without waiting for an answer, he slipped into the stairwell. One of the Yard men in the lobby noticed but made no move to stop him. At the first-floor landing, Banks heard someone wheezing behind him and turned.

'Don't worry, I'm not deaf,' said Hatchley. 'I just thought you might like some company anyway.'

Banks grinned.

'Mind if I ask you what we're doing this for?' Hatchley whispered, as they climbed the next flight.

'To find out what happens,' said Banks. 'I've got a funny feeling about this. Something Spike said.'

'You know what curiosity did.'

They reached the third floor. Banks peeked around the stairwell and put his arm out to hold Hatchley back.

Glancing again, Banks saw Spike point at his watch and mouth something to Shandy. Shandy nodded. They drew their weapons and walked slowly along the corridor towards Jameson's room.

The worn carpet that covered the floor couldn't stop the old boards creaking with each footstep. Banks saw Spike knock on the door and heard a muffled grunt from inside.

'Room service,' said Spike.

The door rattled open – on a chain, by the sound of it. Someone – Spike or Jameson – swore loudly, then Banks saw Shandy rear back like a wild horse and kick the door open. The chain snapped. Spike and Shandy charged inside and Banks heard two shots in close succession, then, after a pause of three or four seconds, another shot, not quite as loud.

Banks and Hatchley waited where they were for a minute, out of sight. Then, when Banks saw Spike come out of the room and lean against the door jamb, he and Hatchley walked into the corridor. Spike saw them coming and said, 'It's all over. You can go in now, if you like. Silly bugger had to try it on, didn't he?'

They walked into the room. Banks could smell cordite from the gunfire. Jameson had fallen backwards against the wall and slid down into a perfect sitting position on the floor, legs splayed, leaving a thick red snail's trail of blood smeared on the wallpaper. His puppy-dog eyes were open. His face bore no expression. The front of his green shirt, over the heart, was a tangle of dark red rag and tissue, spreading fast, and there was a similar stain slightly above it, near his shoulder. His hands lay at his side, one of them holding his gun. Another dark wet patch spread between his legs. Urine.

Banks thought of the chair at Arkbeck Farm, where this man had scared Alison Rothwell so much that she had wet herself. 'Jesus Christ,' he whispered.

'We'd no choice,' Spike said behind him. 'He had his gun in his hand when he came to the door. You can see for yourself. He fired first.'

Two shots, in close succession, followed by another, sounding slightly different. Two patches of spreading blood. 'Our boss tells us we don't want a lot of fuss about this.'

Banks looked at the two policemen, sighed and said, 'Give my regards to Dirty Dick.'

Shandy came back with a not very convincing, 'Who's that?'

Spike grinned, rubbed the barrel of his gun against his upper thigh, and said, 'Will do, sir.'

16

ONE

Banks had always hated hospitals: the antiseptic smells, the starched uniforms, the mysterious and unsettling pieces of shiny equipment around every corner – things that looked like modern sculpture or instruments of torture made of articulated chrome. They all gave him the creeps. Worst of all, though, was the way the doctors and nurses seemed to huddle in corridors and doorways and whisper about death, or so he imagined.

It was Saturday afternoon, 21 May, just over a week since Rothwell's murder and two days after Jameson's shooting, when Banks walked into Leeds Infirmary.

He had spent Thursday night in London, then headed back to Amersham for his car the next morning. After spending a little time with Superintendent Jarrell, Banks and Hatchley had driven back to Eastvale that Friday evening and arrived a little after nine.

On Saturday morning, he had to go into Leeds to consult with Ken Blackstone and wrap things up. After their pub lunch, he had taken a little time off to go and buy some more compact discs at the Classical Record Shop and pay a sick visit before heading back to Eastvale for Richmond's farewell bash. Sandra was off with the Camera Club photographing rock formations at Brimham Rocks, so he was left to his own devices for the day.

Banks paused and looked at the signs, then turned left. At last, he found the right corridor. Pamela Jeffreys shared a room with one other person, who happened to be down in X-ray when Banks called. He pulled up a chair by the side of the bed and put down the brown paper package he'd brought on the table. Pamela looked at it with her one good eye. The other was covered in bandages.

'Grapes,' said Banks, feeling embarrassed. 'It's what you bring when you visit people in hospital, isn't it?'

Pamela smiled, then decided it hurt too much and let her face relax.

'And,' Banks said, pulling a cassette from his pocket, 'I made you a tape of some Mozart piano concertos. Thought they might cheer you up. Got a Walkman?'

'Wouldn't go anywhere without it,' Pamela said out of the side of her mouth. 'It's a bit difficult to get the head-phones on with one hand, though.' She directed his gaze to where her bandaged right hand lay on the sheets.

He set the cassette on the bedside table beside the grapes. 'The doctor says you're going to be okay,' he said.

'Hm-mm,' murmured Pamela. 'So they tell me.' It came out muffled, but Banks could tell what she said.

'He said you'll be playing the viola again in no time.'

'Hmph. It might take a bit longer than that.'

'But you *will* play again.'

She uttered a sound that could have been a laugh or a sob. 'They broke two fingers on my right hand,' she said. 'My bowing hand. It's a good thing they know bugger all about musical technique. If they'd broken my wrist that might really have put an end to my career.'

'People like that aren't chosen for their intelligence, as a rule,' said Banks. 'But the important thing is that there's no permanent damage to your fingers, or to your eye.'

'I know, I know,' she said. 'I ought to think myself lucky.'

'Well?'

'Oh, I'm okay, I suppose. Mostly just bored. There's the tapes and the radio, but you can't listen to music all day. There's nothing else to do but watch telly, and I can stomach even less of that. Reading still hurts too much with just one good eye. And the food's awful.'

'I'm sorry,' Banks said. 'And I'm sorry about that day in the park.'

She moved her head slowly from side to side. 'No. My fault. You had to ask. I overreacted. Is this an official visit? Have you come about the men? The men who hurt me?'

'No. But we know who they are. They won't get away with it.'

'Why have you come?'

'I . . . that's a good question.' Banks laughed nervously and looked away, out of the window at the swaying treetops. 'To see you, I suppose,' he said. 'To bring you some grapes and some Mozart. I just happened to be in the area, you know, buying CDs.'

'What did you get?'

Banks showed her: Keith Jarrett playing Shostakovitch's twenty-four preludes and fugues; Nobuko Imai playing Walton's viola concerto. She raised her eyebrow. 'Interesting.' Then she tapped the Walton. 'It's beautiful if you get it right,' she said. 'But so difficult. She's very good.'

'It says in the notes that the viola is an introvert of an instrument, a poet-philosopher. Does that describe you?'

'My teacher told me I had to be careful not to get overwhelmed by the orchestra. That tends to happen to violas, you know. But I manage to hold my own.'

'How long are they going to keep you here?'

'Who knows? Another week or so. I'd get up and go home right now but I think my leg's broken.'

'It is. The right one.'

'Damn. The prettiest.'

Banks laughed.

'Did you catch the men who killed Robert?' she asked. 'Was it the same ones?'

Banks gave her the gist of what had happened with Jameson, avoiding the more lurid details.

'So one got away?' she said.

'So far.'

'That's not bad going.'

'Not bad,' Banks agreed. 'Fifty per cent success rate. It's better than the police average.'

'Will you get a promotion out of it?'

He laughed. 'I doubt it.'

'Don't look so worried,' she said, resting her bandaged hand on his. 'I'll be all right. And don't blame yourself . . . you know . . . for what happened to me.'

'Right. I'll try not to.' Banks felt his eyes burn. He could see her name bracelet and the tube attached to the vein in her wrist. It made him feel squeamish, even more so than seeing Jameson's body against the wall in the hotel room. It didn't make sense: he could take a murder scene in his stride, but a simple intravenous drip in a hospital made him queasy.

Pamela was right. She would be fine. Her wounds would heal; her beauty would regenerate. In less than a year she would be as good as new. But would she ever recover fully inside? How would she handle being alone in the house? Would she ever again be able to hear someone walking up the garden path without that twinge of fear and panic? He didn't know. The psyche regenerates itself, too, sometimes. We're often a damn sight more resilient than we'd imagine.

'Will you come and see me again?' she asked. 'I mean, when it's all over and I'm home. Will you come and see me?'

'Sure I will,' said Banks, thinking guiltily of the feelings he had had for Pamela, not sure at all.

'Do you mean it?'

He looked into her almond eye and saw the black shape of fear at its centre. He swallowed. 'Of course I mean it,' he said. And he did. He leaned forward and brushed his lips against her good cheek. 'I'd better go now.'

TWO

Why was he born so beautiful?
Why was he born so tall?
He's no bloody use to anyone,
He's no bloody use at all.

Richmond took the Yorkshire compliment, delivered in shaky harmonies by Sergeant Hatchley and an assorted cats' choir of PCs, very well, Banks thought, especially for someone who listened to music that sounded like Zamfir on Valium.

'Speech! Speech!' Hatchley shouted.

Embarrassed, Richmond gave a sideways glance at Rachel, his fiancée, then stood up, cleared his throat and said, 'Thank you. Thank you all very much. And thanks specially for the CD-ROM. You know I'm not much good at giving speeches like this, but I'd just like to say it's been a pleasure working with you all. I know you all probably

think I'm a traitor, going off down south—' Here, a chorus
of boos interrupted his speech. 'But as soon as I've got that
lot down there sorted out,' he went on, 'I'll be back, and
you buggers had better make sure you know a hard drive
from a hole in the ground. Thank you.'

He sat down again, and people went over to pat him on
the back and say farewell. Everyone cheered when Susan
Gay leaned forward and gave him a chaste kiss on the
cheek. She blushed when Richmond responded by giving
her a bear-hug.

They were in the back room of the Queen's Arms on
Saturday night, and Banks leaned against the polished bar,
pint of Theakston's in his hand, with Sandra on one side
and Gristhorpe on the other. Someone had hung balloons
from the ceiling. Cyril had hooked up the old jukebox for
the occasion, and Gerry and the Pacemakers were singing
'Ferry Across the Mersey'.

Banks knew he should have been happier to see the end
of the Rothwell case, but he just couldn't seem to get rid
of a niggling feeling, like an itch he couldn't reach.
Jameson had killed Rothwell. True. Now Jameson was
dead. Justice had been done, after a fashion. An eye for an
eye. So forget it.

But he couldn't. The two men who had beaten Pamela
Jeffreys hadn't been caught yet. Along with Jameson's
accomplice, that left three on the loose. Only a twenty-five
per cent success rate. Not satisfactory at all.

But it wasn't just that. Somehow, it was all too neat. All
too neat and ready for Martin Churchill to slip into the
country one night with a new face and a clean, colossal
bank account and retire quietly to Cornwall, guarding the
secrets of those in power to the grave. Which might not be
far off. Banks wouldn't be surprised if someone from MI6

or wherever slipped into Cornwall one night and both Mr Churchill *and* his insurance had a nasty accident.

Susan Gay walked over from Richmond's table and indicated she'd like a word. Banks excused himself from Sandra and they found a quiet corner.

'Sorry for dragging you away from the festivities, sir,' Susan said, 'but I haven't had a chance to talk to you since you got back. There's a couple of things you might be interested in.'

'I'm listening.'

Susan told him about her talk with Tom Rothwell after the funeral, about his homosexuality and what he had seen his father do that day he followed him into Leeds. 'The artist came in on Wednesday evening, sir, and we managed to get the impression in the papers on Thursday, while you were down south.'

'Any luck?'

'Well, yes and no.'

'Come on, then. Don't keep me in suspense.'

'We've found out who she is. Her name's Julia Marshall and she lives in Adel. That's in north Leeds. She's a school-teacher. We got a couple of phone calls from colleagues. Apparently, she was a quiet person, shy and private.'

'Was?'

'Well, I shouldn't say that, really, sir, but it's just that she's disappeared. That's all we know so far. I just think we should find her, that's all,' she said. 'Talk to her friends. I don't really know why. It's just a feeling. She might know something.'

'I think you're right,' said Banks. 'It's a loose end I'd like to see tied up as well. There are too many bloody disappearances in this case for my liking. Is there anything else?'

'No. But it's not over yet, is it, sir?'

'No, Susan, I don't think it is. Thanks for telling me. We'll follow up on it first thing tomorrow. For now, we'd better get back to the party or Phil will think we don't love him.'

Banks walked back to the bar and lit a cigarette. The music had changed; now it was the Swinging Blue Jeans doing 'Hippy, Hippy Shake' and some of the younger members of the department were dancing.

Banks thought about Tom Rothwell and his father. Susan had been sharp to pick up on that. It didn't make sense, given Rothwell's *other* interests, that he should be so genuinely upset that his son didn't want to be an accountant or a lawyer. On the other hand, perhaps nothing was more of an anathema, an insult, to a confirmed heterosexual philanderer than a gay son.

'Penny for them?' Sandra said.

'What? Oh, nothing. Just thinking, that's all.'

'It's over, Alan. Leave it be. It's another feather in your cap. You can't solve the whole world's problems.'

'It feels more like a lead weight than a feather. I think I'll have another drink.' He turned and ordered another pint. Sandra had a gin and tonic. 'You're right, of course,' he said, standing the drink on the bar. 'We've done the best we can.'

'You've done *all* you can. It's being pipped at the post by Dirty Dick that really gets your goat, isn't it?' Sandra taunted. 'You two have got some kind of macho personal vendetta going, haven't you?'

'Maybe. I don't know. I won't say it's a good feeling, knowing the bastard's got his way.'

'You did what you could, didn't you?'

'Yes.'

'But you still think Burgess has won this time, and it pisses you off, doesn't it?'

'Maybe. Yes. Yes, it bloody well does. Sandra, the man had someone *shot*.'

'A cold-blooded murderer. Besides, you don't know that.'

'You mean I can't prove it. And we're not here to play vigilantes. If Burgess had Jameson shot, you can be damn sure it wasn't just an eye for an eye. He was making certain he didn't talk.'

'*Men*,' said Sandra, turning to her drink with a long-suffering sigh.

Gristhorpe, who had been listening from the other side, laughed and nudged Banks in the ribs. 'Better listen to her,' he said. 'I can understand how you feel, but there's no more you can do, and there's no point making some kind of competition out of it.'

'I know that. It's not that. It's . . . oh, maybe Sandra's right and it is macho stuff. I don't know.'

At that moment, Sergeant Rowe, who had been manning the front desk across the street, pushed through the crowd of drinkers and said to Banks, 'Phone call, sir. He says it's important. Must talk to you in person.'

Banks put his pint glass back on the bar. 'Shit. Did he say who?'

'No.'

'All right.' He turned to Sandra and pointed at his pint. 'Guard that drink with your life. Back in a few minutes.'

He couldn't ignore the call; it might be an informer with important information. Irritated, nonetheless, he crossed Market Street and went into the Tudor-fronted police station.

'You can take it in here, sir,' said Rowe, pointing to an empty ground-floor office.

Banks went in and picked up the receiver. 'Hello. Banks here.'

'Ah, Banks,' said the familiar voice. 'It's Superintendent Burgess here. Remember me? What do you want first, the good news or the bad?'

Speak of the devil. Banks felt his jaw clench and his stomach start to churn. 'Just tell me,' he said as calmly as he could.

'Okay. You know those two goons, the ones that beat up the tart of colour?'

'Yes. Have you got them?'

'We-ell, not exactly.'

'What then?'

'They got away, slipped through our net. That's the bad news.'

'Where did they go?'

'Back home, of course. St Corona. That's the good news.'

'What's so good about that?'

'Seems they didn't realize they'd become *persona non grata* there, or whatever the plural of that is.'

'And?'

'Well, I have it on good authority that they've both been eating glass.'

'They're dead?'

'Of course they're bloody dead. I doubt they'd survive a diet like that.'

'How do you know this?'

'I told you. Good authority. It's the real McCoy. No reason to doubt the source.'

'Why?'

'Ours is not to reason why, Banks. Let's just say that their bungling around England drawing attention to themselves didn't help much. Things are in a delicate balance.'

'Did you know in advance that they were out of favour? Did you let them slip out of the country, knowing what would happen? Did you even try to find them?'

'Oh, Banks. You disappoint me. How could you even think something like that of me?'

'Easy. The same way I think you sent Spike and Shandy down to Kensington to make damn sure Arthur Jameson didn't survive to say anything embarrassing in court.'

'I told you, Jameson wasn't in my brief.'

'I know what you told me. I also know what happened in that hotel room. They shot the bastard down, Burgess, and you're responsible.'

'*Superintendent* Burgess, to you. And he shot first is what I heard. That's the official version, at any rate, and I don't see any reason not to believe it. As our cousins over the pond would say, it was a "righteous shoot".'

'Bollocks. They shot him twice then fired off a round from his gun to make it look like he fired first. Apart from the shots, do you know what gave them away?'

'No, but I'm sure you're going to tell me.'

'They left the gun in his hand for me to see. Procedure is that you disarm a suspect *first thing*, whether you think he's dead or not.'

'Well, hurray for you, Sherlock. Don't you think they might have got careless in the heat of the moment?'

'No. Not with their training.'

'But it doesn't matter, does it? You weren't there, officially, were you? In fact you were ordered to stay on the ground floor. Anyway, I don't think we need to go into all that tiresome stuff, do we? Do you really want me to have to pull rank? Believe it or not, I *like* you, Banks. Life would be a lot duller without you. I wouldn't want to see you throw your career down the tubes over this. Take my word for it, *nobody* will take kindly to your rocking the boat. The official verdict is the only one that counts.'

'Not to me.'

'Leave it alone, Banks. It's over.'

'Why does everyone keep telling me that?'

'Because it's true. One more thing. And don't interrupt me. We found an address book in Jameson's stuff and it led us to an old ex-army crony of his called Donald Pembroke. Ring any bells?'

'No.'

'Anyway, it seems this Pembroke just inherited a lot of money, according to his neighbour. The first thing he did was buy a fast sports car, cash down according to the salesman. Two days later he lost control on a B road in Kent – doing eighty or ninety by all accounts – and ran it into a tree.'

'And?'

'And he's dead, isn't he? What's more, there's no way you can put it down to me. So don't say there's no justice in the world, Banks. Goodbye. Have a good life.' Burgess hung up abruptly, leaving Banks to glare into the receiver. He slammed it down so hard that Sergeant Rowe popped his head around the door. 'Everything all right, sir?'

'Yes, fine,' said Banks. He took a deep breath and ran his hand through his short hair. 'Everything's just bloody fine and dandy.' He sat in the empty office gaining control of his breathing. Susan's words echoed in his mind. *'It's not over yet, is it, sir?'* No, it bloody well wasn't.

17

ONE

Banks sat at a taverna by the quayside sipping an ice-cold Beck's and smoking a duty-free Benson and Hedges Special Mild. When he had finished his cigarette, he popped a dolmas into his mouth and followed it with a black olive. One or two of the locals, mostly mustachioed and sun-leathered fishermen, occasionally glanced his way during a pause in their conversation.

It was a small island, just one village built up the central hillside, and though it got its share of tourists in season, none of the big cruise ships came. Banks had arrived half an hour ago on a regular ferry service from Piraeus and he needed a while to collect his thoughts and get his land-legs back again. He had a difficult interview ahead of him, he suspected. He had already contacted the Greek police. Help had been offered, and the legal machinery was ready to grind into action at a word. But Banks had something else he wanted to try first.

By Christ, it was hot, even in the shade. The sun beat down from a clear sky, a more intense, more saturated blue than Banks had ever seen, especially in contrast to the white houses, shops and tavernas along the quayside. A couple of sailboats and a few fishing craft were moored in the small harbour, bobbing gently on the calm water. It was hard to describe the sea's colour; certainly there were shades of green and blue in it, aquamarine, ultramarine, but in places it was a kind of inky blue, too, almost purple. Maybe Homer was right when he called it 'wine-dark', Banks thought, remembering his conversation with Superintendent Gristhorpe before the trip. Banks had never read *The Odyssey*, but he probably would when he got back.

He paid for his food and drink and walked out into the sun. On his way, he popped into the local police station in the square near the harbour, as promised, then set off along the dirt track up the hill.

The main street itself was narrow enough, but every few yards a side street branched off, narrower still, all white, cubist, flat-roofed houses with painted shutters, mostly blue. Some of the houses had red pantile roofs, like the ones in Whitby. Many people had put hanging baskets of flowers out on the small balconies, a profusion of purple, pink, red and blue, and lines of washing hung over the narrow streets. By the roadside were poppies and delicate lavender flowers that looked like morning glories.

Mingled with the scents of the flowers were the smells of tobacco and wild herbs. Banks thought he recognized thyme and rosemary. Insects with red bodies and transparent wings flew around him. The sun beat relentlessly. Before Banks had walked twenty yards, his white cotton shirt stuck to his back. He wished he had worn shorts instead of jeans.

Banks looked ahead. Where the white houses ended halfway up the hillside, scrub and rocky outcrops took over. The house he wanted, he had been told, was on his right, a large one with a high-gated white wall and a shaded courtyard. It wasn't difficult to spot, now about fifty yards ahead, almost three-quarters of the length of the road.

He finally made it. The ochre gate was unlocked, and beyond it, Banks found a courtyard full of saplings, pots of herbs and hanging plants by a *krokalia* pathway of black and white pebbles winding up to the door. Expensive, definitely. The door was slightly ajar, and he could hear voices inside. By the plummy tones, it sounded like the BBC World Service news. He paused a moment for breath, then walked up to the door and knocked.

He heard a movement inside, the voices stopped, and in a few seconds someone opened the door. Banks looked into the face that he had thought for so long had been blown to smithereens.

'Mr Rothwell?' he said, slipping his card out of his wallet and holding it up. 'Mr Keith Rothwell?'

TWO

'You've come, then?' Rothwell said simply.

'Yes.'

He looked over Banks's shoulder. 'Alone?'

'Yes.'

'You'd better come in.'

Banks followed Rothwell into a bright room where a ceiling fan spun and a light breeze blew through the open blue shutters. It was sparsely furnished. The walls were plastered white, the floor was flagged, covered here and there by rugs, and the ceiling was panelled with dark wood. Outside, he could hear birds singing; he didn't know what kind.

He sat down in the wicker chair Rothwell offered, surprised to be able to see the sea down below through the window. Now he was at the end of his journey, he felt bone-weary and more than a little dizzy. It had been a long way from Eastvale and a long uphill walk in the sun. Sweat dribbled from his eyebrows into his eyes and made them sting. He wiped it away with his forearm. At least it was cooler inside the room.

Rothwell noticed his discomfort. 'Hot, isn't it?' he said. 'Can I get you something?'

Banks nodded. 'Thanks. Anything as long as it's cold.'

Rothwell went to the kitchen door and turned, with a smile, just as he opened it. 'Don't worry,' he said. 'I won't run away.'

'There's nowhere to run,' replied Banks.

A minute or so later he came back with a glass of iced water and a bottle of Grolsch lager. 'I'd drink the water first,' he advised. 'You look a bit dehydrated.'

Banks drained the glass then opened the metal gizmo on the beer. It tasted good. Imported, of course. But Rothwell could afford it. Banks looked at him. The receding sandy hair, forming a slight widow's peak, had bleached in the sun. He had a good tan for such a fair-skinned person. Behind wire-rimmed glasses, his steady grey eyes looked out calmly, not giving away any indication as to his state of mind. He had a slightly prissy mouth, a girl's mouth, and his lips were pale pink. He looked nothing at all like the photograph of Daniel Clegg.

He wore a peach short-sleeve shirt, white shorts and brown leather sandals. His toenails needed cutting. He was an inch or so taller than Banks, slim and in good shape – about all he did have in common with Clegg, apart from the colour of his hair, his blood group and the appendicitis scar. When he went to get the drinks, Banks noticed, he moved with an athlete's grace and economy. There was nothing of the sedentary pen-pusher about his bearing.

'Anyone else here?' Banks asked.

'Julia's gone to the shops,' he said, glancing at his watch. 'She shouldn't be long.'

'I'd like to meet her.'

'How did you find me?' Rothwell asked, sitting opposite, opening a tin of Pepsi. The gas hissed out and liquid frothed over the edge. Rothwell held it at arm's length until it had stopped fizzing, then wiped the tin with a tissue from a box on the table beside him.

'It wasn't that difficult,' said Banks. 'Once I knew who I was looking for. We found you partly through Julia.' He shrugged. 'After that it was a matter of routine police work, mostly boring footwork. We checked travel agents, then we contacted the local police through Interpol. It didn't take that long to get word back about two English strangers who resembled your descriptions taking a lease on a captain's house here. Did you really believe we wouldn't find you eventually?'

'I suppose I must have,' said Rothwell. 'Foolish of me, but there it is. There are always variables, loose ends, but I thought I'd left enough red herrings and covered my tracks pretty well. I planned it all *very* carefully.'

'Do you have any idea what you've done to your family?'

Rothwell's lips tightened. 'It wasn't a family. It was a sham. A lie. A façade. We played at happy families. I couldn't stand it any more. There was no love in the house. Mary and I hadn't slept together in years and Tom . . . well . . .'

Banks let Tom pass for the moment. 'Why not get a divorce like anyone else? Why this elaborate scheme?'

'I assume, seeing as you're here, you know most of it?'

'Humour me.'

Rothwell squinted at Banks. 'Look,' he said. 'I can't see where you'd have any room to hide one, but you're not "wired" as the Americans say, are you?'

Banks shook his head. 'You have my word on that.'

'This is just between you and me? Off the record?'

'For the moment. I am here officially, though.'

Rothwell sipped some Pepsi then rubbed the can between his palms. 'I might have asked Mary for a divorce eventually,' he said, 'but it was still all very new to me, the freedom, the taste of another life. I'm not even sure she would have let me go that easily. The way things turned out, though, I had to appear dead. If he thinks I'm alive, there'll be no peace, no escape anywhere.'

'Martin Churchill?'

'Yes. He found out I was taking rather more than I was entitled to.'

'How did you find out he knew?'

'A close source. When you play the kind of games I did, Mr Banks, it pays to have as much information as you can get. Let's say someone on the island tipped me that Churchill knew and that he was pressuring Daniel Clegg to do something about it.'

'Is that how it happened?'

'Yes. And it made sense. I'd noticed that Daniel had been behaving oddly lately. He was nervous about something. Wouldn't look me in the eye. Now I had an explanation. The bastard was planning to have me executed.'

'So you had him killed instead?'

Rothwell gazed out of the window at the sea and the mountainside in silence for a moment. 'Yes. It was him or me. I beat him to it, that's all. Someone had to die violently, someone who could pass for me under certain circumstances. We looked enough alike.'

'Without a face, you mean?'

'I . . . I didn't look . . . in the garage . . . I couldn't.'

'I'll bet you couldn't. Go on.'

'We were about the same age and build, same hair colour. I knew he'd had his appendix out. I even knew his blood group was "O", the same as mine.'

'How did you know that?'

'He told me. We were talking once about blood tainted by the HIV virus. He wondered if he had a greater chance of catching it from a transfusion because he shared his blood group with over forty per cent of the male population.'

'What did you do once you had the idea of passing him off as you?'

'There was this man we'd both met in the Eagle a couple of times, down there for the Ed O'Donnell Band on a Sunday lunchtime, and he'd boasted about being a mercenary and doing anything for money. Arthur Jameson was his name. He was a walking mass of contradictions. He loved animals and nature, but he liked hunting and duck-shooting, and he didn't seem to give a damn for human life. I found him fascinating. Fascinating and a little frightening.

'It was perfect. Daniel knew him, too, of course, and he told me that Jameson had even approached him for some legal help once, shortly after we met. I thought if you found out anything, that would be it. He might have had something in his files. You know how lawyers hoard every scrap of paper. But there was nothing linking Jameson to *me*. It would only reinforce what you suspected already, that Daniel had had *me* killed instead of the other way round. You weren't to know that I was with Daniel the day we met Jameson, or that I'd chatted with Jameson on a number of subsequent occasions.'

'So you and Clegg were pals? Socialized together, did you?'

Rothwell paused. A muscle by his jaw twitched. 'No. It wasn't quite like that,' he said quietly. 'Daniel had a hold over me, but sometimes he seemed to want to play at being boozing buddies. I didn't understand it, but at least for a while we could bury our differences and have a good time. The next day it would usually be back to cold formality. At bottom, Daniel was a terrible snob. Been to Cambridge, you know.'

'How much did you pay Jameson?'

'Fifty thousand pounds and a plane ticket to Rio. I know it's a lot, but I thought the more I paid him the more likely he'd be to disappear for good with it and not get caught.'

'First mistake.'

'How did it happen?'

Banks told him about the wadding and about Jameson's attitude to the world beyond Calais. Rothwell laughed, then stared at the sea again. 'I knew it was a risk,' he said. 'I suppose I should have known, the way he used to go on about the Irish and the Frogs sometimes. But if you have a dream you have to take risks for it, pay a price, don't you?'

'You needn't try to justify your actions to me,' said Banks, finally feeling steady and cool enough to light a cigarette. He offered one to Rothwell, who accepted. 'I was the one left to clean up your mess. And Jameson killed one policeman and seriously wounded another trying to escape.' The fan drew their smoke up to it, then pushed it towards the windows.

'I'm sorry.'

'I'll bet you are.'

'It wasn't my fault, what Jameson did, was it? You can't blame me.'

'Can't I? Let's get back to your relationship with Daniel Clegg. How did you get involved?'

'We met in the George Hotel, on Great George Street. It was about four years ago. A year or so after I left Hatchard and Pratt, anyway. Expenses were high, what with renovations to Arkbeck and everything else, and business wasn't exactly booming, though I wasn't doing too badly. They have jazz at the George on Thursdays, and as I was in Leeds on business, I thought I'd drop by rather than watch television in the hotel room. It turns out we were both jazz fans. We just got talking, that's all.

'I didn't tell him very much at first, except that I was a freelance financial consultant. He seemed interested. Anyway, we exchanged business cards and he put a bit of work my way, off-shore banking, that sort of thing. Turns out some of it was a bit shady, though I wasn't aware at the time – not that I mightn't have done it, anyway, mind you – and he brought that up later, in conversation.'

'He put pressure on you?'

'Oh, yes.' Rothwell paused and looked Banks in the eye. 'A smooth blackmailer, was Danny-boy. I suppose you know about my bit of bad luck at Hatchard and Pratt's, don't you?'

'Yes.'

'That was five years ago. We'd just moved into Arkbeck then and we couldn't really afford it. Not that the mortgage itself was so high, but the place had been neglected for so long. There was so much needed doing, and I'm no DIY expert. But Mary wanted to live there, so live there we did. The upshot was that I had to pad the expenses a little. If I hadn't been married to the boss's daughter, and if Laurence Pratt hadn't been a good friend, things could have gone very badly for me at the firm then. As it was,

after I left I didn't have a lot of work at first, and Mary . . .
well, that's another story. Let's just say she doesn't have a
forgiving nature. One night, in my cups, I hinted to Daniel
about what had happened, how I had parted company
with Hatchard and Pratt.

'Anyway, later, Daniel used what he knew about me as
leverage to get me involved when his old college friend
Martin Churchill first made inquiries about rearranging his
finances. That was a little over three years back. See,
he knew he couldn't handle the task by himself, that he
needed my expertise. He told me he could still report me
to the board, that it wasn't too late. Well, maybe they
would have listened to him, and maybe they wouldn't.
Who knows now? Quite frankly, I didn't care. I already
knew a bit about money-laundering, and it looked to me
like a licence to print money. Why wouldn't I want in? I
think Daniel just enjoyed manipulating people, having
power over them, so I didn't spoil his illusion. But he
really wasn't terribly bright, wasn't Danny-boy, despite
Cambridge.'

'A bit like Frankenstein and the monster, isn't it?'

Rothwell smiled. 'Yes, perhaps. And I suppose you'd
have to say that the monster far outstripped his creator,
though you could hardly say the good doctor himself was
without sin.'

'How did you arrange it all? The murder, the escape?'

Rothwell emptied his tin, put it on the table and leaned
back. The chair creaked. Outside, gulls cried as they
circled the harbour looking for fish. 'Another Grolsch?' he
asked.

There was still an inch left in the bottle. 'No,' said
Banks. 'Not yet.'

Rothwell sighed. 'You have to go back about eighteen

months to understand, to when I first started using the Robert Calvert identity. Daniel and I were doing fine laundering Churchill's money, and he allowed us a decent percentage for doing so. I was getting rich quick. I suppose I should have been happy, but I wasn't. I don't know exactly when I first became aware of it, but life just seemed to have lost its savour, its sweetness. Things started to oppress me. I felt like I was shrivelling up inside, dying, old before my time. Call it mid-life crisis, I suppose, but I couldn't see the *point* of all that bloody money.

'All Mary wanted was her bridge club, more renovations, additions to the house, jewellery, expensive holidays. Christ, I should have known better than to marry the boss's daughter, even if I did get her pregnant. One simple mistake, that and my own bloody weakness. What was it the philosopher said about the erect penis knowing no conscience? That may be so, but it certainly understands penitence, regret, remorse. One bloody miserable, uncomfortable screw in the back of an Escort halfway up Crow Scar set me on a course straight to hell. I'm not exaggerating. Twenty-one years. After that long, my wife hated me, my children hated me, and I was beginning to hate myself.'

Banks noticed that Rothwell had picked up the empty Pepsi tin and started to squeeze until it buckled in his grip.

'Then I realized I was handling millions of pounds – literally, millions – and that my job was essentially to clean it and hide it ready for future use. It wasn't difficult to find a few hiding places of my own. Small amounts at first, then, when no one seemed to miss it, more and more. Shell companies, numbered accounts, dummy corporations, property. I liked what I was doing. The manipulation of large sums of money intrigued me and excited me like nothing else, or almost nothing else. Just for the sake of it, much of the time. Like art for art's sake.

'I began to spend more time away from home "on business". Nobody cared one way or another. They never asked me where I'd been. They only asked for more money for a new kitchen or a sun-porch or a bloody gazebo. When I was home, I walked around like a zombie – the dull, boring accountant, I suppose – and mostly kept to my office or nipped out to the pub for a smoke and a jar occasionally. I had plenty of time to look back on my life, and though I didn't like a lot of what I saw, I remembered I hadn't always been so bloody bored or boring. I used to go dancing, believe it or not. I used to like a flutter on the horses now and then. I had friends. Once in a while, I liked to have too much to drink with the lads and stagger home singing, happy as a lark. That was before life came to resemble an accounts ledger – debits and credits, profit and loss, with far too much on the loss side.' He sighed. 'Are you sure you wouldn't like another beer?'

'Go on, then,' Banks said. His bottle was empty now.

Rothwell brought back a Pepsi for himself and another Grolsch for Banks. His glasses had slipped down over the bridge of his nose and he pushed them back.

'So I invented Robert Calvert,' Rothwell said after a sip of Pepsi.

'Where did you get the name?'

'Picked it from a magazine I was reading at the time. With a pin. The *Economist*, I believe.'

'Go on.'

'I rented the flat, bought new clothes, more casual. God, you've no idea how strange it felt at first. Good, but strange. There were moments when I really did believe I was going mad, turning into a split personality. It became a kind of compulsion, an addiction, like smoking. I'd go to the bookie's and put bets on, spend a day at the races, go listen to trad jazz in smoky pubs – the Adelphi, the George, the Duck and Drake – something I hadn't done since my early twenties. I'd go around in jeans and sweat-shirts. And nobody back at Arkbeck Farm ever asked where I'd been, what I'd been doing, as long I turned up every now and then in my business suit and the money kept coming in for a new freezer, a first edition Brontë, a Christmas trip to Hawaii. After a while I realized I wasn't going mad, I was just becoming myself, returning to the way I was before I let life grind me down.

'And, sure enough, the money kept coming in. I had tapped into an endless supply, or so I thought. So I played the family role part of the time, and I started exploring my real self as Robert Calvert. I had no idea where it would lead, not then. I was just trying out ways of escape. I told Daniel Clegg one night when we'd had a few, and he thought it was a wild idea. I had to tell someone and I couldn't tell my family or Pratt or anyone local, so why not tell my blackmailer, my confidant? He helped me get a bank account and credit card as Calvert, which he thought gave him an even stronger hold over me. He could always claim he'd been deceived, you see.'

'What about the escape?'

'You're jumping ahead a bit, but as I'd already created Robert Calvert successfully enough, it wasn't very difficult to go on from there and create a third identity: David Norcliffe. As you no doubt know, seeing as you're here. Rothwell was dead, and I couldn't go as Calvert. I had to leave him behind; that was part of the plan. So I shuffled more money into various bank accounts in various places over a period of several weeks. After all, that's what I do best. I've laundered and hidden millions for Churchill and his wife.'

'How much for yourself?'

'Three or four million,' he said with a shrug. 'I don't know exactly. Enough, anyway, to last us our lifetime. And there was plenty left in Eastvale for my family. They're well provided for in the will and by the life insurance. I made sure of that. Believe me, they'll be better off without me.'

'What about Daniel Clegg? What about Pamela Jeffreys?'

'Pamela? What about her?'

Banks told him.

He put his head in his hands. 'Oh, my God,' he said. 'I would never have hurt Pamela . . . It wasn't meant to be like that.'

'How did you meet her?'

Rothwell sipped some more Pepsi and rubbed the back of his hand across his brow. 'I told you the Calvert thing felt very strange at first. Mostly, I just used to walk around Leeds in my jeans and sweatshirt. I'd drop in at a pub now and then and enjoy being someone else. Occasionally, I got chatting to people, the way you do in pubs. I'll never forget how frightening and how exciting it was the first time someone asked me my name and I said "Robert Calvert". I knew it was still me – you have to understand that – we're not really talking about a split personality here. I was Keith Rothwell, all right, just playing a part, or trying to find himself, perhaps. It gave me an exhilarating sense of freedom.

'Anyway, as I said, I used to drop in at pubs now and then, mostly in the city centre or up in Headingley, near the flat. One night I saw Pamela in The Boulevard – you know, the tarted-up Jubilee Hotel on The Headrow. It seemed a likely place to meet women. They stay open till midnight on weekends and they've got a small dance floor. Pamela was with some friends. They'd been doing something at the Town Hall, a Handel oratorio, or something like that. Anyway, something happened, some spark. We caught one another's eye.

'She wasn't with anyone in particular. I mean, she didn't seem to have a boyfriend with her. The next time she was at the bar, I made sure I got there, too, next to her, and we got chatting. I wasn't a great fan of classical music, but Pamela's a down-to-earth sort of person, not a highbrow snob or anything. I asked her to dance. She said yes. We just got on, that's all. We slept together now and then, but both of us knew it was just a casual relationship really. I don't mean to denigrate it by saying that. We had a wonderful time. I was astounded she fancied me. Flattered. It was the first time in my entire marriage that I'd been with another woman, and the hell of it was that I didn't feel guilty at all. She was fun to be with, and we had a great time, but we weren't in love.'

'What came between you?'

'What? Well, we stayed friends, really. At least, I like to think we did. There was her work, of course. It's very demanding and between us we couldn't always be sure we could make time to get together. And Pamela was more outgoing. She wanted more of a social life. She wanted me to meet her friends, and she wanted to meet mine.'

'But you didn't have any?'

'Exactly. And I didn't want to get too well known around the place. It was a risk, playing Calvert, always a risk.'

'Go on. What happened next?'

'I met Julia.'

'How?'

'We met on a bus, would you believe? It had been rain-ing, one of those sudden showers, and I was out walking without an umbrella. So I jumped on a bus into town. Then the rain stopped and the sun came out. I'd been looking at her out of the corner of my eye. She was so beautiful, like a model, such delicate, fragile, sculpted features. I imagined she was probably stuck-up and wouldn't talk to the likes of me. Anyway, she left her umbrella. I saw it, grabbed it, and dashed after her. When I caught her up she seemed startled at first, then I gave it to her and she blushed. She seemed flustered, so I asked her if she wanted to go for a coffee. She said yes. She was very shy. It was hard to get her talking at first, but slowly I found out she was a teacher and she lived in Adel and she adored Greek history and literature.

'Do you believe in love at first sight, Mr Banks? Do you? Because that's what this is all about, really. It's not just about money. It's not just about leaving my old life behind and seeking novelty. I fell in love with Julia the moment I saw her, and that's the truth. It might sound foolish and sentimental to you, but I have never in my life felt that way before. Bells ringing, earth moving, all the clichés. And it's mutual. She's everything I've ever wanted. When I met Julia, nothing else mattered. I knew we had to get away, find our Eden, if you like, our paradise. I had to get a new life, a new identity. Everything was in such a mess, falling apart. No one was supposed to get hurt.'

'Except Daniel Clegg.'

Rothwell banged on his chair arm with his fist. 'I told you! That wasn't my fault. I had to appear to have been violently murdered. By Daniel himself, or by someone he'd hired. And that's exactly the way it would have been, too, if I hadn't been tipped off and made other plans. But Julia knew nothing of that. She's a complete innocent. She knows nothing of the things we've just been talking about.'

'So you invited Clegg over to the Calvert flat to get his fingerprints there? Am I right?'

'Yes. On the Monday. I said I had some business to discuss that couldn't wait and he came over. I showed him around, had him touch things. I'd cleaned the place thoroughly. Daniel was a touchy-feely kind of person. Anything he saw, he'd pick it up and have a look: compact discs, wallet, credit cards in Calvert's name, coins, books, you name it. He'd even let his fingers rest on surfaces as if he were claiming them or something. He handled just about everything in the place. I was much more careful to make mine blurred.' Rothwell laughed quietly. 'He really was a fool, you know. Every time I got him to help me with something illegal, like setting up the Calvert bank account and credit card, for example, he thought *he* was getting more power over *me*.'

'So you must have known we'd find out about the Calvert identity, about Pamela, about Clegg and the money-laundering?'

'Of course. As I said earlier, I had to leave Calvert behind. It was part of my plan that you should find out about him. Another dead end. But please believe me, Pamela wasn't meant to be a part of it, except maybe to confirm the Calvert identity. I mean, I thought she might get in touch with the police if she saw my picture in the papers. Or someone else might, someone who thought they recognized me. It was meant to confuse you, that's all. I left a careful trail for you. I thought it led the wrong way. I knew the police would be able to unlock and interpret the data on my computer eventually, that they would realize I'd been laundering money for Martin

Churchill. I also left a letter for Daniel Clegg in a locked file. I knew you'd get at that eventually, too.'

'That was one of the things that bothered me,' Banks said. 'In retrospect, it was all too easy. And we never found a copy of the letter among his papers. He could have destroyed it, of course, but it was just one those little niggling details. Lawyers tend to hang on to things.'

'I never sent it,' said Rothwell. 'I just created the file so you'd get on to Daniel if you hadn't already. It was a way of telling you his name, but I couldn't make it *too* easy. Then you'd assume he'd had me killed and disappeared with the money.'

'Oh, we did,' said Banks. 'We did.'

'Then why are you here?'

'Because I'm a persistent bastard, among other things. There were too many loose ends. They worried me. Two different sets of thugs roaming the country, for a start. They could be explained, of course, but it still seemed odd. And we couldn't find any trace of Clegg, no matter how hard we tried. His ex-wife said he fancied Tahiti, but we had no luck there. We had no luck anywhere else, either. Of course we didn't. We were looking for the wrong person. But mostly, I think, it was the connection with Julia that really did you in.'

'How did you find out about her?'

'Pamela Jeffreys mentioned her first. She said she thought you were in love. Just a feeling she had, you understand. Then I began to wonder how it would upset the apple-cart if you fell in love as *Robert Calvert*. How would you handle it? Then Tom came back from America for your funeral.'

'Ah, Tom. My Achilles heel.'

'Oh, he didn't realize the significance of it. But you

made him angry. He followed you to Leeds once. He saw you have lunch with a woman. Julia Marshall. You didn't know that, did you? But Tom couldn't imagine the scale of your plans. He's just a kid who caught his father with another woman. He was already angry, mixed up and confused at the way you treated him. He was after getting his own back, but what he saw upset him so much that all he could do was keep it to himself.'

'Christ,' he muttered. 'I didn't know that. He didn't tell Mary?'

'No. He wanted to protect her.'

'My God.' Rothwell ran his hand over the side of his face. 'Maybe you think I reacted too harshly, Chief Inspector? I know we're living in liberal times, where anything goes. I know it's old-fashioned of me, but I still happen to believe that homosexuality is an aberration, an abomination of nature, and not just an "alternative lifestyle", as the liberals would have it. And to find out that *my* own son . . .'

'So you decided it would be best to send Tom away?'

'Yes. It seemed best for both of us if he went away, a long way away. He was well provided for. As it turned out, he wanted to go travelling in America and try to get into film school there. By then I knew I had to get away, too, so it seemed best to let him go. At least he had a good chance. I might have abhorred his homosexuality, but I'm not a tyrant. He was still my son, after all.'

'Tom gave us an accurate description of Julia,' Banks went on. 'He's a very observant young man. We ran the artist's impression in the *Yorkshire Post* and a woman called Barbara Ledward came forward, a colleague of Julia's, then Julia's family. Nobody lives in a vacuum. When we followed up on their phone calls, we found out that Julia had resigned from her teaching job suddenly and told everyone she was going away, that she had a once-in-a-lifetime opportunity abroad but couldn't divulge the details. She said she'd be in touch, then she simply disappeared about three days before your apparent murder. Her family and friends were worried about her. She didn't usually behave so irresponsibly. But they didn't report her as a missing person because she had *told* them she was going away.

'We might have been a bit slow on the uptake, but we're not stupid. All Julia's friends and colleagues mentioned how fascinated she was by the ancient Greeks. She even tried to teach the kids about the classics at school, though I'm told it didn't go down well with the head. He wanted them to study computers and car maintenance instead. We had to assume you didn't think we'd find out about Julia. Oh, you might have suspected we'd find out there was *someone*, but you didn't think we'd try to find her, did you?'

'No,' said Rothwell. 'After all, why should you want to? No more than I thought you would waste time and money doing tests to see if it really was *my* body in the garage. Another risk. I was clearly dead, executed because of my involvement in international crime. What did it matter if I, or Calvert, had a girlfriend? I never thought for a moment you'd look very closely at the rest of my private life.'

'Then you shouldn't have revealed the Calvert identity to us,' Banks said. 'If it hadn't been for that, we might have gone on thinking you were a dull, mild-mannered accountant who just happened to get into something beyond his depth. But Calvert showed imagination. Calvert showed a dimension to your character I had to take into account. And I had to ask myself, what if Calvert fell in love?'

'I couldn't get rid of Calvert,' said Rothwell. 'You know that. I didn't have time. Too many people had seen him. I had to figure out a way to make him work to my advantage quickly. I thought he'd be a dead end.'

'Your mistake. Poor judgment.'

'Obviously. But I had no choice. What else could I do?'

'So how did you handle the killing?'

'Another drink?'

'Please.'

Banks stared out over the pink and purple flowers in the window box at the barren hillside and the blue sea below. Rothwell's mention of the forensic tests galled him. He knew they should have tried to establish the identity of the deceased beyond doubt. Forensics should have reconstructed the teeth and checked dental records. That was an oversight. It was understandable, given the way Rothwell had apparently been assassinated, and given the state the teeth were in, but it was an oversight, nevertheless.

Of course, the lab had been as burdened with work as usual, and tests cost money. Then, when the fingerprints at Calvert's flat matched the corpse's, they didn't think they needed to look any further. After all, they had the pasta meal, the appendix scar and the right blood group, and Mary Rothwell had identified the dead man's clothing, watch and pocket contents.

A red flying insect settled on his bare arm. He brushed it off gently. When Rothwell came back with a Grolsch and a Pepsi, he was not moving with quite the same confidence and grace as he had before.

'I gave Jameson instructions to hold Alison until we got back,' he began, 'but *not* to harm her in any way.'

'That's considerate of you. He didn't. What about his accomplice, Donald Pembroke?'

Rothwell shook his head. He held the Pepsi against his shorts. The can was beaded with moisture and Banks watched the damp patch spread through the white cotton. 'I never met him. That was Jameson's business. He said he needed someone to help and I left it to him, getting guarantees of discretion, of course. I never even knew the man's name, and that's the truth. Pembroke, you say? What happened to him?'

Banks told him.

Rothwell sighed. 'I suppose fate catches up with us all in the end, doesn't it? What is it the eastern religions call it? Karma?'

'Back to the murder.'

Rothwell paused a moment, then went on. 'They held Alison, then when Mary and I got home, they tied her up, too, and took me out to the garage. They had instructions to pick Clegg up after dinner. I knew he didn't like to cook for himself and on Thursdays he always dropped by a trattoria near the office for a quick pasta before going home. That's why I chose that day. I knew Mary and I would be going out for the annual anniversary dinner, and I arranged for us to eat at Mario's. You see, I thought of everything. Even the stomach contents would match.

'They'd already knocked Clegg out and secured him earlier. I even made sure to tell Jameson to use loose hand-cuffs to avoid rope burns on Clegg's wrists. We got him into my clothes as quickly as possible. He was starting to come round. He was on his hands and knees, I remember, shaking his head as if he was groggy, just waking up, then Jameson put the shotgun to the back of his head. I . . . I turned away. There was a terrible explosion and a smell. Then we went through the woods and they drove me to Leeds. I drove Clegg's Jaguar to Heathrow, wearing gloves, of course. Then I left the country as David Norcliffe. I already had a passport and bank accounts set up in that name. I joined Julia here. It was all pre-arranged. It had to be so elaborate because I was supposed to be murdered. I'd read about a similar murder in the papers a while back and it seemed one worth imitating.'

'Well, you know what the poet said. "The best laid plans . . ."'

'But you can't prove anything,' said Rothwell.

'Don't be an idiot. Of course we can. We can prove that you're alive and Daniel Clegg was murdered in your garage.'

'But you can't prove I was there. It's only your word against mine. I could say they were taking me out to kill both of us. I managed to get away and I ran and hid here. They killed Daniel, but I escaped.'

'They killed him in *your* clothes?' Banks shook his head slowly. 'It won't wash, Keith.'

'But it's all circumstantial. Jameson and Pembroke are both dead. A good lawyer could get me off, and you know it.'

'You're dreaming. Say you do beat the murder conspiracy charge, which I think is unlikely, there's still the money-laundering and the rest.'

Rothwell looked around the room, mouth set firmly. 'I'm not going back,' he said. 'You can't make me. I know there are European extradition treaties. Procedures to follow. They take time. You can't just take me in like some bounty hunter.'

'Of course I can't,' said Banks. 'That was never my intention.' He heard the gate open and walked over to the window.

A pale, beautiful woman in a yellow sun-dress, red-blonde hair piled and knotted high on her head, had walked into the courtyard and paused to check on the flowers and potted plants. She carried a basket of fresh bread and other foodstuffs in the crook of her arm. She put out her free hand and bent to hold a purple blossom gently between her fingers for a moment, then inspected the herbs. The sun brought out the blonde highlights in her hair. 'It looks like Julia's back,' Banks said. 'Doesn't tan well, does she?'

Rothwell jumped up and looked out. 'Julia knows nothing,' he said quickly, speaking quietly so she couldn't hear him. 'You have to believe that. I told her I had business problems, that I had to burn a lot of bridges if we were to be together, that we'd be well set up for life but we couldn't go back. Ever. She agreed. I don't know if you can understand this or not, but *I love her*, Banks, more than anyone or anything I've ever loved in my life. I mean it. It's the first time I've ever . . . I already told you. I love her. She knows nothing. You can do what you want with me, but leave her alone.'

Banks kept quiet.

'You'll never be able to prove anything,' Rothwell added.

'Maybe I don't even want to take that risk,' said Banks. By now they could both see Julia and hear her humming softly as she rubbed the leaves on a pot of basil and sniffed her fingers. 'Maybe I'd rather you made a clean breast of it,' he went on, keeping his voice low. 'A confession. It might even go in your favour, you never know. Especially the love bit. Juries love lovers.'

Julia stood up. Some of her piled tresses had come loose and trailed over her cheeks. She was flushed from the walk and some of the hairs stuck to her face, dampened with sweat.

'You must be mad if you think I'd give all this up willingly,' Rothwell said.

'You can't buy paradise with blood, Keith,' said Banks. 'Come on home. Tell us everything about Martin Churchill's finances, everything you know about the bastard. Let's go public, make plenty of noise, sing louder than a male-voice choir. We can make sure he never sets foot in the country even if he turns up looking like Mr Bean. We could offer you protection, then perhaps another identity, another new life. You'd do some time, of course, but I'm willing to bet that by the time you got out, Martin Churchill would be just another of history's unpleasant footnotes, and Julia would be still waiting.'

'You're insane, do you know that? I'd kill you before I'd do what you're suggesting.'

'No, you wouldn't, Keith. Besides, there'd be others after me.'

Rothwell paused on his way to the door and stared at Banks, eyes wide open and wild, no longer calm and steady. 'Do you know what will happen if I go home?'

'It might not be half as bad as what will happen if I let Churchill know you're still alive,' said Banks. 'They say he has a long reach and a nasty line in revenge.' Julia had almost reached the door. 'It wouldn't stop at you,' Banks said.

Rothwell froze. 'You wouldn't. No. Not even *you* would do a thing like that.'

At that moment, Banks hated himself probably more than at any other time in his life. He felt sorry for Rothwell, and he found himself on the verge of relenting.

Then he remembered Mary Rothwell, living in a haze of tranquillizers; Alison, burying her head deep in her books and fast losing touch with the real world; and Tom, flailing around in his own private mire of guilt and confusion. Rothwell could have helped these people. Then he thought of Pamela Jeffreys, just out of hospital, physically okay, but still afraid of every knock at her door and unsure whether she would get back the confidence to play her viola again.

For this man's gamble on paradise, Daniel Clegg lay in his grave with his head blown off, Barry Miller had died on a wet road at midnight and Grant Everett might have to spend the next few years of his life relearning how to walk and talk. Even Arthur Jameson and Donald Pembroke were Rothwell's victims, in a way.

And, much farther away but no less implicated, was a dictator who got fat while his people starved, a man who liked to watch people eat glass, a man who, now, if Banks could help it, would never enjoy a peaceful retirement in the English countryside, no matter what he had on some powerful members of the establishment.

And the more Banks thought about these people, victims and predators alike, the less able he was to feel sorry for the fallen lovers.

'Try me,' he said.

Rothwell glared at him, then all the life seemed to drain out of him until he resembled nothing more than a tired, middle-aged accountant. Banks still felt dirty and miserable, and despite his resolve, he wasn't certain he could go through with his threat. But Rothwell believed him now, and that was all that mattered. This bastard had caused enough trouble already. There was no more room for pity. Banks felt his pulse race, his jaw clench. Then the door opened and Julia drifted in, all blonde and yellow, with a big smile for Rothwell.

'Hello, darling! Oh,' she said, noticing Banks. 'We've got company. How nice.'

PETER ROBINSON

Aftermath

The Inspector Banks Series

PAN BOOKS

'He felt depressed. The elation he had expected to feel on finding the killer somehow eluded him. He had no sense of an ending, of an evil purged. In some odd way, he felt, the evil was just beginning . . .'

Number 35 The Hill is an ordinary house in an ordinary street. But it is about to become infamous. When two police constables are sent to the house following a report of a domestic disturbance, they stumble upon a truly horrific scene. A scene which leaves one of them dead and the other fighting for her life and her career.

The identity of a serial killer, the Chameleon, has finally been revealed. But his capture is only the beginning of a shocking investigation that will test Inspector Alan Banks to the absolute limit.

'It demonstrates how the crime novel, when done right, can reach parts that other books can't . . . A considerable achievement.'
Guardian

PETER ROBINSON

Gallows View

The Inspector Banks Series

PAN BOOKS

A Peeping Tom is frightening the women of Eastvale. Two glue-sniffing young thugs are breaking into homes and robbing people. An old woman may or may not have been murdered. Detective Chief Inspector Alan Banks has recently moved to the Yorkshire Dales from London to escape the stress of city life. But he soon finds himself immersed in crimes that test all his skills and ability to the limit.

In addition, Banks has to deal with his attraction to young psychologist Jenny Fuller. As the tension mounts, both Jenny and Banks's wife, Sandra, are drawn deeper into the case. And Banks realizes that his cases are weaving closer and closer together . . .

'An expert plotter with an eye for telling detail'
New York Times

'The novels of Peter Robinson are chilling, evocative, deeply nuanced works of art'
Dennis Lehane

PETER ROBINSON

A Dedicated Man

The Inspector Banks Series

PAN BOOKS

The body of a well-liked local historian is found half-buried under a drystone wall near the village of Helmthorpe, Swainsdale. Who on earth would want to kill such a thoughtful, dedicated man? A beautiful folk singer with a mysterious past, a shady land-developer, his editor and a local thriller writer soon fall under suspicion. All are figures from the murdered man's previous, idyllic summers in the dale. It is clear that young Sally Lumb knows more than she lets on. And her knowledge could lead to danger.

In his second case, Inspector Banks unearths disturbing secrets behind a bucolic façade.

'Inspector Banks – a man for all seasons, he knows that often the answers to the clues he seeks are hidden in his own heart'
Michael Connelly

PETER ROBINSON

Cold is the Grave

The Inspector Banks Series

PAN BOOKS

Detective Inspector Alan Banks's relationship with Chief Constable Riddle has always been strained. So Banks is more than a little surprised when Riddle summons him late one night and begs for his help.

For Riddle, Banks's new case is terrifyingly close to home. Six months ago, his sixteen-year-old daughter ran away to London, where she has fallen into a turbulent world of drugs and pornography. With his reputation threatened, Riddle wants Banks to use his unorthodox methods to find her without fuss. But before he knows it, Banks is investigating murder . . .

'Watch for those twists – they'll get you every time'
Ian Rankin